Judgment
Wrath of the Lamb

Chronicles of the Apocalypse
Book Four

By Brian Godawa

Judgment: Wrath of the Lamb
Chronicles of the Apocalypse • Book Four
2nd Edition b

Warrior Poet Publishing
www.warriorpoetpublishing.com

ISBN: 9798710885765 (hardcover)
ISBN: 978-1-942858-42-3 (paperback)

Scripture quotations taken from *The Holy Bible: English Standard Version.* Wheaton: Standard Bible Society, 2001.

Get the Theology behind This Novel Series

The Biblical Theology behind Chronicles of the Apocalypse

By Brian Godawa

Brian Godawa reveals the biblical and historical basis for the viewpoint of the Last Days presented in the novel series *Chronicles of the Apocalypse.*

Godawa unveils the biblical meaning of many End Times notions like the Last Days, cosmic catastrophes, the Abomination of Desolation, the Antichrist, the Great Tribulation, and more!

Available in eBook, Paperback & Audiobook

https://godawa.com/get-end-times/

The *Chronicles of the Apocalypse* series

is dedicated to

Ken Gentry and Gary DeMar.

Scholars and gentlemen, both.

ACKNOWLEDGMENTS

Special thanks to my Lord and Savior Jesus Christ for allowing me to combine my esoteric theological interests with my passionate love of storytelling. I never envisioned such privilege or ministry. I do not deserve it.

Perpetual thanks to my wife, Kimberly, my Cassandra, my muse.

I am so grateful for Jeanette Windle for making this entire series so much better because of her loving editorial ruthlessness. Jeanette, your theological understanding, your life experience in missions, your own storytelling choices, and your expertise convince me that God providentially led me to you. I could not imagine a more perfect editor for this project to make it what it needed to become.

My deepest gratitude goes to my long-time friend and scholar Kenneth L. Gentry Jr. for allowing me the privilege of early access to his Revelation commentary *The Divorce of Israel*, which served as a scholarly guide to unveiling the complexities of this most fascinating of all New Testament books.

I cannot neglect to thank Gary DeMar, another long-time friend and scholar whose eschatological work continues to be a trumpet call of sanity in this generation of last days madness.

I would also like to thank my newer friend and scholar Michael S. Heiser, whose work on the divine council, the Watchers, and the Deuteronomy 32 worldview constitutes the other major influence on my interpretation of Revelation.

I believe I have made opposites attract. Christus Victor!

NOTE TO THE READER

Chronicles of the Apocalypse is a standalone series. But this book you are reading is not a standalone novel. It follows *Resistant: Revolt of the Jews* and concludes the series.

In another sense, *Chronicles of the Apocalypse* is the sequel to my Chronicles of the Nephilim series about the biblical Cosmic War of the Seed and the victory of Christ over the Powers. One need not read the previous Nephilim series to be able to understand this Apocalypse series, but the literary and theological connections run deep.

This is the story of the apostle John's writing of the Apocalypse during the time of the Roman Empire, the first major persecution of Christians, and the Jewish revolt of A.D. 66 that resulted in the destruction of Jerusalem and the temple in A.D. 70. My hope is that the ancient world in all its symbolic glory will come alive to the reader as you encounter the imagery in Revelation dramatically unveiled through its Old Testament and first-century literary lens.

I've included numbered endnotes for each chapter that provide detailed biblical and historical substantiation behind the fictional story. As it turns out, half of the text of this book is endnotes. This is my most heavily researched series of novels yet. Though using endnote numbers in a novel text is usually considered anathema, I chose to use them to provide biblical and historical context for those who want to "fact check" the eschatology and dig deeper.

I have tried to be as accurate as I can with the actual historical events and characters surrounding the Jewish revolt of A.D. 66 and the fall of Jerusalem in A.D. 70. However, there are many details we simply do not know with certainty because either the Bible or other historical sources are silent or because there is disagreement over the facts. Because of this, I had to take some creative license to fill in the gaps and simplify for easier reading. But I have tried to remain true to the spirit of the text if not to the letter.

CAST OF CHARACTERS

Some readers prefer to conjure pictures of what characters look like in their own imagination. But this is a sprawling epic with a lot of characters, so I wanted to help the reader keep all the characters straight in their minds as they read. See the color versions of these characters on the Chronicles of the Apocalypse website: http://wp.me/P6y1ub-1uH

I also have artwork of maps, paintings, and illustrations that relate to this story: http://wp.me/P6y1ub-1uJ

Brian Godawa
Author, *Chronicles of the Apocalypse*

MAPS

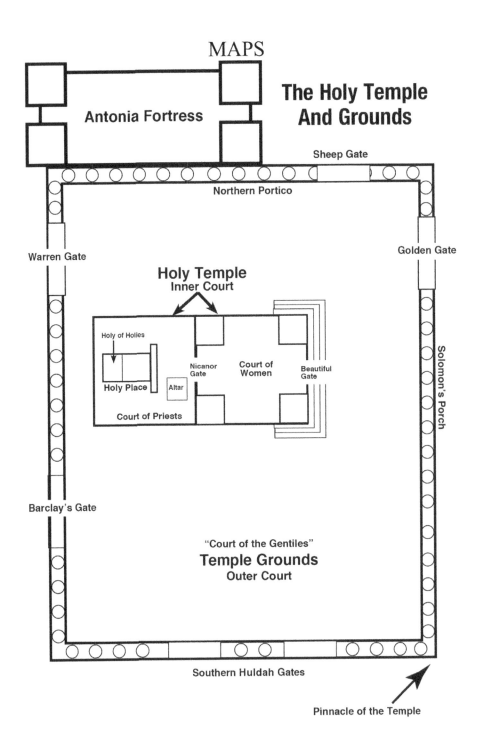

The Holy Temple And Grounds

Antonia Fortress

Sheep Gate

Northern Portico

Warren Gate

Golden Gate

Holy Temple
Inner Court

Holy of Holies

Holy Place

Altar

Nicanor Gate

Court of Women

Beautiful Gate

Court of Priests

Solomon's Porch

Barclay's Gate

"Court of the Gentiles"
Temple Grounds
Outer Court

Southern Huldah Gates

Pinnacle of the Temple

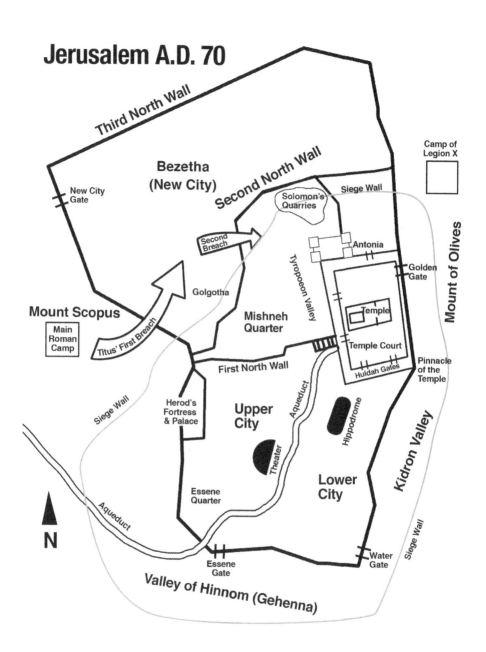

Jerusalem A.D. 70

Third North Wall

Bezetha
(New City)

Second North Wall

New City
Gate

Solomon's
Quarries

Siege Wall

Camp of
Legion X

Second
Breach

Antonia

Golden
Gate

Golgotha

Tyropoeon Valley

Temple

Mount of Olives

Mount Scopus

Main
Roman
Camp

Mishneh
Quarter

Titus' First Breach

First North Wall

Temple Court

Huldah Gates

Pinnacle
of the
Temple

Siege Wall

Herod's
Fortress
& Palace

Upper
City

Aqueduct

Theater

Hippodrome

Kidron Valley

Essene
Quarter

Lower
City

N

Aqueduct

Essene
Gate

Water
Gate

Siege Wall

Valley of Hinnom (Gehenna)

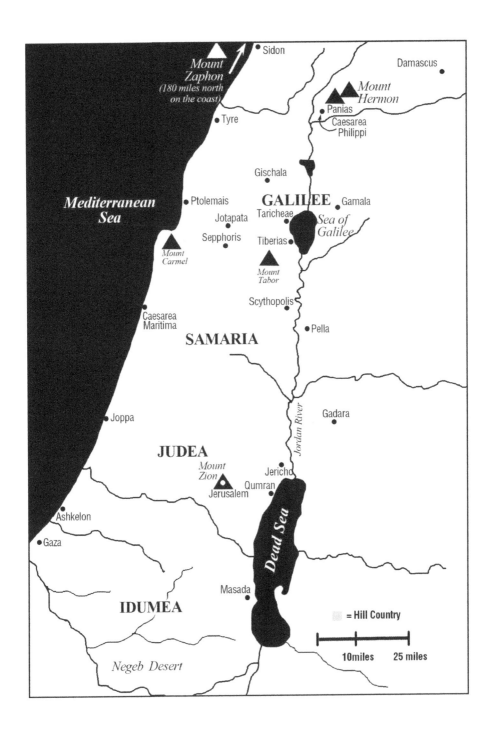

xii

*Aaron shall take the two goats and set them before Yahweh at the entrance of the tent of meeting. And Aaron shall cast lots over the two goats, one lot for Yahweh and the other lot for Azazel. And Aaron shall present the goat on which the lot fell for Yahweh and use it as a sin offering, but the goat on which the lot fell for Azazel shall be presented alive before Yahweh to make atonement over it, that it may be sent away **into the wilderness to Azazel**.*

Leviticus 16:7–10

And they assembled at the place that in Hebrew is called Armageddon.

– Apocalypse 16:16

PART ONE

Azazel

PROLOGUE

Year of the Four Emperors
AD 68 – 69

June, AD 68. Roman General Vespasian has subjugated Judea and its surrounding territories. He prepares to launch a final attack against Jerusalem.

In Rome, Nero Caesar loses control and commits suicide, ending the ancient Julio-Claudian line of Caesars and plunging the empire into chaos. The sixth head of the Beast is mortally wounded. Roman Governor Galba seizes the throne.[1]

Vespasian halts the Judean war and sends Titus to affirm allegiance to the new emperor. But Galba is toppled, and Titus returns to Judea with news of civil and political unrest.

Galba's reign of six months is overthrown by Otho, whose reign of three months is overthrown by General Vitellius. Many fear this is the end of the empire, the death of the Beast.[2]

But a prophecy well-known in the eastern provinces had predicted that the future ruler of the world would go forth from Judea, currently occupied by Vespasian.[3]

July AD 69. Vespasian is declared emperor by his troops. He reluctantly accepts and leaves for Egypt to secure Rome's food source before claiming the throne. The Beast is healed of its mortal wound.[4]

Vespasian leaves Titus in command of Judea with four Roman legions and ten client kings of the nations. These are the ten horns of the Beast.[5] Titus is given the title of Caesar and leads the Imperial forces as that Beast of Rome in the holy land.[6]

3

Jerusalem remains divided three ways in civil war. Simon bar Giora maintains military control of the city with personal plans of revenge against John of Gischala, who retains control of the outer temple complex.[7]

The fanatic Eleazar holds the inner temple hostage with his Zealot forces.

Winter delays the wolves of war. A pall of silence hangs over Judea.

When the Lamb opened the seventh seal, there was silence in heaven for about half an hour. Then I saw an angel came and stood at the altar with a golden censer, and he was given much incense to offer with the prayers of all the saints on the golden altar before the throne, and the smoke of the incense, with the prayers of the saints, rose before God from the hand of the angel. Then the angel took the censer and filled it with fire from the altar and threw it on the Land [of Israel], and there were peals of thunder, rumblings, flashes of lightning, and an earthquake.

Apocalypse 8:1-4

CHAPTER 1

Mount Hermon
December, AD 69

Apollyon, the Angel of the Abyss, sat brooding on his throne of stone in the cavernous mount of assembly in the heart of Hermon.

Seventy gods of the nations, called Watchers, and their divine allies surrounded him, awaiting his decision as he thought through his strategy for their next move. Winter would soon be over, and the armies of Rome, led by Flavius Titus, would finally be able to besiege Jerusalem.

The end of days was at hand.

Apollyon's four strongest angels had been hostages to Yahweh and were recently freed by the enemy at the River Euphrates. The four principalities stood before him now. He looked thoughtfully at each of them: Ares, the Greek god of war; Ba'al, the Canaanite storm god; Ahura Mazda, Persian high god; and Hubal, Nabatean chief of the Arabian deities. All of them were muscular, brutish, and ruthless, exactly what he needed in the patron gods of the Roman legions in order to achieve his purposes. Azazel, patron genius of Titus, stood at Apollyon's right side. Marduk, mighty Babylonian brawler, stood at his left.

Apollyon was the most powerful of all the Watcher gods. He had once been the satan of Yahweh's divine council, a prosecuting adversary. He was a master of the law, Torah. But he impressed himself with the clever irony of taking the visual form of an emaciated, greasy-haired, androgynous cadaver. An incarnation of death and the denial of God's created order.[1]

Apollyon had used that lawful order to his benefit. He had sued Yahweh in his heavenly court, thereby effecting the release of the four principalities and winning the right to punish the Jews based on Torah.

Serves him right, thought the Watcher. The tyrannical patron of Israel had written into the covenant curses for disobedience and was now having to suck it up and enforce those sanctions by punishing his own people seven-fold for their sins: plagues, war, and Apollyon's favorite curse of all—desolation of his house,

5

the holy temple in Jerusalem. It was the earthly incarnation of the covenant, and its desolation was proclaimed by the Nazarene Messiah as well.[2] So now Yahweh had to follow through and allow Apollyon's Gentile armies to fulfill that desolation and trample the Holy Place.

But his victory came at great cost to the Prince of the Power of the Air. A cost that made him boil with anger as he looked out upon his seventy principalities and powers, considering his next move. The great Despot in the Sky had placed a contingency upon the release of the demonic hostages. Apollyon first had to return the two hundred ancient ones that he had released from the Abyss. He had stolen the key to the Abyss from the Foundation Stone in the holy temple and had freed those bound Watchers from their imprisonment in Tartarus to help him accomplish his goal.

The two hundred were the original Sons of God who had rebelled against Yahweh and had come to earth on this cosmic mountain of Hermon. They had taught mankind forbidden knowledge and had violated the earthly-heavenly divide by mating with human women. Their progeny were the Nephilim, the Seed of the Serpent who would wage a war against the messianic Seed of the Woman, Eve. But those two hundred original rebels had been judged at the Flood and bound in Tartarus.[3]

When Apollyon had freed them, he'd also freed an army of two hundred million demons. He'd been forced to return the ancient ones to Tartarus, but not the demons. And those demons were under his control, ready to do his bidding. They filled the land like a plague of locusts, and the Angel of the Abyss was about to call upon them.[4]

But something bothered him like a splinter in his talons. Whenever Yahweh had judged Israel for her unfaithfulness in the past, he'd always protected a remnant for himself. That Remnant was the congregation of true believers. And he would use them like a small speck of leaven in a lump of dough to maintain his kingdom though all seemed lost.

When the antediluvian world was filled with violence, God had spared eight in the ark. When Elijah thought he was alone in contesting with Ba'al, God had spared seven thousand who had not bowed the knee to the Canaanite god. And while Yahweh destroyed the first temple by the hand of Nebuchadnezzar, he had protected Daniel and others in the furnace of fire that was the Babylonian exile.[5]

So where was this Remnant now? Yahweh had supernaturally obscured Apollyon's ability to find them. The Christians had left Jerusalem after Cestius Gallus first surrounded the city two years ago. They had done so in obedience to the Nazarene's warning to flee to the mountains. But where did they go? The highlands of Judea and Samaria or the mountains across the Jordan? Apollyon wanted more than just desolation of the holy house. He wanted to kill the Remnant, the spiritual woman who had given birth to the Messiah and his Gospel. Apollyon the dragon wanted to eat them in a victory feast before Yahweh's face.

But he had to find them first. And there was no one more familiar with the land of Israel than the Canaanite deities most beloved by the great harlot of apostate Israel.

Apollyon spoke up. "Molech and Asherah, scour the mountains on both sides of the Jordan and find me the Christians. Meet the rest of us at Caesarea Maritima. We will lead the Beast to war."

> The dragon who had been thrown down to the earth pursued the woman [Remnant Israel] who had given birth to the male child [Messiah]. But the woman was given the two wings of the great eagle so that she might fly from the serpent into the wilderness, to the place where she is to be nourished for a time, and times, and half a time [3-1/2 years].
>
> Apocalypse 12:13–14

CHAPTER 2

Alexandria, Egypt

Flavius Vespasian fought sleepiness as he waited for an answer from the god. This always happened whenever he engaged in religious ritual. He figured it was the boredom of unbelief. He only did what was required or what maintained proper public service. But he personally had a hard time believing in mysticism over good, hard earthly power and strength. He was a pragmatic man.

Of course, religion had its practical uses as well. The support of the priestly class assured the support of the masses who followed them with unthinking devotion.

Still, a small part of him wondered if there was something to the spiritual world. He had heard many testimonies of such things. He had even experienced some unexplainable oddities himself. Were all the stories of supernatural omens surrounding his own ascendancy to the throne mere self-delusion of believers, or was there something to them?

The Alexandrians had told him that when he arrived in their Egyptian city, the Nile had overflown, a sure omen. While Vespasian was eating on his country estate, an ox had approached him, knelt down, and placed its head beneath his feet. The general had thought nothing of it. He knew animals sometimes did strange things. But while he was still eating, a dog had come over and dropped a human hand beneath his table. A human hand! Vespasian had never found out where the animal had found the thing.

These oddities were not without confirmation. Many years ago, he'd had a dream of a large cypress tree being uprooted and then the next day standing upright again. Vespasian had thought this represented the fall of Tiberius and rise of Caligula. But an oracle had told the general it was his own imperial future. He'd dismissed such an idea at the time. But then he'd had another strange dream predicting that if Nero lost a tooth, Vespasian would become emperor. The next day, Nero had indeed lost a tooth. While Vespasian kept his dream to himself, Nero did not. He had told Vespasian of his own dream of driving Jupiter's chariot

8

to Vespasian's house. To protect himself from Nero's paranoia, Vespasian had laughed it off with a joke and never revealed his secret to the emperor.[1]

But that was not all. When Galba had claimed the throne of Rome, reports were that a statue of the deified Julius turned toward the East of its own accord. The East, where Vespasian was in his Judean campaign.

Even his Jewish "court prophet" Josephus had proclaimed that Vespasian would be the Messiah, come from the East as prophesied in the Jews' own scriptures.[2]

The general had brushed off such ramblings as self-interested flattery. But so many apparent omens were aligning to persuade him that he was wrong. Maybe the gods *were* choosing him precisely because he didn't want it. A bid for impartial justice.[3]

Then last July, after the quick succession of short-lived emperors threatened to collapse the empire, his own soldiers and the military had forced Vespasian at the point of a blade to accept their proclamation of him as emperor. He reluctantly saw the practicality of his military experience in bringing order to the chaos that was collapsing Rome.

Vespasian was currently waiting to receive official approval from the Roman senate to accept his bid for the throne. He had actually disdained such imperial ambitions for years because of his lack of desire for such aristocratic indulgence. He preferred to live out the rest of his life in leisure, drinking wine, eating pig, and making love to his mistress, not political posturing or saving the asses of the entitled ingrates of nobility. He knew he was a boor and was proud of it.

Vespasian glanced around the empty sanctuary of the Serapeum, a temple to Serapis, the hybrid Greco-Egyptian god of the underworld. The architecture was a mixture of Greek and Egyptian styles, functioning much like the deity as a diplomatic unity between the two worlds. He stood in a semi-circular Holy Place with Corinthian-style columns and a square stone altar on the proscenium platform up front with Vespasian's goat sacrifice lying dead upon it. The atrium square outside was lined with red stone obelisks, common in Egyptian occultism.

Vespasian rubbed his eyes and scratched his balding head. Architecture bored him as well. He felt his hefty stomach grumble with hunger. The thought of savoring good meat and wine awakened him more. Then his thoughts drifted to his mistress, Caenis, and he began to fantasize other sensual delights.

A movement to his left drew his attention. A priest approached him from the darkness. These temples all seemed to relish darkness in their sanctuaries. It helped manipulate the emotions.

9

The priest was carrying sacred cakes, garlands, and a bough. When he arrived to hand them to Vespasian as an offering, the legate was shocked to see who it was.

"Basilides?" he said with incredulity. Basilides was the oracle on Mount Carmel in Palestine hundreds of miles away. Vespasian had visited the oracle when he first mustered his forces on the coast of that infernal land.

"Basilides? How on earth did you get here?"

But the oracle would not speak. He simply dissolved back into the darkness. Which was another apparent "miracle" because Basilides had grown old with rheumatism and was unable to walk.

Before he was able to gain his wits, Vespasian noticed someone in the shadows before the altar.

Some *thing* in the shadows.

It looked like the creature was sucking the blood from the neck of the sacrifice. The *thing* stopped and looked at Vespasian. Its glowing lapis lazuli eyes sent a chill down the Roman general's spine.

The creature stood up. It was large, about eight feet tall. And muscular. As a light from a slit window fell across it, Vespasian realized the creature was Serapis, the underworld god. Though the god wore an Egyptian robe and ornaments, he looked Greek with a head of curly hair and Herculean facial structure.[4]

Vespasian found himself out of breath. He bowed to one knee, groaning with his old age, and whispered, "My Lord Serapis. What is your will?"

The deity remained silent for a moment before speaking. "A new god rules. A new dynasty heals Rome." Then he dissolved back into the shadows before Vespasian could question him.

Just like these phantom daemons to speak in riddles and mysteries without explaining them! The ambiguity and uncertain nature of religion annoyed Vespasian. Why could they not just speak plainly? Why must everything be shrouded in mysterious and confusing words? What new god was Serapis talking about? Egyptian? Roman? The sheer number of gods was ludicrous.

He was interrupted by Roman governor Tiberius Julius Alexander entering the room, followed by a group of six priests of Serapis in long-flowing red robes.

Tiberius, a formal military general, bowed and handed Vespasian a senatorial dispatch from Rome.

Vespasian read it. It was short, to the point. And life-changing.

"Well," said Vespasian. "It appears the senate has formally recognized me as emperor."

Tiberius and the priests immediately bowed their heads and went down on one knee. With hand out and palm down, Tiberius said, "Hail Caesar, Lord and Savior."

The priests whispered prayers that sounded like gibberish to Vespasian.

Only then did it strike the general: the cakes brought by Basilides along with the royal bough and garlands—those were a herald of kingship.

The words of Serapis, "A new god rules," must mean that Vespasian was the new god, since Caesar was a god. And his family would be the "dynasty that heals Rome."

Perhaps this religious stuff wasn't so mysterious after all. Perhaps there was something to it.

"Caesar," said Tiberius, "we must present you to the people of Alexandria."

Semyaza and Serapis followed their priests as they led the fat, bald vulgarian king and his toady governor out of the temple into the streets. Serapis had allowed Semyaza's human liege the opportunity to see him for that brief moment at the altar. But now the two gods moved in the unseen realm, invisible to and unheard by the human throngs that filled Alexandria's busy streets.

The Herculean Serapis announced to Semyaza, "I cannot stay. Apollyon wants me to return for my legion in Palestine."

Semyaza didn't bother to respond. He was too angry with his misfortune of being stuck in Alexandria with his oaf of a ruler while Azazel got to plunder the holy land.

Serapis left him and continued to follow Vespasian's escort to their destination in the middle of the city. Semyaza heard trumpets of announcement throughout the city calling the populace to a gathering.

Semyaza had been released from the Abyss with his co-general Azazel. The two of them had been allowed to become the geniuses, or patron deities, of the Flavian father and son. Because of their special appointments, they'd avoided confinement in Tartarus with the others.

At first Semyaza had been satisfied with his guardianship, thinking that Vespasian would be the next Caesar, which would make Semyaza more powerful than Azazel, genius of Titus. But when it became apparent that Vespasian would have to leave Palestine and focus his efforts on taking the throne, Semyaza had realized that Azazel had the much greater assignment. For Titus would be the anointed prince to bring desolation on the wing of abominations to Israel. Titus would receive the greater glory and greater legacy than his father. Azazel would once again best Semyaza in his achievements.

And the fact that father and son were now split up, along with their geniuses, meant that Semyaza and Azazel could not be together to achieve the coup they had planned to spring upon Apollyon during Armageddon. Semyaza had not yet figured out a way to ditch his human and make his way secretly to Jerusalem in time for the end of days.

Semyaza followed Vespasian's entourage into the hippodrome at the center of the city. It was filled with Egyptian citizens awaiting the grand announcement. Semyaza noticed how surprised Vespasian was at the reception. The dull-minded fool. The Roman general knew how to fight a war, but he had no awareness of the civilian world around him.

The Watcher followed the entourage up to a stage in the middle of the stadium, grumbling at the exaltation he was supposed to give the obese old fart of a Caesar.

Vespasian looked out onto the crowds amassed in the hippodrome for his announcement. He was stunned by it all. They had cheered him when he arrived, and he began to feel the excitement of being worshipped.

A priest of Serapis leaned near him and said, "My Lord, we are bringing you some people with infirmities. Just follow along and extend your hand to heal them."

Vespasian looked at the priest, shocked. "What do you mean? I am no miracle worker."

"Today you are, my Lord. It is part of your confirmation. Trust me. Play the part, and they will be healed."

Vespasian sighed. "All right. Get on with it."

He looked out onto the masses, their gullible excitement pathetic to him. But he knew his responsibility for political pandering was only beginning. It made his stomach turn.

Some priests led two men out onto the stage and up to Vespasian. The first one had a crippled hand, bent up into an excruciating crooked position.

Vespasian heard the crowd cheer. He asked the priest, "Do they know this man?"

"Oh, yes, my lord," the priest responded. "Both of these men are well known for years as beggars in the city."

That meant their disabilities were not faked. Unless they had pretended for years? Vespasian shuddered. What had he gotten himself into?

The priest made the crippled man kneel down and place his hand at Vespasian's foot.

"Step on the hand, my lord."

The general hesitated. Wouldn't such an action crush the already crippled hand? Seeing Vespasian's reluctance, the priest reassured, "Just gently, my lord."

Vespasian shrugged and stepped lightly on the man's hand. When he pulled back his foot, the man's hand was normal!

Vespasian was shocked. What was this? The man at his feet couldn't possibly have faked the contortion in which those bones had been.

The priest presented the man's hand to the crowd, and they burst out in massive cheering. That was when Vespasian remembered the dog that had brought a human hand to his table. Was this the meaning of that bizarre omen?

Another priest led a second man up to Vespasian. This man's eyes were clouded over with blindness. The blind man's face grinned in excited anticipation. He muttered, "My Lord, Caesar."

The priest said to Vespasian, "My Lord, if you spit into your hands and moisten this blind man's eyes, he will be healed."

This was getting ridiculous! Where would the priest get such a preposterous idea? Spittle on the eyes? It reeked of theater.

But, of course, theater was what was needed to move the masses. Spitting into his hands, Vespasian wiped the spittle onto the blind man's eyes. The man opened his eyes. The cloudiness was gone.

"I can see! I can see!" the man yelled loud enough for the crowds to hear him. The crowd burst out into an even stronger applause.

Vespasian couldn't believe his eyes. He had seen the man was truly blind. And now he was truly seeing. Vespasian looked at his own hands with shock. *Am I a god?*

The ovation of praise lowered just enough for the priest to stand forward, gesture to Vespasian, and announce loudly, "Behold, the son of Amun-Ra!"

Vespasian would not have thought the crowd could be more out of control. But now they rose to even greater heights of adulation. He'd experienced the feeling of power when destroying an enemy in battle, but this was a different kind of power. It was like nothing Vespasian had ever felt before.

He felt like a god.[5]

Titus was right! After all this time I fought against him, he was right. I will create a new dynasty of Caesars. The Flavians will rule the world. A family of gods.

The cheering crowd drowned his own thoughts in a whirlpool of worship.

Semyaza sighed with disgust. These humans were such puppets. The cripple and the blind fool had been bound by demons. Semyaza had merely put the demons to sleep for a while, which made it look as though the two men had been healed. But the demons would return once the citizenry had moved back into their normal lives. By then it wouldn't matter anymore because the public had such a short memory. They were the easiest thing to manipulate with lies.

Now, thought the Watcher, *If I can only find some excuse to get out of here and return to Palestine.*

CHAPTER 3

Pella
April, AD 70

Cassandra held her year-old infant Samuel in her arms as she watched her ten-year-old adopted son Noah, sparring swords with Michael, the captain of the Kharabu warriors, in the valley just outside the city. The young boy had become quite the swordsman thanks to the help of Michael, who was training the city's males in self-defense. The Roman war with the Jews had not yet found them in their refuge, safely tucked away in the Transjordan mountains.

But the war was not over yet.

The Kharabu were an elite fighting force of forty men, mostly ex-legionaries-cum-Christians, who watched over Pella like sentinels. They had been trained in an ancient form of battle allegedly used by the Cherubim to guard Eden. The Pellans joked about the Kharabu being guardian angels because when they fought, they seemed to glide and float like dancers rather than brute soldiers. And they were virtually unbeatable.

But Cassandra no longer joked with the rest. She had seen what others had not, and she now strongly suspected that the seven captains of the Kharabu were in fact angels.

For one, all seven had the names of archangels from Scripture, like Michael and Gabriel. Such names weren't unusual for Jewish males. But that was only one of many strange coincidences that had led Cassandra to conclude Michael and the six others were *not* earthly beings.

She had seen Michael brutally beaten by a group of bandits and come out without a scratch or bruise. She had seen the seven fight with effortlessness against other warriors. The skills of those seven far surpassed their other Kharabu comrades. There was something more to these captains.

She had also seen Michael engage in long conversations with Moshe and Elihu, the Two Witnesses of the Apocalypse that were specially protected by God in the midst of this time of "Jacob's Trouble." And she knew what the prophet

15

Daniel had foretold regarding Michael the archangel arising to protect God's people at the end of days.

> *"At that time shall arise Michael, the great prince who has charge of your people. And there shall be a time of trouble, such as never has been since there was a nation till that time. But at that time your people shall be delivered, everyone whose name shall be found written in the book."*
>
> *Daniel 12:1*

Christians had escaped Jerusalem and other surrounding cities in obedience to Jesus's words to flee to the mountains. They had gathered in this hidden city that had been destroyed by civil war and rebuilt. They were the Remnant of 144,000 that God had sealed to protect from the judgment coming upon the Jews and their holy city.[1]

Cassandra believed this. But it bothered her that she was safe and protected out here in the mountains while her beloved Alexander was in Jerusalem sacrificing himself for the sake of the Gospel.

"Mother, you're not listening to me."

The voice brought Cassandra out of her thoughts. It was her fifteen-year-old adopted daughter Rachel, sister of Noah. The brother and sister had been among hundreds of orphaned child refugees arriving at Jerusalem a couple years ago from cities destroyed by the Romans. The brother and sister had captured Alexander's and Cassandra's hearts, and once she and the children had arrived at Pella, Cassandra had carried out the couple's plan to adopt the two siblings.

Adoption was a beautiful family experience that reflected God's own heart. Unfortunately, the moment of joy had not lasted long as raising a family of three children alone seemed harder to Cassandra than helping Alexander deal with plague, sickness, and war wounds in Jerusalem.

"What do you mean I'm not listening?" Cassandra asked. "What did you say?"

"I asked you why I cannot go for a simple chaperoned walk with Jonathan."

"I've told you a hundred times," said Cassandra, "this is not the time to consider such things."

"Mother, I'm fifteen years old. If I wait any longer, I'll be an old maid. And what is wrong with Jonathan? He's seventeen, strong, trained in battle, and respects you more than I do."

"Watch your tongue, young lady." Cassandra felt Samuel squirm in her arms. As she rocked him back to slumber, she eyed her adopted daughter. Rachel had matured into a beautiful young lady, a far change from when Cassandra had first met the young girl. Escaping her pillaged city, Rachel had pretended to be a boy to avoid being discovered by men and abused in the midst of war. It was a tragedy countless women had to suffer. Many could not endure it and killed themselves from the shame.

Cassandra had coaxed Rachel out of her shyness and distrust of men, but now she almost regretted it. Her daughter was clearly enamored with this young man Jonathan. And his father had already tried to speak with Cassandra about an arrangement for marriage. Cassandra had put him off under the pretense that she and Rachel's father had to discuss it through long-distance letters. That was only half true. She was avoiding that as well.

Still, Jonathan was a good one. Cassandra had no complaints. Except one. And she voiced it to Rachel. "Rome is still at war with Judea. We are safe for now. But the final battle is coming upon Jerusalem."

"But we're not in Jerusalem," Rachel argued. "We're hidden in the mountains. And protected by the Kharabu."

"Yes. For now. But there is more to come our way, and we must prepare to face greater danger."

"Mother, you keep saying that, but what do you mean? How do you know more will come our way?"

Cassandra had been keeping it from Rachel and Noah. She didn't want them overcome with fear. But the moment of frustration pulled it out of her. "Because the Apocalypse says it will."

Rachel stopped, dumbfounded. She knew about the Apocalypse. Cassandra had told both siblings of her journey with Alexander to find the subversive letter that predicted the end of their world and the coming judgment. They had heard the letter read to the congregation by the lector. But not everything had been explained to the congregation's children.

Still, as Rachel had pointed out, Cassandra's adopted daughter was no longer a child but a young woman and had earned the right to hear the truth. So Cassandra answered by quoting the Apocalypse itself. "And when the dragon saw that he had been thrown down to the land, he pursued the woman who had given birth to the male child."[2]

17

She stopped. She finally had Rachel's attention. "I've explained to you that the dragon is the devil, the serpent, and the woman is the Remnant of true Israel that gave birth to Jesus the Messiah."

"Yes," said Rachel.

Cassandra continued quoting from memory. "'But the woman was given the two wings of the great eagle so that she might fly from the serpent into the wilderness, to the place where she is to be nourished for a time, and times, and half a time.' That's three-and-a-half years."[3]

As Rachel nodded her comprehension, Cassandra continued, "When Rome surrounded Jerusalem, we fled the city, just as Jesus told us to do. That was three-and-a-half years ago."

Cassandra glanced down at her infant son, not wishing to continue. But she did. "'The dragon became furious with the woman and went off to make war on the rest of her offspring, on those who keep the commandments of God and hold to the testimony of Jesus.'"[4]

Rachel was now dead silent. Only the distant sound of clacking swords could be heard in the wind. The girl watched the mock battle between Noah and Michael with an apparent new understanding. A frightful one.

"The devil is not done with us yet," Cassandra said. "And what will you do if you start a family and your new husband is killed in the war with the dragon?"

Rachel's expression turned from fearful to firm. "But you married father during the Great Tribulation." She had picked up a lot of determination from her adoptive mother.

Cassandra answered, "I did so to help him in his ministry, fully expecting that we would both die."

"But you're both still alive."

"Yes. And look at how difficult it is to raise a family without a father. Is that what you want—to raise a family alone?"

"Father is not dead."

"No. But we must accept the inevitable, daughter. He has sacrificed himself for the Gospel, and we cannot be sure he will return. We know that Jerusalem will fall to the Romans, and they have not always been merciful."

"Is that why you're planning to leave us and go to Jerusalem? To die with him?"

Cassandra froze in shock, her eyes widening. After an awkward moment of silence, she demanded, "Where did you hear that?"

"I'm not a moron, mother. I told you, I'm fifteen. I listen. I hear your prayers when you think you are alone."

Cassandra felt trapped by her own words. She had prayed about returning to Jerusalem. About God protecting her children and all the city's orphans whose guardian she had become.

The Kharabu would surely protect them despite the danger.

Rachel's eyes welled up with tears. "Do you not love us, mother?"

Cassandra stood immediately and reached out for her daughter with her free arm. "Rachel, of course I love you with all my heart."

Little Samuel chose that moment to begin squirming again, and Cassandra tightened her one-armed grip on him as she whispered into Rachel's ear, "I would never leave you without protection."

Rachel pulled away from her. "But you would leave us?"

Cassandra's lack of answer appeared to be all the answer Rachel needed. Spinning around, the young girl stormed downhill toward Noah and Michael, still practicing with swords.

Cassandra watched her with sadness. She could not deny her own conflicted feelings for the kingdom of God. Or that her love of family had brought upon her the very grief she'd feared when confronted with the call to sacrifice.

The apostle Paul had warned of this, and now she was experiencing it fully. She had indeed been talking to some of her most reliable friends in the city, preparing to have them watch over her children. They would also be in the protective custody of the Kharabu. But despite her certainty that Rachel, Noah, and little Samuel would be in safe hands, despite the fact that she truly did love her children more than life itself, she still felt guilty that she was willing to leave them in such a time of great peril. What kind of a mother would do such a thing?

Perhaps a mother who felt like a failure in everything she had tried to do for God's kingdom. Or perhaps a wife who felt that she had betrayed her marriage covenant by fleeing to safety and leaving her husband to face life-threatening danger alone. But wasn't leaving her children alone just as bad a betrayal? It seemed no matter what she did, she was leaving loved ones in danger.

Maybe her desire to walk back into the arena of death was her attempt to share the sufferings of Christ like her mentor, the apostle Paul.

Whatever the case, Cassandra felt terrible for not telling Alexander about her intentions to join him in Jerusalem. She knew he would not approve, so she planned to show up and deal with his disappointment at that time. It would be easier to ask for forgiveness than permission.

Down the hill, Rachel had stopped to watch the sparring. Samuel had gone back to sleep. Sinking back down to a crossed-legged position, Cassandra placed her son gently on her lap and pulled out a letter to read.

It was from Alexander. They had written each other regularly over the past year-and-a-half of separation. She cherished every single communication she received from him as sacred. This one was the latest from a month ago. She had read it a dozen times.

> *Alexander, to my dear beloved Cassandra,*
>
> *Grace and peace to you from God our Father and the Lord Jesus Christ.*
>
> *I always thank God when I pray for you and when I think of your love that he has allowed me to experience for a short time on this earth. Our two years of marriage before you left for Pella was the happiest I have ever been in my life. Though we faced the dangers of plague, sickness, and war, we had done so together. And I was never more content than facing it all with you by my side.*
>
> *But God has seen fit to separate us for his purposes. If he chooses to preserve my life through this time of judgment, I will return to you with the most desperate of desire. But if he does not, please know that you have made my suffering more joyous to face.*
>
> *Your love has helped me to understand the love of God in an earthly way. Your zeal for the kingdom has inspired me in times of weakness. I will die with thanks on my lips for the opportunity to have met you and to have enjoyed the privilege of loving you. For without you in my life, I may never have found my Savior.*
>
> *Pray for me as I labor in the city and for the work of the Two Witnesses. And pray for the Christians who are still suffering in the mines at the hands of Jacob.*
>
> *The grace of the Lord Jesus Christ be with you. Send my greetings to Michael and Gabriel and the others. And give my warmest of love to our children, Rachel, Noah, and little Samuel. How I long to meet my infant son for the first time. I love you and miss you with all my heart.*
>
> *Your beloved husband and brother in Christ.*

Wiping tears from her eyes, Cassandra noticed Noah and Michael were done with their practice. They headed uphill along with Rachel. By Noah's untroubled expression, Rachel had not shared their recent discussion with her younger brother. She was acting with more maturity than Cassandra had given her credit.

Was Cassandra making the right choices in her parenting? Was she forcing her own convictions upon her daughter? What if she was wrong?

Just then Cassandra noticed Boaz, the church elder in charge of the Pella congregation, approaching. His elderly frame of over sixty years walked with an unsteady gait.

As he reached Cassandra, he sighed. "I need to take walks to keep my health so I can live to fight this blasphemous heresy of Symeon and his Ebionites."

Michael and her children arrived in time to catch the church elder's words. Cassandra shared a concerned glance with the Kharabu captain as Boaz continued, "I have called a council to deal with the trouble. We can no longer allow them to teach their damnable doctrines in Pella. They are growing dangerously large and upsetting the faith of many with their false Gospel. We must stop them. And I wanted you to be at the council because of your work with the apostle Paul. We need influential voices to counter their lies."

The Ebionites were a contingent of apparent believers who had followed Boaz and the other Christian refugees from Jerusalem to Pella. At first, they'd been a minority residual voice of the Judaizers who'd remained behind. But they had grown to well over a thousand followers. Thank God none of them were elders in the congregation, but their influence was growing.

The Ebionites took their name from the Hebrew word for "poor" and gloried in their pride of poverty as if it were a sign of superior spirituality. They were vegetarians and pacifists who argued against Pella's preparation for self-defense. Most egregious to Cassandra was their denial of the deity of Christ. This alone made them worthy of condemnation and expulsion from the congregation.[5]

Cassandra had despaired that such demonic influence was already plaguing the Christians of Pella. The body of Christ was trying to gather itself together after being almost wiped out by the Great Tribulation. Now they had this spreading cancer trying to wipe them out from within. Even worse, the Ebionites' intent was to become a majority and seize control of the *ekklesia*, or church.

But then again, Jude had warned the church of this very thing. He had said that in the last days there would be scoffers who followed their own ungodly passions. Such worldly people were devoid of the Spirit, perverting the grace of God into sensuality, denying their only Master and Lord Jesus Christ, and causing divisions. That was why Jude had exhorted true believers to contend earnestly for the faith.[6]

Boaz was right. The Ebionites had to be countered. They had to be stopped. Such a battle would delay Cassandra's intentions of getting to Jerusalem. But she owed it to Boaz and the congregation. She owed it to the people who had saved her life and given her a new home where she could raise her children in the Lord.

Cassandra looked down at her precious little Samuel. She owed it to her son, to protect his future. She had to fight for the souls of her people. She had to continue suffering separation from and longing for her beloved.

At least for now.

She returned home to write a letter to her husband.

CHAPTER 4

Jerusalem

Alexander Maccabaeus stood in a small crowd, listening to the Two Witnesses preaching near Golgotha, the "Place of the Skull." It was the location where Jesus had been crucified a generation ago. It had been outside the city walls at the time but was now within the more recently-built second and third walls that encompassed the New City as well. The crowd was several hundred people on the rocky terrain.

The prophetic Witnesses, Moshe and Elihu, had been preaching repentance and judgment to the people of Jerusalem for over three years now. The Apocalypse had foretold that their ministry would be 1,260 days, or three-and-a-half years. The time of the end was near. The Lord was at the door.

Listening to them was one of the ways in which Alexander dealt with his lonely longing for his wife Cassandra. They had been separated for almost a year-and-a-half now, and he missed her deeply. She had fled the city with several hundred orphans of war they had taken under their wing. She had brought the children safely to Pella, where she now raised their own family of Rachel, Noah, and his year-old son Samuel, whom Alexander had never met. His eyes teared up just thinking of them.

Their only interaction was through letters, which he treasured like gold and even carried with him to re-read over and over until the next one came. Hearing the Word of God from the Witnesses at least took Alexander's mind off his loneliness and kept it on God's kingdom and his purpose for being here. He had been called as a doctor to minister to the sick and wounded Jews of the city with the intent of saving as many of them as possible from the wrath to come. Dozens had become followers of Jesus. Some of those had stayed to help him with his work while others had fled Jerusalem to the city of Pella in the Transjordan where his family was safely hidden. He would try to get all of God's elect out of the city before the final battle.

Alexander turned his attention back to the Witnesses. The city had grown weary of their message of judgment, so their audience would normally be a much smaller crowd. But Passover was upon them, bringing thousands of Jews from all over the empire to Jerusalem, most of them less familiar with the Witnesses and therefore more curious. These faithful pilgrims came even though Rome's legions had devastated the land and would soon move on Jerusalem. They believed that they were safe behind the walls of God's holy city. That Yahweh would protect them, especially during their holy feasts of obligation.

Alexander thought of them as captive objects of wrath, just as Jesus had foretold. He also knew that his ministry as a doctor to the sick and wounded was about to become overwhelming. He prayed God would provide help and resources.

As the crowd listened to the Witnesses, many scoffers mocked them saying, "Where is the promise of his coming?" They shouted accusations and blasphemy, claiming that ever since the fathers had fallen asleep, everything continued on as it had since the creation of the covenant.

It had been forty years since Jesus pronounced the destruction of the city and temple. But the stones of the temple were still upon one another, leading many to view Jesus as a false prophet. But the generation to whom Jesus spoke these words had not passed away. No, the day of the Lord was near. And it would come like a thief upon these unprepared fools.[1]

In the same way that the cosmos of Noah's day was destroyed by water, so the present cosmos, the heavens and earth of the Mosaic covenant, was being kept for the judgment of fire. The *stoichea*, the temple and its elements of the old covenant, were about to be burned up and dissolved with that old covenant. The new heavens and earth of the new covenant were going to be consummated in its coming that had been inaugurated with the blood of Jesus on the cross—the blood of the Passover Lamb.[2]

That was the message the Witnesses were now preaching. The Feast of Passover prefigured the Messiah who led a new Exodus like that out of Egypt. Moshe, an elderly white-bearded man nearing seventy wearing only a sackcloth of mourning, had been retelling the story of the Passover from the Torah.

God was bringing upon the Egyptians the last of the ten plagues—a threat to Pharaoh that God would kill all the firstborn in the land. But he'd given the Jews a way out of the judgment—the feast of Passover. Each family was instructed to kill an unblemished lamb and spread its blood over the doorposts of their homes. When the Destroyer came to kill the firstborn, he passed over the houses of the

Jews marked by the Passover lamb's blood. They were covered and protected from death.

Elihu, a handsome dark-skinned Egyptian half Moshe's age and also dressed in sackcloth, now took over, proclaiming to the crowd, "Jesus is the fulfillment of the Passover Feast. Jesus fulfills all the feasts of Israel, for he is Messiah. And Messiah is the final goal of Torah and all its elements."[3]

A heckler in the crowd shouted out, "You speak against Torah! You deny its authority!"

"No," replied Elihu. "The Torah is a mere shadow of authority. Its feasts and obligations are shadows. The very temple and its elements are shadows. Messiah is the reality. Messiah entered the true temple in heaven with his blood. Jesus was sacrificed on the fourteenth of Nisan at the exact time and exact hour of the Passover lamb."[4]

Moshe took over for Elihu. "Hear then the words of the prophet Isaiah about Messiah as the Lamb of God who takes away the sin of the world: 'He was oppressed, and he was afflicted, yet he opened not his mouth. Like a lamb that is led to the slaughter, so he opened not his mouth.

"'He was despised and rejected by men, a man of sorrows and acquainted with grief. He was despised, and we esteemed him not. Surely, he has borne our griefs and carried our sorrows, yet we esteemed him stricken, smitten by God, and afflicted. But he was pierced for our transgressions. He was crushed for our iniquities. Upon him was the chastisement that brought us peace, and with his wounds we are healed. All we like sheep have gone astray. We have turned— every one—to his own way, and Yahweh has laid on him the iniquity of us all.'"[5]

Moshe stopped to let his words sink in. The feasts of Israel were all known to herald the Messiah. By claiming that Jesus fulfilled all the feasts, the Witnesses were claiming that the messianic "age to come" had arrived.[6] Many Jewish leaders of the Great Revolt, whose gangs remained hidden in the wilderness, were claiming to be Messiah rising up to save the nation of Israel. But Jesus was Isaiah's suffering Servant who would save his people from their own sin and usher in a spiritual, heavenly kingdom, not an earthly kingdom through military force. It was something only a remnant of Jews could accept. The majority of them could not. And so they would die in the flames of God's judgment.

Retreating into an alley out of sight of the crowd, Alexander left a small burlap sack with food in it for the Two Witnesses in a hidden location beneath some rocks, as had been secretly arranged in advance. Because of their holy mission, Moshe and Elihu were widely hated, but no one touched them, not even soldiers. Some had claimed they saw invisible guardian angels protecting them. Others had tried to hurt them but were killed in strange circumstances.

Alexander knew God was protecting the Two Witnesses because they were serving as God's legal prosecutors. They were the representation of the Law and the Prophets that witnessed to Israel's unfaithfulness to her husband, Yahweh. Theirs was the heavenly testimony that would justify the capital punishment of Israel as a spiritual harlot. Two witnesses.

If anyone knew that Alexander was helping Moshe and Elihu, they would no doubt hand him over to the authorities to be tortured and executed. He did not have God's guarantee of protection as did the Two Witnesses. So Alexander kept his service a secret.

Alexander was walking back to the hippodrome, where he had established a makeshift hospital for the city's sick and wounded, when he caught sight of a man emerging at a full run from the front entrance of the hippodrome. As the man drew closer, Alexander recognized him as one of his Christian assistants. The doctor had only a handful of such helpers from the brethren these days because that despicable Jacob ben Mordecai had manipulated the Sanhedrin to force the Christians into conscripted labor in the rock mines.

Jacob was an apostate from the Christian faith, and because he was in authority over Alexander's hospital, he sought every way he could to make Alexander and the Christians suffer. In addition to eliminating most of Alexander's assistants, he had also cut back on resources for the sick and wounded. But the heretic's most egregious attack on Alexander had been his attempted rape of Alexander's wife Cassandra. Alexander had stopped him and beaten him bloody in her defense. Cassandra had not pressed charges in exchange for more resources for the sick. But that advantage had soon withered, so it was good that Cassandra had left the city.

Alexander knew that Jacob was intent on not allowing him to ever see Cassandra again. What Jacob could not have, he would seek to destroy.

Spotting Alexander, the running man skidded to a stop and gasped out, "Alexander, thank God you are here! I was coming to find you. We just received news. There's been a cave-in at the mines. Our brethren..."

He didn't have to finish the sentence. Alexander knew. And he dreaded what he would find.

CHAPTER 5

The mines were in the northern part of the city. Alexander ran so hard that his lungs were burning like fire by the time he reached them. A large tent had been erected outside the mine entrance, and through its thin walls Alexander could hear moans of pain and cries for help. He entered to find dozens of victims of the cave-in lying on mats and tables. These were no strangers, but people he knew, Christians who had helped him in the hippodrome.

Blood was everywhere as were crushed legs and arms. These poor men were reaping the consequences of Jacob deliberately sending the Christians to the most dangerous part of the mine.

An on-site doctor was already there overseeing the victims. He said to Alexander, "I have them stabilized. I'll need your help with surgery, but there's one still trapped in the mine. They can't get him out."

"I'll be right back." Emerging from the tent, Alexander broke into a run toward the mine entrance. Inside, he found his way lit by torches. The tunnel was a good thirty feet wide. He passed miners who were waiting for the dust to settle before returning to work. The tunnel eventually opened up into a larger area where the quarrying of limestone was performed.

By now Alexander was several hundred feet in and perhaps a hundred feet below the surface. The further he advanced, the thicker became the dust in the air. Coughing, Alexander pulled his tunic up over his mouth to filter out the dust. Eyes watering, he spotted a large pile of rubble where the cave roof had collapsed. Several miners showed him over to a single worker still trapped beneath a large rock.

Alexander recognized the young man as one of the Christians who had assisted him in the hippodrome. He knelt down on the ground next to the pinned miner. "Brother Daniel."

"Alexander," Daniel responded with difficulty. "How are you today?"

Alexander forced a smile in response to the young man's courageous attempt at humor. "I'm fine."

Daniel let out a groan before gasping, "I'm doing better than you. I'm about to meet Jesus face-to-face."

The young miner's legs and lower torso were crushed beneath the large rock. He was not going to live much longer. Blood was soaking the dirt beneath him.

Alexander fought back tears as he responded, "Daniel, you are a brave man. And you have been a model of Jesus to everyone around you. Thank you for your service and for your example."

"Did the others get to safety?" Daniel asked.

"Yes, they did. We're going to help them."

Daniel grunted in pain, then asked, "Would you pray with me, brother?"

"Of course." Alexander placed his hand on Daniel's shoulder, closed his eyes, and prayed, "Heavenly Father, thank you for saving Daniel from his sins and for the Holy Spirit who is the guarantee of our inheritance. Receive him into your presence. We look forward to the Resurrection and our glorified bodies that will be like Messiah's."

He opened his eyes. Daniel was dead.

Alexander remained kneeling for a few moments in silence before making his way back out of the tunnel.

When he arrived back at the tent, Alexander approached the resident physician and received a report on what surgeries were needed. The two doctors split them up, taking the worst cases first. Only a handful of doctors remained in Jerusalem, and with his Roman military background Alexander was easily the most experienced. His work at the hippodrome had garnered him a reputation of greatest respect among the other physicians, and each helped the others where they could.

Alexander began work on a miner whose left leg was completely crushed. It would have to be amputated. Many others would be crippled by lame arms or legs. He was still examining the patient when a man in his early fifties, somewhat tall and thin with a balding head, entered the tent. Jacob ben Mordecai, Alexander recognized sourly.

"For God's sake, another cave-in?" Jacob's tone held such contempt Alexander wanted to slug him. "I cannot afford this. I am losing too many laborers."

Alexander held his temper firmly in check as he asked peaceably, "May I speak with you after I've completed the surgeries?"

"If you think I have the time to stand around waiting for you, you are mistaken!" Jacob replied. "Come to my home when you're done here."

"Thank you." Returning to his patient, Alexander prepared a bone saw. Two people held the injured man down. A reed had been placed in his mouth to bite down on, and he had been chewing on opium leaves to help with the pain. But these measures would be of minimal help for the trauma of having his leg sawn off.

As an imperial physician in the Roman legions, Alexander had a lot of experience with these kind of surgeries. Over the years he'd worked on soldiers from battlefields with every kind of wound one could imagine. He had seen it all from gashing cuts to crushed limbs to spilled intestines. But these Christian victims were not soldiers. They were simple farmers, shepherds, and tradesmen forced into dangerous hard labor.

Placing the saw on the upper thigh of the victim's mangled leg, Alexander began to saw. The sound of grinding steel on bone mixed with screams of pain penetrated right into his soul.

Come quickly, Lord Jesus! he prayed. *Vindicate your martyrs!*

There would be many amputations today. Some men would not make it. Others would be crippled for life, unable to care for themselves or their families. But did it really matter?

God's wrath was coming upon this city.

After finishing with the cave-in victims, Alexander arranged for them to be brought to the hippodrome where he could care for them during their recovery. Only ten out of twenty-three had survived. Once all were settled, he walked from the hippodrome across the valley into the upper city where the apostate Jacob lived in what used to be the residence of Boaz, one of the elders of the Christian congregation in Jerusalem. After Boaz and the Christians left the city for Pella, Jacob had simply confiscated the residence for himself, as many had done with Christian houses across the city.

It continued to amaze Alexander how the trauma of civil strife and impending war brought out the darker side of souls. Jewish Christians had first been fair game for persecution by their countrymen. Then the Romans had made it acceptable to torture and murder them along with Gentile believers. The theft of their property completed the cycle of violence against followers of Christ.

A knock on Jacob's door was answered by Nathan, Jacob's pepper-haired head servant who sported a scar across his cheek, a sign of his master's lack of restraint. Nathan had a secret connection with Alexander and Cassandra about which Jacob knew nothing. The servant had felt pity for the way Jacob was

29

persecuting the Christians, so over the last year he'd fed helpful information to Alexander.

Unfortunately, he was also a witness to Jacob's attempted rape of Cassandra and had done nothing to stop it. Nathan was a coward with a fragile conscience.

The servant led Alexander into the atrium, where Jacob was tending to his flower bushes, evidently fancying himself an Adam in his own Garden of Eden. These meetings between Alexander and Jacob were rare and full of tension. Because of his political machinations, Jacob was still the authority over the hippodrome hospital. An apostate of hell controlled the resources and food rations of Alexander's ministry of God. Yahweh sure had a sense of irony as he used the perverse to achieve his purposes. Though sometimes Alexander could not understand why.

So he had to trust God.

Jacob eyed Alexander's clothes, blood-stained from his surgeries. "Please don't sit down anywhere. Blood is almost impossible to clean off."

Alexander nodded with acquiescence. "I came here to ask you for favor."

Jacob raised an eyebrow. "You seek my favor?" he demanded with sarcasm, wielding his power over Alexander as a weapon.

"It is not for me. It is for the city. I need you to release the Christians back into my service in the hippodrome."

"You do, do you? And how many of them died today?"

"Thirteen."

"Tragic," said Jacob. But Alexander knew he didn't care. It was, after all, Jacob's intention to make the Christians suffer.

"Jacob, you know Rome is coming to besiege Jerusalem. And that means the hippodrome will be overflowing with sick and wounded. I will not be able to handle the numbers with the handful of assistants that I have. I need the others that are in the mine."

"We are not yet under siege."

"Not yet. But when we are, there is no one else in the city who will volunteer to help the few doctors except the Christians. The more they are killed in the mines, the more Jerusalem suffers."

Alexander could see from Jacob's thoughtful expression that his reasoning was getting through. Surely praise of being the one who provided help to the sick and wounded would appeal to the man's self-interest. He pressed on.

"The city walls have been mostly rebuilt with the stone they've quarried. You don't need the same amount of labor as before. Let me have the Christians back. We will prepare the hippodrome, and you will receive the credit for an efficient help of wounded soldiers in a time of war."

"You make a good argument." As Jacob appeared to consider his words, Alexander relaxed at the moment.

Then Jacob's thin lips curved in a malicious smile. "So, yes, I will release them when the siege begins. In the meantime, why don't you pray that Jesus protect them from accidents in the mines? Isn't he supposed to be your miracle worker?"

Alexander deflated, his stomach sinking to his feet. He had done his best. He had prayed. He had sought to be respectful. He had sought justice. But still he had lost. *Lord, why do the righteous suffer and the wicked prosper?*

"Leave me," said Jacob. "I have work to do."

When Alexander arrived back at the hippodrome, he found a letter waiting for him from Cassandra. Her words alone could comfort him in time of despair.

> *Cassandra, to my beloved husband Alexander.*
>
> *I pray this letter finds you well and fulfilling your calling from the Lord Jesus Christ. It has been so long since I have felt your strong embrace and your healing arms of love around me.*
>
> *Rachel's interests have turned to marriage and Noah is training to fight well with a sword. They are growing up too fast.*
>
> *Your son Samuel is just over a year old now. His presence calms my spirit because he reminds me of you. I pray with all my heart for the day that you will finally meet him. That we will all be reunited.*
>
> *The Ebionites have grown so strong in numbers and effect that they have become a danger to the future of the body of Christ. Pray for Boaz and the elders as they organize a council to deal with their poisonous teachings.*
>
> *May God bless you, my husband. And may he allow us to be together again soon. I love you and miss you and pray for you every day.*

CHAPTER 6

Simon bar Giora and Aaron ben Hyam met with military leaders in a large home in the wealthy Upper City confiscated for Simon's headquarters. These leaders totaled a dozen Jewish captains of thousands and a few officers of their Idumean allies.

Aaron pinned a map of Jerusalem and its surrounding territory on the wall for all to see as they gathered around.

The young Essene monk had been through much with Simon over these past few years, rising to become one of his most trusted officers. He'd been just sixteen when he first contacted Simon several years ago, offering him the wealth of the Qumran community if he would train the monks in the art of war. The Essenes had believed they were God's chosen people, set to take over the holy city and temple once a final battle against the Roman armies purged the corruption of the Jewish priesthood and ushered in the Messiah. Their sectarian scriptures prophesied this victory.

Aaron and his squad had not been at Qumran when the Romans arrived and killed everyone in their small commune on the shore of the Dead Sea, burning it to the ground. So now Aaron and his small band of Essene warriors were following Simon like orphans without a home. They were also orphans of God because everything Aaron believed in had been smashed and destroyed. All their prophecies proven false. All their hopes and dreams ripped to pieces like their scrolls.

Simon felt sorry for his young protégé, but then Simon had experienced his own disillusionment. A life-shattering one that brought kinship with the young monk.

Years earlier, Simon had been captain of the temple guard when he was betrayed by his lieutenant John of Gischala, who'd framed Simon as a traitor, forcing him to escape the city. Simon had become a bandit in the wilderness, leaving everything behind, including a secret love affair with the Herodian princess Berenice, sister of King Agrippa. Gischala had become a military leader in the current Jewish civil war. Trying unsuccessfully to take over the city, he'd wound up in control of the temple complex.

To get his revenge on Gischala was one of the reasons Simon had returned and seized control over the city. His other reason was a certain Roman general on his way to Jerusalem.

"When Titus arrives," said Simon, pointing at the map, "He will no doubt avoid the Kidron and Hinnom valleys. They are too steep for attack. The obvious choice is the western wall up near the New City."

Everyone agreed. Simon said, "We must get ready for the siege with a focus on the western wall."

Aaron looked quizzically at him. "So, you are planning to stay after all?"

Simon had told his army that he wanted to take down Gischala, but then be gone before Rome arrived because it was a war they could not win.

"I have no delusions of defeating Rome," said Simon. "My intentions are for Gischala and Eleazar."

Eleazar ben Simon was the Zealot leader who had taken the inner temple hostage from Gischala, thus breaking up the city into three rival factions led by Simon, Gischala, and Eleazar.

Simon added, "The civil war will destroy this city from within, making it easy prey for Roman desolation. We need to convince the factions to unite against a common enemy."

Simon caught Aaron's look of disappointment. The Essene monk knew Simon was lying. He knew that any plan Simon had for uniting with Gischala was only so that he could get close enough to kill him. Had the young monk not been so loyal to him, he would have called Simon out by now.

The cynical general owed him for that.

Simon said to the others, "I can still leave before the legions fully secure the city. And those who want to die fighting an impossible battle are free to stay and do so."

Simon hadn't figured out yet how he might get at Titus. He would deal with that when the opportunity came.

For now, he just wanted to kill Gischala.

CHAPTER 7

Caesarea Maritima

Julia Berenice watched Flavius Titus reading the Greek scroll of the Apocalypse as he stood beside her brother Herod Agrippa and the captive Jewish general Flavius Josephus. They were in the assembly room of the Herodian palace in the city, just the four of them and their messenger.

Titus's brow was scrunched with incredulity at what he was reading out loud. "Then I saw heaven opened and behold, a white horse. The one sitting on it judges and makes war. His eyes are like a flame of fire, and on his head are many diadems. He will rule the nations with a rod of iron and will tread the winepress of the fury of the wrath of God Almighty."

He stopped and looked at twenty-two-year-old Thelonius Rufus Severus, who had brought him the scroll along with intelligence on the Christian community. "And this unnamed 'King of kings and Lord of lords' is supposed to be the Nazarene Jesus whom they call Messiah?"

"Yes," said Thelonius.

"But you say they are not part of the Jewish revolt?"

"No, my lord, they are not. What you read is a symbolic picture of what happens in the heavenly realm. They believe that their God is commanding the armies of Rome from heaven to do his will and destroy Jerusalem."

Titus read from the scroll again. "Yet, they believe that those armies are gathered to make war against him who was on the white horse. How can they be fighting against him when they are doing his will?"

"It is how they see the sovereignty of their God. He puts into the hearts of his enemies the very desire to carry out his purpose without them even knowing it."[1]

Titus looked at Josephus, who confessed, "I cannot deny that is how our Scriptures speak of the deity. I have openly said to you that I believe our God has gone over to the Romans. You are God's instrument of righteous judgment upon

34

Israel. But the Christians are appropriating the concept and twisting it to their delusions."[2]

Josephus was a Pharisee who had led a Jewish army against Rome. But when he was captured, he had offered to help Vespasian try to convince the Jews to surrender in order to avoid total destruction.

Titus looked back at Thelonius. "But after this god of theirs puts it in their hearts to war, then he judges them for it?" asked the legate.

Thelonius shrugged yes.

"That is a Christian lie," Josephus interjected. "I still believe Vespasian is God's Anointed One, the Messiah."[3]

Josephus's name had originally been Joseph ben Matthias, but when he had been captured by Vespasian, he had prophesied that the general would become both emperor and Messiah. Such flattery had rewarded him with adoption into the Flavian family with his new name of Flavius Josephus.

Titus looked again at the Apocalypse scroll and spit out, "Religious nonsense." He threw the scroll down onto the table. "But you have discharged your duty to me, Thelonius. So I suppose I owe you my side of the bargain."

Thelonius bowed and said, "My lord."

Berenice saw Titus nod to a soldier, who left the room.

Thelonius was the son of Lucius Aurelius Severus, a Vigile prefect of Rome whom Nero had commanded to find the Apocalypse when he heard it prophesied the end of the world and assassination of the emperor. Nero had blamed the Great Fire of Rome on the Christians because of their language of fiery judgment. He had used that as a pretext to hunt Christians down in a systematic persecution that lasted until the emperor's death three-and-a-half years later. Severus had disappeared while trying to find the Apocalypse, and Nero had never received the information he sought.

Once the Flavians ascended to power, Titus had tracked down Severus's son Thelonius and tried to find out what happened to Severus as well as where the Christians were, still believing them to be part of the revolt against the empire. When Thelonius claimed to have no knowledge of his father's whereabouts or activities, Titus had seized his fiancé, daughter of a Roman patrician, holding her hostage until Thelonius should finish his father's commission, uncovering the intelligence Titus sought on the Christians. Pretending to be a believer, Thelonius had infiltrated the Christian community in Jerusalem. He'd even led some orphans to the city of Pella in the mountains where the Christians had fled to safety.

That was over a year ago. Thelonius had lied to the Christians in Pella that he was returning to Jerusalem. Instead, he'd returned to Titus in Caesarea with a scroll of the Apocalypse and intelligence on the whereabouts of the Christians. Then Nero had died, and Titus had put a temporary hold on the war. He'd kept Thelonius in custody in case he needed him again.

He no longer needed him. The Christians were still in Pella where Thelonius had said they were. The son of Severus had betrayed the Christians to save his fiancé. That woman, Livia Marcella Bantius, was presently being escorted into the room by the soldier Titus had sent for her.

She was a beautiful young seventeen-year-old with blond hair and large, bold eyes. Her youth and innocence took Berenice back in time to less complicated days. Days now long gone and destroyed by the responsibilities of life—and politics. Berenice felt like an ugly old hag as she saw her lover Titus stare at the young girl.

At forty-two years of age, Berenice was long past marriageable, but she had kept her beauty and was still able to seduce men like Titus who wanted a woman of maturity and experience over mere childish flesh. Still, age and society were far harsher on women than on men. Even the most privileged of the female sex like Berenice saw their status diminish rapidly with age. And Berenice knew that time was running out for her ambition of becoming empress of Rome.

Berenice was brought out of her thoughts by Livia standing with Thelonius. They had been allowed to cohabit together this last year while waiting for Titus to release them. Berenice's heart melted for the young lovers, for the love she had lost, for the love she would never know.

Titus announced, "I release you from my custody. There is a ship leaving for Rome this evening. You may take it and return home. Get married and enjoy Flavian rule."

"Thank you, Caesar," said Thelonius. "I am indebted to your grace."

Titus left the room announcing, "I have a taurobolium in the camp. I know how you Jews feel about other religions. I do not require your attendance, but you are welcome."

A taurobolium was a pagan blood ritual of the Mithras religion of the legions.

Berenice noticed her brother Agrippa staring lasciviously at her with a smile. He had been conspicuously quiet this whole time, but she knew that he knew exactly what she was feeling. He knew her soul inside and out. Her fears, her ambitions, her desires. He knew her too well. He knew too much. It unnerved her.

After Titus, Josephus, and the two young captives were out of the room, Agrippa whispered seductively to her, "Family love never ages, Berenice. Nor loyalty. Do not forget that. Even if you never become empress, you will always be my sister, my queen."

As his sister, Berenice was a princess who ruled over the Jews in the line of Herod. Herods were hated by Jews because they were Edomites from the detested line of Esau. But their great-grandfather Herod the Great had secured their dynastic rule over Judea in the days of Julius Caesar. And so, though they were hated by most Jews, nevertheless they ruled.

Agrippa and Berenice had an unconventional love between brother and sister. The kind that the world was too ignorant and backward to understand in her enlightened estimation. She had always used her God-given female sexuality to advance her interests in this world dominated by males who were slaves to their libido.

But with her current interest in Titus, something had changed in her. She began to push Agrippa away. Reject his advances. She knew she couldn't do so much longer because in one sense he was right. She had to be loyal to her own. She had to maintain the Herodian dynasty, their future.

And sometimes that required doing things she didn't want to do. Doing things she hated.

Leaving Agrippa, she walked after the others, tossing whimsically back over her shoulder, "Well, my brother, you will always be my brother. But remember to respect me, because one day I may be your empress."

In the unseen realm, Apollyon and Azazel followed Titus and the other human leaders out to the legionary camp along with the Canaanite gods who had returned from their search through the Land.

Azazel spoke with surprise to his overlord. "Of course. It makes perfect sense now. Michael is the guardian prince of Israel. But if the Jewish nation is apostate, then only the remnant believers in Messiah are his chosen people."

"Exactly," replied Apollyon. "And that is why Michael is at Pella, not Jerusalem. He rises up to protect his holy ones in hiding: the Christians."

Azazel said, "That leaves Jerusalem completely unguarded."

"Do not have such a one-track mind," chided Apollyon. "I have plans for Michael and his holy ones. Oh, I have plans."

CHAPTER 8

Berenice and Agrippa stood in the dusty middle of the Roman camp outside the city of Caesarea Maritima. A large area had been cleared, and hundreds of soldiers assembled to watch Titus perform a Mithraic ritual before them all: taurobolium.

Mithras was the god of the Roman legions. He was a muscular warrior deity who was born from a celestial rock, had slayed a sacred bull, and shared in a banquet feast with the Sun. The slaughter of the bull, called the tauroctony, was a picture of the creation of the cosmos. And the taurobolium was a ritual of rebirth for the welfare of the emperor.

Titus approached a large pit in the ground. He wore a silk white toga with its right sleeve thrown over his left shoulder and a golden crown on his head. Designated as Caesar in charge of Vespasian's forces, Titus was about to be baptized for the task ahead of him.

Agrippa leaned in to Berenice and whispered, "Sister, are you sure you want to observe this?"

She gave him a dirty look and returned to watching the ceremony. The truth was that she was not sure. Mithraism was a brutal military cult with origins in Persian mythology. It wasn't the blood sacrifice that bothered her. Jews had their own such sacrifices. It was the idolatry of it all. But it could very well be her future with the son of Vespasian and heir to the throne. She swallowed and forced herself to keep watching.

Titus descended into the pit via a ramp cut into the ground. The top of the pit was covered with slats of wood with punctured holes in them. Through the entrance ramp, Berenice could see Titus kneeling in the pit.

Several priests dressed in white robes led a large sacred bull onto the wooden covering up top. It was draped with garlands of flowers, and its horns were sheathed with gold like the golden crown on Caesar.

With a casual quickness, one of the priests used a sacred spear to pierce the breast of the bull in its heart. The black beast jerked at first in reaction, but the ropes tying it down held firm. It dropped to its knees on the wooden slats, then rolled to its side.

Blood poured from its dying heart onto the wood and through the punctured holes down upon the body of the prayerful Titus. He raised his hands to the bull and lifted his face, receiving the baptism of blood, even drinking in what spilled on his lips.[1]

Blood was never consumed in Hebrew sacrifices. For Jews, the life was in the blood, so they were not to consume it but only to use it as a substitute for their own life. Drinking the blood was abominable to Jews. Berenice turned her eyes away.[2]

"I don't blame you, sister," whispered Agrippa. "It is idolatry. But you had better get used to it if you want to achieve your ambitions. They have just as many festivals and ceremonies as we do, but to their pantheon of gods. Jupiter, Mars, Venus, Neptune, Diana. It's hard to keep them all straight. So much easier having just one god to deal with, wouldn't you say?"

His teasing angered her. He liked to get under her skin. To make her feel unsure or overwhelmed so that she might rely more on him.

He added, "Maybe you and I should try some divination to help prepare you for your future. I can get some pigs and chickens, and we can cut them open, feel their entrails and organs to find omens for the future."

Such superstitions were ridiculous. But he was right. She would have to go along with a whole host of deplorable rituals, most of which were forbidden in the Torah. Some of them were even called "abominations."

Berenice shivered with disgust. She had learned the fine art of compromise from her Herodian upbringing, but sometimes it weighed on her conscience. What integrity did she have? What conviction? Did she believe in anything or nothing? Herods sought power and dynasty. So in the end, did that make power their ultimate deity? The emptiness gnawed at her soul.

She saw Titus walk out of the pit, his hands held out in godlike welcome, his face and white toga drenched red. The thousands of soldiers surrounding the pit cheered and yelled with hands saluted outward, "Hail, Caesar! Hail, Caesar!"

In sharing his father's title, Titus represented the emperor himself, a god. And Berenice knew Titus reveled in the glory. She'd been hopeful when Vespasian had given parting advice to his son to avoid total desolation in his campaign on Jerusalem. Vespasian knew the political ramifications of destroying the heart and soul of the nation. He could lose the Jews as a client state. Yes, they would be enslaved, but they would not be loyal and would remain a thorn in the flesh of the empire.

Titus looked at Berenice and Agrippa, then turned to walk up to a host of tribunes standing next to the Herods.

The blood-soaked general called out, "Quintus Magnus."

A grizzly, one-eyed centurion with graying sideburns stepped forward to attention. "Yes, Caesar." Everything about the man screamed indomitable, even the eye patch. It wasn't a covering of wounded weakness but a badge of marauding experience and meanness.

Titus wiped at blood dripping into his eyes and said, "I commission you to take the First Cohort of eight hundred soldiers to the city of Pella in the Transjordan. Find the Christians and kill them all."

The centurion stiffened with salute and barked again, "Yes, Caesar." He turned to gather his men.

Berenice shared a look of concern with Agrippa. Until now, the Roman general had not displayed such animus against the Christians. She had actually thought he wouldn't bother carrying through on Nero's plans precisely to distance himself from the previous emperor. This was a bad sign. Titus still considered the Christians to be an outgrowth of the Jews, that they were both of the same root. So if he would do this to stamp out the Christians, then her own people did not have much hope of mercy either.[3]

She felt nauseous at the thought of it. And she began to formulate her plans for how she might stop him.

In the unseen realm at the Roman camp, Apollyon summoned the gods of Canaan to his side: Ba'al, Asherah, Dagon, and Molech.

"This is your land," he said. "Go with the Roman cohort and take it back."

Ba'al, the mighty storm god, spoke up, "My lord, why do you require all of us?"

"Because Michael will be there, so you will need all the divine power you can summon in the Land."

The Canaanite deities glanced nervously at each other.

"Will you grant me Driver and Chaser?" Ba'al asked. These were the names of Ba'al's two weapons of power—a war hammer and lightning spear. In the hands of any warrior, they were devastating. In the hands of Ba'al, they could become tools of uncontrollable power. And because Apollyon had previously bound Ba'al's sister Anat into the Abyss for plotting a coup, he could not trust Ba'al before the final battle.

"Not yet," Apollyon answered the storm god. "When you get to Jerusalem."

"Yes, my lord," said Ba'al with a bowed head.

Apollyon watched closely for any hint of reaction. He saw only submission. The storm god was not as devious or calculated as his sister had been.

"I have complete confidence in your ability to accomplish the task," Apollyon flattered Ba'al.

"But, my lord," complained Molech. "We need all the advantage we can get. Michael is the mightiest of the heavenly host of Yahweh. We don't know how many others he will have with him."

Apollyon grinned. "And that is why I am sending you, the strongest of this Land, against him. If all of you cannot take him down, then you are not worthy to fight at Armageddon."

They all accepted the chastisement.

"You will do fine," he concluded. "I have faith in you."

The Canaanite gods did not appear so confident.

He tried to inspire them. "Ba'al and Asherah, you ruled as husband and wife over apostate Israel from the judges to Josiah. Dagon, your Philistines made magnificent trouble for King David. You almost crushed him."

"Almost," complained Dagon.

"And you, Molech," said Apollyon, "You brought child sacrifice to Israel when no one else could."

Molech smiled, self-satisfied, his eyes glittering with thoughts of the heinous things he loved to do to children in the valley of Hinnom, also known as Gehenna.

"You are all principalities and powers over this land and her rulers."

Dagon said, "With due respect, Master, Messiah did take our inheritance away."

"In heaven," corrected Apollyon. "But you're still here. We still have some time—and power. Now go with the legions of Rome. Imprison the prince of Israel and destroy his Christians."

CHAPTER 9

Thelonius and Livia followed the band of sailors and their captain through the dock of the huge, circular manmade harbor that was the port of Caesarea Maritima. They walked past concrete walls with arched colonnades. It was a Hellenistic architectural achievement of Herod the Great. A hundred or more ships rested at dock. Merchants with trade from all over the world passed through here. The ship they were going to was loaded with olive oil, wine, and other niceties of the Mediterranean East.

They arrived at a hundred-foot-long corbita, a workhorse of the sea with strong, sturdy frame that was built for speed to outrun pirates. As the crew busied themselves preparing to take sail to Rome, Thelonius pulled his fiancé aside to speak to her.

"Livia, my dear, do you know I love you?"

"Of course I do." Her eyes began to tear. "This year with you in captivity has been the happiest of my life. You saved me. You have proven your love beyond exception."

"I would do it all again," Thelonius went on.

"I know."

"But Cassandra saved my life—and my father's soul. And I have betrayed her. If I do not go and warn her of the Roman attack that is coming, I could not live with myself. I would not be the man you deserve."

They had planned on this subterfuge for months while in Roman custody. But it was much harder to leave her again than he thought it would be. It meant more months apart from his beloved.

Livia smiled through her tears. "That is why I love you. Because of your integrity. I do not deserve you, Thelonius Severus."

"It is I who does not deserve you. I will join you as soon as I can. You'll be safe." Thelonius had paid the ship's captain to watch over her.

"I will wait for you," she said. "As long as I can. But I cannot guarantee what my father will do."

Livia was referring to the fact that her father wanted her married and if he could not have assurance of when Thelonius would be back, he was liable to find another suitor for her and marry her off. The stark realities of life did not always bend to the romantic desires of lovers.

He said, "I understand."

She grabbed him tightly and kissed him with desperation. Her kiss was deep and full of longing. Thelonius questioned whether he was making a mistake. Whether he shouldn't just walk away from all of this and go back to Rome with the woman of his dreams and live a safe, comfortable life of ease.

To leave the Christians to die without warning.

She pulled away. "Go, now. Or I will change my mind."

Thelonius looked around the ship. No one was looking their way. The few on deck were too busy with their preparations. He silently slipped back onto the deck and into the shadows.

But he didn't leave just yet. He stayed and watched his fiancé as the crew unmoored the ship and it left the dock. He watched her as the ship moved out into the harbor and then drifted onto the dark horizon away from him. Away from happiness.

He watched until he could see the ship's shadow no more.

Then he walked back into the city to find a horse and make his way to Pella where Cassandra was.

He had to warn her of the coming terror.

He had to redeem his soul.

CHAPTER 10

Pella

Alexander, to my dear beloved Cassandra,

As I write these words, I am filled with longing and affection for you and for our children. I pray for you all daily.

My mind has lingered over your words about the Ebionites in Pella. Your presence there is more important than mine is in Jerusalem. The war against false teaching is far more important than any earthly war that destroys mere physical bodies and cities.

False teaching destroys souls. If these Ebionites become a majority, they could take control of the congregation of Pella and destroy the Faith like weeds in a garden. The kingdom of God would be choked to death before it has a chance to bloom.

My heart rejoices that you are there because I trust no one else to have your heart of conviction for doctrinal truth and the purity of the church. Serve the elders in their quest to protect the flock.

May God use you for his purposes.

Cassandra sat in the congregation of several hundred Christians packed into the Greek temple at the center of the city. Her husband's letter haunted her thoughts. He had no idea she was planning to go to Jerusalem to be with him. She had never told him. So he had no idea that his words of praise were more like words of rebuke in her conscience. What was God's purpose for her?

She looked around the temple. The Christians had shorn the pagan structure of idolatrous images and converted its use into a congregational hall for the faithful worship of Yahweh. Hundreds of others stood outside trying to hear whatever they could. This was a meeting that would determine the very survival of the ekklesia in Pella.

Rachel had volunteered to watch over little Samuel at home so that Cassandra could focus uninterrupted attention on this life-changing historical moment.

Boaz stood at the lectern, leading the council of Pella. They were holding an examination of the Ebionites and their doctrine that was spreading through the city, threatening to poison the congregation of the Lord. Cassandra was thankful that none of the Ebionites had been allowed to become elders, or they might have sabotaged this trial.

Symeon ben Clopas represented the group. He stood in the dock before the elders with his manuscript in hand for reference. It was their "Gospel of the Ebionites," also known as the "Hebrew Gospel." Symeon and his followers had claimed that it was Scripture with the authority to match "the Four," that is, Matthew, Mark, Luke, and John.[1]

In his sixties, Symeon had long graying hair, unwashed and pulled back from his wrinkly face. He had the look of a rugged worker, like a brick-layer, but he had the mind of a steel trap, and his charisma had captured the hearts and souls of many weak men and women who were in bondage to their flesh.

It was all Cassandra could do to maintain her own calm. This false teacher and his followers had joined the Christians from Jerusalem to Pella because they had recognized the warning of Jesus to flee the city from the wrath to come. They acknowledged that the Mosaic priesthood and its sacrifices had come to an end with Messiah's death, resurrection, and ascension, which was all well and good.

But that was where they separated from the Faith once-for-all delivered to the saints. Boaz now explained the doctrines promoted by the Ebionites that were cause for condemnation and removal from the congregation.

"The topics of concern that we will examine are several. The Ebionites claim their Gospel has apostolic authority and that the Pauline letters are corrupt theology without apostolic authority. They claim that Christians are required to obey Torah, including circumcision and sabbaths. And lastly, they deny the divinity of Jesus as the Son of Man."

That was enough to stir the audience. Some congregants became agitated, some Ebionites whispered complaints. The elders quieted everyone down.

Boaz continued, "I will start with this last doctrine first. Symeon, is it true that you teach that Jesus the Messiah was not Yahweh in the flesh?"

Symeon stood silent for a moment before speaking. He was a master of emotional manipulation. He used the silence as a means of building anticipation and sounding like a wise sage through few words.

Finally, he spoke, "We Ebionites believe that Jesus is the Messiah, the anointed one foretold by Moses and the prophets. That he fulfilled Torah as the Son of Man and died for our sins. But as to his person, was he 'God on earth'?"

He stopped for a moment and looked around the congregation as everyone waited breathlessly for his answer.

"I answer: What do the Scriptures say?"

The crowd mumbled agreement.

Symeon continued with a proud smirk of control on his face. "The Psalmist says of Christ, 'Yahweh said to me, "You are my son. Today I have begotten thee.'" Now the Gospel of Matthew says that Yahweh spoke these words from heaven at the baptism of Jesus by John. So the baptism marks the point where the perfect and obedient Son of Man was adopted as the Son of God. Jesus was not Yahweh in the flesh, for Yahweh would not adopt himself."[2]

Protesting broke out from the Christians in the audience. Cassandra joined in. This was the most serious of all the Ebionite heresies. It alone was enough to brand Symeon a false teacher and expel him. They didn't need to explore any further.

But Boaz was a fair man. He would follow proper procedure and allow Symeon the chance to defend each of his aberrant doctrines with the intention of leaving no heresy unchallenged.

Boaz proclaimed, "Symeon, the elders of this church do affirm the truth that Jesus was Yahweh in the flesh. We furnish you with this list of scriptures that constitute many convincing proofs." An elder handed Symeon a short scroll for documentation. Symeon didn't bother to even look at it. His countenance seethed with defiance.

Cassandra felt her own pride rise within her in response.

Boaz concluded, "But the simple words of our Lord Jesus are words enough to prove his identity with Yahweh. For when the Jews claimed special status as Abraham's children, Jesus replied, 'Before Abraham was born, I Am.' And those Jews picked up stones to stone him because they knew he was making himself out to be God. The name of Yahweh alone was I Am. So if you claim to follow the Messiah, then you must accept his teaching about himself as the Great I Am, Yahweh in the flesh."

Now the Ebionites broke out in disagreeing chatter. They were interspersed throughout the crowd, giving them the appearance of more numbers than was actually the case.

But that was not what took Cassandra by surprise. What did was seeing the Roman Thelonius Severus enter the congregation and make his way up to Boaz and the elders.

She watched them closely. She could not hear what he was telling them over the din of the crowd. But she could tell it was not good.

Her thoughts swirled in confusion. How did the Roman get here? He had left her over a year ago to go to Jerusalem, but Alexander had said Thelonius never arrived. She'd thought he'd been captured or killed by bandits or by Rome. She wanted to run up to Thelonius and find out what was going on. But that would be out of order. She stayed silent.

After the noise had settled, Boaz took the podium with a grave look on his face. He announced to the congregation, "My brothers and sisters, we must postpone this council on the issue of the Ebionite doctrines."

Bursts of disagreement broke out in their midst.

"Please, please!" he shouted. They quieted down.

"Our trusted brother, Thelonius Rufus Severus, has just told us that there is a Roman cohort of eight hundred legionaries on their way to Pella…" he paused and swallowed, "…to kill us all."

Cassandra's heart sank. The crowd degenerated into panic. Many exclaimed their fear. Some barked out questions. A significant number trampled out to get back to their houses and their families. Symeon left with them.

Someone yelled out, "How do you know this?"

Cassandra took the moment to slip through the departing crowd to the front. Thelonius acknowledged her with a glance and slight nod as he spoke to the elders. "I was in Caesarea Maritima when General Titus gave the command."

Another moment of dread fell upon them all.

"What shall we do?" asked one elder.

"We pray for God's protection," another responded. "But we do not fight. We are not in revolt against Rome."

Thelonius said, "Fighting back is not revolt. It is self-defense. Titus will not solicit surrender. He has ordered the murder of all Christians."

"We thought the Beast was dead with Nero," said someone.

"We must flee deeper into the mountains," said another.

"How much time do we have?" asked Cassandra.

"A few days at most," said Thelonius.

Boaz spoke up. "We cannot run and hide. We have been preparing for just this sort of thing."

"They are experienced, hardened soldiers," said an elder. "Eight hundred legionaries. We have maybe a thousand fighters. Even with our training and the few Kharabu warriors on our side, we don't stand a chance against them."

"We don't trust chance," said Boaz. "We trust Yahweh. Gather all able-bodied men and boys into the town square." He turned to another elder. "Tell Michael and his Kharabu to meet us there. We must begin plans to defend the city."

Cassandra remembered the words she'd told Rachel. The dragon was coming after the Woman in the wilderness. The War of the Seed of the Serpent with the Seed of the Woman was approaching its climax. She had been wondering what form that attack would take. Now she knew.

The elders were the last to leave the building, leaving Thelonius and Cassandra alone. Thelonius knew this was his opportunity to confess to Cassandra. But he wasn't sure he could do it.

"What happened to you, Thelonius?" He could hear puzzled concern in Cassandra's voice. "You never went to Jerusalem. We thought you were dead."

Thelonius couldn't look her in the eye. His face felt flush with guilt. "I told you that I knew a woman in trouble in Rome."

Cassandra nodded. "Did you leave to help her?"

"She is my fiancé."

Cassandra looked startled. "Thelonius. Why didn't you tell us?"

He wanted to tell her. He was going to confess everything. His betrayal. All the lies. But he couldn't.

Instead, he said, "I don't know why."

A useful lie came to his mind. He acted like he was finally revealing the real reason. "She's not a believer."

He knew that would make sense to Cassandra. Paul's command to Christians was to avoid marrying unbelievers. The apostle taught that it was an unequal yoking. He even used an extreme metaphor that such a marriage was like uniting the temple of God with the temple of Belial. So it would make sense to Cassandra that Thelonius would hide his guilt in such a situation.

Except the truth was that Thelonius was not a Christian either. He had only pretended to be one so he could get closer to them and fulfill his obligation to Titus. He was a traitor to the innocent.

But his beloved was more important to him than anything in the world. And he would do anything to save her from suffering at the hands of that Roman beast.

Anything. Even giving up the Christians. It had been an impossible choice, so how could he be blamed?

"What is her name?" asked Cassandra.

"Livia Marcella Bantius." Thelonius brightened at the mere mention of her. "She is seventeen years old, the daughter of my father's friend. I've known her and loved her since I was a young boy."

"But you left her to come warn us."

Thelonius saw the gratitude in Cassandra's expression. But he was not being as sacrificial as she thought. He was expiating his own guilt.

"She is safely on her way to Rome. I could not live with myself if…" He was about to tell her the truth, but he told a half-truth instead. "…if I did not help you. I owe you my life."

Cassandra had rescued Thelonius from the Great Fire of Rome over six years ago. He had been backed up against the Tiber with the flames about to catch him when Cassandra saved him with one of her father's boats on the river.

Cassandra matched his smile. "Thelonius, God saved you from the fires of Rome for his purposes."

His purposes? The very possibility of it haunted Thelonius. He had been around Christians and their teachings long enough that such beliefs played with his mind at times. What if it was true?

Cassandra continued, "You may have saved us with your warning. Now go. Return to your fiancé. And may God bless your new life with her."

For some reason, his guilt did not feel expiated. And a new lie came to his mind as out of nowhere. He blurted it out without thinking, "No. I didn't come just to warn you. I came to fight with you. To defend Pella."

"You would risk your life and future for us?"

He still could not say to Cassandra what he most needed to say. He just wondered what he had gotten himself into. Then it occurred to him that he could stay long enough to prove to her that he was fighting for them and then slip away before battle. She would think he'd been killed, and he would never have to tell her the awful truth and break her heart.

"Oh, Thelonius. You are a good man."

No, I am not, he thought. *I am not a good man at all.*

CHAPTER 11

Jerusalem

Jacob ben Mordecai had been ruminating in his home in the Upper City for some time now. But he finally made his decision. It was a dangerous one, but this was a time of constant danger where every move one made could have life or death consequences. Jerusalem was about to be attacked by the abominable Roman armies. Control of the city was split into three factions. Simon owned the city proper, Gischala controlled the outer temple complex, and Eleazar occupied the inner temple. Their rivalry had torn the city apart. Jew hated Jew and were even killing each other. All while the Roman eagle was about to swoop down with desolation in its wings. The civil war was ruining the defense of the city. If they didn't unite their forces soon, they wouldn't be able to hold the walls.

Jacob wanted to live. He wanted to survive this war. So he would do what he must to ensure his future. He figured that there was one way to make military unity more likely. And that was to get rid of one of the three parties of division. Diplomacy was easier to manage between two parties than three. And of the three parties, the one least powerful and least capable of withstanding the Roman armies was Eleazar. His Zealots were fewer than Gischala's soldiers, and he was more of a fanatic, less reliable. If Eleazar's forces were taken out of the way, Gischala would be consolidated and stronger, more capable of defending the temple alone than with Eleazar stabbing him in the back.

Jacob had decided to help Gischala eliminate Eleazar.

This would gain the favor of Gischala for Jacob. But he would do so secretly and without Simon's knowledge just to hedge his bets between the two of them.

The danger was compounded by the fact that the Passover was tomorrow and Jerusalem was overflowing with pilgrims from all over the land. Tens of thousands of Jews filled the city for this most important of feasts.

More civilians meant more innocent deaths in the wake of a battle. But more civilians also meant more of a chance for subterfuge, the ability to surprise Eleazar

50

in a way they could not without them. Sometimes innocent casualties were simply the necessary collateral damage of war.

He called to his head servant, "Nathan! Prepare a guard for me to visit the temple mount."

But first, he had to stop by the hippodrome and check on the Christian doctor Alexander. If Jacob's plan went as anticipated, there would be a battle between Gischala and Eleazar with many casualties. He wanted to make sure that the medical services that Jacob was in charge of would be ready and exceptional and that Jacob would be rewarded accordingly.

Jacob said to Nathan, "Just two guards. My visit will be incognito. I cannot afford to have Simon find out about it."

Jacob and his two escorts walked over to the hippodrome and entered the large arena, only to find a handful of assistants managing the entire hospital. They looked woefully unprepared for what was about to happen.

Jacob pulled aside one of the assistants, an older woman, who was so busy she didn't recognize Jacob.

"Where is Alexander?"

"He's working in the mines."

She tried to return to her work, but he held her and demanded, "The mines? What is he doing working in the mines?"

"That's what we all said. But he wouldn't listen. He's been working there the last few days."

Jacob stormed out of the arena and pushed his way through the crowds of the Tyropoeon Valley on his way to the mine.

When he arrived, Jacob marched right down into the cave without stopping, all the way down until he found his target deep in the bowels of the mine.

Alexander was using a pick axe against the limestone walls along with dozens of his fellow Christians. He was sweaty and covered in dust with a scarf covering his mouth. But Jacob would know that creature anywhere. He had become obsessed with the Christian doctor as an object of revenge. His intent had been to make Alexander miserable, but it seemed the doctor had outdone Jacob's intentions.

"Alexander, stop working!" Jacob yelled above the noise of iron chipping stone. He broke off to cough from the dusty air he was breathing in.

Alexander stopped swinging his pick and turned toward Jacob. So did those around them.

"What in hell are you doing?" Jacob demanded.

Alexander glanced around. "This isn't quite Gehenna, but it's close."

Jacob was not taking the humor in stride. "I need you in the hippodrome performing your medical duties. You are risking your life and the lives of countless others if you die down here."

Alexander stood firm against him. "These are my brothers down here. They are my purpose for being in this city. Whatever you do to the least of them, you do unto Jesus. And that includes me."

Jacob burned with anger. The doctor was deliberately using a phrase that the Nazarene had used to condemn those who mistreated Christians during the Great Tribulation.

Dirty little satan, thought Jacob. *How dare he make such an accusation.*

"My lord," said Alexander, "I will gladly return to my duties in the hippodrome—if I can bring these assistants with me. There are only fifty of them left, and they are already trained to provide the best care possible for the sick and wounded. Is that not what will bring you the recognition you are looking for?"

Jacob felt uncomfortable under the eyes of those standing around him. The very ones whose lives were being bargained with.

But now Jacob fully understood the doctor's intentions. His care of patients was second to his commitment to protect his fellow believers. They were everything to him.

Alexander was the best of only a few doctors available, and he would need all the help he could get from his trained Christian assistants for the wave of casualties that was coming. Jacob could no longer hold back if he wanted to come out of this clean.

"All right," said Jacob with a dismissive wave of his hand. "You may bring your Christian helpers back to the hippodrome."

Alexander beamed a smile as he looked around at his fellow dirt-covered Christian miners. Surrounding the doctor, they hugged him with gratitude.

Jacob hated their camaraderie, their love for one another. It was unnerving.

Alexander broke away from his men and approached Jacob. "Thank you, my lord. You will not regret this."

"I had better not."

Jacob stomped back up the tunnel. He coughed again and pulled his cloak up to cover his mouth.

Jacob couldn't tell Alexander that his betrayal of Eleazar was going to provide the doctor with many wounded sooner than he realized.

Jacob and his two men arrived at the Hall of Unhewn Stones on the west side beneath the temple mount. Jacob gave a message to the guards there to give to Gischala.

His bodyguards waited outside as Jacob was brought into the hall alone where Gischala met him with two of his captains.

The large semi-circular room was usually used for sanhedrin deliberation but was empty now as Jacob offered Gischala his plan.

"I know how you can eliminate Eleazar and take the inner temple."

Gischala eyed him suspiciously. "And why would you want to betray one of your countrymen into my hands?"

"You are one of my countrymen," he replied. Gischala nodded agreeably.

Jacob continued. "The fact of the matter is that Eleazar is a fanatic who endangers the whole city. He is a mere impediment to your superior forces, which makes him an aid to the Roman abomination."

"True enough," replied the warrior.

Jacob added, "I want Judea to win this conflict, not lose it by cutting our own throats with civil war."

"What about Simon?" queried Gischala. "We are also at odds."

"That is more complicated. But Eleazar is a simple matter. And I have a simple way for you to take Eleazar out of the equation."

Gischala gave a look at his captains. "Our stone miner and medical coordinator is apparently a military strategist as well."

They chuckled.

Jacob spoke up with confidence. "Thanks to my mining, I have an intimate knowledge of the underbelly of this entire city. And I know how to get into Eleazar's hideout in the inner temple."

Gischala gave him a look of serious interest. Now Jacob would finally have the respect he needed for his own intentions.

He said, "Eleazar will obviously have guards over every tunnel he knows beneath the temple. But Eleazar has never been to the mine. So Eleazar does not know of my tunnel."

CHAPTER 12

*The fourth angel blew his trumpet, and a third of the sun was
struck, and a third of the moon, and a third of the stars, so that a
third of their light might be darkened, and a third of the day might
be kept from shining, and likewise a third of the night.*

Apocalypse 8:12

The Feast of Unleavened Bread

The Passover had come on the fourteenth of the month of Nisan. For the next
seven days, the pilgrims of Jerusalem would be celebrating the Feast of
Unleavened Bread. They would bake and eat the prescribed food as a
commemoration of the haste with which they had to leave Egypt in the Exodus.
The feast would end on the seventh day with a celebration at the temple.[1]

Gischala had an agreement with Eleazar to avoid battles during feasts and
religious duties of the priesthood. This way the people would not rise up against
them both for violating Torah and the sacred space of the temple would not be
polluted with the blood of war.

For that reason, Eleazar had opened the gates of the temple for the faithful
to enter during the festival. It was the last day of the festival and a time of
celebration in the temple courts. The moon was starting to leave its full phase but
still lit up the temple mount with heavenly glow on this hot summer night. People
packed into the outer courts, chattering, dancing, and singing in their various
families and communities.

Groups of men came to present themselves before the Lord in the temple's
inner court. Disguised as one of them, Gischala looked up on the battlements of
the temple to see a few unsuspecting guards. Eleazar was keeping his part of their
agreement.

Unfortunately for Eleazar, Gischala wasn't. He whistled. The hundred men
who had just entered the temple with him threw off their cloaks to reveal armor

and weapons ready for battle. There were only about fifty of Eleazar's Zealots casually overseeing the inner court. Gischala's men dispatched them quickly before they could even notify their fellow Zealots of the attack. Hundreds of them had joined the festivities outside, and the rest of them were camped out in the compartments below the temple.

A trumpeter blew his horn for attack.

In the crowded outer court, three hundred other men rushed forward and broke into the temple to join Gischala.

They pushed the gate shut behind them.

Jacob had earlier revealed to Gischala a secret tunnel route that led from his mine to the inner temple. A horde of Gischala's soldiers had been quietly waiting there to attack. When they heard the trumpet, they burst out of hiding, filling the hallways and compartments with brandished weapons.

Eleazar's men were taken by surprise. Those who had been sleeping were thrust through with swords before they could awaken. Others who were awake sought to fight back but were overwhelmed by the numbers and lack of preparation.

Not all were zealous in their loyalty to Eleazar. While half of the Zealots were cut down, the other half surrendered.

The floors of the tunnels and rooms beneath the temple ran thick with the blood of the conquered forces.

Up above in the inner court, Gischala stood victoriously on the steps, surrounded by his armed men.

At last, a handful of warriors came from below dragging the beaten body of Eleazar out of the hall and up to the foot of the steps. They dropped him to the ground. Grunting in pain, he looked up at his conqueror descending the steps in the moonlight to meet him.

When Gischala came near to Eleazar, he sat down on the last step to talk out of earshot of his men.

Eleazar spoke painfully, holding his side of broken ribs. "Traitor. You pollute the temple with the blood of war."

Gischala smiled, looking around at his men. Then he whispered to Eleazar, "This is *my* temple. You polluted it long ago when you took it from me."

Eleazar coughed up blood. Gischala said, "Can you see the moon and stars tonight, Eleazar?"

The Zealot refused to look at the sky. He kept staring at his captor with hatred in his eyes. Gischala added, "A third of the heavenly bodies over Jerusalem are struck tonight. A third of the sun has gone dark. Two thirds remain."

Gischala was using the language of prophecy that Eleazar knew all too well. Covenantal language. The description of the heavenly host going dark or being struck or falling from the sky was a way of describing the fall of powers, whether in heaven or on earth. In this case, it was earth as Eleazar represented one third of the rulers who had power over the holy city.

Gischala leaned in and growled, "I trained you when I was captain of this temple. When I stood against Florus on this very spot, against the abomination of Rome, you didn't stand with me. You watched as I became a fugitive so you could take my place. And then you dared to stand against me when I returned. Well, you fought on the wrong side of this conflict. Now it is time for you to stand and face God."

Eleazar spat on Gischala, who pulled back and wiped the spittle from his cheek.

Standing up, Gischala declared, "Hang him from the Beautiful Gate."

His men cheered and dragged Eleazar over to the front gate of the temple, now opened, where they threw a rope down and pulled their captive up into the air.

As Eleazar's body jerked with its last spasms of life, Gischala looked out onto the crowd of Jews that had amassed below the steps. They had been silenced by what was transpiring before them.

Gischala announced, "The Zealot Eleazar, traitor to our people and our cause, is dead! I have cleansed the temple of his corruption. Now the inner and outer temple are one and I am its guardian! To all those of his men who remain, I give amnesty! Join us as one to protect the temple from the nations who would defile God's holy house!"[2]

His men cheered. The crowd joined in. Soon, chants of "Gischala! Gischala! Gischala!" could be heard outside the walls in the streets of Jerusalem—and no doubt in the ears of Simon bar Giora.

CHAPTER 13

Then the sixth angel blew his trumpet, and I heard a voice from the four horns of the golden altar before God, saying to the sixth angel who had the trumpet, "Release the four angels who are bound at the great river Euphrates." So the four angels, who had been prepared for the hour, the day, the month, and the year, were released to kill a third of the people. The number of mounted troops was twice ten thousand times ten thousand; I heard their number. And this is how I saw the horses in my vision and those who rode them: they wore breastplates the color of fire and of sapphire and of sulfur, and the heads of the horses were like lions' heads, and fire and smoke and sulfur came out of their mouths.

Apocalypse 9:13-17

Road to Jerusalem

Apollyon stood with Azazel on a high place on the hillside above Gibeah about four miles outside of Jerusalem.

Azazel breathed in the air with relish. "Ah, the desert of chaos. It feeds me."

Apollyon gave him a suspicious glance. Azazel was referring to the fact that the Jews called the desert the dwelling place of Azazel and his goat demons.[1] It had been the satyr's domain for so long in the past, and he surely wanted to take it back from Apollyon if he had the opportunity.

That was one of the reasons why the Angel of the Abyss had separated Azazel from his co-captain Semyaza by sending the latter to watch over his human ward Vespasian. Despite their importance to his plans, Apollyon had to head off the possibility of a coup, so it was worth keeping them apart.

To release the captive four angels at the Euphrates, Apollyon had been required by the divine council to return the two hundred ancient ones back to the Abyss. But he had kept these two mighty leaders from that requirement, replacing them with two others.

57

Apollyon looked out upon the snaking column of legionary soldiers winding its way through the valley toward its destination: Jerusalem. In the lead were the auxiliary forces from among the nations. Then the three legions followed by their imperial legate Titus. The fourth legion was going to meet them from the direction of Jericho. In all a total of over sixty thousand troops descending upon Jerusalem like a plague of locusts. Or more precisely, a plague of locust demons.

Apollyon, the Locust King, considered the irony with amusement. In the unseen spiritual realm, the picture was a bit more impressive. The seventy gods of the nations went before the horde dressed in their heavenly armor and ready for war. The number of mounted troops following them was more like two hundred million. Apollyon snorted with satisfaction at yet again mocking the Most High, who often referred to his heavenly host as "ten thousand times ten thousands of his holy ones."[2] That would be a mere hundred million. Well, Apollyon had *twice* that number in his demon army of "unholy ones" that now infested the legions of Rome. Through spiritual eyes, these blasphemous creatures were frightening exaggerations of their earthly counterparts. Their horses wore breastplates of fire, sapphire, and sulfur. Their heads were lions' heads. Fire, smoke, and sulfur came out of their mouths. And their tails were like serpents with heads.[3]

"What of the northern army?" asked Azazel. He was referring to the three thousand Roman legionaries who guarded the Euphrates River in the north.

"Oh, they are on their way," answered Apollyon. "I wouldn't miss that symbolic opportunity for anything." He was referring to the fact that his four captive angels were previously released at the Euphrates River, which was the unleashing of Apollyon's restrictions to be able to launch this final campaign upon Jerusalem. Every significant enemy of Yahweh had invaded Israel from the northern regions. Assyria, Babylon, Persia, Greece. So the Euphrates River as the northernmost border of the Promised Land had become a consistent symbol used by the Hebrew prophets to express impending judgment by Yahweh.[4] Apollyon was certainly not going to break that delicious prophetic pattern.

"Mark my words," said Apollyon to his watching accomplice. "I'll be done with these Jews within five months, and by then another third of their population will be dead, their city and temple desolate."

CHAPTER 14

Pella

Cassandra sat on the left side of the congregation holding her sleeping infant. Rachel sat beside her as they all listened to Boaz preach a sermon. Women and children sat separate from men just as in Jewish synagogues. Cassandra's attention was distracted by Rachel's gaze at a young man sitting near Noah on the opposite side of the converted synagogue. He was gazing back at her daughter.

Jonathan. The young man on whom Rachel's thoughts of marriage had centered no matter how much Cassandra discouraged them. The youth was admittedly quite handsome. Sweeping hair, good complexion, quite masculine for his age. He had been training to become a warrior. He wasn't a worthless suitor if it came to that.

But it wasn't going to come to that. Cassandra elbowed her daughter and whispered in her ear, "This is a house of the Lord."

She instantly regretted saying that. It sounded like her own mother.

She refocused her attention on the sermon.

In light of the danger of the coming Roman army, the Christians of the city had begun a prayer vigil that went around the sun dial. They'd also prepared a hiding place for the women and children when the time came. But first they prayed, appealing to the Lord to save them from the wolf at the door. Meanwhile, those who were capable prepared to defend them at that door.

The elders had taken time for a sermon of encouragement before giving instructions on their defense strategy. Boaz explained how the Feast of Unleavened Bread currently going on in Jerusalem was a "type" or prophetic picture of the Messiah. The feasts of Passover and Unleavened Bread were linked because the latter followed right after the former.

But the Jewish Christians would not join their brethren in celebrating these feasts in Jerusalem this year. Jesus had warned his followers to stay away, and all the feasts were about to come to an end anyway.

So Boaz told the story of the first Passover in Egypt and the deaths of the firstborn to commemorate the event. Cassandra looked down on her own first born, Samuel, still sleeping soundly in her arms. How precious he was to her. And how horrible it would be to lose him. She could not imagine the pain.

Looking across the synagogue, she saw Thelonius listening with a painful expression of his own. He too was making a sacrifice to defend Pella.

In the Torah story, once Pharaoh had let the Jews go from the land, the Egyptians out of anger had forced the Israelites to leave in haste—so much so that they did not have time to bake bread for the trip. This was described as not having enough time for the leaven in the dough to rise. Thus the feast of Unleavened Bread in their exodus of haste.[1]

Yahweh then led the Israelites through the desert in a pillar of cloud by day and a pillar of fire by night all the way to the shore of the Red Sea. It had taken seven days for them to get there. The feast lasted seven days in commemoration of the event.

Boaz retold the narrative of the sons of Israel backed up against the sea with the Egyptian army coming after them and how Yahweh delivered the Israelites by parting the waters with the blast of his nostrils. The Israelites walked through on dry land, but when the Egyptians came after them, Yahweh returned the waters to their place and drowned the Egyptians, thus delivering the children of Israel.

"The Psalmist wrote of Yahweh's deliverance at the Red Sea," said Boaz, "'You divided the sea by your might. You crushed the heads of Leviathan. You gave him as food for the creatures of the wilderness. Yours is the day, yours also the night. You have established the heavenly lights and the sun. You have fixed all the boundaries of the earth.'"

He paused to let the poetic words sink into his audience. Cassandra loved the creation imagery as a symbolic portrayal of the origin of the covenant, the creation of the Mosaic cosmos. Boaz continued, "Yahweh displays power over the waters and over Leviathan, the sea dragon of chaos. He crushes Leviathan's many heads and pushes back the waters of chaos to establish his covenant order."[2]

Cassandra knew that beautiful theme well: order out of chaos.

"That covenant was the old order of the cosmos. David used the language of creation to express the covenant for Sinai that came shortly after the Red Sea deliverance. The establishment of Yahweh's covenant order was the creation of the heavens and the earth, the lights above and the boundaries of the land, the first words of the scroll of Genesis."[3]

Cassandra's mind wandered. In the same way that the creation of the covenant was described as the creation of the heavens and earth, so the temple had become the incarnation of that cosmos. So much so that when the first temple was destroyed by the Babylonians, the prophet Jeremiah had described it as the destruction of the heavens and the earth as though the earth was going back to its pre-created state of chaos.[4]

> *I looked on the earth, and behold, it was without form and void; and to the heavens, and they had no light. The mountains were quaking, and all the hills moved to and fro. There was no man, and all the birds of the air had fled. The fruitful land was a desert, and all its cities were laid in ruins before Yahweh, before his fierce anger.*
>
> *Jeremiah 4:23–28*

Yahweh had judged Israel in his anger by destroying the first temple as the incarnation of his cosmos, something he was about to do again. Her thinking was right in line with Boaz's words that rang through the congregation. "The new heavens and earth has been inaugurated in the new covenant by the death and resurrection of Messiah. Jesus, our Passover lamb, is also our new deliverer. Jesus is our unleavened bread. The leaven represented the sin of Egypt, so the bread contained no leaven. So Messiah had no sin in himself. The stripes on the matzah are symbolic of the stripes on Messiah's back that heals us from our sin. He is the bread of life, which a person may eat of and never die. As the Israelites were fed the manna in the wilderness, so Jesus is the bread of God that comes down from heaven.[5]

"And like the Red Sea deliverance, Jesus showed his power over the waters when he calmed the storm and walked on the sea. As Moses was faithful over God's house, the tabernacle, so Jesus is faithful over his house, the new tabernacle of God, his people.[6] Jesus is the new Moses of a new covenant, a new heavens and earth.

"Did not the prophet Isaiah write of this new covenant? 'For behold, I create new heavens and a new earth, and the former things shall not be remembered or come into mind, for behold, I create Jerusalem to be a joy.'"[7]

Little Samuel squirmed in Cassandra's arms. She hoped she had enough time to hear the end of Boaz's exhortation before he awoke. This was her new life of balance between spiritual interests and earthly family. She loved both, but they tended to compete with each other for her attention.

Boaz concluded his sermon, "Brothers and sisters, the Apocalypse has assured us that the new heavens and earth is the new covenant in Messiah that has come down from heaven. We, the bride of Christ, are the new Jerusalem, created to be a joy. And when the old covenant temple is destroyed, the old heavens and earth will finally be obsolete."[8]

Cassandra's earlier remarks to Rachel were confirmed in Boaz's final words. "The dragon of chaos has pursued the bride into the desert. But trust in the Lord, for as the apostle Paul assured this generation, the God of peace will soon crush the dragon under our feet.[9] Ours is not a battle against flesh and blood, but against principalities and powers of this present darkness, against the spiritual forces of evil in the heavenly places."[10]

Awakening in Cassandra's arms, Samuel began to cry. She made her way out of the building to avoid disrupting the service. But as she left the congregation, she could hear Boaz describe the spiritual armor of God: the shield of faith, the sword of the Spirit, and other pieces. She could not help but think of their heavenly guardians, the Kharabu, who at this very moment were outside the perimeter of Pella preparing to defend the city against both the heavenly and earthly powers that were on their way to murder all the Christians.

Once Samuel had calmed down, Cassandra returned to the service. Only then did she notice that Noah was no longer sitting with Jonathan and the other men.

Thelonius saw Cassandra re-entering the service and looking around for someone. But his mind was taken up by the sermon. There was something in the words that touched his soul like never before. He was still pretending to be a Christian while trying to salve his conscience for betraying Cassandra and these good people. Why had it not been enough for him to merely warn them and then leave? What had made him commit to defend them when he only wanted to return to his beloved Livia? Now leaving them before the battle would make him a coward as well. His father had raised him to be strong. Romans were not cowards.

But he was not going to fight and die at the hands of his own people for something he didn't believe in.

Nevertheless, the sermon was bothering Thelonius.

He had been familiar with the story of Israel's exodus and Red Sea deliverance. He had heard about Jesus as a spiritual type of the Passover lamb and unleavened bread. It had all been so much foreign religious mythology to him.

Until now. For some reason as he listened, the story came alive in a way he could not explain. He saw the pillar of fire in his imagination, and his heart shuddered with awe. He felt the fear of the Jews backed up against the sea. The evil of the Egyptians became palpably real.

And he knew earthly Jerusalem was Egypt. He knew these Christians were God's people in a new exodus.

Something was happening to him. It wasn't a rational process. He wasn't reasoning through a logical argument to a reasonable conclusion. He was inhabiting a story. He wasn't finding truth. Truth was finding him. It was as though a lamp was lit inside of him and he could suddenly see in the dark like he had never seen before. Clarity.

The gods of his fathers were manmade idols. His religion, his empire, was a fraud. Words flooded his thoughts that he had heard Boaz quote from their Scriptures:

> *"Truly, truly, I say to you, it was not Moses who gave you the bread from heaven, but my Father. For the bread of God is he who comes down from heaven and gives life to the world. I am the bread of life; whoever comes to me shall not hunger, and whoever believes in me shall never thirst."*[11]

All his life Thelonius had felt hungry. Like something was missing. He thirsted for meaning and purpose. Rome was supposed to be the polis, the sacred city that gave significance to the individual citizen. But it only took away his significance as his identity was submerged into the collective. And that collective was a beast, a seven-headed dragon that left him perpetually empty, hungry, and thirsty.

But now for some reason, he felt filled even as at that very moment he was no longer a Roman in his soul.

Rome was his Egypt. He believed in the Bread of Life.

Was this what had happened to his father?

Was this what the Christians had called the baptism of the Holy Spirit? God's spirit opens your eyes. He grants you repentance. He resurrects your dead soul from the grave of sin.

Thelonius's mind went instantly to his fiancé Livia. He had to write her. And he had to tell Cassandra. What would she do when she found out that he had never been a Christian? That he had been lying about everything? Would she believe anything he told her ever again?

Cassandra interrupted his thoughts. The service had ended, and people were socializing before leaving for their homes.

"Thelonius. I need your help."

"What's wrong?"

"Noah has slipped away, and I think I know where he is. I need your help to find him."

• • • • •

Michael walked along the valley just outside Pella with his six Kharabu captains, Gabriel, Uriel, Raphael, Remiel, Raguel, and Saraqel. Back inside the city their thirty other warriors were gathering the capable male citizens in preparation for battle. They were fortifying the old Hasmonean fort on the southern hill and practicing strategic maneuvers in anticipation of the coming storm.

The fort was just across the wadi south of the city hill. It was originally a well-fortified limestone castle on a high butte, but after its destruction over a hundred years ago, it had never been rebuilt. These crumbling ruins were all they had left. The castle would be their last resort.[12]

There were less than a thousand men and boys who could fight. While the Roman cohort on its way to Pella was only eight hundred, they were eight hundred well-trained, battle-hardened legionaries led by countless principalities and powers in the heavenlies. The Christians of Pella were mostly plebeians with bows for hunting and limited swords. They had trained for over a year, but they had no real battle experience. And the forty Kharabu warriors would not be enough to counter that imbalance of experience and weapons.

"We can hide most of the women and children in the caves of the cliffs," said Uriel. "But not all." He was referring to a system of caves linked by tunnels that were hidden in the sharply-rising north face of the western wadi. The rest would go into the southern fort, leaving the city itself open to plunder.[13]

"We must set traps," said Gabriel, looking at the tree-lined range of foothills that led back to the Jordan River.

"I have a few ideas," replied Michael.

Gabriel smirked. "If the gods who are coming are the ones I think are coming, we archangels have an ancient land dispute we're finally going to settle."

He was referring to the Canaanite gods whose claim on this territory gave them the strongest possible power to attack the angels. There were four of them left, and it would not be an easy battle.

Uriel said to Gabriel, "I bet I take out more Watchers than you."

Gabriel snorted. "Only because you have Rahab, which is not really fair." Rahab was the name of Uriel's ancient whip-sword, forged of heavenly metal in the coals of the primordial Mount Sahand. Rahab was also another name for Leviathan the sea dragon.[14]

Michael rolled his eyes. These two had been friendly competitors with each other for eons.

"Okay," said Uriel. "I'll tell you what, I'll give you Rahab as a handicap, and I'll just use my two swords. Would that even up the stakes for you?"

Gabriel smiled. "Indeed it would. But I do fear for your own handicap of impaired mathematical counting."

"I cannot believe you are bringing that up again. I think you have unresolved issues."

"Only with your counting skills."

"All right, you two," said Michael. "I will verify the counting of the enemies you vanquish."

Uriel took off the belt that held the whip-sword rolled up in a special leather case. He handed it to Gabriel, who buckled it on and pulled out the weapon. It unfurled as a ten-foot-long flexible metallic blade that could be used like a whip, cutting through just about anything on earth and most things in heaven.

Gabriel snapped it with precision at a thick tree branch. The blade cut through the branch as if it were a twig. Gabriel looked over at Uriel with satisfaction.

"Finally," he said. "It's my turn." Gabriel had forged the weapon himself. It had been passed down through generations of human giant killers from Lamech to Shem to Caleb to Ittai the Gittite until it came into the possession of Jesus, who had given it to Uriel.[15]

Michael said, "If you two are finally through with your bickering, let us get moving and set our traps."

Their task was interrupted by the arrival of a young boy carrying a gladius and wearing a leather helmet that was a bit too big for his head.

"Noah!" cried Cassandra as she and Thelonius overtook the boy from behind.

Michael smiled and stepped out from the captains. Noah went straight to him.

"Please let me join the army," said Noah, exasperated.

He was still breathing heavily from his brisk walk. And Cassandra was breathing even more heavily as she and Thelonius arrived beside her son.

"Noah, I have told you a thousand times, you are too young for battle."

65

The little warrior argued back, "And I have told you a thousand times that they need everyone who is able."

"Do not talk to your mother that way." Cassandra turned to Michael. "I apologize for my son's disrespect."

Noah looked pleadingly into Michael's eyes. "You have taught me all these months. I'm good. You said so yourself. I could kill Romans."

Cassandra tried to pull Noah away while still apologizing, "I am so sorry to take your time. My son is zealous and not a little naïve."

Noah pulled back, unwilling to leave with her. "I am not naïve. I know exactly what soldiers do. I watched Romans kill my mother and father!"

Cassandra stopped tugging at him. Michael could see her eyes filling with tears. He knew Noah was not going to give up because he was driven by the most primal of desires: revenge.

Michael looked sternly down at Noah. "Young man, your mother is right. You do not talk to her with such disrespect."

Noah was stunned silent at the rebuke. Michael added, "If that is how you treat her, am I to expect the same disrespect if I was your commander?"

He could see he was getting through to the young lad. Noah turned back to Cassandra and apologized. "I'm sorry, Mother. Please forgive me."

She looked at Michael, who winked at her before turning back to Noah. "You are a good fighter for your age. But you are not ready yet."

He saw the boy's eyes turn as sad as a sacrificial lamb. It tugged at the commander's heart. He went on, "However, I think I may have a way to satisfy all parties in this dispute. I do have a task that would properly fit your level of skills, our defensive needs, and your mother's concerns."

Noah's eyes brightened with excitement. "Real defense?"

Michael looked over at the fortress across the valley. "Yes, real defense."

Noah looked at his mother for approval. She appeared unsure.

Thelonius stepped forward and asked, "Commander, I have Roman legion experience. May I lead a squad of defenders?"

Michael considered the request. He recognized the Roman as Cassandra's old friend who had disappeared a year ago. But Michael knew the young man was now different. He could see that Thelonius was newly regenerate. The Spirit of God had baptized him into the body of Christ.

Michael said, "You and I will talk."

He suddenly noticed Cassandra looking up in the sky behind him. He knew what her spiritually sensitive eyes were seeing: Jesus on a white horse in the

66

heavens, surrounded by his army of martyred saints, on their way to Jerusalem for their vindication. When she looked back down at Michael, he looked away from her as if he were unaware. It was not yet time to reveal his true identity.

Michael ordered his captains, "Tell the others it's time to evacuate the women and children."

• • • • •

Cassandra, to my beloved husband, Alexander.

The time has come for me to share some grave news with you. We have discovered that Pella is being targeted by the Romans for destruction.

I do not want you to despair. Only pray. Michael and the Kharabu have prepared for this, and they have trained our men as best they can. We are not without protection or strategy. And certainly not outside of God's will.

Now it is my turn to tell you that if I do not survive, I want you to know how much you mean to me.

I first fell in love with you because I saw a man of healing and compassion in a world of suffering. Even though you say that I led you to the Gospel, you were the one who taught me about God's grace. I had been a bitter soul longing for revenge until you came into my life. Thank you for teaching me to love and forgive.

You have spoken of your desire to be more of a warrior or a man of action. Alexander Maccabaeus, you are the most heroic man of action I have ever known. You save bodies and souls. You are God's warrior. You are my man, and I thank you for loving me and for protecting me and for making me feel beautiful. Thank you for being a man of God that I can look up to and respect beyond all other men.

I vow to you that I will do everything in my power to protect our children. I pray that God the Father watches over you and brings you home safely. And if he does not, then I will go and find you and bring you back myself.

The grace of our Lord Jesus Christ be with you.

• • • • •

Thelonius Severus to Livia Bantius, my precious betrothed.

I write this letter to you with a heavy heart. So much has happened since we parted at Caesarea. I miss you and dream of you, of the warmth of your embrace, the softness of your lips, your touch.

I am sorry to say that my time here in Judea has been extended. I am not sure how long it will be or if I will survive. I wanted to tell you what has happened to me so that you will never doubt my unending love for you.

I arrived at Pella and warned them of the coming Roman attack just as we had planned. But then something happened to me before I could leave and follow you to Rome. I cannot explain it fully in words, but I will try.

I was listening to a sermon in their gathering, and God's Spirit fell upon me. I don't know how, and I don't know why. I only know that I met my Creator. I became a Christian.

And that is why I must stay a little while longer before I return to you. I need to learn more about what has happened to me, and I need to help defend these beautiful people from the attack that I helped bring upon them. It is no longer enough for me to merely warn them. I must act and take true responsibility for what I have done to them.

I know this will be difficult for you to accept. But please believe me when I tell you that my love for you has not wavered or lessened in the slightest. In fact, it has only increased.

This is because I have found a higher love, the love of my Creator that gives meaning and purpose to our love. And only by obeying that higher calling can my life—can our life together—have any lasting meaning here on earth or beyond. I want you to know this love as well.

Please wait for me. But if you cannot, I will understand.

I am forever yours in the love of Jesus Christ, my Lord and Savior.

CHAPTER 15

Jerusalem

Alexander held a small sack of food in his hands as he watched the Two Witnesses speaking at the Huldah Gates to the temple. He was waiting for an opportunity to sneak the sack unnoticed into the usual pre-arranged location for the Witnesses to grab after their sermon.

Very few locals stopped these days to listen to the Witnesses. Most just wanted to live their lives, eating and drinking, marrying and giving in marriage, without being condemned by those they saw as fanatics. But with the large number of pilgrims here for the feast, the message of Moshe and Elihu was being broadcast like farmer's seed, even if done so upon stony hearts.

The Two Witnesses were recounting the judgment upon "Babylon" from the Apocalypse. Elihu spoke in a mighty voice to the crowds of people passing by. "This holy city Jerusalem was supposed to be a dwelling place for Yahweh, but she has become Babylon the Harlot, a dwelling place for demons, a haunt for unclean spirits. For all nations have drunk the wine of the passion of her immorality. And the kings of the Land have committed spiritual immorality with her. They have lived in luxury with her, but they will weep and wail over her when they see the smoke of her burning."[1]

The Witnesses had often said that the Harlot was a symbol of Jerusalem as led by her apostate priesthood. The kings of the land of Israel, that is, her religious leadership, had benefited from Jerusalem's wealth and glory. But they were also guilty of the blood of the Christian martyrs. The metaphor that the apostle John had used was that of drinking their blood like wine. That leadership was responsible for aiding the Roman persecution of the Christians by Nero throughout the empire. The persecution had stopped with the death of Nero, but it was too late. Their fate was sealed.[2]

Moshe joined in. "Fallen, fallen is Babylon the Great. Alas! Alas! You great city, you mighty city, Babylon! For in a single hour your judgment will come.

And the merchants of the land weep and mourn for her since no one will buy their cargo anymore!"[3]

The prophet began to announce a list of merchant goods like gold, silver, jewels, pearls, and fine linen. Alexander recognized that they were the same goods described by Ezekiel in his prophecy against Tyre. Solomon had covenanted with the pagan city of Tyre to build the first temple, which resulted in those same goods being listed in the temple manifest. To this day, the temple only used Tyrian currency, which contained the idolatrous image of Ba'al on it. In its successful economic influence on the merchants of the land, the temple and all the goods sold within it had become thoroughly polluted with spiritual corruption.[4]

Moshe stood back, and Elihu concluded their jeremiad. "So will Babylon the great city be thrown down with violence and will be found no more, and the voice of bridegroom and bride will be heard in you no more. For in her was found the blood of prophets and of saints and of all who have been slain on the Land. Rejoice over her, O heaven and you saints and apostles and prophets, for God has given judgment for you against her!"[5]

Jerusalem had always been known as "the great city" in the eyes of God and his prophets. She was, spiritually speaking, the center of the earth.[6] But because this generation had crucified their Messiah, they would be guilty of the blood of all the prophets and would reap judgment for that bloodguilt unlike any generation before or after.[7]

Alexander had moved over to the wall, looking around to make sure no one saw him. He reached down and inconspicuously slipped the small sack into one of the large cracks that had been created in the crumbling wall. He then moved on. He'd seen the Witnesses take note of his arrival. Once they'd finished and the people had dispersed, they would make their way over to retrieve the hidden package of food from the hole in the wall.

Alexander had made it all the way to the bottom of the steps when his way was blocked by a group of temple guards.

The lead guard said, "You are under arrest."

"For what?" he asked.

Two other guards grabbed him.

"Why are you arresting me?" he repeated.

"Conspiring with the Two Witnesses."

They must have been watching Alexander's every move. He'd thought he had successfully hidden the food in the wall without being seen. He had escaped their detection for months. But he had finally gotten caught.

They must be dragging him to his death.

• • • • •

John of Gischala descended the damp stone staircase into the dungeon below the temple mount. A prison guard opened an iron door that led Gischala into the long line of cells carved out of the rock and caged in by iron crossbars.

The cell door clanged shut behind him, and he was led by the prison captain past cells of various prisoners from religious Zealots to hardened criminals, until he found the one he was looking for.

The captain opened the door for him, and he entered. He saw Alexander Maccabaeus sitting in the corner of the cold, dark cell, his legs crouched up beneath his encircling arms.

Gischala had told them to be neglectful of this one in order to break him. He walked up to Alexander and towered over the doctor who trembled from cold and hunger. The doctor looked up at him with a steady, determined glare, despite his physical maladies.

Gischala considered the prisoner's courage to be impressive. He said, "You are the doctor at the hippodrome hospital."

"Yes."

Gischala narrowed his eyes. "You have been arrested for conspiracy. What do you have to say to your charges?"

Alexander coughed before speaking. "Conspiracy? I'm guilty of conspiracy for feeding poor people?"

"It is illegal to aid those two madmen in any way, including food, shelter, or provisions."

Alexander's steady gaze was unfazed by the accusation. "Why don't you just arrest them or kick them out of the city?"

Gischala gritted his teeth at the jab. He couldn't do a thing directly to the two madmen, and this little weasel knew it. The general had been able to bar them from entering the outer temple courts, but he could not arrest them or do violence against them. Soldiers had been foiled when they tried. Some dropped dead. Others caught plagues. Still others went mad, claiming guardian angels watched over the so-called prophets. Hysterical gossip had spread so fully amongst the populace that no one would dare touch them out of fear for their own lives.

Gischala knelt down to Alexander's level and spoke with a menacingly soft voice. "What is their secret?"

The prisoner looked away, making no response.

"Everyone has a secret. Where do they get their powers, and how do I stop them?"

Alexander looked up again at Gischala. "You cannot stop them."

"Maybe not. But I can stop you. Then who will help them?"

"I think they've made it clear there is only one who is helping them."

The prisoner was implying God himself was on their side, which was something Gischala could never believe in a thousand years. Yahweh was on *his* side. So the two madmen had to be from the devil. Their powers were sorcery. He was sick of their demonic disturbances and traitorous hatred of the holy city, their vile blasphemies against temple and Torah. They had been untouchable for over three years. Three-and-a-half years. It was time to get rid of them, and this Christian traitor was Gischala's opportunity to do so.

He heard the prison door to the dungeon at the end of the hallway open again. He ignored it. "I will make you suffer. You will speak."

Alexander replied, "You will get nothing because I have nothing. Jesus is everything."

Gischala stood to his feet.

"General," came a voice from behind him.

Gischala turned to see Jacob ben Mordecai at the cell door.

"I heard about your prisoner. I'm not sure you realize…"

"I know who he is."

"Well then, you know how crucial he is to your interests. To the interests of our wounded soldiers in this coming war."

"Do we not have other doctors?"

"Perilously few. And Alexander has the loyalty of most of them because of what he has already done for this city. He is a hero to the people. Killing him will be politically disastrous."

Gischala stared at the doctor while still speaking to Jacob. "So the people love him."

"I believe so, my lord," replied Jacob. "I despise him as much as you do. But his death will work against you."

"Well then," said Gischala to Alexander, "since you care so much for your patients, I won't kill you. I will keep you alive down here. I will use what few other doctors we have to attend only to my soldiers and leave the citizens on their own. Perhaps the knowledge that your insolence causes their increased suffering might persuade you to change your mind."

Gischala saw Alexander return his threat with an angry glare.

"If you tell me the secret of the Witnesses, I will let you return to the hippodrome and to your work." He added with sarcastic flare, "Pray to your Jesus about that."

Turning, he left Alexander to the damp cold floor of his cell.

Jacob followed Gischala and informed him, "The Romans have arrived. They are setting up camp on Mount Scopus and the Mount of Olives."

"Yes," said the general, glancing back at Alexander. "The great suffering is about to begin."

CHAPTER 16

Berenice and Agrippa walked through the Roman camp to meet Titus at the far eastern edge. They were just one mile northeast of Jerusalem on Mount Scopus, overseeing the city.

A legionary camp was called a "castrum." It consisted of a square plot of soldier's tents arranged in an orderly geometric fashion around the general's residence in the center. This castrum was large enough to contain three legions— V, VII, and XV—along with their auxiliary forces for a total of fifty thousand soldiers. Legion X and other auxiliaries were across the eastern side of the city on the Mount of Olives, ten thousand in number.

It had taken less than a day for the soldiers to set up camp. They were now busy taking a couple additional days building an eight-foot-tall stone wall with moat around the perimeter of the camp as a standard defensive precaution. They were getting ready for a long siege.

Just outside the wall, the Herod siblings met with Titus, Josephus, and some tribunes. Tiberius Alexander, Roman governor from Egypt, stood firmly beside the general as his second-in-command. He eyed Berenice with a skeptical look.

Berenice despised the man. He had been born to a wealthy Jewish family, but had rejected his heritage, had become procurator of Judea under Claudius, and had ended up a brutal oppressor of Jews in Alexandria. Tiberius was fifty years old with short-cropped hair and a muscular physique. He reminded Berenice of a bird of prey that shadowed Titus everywhere, ready to protect him and eat the scraps from his master's table.

At their elevation, Berenice could see into the city as well as into the temple courts. The white marble walls of the inner temple and its golden trimming gleamed in the sunlight. Berenice felt her stomach churn at the prospect of what was coming.

Josephus was the first to speak, pointing toward the city. "The most accessible part of the wall will be the northwestern section just north of the Herodian palace towers."

Titus looked to Agrippa for confirmation. Herod nodded. "The terrain is higher there. It would require less of a ramp to build."

74

Titus turned to Tiberius. "Start clear-cutting the nearest forests to procure the ramp materials."

"Yes, General." Tiberius left them to make the order.

Titus then asked the Jews, "But what is the intelligence report of the forces inside the city?"

Agrippa said, "The civil war continues. John of Gischala holds the temple complex against Simon bar Giora who controls the city. As you can see, we arrived during the Feast of Passover and Unleavened Bread."

Berenice saw that the pilgrims who were staying outside the city had all moved inside at the presence of the Roman forces. They were like trapped birds in a cage. Several hundred thousand of them.

Josephus added, "That means the city will be over capacity with civilian population, causing stress on both their food supplies as well as simple law and order. The sooner you attack, the speedier will be your victory."

Berenice countered, "But with haste there is a greater danger of more innocent victims."

Titus considered their arguments silently.

"If you spare the city," said Agrippa, "I can assure you complete submission from the Herodian throne presiding over the aftermath. Better a submissive ally than a conquered foe."

Titus said, "I will not destroy the city—if the Jewish forces are not incorrigible. It is up to them what treatment they receive."

That was not comforting to Berenice for she knew just how incorrigible her people were. She also knew Simon bar Giora—intimately. They had been lovers years ago, and she knew his soul. She would never forget. He was the closest thing to true love that she had ever experienced. Even to this day, she remembered those years with melancholy loss. She imagined where he was inside the city right now and what he might be doing, and her heart welled within her. She had never fallen out of love with Simon bar Giora.

Simon was a man of tenacious integrity. He had guarded the temple from corruption, and when he had been framed and chased out of the city, she knew he'd carried with him a desire for revenge against his betrayer Gischala. But a threat against the temple by the Roman abomination would drive him to a much higher commitment to the sacred house of God.

Unless he had changed after all those years as a fugitive in the desert. She'd heard he had become a bandit, but gossip was never reliable. Had he changed? Was character destiny? Or could even the truest of men lose their way?

• • • • •

The moon had arisen, and the Roman soldiers were safely behind their camp walls for the night. Berenice paced about in her tent with her brother watching her every step.

"I cannot believe you would advise immediate attack," she complained. "There is no telling how devastating that would be on the unprepared civilians. There is more chance of chaos and therefore more casualties."

Agrippa disagreed. "Swift judgment is quicker with less damage."

"Sometimes I don't know if you even want a people to rule over," she said.

He replied, "Sometimes, I think your divided loyalties paralyze you. You still love Simon, don't you?"

She wouldn't answer him.

"I think you do not realize how changed of a man he really is. You think he will fight to the end for the temple he used to guard. But he is not that man anymore, Berenice. He is a mercenary without a soul. He believes in nothing."

"How would you know?"

"Because I met with a young man who was personally trained by Simon. An Essene warrior-monk named Aaron ben Hyam. I pled with him to find Simon and bring him to Jerusalem because I thought he could protect it, keep it from being totally destroyed."

"Qumran," she mused. It came clear to her now. "That is why you did not tell Titus of Qumran when we were in Perea."

"Evidently, it didn't help," he said, "because Titus found the commune and killed them all anyway. But Aaron and his squad of warriors were not there at the time."

Berenice couldn't believe what she was hearing. "So you found the monk and that is why Simon came to Jerusalem."

He answered, "I don't want the Jews to win. I just don't want to lose the temple. It is the key to Herodian rule. We control the temple, and with it, religious authority over the nation. If we lose the temple, we lose the nation."

She shook her head. "And you claim that I am double-minded. You are fighting on both sides."

"Out of love for both sides," he said. "But I am loyal to Titus."

"And I love him," she said.

"As you should. Or you will never rule by his side."

"Brother, I am not sure that you will ever know what real love is."

"Let us hope not. Because it has made you weak, sister." Berenice felt her anger rising. Agrippa continued, "The only love I trust is the love of family."

He stepped closer. Berenice saw that his face was soft now, inviting. He looked her up and down, and a feeling came over her of complete repulsion. She had been withdrawing from his affections, but this was the first time that she saw who he really was. And who she had become. It overwhelmed her with disgust and self-loathing. She reached for the only way to get rid of him quickly.

"Titus is on his way to see me. You need to leave now."

He straightened up and withdrew into a cool disposition. "Well then, my sister. Do what you must for Herodian legacy."

He left her.

A wave of guilt came over Berenice. Was he right? Was she so self-deluded that she had started to believe her own lies? Had she lost her way?

She got up to watch her brother walk away in the moonlight.

When she turned back, she saw Titus standing inside the back of the tent. She jumped with a shriek. "You were outside the tent all along?"

He nodded.

She ran through the conversation in her mind, everything she and Agrippa had spoken of. Had she said anything incriminating? Had her brother?

She felt safe when she remembered her words of love for Titus and how she'd turned away Agrippa's advances.

Titus stepped close to her, caressed her shoulders. "So tell me about this man Simon bar Giora."

Berenice felt a twinge of danger. She smiled. "Are you jealous?"

"Among other things."

Perhaps she was not so vulnerable after all.

"Despite his protestations, my brother is sentimental at heart. I do not love Simon bar Giora. He was part of a world that is long gone. One that I would never want to return to."

"Tell me about him as a leader."

She pulled softly away from him and turned to pace around. It felt more removed, less emotional. "He was a captain of the Temple Guard. A good warrior. I had an affair with him."

"That was beneath you."

"It was a dalliance of mischief. I enjoy violating taboos."

She said it seductively. She saw him move slightly toward her with desire. She jerked back into a matter-of-fact attitude and turned her back in musing. "He

77

was useful for Herodian interests in the temple. As you no doubt overheard my brother say, the temple is the key to the nation."

She turned back around to face him again. "Which is why you should not try to destroy it. Or you will lose the very thing you seek to control."

Titus smirked. "Jews are a stubborn people."

"My people have a long history of impossible rulers."

"Your people have a long history of being impossible to rule."

"For despots and tyrants."

He gave her a scolding look, but then sighed. "Berenice, my father is a simple man. A fair man. He cares little for politics. As Caesar, he has no desire to oppress those over whom he rules, especially the Jews."

"And what of his sons?" She knew that the heirs of thrones often reversed previous policies of their fathers.

She could see he felt slighted at the remark.

He turned firm. "The Flavian dynasty will be just." His look turned pleading. "Help us to make it so."

What did he mean by that? Was it a generic appeal to an allied leader or a hint of her future with him?

She said, "Apparently, according to my brother, I cannot help you much when it comes to Simon bar Giora because he is no longer the man of conviction and honor that I knew. I have no understanding of the mercenary mindset. I can only tell you what you already know. Haste in your attack on the city or a focus on the temple as a target will unite the divided factions of all those 'stubborn' Jews as you call them. Then you will have an historic catastrophe on your hands. Is that what you want?"

Titus stared at her now. He whispered, "To whom are you loyal?"

She was taken aback by the question. So he *had* heard everything she and Agrippa had said. She responded with a sense of indignation. "I care about the innocent victims of war. If you treat them with mercy, you will foster their loyalty."

He repeated himself louder now. "To whom are you loyal?"

If she said, "My nation," she would be disloyal to Rome. If she said, "Rome," she would be a traitor to her own people. She said the only thing she could say. "You."

He grabbed her arms and shouted again. "TO WHOM ARE YOU LOYAL?"

Her arms hurt. She stiffened and teared up with fear.

"TO WHOM ARE YOU LOYAL?"

She blurted out again, "You! I am loyal to you!"

He stared into her eyes searchingly. Then he kissed her hard on the mouth. Deeply. He pulled at her clothes with desperation.

She felt herself relax like a silken sheet in his arms. All fear fell away. And once again she experienced the exhilaration of complete surrender to his power.

Outside the back of the tent, a new eavesdropper adjusted his stance for a better look through the hole in the tent flap.

Herod Agrippa smiled to himself as he watched the two lovers lose themselves in each other. *So there is a benefit to my sister's rejection of me. Her weakness may be a strong asset, not merely for the Flavian dynasty but the Herodian dynasty as well.*

CHAPTER 17

Pella

The angels Uriel, Gabriel, and Raphael hid amongst the stone and foliage near the banks of the Jordan River. They watched the eight hundred legionaries pass them by on their way into the Pella Valley just a mile-and-a-half away. They were led in the unseen world by four gods of Canaan: Ba'al, the mighty storm god; Asherah, Tyrian battle maiden called "Great Lady of the Sea"; Dagon, notorious deity of the Philistines; and the despicable Molech, abomination of the Ammonites.

Uriel whispered to the others, "Anat is not with them."

Gabriel whispered back, "She was sent to the Abyss with the ancient ones."

"Well, that makes our task more enjoyable," quipped Uriel. "I hated her most."

"More enjoyable you say," added Gabriel. "But not much easier."

The archangels were normally very capable of overcoming the gods, but these four Canaanite deities would be fighting furiously for their lives. Messiah had legally disinherited them from their Land, so they had nothing left to lose but their eternity—and that was everything to them.

Michael and the three other archangels were with the human Kharabu warriors protecting the Pella Christians from the Romans. This split up the supernatural forces, but the survival of the Christians was equally as important as the death of the gods. It would do no good to bind the Watchers *into* the earth if the Kingdom of God was crushed before it could expand *upon* the earth.

"Let's go," whispered Uriel.

• • • • •

Quintus Magnus led his cohort through the valley that lead to the city of Pella. The fifty-mile march had taken them six days through mountain passes and several skirmishes with wilderness rebels. Ahead of them was a forest from which the Christians could ambush them.

Let them try, he thought. *We will rip them to shreds.*

He had given the order to his men that there were no restrictions. They were to kill every man, woman, and child. Plunder the city for anything they wished. Then raze it to the ground in flames, salting the ground as a symbol of the complete annihilation of the Christians forever.

Quintus himself cared nothing for the spoils or for these worthless fanatics. He wanted a speedy massacre so he could get back to join the siege of Jerusalem. That would be the real challenge.

He did wonder why this insignificant little group of people was so important to Titus. Quintus was the Primus Pilus, the most senior centurion of his legion, and one of the general's most experienced and trusted leaders. Titus wouldn't send him and the First Cohort unless he wanted absolute assurance of victory.

But this task was a bit like ordering a gladiator into the arena with a dog. It seemed like overkill to Quintus.

The sound of distant thunder in the east made him consider their timing. Black storm clouds were coming, but they were far enough away. There was plenty of time to take this target before the storm got close enough to cause any trouble.

They marched through the forest and kept alert for any traps or surprises. A forest was the perfect place to hide an ambush.

But there were none. They made it through to the other side that opened up to the wide valley. On the southern side was an old, dilapidated Hasmonean fortress on the top of a steep hill. Quintus saw lookouts on the battlements alerting their fellows inside of the arrival of their enemy.

On the north side, he saw another hill upon which the city of Pella stood.

He announced to his centurions riding with him, "They've seen us in the fortress. Let us take the city first and burn it to the ground."

Quintus was confident that the Pellans did not know the Romans were coming. So they would not know what hit them.

One of his centurions mocked, "Let them come out of their little fort and attack us while we are raping their women!"

The centurions gave orders to their bannermen, who promptly alerted their soldiers with the appropriate flags. They marched in formation toward the city and passed right by the weakly fortified castle on the hill.

The cohort made their way up to the city, ready for slaughter. Quintus saw no civilians outside the city.

When they reached the top and entered the city, no one was there. Pella was completely empty.

Quintus shook his head. He said to his centurions, "They must have discovered us coming."

One of his centurions queried, "They couldn't have gotten far in such little time. Women, children. Could they all be in the fortress?"

Quintus stared at the old Hasmonean fort across the valley.

"No," he said. "It's not large enough for the population, and it's almost in ruins. They wouldn't consider it enough protection."

He turned back into the city and narrowed his eyes in thought. "I think they're hiding here."

His leaders appeared surprised. One of them laughed. "They're like children playing hide and seek. Well, let's go find them."

Another centurion asked, "Why not surrender? They don't know our intent."

"We will find out soon enough," said Quintus. "Break up into contubernia and search for hideaways, cellars, underground shelters." Contubernia were groups of eight soldiers led by an officer called a decanus.

"Do what you will with them," added Quintus. "But kill them. If it turns out they've run away into the hills, we'll hunt them down."

The cohort broke up into groups and began searching through the alleys and buildings for their hidden targets.

As one of the cities of the Decapolis, Pella had a Hellenistic heritage that had resulted in Greek architecture and planning. There were temples, theaters, and colonnaded streets of stone and marble. The orderly beauty combined with the lack of people gave it an eerie atmosphere as though its inhabitants had vanished without warning. Houses and markets were still full of foodstuffs, clothes, and even beasts of burden. If the citizens were not hiding here, they must have picked up and ran without preparation.

• • • • •

A group of eight Romans walked through a large temple to Jupiter in the middle of the city. The decanus looked around with wonder. All the Greek images of worship had been taken down. It appeared that the structure had been converted into a different purpose. He had heard that Jews and Christians despised images and all other gods but their own. It seemed like an arrogance unbefitting a powerless people. It seemed atheistic.

As the decanus stood in the middle of the grand hall looking up into the ceiling high above him, he heard the sound of a bird whistle. He knew what that meant. But the Romans didn't have time to raise their shields or draw their weapons. From behind the pillars all around them, a group of shadow warriors drew their bows and pierced every member of the squad with deadly aimed arrows.

As the decanus lay dying on the floor, gasping for breath, his punctured organs bleeding out, he saw the face of a warrior in strange armor looking down upon him. The Roman managed to grunt out, "Who are you?"

The warrior smiled and said, "You had best concern yourself with who your Creator is, because you are about to meet him and stand to account for everything you've done."

• • • • •

Another Roman contubernium found a large sewer entrance that led beneath the city. Such water canals were often a place of hiding for civilians trying to escape capture. The eight legionaries drew their weapons, raised their shields, and entered the darkness with a lit torch in search of refugees.

They had no plans for capture.

A single warrior, Saraqel the archangel, entered the sewer behind them. A small squad of Pellan warriors who were with him waited outside, guarding the entrance.

They heard the sounds of surprise, then grunts and clangs of battle.

And finally the silence of death.

A lone pair of footsteps echoed through the watery tunnel as Saraqel exited back into the daylight, his sword dripping with gore and a satisfied look of victory on his face.

"Time for the rendezvous," he said, and they slipped back out into the city.

• • • • •

Thelonius led a squad of warriors hiding in a back alley of one of the upper-class districts. He had been given command of a group by Michael, and they had prepared for this moment.

He'd wanted to explain to Cassandra what had happened to him. But there wasn't time, so it would have to wait until after the battle. If he survived. He prayed that he would.

Now he sat hidden on a rooftop watching a group of eight Roman soldiers tread cautiously through the alleyway below.

He glanced over at the young man Jonathan hiding next to him. The kid looked scared, but he had been brave. Thelonius had deliberately chosen Jonathan for his squad to protect him. He hoped the young man would survive because Thelonius knew he was a suitor for Rachel, and Thelonius thought Jonathan would make a fine husband—if Cassandra would only give Jonathan the chance.

A small group of five Pellan Christians appeared at the other end of the alley as though accidentally stumbling upon the Romans. When they saw their enemies, they fled, causing the Romans to take chase.

With their senses focused on their prey, the Romans were unprepared for the trap that collapsed beneath their feet, plunging them into a ten-foot-deep pit.

Thelonius and his fellow Pellans on the rooftops then stood up and launched javelins and arrows into their captives, killing them all.

Their next orders: move to their rendezvous point.

Other squads of hidden defenders executed similar ambushes all over the city. It was the way that Michael had determined they could best fight the more experienced Roman warriors. By hiding out and using the element of surprise upon small groups of soldiers, they were able to achieve what their lack of trained fighting skills could not.

A hundred legionaries had fallen victim to these guerilla tactics in sporadic attacks across the city before the Romans caught on and announced with trumpets their withdrawal and assembly into the city square.

•••••

Seven hundred legionaries reached the square and immediately organized a square formation, shields edge-to-edge, thrusting spears pointing out toward their hidden enemies. In the center Quintus Magnus assessed his options for dealing with these annoying gadflies.

He yelled out a command. "Let us burn this dung hill to the ground!"

The gods were there in the city square as well, but unseen and unheard by human senses. Ba'al yelled out in the heavenlies, "Come out and play, Michael! No more of your little tricks!" The sound of thunder, still miles off, punctuated the god's voice with exclamation.

But no angel showed himself in response to the challenge.

"Coward," Ba'al grumbled. Asherah, Dagon, and Molech held their weapons tight but found no use for them.

A decanus and his group of eight arrived late to the square and announced to Quintus, "Commander, they are escaping the city into the valley!"

Quintus yelled the order, "Let us go catch these mice!"

The square of soldiers immediately broke up into their smaller units for swift travel and jogged out of the city down into the valley after their prey.

As they descended the city hill, Quintus saw the defenders fleeing further down on the valley floor into a nearby wadi, a dry riverbed that emptied out into the valley. There were several hundred of them scurrying like scared rodents to get away.

Quintus knew they were mostly farmers and simple people. They wouldn't last ten minutes before the Roman line. But their surprise tactics in the city made him pause. Someone with real military strategy was leading them. And these simple men had killed almost a hundred of his legionaries with their dirty tricks. They had been preparing for this. How did they know?

He would have to be more careful.

By the time the legionaries got down into the valley, the Pellans had a good fifteen-minute lead. Unlike their quarry, the Romans did not know the terrain. And because of their weighty armaments, legionaries could not travel as swiftly as these light-armored Jews. It might take an hour or so to catch up with them. But the Romans had endurance. They would eventually catch the Christians, and when they did, there would be hell to pay.

The Romans entered the wadi after the Christians and jogged up the dry riverbed.

The gods of Canaan followed their human counterparts from a distance. Michael would be guarding the Christians, so Ba'al and his comrades would eventually face him. There was no need to rush ahead. They could be running into a trap. Let the humans hit it first.

Unfortunately, the trap was not before the gods, but behind them. Uriel, Gabriel, and Raphael exploded from the brush and launched at the gods as they passed by. Uriel hit Ba'al's legs, and they rolled into the dirt. Gabriel took down Asherah and Molech. Raphael landed on Dagon's back, dragging him to the ground.

At that moment an earthquake shook the land around them. The Roman soldiers were brought to the ground at the power of the quake.

Then a chasm opened up in the earth not far into the wadi from the valley, separating the gods from the Romans ahead of them. It looked like a huge gash in the ground across the width of the wadi and twenty feet wide.

In the fortress, many Pellans steadied themselves during the quake. Some fell to the ground from the force. Pieces of rock fell dangerously from the weakened walls, but thankfully, no one was hit by them. God was watching over them.

Cassandra leaned out over the battlement, cautiously balancing herself and little Samuel, who was resting in a sling around her hip. At her side, Noah reached to steady her, keeping careful watch over his two charges. Rachel watched from further along the parapet.

The Hasmonean fort was not manned by soldiers but housed the other half of the civilian residents not hiding out in the caves. Cassandra was among many who were watching the chase from their distant perch above the valley.

Noah and dozens of other boys not quite ready to join the battle had been given the task of protecting the families in the fort. Noah pulled Cassandra back away from the battlement wall. "Mother, don't stand too close to the wall's edge. You could be a target."

Cassandra smiled and stepped back. "Thank you, son." She was so proud of her little man. He was taking his new responsibility with more maturity than she had given him credit for. The fort was truly their last line of defense, and it gave Noah and the other eager lads a chance to be the men they were aspiring to be, though the chances of castle battle were not likely unless the Pellan warriors failed in their strategy. And if they did, then it would be all over for everyone anyway. They had gambled everything on their strategy.

Cassandra looked back out onto the plain. She heard Rachel call over to her, "Mother, do you see Jonathan?"

Cassandra shook her head no. She didn't want to feed hope or fear in Rachel.

Cassandra had been gifted by God with the special ability of a seer or a "sensitive." She could see into the spiritual realm. While the other Pellan refugees saw the Romans chasing their husbands, brothers, and sons through the wadi, she alone saw the battle of gods that was occurring at the crevice in the valley. She turned back and yelled to those waiting anxiously down below the parapets, "Pray! We must pray for Yahweh's victory over the forces of darkness!"

Many were already on their knees. The rest joined them. When Cassandra bowed her head, she saw Samuel's little eyes looking up at her with a strange sense of calm. They had just experienced a massive earthquake, and he wasn't even crying. It was as if this little infant trusted Yahweh. Like he knew who was in control.

Had he been gifted as a seer like Cassandra? She drew strength from the moment and prayed with all her soul. And finally, she was certain of what she had strongly suspected all this time. The Kharabu captains were in fact the archangels of Yahweh.

CHAPTER 18

Ba'al drew a battle mace and faced off against Uriel near the gaping crevice in the valley of Pella. He laughed. "So Yahweh sends the smallest twit of an angel against the mighty storm god?" Roaring, he flexed his bulging muscles at Uriel.

The angel smoothly drew both swords from their sheathes on his back and got into a defensive posture. "Don't forget, gas bag, you're also the god of broccoli."

Ba'al blew up with rage at the comment and swung his mace at Uriel, who dodged it with ease. The verbal insult was a reference to Ba'al being the god of vegetation as well as storm. The brute had always had a short temper and a lack of humor, so stabbing at his pride was the easiest strategy for Uriel to get him off balance.

But then Uriel was thrown off balance when Molech attacked him from behind with a flaming torch. The archangel felt the heat and spun around, his swords blocking the torch's thrust. His blond hair was singed from the close call.

Molech was a despicable deity with his reputation as a lover of child sacrifice. He spent much of his time in the underworld, so his skin was pasty and wrinkly. He looked a bit like a mole to Uriel, which could distract from the monster's treacherous skills. And Molech was driven by revenge against Uriel for what he had done during the days of Messiah in the valley of Hinnom.[1] This was going to be much more difficult than Uriel had anticipated.

"What's the matter, angel?" Molech demanded. "I don't see you joking anymore."

Gabriel faced off against the huge battle maiden Asherah, the Canaanite Queen of Heaven. Gabriel unfurled Rahab and lashed at the goddess. But she was very good with a shield and sword herself and blocked each attack of the long, flexible, heavenly blade.

Gabriel saw Dagon approaching him with his trident, and he realized that the archangels had underestimated the numbers they would need to take these divinities out.

During the earthquake, Raphael had lost his footing and Dagon was able to skewer him with his heavenly trident. Its three prongs were more than a spear. Much like Poseidon's weapon, Dagon's trident could incapacitate an angel with an occult power that was like poison. Raphael had been pierced and pushed into the crevice. He hung from a ledge. Beneath him, the chasm led deep down into the Abyss.

Though angels and Watchers were immortal, they were still created beings. They had heavenly flesh that had supernatural properties, but it was still flesh and as such could suffer pain and desecration at the hands of other divine beings. Raphael was now trapped in the very pit where they were trying to bury the gods, hanging on for his life.

Gabriel could not fret for Raphael. He had to win this battle that now pitted him and Uriel against the four strongest gods of Canaan.

But as far as Gabriel was concerned, there was no better angel to be paired with than his little spiritual brother Uriel. Sure, they bickered like family siblings, but in battle when the odds turned against them, they acted like the family they were. They had each other's back.

And the odds had just turned against them.

•••••

Quintus and his soldiers had followed their Christian prey a good half-hour through the wadi. They were now in a high-walled ravine with nowhere for the Christians to flee but forward. Miles ahead in the distance, Quintus saw the dark-clouded rainstorm continuing to advance their way. But they still had time. And the Romans were now within striking distance of their enemy.

Quintus saw the Christians faltering not far ahead now and was about to bark orders to his men. But he had failed to look above them on the ravine ledges.

Suddenly, a wave of arrows came down upon the Romans from hidden bowmen above. A trap.

A dozen soldiers were hit. But the legionaries were experienced. Almost immediately, they raised their full-body shields in protection and gathered again into testudo formation.

Quintus's horse was struck by several arrows and went down. Quintus rolled to safety behind his footmen. The moment of confusion halted the Romans.

The Christians ahead of them had also turned, launching a volley of darts as well. The legionaries were being attacked on three sides.

Quintus noticed an officer standing in front of the enemy that had turned upon them. He was well-built with black wavy hair and handsome features. He wore strange armor Quintus had never seen before—and Quintus had been all over the world with the military.

Whoever this mystery soldier was who helped these pathetic Christians with their devious tricks, Quintus would reserve the worst fate for him.

The commander yelled, "Return fire!" The Romans released their own missiles until the ambushers above them shrank away.

"Forward!" Quintus yelled again, and the legionaries jogged with shields in protective positions.

The Christians had been more clever than Quintus had been willing to grant them. He had lost a few more men, and they had lost some gained ground, but he refused to slow down. It was only a matter of minutes before these pesky rodents were caught and exterminated.

•••••

At the crevice, Uriel swung his two swords, one in each hand, with a smooth water-like fluidity. He blocked Ba'al's mace and Molech's torch with each attack. But Ba'al's strength was mighty. Uriel had to shift his position and change arms of defense because Ba'al's hits would jar Uriel's arm to the bone, weakening his strength with each blow. He would not be able to keep this up much longer. He would have to take down one of these monsters soon or he would break under the sheer stress of Ba'al's force.

Gabriel swung Rahab wide, its ten-foot arc keeping Asherah and Dagon at bay. It snapped off Asherah's shield, cutting clean through the defensive armament and splitting it in half. Rahab had a nasty bite. Stumbling backward, Asherah almost slipped into the crevice behind her. But Dagon was there in a flash, jerking her back from the precipice.

Gabriel glanced over and saw an opportunity to help Uriel. Ba'al's back was to Gabriel, so the angel snapped his blade toward the behemoth and caught his left arm, slicing through the massive muscles. The storm god roared in pain, his left arm now rendered useless.

Uriel took that moment to focus on Molech. He used his swords in rapid sweeps to disarm the deity and knock him senseless to the ground. Drawing some

90

Cherubim hair from a pouch on his belt, Uriel wrapped it around the Watcher's hands and neck. Cherubim hair was the only cord that the Watchers could not break. So it was the archangels' binding of choice.[2] Uriel pulled Molech up and gave him a hard, swift kick to the butt, launching the god into the crevice that led down to the Abyss. His pathetic scream empowered the archangels.

Gabriel spun back around toward Asherah and Dagon and cracked his whip-sword at them.

But Dagon was ready. He raised his trident and used it as a pole to block the sword, causing the blade to wrap around it. Dagon then jerked the trident back, pulling Gabriel off his feet and slinging him behind the Philistine monster—down into the crevice.

Gabriel held on to the sword handle with both hands and hit the rock wall inside the chasm.

He dangled over the precipice at the mercy of Dagon's hold. Below him, the darkness of the Abyss clawed at his feet.

But he knew Dagon would never release his trident and lose it in order to defeat the angel.

Giving up his plan, the Watcher pulled Gabriel up and out of the crevice. This time he arced the angel high and slammed him to the ground. Gabriel was knocked dizzy for just a second.

Enough time for Asherah to rush him.

• • • • •

Quintus and his soldiers had repelled the attack of arrows from above. They pushed forward, shields up. He wanted to grab these tricksters by the throat and strangle them one by one.

Then he heard a horn blow from the Christian position and suddenly realized that the arrow attack was only a distraction. A sound of rumbling overhead drew his attention upward. On both sides of the ravine, a pile of boulders had been released with a manmade break.

An avalanche of rock now fell upon the legionaries, threatening to crush them from two sides. Quintus screamed, "Retreat!"

Everyone but the front line was able to pull back out of the way.

Rocks of all sizes pummeled the men, who tried to dodge them or block the barrage with their shields. Quintus saw his advance guard engulfed in a landslide of stone.

When the cloud of dust had settled, he discovered that twenty of his soldiers had been crushed to death.

The trick had only served to make Quintus angrier.

These Christians had used dirty tactics to kill or wound close to two hundred of his men. Who was leading them with such skill? It was embarrassing. And it meant he would no longer show mercy. He would no longer put them swiftly to the sword. He was going to take his time, torture each and every one of them, crucify them all for the trouble they had caused. And he would crucify all their women and children as well.

Let them and all their families rot in the sun facing each other. Let the birds of prey gouge out their eyes and pick at their dying flesh.

Quintus regrouped his six hundred soldiers. They climbed over the dam of rock and began to jog in formation toward their imminent victims.

He would fall prey to no more tricks.

• • • • •

Back at the crevice, Gabriel had barely shaken off his dizziness from being slung onto the ground by Dagon. He looked up to see Asherah running at him full force, screaming a war cry with her sword held high, ready to cleave Gabriel in two.

Then a sword came flying out of nowhere and hit the goddess in the ribs, making her tumble into the dirt. As she landed at Gabriel's feet, he saw Uriel with one sword, now facing off against Ba'al.

"You're welcome!" the blond angel yelled out. He grabbed his other sword with both hands, holding off Ba'al's pounding mace with even less protection than before. Ba'al's left arm had been cut, but he was right-handed and swung with angry vengeance.

Gabriel withdrew the sword from Asherah and pulled out some binding from his pouch to hogtie the wench goddess.

When he had finished, he looked up to see Uriel fall to the ground under Ba'al's mighty swing.

But the monster didn't finish off the angel. Instead he whistled to Dagon, who was about to attack Gabriel. The two of them then turned completely around and sprinted toward the crevice.

Their divine muscles pounded the ground, and they launched into mid-air, just barely making it to the other side of the twenty-foot divide. They rolled in the dirt, got up, and bolted off into the wadi after the Roman legions.

They were going to empower the Romans to kill the Christians.

Gabriel dragged the squirming Asherah over to the crevice. He called out, "No need to chase them down. They'll be coming back. Whether they want to or not."

He looked down at the goddess, muttered, "Enjoy your prison, tramp," and threw Asherah into the pit.

He walked over to the exhausted Uriel.

He handed him his sword. "This does make us even—so far. One for one."

Uriel stood, brushing himself off and taking the sword. "If it weren't for my sword stopping Asherah…"

Gabriel interrupted him, "If it weren't for my slicing Ba'al's arm…"

The blond angel nodded with a shrug. "Fair enough. We're even. Now let's get ready for these two sons of Belial."

• • • • •

In the wadi, Thelonius followed Michael as he led the several hundred Pellans as fast as he could through the ravine. The walls were highest and steepest here.

That avalanche was their last stratagem. They had no more left. They had killed almost two hundred legionaries with Michael's superior military leadership. But it wasn't enough. Hundreds more Romans kept coming, and they were almost upon them. Thelonius didn't see how they would get out of this.

Thelonius jogged close to Michael and was about to address him when Michael stopped the Pellan men with his hand in the air. He turned to face them. They were sweating heavily and exhausted from running. Some of them knelt on the ground, they were so tired. Most of them looked like they wouldn't be able to run any longer.

"What will we do, commander, fight?" Thelonius asked Michael.

Someone else shouted out from the crowd, "We can't win!"

"Have we not trained you?" Michael demanded.

"We did well in the city," Thelonius responded. "But we're still no match for them in open combat. Even with the Kharabu at our side." The thirty Kharabu warriors surrounded Michael along with three of his captains— Saraqel, Raguel, and Remiel.

93

Thelonius saw a lack of fear in the looks of the Kharabu.

Then Michael told them, "You have fought bravely, men of Pella. And you are correct. We cannot win this battle. You have been brought to the end of yourselves. Now you have no one to rely upon but the Lord."

Another shouted, "They are almost upon us! Around the bend!"

Michael pointed to the rock walls, where Thelonius saw ropes dangling from small cave openings all around them. "Then you had better climb quickly and get inside the caves."

"But we'll be trapped!" Thelonius exclaimed.

"No," said Michael. "You will be delivered by the hand of the Lord."

Thelonius looked over at young Jonathan, who looked as confused as the rest of them. This plan was clearly something Michael had hidden from them. Cassandra had often speculated to Thelonius that Michael and his captains might be angels in disguise. Thelonius prayed that she was right.

"They haven't failed us yet," Thelonius said. Following Jonathan over to one of the ropes, he started to climb.

· · · · ·

Quintus and his legionaries had left the avalanche of rock behind them. They had lost some time and distance to their prey from that last stunt, but not much.

The Christians were running out of tricks. The Romans were ready for anything.

As they rounded a bend in the ravine, they came to a halt. The Christians were nowhere to be seen. They could not have possibly traversed the half-mile that Quintus could see into the distance.

He looked around at the walls. They seemed too steep to climb. Was this another trick? He and his men searched for signs of subterfuge.

"There's one!" a legionary cried out. He was pointing to a small opening in the rock wall thirty feet up. Quintus saw a rope pulled up and vanish into a hole. Then a rock moved to cover the opening.

Well, if those cowardly Christians really thought hiding in caves would protect them from his legionaries, they would soon learn that they'd simply trapped themselves. Quintus looked ahead for a path up the cliff face. That was when he saw the Christians' strange lead warrior again. This time he was simply standing alone in the middle of the wadi, his dark, wavy hair tossed around by a wind coming from behind him.

What was the fool doing? Giving himself up?

Then Quintus looked past the warrior and saw in the distance above the steep walls of the wadi dark storm clouds still pouring rain as they had been doing all day. He reconsidered where they were standing—in the middle of a wadi. Wadis were dry riverbeds in the mountains where flash floods could rage without warning, created by water built up from heavy rain storms—like the one in the distance.

His glance dropped down from the sky, and he saw rushing toward them a ten-foot wall of water. And the legionaries were trapped between two tall barricades of rock on either side.

Quintus yelled, "Climb! Climb!"

He found a scalable portion of the ravine that he could scramble up and did so as fast as he could.

Other soldiers followed suit. Still others ran the opposite way as though hoping to find somewhere, anywhere, that offered safety from the rushing waters.

No one could outrun the deluge.

Quintus looked back. The lead Pellan warrior was still standing in the path of the water. The fool was committing suicide. It didn't make sense.

The centurion saw the water pass over the strange warrior and consume him in its wake. *Good riddance*, he thought.

Quintus had made it up a good twenty feet when the water hit his location. The splash of a wave slammed into the rock below him. He felt his legs pulled by its force.

But he held on as the wave passed.

The power of the surging flood was unstoppable. Nothing could stand in its wake or survive its fluid fury. Glancing down, Quintus saw many of his soldiers being swept away, caught up and drowned in the torrent.

He would surely lose most of his men. They would no longer have the numbers to be able to carry out Caesar's command to kill the Christians.

Now, the hunters would become the hunted.

• • • • •

Cherubim hair in hand, Uriel and Gabriel waited for their enemies to be returned to them in the flood waters. They'd positioned themselves with their backs against a large boulder not far up the wadi, beyond the long chasm in the ravine floor into which they'd tossed Asherah and Molech.

95

Michael had planned this preternatural event as their last resort. Just as at the time of Noah's Flood, the Watchers were stronger in the desert of chaos, but weaker in water.[3] The archangels had bound the original two hundred Watchers into the earth at the Flood. In a similar way, Uriel and Gabriel would do so now.

The tidal wave of water soon crashed around a bend in the wadi on its way toward them. Bracing themselves against the boulder, the two angels were slammed by the powerful force of the swirling torrent. Corpses of legionaries swept past them in the current. As with the Egyptians during the Exodus, there must have been several hundred drowned soldiers. Uriel treasured the poetic justice of it all.

He then spotted the larger bodies of the two Watchers, Ba'al and Dagon, flailing helplessly toward them. Michael was not far behind.

Launching away from the boulder, the two angels swam toward the incapacitated gods to bind them. But now they too were caught in the tsunami of water. As the raging current swept them down the ravine toward the open valley, the water reached the huge crack in the ravine floor. The tidal wave spilled over the rim in a mighty cascade.

Everyone—legionaries, Watchers, and angels—were sucked down into the fissure like some monstrous throat devouring the flood waters.

On the battlement of the Hasmonean fortress, Cassandra had glanced up from her urgent prayers in time to see the flash of sunlight on tossing water as a towering wave rushed like a baptism of judgment down the wadi into which Roman warriors had vanished. But the wave never reached the valley. Around her, Cassandra heard astonished exclamations and even screams.

Only Cassandra's supernatural sight had shown her what was really happening just inside the opening to the wadi—a massive crevice in the earth that was swallowing up the raging torrent. Cassandra kept her vigil until she saw four beings crawl exhausted but victorious out of the crevice—the Kharabu warriors Michael, Uriel, Gabriel, and Raphael.

Down by the fissure, Uriel complained to Michael, "Did you help Gabriel bind Dagon? Because if you did, then that means I won the bet. I bound two gods by myself."

"I did not help Gabriel," said Michael. "I was busy finding Raphael."

Raphael was only now starting to overcome the poison of Dagon's trident. He stumbled. Michael helped steady his fellow wounded warrior.

"So we are tied, little guy," said Gabriel to his competitor.

"We're not done yet, big guy," said Uriel.

"That is beyond dispute," said Michael. "But I have an urgent mission for Uriel."

A half-hour later, a rain storm arrived in the valley along with hundreds of Pellan Christian men who came jogging out of the flood-swept wadi and up to the fortress gates led by the Kharabu. Cheers for God's deliverance resounded throughout the fort.

Up above on the battlement, Rachel stood close to Cassandra, her head scarf extended to shield Samuel from the rain. To Cassandra, the rain was like a cleansing flood washing away the evil that had threatened them—and with it their fear. Many all over the fortress had their hands raised to heaven in worship to the true storm God.

Below, Noah was among the young "guardians" who stood proudly, if soaked to the bones, to receive the incoming soldiers. As the Pellan warriors passed through the fortress gates, Cassandra saw Noah beaming as Michael greeted him and the other young lads with gratitude. Yes, her son was becoming a young man.

"Jonathan!" At Rachel's exclamation, Cassandra glanced beyond Noah to see her daughter's suitor among the crowd of warriors entering the gate. He strode shoulder-to-shoulder with Thelonius, both smiling proudly. Alive.

So the young Jewish warrior as well as Thelonius had survived the battle. *Impressive.* But Cassandra leaned over as Rachel began waving desperately and hissed, "Now is not the time. We are still in danger."

Rachel backed down with a frown of disappointment.

Overhead, the storm passed quickly over the valley, and the rain stopped as suddenly as it had begun. The warriors gathered the civilians around. Then Michael announced that the surviving Romans who had escaped the waters were so few that they ran in fear of being captured. Pella had won the battle.

Cassandra was not satisfied with the news. She asked Michael, "But won't they return with greater numbers?"

Michael smiled. "Fear not. Yahweh will protect you."

She didn't want to know how. She trusted the commander of the Kharabu. He had always proven himself worthy through the years. This would be no different.

But the deliverance of Pella only made Cassandra more determined to let her husband know that his family was alive and safe. Unfortunately, they had received word that Jerusalem was now surrounded by Roman armies. And she had not received any letters from Alexander for some time. She wasn't sure he was even alive. She had to know.

As dangerous as it was, she had to get to Jerusalem.

And when the dragon saw that he had been thrown down to the earth, he pursued the woman who had given birth to the male child. But the woman was given the two wings of the great eagle so that she might fly from the serpent into the wilderness, to the place where she is to be nourished for a time, and times, and half a time. The serpent poured water like a river out of his mouth after the woman, to sweep her away with a flood. But the earth came to the help of the woman, and the earth opened its mouth and swallowed the river that the dragon had poured from his mouth. Then the dragon became furious with the woman and went off to make war on the rest of her offspring, on those who keep the commandments of God and hold to the testimony of Jesus.

Apocalypse 12:13–17

CHAPTER 19

Jerusalem

Jacob followed Gischala and two hundred armed Zealots through the underground horse stables below the temple mount. This was a vast, arched cavern built by Herod for horses and chariots. They were only a quarter full. Famine and civil war had taken its toll. Jacob thanked God they were not planning on engaging in any field battles beyond the walls because the Jews would clearly not do well against Roman cavalry with such insufficient cavalry of their own.

The company marched through the tunnel on their way to a secret entrance in the residential area southeast of the temple. They exited the tunnel into a government building. The soldiers checked their weapons and waited for Gischala's command while Jacob snuck out ahead into the streets to reconnoiter.

Their target was a small marketplace with little activity going on. Only a handful of stands were open, and most of these were leatherworks or pottery. There was so little food to go around that many merchants were saving as much as they could for themselves during the siege.

But the market square had a large platform in the middle where the Two Witnesses were spewing their hateful message to the few who would listen, just as Gischala's spies had told him.

Above the city, the sky had gone dark with storm clouds and rumbling thunder. Jacob could see the rains coming their way. It would make things messy, but it might also keep the incident from drawing too much public attention. Especially if anything went wrong.

Gischala had become fed up with the two false prophets, especially since he'd proved unable to find out anything about their secret power from his captive Alexander. So Gischala had left the doctor in the dungeon, deciding instead to lead an entire armed company to take out the Witnesses. He reasoned that whatever sorcery these two troublemakers had been able to conjure in the past few years, it would surely not be enough to stop two hundred armed soldiers from overwhelming them.

Despite his Jewish faith, Gischala didn't believe that there was such a thing as guardian angels watching over them. Such were the fantasies of heavenly imagination and storytelling, but certainly not earthly reality.

Jacob was not so sure. And he felt that even Gischala was hedging his bets just in case. A handful of so-called invisible guardians would find their hands full of these experienced visible warriors.

Just in case.

So here Jacob was, forced to help Gischala hunt down the Christian prophets and confirm their location for Gischala's strike force.

Marching out into the market square, the warriors surrounded the platform where the Two Witnesses were preaching. Gischala stood back with Jacob, watching to see what happened next.

The sky released its floodgates and poured down upon city. The few tradesmen still lingering had packed up at the sight of rain, and now fled the scene with the arrival of the soldiers. No one wanted to be collateral damage.

The soldiers held their shields high and their swords firmly in their grips despite the pounding rain that drenched them all.

To Jacob, the Two Witnesses looked like cornered and drowning rats in their soggy sackcloth clinging to their frail bodies beneath the wind and rain that pelted them with fury. The last three years had not been kind to the two of them as they scrounged for scraps to live. Even the younger and stronger Egyptian had withered in his strength.

Jacob glanced over at Gischala, who waited to give his command. Was he reconsidering his plan? Could these two false prophets also command the weather?

Then suddenly the rain stopped. Rather, it moved onward through the city, carried along by fast-moving summer storm clouds.

Jacob saw a grin of confidence cross Gischala's lips. The luck of the Witnesses had just changed. The two men looked up, then knelt down, bowing their heads in prayer. Or were they baring their heads to be removed by swords?

"Zealots!" Gischala yelled out. The soldiers readied their battle stance. "Forward!"

The warriors inched forward cautiously, preparing for an unforeseen attack. They too had heard the rumors and gossip about those who had previously tried to harm the Witnesses.

But Jacob did not see any of them falter as if seeing alleged invisible guardians. They stepped up the stairs with unified precision. They were now a mere thirty feet from their weak and unarmed targets.

Jacob reconsidered his own fears. Perhaps their special protection had been taken away. Perhaps their luck had run out.

Before he could think any further, he heard the sound of rumbling thunder, the last of the passing storm, followed by a blinding flash in the sky above.

A fiery bolt of lightning punched through the clouds and hit the circle of soldiers. But this was not a typical lightning bolt that vanished upon impact. This one seemed to hang from the sky with its flaming fury and then move around the band of soldiers, burning them to death in a circle of fire.

Zealots screamed in agony as their flesh roasted on their bodies. Most dropped their weapons and shields. Some ran wild without direction before dropping dead in a sizzling, smoking heap. But all of them were burned to cinders by the flames.

And then the fire was gone, It went back up into the sky, followed by a crack of thunder so loud Jacob covered his ears.

When he looked back up, he saw the circle of two hundred Zealots, now smoldering corpses, surrounding the Witnesses—who remained untouched by the catastrophe.

Jacob peed in his tunic with fright. He looked over at Gischala, whose face was frozen in shock.

Whatever they had just seen—sorcery, a freak of weather, a miracle—it had completely obliterated Gischala's forces with pinpoint accuracy while leaving the Witnesses alive.

Whatever it was, this was no coincidence nor luck.

Gischala turned and ran back to the temple. Following, Jacob caught up with him. Gischala's expression was full of confusion, but he said nothing. It was as though he'd been made mute by the sorcery. Unable to even respond. His only concern was to get as far away from this scene as possible.

And Jacob knew Gischala would never try to touch the Two Witnesses again.

For his own part, Jacob was shaken to the core. Was he on the wrong side of this war? He was helping Gischala for the sake of the city, but he had just seen Gischala's power burn up in a flash of fire. Jacob had despised the Christians, seeking to punish them for their treason against the temple and against Torah. But why were the demon-possessed prophets being protected?

He felt futility come over him. Despair.

What side was he on?
What side was God on?

CHAPTER 20

Transjordan Mountains

Quintus Magnus dragged his feet through the dirt of the desert highlands of the Transjordan. He had led his seventy soldiers who'd survived the flash flood near Pella deeper into the mountains to regroup and make their way to Jerusalem.

The plan was to face the shame of failure before Titus, then request a full legion to return and take swift and ruthless revenge upon the Pellan Christians. The centurion knew Titus well enough to feel assured the general would let Quintus redeem his failure.

But they had to find their way to Jerusalem first. And something was wrong. They had a scout who knew these mountains, and they had been following the setting sun toward the west. But for some strange reason, they had been marching for two full days but still seemed deep in the mountains, miles away from any life.

It didn't make sense to Quintus. By all accounts, they must have travelled thirty or forty miles easily, which should have placed them on the other side of the Jordan River on their way to Jerusalem.

But here they were surrounded by the same desert mountains of the Transjordan without any sign of the Jordan Valley.

What was happening? They had lost most of their food and water rations in the flash flood, so they had run out after two days. They could not survive much longer without water. And they were lost.

Were they hallucinating? No, that wasn't possible. They were all following the sun in its westerly direction. They couldn't possibly all be having the same hallucination.

Quintus coughed through a parched throat and croaked out, "Scout, come here!"

The scout, a small, blond legionary, approached with a map he'd pulled from his pouch.

"Where do you reckon we are?" Quintus asked.

Opening the parchment, the scout pointed to a place on the map. "I recognize these hills. We should be about here. The Jordan should be just past these couple ranges."

"Then we march on," said Quintus, squinting up into the sun in its westerly course in the sky. "Unless the gods have swapped the heavens and made the sun to rise in the west and set in the east."

The scout chuckled. "We should reach the Jordan by tomorrow."

Quintus noticed a rock formation on the hill above them. It was a large one shaped like a human head watching them. His mind filled with confusion.

He had seen that formation the day before. That very same human-looking head. How could it be? Was it a similar formation in a different location? Was it just a coincidence? Or had they been traveling in a circle? But he had carefully watched the sun descending in front of them directly west. They had always been traveling directly west.

Unless the gods had swapped the heavens.

Dehydration was making him think crazy thoughts. He had to push on. He gestured to his men behind him to keep moving.

They plodded forward. A soldier dropped to the ground in a heap. He was dead of exhaustion and lack of water. The other soldiers ignored him. This was no time for heroics. They had to survive or all die out here in the wasteland.

Up front, the small scout pulled out from the slow march to make sure the others were following.

Unlike the others, the scout did not seem to be dehydrated. His lips were not cracked dry, his eyes were not cloudy, and his steps were not stumbling.

He was in fact the angel Uriel in disguise.

He looked up into the bright, burning sun in the sky. Only he knew that God had swapped the heavens to make the sun rise in the west and set in the east—or at least to the eyes of these hallucinating legionaries.

Returning to the front of the line, Uriel continued to lead the soldiers deeper into the eastern mountains of Arabia and away from their only hope and source of life, the River Jordan.

CHAPTER 21

Jerusalem

Alexander felt groggy and dizzy with a headache. All his joints ached from the cold, damp environment of his dungeon cell. He drifted in and out of sleep in a dehydrated daze. When he was awake, he would pray. Prayer was one thing imprisonment could not stop. In fact, he had never prayed so much in his life. He had always been a man of action, trying to love his neighbor through the sharing of the Gospel or the healing of medicine. His biggest spiritual weakness was his prayer life.

Not anymore. Incarceration left one with nothing but solitude and time. The options were limited. Focus on your cage and destroy your mind with madness. Focus on your captors and destroy your soul with bitterness. Or focus on your God and refresh both mind and soul with the freedom of prayer.

Alexander prayed for the lives of those in his infirmary as well as the Christians who were helping them. He prayed for his wife and three children in Pella—that the Lord would protect them and watch over them along with the other Christians of that city. He prayed that God would give him the faith to accept whatever suffering he would have to experience. He prayed for another chance to minister to his lost brethren in the city before they were consumed by the fires of judgment. He prayed that God would free him from this prison so that he could accomplish his ultimate goal of helping the newly saved elect to escape Jerusalem.

He felt himself drifting away from his prayer into a dream sleep. He had read and studied the scroll of the Apocalypse so much that he sometimes dreamed of its visions as though he were there with the apostle John.

He had another one of those dreams.

Alexander felt himself carried away by the Holy Spirit to a great, high mountain. Mountains were the meeting places or residences of gods. They were symbols of the cosmic order. Jesus had looked upon Mount Hermon, the mountain of Bashan, and had declared that he would build his kingdom upon the destroyed ruins of that rock. Mount Hermon was the primeval mountain of rebellion where the fallen Watchers had come down. Jesus had dispossessed that cosmic kingdom of darkness.[1]

Alexander sensed that the mountain in his dream was Bashan because he could see the new Jerusalem, God's holy city, coming down out of heaven in victory upon it. Or was it a symbol of Mount Zion, highest of spiritual mountains, of which Bashan was envious?[2]

He heard a loud voice from the throne of God declare, "Behold, the temple of God is with man. He will dwell with them, and they will be his people, and God himself will be with them as their God. He will wipe away every tear from their eyes, and death shall be no more. Neither shall there be mourning nor crying nor pain anymore. For the former things have passed away. Behold, I am making all things new. It is finished. I am the Alpha and the Omega, the beginning and the end."[3]

Alexander felt the weight of his present suffering lift from his body in the presence of this vision of glorious splendor. The new creation had come in Christ's death, resurrection, and ascension. It was the voice of his savior coming from that throne. Jesus had finished the atonement as prophesied by Daniel. He had instituted the new creation. In Christ, all believers were right now part of that new creation, the new covenant. It was spiritually and cosmically understood as a new heavens and earth that had been inaugurated at the cross.[4]

The new covenant kingdom had come down out of heaven to the earth itself. It was a kingdom where God's Holy Spirit dwelt in his people through faith in Jesus. Those people were the new heavenly temple of God's presence that would replace the old earthly temple about to be destroyed.[5] And that spiritual kingdom would eventually wipe away every physical tear and pain. Even death had been defeated at the cross and would one day be no more. Death had lost its sting. Alexander was experiencing the first stages of that expanding new mountain that had begun as a rock cut without hands but would ultimately fill the whole earth. A kingdom that had already started as the smallest of seeds but would one day become the biggest tree of all.

The kingdom of God had come to earth in the work of Jesus Christ, establishing a new covenant. But its full expression was yet to be manifested in history. Even the Great Tribulation that had almost wiped out the Christians would not be victorious because God's plans could not be thwarted. As Daniel had prophesied of Messiah when he ascended to the throne of David at the right hand of God, "to the Son of Man was given dominion and glory and a kingdom, that all peoples, nations, and languages should serve him; his dominion is an everlasting dominion, which shall not pass away, and his kingdom one that shall not be destroyed."[6]

Alexander looked up at the visionary new Jerusalem in his dream. It was a huge cube of a city that the apostle John had measured to be 12,000 stadia along each side. This was the approximate size of the inhabited world, the Roman empire. The kingdom of God would eventually fill the whole world that was now under Rome's dominion.[7]

The city had a divine radiance like that of rare crystal jewels embedded in its high and impenetrable walls, having been measured for protection by Messiah himself. The walls kept out the detestable enemies of God, unlike the walls of the earthly Jerusalem that were soon to be breached by the abomination of desolation.

Twelve gates guarded by twelve angels led into the city. On the gates were inscribed the names of the twelve tribes of the sons of Israel. This represented the patriarchs of the faith rather than their fleshly descendants. The 144,000 Jewish Christians who were saved through their faith in Jesus were those from the twelve tribes, the believing Remnant. The foundation of their election was not in ethnic heritage, but in the transformation of those twelve tribes into the twelve apostles of faith, who were represented as foundations of the wall of the city inscribed with their names. A new people of God required a new foundation in this new city with a new priesthood of all believers in Christ. That new priesthood was symbolized by twelve jewels of the high priest's breastplate embedded in that foundation.[8]

The fact that the gates were spread out over all four walls of the city was a symbol of the four points of the compass. God's messengers would draw people from the four winds into Christ's new Jerusalem. The words of Jesus echoed in Alexander's mind:

> *And he will send out his messengers with a loud trumpet call, and*
> *they will gather his chosen from the four winds, from one end of*
> *heaven to the other...*
> Go therefore and make disciples of all nations.
>
> *Matthew 24:31; 28:19*

Suddenly, Alexander was inside the visionary city. It was both city and garden. The river of the water of life flowed through the very center of the city from the throne of God and of the Lamb. The apostle John had explained to Alexander that this river was the Holy Spirit, the living water that nourished all believers in the body of Christ.[9]

107

But it was also symbolic of the rivers of Eden that were restored spiritually with the new covenant, along with the tree of life that grew on either side of the river, bringing the Gospel of healing to the nations.[10] That tree of life, originally guarded from human access, was restored spiritually in the tree of Christ's crucifixion.[11] The tree of death had become the tree of life. Christians now ate of that tree and escaped the curse of sin.[12] The restoration of Eden had been inaugurated with the new Jerusalem of the new covenant kingdom.

Alexander looked around him. He saw no temple in the garden city because the Lord God Almighty and the Lamb were its temple, residing in the body of Christ.[13] All believers were now living stones being built up into the new spiritual house of the Lord.[14]

The body of Christ was the new spiritual temple residing in the new heavenly Jerusalem of the new covenant on spiritual Mount Zion. The writer of Hebrews had explained it that way.

You have come to Mount Zion and to the city of the living God, the heavenly Jerusalem, and to the assembly of the firstborn who are enrolled in heaven, and to Jesus, the mediator of a new covenant.

Hebrews 12:22–24

Alexander felt overwhelmed by the beauty and peace of it all. This vision of the heavenly city and temple established through Messiah's humiliation and glory would remain forever, even after the earthly city and temple were destroyed. The heaven and earth of the old covenant were about to be destroyed and replaced by a new heaven and earth of the new covenant. What had begun in the heavenly realm through Christ's death, resurrection, and ascension would be consummated in earthly history.

Alexander's peaceful dream was interrupted by the sound of an iron cell door clanging shut. He opened his eyes. Through his bleary vision, he saw two men before him. Gischala sat on a stool. Behind him stood Jacob, watching like a vulture.

With his foot Gischala pushed forward a platter of bread and vegetables that had been placed on the floor. Next to it he set a large chalice full of wine.

Alexander felt his mouth start to salivate at the sight and smell. He hadn't eaten in so long.

Gischala said, "Eat slowly. You don't want to throw it up."

But Alexander already knew that. It was a temptation for a starving person to gobble up a meal too quickly, causing their sick body to reject it. One had to reintroduce healthy food slowly to an unhealthy body.

Alexander eyed his visitors suspiciously. If the food was poisoned, so be it. He would embrace his destiny with faith in God's provision. He picked up the chalice first and took a gulping drink.

His voice croaked out, "What do you want?"

Gischala stared at him. "I want you alive."

CHAPTER 22

Pella

Apollyon walked past dozens of dead bodies lying along the valley deep in the Transjordanian mountains. Birds of prey picked at the dead flesh. Others circled overhead, awaiting their place at the dinner table of human corpses.

These were the last of the cohort of legionary soldiers that had been sent by Titus to destroy Pella and kill the Christians. Yet they were a hundred miles east of the city into Arabia. They had marched away from the city and away from Jerusalem into the eastern wasteland.

The muscular deity Marduk stood near Apollyon as bodyguard. They had ridden his storm chariot here pulled by his four stallions of hell. Marduk tended to them now in preparation for the return ride. Each was a different color. The one named Slaughterer was red, Merciless pale, Overwhelmer white, and Soaring black.[1]

Five other gods walked amongst the dead, searching for survivors. There were none. The soldiers had all died of dehydration in this desert mountain range—and within walking distance of a small brook on the other side of the ridge. Experienced legionary warriors who could easily have followed the sun west had marched the opposite way right to their deaths like a herd of swine off a cliff. It was absurd.

"This was Michael's doing," grumbled Apollyon. He stopped when he found the dead cohort commander, a grizzly one-eyed centurion with an eye patch. His good eye was frozen open, staring into the Abyss of death. Apollyon muttered to himself with disgust, "Blind leading the blind." He thrust his sword into the good eye for final measure.

He whistled for the other gods to follow him back to the city of Pella.

They traveled along a ravine to the west. As they passed through the gauntlet of rock, Apollyon saw the water damage and the bodies of some dead legionaries along the way. He deduced the flash floods that often ran through these wadis had

110

apparently been used as a miraculous defensive tactic by the angels to protect the Christians.

Clever! And I suspect there is more to be disappointed by.

When they arrived at the valley of Pella, Marduk rode his chariot up to the large crevice just inside the wadi where it emptied into the valley. The Babylonian storm god pulled his horses to a halt near the rim.

Apollyon looked into the fissure, then up the wadi. He could surmise what had happened. Michael had drawn the Romans and their Watchers into the wadi, where the archangel must have brought a flash flood down upon them, sweeping the Watchers into the crevice, where they'd been bound into the Abyss.

Clever indeed.

The five other gods caught up to them in their chariots.

Marduk got his attention, "My lord."

Apollyon looked up at the city above them. Seven figures stood a distance apart from each other at the top of the hill. They were armed and ready like sentinels guarding the city. Even at this distance, Apollyon knew who the seven were.

He looked back into the fissure and said, "I underestimated the prince of Israel. I didn't anticipate this strategy. As much of an overkill as it is."

"Shall we attack, Master?" said Marduk. He calmed his restless steeds, who were snorting smoke, ready for battle.

"No, you fool. Those are the seven archangels."

Marduk placed his hand on his mace with pride. His armor gleamed in the hot sun. "We are seven."

Their attention was suddenly drawn to the sky above the city, where a tumult of swirling clouds opened up to reveal a sight even more frightening to the gods. The heavenly host from the throne of God, ten thousand times ten thousand holy ones, were arraigned on chariots of fire and ready to descend. It sent a chill of fear through Apollyon's spine. It was the same vision he had seen at the Mountain of the Amorites when he had attempted to take the angels hostage.

"We wouldn't stand a chance against the heavenly host. I cannot afford to lose any more battles." Apollyon stared up at the archangels. "Besides, if Michael is going to put all his forces into defending this puny congregation of insignificant Christians, that only makes Jerusalem an easier victory."

Marduk grinned with acceptance. Apollyon didn't want to mention that the loss of Ba'al was also a convenience since he had not trusted the brute or his sister

Anat. He had suspected they were plotting a coup. But now both of them were gone and with them all concerns of mutiny against the Angel of the Abyss.

Apollyon gestured for the other deities to follow him back to Jerusalem.

CHAPTER 23

Jerusalem

In his dungeon cell, Alexander finished half his food and saved the rest for later. He had eaten in silence as Gischala watched him with an odd curiosity in his eyes.

Something had happened to change the warrior's disposition toward him. But Alexander had no idea what it was.

Finally, Gischala spoke. "This Messiah you follow. The Nazarene." He paused thoughtfully. "The prophet Zechariah spoke of Messiah, the branch of David. He said that when Messiah came, his rule would be from sea to sea and from the Euphrates River to the ends of the earth. That he would set the prisoners free and restore the stronghold of Israel. *Your* messiah is dead."[1]

"He is alive," Alexander corrected calmly. "He has resurrected from the dead. He is the resurrection of Israel."

Gischala opened his arms in a gesture all around him and demanded with disdain, "Then where is he?"

"He is coming."

Gischala sighed. But he didn't look angry. He seemed to be actually trying to understand.

Alexander said, "Messiah does rule over all the earth, seated at the right hand of God in heaven. And he did set prisoners free from sin. But the tribes of the Land missed him because they were looking for an earthly kingdom as opposed to a spiritual one. The rest of that prophecy you quoted says, 'Behold, your king comes to you, righteous and having salvation, humble and mounted on a donkey. And he shall speak peace to the nations.' These were the very actions and words of Jesus. And his kingdom is not of this earth."

Jacob, remaining quiet until now, jumped in. "And what of the temple? Zechariah said Messiah would build the temple of Yahweh with the help of foreigners. That he would rule as king with a priest on his throne. Where is this king and priest and temple?"[2]

"Jesus *is* building his temple," said Alexander. "A spiritual one with believers as living stones. Both Jew and Gentile alike. Jesus is not only the prophet Moses foretold. He is also a priest according to the order of Melchizedek, and he is king from the line of David."[3]

"I've heard all that before," said Jacob dismissively. Alexander guessed he was referring to a discussion Cassandra had once told him she'd had with the apostate.

Gischala appeared not to have heard it before. "But we are still a scattered people," he complained. "Zechariah also wrote that Yahweh would gather his people from among the nations. Look at us. We are more divided and scattered to the four winds than we have ever been."[4]

"No. Yahweh has been gathering his people from the four winds, from every tribe and nation, for the past forty years. In Messiah, believing Jews *are* the Restoration of Israel. They are the Remnant of Zechariah, and they were gathered in protection from the wrath to come."[5]

"In Pella," said Jacob with more contempt. "Are you so sure they are protected?"

Alexander hadn't heard from Cassandra in a month. Their letters could no longer get through the Roman blockade. He truly didn't know if the Christians were still safe. He felt the bite of fear. He prayed for faith.

"Perhaps," said Gischala, "the Day of the Lord may be the one thing upon which you and I agree. All the nations are gathering against Jerusalem to battle just as Zechariah predicted." He was referring to all the nations that comprised the Roman armies now surrounding them. "Then Yahweh will come and all the holy ones with him."[6]

Gischala stared off into the distance as he recounted the prophecy of the end of Zechariah with sober reflection as if he was seeing it in a vision. "Two thirds of this people shall be cut off and perish. Only one third shall be left alive. Then Yahweh will go out and fight against those nations. And on that day, his feet shall stand on the Mount of Olives. And it shall be split in two from east to west by a very wide valley."[7]

Alexander was following the general's words closely. The symbolism of Yahweh "coming down" to earth to strike it was a common metaphor used by the prophets to indicate Yahweh's use of one nation to judge another through his sovereign control. The prophet Micah described the Assyrian invasion of the northern tribes as God coming down from heaven and treading on the mountains, making them melt like wax and splitting the valleys like poured out water. So too, this splitting of the Mount of Olives was not literal, but symbolic of a spiritual division.[8]

Alexander had so much he wanted to say to his interrogators. The Messiah had come and stood on the Mount of Olives forty years ago and had proclaimed the very judgment that Zechariah and the other prophets had forewarned: that the Day of the Lord was near. This judgment would truly split the people in half, spiritual Jerusalem from earthly Jerusalem, believers from unbelievers, by an impassable valley.

But Alexander chose instead to focus on the revelation given to the apostle John, who had quoted this very prophecy of Zechariah as being the theme of the entire Apocalypse. He said, "You have left out the key to the Day of the Lord in Zechariah."[9]

Gischala looked at him quizzically. Again with more curiosity than hostility as if he were truly listening. Was the Holy Spirit working on the warrior?

Jacob stood with arms still folded and mind still closed.

Alexander quoted from Zechariah again, "I will pour out on the house of David and the inhabitants of Jerusalem a spirit of grace, so that when they look on me, on him whom they have pierced, they shall mourn for him, as one mourns for an only child, and weep bitterly over him, as one weeps over a firstborn. But I will cause the Remnant of this people to possess all these things."[10]

He stopped to let it sink into his captor. "There are two Jerusalems: the earthly city of people who pierced Messiah on a cross and the heavenly city of the Remnant who received the Holy Spirit through faith. Jesus, the firstborn Son of God, is coming on the clouds of judgment to earthly Jerusalem. All the tribes of this Land will mourn as the heavens and earth are shaken and your cosmos is split apart. But the Jerusalem that survives, the Jerusalem that 'shall dwell in security' is the heavenly city of the new covenant. That is why Zechariah says, 'On that day, living waters shall flow out from Jerusalem.' The living water is the Holy Spirit given to those who have faith in Jesus as Messiah and Lord. That is the Jerusalem that remains, the heavenly one that consists of the Remnant."[11]

"So much for your loving, forgiving Messiah," complained Jacob. But he was shut up by the raised hand of Gischala quieting him. The warrior was clearly trying to think, to process what he had heard. As he did so in silence, Alexander prayed for his salvation.

Jacob's insult was a desperate attempt to discredit the grace of Jesus as God's suffering Servant. It was always the way of unbelievers who didn't want to be accountable for their sins. Cast aspersion on God's love by drawing attention to his judgment. As if the two were contradictory. As if God could not be loving if he judged sin.

But justice and mercy were not contradictory in Christ. God had always foretold the coming of Messiah as both a time of salvation and of judgment. Salvation of the Remnant and judgment of the rest. Elijah had come to prepare the way for the Lord. John the Baptizer had turned the hearts of the fathers and children, but he had also declared that the Day of the Lord would burn like an oven. The wrath to come.[12]

Isaiah's proclamation of Messiah's Jubilee year of forgiveness was intimately connected to his day of vengeance. Jesus had proclaimed the fulfillment of that Jubilee in his own ministry and the day of vengeance in the fall of Jerusalem.[13]

> But when you see Jerusalem surrounded by armies, then know
> that its desolation has come near...for these are days of
> vengeance, to fulfill all that is written.

Luke 21:20-22

No, God's love and wrath were not at odds. In the Son, justice and mercy kissed.[14]

Gischala raised his head with decision. It was evident he had made up his mind. Alexander hoped it would be merciful.

"You speak of a suffering messiah," said Gischala, "a spiritual kingdom, a spiritual temple, a heavenly Jerusalem." He paused again as though trying to accept his own words. "But I believe in earthly salvation, an earthly Jerusalem and temple. I will liberate captives from our prison. I will restore this stronghold, win this war, and build the temple. And all Israel will be gathered to it."

Alexander filled with dread. This man before him, this monstrous leader, saw himself as the anointed one to deliver Israel. Gischala had fallen to a delusion that even Jacob was unwilling to challenge.

Everything was going to get much worse.

Gischala said, "And I am going to start with releasing you, Alexander. But you will not return to the hippodrome. You will remain in the temple to help with my wounded soldiers. I am told you are the best of the few doctors remaining. Well, I need the very best to minister to my forces if I am to win this battle."

CHAPTER 24

Pella

Cassandra paced around desperately in her small home in Pella. She couldn't get Samuel to stop crying. She tried to feed him, but he wasn't eating. She changed him, she rocked him in her arms, tried to sing sweet hymns to him. She couldn't figure out what was wrong. He had kept her up all night with his fussing, and now his crying worked to make her feel like she was going mad.

Noah had escaped to go play with his friends outside. Rachel was watching over the orphans housed in a converted Greek building. Cassandra was all alone with Samuel, and she felt guilty for her thoughts of self-pity.

And the maidservant was late returning from the water well. The congregation had provided the help for her because of Cassandra's extensive responsibilities overseeing the care of the orphan children from Jerusalem.

Cassandra bit back her own tears. She missed Alexander deeply. She wanted to see him, to return to his side. To support him in his ministry for the kingdom of God. But her children needed her too. Little Samuel required constant attention. Rachel was a young woman come of age for marriage. Noah needed a father's strong arm to temper his growing anger.

The war orphans needed her oversight as well. She had been given charge of the children she had rescued from Jerusalem. Families in the city had adopted most of the two hundred orphans, but there were still fifty left in Cassandra's direct care.

Still, she had made arrangements for both her own and the orphan children to be cared for until she returned from Jerusalem. Now she needed to get to the city meeting to find out what the elders and leaders were planning next. But not with a crying infant.

She whispered into the air, "Where are you, Magdalena? Hurry up."

She continued to pace back and forth, rocking the bawling Samuel, looking out the window for the maidservant's arrival, and feeling terrible for wanting to get away.

At last she saw the young woman approaching the house with a pot of water on her head. Magdalena was one of the older war orphans that Cassandra and Alexander had rescued. Fifteen years old with long, brown hair and a lanky body, she had been so grateful that she had jumped at the chance to be Cassandra's maidservant, counting it an honor. The only problem was that Magdalena was always a bit pokey and slow at what she did.

Cassandra opened the door for her. Once Magdalena had put the water down, she handed the maidservant her crying son. "I'm late for the city meeting."

She rushed to the door but stopped when she noticed that Samuel had stopped crying. Cassandra looked back at him, now nestled calmly in Magdalena's arms. *My own son can detect my desire to leave. He hates me for it. Well, I don't blame him. I am a terrible mother.*

She gave Magdalena a smile as fake as it felt. "I'll be back as soon as I can." She closed the door behind her.

When Cassandra arrived at the temple, she was heaving for air. She had run all the way and was happy to discover that she had only missed the introductory meeting procedures led by Boaz.

She noticed the seven Kharabu captains up front. Michael was addressing the congregation of hundreds of citizens. "The seven of us are leaving Pella temporarily on a mission."

The citizens broke out into a rumbling of fearful chattering.

Boaz stepped forward and quieted them, waving his arms downward.

Cassandra found Thelonious standing at the back. She stood next to him.

Michael continued explaining to the crowd, "Fear not, Christians of Pella. You will be safe. There will be no more Roman attacks on this city."

A citizen yelled out, "How can you know that?" Others in the crowd called out their agreement with the query.

Michael said, "I have intelligence of which I am very confident. You will not be in danger."

"What is your source?" asked another voice in the crowd.

"I cannot reveal my source. You must trust me in this. Have we Kharabu not proven our word to you all these years?"

At that, the citizens gave hearty agreement and even shouts of gratitude. One voice called out, "What is your mission?"

Michael smiled warmly. "I am afraid I cannot reveal that either."

Boaz stepped out now and asked, "When will you return?"

"I do not know," said Michael.

The crowd became upset again.

"You must trust the Apocalypse. The devil's time is short. Are you not the 144,000 sealed on your foreheads with the name of the Father and of the Lamb?"

The crowd chattered with approval. Some shouted, "Praise Jesus our Lord!"

Cassandra could not get out of her mind what she thought their mission might be. If these seven were the angels she suspected, then she also suspected where they might be going. She turned to Thelonius and whispered to him, "Can I ask you a favor?"

"Of course," he answered.

After Michael had reassured the city, he and his six captains left the temple and made their way to their horses at the stable just down the street.

When they entered the building, Cassandra and Thelonius were there to greet them.

She wasted no time. "You're going to Jerusalem, aren't you?"

The captains looked at one another, caught. Michael smiled affectionately at her. "Cassandra, you cannot come with us."

Her composure dropped with disappointment. He explained, "You have been a good and faithful servant to the Father all these years. I would not refuse to bring you with us if I thought I could keep you safe. But that is not the case. Your family is now your calling."

She sighed, and her whole body seemed to deflate with resignation. Thelonius held her up from melting to the floor in despair.

She said, "I need to know if Alexander is still alive. I need to see him."

"Trust in the Lord," Michael responded.

At times like this, such words sounded trite. A kind of resignation to the fact that there was nothing left to do, so one might as well just trust in the Lord.

Cassandra pulled a rolled parchment out of her cloak. "If he is alive, will you at least deliver this letter to him? I miss him so deeply."

Michael felt the wound of her soul. Those two had gone through hell on earth together. It pained him to keep them apart. "Of course I will."

He reached out and took the letter. "Forgive me, but time is short. We must leave."

Cassandra and Thelonius moved aside and let them pass the stalls on their way to their own horses.

She called out to him, "Michael."

119

He turned back to see her smiling, but with sad eyes. She said, "I don't think there are any better princes in heaven than you seven guardian angels."

Michael smiled. The other angels looked askance at each other. Her face seemed to reveal that she wasn't speaking metaphorically. She must have seen them battling the gods in the valley.

Michael turned back and led his Kharabu warriors to their horses for their journey southwest.

CHAPTER 25

Jerusalem

Jacob walked among the tombstones of the necropolis not far from Golgotha in the western end of the city. He passed along a line of caves marked out for the wealthy. They would lay the bodies of their dead loved ones on shelves until the flesh rotted from the bones. Then they would put the bones in small stone boxes called ossuaries. This way they could store entire families in the crypt so that when the resurrection occurred, they would arise together.

Despite the hope that pervaded this belief, the cemetery still gave Jacob a feeling of despair. Was he afraid of death or the afterlife? He wasn't sure which.

He found the Two Witnesses preaching outside the tomb of a rich Pharisee, Joseph of Arimathea. He'd known they would be here today because it was Sunday, the Feast of First Fruits, the anniversary of their resurrection hoax. This had been the temporary grave where the Nazarene had been laid before the disciples stole the body on the Feast of First Fruits forty years ago. Three days after he was buried. Another attempt to manufacture fulfillment of the Nazarene's own predictions.

For just as Jonah was three days and three nights in the belly of the great fish, so will the Son of Man be three days and three nights in the heart of the earth.

Matthew 12:40

A handful of visitors listened to the two preachers in sackcloth. Jacob had anticipated few would be listening to them, not just because this was a cemetery, but because their message was mostly ignored by the populace.

Though he despised these two for their arrogance and rejection of temple, Torah, and Land, Jacob could not deny that they were somehow supernaturally protected. The image of fire from heaven engulfing a company of soldiers was burned into his memory with fear and dread. What if they were Yahweh's prophets after all? What if the people were not listening to them with the same results as when they didn't listen to Isaiah or Jeremiah or Ezekiel?

"Go, and say to this people: 'Keep on hearing, but do not understand; keep on seeing, but do not perceive.' Make the heart of this people dull, and their ears heavy, and blind their eyes; lest they turn and be healed."

Isaiah 6:9-10

Jacob put it out of his mind. The ramifications were too frightening. He had come too far to entertain such heretical thoughts. And he was here to hedge his bets anyway. He was going to play both sides.

The young, dark Egyptian Elihu proclaimed to those few surrounding him, "Jesus is the fulfillment of the Feast of First Fruits. He died on Passover as the Lamb of God. His death, like the Feast of Unleavened Bread, brought about a new exodus. And he rose from the dead on the third day as the first fruits of the resurrection to come."[1]

People in the city were supposed to be bringing stalks of barley to the temple as wave offerings. These should have been taken from the first fruits of their harvest as a sign of the greater harvest to come. But because Rome had surrounded the city and locked them inside, the Jews could not access their fields and thus had no stalks of grain. What they didn't realize was that their lack of first fruits was a picture of their own dark fate.

Elihu quoted from the book of Daniel, "And many of those who sleep in the dust of the earth shall awake, some to everlasting life and some to shame and everlasting contempt."[2]

The Witnesses were claiming that Daniel's resurrection was a picture of the raising of his Remnant out of the dead nation of apostate Israel, not unlike Ezekiel's resurrection of the dry bones as a picture of the Remnant return from exile. But in this case, the newly raised Remnant consisted of believers in Jesus as Messiah. The rest were condemned.[3]

Old Moshe now took over. "The prophet Isaiah wrote of the new exodus achieved by this resurrection: 'The root of Jesse will come, even he who arises to rule the Gentiles; in him will the Gentiles hope.' That root of Jesse is Jesus of Nazareth who rose from the dead. Isaiah goes on to say of him, 'And in that day the Lord will extend his hand yet a second time to recover the Remnant of his people.' So Jesus raises his Remnant through faith."[4]

Jacob understood what the Two Witnesses were claiming, and it was scandalous to the Jewish mind. Their argument was that Jesus had reorganized the people of God around himself as the faithful Israelite. Jesus was the Israel of God in whom all the promises to Israel were fulfilled. The "resurrection" of Israel out of their continuing exile was fulfilled in Jesus's resurrection from the dead. Those who believed in Jesus were included in that resurrection because of their life-giving faith from the Holy Spirit. Jesus had said that the dead were already coming alive spiritually as they heard the Gospel of salvation. But one day there would be a bodily resurrection of both the wicked and the righteous, which would be the final harvest.

Jacob waited until the Witnesses were finished with their sermon before he approached them with his urgent request.

Moshe and Elihu looked at him cautiously. He had been their enemy all these years, but he had also helped the women and children and orphans of the city by overseeing the hospital in the hippodrome. Jacob had helped the doctor Alexander to accomplish his medical mission of aiding the suffering citizens. So the Witnesses had an uneasy alliance with Jacob.

"What is wrong?" asked Elihu.

"Alexander Maccabaeus needs your help."

• • • • •

Alexander had set up an infirmary for Gischala's soldiers in the upper story of the royal portico on the southern wall of the temple mount. Its location was on the side of the temple complex least likely to be attacked. He had organized for over three hundred beds and as many supplies as could be gathered. Gischala had two other doctors who supported the rebels' cause and Alexander was able to gain the general's approval of a dozen or more volunteers from his army to train in medical assistance.

Alexander would not turn down a request to help anyone who was wounded, be they civilian or soldier, Herodian or Zealot. His calling was to heal.

But his heart was with the hippodrome. He couldn't help but think of how the innocent would suffer without adequate help. His assistants would be able to keep the wounded and sick for a time, but when the casualties of war started, they would become overwhelmed. And his surgery skills would be desperately needed. The truth was, he cared most for the civilians and innocents of the city. He prayed that God would release him to return there. He prayed for a miracle as he checked the bandage on the arm of a wounded soldier. There were twenty of them from previous battles at various stages of need. Some had lost or broken limbs. Others had stab wounds, lacerations, and contusions.

"Doctor," came a voice behind him. Alexander turned from the patient to see Gischala looking pale and nervous.

"I am releasing you to return to the hippodrome."

"Why?" asked Alexander. He immediately realized that his surprise might sound like he was complaining. Gischala just didn't look right in his disposition.

"You've set up the infirmary here, and I'm sure our doctors can take it over with competence. I want to thank you for your concern and help."

Alexander picked up his pack of tools and personal effects and followed Gischala down the stairs to the Huldah Gates.

The general was acting so strange—as though he was going to spring a trap—Alexander wondered if Gischala might be planning to execute the doctor. But why would he do such a thing?

What was going on? What had gotten into the general? Why was he acting like a frightened soldier following someone else's orders?

When Alexander exited the gates, he saw Moshe and Elihu were waiting for him. Was this the answer to his questions? Alexander turned to look back at Gischala, who had stopped and appeared to stand back protectively inside the gates. The general gestured with open arms to the Two Witnesses as if to indicate he was releasing Alexander into their arms.

Alexander looked back at Moshe and Elihu, confused. The Two Witnesses had smiles on their lips. Why? Gischala hated these two with everything in him. He had sought their secret from Alexander to get rid of them. And now he was releasing the doctor to them like a gift.

Or was it a ransom?

The two prophets hugged him. Elihu said, "Let's get you back to the hippodrome. The sick and wounded need you."

Alexander knew something very serious must have occurred to cause Gischala, a warrior of fearless zeal and violence, to hand over an important hostage to his hated opponents.

As they walked back to the arena, he asked the Witnesses, "What did you do to persuade Gischala to release me? He wanted you dead."

The two prophets looked at each other as if to consider how much to tell him.

Moshe finally said, "I'm surprised at you, Alexander. By now I would think you would know we don't do anything. It's Yahweh who persuades."

Elihu added impishly, "We're just messengers."

Moshe concluded, "Though it did have something to do with a little fire from heaven."

CHAPTER 26

Simon and Aaron stood on the battlement of the northwestern wall near the tower of Psephinus and the northwestern gates. The sun was low on the horizon, and they could see smoke rising from the cooking fires of the Roman camp, just a mile away protected by its own wall and guard. Simon had been alerted by the Romans that there was to be an offer of terms.

This will be interesting.

Aaron nudged him and pointed down by the wall. Simon saw three men on horses followed by a contingent of perhaps a hundred cavalry. The horsemen cantered along the wall as if examining the structure. They were within arrow striking distance.[1]

Then Simon saw who the three leaders were. "Josephus and Herod Agrippa," he said with surprise. "Is that...?"

"Titus Caesar," said Aaron. The general was riding a white stallion.

Simon felt his teeth clench tight.

"Strange," added Aaron. "He has no armor or helmet on."

Simon said, "He risks safety for his pride."

Archers along the parapet prepared arrows. Simon waved his hand to hold them back. He wanted to hear what the Roman beast was going to offer.

Titus and his squad arrived at the tower and halted.

Josephus was the one who called out, "Where is Simon bar Giora?"

"I am here!" Simon shouted back, now standing tall to be seen.

Titus locked eyes with the Jewish general. Even at this distance, Simon felt like they were in each other's face, each daring the other to attack. Could Titus sense Simon's burning hatred? Did Titus know the pain he'd caused this once-devout, once-loyal captain of the temple guard? Herod knew. Berenice knew. This monster had to know.

Josephus shouted again, "I am Joseph ben Matthias, former general of the Galilean forces and captive of Rome. I am here to offer you Caesar's generous terms!"

Aaron muttered sarcastically, "How like a god, this Caesar."

Simon smirked. "And Joseph, his prophet."

Josephus continued, "Surrender the city now and spare the lives of all. Caesar has no desire to pollute the holy city or temple. But if he is resisted, he will do as he wills."[2]

"Blasphemer!" Aaron spat out.

Josephus continued, "I swear to you that he is merciful and true to his word as he has been to me."

Josephus stopped as though expecting a reply of some kind. But Simon decided to remain silent. He wanted to intimidate his opponent. To speak was to reveal. Simon wanted to conceal.

Agrippa joined in on the pleading. "Simon, you cannot win this war. You will lose. All the Land is beneath the boot of Rome. Would you preside over the desolation of the holy city as well?"

"No! But you would, traitors!" Aaron yelled out.

Josephus responded, "I am no traitor to my people. I am here to testify to you of Caesar's grace toward us. I believe that God has gone over to the Romans and is chastising Israel for her disobedience. But there is still time to repent. To turn away wrath!"

He paused before adding deliberately. "Thousands of innocent Jews have already been killed or captured. I beg of you, Simon, do not let thousands more die."

Josephus stopped again. Again, Simon said nothing. He stared at Titus with all the hatred in his soul.

Josephus concluded, "All Caesar asks is that you consider his proposal by meeting with him in person with your council for negotiation. What is your response?"

Simon said nothing. Instead, he and Aaron slid down ropes and mounted their horses, left ready at the interior base of the city wall.

Josephus saw the gates opening. He glanced at Titus. Was Simon more reasonable than the fanatics Gischala or Eleazar?

A legionary shouted out, "Caesar! Behind us!"

Josephus turned. A sizeable contingent of Jewish horsemen had snuck out from somewhere—perhaps a secret gate in the city wall—and had managed to place themselves between the Roman cavalry and their camp. Josephus panicked. He jerked a look back to see that the northwest city gates were now open enough for another contingent of horsemen to charge out, launching an attack on Titus and his men. They were wedged before and behind.

Josephus noticed that Simon was leading the attack force that had emerged from the city gates.

Titus yelled, "Retreat!"

The Roman cavalrymen turned about and faced head on the Jewish warriors that were behind them. They clashed in battle.

Titus cut through the Jews with his sword upon his mighty white steed. The man was like a windmill of fury. His lack of armor made him more agile. But it also made him more vulnerable.

The archers on the wall released a volley of arrows at the fleeing Romans.

But they were too late. Titus and his cavalry were well on their way back to the safety of their camp, and Titus had escaped unscathed.[3]

Simon and his men met with the other contingent who awaited his command. "Let them go. He has my answer."

"Simon," called Aaron, sitting nearby on his horse. He gestured to the northern side of the wall behind them.

A fourth contingent of horsemen now entered the field, racing toward Simon and his men. But they weren't Roman, and they weren't Simon's men.

"Gischala!" yelled Aaron.

Simon shouted, "Engage the enemy!"

His horsemen turned to do so, but they didn't have the time to get mobile. Gischala's forces hit them like a wave.

The sheer force of a cavalry attack was overwhelming on whomever was on the receiving side. Horses crashed into one another. Swords and spears clashed between Jews.

Simon found Gischala in the battle about fifty feet away. He thought as if to project to his opponent, *If this ambush is your idea of our final confrontation, so be it. This will be your death.*

Gischala turned toward Simon as if he had heard his rival's thoughts. The two men began working their way through the battle with intent fixed upon one another. Simon's attention was taken by an attacking Zealot with spear. He dodged it, grabbed the shaft, pulled the soldier close, and plunged his sword into his chest.

When Simon looked back up, Gischala was almost upon him. But before they could meet, Gischala's horse was pierced with a lance, and he fell to the ground.

Simon dismounted. He wanted to face this creature man-to-man and see his face as his life bled out of him. In the past, Gischala had been a superior fighter to Simon. He had even taught him a move or two. But Simon had survived in the wilderness for years now and had gained much battle experience that was superior to his sparring practice of the past. All the bitterness of Gischala's betrayal boiled over into a force of strength in Simon's arms.

He would cut Gischala down and spit on his corpse.

The two warriors were now within twenty feet of each other. Simon felt something hit his leather armor from behind. He spun around, sword raised, but no one was there. He turned back to face his nemesis.

Gischala had rolled away from his fallen horse and was back on his feet. He glanced over at Simon, then yelled to one of his soldiers on a horse. The soldier galloped up to Gischala, and the general jumped onto the horse behind the rider. They galloped away. A horn blew, and Gischala's men followed him back into the secret gate out of which they came.

Cockroach, thought Simon. He mounted his horse.

Aaron was there. "Shall we give chase?"

"No," ordered Simon. They would return to the walls and regroup.

Aaron lifted his horn and blew.

Then he raised his eyebrows in concern and pointed to Simon's shoulder. "Do you know you have an arrow sticking in your back, general?"

Simon turned his head to see the arrow sticking in his leather backplate up on his left shoulder blade. Suddenly, he felt the pain of it. He had been so focused on the battle that he'd hardly realized he was hit. A random arrow accidentally released from his own side.

"That would have been a disadvantage," said Simon. The smallest thought entered his mind that Gischala's fleeing might have saved his life.

Aaron said, "We had better get that taken care of."

This was the first skirmish of the siege. Simon considered it a taste of what was to come. He would have to be very strategic to win this war on two fronts: the war without and the war within.

Or maybe he wouldn't make it past this battle. He suddenly realized that the arrow he'd been hit with must have been poisoned. He swooned and fell to the ground in a drugged stupor.

CHAPTER 27

Alexander and his Christian assistants rushed around the hippodrome tending to the needs of the sick and dying. Because of the earlier destruction of the city's food silos by warring factions, food rations had been cut in half for everyone. The Romans had confiscated all the farms outside Jerusalem and blocked any access from the citizens to leave the city. The first to fall sick and begin dying from malnutrition were the elderly.

Within the week, hundreds of them filled beds in the sick partition of the hippodrome. Dozens had already died. Alexander did all he could to care for them and comfort them before their end. He had no extra rations, and there was no medicine to cure hunger. He knew this was going to get worse. Much worse.

Alexander heard the announcement of the arrival of some men wounded in a skirmish. He ran to the entrance to see a dozen soldiers entering the stadium. He recognized General Simon bar Giora being held up by the young Essene warrior-monk Aaron ben Hyam.

Aaron's look at Alexander was not pleasant. They had last met on the road to Jerusalem, where Alexander and Cassandra had shared the Gospel with the young monk. Aaron had reacted in anger and impatience with Cassandra's zeal.

Alexander barked to his assistants, "Help these soldiers and let me know if there is any surgery needed." He turned back to Aaron and Simon. "What is wrong with the general?"

Simon looked dizzy, but he could still speak for himself. "I've been hit with a poisoned arrow."

"Follow me," said Alexander. He rushed the general over to his drug tent at the closest end of the arena.

Alexander asked him, "Was it a Roman arrow?"

"No," said Simon. "An accident. My archers. So I know it's viper's poison."

They arrived at a small tent with some beds arranged outside it. Alexander said, "Sit on this bed and remove your tunic and wrapping of the wound. I'll be right back."

He went into the tent to retrieve a device he had made based on the Roman physician Celsus's medical research.

130

Alexander came back out to see Simon bare-chested on the bed. The doctor looked at his shoulder where the arrow had hit him.

Simon said, "The wound itself is not deep. My armor protected me."

The general was right, Alexander saw. The wound wasn't deep. But it was discolored and agitated from the poison.

Alexander explained what he was doing. "This is a suction cup device that will suck out the venom from the wound. It will be too late to get it all, but hopefully enough to help you."[1]

"I've already been bitten by vipers in the desert," Simon said. "My body is used to it."

Alexander placed the little bronze cup device over the arrow wound. "You'll feel some discomfort as the cup sucks blood and venom out." He pulled a plunger device attached to the cup, and Simon winced at the pain.

"I need to do this several times," said the doctor. He withdrew the plunger and pulled up the cup. It had some blood in it that he dumped on the ground before returning to plunging and sucking.

When Alexander had finished, Simon rose to his feet. "Thank you for your help, doctor. I need to return to my men." But as he started to leave, he stumbled like a drunk. Aaron caught him.

Alexander said, "You are not leaving yet, General. You may have some tolerance to the poison, but enough of it got into your system to cause you problems. Please, just rest here until evening. I want to keep an eye on you to make sure no other complications arise."

"My men need me," said Simon.

"And they won't have you alive if you act foolishly and don't follow my directions."

Simon sat back down. Aaron smiled. "Doctor, you've accomplished what no other man has been able to with this stubborn rock badger."

Alexander said, "Let us pray I am able to do what no other man can do with your fellow wounded soldiers. If you'll excuse me, I have some surgeries to attend to."

Alexander left them and returned to the other wounded men.

Most of the injuries were manageable except a sword wound that had slashed deep into one soldier's torso. Alexander had fed the victim some opium poppies to ease the tremendous pain of placing his bowels back in place and searing his laceration with a red-hot iron.[2] Despite the anesthesia, the scream of the poor soldier echoed through the stadium.

He died shortly after.

Alexander finished his duties by the end of the day. The sun was going down, and he decided to make a visit to Simon.

When he arrived at the bed, he saw Simon and Aaron were gone. It didn't surprise him in the least. What did surprise him was that he found the general and his Essene lieutenant over by the soldiers' beds, checking on their well-being.

Alexander approached the two men as they finished talking to one of the wounded. "General. I see you care more for your men than for your own welfare."

Simon turned, and Alexander saw that the general actually looked well. He had weathered the poison quickly.

"I told you, doctor, I have a tolerance for viper poison. It's the sting of human serpents that is the hardest to overcome." Simon and Aaron shared a knowing smile of inside meaning.

"Let me check your wound."

They returned to Simon's bed, and Alexander unwrapped his shoulder. The wound was looking better. The infection was leaving.

"Praise God for your healing," Alexander said and wrapped him back up.

Simon said, "So, doctor, I've been warned of your Christian heresies."

Alexander asked, "Are you afraid of my sting?"

Simon chuckled. "No. And do you know why?"

Alexander stopped and looked at him curiously.

"Because I've seen the way you've treated my men and the way you've cared for the innocent sick and dying in this stadium. As a matter of fact, besides Aaron here, you are probably one of the only men in this city I trust will not betray me."

Alexander said, "It is only because Jesus the Messiah cared for me when I was wounded in my soul."

Simon gave him another smile. "So tell me about this heresy of yours. What makes a man of compassion and healing so dangerous?"

Alexander considered how to phrase his words before speaking. "I suppose it's the same thing that made Jeremiah, Isaiah, Ezekiel, and all the prophets so dangerous to Israel. Jesus prophesied judgment upon this adulterous generation because they did not recognize their visitation of Yahweh.[3] He is going to destroy the earthly city and temple with its covenant and replace it with a heavenly city and temple, a new covenant forever."

He saw Simon considering his words with arched brow. Aaron remained angrily silent.

Simon noticed this as well. He said to Alexander, "It appears you have done the impossible twice. You've gotten me to obey you, and now you've gotten Aaron to remain silent on religion."

"We have already had an extended debate on the issue," Alexander demurred.

"You two know each other?"

Aaron sighed. "My men saved him and some others from bandits in the desert a while back."

Simon looked back and forth between them. "I take it your debate did not end well."

Alexander said wryly, "I'd say Aaron was not used to women being quite so bold and engaged as my wife was."

Simon grinned at his lieutenant. "Ah, yes, my good monk here is not used to dealing with women unless they are washing his clothes or cooking his food at the community."

Aaron steamed with anger. Simon slapped his back with humor. "Don't worry, Aaron, I won't tell any of the other men that you couldn't handle a woman."

Then the general turned back to Alexander. "Where is your wife?"

"She is safe in the mountains with our children."

"Yet you remain here in danger of your life?"

"Jesus gave his life for me. The least I can do is bring his healing of both body and soul to those of this condemned city." He would not tell the general of his plans for escape with the Christians.

Simon stared at him, impressed. "And that, my dear doctor, is why I am going to appoint some of my guard to watch over you and protect this infirmary. I thank you for your service, and I only hope to find more heretics like you who are men of such worthy character. But I am afraid my unusually silent lieutenant and I must return to my headquarters to prepare for the visitation of the Romans upon this city."

CHAPTER 28

Jordan Valley

Cassandra held the blanket tightly around her shoulders. The night was a bit chilling for summer. But she couldn't make a fire for fear of being discovered. The insects in the foliage around her—cicadas and crickets—blended into the sound of the Jordan River nearby to lull her into sleepiness.

She had traveled a good twenty miles through the valley on horseback already. She had done everything she could to stay concealed. The Kharabu had taught her much over the past few years. She had watched them track others and avoid being tracked. She had asked questions about safety and self-defense and had practiced in preparation for the very conflict that now consumed the Land.

She tried to console herself that she had left her children in the very capable and loving hands of the Pella congregation. She wasn't abandoning them. She was simply leaving them with others until she returned. And Thelonius had promised he would keep a protective eye on them as well. He was staying in Pella to help guard the city in the absence of the Kharabu leaders.

Or was she just deceiving herself? For the mind is never so clever as when it is involved in the act of self-justification.

She was going to Jerusalem to find her husband. To see if he was still alive and to help him if she could. She had made a covenant in marriage to be Alexander's helpmate in the ministry God had given him. She had no right to force that calling upon her children, to place them into that danger. Leaving them with those in safety was the most loving and motherly thing she could do to protect them.

She was walking into a den of lions, the furnace of fire. But she was no prophet of God like Daniel. Jesus had told his followers to flee Jerusalem, not to enter it. For just like the Babylonian exile, of two men in the field, one would be taken into captivity and one left. If two women were grinding at the mill, one would be taken away into exile and one left.[1]

Cassandra prayed, asking Yahweh to allow her to be one of those who was left behind to survive the desolation.

Or would those who were not taken simply be executed in the aftermath? If Jerusalem did not surrender, the Roman policy would be to enslave the choicest and slaughter everyone else in response to stubborn resistance.

She was ready to die, ready to give her life for the greater cause of the Gospel. She had learned such an attitude from her mentor, the apostle Paul.

> *For I am already being poured out as a drink offering, and the time of my departure has come. I have fought the good fight, I have finished the race, I have kept the faith. Henceforth there is laid up for me the crown of righteousness, which the Lord, the righteous judge, will award to me on that day, and not only to me but also to all who have loved his appearing.*
>
> *2 Timothy 4:6–8*

She mused over the words of her old friend. *Those who have loved his appearing.* That appearing was at hand. The *parousia,* the coming of his presence.[2]

The end of all things was at hand. These were the last days of the old covenant, the end of the age. The messianic age had arrived in Christ.[3] Paul had declared that God's wrath on the people and city was to be complete and "to the utmost."[4] Like the wilderness generation of old, this adulterous generation had filled up the measure of their sins.[5]

Her chances of surviving were not high.

She thought of the crown of righteousness laid up for her. But before she could drift off to sleep, she felt a strong hand cover her mouth from behind. She was lifted roughly from the ground in the strong arms of a dark stranger.

• • • • •

Michael and the four other archangels warmed themselves at their fire. They had made a small clearing to sleep. Raphael was in the brush guarding their perimeter.

Uriel and Gabriel were quietly debating one of their many differences of opinion.

They were interrupted by Saraqel entering their camp carrying a squirming Cassandra.

"Put me down. I can walk," she complained.

Saraqel said, "I'm tired. I don't want to chase you if you run."

"I'm not going to run! You're treating me like I'm the enemy."

As Saraqel set her down, she saw the six other Kharabu staring at her.

Uriel said, "You may not be the enemy, but you didn't do what Michael told you, and you've been following us like a spy."

She gave him a sour look. "Like a spy? I was following you for safety."

She looked to Michael for approval.

Michael approached her and said, "Cassandra, you cannot go with us to Jerusalem. We've told you this repeatedly. We have a mission."

"I'm not asking for you to protect me. You just don't understand marriage. You're a bunch of..." She stopped herself. Michael and the others stared at her expectantly. Would she say it? They almost dared her to with their looks. But she said, "bachelor warriors" instead of "angels."

Michael smiled at her. "Indeed we are. But may I suggest to you, Cassandra, that in your zeal for the kingdom of God, you may have misunderstood your highest calling."

"What do you mean?" she said.

"Well, it is true that Yahweh has a special love for those who are martyred for the faith in these last days. He promises them blessing and reward. Theirs is the first resurrection. And you, like your husband, are not afraid to shed your blood for the sake of the Gospel. This is an honorable heart that you have. But I need to tell you something, Cassandra. Jesus does not want *you* to be a martyr."

Her eyes became misty with sadness.

He continued, "He does not want you to die for the past. He wants you to live for the future."

Her look of confusion began to clear up. She listened with all her heart.

Gabriel was sitting behind Michael with his hands warming in the fire. He said to her, "Remember when you and I first met on your father's merchant ship?"

It was his first mention of such an encounter. Suddenly, she remembered as if being hit by an arrow.

All this time she had been around the Kharabu captains, and she had never recognized Gabriel as that angelic visitor on the corbita all those years ago. Now all of a sudden, she did. It was as if she had been blinded to his identity by some kind of enchantment.

But not any longer. Her eyes were opened.

She'd planned to kill herself that night. She was going to cast herself into the sea to avoid being used as a tool to hunt down other Christians. Gabriel had appeared as a shining one and stopped her.

Gabriel now said, "Do you remember what I told you then?"

"That Yahweh had a plan for me. That I was to bring salvation to many."

"You remembered." He smiled at her. "Now you must believe it."

She wanted to. She had to. But she couldn't help thinking how like a failure she had felt. Had she been pursuing a false glory in wanting to be a martyr? Accepting God's call to be a martyr was one thing, but pursuing it for spiritual pride was another.

Michael said, "When the Son of Man ascended to David's throne at the right hand of God, he was given dominion and glory and a kingdom that all peoples, nations, and languages would ultimately serve him. Soon the saints of the Most High will receive that kingdom of dominion to possess it forever and ever. And the kingdom will grow by raising families to multiply and fill the earth, obey the Lord, and disciple the nations. They must be taught to observe all that he has commanded.[6]

"Go back now to your family. Take dominion. The time to die for the faith is over for you. Now live for the future. Build the kingdom."

Of course. It was what Daniel had prophesied and Jesus had affirmed. The kingdom of God would start as a small stone that would take down Rome and, in her, the foundation of previous Gentile kingdoms that had held Israel captive— the times of the Gentiles.[7] That stone would grow to fill the earth as a mountain. It would start like a small bit of leaven in a lump of dough that would eventually leaven the entire loaf.

Yes, the end of the age had arrived. But it was also the beginning of the age to come, the new Jerusalem come down out of heaven. Cassandra knew the promise Isaiah had given of the last days where the nations would be drawn to his holy mountain and they would ultimately beat their swords into plowshares.[8] Those nations were flowing right now into the New Jerusalem of Christ through the Gospel that had reached all the earth.[9]

Cassandra was living prophecy. And she had shamefully forgotten it. She had focused on God's judgment in these last days of the old covenant instead of the peace of God's kingdom embodied in the new covenant. Her new life in Pella was her calling. To raise her family for the kingdom of God under the lordship of Jesus Christ.

She broke down in the weeping of repentance. She gave up her pride and her will and gave in to Yahweh's calling. It was bittersweet because she knew she might never see her beloved Alexander again in this life. But she could see her beloved children and their life, a world transformed by the spread of the Gospel that would change their children and their children's children.

The time to die for the faith is over for you. Now live for the future.

All the weight of the world came off of Cassandra and went onto God's shoulders. She felt her knees get weak with surrender. It was not up to her after all. Not even her own faith. It was all a gift of God from beginning to end. And God's kingdom would never be destroyed.[10]

She whispered to Michael, "I'm so tired. I need to sleep."

"Yes, you do," said Michael with a smile. He led her over to a blanket on the ground. "One of us will bring you back to Pella in the morning. And fear not, your husband is alive. I will get your letter to him."

Cassandra snuggled up and fell into a sleep deeper than she had experienced for so long. After several years of running and fighting, she finally felt at rest. In the midst of the cosmos coming apart, she felt strangely at peace.

> *It shall come to pass in the last days*
> *that the mountain of the house of Yahweh*
> *shall be established as the highest of the mountains,*
> *and shall be lifted up above the hills;*
> *and all the nations shall flow to it,*
> *and many peoples shall come, and say:*
> *"Come, let us go up to the mountain of Yahweh,*
> *to the house of the God of Jacob,*
> *that he may teach us his ways*
> *and that we may walk in his paths."*
> *For out of Zion shall go forth the law,*
> *and the word of Yahweh from Jerusalem.*
> *He shall judge between the nations,*
> *and shall decide disputes for many peoples;*
> *and they shall beat their swords into plowshares,*
> *and their spears into pruning hooks;*
> *nation shall not lift up sword against nation,*
> *neither shall they learn war anymore.*
>
> *Isaiah 2:2–4*

CHAPTER 29

Jerusalem

The Romans had been working for days clear-cutting all the trees within miles of the city and leveling the ground that led up to the city wall on the Mount Scopus side. They used trees, dirt, and stones to fill in gullies and ravines, creating a ramp a hundred feet wide. This would provide enough space for a sustained flow of infantry to pour into any breach they might accomplish.

Jews watched from their positions high on the walls. As their work moved closer to the wall, the legionaries creating the ramp were protected from projectiles of all kinds by large shields of timber. Further out, other soldiers were constructing hundreds of catapults, ballistas, and several siege engines in preparation for attack. Always out of range of arrows, but always within sight to inspire dread.

And it was working. A hundred Jews had congregated outside the walls, rejected by their fellow fighters inside the walls because they had counseled surrender to Caesar. Guards up on the walls cast aspersions and rocks down upon them as they prepared to approach the Romans to ask for clemency.

One of the Roman centurions on guard was given intelligence on this group and brought a century of soldiers to escort them to Roman custody.

But when they met the fleeing Jews away from the walls, the apparent refugees turned on their escort, pulling out hidden weapons.

The Romans were overtaken by the surprise and fled back to camp. Twenty of them had been killed in the trap.[1]

This was the story that was relayed to Titus as he looked out on the surviving legionaries who stood at attention before him.

He spoke to them, "Those Jews, whose only leader is despair, engage with forethought and intelligent strategy. While Romans, whom fortune has always favored for your discipline, now become so rash that you venture into battle without my command. By law, the punishment for such subordination is execution of every member of your squad."[2]

139

The scolded soldiers tried to remain stoic in acceptance of their fate. The centurion who led them could produce no plea on their behalf as their leader. He'd led them into the trap, and they'd followed. The law was clear. And they all knew it.

Tiberius stepped up beside Titus and whispered to him, "Caesar, may I advise?"

Titus nodded. Tiberius said, "The battle has not even begun. The soldiers are restless and ready to fight for you. I believe they were impatient, not disobedient. You are within your rights to execute justice upon these fools. But if you kill them so early in this siege, it may work against you. It may dull the hunger for glory in the ranks."

Titus lifted his brow in recognition of the logic. A stern general inspired the loyalty and respect of his soldiers. But a cruel one bred fear and mutiny.

Tiberius concluded, "I suggest you show mercy. Like a god. Pardon the men and you may find them more zealous on your behalf when the time comes."

Titus thought it through. Tiberius was right. He turned back to the centurion. "Tell your soldiers that I will withhold their execution out of my grace and mercy. But you will take over latrine duty until I say so."

The centurion relaxed with relief, but then stiffened and saluted. "Hail, Caesar! Just and merciful. We are your most loyal soldiers."

He turned around to announce to the men their new duties, and Titus returned to his war tent for a meeting with his generals.

• • • • •

Apollyon stood in his war chariot on the ridge overlooking the Roman camp with Jerusalem beyond. He had returned with Marduk and the five other gods from Pella. The four war horses snorted smoke and stomped the ground restlessly. The remainder of the Watchers arrived and joined them on the ridge.

Marduk said, "The ramp and the catapults are almost completed. Soon, the battle begins."

"Yes," said Apollyon. "The end is near."

Zeus stepped near to the chariot. "My lord, where are the gods of Canaan? Are they coming?"

"No," snapped Apollyon. "But the problem is taken care of. Now we set our sights on Jerusalem."

The truth was that Pella had been a colossal failure for the Angel of the Abyss. He had lost four powerful deities there, and he could not afford to lose any more. But he had the other sixty-five gods assembled for war. His locust demons filled the land, the legions, and the city with chaos and uncleanness. And the archangels would not be there to defend the city. He had to focus.

"Gods of the nations, take your positions and prepare to unleash hell upon Jerusalem. When we have won, we will inhabit Yahweh's temple as our own!"

The gods cheered. But Apollyon thought, *And then I will destroy it. I will not leave one stone upon another.*

· · · · ·

Titus unrolled a map of Jerusalem out on a table in his war room at the center of the Roman camp. Agrippa and Josephus had crafted it from their intimate knowledge of the structures and layout of the city.

Agrippa stepped up beside Titus and Tiberius. "The key to the city is below. There is a network of underground tunnels with exits out beyond the walls." One tunnel was sketched out as a light line on the drawing to illustrate its rough location beneath the structures and streets. Agrippa pointed to the western wall. "Your best insertion point for troops would be here—the tunnel north of Herod's palace. I will show you the hidden entrance."

Titus saw that the tunnel to which Agrippa referred would angle back into the New City close to where they were building the ramp. He said, "But surely the tunnel will be guarded."

Agrippa said with a smirk, "Select few are privy to all secrets of the aristocracy."

Titus looked to Josephus for approval. He nodded in agreement and said, "Your only concern will be navigation through the city. Unfortunately, the streets are a labyrinth and difficult to know unless you have lived there."

"Solved," said Titus.

Agrippa and Josephus looked at each other with curiosity. Agrippa asked, "Do you have a mole?"

Titus smirked and said, "Select few are privy to all secrets of Caesar."

CHAPTER 30

Jacob climbed the stairs to the top of the tower at the southern pinnacle of the temple. He arrived at the top with a rapid heartbeat in his chest and labored breathing from the flight of stairs that led four hundred feet above the Kidron Valley.

He walked out onto the parapet. No one was here. Good. It was his favorite place to come to refresh himself or think through problems and issues. As he looked out over the city of David, the city of God, he felt that he could think more clearly. Like he was above it all, looking down from God's own heights.

This was the southwest corner of the temple complex. To his left was the rocky Kidron valley outside the walls. To his right, the Upper City where Herod's elaborate palace stood. The people far below on the pavement outside the temple looked like little animals scurrying every which way.

This was his beloved holy city. But now it was a city under siege. He could see the Roman encampment on the Mount of Olives just above the Kidron Valley. The main camp on Mount Scopus was a mile from the other side of Jerusalem. They were surrounded.

He needed to breathe the fresh air up here. Down below in the foul stench of the city, he had felt he was suffocating. The population was overflowing with several hundred thousand people now trapped inside the walls because of the legions surrounding them. Many were living in the streets because all the residences and inns were filled. Garbage was piling up everywhere. Even public defecation was a problem. It both literally and metaphorically reeked to high heaven in Jacob's nostrils—and no doubt God's as well.

From his vantage point, Jacob saw the charred remains of food stores in the city that had been burned down over a year ago. In the intervening time, the last of the city's resources had finally been consumed and starvation had set in. Fights were breaking out in the streets over food. They would not last much longer.

Jacob's thoughts returned to his earlier years when he had been naively fooled into the Nazarene's false teachings. But he had eventually returned to the Hebrew roots of his faith. He had come to the conclusion that the Way of the Nazarene was a lie. Jacob had become a staunch enemy of the Christians, fighting their pernicious heresies against Torah, temple, and Land. He had fought for circumcision, sabbaths, and dietary restrictions, the marks of covenantal membership.

Jacob looked across the city streets to the hippodrome, the source of his survival and the pain of his unhappiness. The doctor Alexander and his shrew of a wife had created the hospital there and had become a thorn in his flesh. He had done everything he could to rid the city of their vile influence. But their medical services had been too important to the populace—and to his own survival. It bothered him deeply that they had nursed him back to health when he had caught the plague. They'd said it was a miracle healing of Jesus, which only served to anger him.

What kind of a God would allow such suffering anyway? If these Christians were his children, then why had he almost wiped them out with a great tribulation? Which also raised the question of why Yahweh allowed his people the Jews to suffer so greatly beneath the foot of Rome. *Is he chastising us for our disobedience?* Cassandra had made this argument to him on this very spot not long ago.

Jacob could not deny that he was strangely attracted to Cassandra. He hated what she was, but he craved her with perverse desire. Maybe it was to subjugate her beliefs to his own. Or maybe it was to defile her self-righteous holiness. Put her in her place, make himself feel better. He had tried to take her by force, but once again, he'd been stopped by unfortunate circumstances. It seemed that everything he tried to do to stop Cassandra and Alexander backfired on him. He couldn't get them to leave the city with the others. He couldn't keep the Christians working in the mines. He couldn't catch Cassandra when she escaped to Pella.

The worst example of this frustration was the Two Witnesses. Those scourges of the people were closely connected to Alexander and Cassandra, and no one could touch them. What Jacob had witnessed earlier had burned into his soul with fear and dread: two hundred warriors destroyed by fire from heaven. *Two hundred warriors.* He had seen it with his own eyes, and he could not get it out of his mind.

The ramifications haunted him. If God himself was truly protecting the Witnesses, if he was behind their message of destruction of city and temple, if they were right that this generation was guilty of crucifying the Messiah, then the blood of all the prophets ever shed in the Land was indeed upon their heads. There was no way out.

If the Witnesses were truly God's prophets, then God was divorcing Israel after the flesh to marry a new bride, Israel after the Spirit. But that would make everything Jacob had believed a lie. A lie for which he had stolen, lied—and even killed.

Worse, Jacob would be the most cursed of all, unable to be restored, because he had crucified the Messiah all over again by returning to an obsolete covenant.[1] By not treating the Christians with acceptance and mercy, he would be guilty of not treating Messiah with acceptance and mercy. Jesus's parable of the sheep and goats came to his mind.

"Truly, I say to you, as you did not do it to one of the least of these, you did not do it to me."[2]

"But I helped Alexander," Jacob complained to the air. "I fed his people. I got him out of prison with the help of the Witnesses. I took his Christians out of the mines and brought them back to the hippodrome."

Except that everything Jacob had done from the hippodrome to the food and financial support was only a calculated strategy to benefit himself. His own words rang hollow in his ears. He had never done anything in this life for God or anyone else other than himself. He had lived a lie under the guise of religious duty. Even his love of country and city and temple was a love for what it had given him: prestige, privilege, power.

His religious obligation was a burden of weight upon him he could no longer bear. He had struggled to be a good Israelite, one who kept the Torah and made sure others did as well. But he knew his heart was not circumcised. He knew the works of Torah could not save him from his own vile unclean heart.

For what shall it profit a man, if he gain the whole world, and lose his own soul?[3]

"I am accursed," he said. "Anathema."

He climbed up on the ledge of the tower wall and cast himself down into the rocky bottom of the Kidron valley four hundred feet below.

CHAPTER 31

Pella

Uriel had dropped Cassandra back at Pella and returned to his squad of Kharabu on their way to Jerusalem.

Her heart racing, Cassandra hurried straight to her house. All she wanted was to see her children. She felt a longing for them like never before.

She burst through the front door to find her maidservant Magdalena feeding Samuel. "Mistress, you've returned!"

"Yes. Yes, I have."

"Mother!" Rushing into the front room of their small home, Noah and Rachel ran into Cassandra's arms. She hugged and kissed them as though she'd come back from the dead.

She rustled Noah's untidy hair. "My little warrior." She held Rachel away from her to look lovingly into her daughter's teary eyes. "My responsible young woman."

Rachel hugged her back fiercely. "I thought we'd never see you again!"

"My dear, dear children. I am here to stay. With you. I will never leave you. I love you all so dearly." Cassandra moved over to receive Samuel from Magdalena. Holding him tight, she looked into his cooing face and kissed him. In his eyes she saw the future. A future of hope growing out of despair. A seed blossoming into a beautiful tree of bountiful fruit.

She looked back at Noah and Rachel. "I guess I never wanted you to grow up."

They both sighed and rolled their eyes. Noah complained, "We know."

"But yesterday, I realized that you are growing up. And you know what? I decided that I'm going to let you."

Both of their eyes brightened.

Rachel wasted no time with her response. "Does this mean you've changed your mind about Jonathan?"

Cassandra sighed. "Somewhat."

Rachel squealed with delight and hugged Cassandra again. "I love you, I love you, I love you."

Cassandra couldn't help but laugh.

And then a tiny pain pricked her heart. Her own pain of unfulfilled longing for her beloved husband and friend with whom she might never spend time again.

There was a knock at the door. Noah hurried over to open it. "Thelonius!" he yelped at the sight of the Roman. "Am I late for my guard duties?"

"No, I just came to see if there was anything you all needed with your mother gone." Looking past the young boy, Thelonius exclaimed, "Cassandra! You're back. Thank God. What happened?"

She smiled. "I had to learn what I should have known all along. My calling is here to raise my family for God's kingdom."

"But what about Father?" Noah's eyes turned sad.

Cassandra touched him reassuringly. "We must pray for him. Pray that God protects him and returns him to us. But more importantly, that God's will be done. It's what your father wants."

Noah was not satisfied. "Will we see him again?"

Cassandra smiled painfully. "Yes, Noah. We will see him again." She decided not to finish her sentence with "in glory." After all, there was still hope that Alexander might survive and find his way back to them. A very small hope. But if the smallest grain of faith could move a mountain, then such hope was enough for her.

She hugged Noah and Rachel again along with little Samuel in her arms. "Oh, I missed you all so much."

As she released them, she took note of Thelonius's troubled expression. He asked, "Cassandra, can I speak to you alone?"

Handing Samuel back to Magdalena, Cassandra followed Thelonius up onto the house roof.

As she looked out upon the city, Cassandra saw even this aspect of her life in a fresh new way. The city was no longer a refuge. It was her home. No longer did she see the Remnant of believers as the last of the faithful on the verge of annihilation, but as the first fruits of an everlasting dominion of God's kingdom. No doubt it would take untold years and much suffering of growing pains through history. But Jesus Christ was seated at the right hand of God ruling over all the earth. The war that was upon them would remove the old covenant forever and vindicate his reign that the apostle John had written would last a thousand years.

An obvious symbol for a vast amount of time. His spiritual kingdom would grow from this smallest of seeds in the garden to the largest of trees in whose branches all the birds would make nests. The Gates of Hades would not prevail over the Church of Jesus Christ, his holy congregation.[1]

Thelonius broke her out of her thoughts. "Cassandra, I am not who you think I am."

She searched his face for understanding. "What do you mean?"

Thelonius looked away in guilt. "I have not told you everything about my fiancé or why I was here in Judea." He swallowed hard before adding, "I lied to you. I betrayed you."

"What?"

He looked away again in guilt. "I told you that Livia wasn't a Christian. Which is true. But neither was I."

Cassandra was not sure she'd heard correctly what he had said. "You're saying you are not a Christian?" It didn't make sense to her. Like a person speaking a foreign tongue.

"I *was* not a Christian. And the reason why I was here in Judea was because Titus was holding Livia hostage."

"Oh, Thelonius. Why?"

He appeared to be fighting to say every word. "He kept her in custody until I brought him the answers my father was commissioned by Nero to find."

Cassandra felt her stomach drop. Her mind became dizzy. She knew what Severus had been looking for when he was alive. She had been his servant years ago when he was on a journey to find the Apocalypse and its author and to kill him. But there was a third thing Severus was commissioned to do that he'd never done for the emperor.

Thelonius now said it. "I had to tell Titus where the Christians were hiding."

Stunned, Cassandra took a step away from him.

"I pretended to be a Christian in order to find you and gain your confidence."

She trembled with shock. She had left her children in this man's hands. She had trusted him.

Her voice shook. "Pretended? So it was all a lie?"

"At first it was. But what else could I do? He threatened to kill my fiancé, Cassandra. Titus threatened to kill Livia if I didn't bring him intelligence on the Christians."

Cassandra thought hard about it. Thelonius was now looking into her eyes with total honesty and vulnerability. He pleaded with her. "It was an impossible choice. What else could I do?"

Cassandra's thoughts swirled in her head. Would she have done the same to save Alexander? Was it really impossible to compare one life to the lives of many? A dozen of their men had died in the battle with the Roman legion. They had paid the price of Thelonius's treachery.

But her feelings of betrayal were countered by her knowledge of God's faithfulness. His will could not be thwarted. Like Joseph's brothers throwing him in the pit, God had used even this betrayal to accomplish his purpose of protecting his people. Joseph had said, "You meant it for evil, but God meant it for good to save the lives of many."[2]

Thelonius's words brought her back. "But Cassandra. Something happened to me when I returned to Pella to warn you of the Roman attack. God's spirit broke me. I became a believer."

"You became a believer?"

"Yes. I repented of my sin, and I am a follower of Jesus. That is why I stayed to fight for Pella. I have been redeemed by the blood of Christ."

"Why didn't you tell me then?" she asked.

"I wanted to. But the attack occurred, and there wasn't time."

She stared at him.

How could she believe him now after all his lies?

Did his actions prove a true change of heart?

They had to.

The fact that Thelonius had stayed to fight for Pella and risk his life with those men who'd died indicated true repentance, behavior that showed a changed heart. He had repented of his betrayal. He had warned the Pellan Christians, and he had accepted death on behalf of those he had once deceived.

She believed him now.

It was painful to say, but she said it. "I forgive you, Thelonius."

He looked at her as if he couldn't believe what she had just said.

Then he broke down weeping. He fell to his knees, clinging to the edge of her robe like the Prodigal Son at his father's feet.

Cassandra pulled him up. His blurry-red eyes looked determinedly down into hers. He said, "I am going to Jerusalem. I am going to find Alexander for you."

"No," said Cassandra. "You have already paid your debt."

"Not to everyone," he countered.

Thelonius stepped away from her. Cassandra could see that his mind was made up. He was going to jump into the furnace of fire, and she was not going to be able to stop him.

PART TWO

Armageddon

CHAPTER 32

Jerusalem
May, AD 70

And they assembled them at the place that in Hebrew is called Armageddon...
...and God remembered Babylon the great, to make her drain the cup of the wine of the fury of his wrath. And every island fled away, and no mountains were to be found. And great hailstones, about one hundred pounds each, fell from heaven on people; and they cursed God for the plague of the hail, because the plague was so severe.

Apocalypse 16:16, 19-21

Simon and Aaron stood on the top of the hundred-foot-tall tower of Psephinus on the northwestern wall, which overlooked the earthworks being built by the Romans. The rampart had come to within a hundred feet of the wall. All the workers had withdrawn.

About three hundred yards from the city wall, Titus and Tiberius sat on their horses beside a line of a hundred catapults and ballistas, huge machines of ruthless Roman ingenuity built from wood and iron. Many of the siege engines were fitted to throw javelins and darts the size of a large man. These could penetrate wood or rip through a dozen soldiers with one fling from the ballista. Some of them were shaped like large crossbows mounted on a stand that took two or three men to operate—one to load the dart and two to crank back the lever that stretched the bow string.

But the crowning achievement was the twenty or so catapults that ejected huge stones, a hundred pounds each, at their targets. About the size of an elephant, these were triangle-shaped wooden levers mounted on wheels. Several soldiers cranked back the long arm connected to a spring mechanism. Several others then placed their heavy payload into the bucket at the end of the arm and painted the stone with whitewash. It looked like a large spoon ready to fling a payload of ice at the enemy.[1]

The catapult crews placed their stones and darts in place, drew back the spring mechanisms, and awaited the command of Titus.

Simon muttered to Aaron, "Get ready for a very large hailstorm."

Moshe and Elihu watched from the battlement some way down the wall from Simon and Aaron. They could see what the rest could not: a line of almost seventy gods of the nations dressed in their heavenly armor. The gods stood in the unseen realm amidst the Romans, a parallel of worlds as if two wars were going to occur simultaneously, on earth as it was in heaven.

The gods were led by Apollyon, who stood beside his bodyguard Marduk on his war chariot, bridled to his four horses of hell. On his back Apollyon had Ba'al's war hammer, Driver, and in his hands he carried Chaser, Ba'al's heavenly spear of lightning. Apparently something had happened to Ba'al and the other gods of Canaan because they were nowhere in sight.

And there were certainly no angels to defend Jerusalem because the shekinah presence of Yahweh had long since left "the great city."[2] Jerusalem had become Babylon, Sodom, and Egypt and was about to be judged as an enemy of God. The nation of Israel was an unfaithful harlot who rode the Beast of Rome and had been divorced by her husband, Yahweh. Moshe and Elihu were the Two Witnesses required by Torah to declare her guilt before Yahweh and his divine council. And now Yahweh was going to stone that unfaithful harlot to death and marry a new bride.[3]

But this was also a battle of cosmic mountains: Mount Bashan, the mountain of the gods, against Mount Zion, the mountain of Yahweh, God of gods.[4] But the earthly Jerusalem was not the heavenly Jerusalem. God had relocated Mount Zion to the body of Christ, God's new temple consisting of the Remnant of Messiah.[5] The destruction of the earthly city and temple was to be the sign that the Son of Man was in heaven on the throne of David and the new Jerusalem was come down out of heaven. It would historically vindicate the new covenant inaugurated in Christ's blood and consummated in his *parousia*. God was draining the cup of the wine of the fury of his wrath.[6]

Moshe said one word out loud that summed it all up: "Armageddon."[7]

The Two Witnesses heard the trumpet call from Titus's herald. Then the catapults released their payloads upon the city.

Simon was right. It was like a thunderstorm of hundred-pound hailstones that crushed everything in its wake. Rocks hit the wall, shaking it to its foundations, throwing soldiers on the parapet to the ground. Arrows pierced human targets and launched them fifty feet into the air with their force. Other stones struck deeper into the city, destroying houses, killing entire families. Whatever parts of the New City had been rebuilt from its previous destruction would eventually be reduced to rubble.

And the Romans were alternating, half loading and half launching, so that it created a constant stream of rocks and bolts pounding away at the fortification without rest.

Jacob's quarrying of new stone for wall reinforcement had helped the strength of the Jewish bulwark, but only so much. Simon was not sure how long these walls would hold. He knew they would not hold forever.

A reminder of that slimy opportunist's odd death. Simon would never have even learned of Jacob's demise among thousands of casualties in the city if a passing soldier had not witnessed the Pharisee's fall from the temple tower and recognized the battered corpse splattered on the rocks below. Had the man slipped? Been pushed? Or just given up in despair like so many others of the city's citizens?

Either way it was no great loss to neither the city nor the Jewish cause.

Moshe and Elihu saw the gods of the nations in the heavenlies pounding away at the spiritual wall as well. Their blows matched the blows of the catapults. As above, so below.

But they could also see the myriad of demons that infested the Roman forces. Turning, twisting clouds of shadows moved in and around the soldiers like a plague of locusts unseen by other humans. They were strange hybrid monsters with human heads and breastplates of iron, the noise of their wings like that of many chariots. In fact, the whole Land of Israel was polluted by these evil spirits. Hundreds of millions of them. The demonic spirit cast out by Jesus in his ministry had returned sevenfold. Their fury was as frightening as anything the Two Witnesses had ever seen. Without the heavenly host here to stop them, the end was near.[8]

At that moment, Moshe and Elihu caught the eyes of Apollyon. Eyes of flaming hatred. Though the god was commanding his forces a hundred yards away, the two prophets could see his ugly, long androgynous features and tattered, scraggly hair as though they stood directly in front of him. His voice spoke inside their heads.

I will have you soon. You will be mine. All this will be mine.

The Two Witnesses climbed down the wall and made their way back into the city. They were unafraid of the hailstorm of stone. Their time would not come until Yahweh allowed it.

CHAPTER 33

Alexander tended to the wounded as they were brought into the hippodrome. There were crushed arms, legs, and head wounds from the collapse of buildings hit by the catapult stones. Dozens of victims were wheeled in or carried by family members. Many others had died in the onslaught.

The Christian medical assistants brought the wounded citizens to beds, and the few doctors cared for them. Alexander headed up immediate surgery for some, stitching up gashes, setting broken limbs, cutting off others that were mangled beyond repair.

Screams of suffering from the wounded in surgery filled the stadium. Behind it all was the constant concussive sound in the distance of boulders demolishing buildings in the New City. Every crashing impact made Alexander cringe, wondering who might have been killed or wounded by the hit. For now, the hippodrome was too far for the catapults to reach with their devastating ammunition. But he knew that would change if the Romans broke through the outer wall and took over the New City.

This was one time when Jacob ben Mordecai might have made himself useful in helping with an evacuation plan. But Alexander hadn't seen his nemesis in weeks and had heard rumors that he'd been among the siege's casualties. It was hard for Alexander to muster up sorrow for the Judas except at the loss of any further rations and medical supplies the man might have provided.

"Please, doctor, save my father," cried a boy behind him.

Alexander turned to see two men placing an unconscious man gently on a bed. Alexander examined him. The patient was husky and had the rough hands of a farmer. The doctor noticed that the man's head was swelling and he was struggling to breathe. His larynx appeared to have been crushed.

"What happened, young man?"

The boy looked no older than ten. Noah's age. He was dark-skinned with black hair and innocent eyes. He shook with fear. "The place we were staying in was hit by one of the flying rocks. Everything crashed in on us. My father was hit in the head and throat."

The man did not have much chance of surviving.

157

He asked the boy, "What is your name?"

"Samuel."

It was a popular enough name. But the irony was not lost on Alexander that it happened to be the name of his own son. He could not help but think of his sons and how they would grow up without their father. He was not going to let that happen to this one.

Alexander pointed to a waiting area. "Samuel, go over there and pray." He could not allow the child to see what he was going to do. And he certainly was not going to tell him the great risk that it was.

The boy obeyed, and Alexander reached into his bag for tools. First importance: breathing. He needed to get air into the man's lungs. He felt the larynx where it had been crushed. He felt several ridges below the larynx on the windpipe. He took a scalpel and cut through the throat, performing an emergency tracheotomy he had learned from reading Asclepiades. He slid in a wooden reed as a tube in the hole to keep the airway open.[1]

The man finally began to breathe. Now for the hard part. Alexander yelled out, "I need help over here now!"

"I'll help, doctor."

Alexander turned at the familiar voice to see Thelonius Severus with surgical gown on, ready to help him.

"How in the world did you...?"

"I'll explain later. What do you need now?"

Alexander shook off his confusion and returned to the emergency at hand. "Hold him down. He's comatose, but I have to drill into his head to relieve the pressure. He might have a seizure."

Thelonius held him dutifully while Alexander pulled out a small hand drill created for this sort of task. He had heard of this remedy for swelling brains but had never done it before.

"Please, Jesus," he prayed out loud, "Keep this father alive for his son."

"Amen," Thelonius said.

Alexander found the swollen area of the man's head and first clipped away some hair so he could have straight access to the skull. He put the drill in place and began to crank it.

The sound of grinding skull did not even faze the doctor. He was only thinking of the boy and how he must not lose his father.

He had to go slow enough so that when he broke through, he would not harm the brain.

He felt a slight breakthrough and stopped when blood squirted out. He unwound the drill and let the opening drain, relieving pressure on the brain.

After the swelling went down, Alexander bandaged the man's head and checked his pulse again. He was alive. He felt a sigh of relief.

Thelonius said, "Doctor."

Alexander looked up, only to be surprised by Samuel standing there in tears. "Will he be all right?"

"For now," said Alexander. He couldn't lie to the boy. "But time will tell." The boy quickly reached out and hugged Alexander tightly. "Thank you. Thank you so much."

The father would be dead in a few days. Alexander felt a pang of deep loneliness come over him. He missed his children. He missed his wife. Saving these lives seemed so futile, knowing their ultimate fate at the hands of the Romans. But his calling was to relieve suffering, not figure out the secret plans of God.

Alexander had arranged for his two doctors and multiple assistants to work in shifts so that each of them would get rest. Without enough rest, they would be useless in helping the patients, even dangerous.

By nightfall, the steady stream of wounded had reached near a thousand. The relentless barrage of catapults continued, but many people had moved out of the range of the stones to protect themselves and their families. Alexander and Thelonius took a break together and ate some bread and figs for strength in the doctor's tent.

"I took the tunnel we used to escape to Pella," said Thelonius. "It leads outside the Roman perimeter."

"Why did you come back, Thelonius? I thought you would be in Rome with your fiancé."

"I have several things I must first redeem."

"What do you mean?"

"To begin with, I have a letter for you from Cassandra." Thelonius reached in his cloak, pulled out a crumpled parchment, and handed it to the doctor.

Alexander stared at the parchment. It was like a ray of hope in this dark pit of despair.

"Do you mind?" he asked.

"Please do," said Thelonius.

Opening the letter, Alexander read it silently, tears building in his eyes.

Cassandra, to my dear beloved Alexander,

I have something to confess to you. I have tried many times to come to Jerusalem to see you, but the Holy Spirit has kept me here in Pella. I am sorry that I never told you because I was afraid you would not allow me to join you. Please forgive me.

I have finally learned in my stubbornness the lesson of his calling upon our family, that is to build the kingdom of God for the future. I am asking the Father to spare you for the sake of your family so that we will see you again in this life. But his will be done.

And should he choose a different course, I am content in Christ, knowing that whether in life or death we glorify him, and I believe that no matter what happens, we will share in the resurrection of glory to come.

I treasure our few short years together more than all that came before it. Thank you for loving me with such kindness and patience.

I have been faithfully praying for your labor and that of the Two Witnesses. Pray for us as we are finally convening a council to address the false teaching of the Ebionites.

I have asked Thelonius to deliver this letter to you. And now I want to ask you to do something very important to me. I want you to forgive Thelonius for what he is going to tell you. I have forgiven him, and I have entrusted him to you in the Lord Jesus Christ.

May the grace of our Lord watch over you, my husband, my lover, my friend.

All the emotions of love and gratitude that had welled up within Alexander were suddenly spinning out of control with the confusion of his wife's last request.

I want you to forgive Thelonius for what he is going to tell you.

What did Thelonius do that required forgiveness? What had he done?

Alexander gazed at Thelonius with scrutiny. The Roman glanced away in shame before finding the courage to face the questioning doctor.

"I have a confession to make," he said.

CHAPTER 34

The Roman catapults had been pounding away for two days at the walls and city. The stone was starting to disintegrate. If they kept it up, the Romans would break through in a day or so. But they were running out of large payloads and were flinging smaller rocks now, fifty pounds in weight and less.

Simon and his soldiers had been sheltering themselves at the base of the inside walls, fifteen feet thick, the safest place during the bombardment. There had been little they could do but wait.

Without warning, the barrage of pounding just stopped and the skies became clear of flying projectiles. The Jewish soldiers were surprised by the sudden silence. They had been under such constant noisy attack for the past two days that their eardrums felt assaulted. But the new quiet was foreboding. They looked at one another, wondering what was next.

Simon knew. He barked out a command, "Archers to the walls! Infantry behind them!"

The soldiers obeyed, gathering in their respected places on the battlement.

Aaron followed Simon to the top to see two large siege towers being wheeled to the walls on the rampart. They were over seventy feet tall, thirty feet higher than the city walls. The rolling towers were somewhat pyramid-like in shape to keep from easily toppling. The structures were covered with metal plates to protect against the flaming arrows that the Jews now launched at them to no avail.[1]

Simon saw that each tower was filled with hundreds of soldiers with hundreds of others pushing the structures forward. The Romans only needed to get within a hundred feet of the walls because each tower had a large drawbridge that would come down to close the gap and allow the legionaries to cross over to the walls and invade the city.

Simon and Aaron were near one of the towers as its drawbridge came down on the battlement. Simon noticed that the bridge had just barely caught the edge of the stone wall, a wall that had been crumbling beneath the weight of catapulted boulders.

It was a gift from God.

He turned to his new bodyguard, a huge six-foot-tall muscular bald Jewish warrior who carried a large sledgehammer. He shouted, "Simcha! Break the wall beneath it!"

Simcha moved quickly to the bridge mount. Dozens of legionaries were spilling out onto the bridge a hundred feet away and starting to cross.

Simcha took his sledgehammer and pounded at the stone edge where the bridge mount lay. It began to crumble.

The legionaries filled the drawbridge on their way to the wall. They were moving carefully, full shields up, prepared for confrontation. But they were not prepared for what happened next.

Simcha managed to dislodge a large chunk of stone at the edge of the wall. The weight of the soldiers on the bridge added more stress, and the stone just broke away, taking the wooden bridge down with it. The structure plummeted fifty feet to the ground with a crash. Legionaries slid to the bottom of the moat surrounding the wall.

The Jews around Simon and Aaron cheered.

The weight of the drawbridge pulled the tower forward, tipping it toward the wall. The creaking sound of wood cracking under the strain coupled with the screams of soldiers inside was silenced when the tower crashed into the wall.

Simon's men cheered again.

But not Simon. He saw the other siege engine drop its bridge to the wall, the Jewish defenders meeting the Romans halfway across.

Forces clashed as the Jews sought to keep the invaders from setting foot behind the walls. Once they broke through, it would be near impossible to hold them back.

They had to hold them back.

Simon yelled, "Soldiers! Attack!" His company of men ran along the walls to reinforce their brothers.

But it was too late. The Romans had breached the wall. They were rushing in like a flood now, battling on the narrow wall top, pushing the Jews further back.

Simon could see the outer wall was lost.

He shouted, "Retreat to the second wall!" Aaron blew his war horn for retreat, and the men obeyed, dissolving away from the marauding Romans.

Simcha was not quick to retreat. He battered and pulverized Romans with his sledgehammer.

Simon yelled, at him, "Simcha! Enough! Retreat!"

The Jewish giant obeyed and slid down a ladder to the ground. He joined Simon and Aaron as they ran through the New City to the second wall.

The Romans chased the fleeing Jews. There were a couple hundred in the first wave of legionaries with more flowing in at the breach.

The Romans were several hundred yards behind. Their heavy armor weighed them down and slowed their pace.

By the time they made it to the gates of the second wall, the last of the Jewish warriors, Simcha, had made it through.

But it appeared that the gates would not be shut in time.

Despite their exhaustion, the legionaries took their opportunity to try to make it through and keep the gates open for their comrades.

But when they made it to the opening, the Jews suddenly poured boiling hot fenugreek down upon them from the walls, scalding them to death. Fenugreek was particularly odious because it was green gunk that stuck to clothes and bodies, burning through both fabric and skin.[2]

One of the Jews yelled out, "There's your warm welcome!"[3]

A second wave of legionaries aligned themselves into testudo formation with shields overhead for protection as they approached the closing gate.

But another helpful trait of fenugreek was that it was slimy. So when the Romans reached the ground where the fenugreek had been poured out from above, the soldiers slipped and lost their footing. Shields went down as men fell to their butts on the ground. The testudo formation broke open, making the soldiers vulnerable to attack from above.

It was just the opening the Jewish archers needed to drown the century of legionaries in a wave of arrows.

Not one of them survived. Their bodies were so full of arrows, they looked like macabre human porcupines.

The gates were closed and barricaded.

The Jews on the wall laughed and insulted the arriving Romans, who found their fellow soldiers lying dead in their tracks.

Inside the wall, Simon turned to Aaron. "We can yield no more ground. We must hold the second wall or we fail the seige."

Aaron responded, "We must end our civil war and unify with Gischala or we will all die."

CHAPTER 35

Pella

Cassandra sat near the front of the audience in the converted temple of Jupiter. The city and church elders had convened the church council to finish examining the Ebionite beliefs that were causing division within the congregation.[1] They usually adjudicated at the gates of the city, but because of the large number of citizens in attendance, several thousand, the size of the church building was more appropriate.

The Pella council had previously been interrupted by the arrival of the Roman cohort that had tried to kill them. But with their miraculous deliverance, the Christians sought to return to their duty to protect the flock from spiritual assault.

Cassandra agreed with Boaz that false teachers and their doctrines were as dangerous for the survival of the body of Christ as was the siege of Jerusalem. For what good would it do if the Church survived persecution but embraced lies and deception? A church without the true Gospel would not be a vessel of redemption but of damnation.

The apostle Peter had warned them all of this very thing in these last days.

> There will be false teachers among you, who will secretly bring in destructive heresies, even denying the Master who bought them, bringing upon themselves swift destruction. And many will follow their sensuality, and because of them the way of truth will be blasphemed. And in their greed, they will exploit you with false words. Their condemnation from long ago is not idle, and their destruction is not asleep.
>
> 2 Peter 2:1-3

Boaz led the examination along with a dozen of other elders seated at the front of the congregation. Symeon, leader of the Ebionites, sat before the council as a court of law. His long, greasy white hair and unwashed, unkempt appearance

164

reminded Cassandra of a madman. Which was deceptive because Symeon was no madman. He was diabolically cunning.

All of Symeon's followers came, a thousand of them. But they were only allowed a few hundred seats in the court. The rest stood outside with the overflow into the surrounding temple grounds. Cassandra was worried. The false doctrine of the Ebionites threatened the very survival of the church. They were a growing vocal minority that sought to take over the congregation if their numbers reached a majority.

Prayer and proper assembly procedure had all been followed. Boaz was now engaging the first question of Symeon. Boaz kept it simple and clear.

"In our previous assembly, we already addressed the issue of the divine person of Jesus. I remind this council that the Ebionites do not confess the Son of Man as being Yahweh in the flesh. They affirm only that he was merely a man, adopted by the Father to be Messiah.

"Our apostolic confession is affirmed in the opening of the apostle John's Gospel: 'In the beginning was the Logos, and the Logos was with God and the Logos was God. And the Logos became flesh and dwelt among us, and we have seen his glory, glory as of the only Son from the Father.'"[2]

Logos was the Greek word that philosophers used to describe the divine Reason or underlying order of the cosmos. Christians subverted it by infusing the word with new meaning of God's message, his wisdom, and the fulfilled promise that he would dwell within them as in a tabernacle.

The Ebionites did not like the Gospel of John. They had their own scripture they called the Gospel of the Hebrews that countered it.

Symeon responded, "We Ebionites do believe in Jesus as Messiah, even if we may have minor disagreement over the nature of his person. But we do believe."

Boaz moved the examination forward. "Is it true, Symeon, that you promote Torah observance as a requirement for inclusion in the Body of Christ?"

Symeon said, "Only for Jews, not Gentiles."

"Defend your doctrine."

Symeon paused. He stood up and paced around, mimicking the great philosopher Apollonius of Tyana. He had performed this same exact theatrical act last time they'd begun the council. Cassandra considered him to be a demagogue and an unoriginal one at that.

"We believe that Torah is obedience to Yahweh. God himself said that his statutes were forever, 'an eternal covenant for generations.'[3] Now, we readily accept Gentile believers into the *ekklesia* through faith." *Ekklesia* was the Greek word that meant congregation of the Lord, or church, under both old and new covenants.[4]

"But surely the arrival of Jesus as Messiah does not eradicate the Jewish identity as God's chosen people. We simply see two promises to two people, one to the Jews and one to the Gentiles. After all, the new covenant that the prophet Jeremiah foretold was to be made with the houses of Israel and Judah. We don't stop being Jews when we believe in Jesus. Did not Jesus himself say that not one jot or tittle of Torah would pass away until heaven and earth passed away? Yes, we heartily affirm with Jesus that Torah is still binding on Jewish believers in Messiah."[5]

Boaz quieted the murmuring of the crowd. Then he announced, "The question of Torah has been an ongoing issue of difficulty in the congregation of the Lord ever since the apostles first proclaimed the Gospel. We struggled with this in Jerusalem before the flight to Pella. So the elders have decided to call as prosecutor someone who is uniquely qualified to address this problem: Cassandra Maccabaeus."

The crowd murmured with scandal. Symeon and the Ebionites were particularly loud and disagreeable. Though God had included females in baptismal rites, prophecy, and other spiritual gifts in the ekklesia for the past forty years, some still thought they should not be allowed public recognition. Boaz saw no problem with it.

He said, "Cassandra traveled and ministered with the apostle Paul, who wrote and taught extensively on the issue of Torah. She comes to us with expert testimony."

Symeon blurted out, "Women are not to exercise authority over men! It is unnatural!"[6]

Boaz replied, "Cassandra is not exercising authority. The elders have examined her and found her worthy to testify. She is submitted to our authority."

Cassandra walked up to the front. She saw the sour look on Symeon's face. She had expected it. It made her feel good. She had to be careful not to let her pride rise up. Or her anger. She had learned her lesson a few years back when this had all started. She had lashed out in self-righteous condemnation of her fellow Jews. They had martyred her parents, and she had been happy to see God's judgment coming upon them. But the Holy Spirit had broken her, changed her heart. And now she wanted to save as many as possible from the wrath to come.

Heretics and false teachers, however, were a scourge. The apostle Peter had written of them as blasphemers, like irrational animals born to be caught and destroyed. Accursed children following the way of Balaam. Waterless springs and mists driven by the storm, for whom the gloom of utter darkness has been reserved.[7] False prophets and teachers had to be stopped and cut off before their poison corrupted the body of Christ.

In contrast with her past incivility, Cassandra tried to speak firmly yet graciously to the elders and crowd. "Symeon speaks of the need to maintain Torah. Yet he also claims to believe in the inclusion of Gentiles into the ekklesia. This is the problem that the apostle Paul wrote about. How can you *include* Gentiles into the body, but continue to engage in rituals that *exclude* Gentiles from the body? It is a contradiction. The very essence of Torah holiness, whether it is diet, sabbaths, or circumcision, is separation from the Gentiles. But Paul the apostle wrote that Jesus has made us both one and has broken down in his flesh the dividing wall of hostility between Jew and Gentile by abolishing the law of commandments expressed in ordinances that he might create in himself one new man in place of the two.[8] There are not two promises to two peoples. There is one promise to one people of faith, both Jew and Gentile.

"Jesus has made Torah obsolete. And what is Torah? It is the heavens and earth of Yahweh's old covenant. The temple in Jerusalem is the earthly incarnation of that old covenant heavens and earth. So when Symeon quotes Jesus that not one jot or tittle will pass away from Torah until heaven and earth pass away, he is correct. The new heavens and earth of Isaiah have arrived in the new covenant of Christ's blood. And it will be consummated at Christ's *parousia* with the earthly destruction of the temple, which is the passing away of the old covenant heavens and earth.[9]

"This is why the writer of Hebrews tells us not to turn back to the shadows of Torah and temple that looked forward to Messiah, the reality. Jesus Christ is greater than the angels, greater than Moses and Aaron, than the temple itself.[10] In Christ, God's eternal covenant of perpetual statutes is fulfilled forever. Because Torah is fulfilled in him, he has abolished it for us.[11]"

Symeon was allowed to respond. He spoke to the elders up front, taking pains to avoid looking at Cassandra. "We Ebionites anticipate that Jesus is coming to the temple in Jerusalem, but not to destroy it. Rather as our new high priest, he will rebuild an eschatological temple, establish a new priesthood, and reinstitute the sacrifices as Ezekiel prophesied."

Cassandra was not going to let him get away with that. She said, "Jesus is building the eschatological temple right now. The body of Christ all over the world is the new temple without land or boundaries. We are living stones in that spiritual temple. Paul wrote that Gentiles are no longer strangers and aliens but fellow citizens with the saints and members of the household of God, built on the foundation of the apostles and prophets. Christ Jesus himself is the cornerstone in whom the whole structure, being joined together, grows into a holy temple in the Lord. The Shekinah glory has left the earthly temple and now resides in us because we are the new dwelling place for God's Spirit.[12]

"It is blasphemy to claim that Jesus would reinstitute sacrifices in an earthly temple after he paid the price with his eternal sacrifice in the heavenly temple. It would be a denial of the once-for-all sacrifice of Christ. A denial of the Gospel itself."

"Elders, if I may," said Symeon. "This woman continues to quote the apostle Paul. But we Ebionites do not acknowledge Paul's writing as God-breathed precisely because he rejects Torah."

The crowd went wild. Cassandra knew that this would not go well for the Ebionites.

Symeon went on, "Even if we ignored Torah, the promise of God goes back further in history to our father Abraham. And it is there where the eternal covenant is made to Abraham and his seed, his offspring. If I may quote the Scripture, 'Behold, my covenant is with you, Abraham, and you shall be the father of a multitude of nations. And I will establish my covenant between me and you and your seed after you throughout their generations for an everlasting covenant. And I will give to you and to your seed after you the land of your sojournings, all the land of Canaan, for an everlasting possession.'"[13]

"Now, it seems to me that God's covenant with Abraham and his seed is an everlasting one rooted in circumcision. A covenant where he promises not only that we will number as the stars of heaven, but that we shall possess this Land forever. God will not reject his people, will he? I think not. For the gifts and the calling of God are irrevocable."

Cassandra immediately thought, *Good. I've got him now. He's denied justification by faith.* She turned to the elders and prepared to make her final argument—to cut off the head of the snake.

CHAPTER 36

Jerusalem

Simon, Aaron, and Simcha entered the Antonia fortress, cautiously looking around. The middle of the fort was a large, open courtyard with four seventy-five-foot-tall towers on each corner. The walls themselves were sixty feet in height, and they shielded a series of rooms all about the palatial structure. The fort was on the northwestern corner of the temple mount, so it would most likely be the focus of attack for the Romans to get to the temple. Since Gischala controlled the entire temple complex, the Antonia was his to defend.[1]

Simon had risked this meeting on Gischala's turf because the time had arrived for putting aside their personal grievances. They had to stop this civil war. They had to unite against Titus or they would fall beneath the trampling feet and iron jaws of Rome.[2]

Or at least that is what Simon wanted Gischala to think. Simon wanted to somehow find a way to kill Titus, and the Zealot might help make that goal possible. The slaughter of the Essene community by the Roman general had felt like the massacre of Simon's own family. That group of naïve, idealistic monks had changed his life. Young Aaron beside him had taught Simon to see the world differently. But Titus had so completely destroyed the community of Qumran that everything they believed in was gone, burned up in the wreckage of their Dead Sea village.

Simon still thought he could avoid the rest of the war. Even at this late time, it was not impossible to escape back out into the wilderness. He had planned to run to Masada, a truly impregnable fortress where he could withstand any enemy siege. But that was for later. For now, he had to gain Gischala's trust. Because the only other person Simon was more intent upon killing than Titus was Gischala. He was still plotting a way to catch Gischala unaware and get his final revenge upon the creature for everything he had done to Simon, to the only woman Simon had ever truly loved, and to the temple that Simon had once believed in.

169

Aaron alerted Simon to the arrival of Gischala walking toward them all alone, a gesture of good faith—backed up by corridors of soldiers surrounding the courtyard around them.

Gischala approached Simon and his two companions with open arms, trying to gauge their intent. The young monk he knew about, but the huge bodyguard must be a new addition. Gischala stared up at the six-foot-tall brute bulging with muscles and said, "Well, a call for a truce is just in time, considering my chances of surviving this one."

Simcha grinned.

Simon did not appear in a mood for humor. He said, "We must put aside our differences and unite. If the Romans take the temple, you know what they will do to it. Abomination and desolation."

"Ah, yes," said Gischala. "We have Antiochus Epiphanes to blame for that strategy." In the days of the Maccabees, three hundred years ago, the Greek ruler Antiochus had defiled their temple, had set up a statue of Zeus in it, had used the holy altar to sacrifice to pagan gods, and tried to force the Jews to go against their own religion. It had become the model of abomination that Jews considered the highest unholy crime possible by Gentiles.

Gischala said, "But I am afraid that we both have a common problem in this city that will not go away. The Two Witnesses."

He saw Aaron sigh with regret. The two so-called prophets had been spewing their hatred for the past three-and-a-half years in Jerusalem. Because of the incident of the fire from heaven, Gischala considered them more dangerous than Simon.

Gischala went on, "I believe they may be in collusion with Rome, feeding Titus intelligence on our forces to aid him in the overthrow of the city."

Simon appeared to be thinking the accusation through. He said, "They have spoken of Yahweh using the Roman military as his anointed means of purpose."

Gischala nodded.

Simon said, "I have avoided them at the behest of my lieutenant." He gestured to Aaron. "My soldiers are afraid of them, the rumors surrounding their unexplained powers. The drought, the plagues."

"Sorcery," said Gischala. "We have left them alone, thinking they would go away or be ignored. But have you noticed that since the war began, their message has become stronger, more unrepentant. We have allowed demons to fester in our midst. We must exorcise them and free ourselves from their collusion with Rome."

Simon glanced at Aaron for his input. The young monk said, "Whether they are demons, magicians, or deceivers, they are dangerous. They may try to claim to be the two messiahs that the prophet Zechariah foretold, a kingly one and a priestly ally. The scrolls of my community predicted the same."[3]

Gischala knew the prophecy to which he was referring. Zechariah had foretold the Day of the Lord when all the nations would come against Jerusalem, ruled by an anointed king and a priest.[4]

> 'Thus says Yahweh of hosts, "Behold, the man whose name is the Branch: for he shall branch out from his place, and he shall build the temple of Yahweh. It is he who shall build the temple of Yahweh and shall bear royal honor, and shall sit and rule on his throne. And there shall be a priest on his throne, and the counsel of peace shall be between them both." '
>
> Zechariah 6:12-14

Aaron continued to explain, "If the Two Witnesses should claim themselves anointed as the king and the priest, they would have the last three-and-a-half years of signs and wonders to back up their claims. We could see them quickly turn from madmen howling in the wind into messianic pretenders with a large following."

Excellent, thought Gischala. *These Essene delusions fit right in with my plans.*

"Gischala, will you join with me against these enemies within and without?" Simon asked.

Gischala could see Simon's jaw tightening. It must have taken everything in him to suppress his true feelings and make that offer. Gischala knew the hatred that boiled below the surface. He carried it as well.

He said, "I will consider it. After you deal with the two demons within your own domain of the city."

He could see the concern that came over Simon. Addressing the Two Witnesses was about the only unknown danger in this campaign. Gischala decided not to tell his potential "ally" about his own experience doing so. How the fire from heaven had almost burned him alive with the two hundred soldiers. He would let Simon discover that for himself. And maybe Gischala would never have to bother with Simon again.

Simon said, "I will deal with them," and he left with his Essene and bodyguard.

"Or they will deal with you," muttered Gischala to himself.

CHAPTER 37

The streets of the Mishneh Quarter by the western wall of the temple were empty. The night winds blew through the Tyropoeon Valley, and the stars above glittered like the gods. A shadow moved through the alleys of the marketplace. A cloaked figure on a mission.

The figure reached up to the awning above an inn and tied a red cloth to one of the timbers. It was small but certainly visible should anyone look for it.

The shadow character then moved on down the street for a new location with a cluster of additional red cloths in hand.

• • • • •

At sunrise, Simon was called to the second wall by his lookouts. When he and Aaron arrived, they saw that the catapults and ballistas had been wheeled into the New City and were now preparing to target the Mishneh Quarter with their stones and arrows. The damage would be devastating.

Many of the survivors from the New City had found refuge behind the second walls—those few thousand who had not already fled or been taken captive by Titus.

Aaron said with irony as he gestured toward the enemy lines, "And I thought we could not be more pulverized."

Simon saw that the Romans had wheeled in a large battering ram the size of a small house. Its structure was covered with a brass-pounded triangular roof, and a huge timber post with an iron ram's head at the fore. The catapult stones would be like pebbles compared to the damage that a battering ram of this size would do to a fortification.

And the Jews were about to find out quite soon what that damage would be.

Aaron held up a Roman arrow with an attached message to it. He handed it to Simon.

"Indeed," said Simon as he read. "Titus will not bombard the temple with his catapults out of respect for our religion." He crumpled the message in his hand

173

and said with a sarcastic edge, "The rest of the city, however, will not fare so well."

"How gracious a beast," echoed Aaron.

$$\cdots$$

In the unseen realm, Apollyon and Marduk overlooked the second wall from behind the Roman lines. The gods of the nations stood behind them awaiting his command.

Apollyon said to Marduk, "Go, my victor. Split those gates as you split Tiamat."[1]

"Yes, Master."

Marduk got off the chariot and marched down to the closed gate.

Azazel, the guardian Watcher of Titus, gave Apollyon a jealous look.

The Angel of the Abyss said, "Do not worry, ancient one. My plans for you remain. You'll have your glory soon enough."

A company of Romans pushed the wheeled ram toward the gate, chanting in unison, "Here comes Victor! Here comes Victor!"[2]

Aaron understood Latin. He said, "So the Romans name their phalluses with a confident pride."

Simon didn't hear him. He was wondering why Titus was not first engaging in a catapult storm to provide cover for the ram. That was unusual. The general always sought to pound the will of his enemies before such an attack. He had promised he would not bombard the temple. But the city was still fair game. Was Titus trying to avoid mistakenly hitting the temple?

Aaron broke his concentration. "General."

Simon shook himself out of his thought and yelled to his men, "Archers! Release!"

A line of archers launched their missiles at the men pushing the ram from behind. Some Romans fell. But others carried large shields of wickerwork to protect the rest. The ram kept coming like a predator with its eyes focused tenaciously on its prey.

The battering ram arrived at the gate and began to immediately swing back and forth, smashing away at the huge brass-covered wooden gates. It would not take long.

In the unseen realm, Marduk pounded on the gate with his war mace. There was no pagan deity mightier than this denizen of Mesopotamia. And Apollyon enjoyed the poetic touch of using the most high god of Babylon, the same city that Yahweh now symbolically called Jerusalem.[3]

Apollyon telepathically spoke to the deity at a distance. *Welcome home, Marduk.*

In the earthly realm, Jews on the walls poured boiling oil down upon the roof of the battering siege engine. Some legionaries were scalded inside, but the remainder continued to bash away with the iron ram's head.

Back and forth it swung. With each hit, the sound of creaking, cracking timber increased.

Pounding. Pounding. Pounding.

Victor was unstoppable.

A fiery arrow set the oil ablaze, and the ram began to burn. But the housing kept the men inside safe enough to finish their task.

Pounding. Pounding. Pounding.

Simon was still trying to figure out the strategic purpose behind the Romans' lack of prior bombardment. He wondered aloud to Aaron, "Why has Titus withheld the catapults?"

• • • • •

Tiberius Alexander, Titus's right hand, waited in silence with a long line of several hundred legionaries in a single tunnel beneath the city. They had entered the secret passageway according to the directions of Agrippa and Josephus and were now below the Mishneh Quarter behind enemy lines.

They heard the pounding of the battering ram assaulting the gates somewhere up above.

Tiberius announced, "That's Victor! Let's move!"

He led the long line of armed soldiers to an exit above. The men behind him marched silently, malevolently.

Tiberius pushed aside a board that covered the tunnel entrance and led the men out. They exited in the midst of a garbage dump behind a marketplace.

He held the line when a small boy no more than four or five stood up right in front of Tiberius. The lad looked sickly and malnourished, dressed in rags. He had been scrounging for food. But now he just stood still with mouth frozen open in silence at the sight of the tall tribune standing before him.

Tiberius smiled down at the boy.

He gently raised his hand to pat the boy's head.

Then without warning, he snapped the child's neck.

He tossed the broken body into the garbage and led his company out of the alley.

He halted again at the opening to the street. The line of three hundred legionaries stayed stone-silent behind him, two-by-two, following command.

Tiberius peeked out and saw what he was looking for: a small, red cloth tied to the timber of a porch awning in the marketplace. It was their signal for direction. He waved to his men, and they moved out into the empty streets, drawing their swords.

He looked for the next red cloth to guide him to their target: the second wall gate inside the Mishneh Quarter.

• • • • •

Victor was making headway. The gate yielded beneath the relentless pounding of the ram. Its bar braces cracked.

But the ram was burning out of control, and the Jewish archers on the walls hindered Roman reinforcements with their relentless missiles.

Inside the wall, a contingent of several hundred Jewish warriors were ready to rush through the gates as soon as they opened. Their goal was to tip the ram over and meet any arriving Romans with a sledgehammer, led by the mighty Simcha.

Up above, it finally came to Simon. The reason why Titus did not assault them with catapults was to protect something *inside* the walls. Sabotage.

Before he could alert his soldiers, he saw a line of legionaries fill the square. "BEHIND YOU!" he shouted to his men.

The Romans hit them like a flash flood. The battle for the gate was on.

Outside in the unseen realm, Apollyon saw Marduk pushing on the gates with all his strength, his feet digging into the ground behind him, his muscles bulging with exertion.

The bronze was bending, the wood cracking open. The mighty deity stopped pushing and withdrew his mighty cleaver that he had used on Tiamat. This would split open heaven and earth.

But up above the raging deity, clouds swirled like a whirlpool of fury.

Apollyon knew what that meant.

The heavens were opening.

He shouted to Azazel, "Hold the line!" He whipped his chariot horses and charged for the gates.

Behind the second wall, Simon jumped to the ground with Aaron and others. They engaged the Romans with a crash. Simcha was a one-man battering ram, swatting Romans aside with his sledgehammer like Samson of old.

But Simon's numbers were not enough to overwhelm his enemy.

These Romans seemed to be handpicked fighters with superior skills.

They were pushing forward, cutting down Jews with astonishing ease.

Simon thought, *This is it. We have lost the second wall.*

Outside the gates, Apollyon raced toward Marduk's position. He saw him suddenly surrounded by a company of heavenly host, *malakim.*

Why were they here? He had been assured that Yahweh's protection had been withdrawn. It didn't make sense.

It was just like Yahweh to break a covenant. No respect for the rules of engagement. Just like the holy wars of Joshua's conquest.

He screamed into the wind, "When this is over, Yahweh, I'm charging you with war crimes!"

Marduk's demon horses plowed through the line of angels, crushing them beneath their hellion hooves. They were no match for his mighty stallions of the Apocalypse.

"Get on!" he yelled to Marduk.

The behemoth jumped onto Storm Demon, and Apollyon bolted out of the battle zone before the malakim could regroup and attack.

At the same moment behind the gates, just as Simon was sure the wall was lost to the Roman invaders, he was shocked to see Gischala leading a force of horsemen from the temple behind them.

The first thought that came into Simon's head was that Gischala was ambushing Simon like before.

Instead, the Zealots attacked the legionaries from behind, catching them in a wedge.

The numbers and strategy had just turned against the Romans. They began to buckle.

Gischala had obviously reconsidered his demands to Simon for joining him. The time for infighting was over. Gischala had placed a condition of becoming allies upon Simon confronting the Two Witnesses. But before Simon had a chance to do so, Gischala must have decided not to wait this time.

Thank God, thought Simon.

Then he saw other Jews joining the fight as well with pitchforks, hoes, and hammers. The citizens were joining their fellow soldiers in a desperate bid for survival.

The braces to the gates broke open beneath the flaming ram. The gates swung inward.

But the Romans inside were so overwhelmed that they bolted for the opening to run back to their camp.

They would not be leading their comrades inward to victory after all.

•••••

In the unseen realm behind the enemy lines, the seventy gods ran toward the gates to join the heavenly battle and defend their Master.

But they weren't prepared for the seven archangels and a legion of malakim who rose from their hidden positions beneath the debris of the annihilated New City. Five thousand angels.

Watcher, malakim, and archangel clashed on the spiritual field of battle. Malakim were no match for the gods. But archangels were.

Watchers fought like cornered rats, brandishing their heavenly weapons with furious rage against their adversaries, cutting down hundreds of angels with divine fury. They were fighting for their lives.[4]

But the numbers were simply not equal.

And their confusion over the presence of the heavenly host threw them off. The angels were not supposed to be here.

In the earthly realm, Titus saw the fleeing Romans exiting the gates, chased by the Jewish defenders.

He yelled out to his bowmen, a contingent of Jewish archers under Agrippa's command, "Archers! Defend the legionaries!"[5]

The archers lined up to release their arrows.

They were about to slaughter their fellow Jews. But these soldiers had long ago overcome their hesitation when they helped wipe out the Jewish cities of the Land on their way to Jerusalem.

They launched a volley into the air and pushed back the Jews from catching the fleeing Romans.

And they captured a good number of those Jews, wounded and not, as the battle had been stayed.[6]

• • • • •

Apollyon and Marduk had raced the chariot away from the front lines of battle along the wall to escape the angelic ambush. Malakim could not stop Storm Demon and its four trampling horses from hell.

But when he circled back to his generals, Apollyon discovered only three of them still there. And they were beaten bloody from battle.

Azazel, Zeus, and Ares approached the chariot as it stopped, its horses snorting the smoke of their furious ride. All around them were broken and hacked bodies of malakim, taken down by the Watchers in defense.

"It was a trap, my lord," said Zeus, breathing with the exhaustion of battle.

Ares explained, "The archangels led a legion of malakim against us. We held them off as long as we could, but we were severely outnumbered."

"I thought Jerusalem was ours to plunder," said Azazel. "Why would Yahweh do this?"

Apollyon had an idea, but he kept it to himself.

Zeus asked, "Michael and his heavenly host were supposed to guard the Christians, in Pella. Is Michael rebelling from Yahweh?"

"I don't think so," said Apollyon thoughtfully. Then he changed the subject. "Where did they take the captives?"

"Out of the New City," said Azazel, pointing to the demolished gate.

Apollyon sighed and closed his eyes tight with revelation. "I know exactly where those godlickers took them. Follow me."

He snapped the reins, and the chariot launched for the gate out of the city.

• • • • •

Titus cursed as he looked over his Jewish captives from the battle. A hundred of them. He ordered Tiberius, "Get them ready for the punishment we talked about."

Titus had decided it was time for psychological warfare that would raise the stakes on these obstinate rebels.

• • • • •

Behind the gates, Simon and Aaron considered their strategic options as soldiers tended to the wounded and replaced the broken wooden braces with heavy iron ones. They would reinforce the gates against any future attempts to replay this near-successful breach.

Aaron saw a legionary lying on the ground in a pool of blood. The Roman stirred, and Aaron plunged his sword into the soldier's chest, killing him for good.

Simon knelt beside a Jewish comrade who had been slashed in the arm. He held a cloth over the wound, compressing it. "Keep pressure on it until you get stitched up. You'll be fine."

"Thank you, General," said the young man. He looked no more than sixteen years old. Beside him was another young man, more like a boy, dead from his wounds.

Simon felt an overwhelming sense of despair at how many young men— the future of the nation—had already been killed in this war. If they didn't hold the city, their entire seed would be wiped out.

His eyes focused on two men standing at the edge of the crowd of citizens who had come to see what was happening. He recognized them as the Two Witnesses, Moshe and Elihu.

"General." The voice was firm. Simon turned back. Gischala sat strong on his neighing horse, looking down upon Simon.

Simon stood. "Thank you for your help. We would have lost without you."

"Yes," said Gischala with an air of superiority, "you would have."

Simon chose not to address the insult, but to absorb it.

Gischala responded diplomatically, "You were right. We must put aside our differences and unite immediately. Or we will lose everything."

Simon said, "You were right as well. There is a mole in the city."

He held up a handful of red cloths in his hand. "One of my men found these signaling the way from a tunnel entrance to these gates."

Gischala said, "Traitor."

"Or traitors," said Simon. He looked back, scanning the crowd. "I have a couple of suspects I need to speak with immediately."

The Two Witnesses were gone.

CHAPTER 38

Pella

The council of Pella continued its examination of the Ebionites in the congregation at the center of the city. Symeon had last brought up the promise to Abraham as an argument that Yahweh would not cut off his seed and that the Jews would inherit the Promised Land forever.

Cassandra was still addressing the elders at the front. She had so much she wanted to say but had to focus on the most important truths. She had first started with the conditionality of the covenant. El Shaddai had said that if Abraham or his seed broke the covenant, they would be cut off.[1] This was exactly the same as Jesus's parable of the tenants that described God returning to Israel to destroy this generation and let out the vineyard of his kingdom to others.

> *"Therefore I say to you, the kingdom of God will be taken away from you, and be given to a nation producing the fruit of it."*
>
> *Matthew 21:43*

She had affirmed that Abraham was to be a father of many nations, but that this was a reference to the inclusion of the Gentiles into the body of Christ. She quoted Paul's letter to the Galatians.

> *And the Scripture, foreseeing that God would justify the Gentiles by faith, preached the gospel beforehand to Abraham, saying, "In you shall all the nations be blessed." So then, those who are of faith are blessed along with Abraham, the man of faith.*
>
> *Galatians 3:8-9*

This brought Cassandra to her penultimate argument: that the children of Abraham were not fleshly descendants but faithful believers. As Paul had repeatedly argued through his letters, those who are of faith are the true children of Abraham.

For not all who are descended from Israel belong to Israel, and not all are children of Abraham because they are his seed, but "Through Isaac shall your seed be named." This means that it is not the children of the flesh who are the children of God, but the children of the promise are counted as offspring.

Romans 9:6-8

The unbelieving Jews were not God's chosen people to whom he kept his promise. Only the believing Remnant were. The rest would be judged and cut off like Ishmael. And that was what they were in the middle of right now. The Ebionites had joined the 144,000 elect to come to Pella, but they were not part of the elect. The Christians had to clean God's house.

Cassandra drew to her conclusion. "Perhaps most important of all, the apostle declared that 'the promises were made to Abraham and to his seed. It does not say, "And to seeds," referring to many, but referring to one, "And to your seed," who is Christ.' So we must conclude that only those who are 'in Christ Jesus' are sons of God through faith, heirs according to promise. The eternal covenant to Abraham is fulfilled in Christ and only Christ. To apply the promise to Abraham to fleshly descendants is to deny the Gospel of justification by faith.

"But the Ebionites may then ask, what about the promise of land inheritance? Was not this nation to inherit the Land of Israel forever? Well, that land inheritance was connected to the old covenant that was replaced by the new covenant. Jesus is the seed of Abraham. Jesus is the eschatological temple. He is also the resurrection and the life. *He* is our inheritance. For Messiah inherited all the nations. His people are no longer confined to a single parcel of land in Canaan, they are over all the earth. *Jesus* is the Land. So the new covenant is a spiritual transformation of the old covenant from earthly people, city, temple, and land into a heavenly people, city, temple, and land."[2]

Cassandra heard scoffing from the Ebionites, but more positive chatter from the rest of the audience. She felt that she had done as well as she could. She only hoped the elders were listening. She left it up to God and sat down.

Boaz took the podium. "The elders will now meet in assembly. Let us return tomorrow to discuss our conclusions. You are dismissed."

Cassandra looked over at Symeon, who was giving her the evil eye. He was so full of hatred it was almost tangible.

Good, she thought. *I must have been filled with the Spirit.*

CHAPTER 39

The Valley of Hinnom

Apollyon and Marduk rode Storm Demon to the southern valley outside Jerusalem. The Valley of Hinnom—also known as Gehenna, the Valley of Slaughter. An earthquake had occurred two years ago that had opened a chasm in the spiritual realm of this accursed valley.[1]

They rode up to the edge of the crevice. Apollyon got off the chariot with Marduk. The Master reached down and picked up a heavenly sword used by one of the Watchers. Other heavenly weapons were strewn about, left from the captives.

Azazel, Zeus, and Ares arrived on foot. "Master," Azazel said, gesturing to the top of the city wall towering a couple hundred feet over the valley.

Apollyon looked up to see the Two Witnesses looking down on them. Four archangels stood watching over the humans in the unseen realm. It confirmed Apollyon's theory: the angels had come to protect the Two Witnesses, spokesmen for Yahweh's divine council.

But that was not all.

"You can have the gods of the nations," Apollyon muttered to Yahweh. "I get everything else."

The Watcher walked up to the chasm ledge, looking down into the pit of darkness.

Human eyes would not be able to see very far, but Apollyon could see—all the way to Sheol.

The archangels had ambushed his gods, dragged them here, and cast them into the Abyss, where they would be bound and punished as Isaiah had promised.

The land is utterly broken,
the land is split apart...
On that day the Lord will punish
the host of heaven, in heaven,
and the kings of the land, on the land.

184

They will be gathered together
as prisoners in a pit;
they will be shut up in a prison,
and after many days they will be punished.

Isaiah 24:20-22

Apollyon knew this day had been coming. The principalities and powers had been given the Gentile nations to rule over at Babel. God had given the pagans over to their false gods and depraved idolatry. He'd let them fill up the measure of their sins. At his resurrection, Messiah had stolen back the inheritance of the gods. This was the triumphal procession of his victory. He was completing what he had begun at the cross.

The words of the psalm haunted Apollyon like a heavenly assassin.

God has taken his place in the divine council;
in the midst of the gods he holds judgment:
"How long will you judge unjustly
and show partiality to the wicked? Selah
Give justice to the weak and the fatherless;
maintain the right of the afflicted and the destitute.
Rescue the weak and the needy;
deliver them from the hand of the wicked."
They have neither knowledge nor understanding,
they walk about in darkness;
all the foundations of the earth are shaken.
I said, "You are gods,
sons of the Most High, all of you;
nevertheless, like men you shall die,
and fall like any prince.
Arise, O God, judge the land;
for you shall inherit all the nations!"

Psalm 82:1–7

The Angel of the Abyss knew that though his generals had been taken, *he* still had authority. He had the legal right to destroy this city, and Yahweh was not taking that away from him. He had sued in the heavenly court, and he had won that right.

Apollyon looked back up at the Witnesses through gritted teeth. Then past them up into the heavenly throne above the waters. "Take what you will, tyrant of the cosmos. I am not without allies. I still have my locust demons—and one last measure."

He turned his attention to Marduk. "Turn this chariot around. We have a ride ahead of us."

He turned to the others. "Azazel, continue with our plans for your prince of desolation.[2] You are in charge until I return."

He looked up at the Witnesses and their guardians again and continued his orders, "And for this to work, I need to lance two particularly annoying boils of pus."

CHAPTER 40

Alexander and his medical assistants had taken care of the new patients who had been brought to the hippodrome from the battle of the second wall. With the help of Thelonius and the other two doctors, they had sewn up lacerations, set broken bones, and watched helplessly as too many died from their wounds, hundreds of them. But the survivors were now resting, healing in their beds. A moment of calm before the next big storm.

When Thelonius had told Alexander of his betrayal of them all, the doctor had thought he had a slight understanding of how Jesus had felt to be betrayed by Judas. Thelonius was not who he had said he was. It had all been a lie. And they had opened their hearts, their homes, their lives to him, like prey baring its throat to a predator.

Upon learning of Thelonius's conversion, it was not as easy as Alexander had thought it would be to forgive. Thelonius had manipulated the Christians into danger all for his own interests. And now that the Roman spy was a Christian, Alexander was supposed to just accept him as if he had never done those things?

Paul of Tarsus had persecuted and murdered Christians, but then he had become an apostle of the Faith. If the "chief of sinners" could be redeemed and forgiven, then why not Thelonius?

If *Alexander* could be forgiven, then why not Thelonius?

Still, Alexander found himself scrutinizing the Roman. Questioning his motives in everything. Forgiveness was not as easy as he had thought it would be.

But as Thelonius helped him in his duties, Alexander remembered how the Roman had truly changed. The son of Severus had given Titus the location of Cassandra and the Christians. But then he'd warned those same Christians, even risking his life in battle to defend them. And now he risked his life again by coming to Jerusalem.

Or was that a lie as well?

Alexander had taken some time to share with their fellow countrymen the good news of Jesus the Messiah through the seven high feasts of their Faith. He had been explaining how Messiah was fulfilling the feasts to completion in their generation. He had explained Jesus as the Passover lamb, sacrificed for our sins.

As the Feast of Unleavened Bread commemorated the exodus out of Egypt, so Jesus had become the bread of heaven who was leading the new exodus out of the Egypt of apostate Israel. His resurrection from the dead was the first fruits of the resurrection to come, just as the Feast of First Fruits had foreshadowed the harvest.[1]

And now Alexander had just finished explaining the typology of the Feast of Pentecost that had been celebrated earlier in the month. Also known as the Feast of Weeks, Pentecost was celebrated fifty days after the start of First Fruits. It was always on a Sunday, and it marked the beginning of the summer wheat harvest.[2]

That new beginning had originated in the first Pentecost that had occurred fifty days after the sons of Israel had left Pharaoh's Egypt. On that very day, Yahweh had given the ten commandments to Moses on Sinai and created the "heaven and earth" of the old covenant.[3]

But forty years ago today, a new covenant had been inaugurated. After the death and resurrection of Jesus on the Passover, a new heaven and earth was inaugurated on the day of Pentecost, a new covenant with his people.

Alexander had told his audience of that first fruits of the kingdom. The gathering of the disciples at the temple, the Holy Spirit filling and baptizing the believers in tongues of fire, the shekinah glory. He had explained how scattered Jews from every nation on the face of the earth had come to Jerusalem and were participating in the restoration of Israel. They were the Remnant of God, and they were united with Gentile believers just as the new covenant had promised.[4]

That first Pentecost of the new covenant in the days of the apostles marked the beginning of Yahweh building his new temple, a spiritual one made of spiritual stones of believers founded on the spiritual cornerstone of Christ.[5] It began the transition period of the Last Days that Peter had proclaimed on that day forty years ago.

> But this is what was uttered through the prophet Joel:
> " 'And in the last days it shall be, God declares,
> that I will pour out my Spirit on all flesh,
> and your sons and your daughters shall prophesy,
> and your young men shall see visions,
> and your old men shall dream dreams;
> even on my male servants and female servants
> in those days I will pour out my Spirit, and they shall prophesy.
> And I will show wonders in the heavens above
> and signs on the earth below,

blood, and fire, and vapor of smoke;
the sun shall be turned to darkness
and the moon to blood,
before the day of the Lord comes, the great and terrible day.

Acts 2:16–20

The last days of the old covenant had begun at Pentecost with the outpouring of the Holy Spirit. The old covenant had been written on tablets of stone. The new covenant was written on hearts of flesh.

And the usual prophetic symbolism of cosmic collapse, the darkening of the sun and the turning of the moon to blood, were the poetic expressions of the Day of the Lord for Jerusalem within that generation. It was a day where the destruction of the old covenant temple would consummate the transition to the new covenant, from old heavens and earth to new heavens and earth.

They were in the middle of that great and terrible day. Would they call upon the name of the Lord?

Alexander could see that those who were able to listen had been doing so. These concepts were not new to them. Only their fulfillment was. Some faces appeared to indicate that it was making sense.

Some voices indicated otherwise. "Stop preaching to us your Christian fire and brimstone from heaven! Just heal our bodies and let us get out of here!"

Another shouted, "Messiah would not let this happen to us!"

A third yelled back at them, "Shut up and listen to the man! We deserve everything we get from the hand of God!"

Alexander was about to discuss the last three feasts when he was interrupted by the surprise of Moshe and Elihu entering the hippodrome.

The audience of several hundred patients fell silent as the two approached them. Everyone knew who they were and was afraid of them. The rumors and gossip of all the strange things that followed the Two Witnesses were not just known through word of mouth. Some of these people had seen the signs and wonders with their own eyes. Wherever the Witnesses went, they spread fear.

Elihu spoke to the patients, "The doctor is correct. The harvest is upon us. The Son of Man is like one who sows good seed into the field of the world. But sons of the evil one are like tares or weeds sown by the devil in that same field. So the harvest is the end of the age that has now come upon us. The Son of Man will separate the wheat from the tares. And the tares he will gather out of his

189

kingdom, and he will throw them into the fiery furnace where there shall be weeping and gnashing of teeth. But the righteous will shine like the sun in the kingdom of their Father."[6]

The patients were painfully silent with the implications. Some could be heard weeping.

Moshe added, "The Son of Man has a sickle. And the hour to reap has come for the harvest of the land is fully ripe. Are you wheat, or are you tares?"[7]

Moshe stopped his preaching when he saw Simon arriving in the hippodrome entrance with a company of two hundred guards. The monk Aaron rode beside him.

Moshe shared a knowing look with Elihu.

Simon and Aaron dismounted their horses and approached.

Simon said, "I need to speak with the four of you."

Alexander had taken Simon, Aaron, Thelonius, and the Witnesses to his tent for privacy. Simon's guards stood at attention by the entrance of the hippodrome with arms displayed, ready for orders.

Simon appeared agitated. He said, "We have been betrayed by a spy. He, *or they*, helped guide a company of legionaries through the city to ambush us behind the wall." He was looking straight at the Witnesses.

Elihu shook his head with incredulity. "And you think we are the spies?"

Aaron jumped in, "Your constant sermon is that Rome is God's chosen army to destroy city and temple."

"And so it was Jeremiah's sermon as well," said Moshe. "Was Jeremiah a spy of Babylon—or a prophet of God?"

Aaron's face turned sour. Moshe had forced him onto the horns of a dilemma. However Aaron answered, he would condemn himself. If he admitted Jeremiah wasn't a spy, then he would have to admit that the Witnesses were not either. But if he claimed Jeremiah was a spy, then he would be denying God's prophet. Jeremiah had prophesied that Yahweh was coming to judge Jerusalem through the armies of Babylon. Ezekiel had said that Yahweh put his own sword in the hands of Nebuchadnezzar to scatter the Egyptians as well. And then Isaiah wrote that Yahweh had mustered the Medes as his own army to punish Babylon. In the providential hands of Yahweh, these tyrants were not the gods they supposed themselves to be.[8]

Simon stared intensely at Moshe and Elihu. "Aaron here has advised me more than once to stay away from the two of you. It seems you are dangerous on a level that we cannot understand. So I want to know, are the rumors true? What will happen if my soldiers arrest you?"

"What did Gischala tell you?" asked the dark-skinned Elihu.

"Nothing. All I have is gossip and rumors. Whispers of angels and demons. Claims of sorcery."

"Did Gischala put you up to this?" Moshe asked. "To deal with us?"

"Yes."

Elihu and Moshe shared a glance. Elihu said, "What Gischala tells you may not be as important as what he does not tell you."

"Do you think we are sorcerers?" asked Moshe.

Simon thought for a moment, then said, "No. But I do not have the luxury of theological speculation. I have a city to save. And traitors to stop."

Moshe got to the point. "We are not spies for Rome, General. And the Christians are not your enemies. Yahweh will pour out his wrath upon Rome just as he does Jerusalem. The prophet Zechariah was clear in his condemnation: 'And this shall be the plague with which Yahweh will strike all the peoples that wage war against Jerusalem: their flesh will rot while they are still standing on their feet, their eyes will rot in their sockets, and their tongues will rot in their mouths. And on that day a great panic from the LORD shall fall on them.'"[9]

Again, Simon stared at the Witnesses, deep in thought, trying to decide what he was going to do.

Finally, he spoke up. "I believe you. Unfortunately, that leaves me without a suspect and the strong possibility that Titus will use the strategy again—more successfully—if he is shown other tunnels by the Herods."

"Have you considered Gischala?" asked Alexander. "He seems to have the most to benefit from your defeat."

"And the most to lose as well," said Simon. "Gischala cannot hold the temple alone. No. I have a better idea for how to draw out this rat of a traitor."

He also had a better idea as to who the true traitor was, now that he'd had opportunity to ponder. At least two people within the Roman camp knew more about Jerusalem's secrets than even Simon—his erstwhile lover Berenice and her brother Agrippa.

Still, if the siblings had turned those secrets over to Titus, they had not been wandering Jerusalem's night streets with patches of red cloth. Someone with intimate knowledge of the city had done that. And whether their accomplice remained within the city or had long since fled back to the Romans, an accusation to that effect could have its uses to Simon.

Simon stood up. "Doctor, I leave you to your duties for the city. And you two," he paused, looking thoughtfully at Moshe and Elihu, "I leave you to God." Aaron at his heels, he turned and left.

CHAPTER 41

The entire populace had been called to assemble in the outer court of the temple. Gischala, now in a truce with Simon, had agreed to allow the men of the city to represent their families for the announcement that he and Simon were about to make. The courtyard was filled with tens of thousands, and the air was filled with anticipation—and fear.

Alexander and Thelonius were near the front of the temple steps, where Gischala and Simon, Aaron and Simcha now stood. The Jewish generals were backed by several thousand of their soldiers surrounding the inner temple. They had managed to quiet the crowd.

Gischala spoke first. "People of Israel, as you now see, Simon and I have entered into a truce to protect this city and temple from the abomination of desolation at the gates."

Cheers in the masses forced him to wait to be heard again.

"We are prepared to fight to the death to defend you and God's own honor. But we have a danger in our midst that jeopardizes everything, even our very survival. A traitor inside this city has given intelligence to Titus that almost led to the loss of the second wall and which threatens further breaches of our defenses."

Anger and murmuring broke out as Simon held up a piece of red cloth and waved it back and forth.

"Perhaps one of you saw the traitor who marked the way for the Romans with such cloths as this. We are calling upon all of you to find this person and turn him in. If he continues to help the Romans, we could lose this war."

More agitation in the crowd.

"But I appeal to that person right now. If you turn yourself in, we will grant you leniency. But now is your only moment. For the sake of this city, your people, and your God, give yourself up now and save us all."

He stood silently as the crowd looked around, murmuring. People were asking one another if they knew anything. Had they seen anything suspicious? Had anyone boasted about their betrayal? Hinted at it?

There was no surrender.

Gischala surveilled the crowd with a cold-eyed, stony expression. But Simon's face betrayed his fury. He stepped forward and spoke with a harsh anger that made Alexander shudder.

"One man, this Achan in our midst, betrays the entire city because of his actions. Now the entire city will suffer. Food rations will be cut in half for everyone until the traitor hands himself in."[1]

The crowd burst out in shock. Alexander could see that even Gischala and Aaron were surprised at the extreme course. They had already been on half rations for months now. To halve them again would be devastating.

The crowd became unruly.

Gischala ordered his men to present arms.

The crowd backed down.

But no one handed themselves in.

Soldiers surrounded the entire courtyard in the pillared porticoes. Alexander felt the fear that washed over the masses. It was dangerous. An angry crowd could turn into a mob, and a mob was hard to stop even with armed soldiers.

Gischala managed to calm them down with assurances of safety if they only obeyed.

And still no one came forward.

Alexander saw Simon and Gischala talking to each other about their next course of action.

Suddenly, Thelonius stepped forward from the crowd and mounted the steps.

The guards surrounded him with weapons drawn, protecting the generals.

But they were waved aside.

Alexander watched Thelonius with confusion.

The young Roman spoke to the generals.

They alerted some guards who came and bound Thelonius in chains and began to whisk him away.

What have you done, Thelonius? thought Alexander.

Gischala then announced, "The traitor has handed himself in!"

The crowd yelled, but more with anger at the traitor than with relief. The guards whisked Thelonius away so that a riot would not break out to lynch the confessor.

Alexander could not believe what he had just witnessed. He had been having trouble trusting Thelonius. But this?

Was the Roman's newfound belief in Jesus a motivation? If he believed the city would fall as Jesus predicted, was he trying to help the prophecy? Had Thelonius turned from a secret unbeliever into a secret fanatic?

Alexander felt sick. A wave of dizziness overcame him.

Alexander could only mutter in unbelief. "Thelonius, what have you become?"

CHAPTER 42

Pella

Cassandra sat expectantly, awaiting the decision of the Pella council over the Ebionite affair. The elders and citizens had returned to the temple after a day's consideration. The number of people in the audience was overwhelming. Maybe two thousand or more filling the streets. This was an important day for the future of the kingdom. Cassandra prayed for God's will to be done.

Boaz took the podium again to speak for the council of elders behind him. The masses immediately quieted down in anticipation of the verdict. He said, "I want to give an exhortation to the ekklesia here to endure in faith to the end. We are in the last hour of the end of the age. Like the children of Israel in the wilderness, so we have lived through forty years of waiting to enter our promised land. During his ministry, Jesus called this generation an 'adulterous and wicked' one for rejecting him as they had rejected him in the generation of Moses. And like those days, God will judge this generation before he allows us to enter into that kingdom in full.

"We have lived in a tense period of transition between covenants. The old covenant has become obsolete. It has grown old and is ready to vanish away with the destruction of the temple.[1] At the same time, the new covenant has been inaugurated but not yet consummated, leaving some believers confused and fueling false teachers who try to pour new wine into old wineskins. This has caused the very trouble that we have dealt with from the start regarding the Judaizers, who sought to place a burden upon believers that was too great to bear.

"But soon the old will vanish with all its elementary principles, its *stoicheia*.[2] As the writer of Hebrews has written, the Lord says yet once more he is about to shake the heavens and the earth. This phrase, 'Yet once more,' indicates the removal of things that are—that is, things that have been made, the temple and all its elements—so that the things that cannot be shaken may remain: the new covenant kingdom and its superior *stoicheia*. Therefore let us be grateful for receiving a kingdom that cannot be shaken, and thus let us offer to God acceptable worship with reverence and awe, for our God is a consuming fire."[3]

The entire crowd with the exception of the Ebionites broke out with praises that lasted for several minutes. Expressions in the congregation displayed awe of this moment of history in which they lived. A moment of transition between covenants that heralded a change of cosmos.

When they quieted down, Boaz continued. "The elders have concluded that the Ebionites promote false teaching by their doctrines that deny the godhood of Messiah and the God-breathed letters of the apostle Paul. Their enforcement of circumcision and Torah as justification severs them from Christ and crucifies the Son of God all over again. They are shipwrecked as regards the faith, and we hereby cut them off from the congregation of the Lord."

More murmuring broke out in the crowd. The Ebionites were not pleased. Boaz concluded, "We have given them five days to gather their belongings and leave the city. May Yahweh protect his sheep."[4]

The chatter in the crowd grew. Cassandra sighed and prayed a prayer of thanks to the Father. It felt like they had dodged an axe. When this was all over, the ekklesia would grow with the protection of the Holy Spirit over her. The Church would not die out or apostatize.

But it was not over yet. The shaking of heaven and earth was about to occur, and it would be devastating.

CHAPTER 43

Jerusalem

Thelonius groaned and shifted his position where he lay on the floor of the dungeon below the temple mount. He had been in the cell for five days now. He was dehydrated and starving. But he'd had a lot of time down here in the dark to think about his life and the choices he had made. He knew it was all coming to an end. Would his beloved Livia ever find out what had happened to him? Would she live a lonely life, waiting for years for his return before resigning to his fate? Would she find someone else to love? He prayed she would.

He drifted in and out of foggy wakefulness and restless sleep. The sound of a guard's voice and the opening of the cell door awakened him. "Thelonius Severus."

He rubbed his eyes as a figure approached him.

The figure sat down next to him and leaned in close. It was Alexander. The doctor pulled out a small water skin from his cloak and lifted it to Thelonius's mouth to drink. He did so, gulping the life-giving water desperately.

"Slowly," said Alexander.

Thelonius looked up at him. "Thank you," he whispered back.

Alexander reached into his cloak and pulled out some pieces of bread. Snatching the bread, Thelonius stuffed it into his own cloak in several places. All but the last piece, which he jammed into his mouth. He was so hungry he almost swallowed the sustenance whole.

Alexander watched his captive ally chewing the bread with desperation. The doctor had thought through the incident with much prayer. He knew Thelonius was not the spy. He said, "So you lied about your identity again."

Thelonius stopped eating. He searched Alexander's face for his intent.

Alexander added, "But this time you did it to save others instead of yourself."

Thelonius smiled. "The best lie is a half-truth. I told them I was an agent of Caesar. Unfortunately, my confession didn't match their evidence, so I'm not sure what they are going to do next."

Alexander said, "You saved the innocents from starving. You've given them a few more days to live. But you know how this ends."

Thelonius stared into his eyes with conviction. "So do you. Yet here you are."

The implication was obvious. As Alexander sought to snatch some from the fire, Thelonius sought to help him in the face of great odds against them.

Alexander said, "You sacrificed yourself. But the real traitor remains hidden."

"The real traitor was never going to reveal himself. You know that." He returned to his bread.

Alexander turned dour. "The Romans returned to the gates of the second wall the next day and broke through with their battering ram. They burned down the wall and now occupy the Mishneh area and the Tyropeon Valley. Simon has been pushed into the Upper City. Gischala still holds the temple mount. It will not be long."

Thelonius quoted the Apocalypse, "Alas. You great city, you mighty city, Babylon. For in a single hour your judgment has come."[1]

Alexander reached into a hand bag and pulled out some parchment along with ink and a quill. "I thought you would want to write a letter to your beloved."

Thelonius sighed. He lifted his trembling hand to show Alexander. He had been beaten badly by his captors. "Would you be my scribe?"

Alexander solemnly nodded and set up his ink bottle and quill for transcription. He could not help but think of his own beloved Cassandra and how he had not heard from her since the Roman blockade. He would write a letter for her as well—in case he didn't make it.

Thelonius started to choke up when he thought of Livia. Oh, how he missed her. If only he'd had one more day with her. If only he could tell her he loved her one more time in person. Touch her, smell her, embrace her. Just one more time.

But it was not to be.

"Thelonius Severus, to my most loved Livia Bantius." He waited for the scratching of pen on parchment to catch up with him. "I am writing to you from prison in Jerusalem. I have done no evil but have been caught in the crossfire of war. My execution shall shortly take place. I do not know the day or hour, only that I will never see you again in this life. And that is a fear that far outweighs death. Do not mourn long for me. God has allowed me the grace to be able to right the wrongs I have done.

"As I wrote you in a previous letter, I have come to know the saving grace of Jesus Christ. I want you to know this love and forgiveness as well. This savior is not only for Jews, but for all peoples and nations. But unlike Rome, his kingdom does not conquer and enslave through the sword. Rather, it converts and changes hearts through freedom from sin. His dominion is an everlasting dominion which shall not pass away and his kingdom one that shall not be destroyed.

"Livia, the gods are not our creators but tainted projections of our own humanity. Though we knew the Creator, we did not honor him as God. We exchanged the glory of the immortal God for images resembling mortal man and other creatures. We exchanged the truth of God for a lie and worshipped creation rather than the Creator. So God gave us up to the lusts of our hearts and depraved minds.[2]

"When I was an unbeliever, I told you that Jesus was just another charismatic leader with the gift of persuasion who had managed to fool some Jews into thinking he was God on earth. Now I know him as my resurrected Lord and Savior. He has baptized me in his Holy Spirit, brought me out of the domain of darkness, and transferred me into the kingdom of his beloved Son. Join me there, Livia, and you will find redemption and forgiveness of your sins.[3]

"The doctor I told you about, Alexander Maccabaeus, writes this letter for me as I am unable. And he will seek to deliver it to you. He is the one I betrayed the most, and yet he is the one who has forgiven me most. Ask him anything. I have trusted him with my life."

Thelonius noticed Alexander wipe tears from his blurry eyes.

"Fear not, Alexander, I go to my reward. I only ask that you tell Livia the truth about me. The whole truth. Leave no sin out, for I have nothing to hide. Let grace abound even more."

Alexander finished the letter, and Thelonius signed his name with his trembling hand.

He then looked up at Alexander and said, "Thank you, my brother, for all you have done for me."

"All you have done for me," replied the doctor. "And for the kingdom of God."

"I have not done enough. I only wish God had given me more time to save more people from the fires of Gehenna to make up for those I sent there."

"It is not up to us to save anyone, Thelonius. We trust and obey."

"His will be done," agreed Thelonius. "Please greet Cassandra with my love. She trusted and obeyed, and Jesus saved me."

They embraced one last time.

CHAPTER 44

Simon was awakened by Aaron in his war room. He had fallen asleep on the map trying to consider every possible strategy for achieving his goal and leaving the city. It became more difficult with each advance of Titus's forces. These had breached the second wall and occupied the Tyropoeon valley adjacent to the temple.

At least he'd uncovered the traitor who had helped Tiberius gain access to the city center. That this would prove to be a Roman spy was rather unexpected, but the traitor's confession of past visits to Jerusalem explained his knowledge of the city's streets and alleys.

In truth, he could almost wish the spy had not given himself up, since this had prevented Simon from enacting further reduction of the city's food rations. As a result, now even his own men were going hungry.

Simon was now headquartered in the tower of Phasael, one of the three strongest fortifications of Herod's palace on the western wall of the city. The palace had been thrashed by Zealots and Sicarii, but the three towers would most likely never be breached. They were towers of great strength.

"Simon, come quickly," said Aaron. "You have to see this."

Simon shook himself awake and followed his lieutenant to the other side of the tower.

They entered a room, and Aaron led Simon up to a small window. They were about a hundred feet high and could easily see the entire city, including the Mishneh quarter just adjacent to the Herodian palace they guarded.

Simon looked out and saw a horrible sight. Titus had crucified his hundred captured Jewish warriors. They were lined up along the wall on timber-shaped "Xs" and "Ts". Most of them were still alive, suffering in great pain and agony. Crucifixion could take days for the victim to finally suffocate or dehydrate to death. It was one of the most vicious forms of punishment imaginable. And Titus was using it to strike fear into the hearts of the surviving Jewish defenders of the city.[1]

Simon whispered painfully, "Are there no bounds to his cruelty?"

Aaron hissed, "Titus is a son of the devil."

Simon turned and marched out of the room. Aaron briskly followed him down the stairs.

He asked after him, "What are you going to do, sir?"

"Give Titus my response."

· · · · ·

Berenice lay in Titus's bed and wept. She had tried to stop Caesar, persuade him to use a different strategy. It had been futile. War brought out the worst in men. No behavior was out of bounds. Everything was possible, no matter how evil or inhuman. The absolute worst of human nature expressed itself in such times.

When Titus had crucified the hundred Jewish warriors, Berenice had refused to sleep with her lover, so he'd taken her by force. He had never been so violent with her before. She had used make-up to disguise her black eye, and covered her bruised arms with long sleeves. She was frightened to the core of her being.

They had shared a passionate sexuality that she'd thought helped her to influence the power of the beast. But now she was reminded that power was an untamable god. And she wept for herself as much as for her countrymen.

The sound of a distant Jewish ram's horn caught her attention. She immediately snapped up, put on her tunic and robe, and ran outside to see what it was.

She arrived outside the war tent just behind Titus, who was standing with Tiberius, Josephus, and Agrippa. They looked out onto the second wall that guarded the Upper City a couple hundred yards away.

Simon and his lieutenant stood on the battlement with his guards. Beside each soldier was a captured Roman legionary bound in ropes. There were about fifty of them.

"Flavius Titus Caesar!" Simon yelled with a voice full of fury and ironic contempt, "Your display of might is terrifying! We offer a sacrifice to you as Imperator, the son of Caesar, son of the gods!"

He gestured to his men, who then got behind the captives and pushed each of them off the wall into the valley.

The fall of all fifty captives was stopped short by the ropes around their necks. They jerked to a bouncing halt, snapping their spines and killing them all instantly.

Berenice felt her own soul break. Romans or not, these were human beings extinguished in an act of revenge. This was the world she was trying to negotiate. A world of vengeance and unimaginable horror. It continued to tear her apart.

Titus said, "I will drag Simon bar Giora alive through the streets of Rome." Then he noticed something. "There is a sign on one of the bodies. What does it say?"

Josephus read it. "Spy."

Titus stepped forward, looking closer at the corpse of the spy. "He looks familiar."

Josephus said, "I believe it is the Roman Thelonius Severus."

"The one who helped us find the Christians?" asked Titus. "I thought he returned to Rome."

Tiberius said dryly, "Apparently not."

"Well, whatever the case, I reject their sacrifice." Titus was smirking, trying to make light. Tiberius dutifully smiled.

The dark humor faded. "Start the catapults again. Let us see how they hold up beneath the wrath of their new god."

CHAPTER 45

Mount Hermon

Apollyon stood at the summit of Hermon with Chaser, Ba'al's heavenly spear, in his hands, pointed to the heavens. Marduk waited for him at the base of the mountain with his chariot and horses.

Black storm clouds swirled overhead with rumbling thunder ready to split the sky. His eyes closed tightly, Apollyon continued to chant the words of the ancient tongue. He had been engaging in an occult incantation of allurement since the sun had gone down.

He was drawing forth his final army.

The angels had ambushed the gods of the nations in Jerusalem, so he could only imagine what surprise was waiting for him inside Yahweh's temple. Evidently, the heavenly despot had gone back on his word and was not going to let the dragon take his prize without a fight.

But it was not hard to figure out. The temple housed the Holy of Holies, the very throne of God. So Apollyon expected Yahweh's throne guardians to be awaiting him in the unseen realm of Jerusalem's temple mount: seraphim, cherubim, and ophanim. These were the mightiest of Yahweh's heavenly host. It would not be an easy task to get through them to the temple. Apollyon would have to match them in force and power.

So he was on his cosmic mountain drawing throne guardians from every Gentile nation on the earth: Greece, Egypt, Assyria, Mesopotamia. He owned them all. He was the god of Rome. And he would call upon the mightiest of his servants to counter the mightiest of Yahweh's.

A huge bolt of lightning shot down from the heavens and connected to the spear like a surge of conducting energy. The heavenly weapon absorbed the lightning, and Apollyon absorbed the power into his being.

He shouted their names into the storm. The winds took his command to the four corners of the earth. "Griffins! Sphinxes! Lamassu! Mushussu! Come forth to your lord Apollyon. Prepare for battle!"

It would take some time for the divine creatures to come from the four winds, but they would hear the call, and he would soon have his army of mighty throne guardians for his final battle.

CHAPTER 46

Jerusalem
July, AD 70

Berenice, Agrippa, and Josephus followed Titus and Tiberius around the conquered area of the Mishneh quarter as the catapults were wheeled into place. They surveyed the walls of the temple mount, as impregnable as the outer city walls. They inspected the Antonia fortress on the northwest end of the temple. They ended up before a large granary that had been burned to the ground some time ago.

Titus asked Tiberius, "Did we burn these down?"

"No, my lord."

Titus displayed curiosity. "I saw some others in the New City that were also destroyed. Not by us."

Josephus offered the explanation. "The consequence of civil war. They were burning each other's food supplies in vengeance."

"And what of the quarters they hold now?" Titus asked.

"Most of those have lost their food supplies as well," said Josephus.

Titus muttered with contempt, "Fools." Then he turned to his tribune. "Tiberius, let us have a feast in the officer's mess hall tonight."

"Yes, Caesar." Tiberius rode off to the New City, where Titus's new headquarters remained safely behind the battle lines.

• • • • •

The sound of catapult stones hitting structures in the Upper City could be heard even this distance away in the New City. Berenice sat beside her brother and Josephus at Titus's table in the officer's mess hall. The tables were stocked with pork, fowl, vegetables, figs, and wine.

Berenice winced at the pig roasted whole sitting before them. It was unclean meat and forbidden by her religion. But her brother had no shame in taking the pork and mixing it in with his fowl. He had always had trouble keeping kosher diet because of his love of food and drink. He would play the part in Jewish public, but they were in Roman company now, and it wouldn't even be noticed. Except by Berenice and Josephus, who, because of their own compromise with Rome, could say nothing.

Berenice could not help but think of the Maccabees and how they had died rather than eat the pork forced upon them by the Greek pagan king Antiochus Epiphanes. Their conviction of conscience had eventually led them to the courage of victory against their oppressors. She felt ashamed at the memory of her ancestors. Was this a portent of failure for this generation?

One of the tribunes approached the table and saluted Titus with hand out. "Caesar," he asked, "will you be using Victor against the Antonia soon?"

Titus took a deep gulp of wine. "Eventually."

They had rebuilt the huge battering ram of that nickname with the iron head that had survived the ashes of its destruction at the walls. The tribune gave him a curious look.

Titus explained, "Evidently, the warring factions within the city destroyed their own food supply some time ago. They are already starving to death. So I am going to let them do so."

Berenice felt fear flood her body. The three Jews looked at one another with shock. She blurted out, "Caesar, please! You cannot do that."

Titus looked at Josephus. "You will have your temple." He shifted his gaze to Berenice and Agrippa. "And you will have a broken people easily ruled."

Berenice heard her brother mutter to her, "Dead people are not ruled." She pled with the imperator, "It will be innocent women and children who suffer most!"

Tiberius joined in with gruff dismissal, "Innocent women and children had their chance to leave the city long ago. Many already have."

Berenice felt the food in her stomach rise up in her throat.

Titus added with a grim smirk, "I have heard your god rained down bread from heaven in the past. Let us see if he cares enough to do so again."[1]

Berenice looked away. She couldn't look into his face. He had become the shadow of an ugly creature to her.

Titus said to Tiberius, "Take two legions of soldiers and build a stone blockade around the entire city. Man it with sentries all about. I don't want anyone trying to escape now."

"Yes, Caesar," came the reply. And he left immediately.

Berenice's only thoughts were horror. She had sought to sympathize with Rome, to build a bridge. She should have built a wall.

Am I a traitor to my people? How many will starve to death because of what I have done? Can God above forgive me?

CHAPTER 47

The night was cool, the moon waxing overhead. Apollyon had not yet returned with Marduk to Jerusalem, so his remaining principalities prepared their master's plan. Ares and Zeus crept silently behind enemy lines of the Lower City in search of the Two Witnesses. Azazel stayed with his ward Titus in the newly conquered Mishneh quarter.

Ares and Zeus found their targets approaching the north wall, still guarded by the four angels: Michael, Gabriel, Uriel, and Raphael. The Watchers stayed hidden in the shadows, awaiting their moment.

$\bullet\ \bullet\ \bullet\ \bullet\ \bullet$

Simon and Aaron sat at a fire with Simcha and some of their soldiers by the gate of the Upper City. Simon would often sit and visit with his men to encourage them. But tonight was a difficult one. Boulders were flying into the city from the Roman catapults, demolishing structures with loud crashes.

Aaron had been trying to distract them with a description of his strange disciplined life at Qumran—endless baptisms, scribal duties, and the austere life of monks. But when one of the soldiers asked what had happened to the village, the atmosphere quickly turned dour as Aaron admitted the community's fate at the hands of the Romans.

One of the soldiers stood up and sniffed the air deeply. "Do you smell that? It's food cooking."

Simon could smell it now. The scent was wafting over the wall.

Another soldier said, "It's coming from the Roman camp."

A third complained, "They're taunting us. They know we have no rations left."

A teenaged soldier held his stomach in pain and groaned. Simon placed his hand reassuringly on the lad's shoulder.

Aaron whispered to Simon, "We won't last long without food."

Simon whispered back, "What about your faith, monk? Won't that last you?"

Aaron looked away.

The Two Witnesses walking on the wall above them captured everyone's attention. The older one proclaimed, "Woe! Woe! Woe to the city again and to the people and to the holy house!"[1]

The younger one picked up the lament, "Woe! Woe! Woe to those who dwell on the land. Two angels have blown their trumpets. The second woe is passed. The third is coming."[2]

A soldier complained, "What the hell are they talking about? Will someone shut them up?"

Another shouted, "We have tolerated their loud mouths long enough!"

Another yelled, "Three-and-a-half long years! 42 months! 1260 days! They're driving me mad with anger!"[3]

Then, as if the two prophets had heard them, the Witnesses stopped and looked down upon the soldiers. Moshe announced, "Woe! Woe! Woe to us as well!" They turned back to face the Romans outside the walls.

One of the Jewish defenders shouted back, "Woe to your wives, who are less nags than you are!"

A burst of laughter rang out amongst the soldiers.

As Simon and his men mocked the Witnesses, they had no idea what was happening in the unseen realm. The two prophets were flanked on the battlement by two angels on each side. As Elihu and Moshe proclaimed their woes, Ares came at them from one side of the battlement and Zeus from the other.

The two gods drew the angels into combat.

Zeus was the Greek king of the gods and Ares the mighty Greek god of war. But they would be no match for the four archangels who protected the Witnesses.

It was an act of suicide.

Ares attacked Michael and Raphael. Zeus charged at Gabriel and Uriel. Swords clanged with the sound of thunder in the heavenlies.

The angels pushed each of the gods back. But because the battlement was narrow, they could only face their enemies head on.

Ares swung his weapon with a fury never before seen by Michael and Raphael. They barely kept up with the strikes. It was as if Ares had summoned every ounce of strength in his being for one final charge.

Zeus called down bolts of lightning from heaven and launched them at his opponents. Gabriel and Uriel had to deflect the incoming blasts with their own heavenly blades. But the surges worked to weaken their arms.

That was when the angels realized they had been drawn away from the Two Witnesses, who now stood unprotected on the battlement.

Uriel shouted, "The Beast!"

At that moment they turned to see Azazel far behind the Roman line direct two catapults at his intended targets.

The stones launched.

The gods jumped off the wall onto the Roman side.

Before the angels could return to their wards, the two catapult stones hit the Two Witnesses, propelling them into the air, off the wall, and down to the ground forty feet below.

They landed with a splatter of blood not far from the Jewish defenders' campfire.

The angels jumped down to the ground near them.

The sound of Michael's guttural yell of agony resounded in the heavens.

The Witnesses were dead. Yahweh's anointed messengers. And under Michael's watch, no less.

The Apocalypse had foretold this day. But it still burned with pain in Michael's heart, in the hearts of them all. The prophets of every age were special to Yahweh, along with the martyrs. Most of the prophets, like Elihu and Moshe, had been martyred.

These two would be the last of that great line before the Day of the Lord was finished.

In the human realm, the Jewish soldiers went quiet. Everyone looked at one another in shock as if to question whether they had all just seen the same event.

They had.

Jumping up, Simon and Aaron ran to the two prophets, who were lying on the ground a few feet apart.

Simon looked down upon them both. The catapult stones that had struck the prophets were about the size of pumpkins, large enough to kill on impact, but not crush their victims to mush. He couldn't believe it. These two had spoken in the name of Yahweh. As the heckler had shouted, for three-and-a-half years they had stopped soldiers dead, called down fire from heaven. And now a freak occurrence had killed them both instantaneously as if they were just like anybody else?

Did that mean the Two Witnesses' words were empty? Their deeds mere sorcery? Or did it mean their work was done?[4]

Was it really a freak occurrence?

212

"Are they dead?" a soldier yelled out.

Simon said, "Yes."

"Thank you, Jesus!" yelled a heckler.

Dozens laughed. Many stood and applauded, mocking the two prophets' demise.

Another heckler yelled out, "So the Romans are good for something after all!"

More laughs. Soldiers got up and came over to see the bodies.

Simon ignored their gaiety, overwhelmed with a memory as he studied the still face of the older prophet. Years ago when Simon was captain of the temple guard, this man's name had been Joshua ben Ananus. He had changed his name later to Moshe as a symbolic reference to Israel's lawgiver. Simon remembered scourging Joshua with such brutality that his back had been opened, exposing the bone. He had broken the preacher's jaw for spewing his vile calumnies upon the city and temple.

And now here they were, about to have city and temple destroyed just as this poor dead fool had said. Or was he a prophet, killed like all prophets of Israel?

Soldiers had now surrounded the two bodies. Simon tried to push them back from the corpses, but they were becoming a mob. He had lost control of them.

Someone removed the stones from the bodies. Their chests were crushed but still intact. Was that sorcery too?

One of the mob yelled, "This deserves a celebration!"

The soldiers cheered.

He yelled again, "A triumphal procession! In honor of Caesar!"

Laughs were accompanied by even more cheering and rowdiness.

Four men knelt down to pick up the bodies by their arms and legs. They were going to drag the dead men through the streets.

But without warning, the four who had touched the fallen prophets dropped the bodies and screamed. It was enough to stop the crowd.

Soldiers backed away from the four men, who were holding up their hands in horror.

They each had blackened, pus-filled skin on both hands and arms. It looked like gangrene had infected them instantaneously.

But that isn't possible, thought Simon.

Someone yelled, "Plague! They have the plague!"

The soldiers backed away in fear.

The four men stumbled in pain and fell to their knees.

Then they dropped to the ground on their faces, all four of them. Dead within a minute of touching the Two Witnesses' bodies.

The rising mob of violence had suddenly become a scattered crowd of fear.

Simon and Aaron alone still stood over the bodies. Simcha joined them but stayed at a distance.

Simon thought about the last words one of the Witnesses had said. "The second woe is passed. The third is coming." What did he mean by three woes? Simon looked back up at the top of the wall as if some monster was about to appear there. He shook his head to release the crazy thought.

He looked over at Aaron. The Essene monk returned his glance with affirmation. *No, you are not crazy.*

Simon said, "We leave them where they lie."

Aaron nodded fearfully in agreement.

And when the Witnesses have finished their testimony, the beast that rises from the Abyss will make war on them and conquer them and kill them, and their dead bodies will lie in the street of the great city that symbolically is called Sodom and Egypt, where their Lord was crucified.

Apocalypse 11:7–8

CHAPTER 48

Alexander had heard of the deaths of the Two Witnesses, but with the numbers of wounded and starving Jews that were filling up the hippodrome, he could not get away to see it for himself for several days. The gossip was that the Jewish defenders had left the corpses in the street because some soldiers had died of plague trying to pick them up.

That was three-and-a-half days ago.

But now he'd finally found some time to get away, and he headed to the gates of the Upper City.

Upon his arrival, Alexander found the square full of citizens dancing and celebrating. He felt sick to his stomach. They should have been mourning for their souls and for the destruction that was coming upon them. Instead, they were giving each other gifts and partying over the death of God's prophets.

Pushing his way through the crowd, Alexander found the dead bodies still lying in the street. He fell to his knees between them and wept.

Then he noticed something. The corpses did not smell. He looked at their faces. After all this time, their flesh had still not decayed.

The crowd around him kept their distance for fear of catching the plague. But Alexander didn't care anymore. He didn't even consider burying the bodies because he knew what was going to happen. He had read the Apocalypse.

Someone yelled out, "Hey, doctor, can you fix them?" People laughed.

Another shouted, "Don't touch the bodies! You'll be sorry!"

More laughter rang out. Ignoring the mirth, Alexander stood back from the two fallen prophets.

Someone heckled him, "So Jesus won't protect you either, eh?"

But the crowd's laughter was cut short as the ground beneath them began to rumble.

A cloud passed in front of the sun, casting the entire area in a shadow of darkness.

Then a ray of light burst through the cloud and fell upon the Two Witnesses.

Before the eyes of all the celebrants, the two corpses suddenly filled with breath and stood up, their broken chests healed.

The crowd went silent save for a few shrieks from women who fainted in fear.

Someone screamed, "They're alive!"

The Two Witnesses did nothing. They merely looked up to heaven.

Another yelled out, "Are they going to kill us?"

Alexander heard a loud voice from heaven say, "Come up here!"

As the people looked on, the Two Witnesses ascended to heaven, surrounded by Yahweh's shekinah glory. More women screamed and fainted.

A stampede began as the terrorized crowd tried to get away from this frightening wonder. Then the soft rumbling in the ground gave way to a full-blown earthquake. Alexander felt the shock go through him. He stayed down in the dirt. The ground seemed to ripple like a rug being shaken in the wind.

Those running away fell to their hands and knees. Alexander could see buildings around them collapsing. With an earthquake this devastating, thousands would be killed. He only hoped the Romans were experiencing an equal amount of damage.

When the ground settled down again, Alexander heard the cries of pain and regret as people ran back to their homes to see if their loved ones were alive and okay. But he knew seven thousand of them would not survive—one tenth of the city's population. The Apocalypse had foretold it.[1]

He got up, brushed the dirt off himself, and returned to the hippodrome, thinking over the spiritual meaning of everything he had just witnessed.

Years ago on the isle of Patmos, the apostle John had told Alexander and Cassandra that the Two Witnesses were symbolic of the martyrs in Christ for whom much of the Apocalypse was a vindication. As Jesus had prophesied in his sermon on the Mount of Olives, this generation of spiritually blind Jewish religious leaders, as Israel's representatives, would have the blood of all the martyred prophets upon them because they would kill their Messiah. The "great city" Jerusalem—the spiritual successor to the demon-ridden Babylon of old—would suffer destruction for that bloodguilt. Those martyrs would be vindicated.

I saw Babylon the great, mother of harlots and of the Land's abominations." ... And in the great city was found the blood of prophets and of saints, and of all who have been slain on the Land... Therefore, Rejoice over her, O heaven, and you saints and apostles and prophets, for God has given judgment for you against the great city!

Apocalypse 17:6; 18:24, 20

The Greek word *martyr* meant "witness." John had explained to them that the Two Witnesses would represent Moses and Elijah. The Law (Moses) and the Prophets (Elijah) of the old covenant had borne witness to the coming Messiah. So these two were the witnesses in the heavenly court that had convicted Israel of her spiritual unfaithfulness to Yahweh.

Their ministry of 42 months, or 1,260 days, aligned with the trampling of the holy land and temple by the Roman Beast for three and one-half years—time, times, and a half-time.[2] That time had come to an end. The first prophetic "woe" had been the release of the locust demons from the Abyss. The second woe was this resurrection of the Witnesses.[3] The seventh trumpet was about to sound, the third and final woe.

The death and resurrection of the Witnesses was a symbolic picture of the first resurrection of all the martyrs that John had written of in the Apocalypse, a spiritual resurrection that would come out of the death of the body of Israel. The prophet Daniel had written of this resurrection as well.[4]

And many of those who sleep in the dust of the earth shall awake, some to everlasting life, and some to shame and everlasting contempt.

Daniel 12:2

In the same way that Ezekiel's valley of resurrected dry bones was a prophetic vision of Israel's return from exile at the hands of Babylon, so the resurrection of the Witnesses was a prophetic vision of the body of Christ overcoming their martyrdom and near-extinction at the hands of the Jews, the new Babylon. This generation of Jewish apostates would die in shame and contempt. The Remnant, or body of Jesus Christ, would arise out of tribulation to spread the Gospel upon all the earth.[5]

Alexander's stomach hurt with hunger pains. As he arrived back at the hippodrome, he prepared for the final trumpet, the last woe.

CHAPTER 49

August, AD 70

I looked, and behold, a black horse! And its rider had a pair of scales in his hand. And I heard what seemed to be a voice in the midst of the four living creatures, saying, "A quart of wheat for a denarius, and three quarts of barley for a denarius, and do not harm the oil and wine!"[1]
Apocalypse 6:5–6

A month had passed since Titus first built a wall around Jerusalem to ward off escapes and imposed his strategy of starving the inhabitants. Each passing day made the burden on Berenice's heart only heavier. She felt so guilty for her part in the suffering that she found it difficult to eat her own meals. She was losing weight and looking sickly because of it.

She had helped to process hundreds of Jewish deserters, most of them innocent men, women, and children willing to risk enslavement to the Romans rather than face the famine that was raging within the city walls. With every story she heard, Berenice fell into a deeper depression.

She currently sat with a small, impoverished family consisting of a husband, a wife, and their daughter who'd been recently captured outside the walls trying to escape Jerusalem. They were now in the internment camp near the New City gate that housed several thousand deserters. Berenice was interviewing them after giving them some bread and water. The poor little girl was so malnourished that she looked like a sleepy skeleton. Flies buzzed around her as though her own flesh were dying. It was all Berenice could do to keep from breaking out in weeping at the sight of her. She was determined to be strong, to hold in her emotions. Weeping would be of no help to these suffering innocents.

The parents were in little better condition. The husband, emaciated with hollow eye sockets, explained what they had experienced and seen behind the walls. "We gave all the money we had left for one measure of wheat. We had closed our doors and windows to bake a small loaf and consume the last morsels of our food before dying. We didn't want anyone to smell it and find us. But they did. Robbers came in and took everything. They picked the food right out of my daughter's mouth as she was trying to swallow. They pulled my wife's hair out." He started to choke up.

The wife held her hand out to stop him from saying more. She had a bald spot on the left side of her head and a broken nose from being raped. But even now she was too dignified to let such indignity be known in front of their dying child.

Berenice asked, "How did you survive after that?"

The husband said, "We did what many others were doing. We ate wisps of hay and grass that we could find and then ate our leather sandals and girdles that we owned."[2]

Berenice looked down at their bare feet. They were bruised and bloody from running over rocks and rough ground outside the wall.

"We fared better than others."

"How so?"

"My next-door neighbor was impaled to force him to confess where he had hidden a handful of barley."

Berenice took a deep breath to calm down.

Then the man looked around to make sure no one could hear them. "The rich who are escaping the city have had it much harder than us, though."

Berenice couldn't believe what she was hearing. Could it get much worse? The rich never had it harder than the poor when it came to difficult times. They always paid their way out of things that the poor could not.

She listened with dread as he explained.

"The Arab soldiers outside the walls learned that rich Jews were swallowing gold coins before escaping. The Jews would then pick them out of their own excrement to have some means of bribery to help themselves. When the Arabs found out, they cut open the bellies of those who wore wealthy apparel to get their gold."

Berenice found herself audibly gasping at the horror. "They kill them and cut them open?"

"No. They cut them open while still alive and fish through their intestines."

Berenice immediately got up and walked over to a Roman guard that Titus had given her. "Get the imperator, immediately. This is an emergency. Tell him to bring a full century of soldiers."

The guard left her.

• • • • •

Titus met Berenice at the edge of the internment camp with legionaries. He was annoyed.

"I'm trusting you, Berenice. This had better be important."

"Thank you, Caesar. I am confident you will find it more than important."

She told him what the starved man had told her and where the diabolical deeds had been taking place—outside the internment camp in an empty field on the far eastern, abandoned part of the New City.

Berenice followed Titus and his century to where a contingent of a thousand Arab auxiliaries were camping out. As the Roman general led the way into the midst of their tents, the Arab auxiliaries jumped to attention and saluted Caesar.

He said nothing but walked on past them with his guard and over to the empty field. The legionaries carried torches, but they couldn't see what was out there until they were upon it.

Berenice gasped. It was a pile of hundreds of dead Jews, perhaps even thousands, with their bellies cut open and their intestines hanging out.

The starved Jew had spoken the truth. Berenice vomited on the ground.

She looked up at Titus, who boiled with anger.

She said to him, "The punishment for insubordination is execution."

She wanted to see them all die. Arabs had a peculiar hatred for Jews. Arabs were the sons of Ishmael, the rejected ones. Yahweh had chosen Isaac over Ishmael, so the Ishmaelite Arabs had always carried an animosity toward the sons of Isaac, the true heirs of Abraham.

Titus whispered to her, "You are right. They deserve it. But if I kill them, there will be more dead Arabs than Jews, and that will not go over well with the rest of my legions."

He turned and led her over to the Arab commanders. There were several thousand Arabs in this auxiliary unit. She felt intimidated by their presence. They stared at her hungrily. She stayed close to Titus, who stood firm and announced to the officers, "This barbarism is unacceptable to Caesar. You will cease it immediately and report to me any soldier who continues to engage in this behavior. Anyone who is caught from now on cutting out the bowels of Jews will be executed. Am I understood?"[3]

The handful of Arab leaders saluted and said, "Hail, Caesar!"

Titus turned and led Berenice and his century out of the area back to his headquarters.

She whispered to him as they marched along, "You admit it was barbaric. But you refused to execute justice."

Titus shrugged. "Arabs are wild donkeys. Uncontrollable. I must tread carefully."

"But is Caesar not a god?"

"Not even a god can stand before the mutiny of a mob."

That was just the inspiration Berenice needed. If these Arab sons of perdition could disobey Caesar, then so would she.

CHAPTER 50

Simon led Aaron and a guard of a hundred soldiers to the hippodrome. He passed through streets filled with garbage, rubble, and emaciated corpses. Some neighborhoods were darkly quiet, others punctuated with screams of pain and suffering. The past month of silence from Titus had worked its psychological effect upon him, upon everyone inside Jerusalem. The imperator had stopped the catapults, built a wall around the entire city, and waited for them to starve to death. The warring Jewish factions inside had burnt their food stores months ago, and their rations had run out. The fact that they were now unified did not help them produce more food. They were all dying.

We have brought this on ourselves, thought Simon. *We have slit our own throats.*

Lawlessness had taken over. Robbers and bandits led gangs of marauders through the streets, stealing the last scraps of food from dying families. Simon could not control his own men from joining in the looting. After all, if the soldiers did not eat, they could not defend the city. They had to have priority over the citizens.

To salve his conscience, he ordered his men to withhold from such crimes. To avoid mutiny, he turned a blind eye and deaf ear to what they did in his absence.

But one thing haunted Simon's soul more than the anarchy; the last thing he had heard the Two Witnesses proclaim before they were killed. It was a cryptic prediction that he had dismissed in the face of his immediate concerns of war. But the more he thought about it, the more he wondered if he ought to have listened to them. They had been right about so many things. Could false prophets have that kind of accuracy?

After he'd left their dead bodies in the streets, Simon had heard that the prophets were said to have been resurrected and ascended into heaven. If only he had been there to see for himself. If it was true, it would be a miraculous confirmation of their message, would it not?

Still, Simon knew the propensity of people to exaggerate and see things to confirm their biases. Ascension into heaven was a common occurrence in legends and myths.

Then someone had told him that Alexander was there. That the Christian doctor had seen it happen. A man whose integrity he trusted above his own allies. Simon wanted to find out what the doctor knew, what that last cryptic prophecy meant. Everything around him was breaking down. He was losing control. He was desperate for any help he could get.

Simon and Aaron entered the hippodrome. As they walked out onto the arena, the sight and smells around them arrested Simon. He covered his nose at the stench. Thousands of sick and wounded filled the southern half of the stadium floor. There were three times as many patients as beds. People were lying on mats, many of them in the uncovered dirt. Most were simply not being helped. It was completely unmanageable.

The northern half of the stadium contained piles of dead bodies, a hundred or so of them.

"This is not a hospital," Aaron muttered. "It's a cemetery."

Simon saw Alexander coming toward them with some assistants. "General, to what do I owe this visit?" the doctor asked.

"I want to ask you something," said Simon. "But I was unaware of your situation here. They are dying faster than you can bury them."

Alexander looked around. "Oh, we stopped burying long ago. There is no space for graves. We have to dump them outside the walls. Those that you see are the ones who died today."

Burial for Jews was a sacred right. Leaving bodies to rot in the open air was often a symbolic form of judgment upon one's enemies. So for the Jews to do this to their own meant they had lost all hope.

Alexander said, "People have stopped coming here. They are dying in their homes now. We were just about to carry those bodies to the wall."

Simon turned to his soldiers. "Everyone, start piling up the dead in these carts. Let's help the doctor clear them out."

The soldiers reluctantly moved to obey. They filled a dozen donkey-drawn carts with bodies. They would pull the carts out to the city wall.

"If you will follow me, I will show you where the bodies are to be dumped." Alexander gave his assistants a few instructions, then led Simon out of the hippodrome. Lashing at the donkeys, the soldiers maneuvered the carts to follow.

The route took them past destroyed buildings and piles of stinking rubbish. As they walked, Simon said, "I actually came today because I wanted to ask you about the Two Witnesses."

"So their preaching has not left you?" Alexander responded.

Simon didn't answer him. Instead, he said, "I understand you were there after they died. Did you steal the bodies?"

Alexander laughed. "They said the same thing when Jesus rose from the dead. There were hundreds of witnesses, General. We all saw them rise and ascend into heaven. Some heard the voice of God call them up. Others heard thunder."

Simon would get nowhere with this. He said, "I heard them say something before they were killed. I wanted to ask you what it meant since you were associated with them."

"What did they say?"

"Something about a third woe that was about to happen. Something with a final trumpet."

"And you want to know what the final woe and trumpet are—to prepare for them or to leave while you can?"

Simon changed the subject. "Is the final woe the starvation of the city?"

"No. The three woes correspond to the last three of seven trumpets of judgment upon the Land and people. You've experienced the previous judgments throughout this war. The Witnesses explained them when they were alive. The last trumpet is the conclusion."

Simon asked, "And the conclusion is…?"

Alexander quoted from the Apocalypse: "Then the seventh angel blew his trumpet, and there were loud voices in heaven, saying, 'The kingdom of the world has become the kingdom of our Lord and of his Christ, and he shall reign forever and ever.' The nations raged, but your wrath came, and the time for the dead to be judged, and for rewarding your servants, the prophets and saints, and for destroying the destroyers of the Land."

Simon expected an explanation, but Alexander walked on without giving it. Simon got impatient. "But what does it mean?"

"As Messiah, Jesus has inherited all the nations. Those who rejected him will know the wrath of God. And when this is all over, the kingdom of God will be established on the ruins of this destroyed Land. There is no escape, Simon."

It still sounded like so much delusional nonsense to Simon. But before he could figure out his next question, they had arrived at the city walls where a ramp to the top had been created for the wagons. The soldiers walked the donkeys up the steep incline. Simon and Alexander followed, arriving at the ledge that overlooked the Valley of Hinnom.

What Simon saw was more horrible than the sight in the hippodrome. The entire valley was filled with dead bodies, hundreds of thousands of them, all along the wall where people had been dumping them. The largest pile of corpses was here in the Valley of Hinnom, the place they called Gehenna.[1]

Heaps of rotting human flesh below were surrounded by clouds of flies, packs of rodents, and birds of prey. The stench was unbearable even way up high on the wall. Simon had fought in many a battle and had seen his share of atrocities, of the barbaric things men could do to one another. But he had never seen anything like this before. The sheer numbers of the dead were staggering. Starved skeletal remains of people who had been robbed of every ounce of their humanity.

The words of Jeremiah the prophet about this very valley echoed in his mind:

> "Behold, the days are coming, declares Yahweh, when this valley will no more be called the Valley of the Son of Hinnom, but the Valley of Slaughter; because there is no room elsewhere. And in this place I will make void the plans of Jerusalem, and will cause their people to fall by the sword before their enemies. I will give their dead bodies for food to the birds of the air and to the beasts of the earth. And I will make this city a horror."
>
> Jeremiah 7:31–33, 19:7-8

Jeremiah had been describing the Babylonian invasion and destruction of Jerusalem and the temple in the days of Nebuchadnezzar. This valley had become cursed with the bodies of the judged dead. That was the meaning of *Gehenna*. And now the Valley of Hinnom had become once again the Valley of Slaughter.[2]

Suddenly, everything Simon had been seeking in this war became as nothing. His entire selfish life—an empty mockery of meaning—passed before his eyes. Money, power, glory. Revenge. None of it mattered. Everything was vanity and chasing after the wind.

Simon turned to see Aaron staring out onto the horizon where the sun burned like Yahweh's justice. Simon asked him, "Remember what I said when we met?"

Aaron replied dryly, "You didn't believe in causes, and you didn't live on faith."

Simon said simply, "I was wrong."

Aaron gave him a surprised look. Simon continued, "I see now the life of cowardice I have lived."

"What are you talking about?" Aaron demanded. "You are the hero of this nation."

"Revenge is a coward, Aaron. And I am its foolish lover. I think I finally understand what your community was seeking: the holiness."

Holiness was that which was set apart unto God. Yahweh created humans in his image, setting them apart from all of creation to be his image-bearers—his representatives—on earth. The monks' motivation in separating themselves was to focus exclusively on Yahweh by punishing their flesh.

"I want to become an Essene," said Simon. "Baptize me."

"The Essenes are dead," said Aaron, his eyes not turning from their gaze into the desert of Azazel.

"But you are alive," said Simon.

"No, General. All that I was is dead. There is no Qumran, no Sons of Light, no end of the world, and no coming Messiah. There is only war. Never-ending war between the strong and the weak."

How tragic it was that the very thing that had brought faith back to life in Simon had killed faith in Aaron.

· · · · ·

Simon was baptized by one of Aaron's fellow Essenes in one of the many ritual mikveh pools in the Essene quarter of the city.

When he came up out of the water, he expected to feel holy, born again. But something inside him told him he was not. Had he swung from one extreme of the flesh to another?

He decided that instead of escaping the city, he would fight to the end and give his life for the hope of achieving that holiness, to again be a part of something bigger than himself.

CHAPTER 51

Gischala marched through the passageway beneath the inner temple with his eight captains of thousands. They carried torches that lit the moss-covered stone arches with an eerie glow.

One of the captains, a bearded older warrior, complained, "General, our rations are gone. The troops are demoralized. All they can think of is food."

Gischala considered his words. "How many doubt my leadership?"

The captain became skittish, unwilling to say.

"I asked you a question, soldier. I want the truth."

"A third distrust you, my lord. And growing."

Another captain offered, "Loyalty fades quickly with empty bellies. It would take a miracle to revive their spirits and renew their devotion."

Gischala stopped them. They had arrived at a large room with a double-sealed door guarded by two sentries.

Gischala said, "Well then, captain, a miracle is what we shall have."

He ordered the guards aside and unlocked the doors. He swung them open to reveal a large storage room filled with foodstuffs.

The captains froze with shock. There was enough to feed an army. Smoked shanks of beef, jars of wine, piles of dried fruits and vegetables.

The skittish captain muttered, "The temple stores."

"Opened for the army of the temple," said Gischala. "I've also stopped the daily sacrifices."

The captains looked at one another. "But general," cautioned the bearded captain, "Messiah alone can stop the sacrifices."

"Exactly," said Gischala. "And when men are starving to death, they are, shall we say, most suggestible to compliance. Leave that to me."

From the time that the regular burnt offering is taken away and the abomination that makes desolate is set up, there shall be 1,290 days.

Daniel 12:11

1,290 days earlier, the abominable Roman armies had arrived and set up in the holy land to start their desolation of Judea that ultimately led to the temple.[1]

• • • • •

Gischala's forces of eight thousand men assembled outside the Beautiful Gate and surrounded the inner temple. They were losing their morale and strength to fight the Romans. Their hunger, however, made them more volatile with one another, and fights broke out that had to be squashed before they became something bigger.

Gischala stood ready behind the gates as twenty men pushed them open.

A hush went over the crowd as Gischala stepped out onto the top steps of the temple gate dressed in kingly robes with a royal purple cape and a golden crown on his head.

He spoke with a strong voice. "My soldiers! My loyal ones! Taste and see that the Lord is good! Have faith in me and you will receive manna from heaven!"

As he said this, a series of dozens of soldiers began exiting the gate carrying tables loaded with food, all the food that was in the stores below. Others carried jugs of drink.

The soldiers went wild.

Gischala calmed them down and said, "The Lord has provided plenty of food for everyone! Do not stampede. You will all get your turn! Trust me! Trust in the Lord!"

The soldiers cheered again as more tables were brought out overflowing with food. Lines of others brought spits of cooked meat, cows and bulls from the sacrificial offerings. The smell of the meat stirred the masses even more. Gischala had to remind them, "There is plenty for all! Do not rush!"

The men lined up to get their fill. Spirits had risen. Hope had returned. There would be a great celebration this day. But it would not last long, and Gischala knew it. He was taking a big gamble.[2]

The bearded captain whispered to Gischala, "That is the last of the temple reserves. What will they do when they discover there is no more?"

Gischala whispered back, "The citizens will provide us more. Prepare a scout party of five hundred who have had their fill. It is time for us to extract more tribute from those whom we protect."

• • • • •

228

The night was bright and clear. All was quiet about the Huldah Gates of the temple. Until the doors opened and a flurry of armed horsemen launched out into the night. Five hundred of them, divided into groups of five or ten, splitting up into the city to procure more food. The soldiers were well-fed now, strong and ready to plunder.

Gischala led one of the groups of five men. He galloped into the Upper City district where more of the wealthier Jews lived, better targets for robbing.

As he entered one of the neighborhoods with which he was familiar, he noticed a group of three bandits rushing from a house with sacks on their backs.

Gischala whistled. His four men spurred their horses to catch the thieves. Getting off his horse, Gischala walked into the open door of the home. Lamps were still lit, but the pall of silent death lay over it all.

He walked into the main room to discover a mother, a father, and two young children tied up with their throats slit.

As he walked back out, his men dragged the thieves up to him. He discovered that they had stolen a single loaf of bread and some personal items.

Four murdered innocents for a single loaf of bread.

He said to his men, "Cut their throats."

They obeyed and drew their blades across the throats of the squirming criminals, who fell to the ground with spreading pools of blood around them.

Gischala and his men moved on.

The streets were mostly quiet. They approached another home and kicked in the door, only to find a family of six, dead. They were not the victims of bandits but simply starvation. Their emaciated remains looked like they were already skeletons though they had only begun to decompose.

Gischala covered his nose at the smell and left the home. There was obviously no food here.

Down the next block, Gischala was surprised to see a home with smoke coming from its chimney. Smoke with the scent of cooking meat.

Well, that's daring, he thought as they approached the home.

Dismounting, the five men approached cautiously. Gischala braced himself for some kind of trap.

But there was none.

At Gischala's order, his men kicked in the door and entered. Within a few moments, Gischala heard a man cry out. It was one of the Zealots. Was it a trap after all?

The other four men stumbled out of the house. One of them vomited. The others were so shocked they could not speak. They just shook their heads in disbelief as if they had seen a phantom.

Gischala got off his horse and entered the home, drawing his sword. What could have frightened four armed warriors ready for battle? He was afraid of nothing.

When he entered the small kitchen, he saw a woman sitting at her table chewing on a piece of meat.

On the platter before her was the charred body of an infant.

She looked up at Gischala and spoke as if she were completely sane. "Welcome, soldier. Would you like to share a bite to eat with me?"

Gischala asked in horror, "Where did you get that?"

"This?" She looked down at her victim. "Oh, this is my son. I just finished roasting him, and I have no one with whom to share a meal. You wouldn't leave a woman alone to eat, would you?"[3]

Gischala's face froze with terror. He muttered, "Dear God," and backed out of the room slowly, not knowing of what other insanity she might be capable.

It dawned on Gischala that the starvation had brought upon the city a kind of madness that turned normal, peaceful citizens into demon-possessed monsters. It was as if the whole city had become demon-possessed. A haunt for satyrs, jackals, hyenas, and every unclean spirit.[4]

Well, then, we will have to deal with these inhuman monsters with inhuman treatment.

They proceeded to ride through the streets pillaging without mercy. The food they were procuring was minimal—scraps and crumbs—but it was better than nothing. Gischala told himself they were putting these possessed creatures out of their misery. Like rabid dogs. It made him feel better about his own brutality.

Gischala had lost track of the time. And where he was. He looked about him. A couple of his men had just hacked to pieces two men who had refused to give them the food they had hidden. Their bodies lay in the street as their wives and children wailed in pain over them.

Gischala looked up and noticed a group of ten other soldiers on horseback down the street. He squinted in the moonlight. They were not his men. And they were coming his way.

He recognized the young man in the lead. It was the warrior-monk, Aaron ben Hyam.

CHAPTER 52

Aaron ben Hyam had been on security rounds in the city, trying to keep some order in the midst of the growing chaos. He had led his ten warriors through the Essene quarter when he entered into a thoroughfare and saw two men cut down dead in the street by a group of soldiers on horseback. Their wives and children ran to the dead men, wailing and tugging at their bodies.

Then Aaron noticed the leader, a man whose stature and face was very familiar.

John of Gischala.

Their eyes met, and Aaron realized this would be his opportunity to kill the monster who had caused so much pain and misery in this city. Aaron had long ago given up believing in God's providence, so this had to be luck. Yes, Simon had made a treaty with Gischala to join forces against Titus. But this son of Belial deserved to die, and Aaron was willing to take the flack for it. He narrowed his eyes and launched after his target.

He saw Gischala notice him and yell to his men.

They drew chase.

Aaron could see by the way Gischala was fleeing that he was not sure of where he was. As if he had gone on a scouting mission and was lost. Good. Because Aaron knew this Essene quarter like the back of his hand.

He was already gaining on them.

They cut through a small alleyway. Aaron was in the lead. He saw the last soldier in Gischala's team miss a low-hanging pole and get smashed off his horse to the ground.

Aaron's horse trampled over the poor fool and kept hard on the trail.

Four of them left. It would be an easy kill. And an easy task to bring Gischala's body to Simon so that he could take over the temple as well as the city.

Yes, perhaps this was truly good luck.

They broke out onto a market street closed down for the night. Aaron saw Gischala look up. The huge aqueduct towered above them, bringing water from Solomon's pools in the south all the way to the inner temple. Gischala was lost and was trying to find his way back to the temple. The aqueduct would lead him there.

But to Aaron's surprise, his quarry split up. Two followed the aqueduct. Gischala and the other man went back into town. He must have thought the aqueduct was too much in the open and that maybe he could lose Aaron in the labyrinth of the alleyways.

That was not going to happen. The warrior-monk gestured for the other half of his men to follow the two under the aqueduct. Aaron and four others followed Gischala.

As Aaron broke onto the main street, he saw Gischala make an unusual move. He and his fellow horseman rode their steeds right into a government building.

Aaron and his three followed.

He rode his horse up the marble steps of the building. The marble was slippery on the clacking hooves of the horses.

One of Aaron's men's horses slipped and fell to its side, injuring itself. He was out.

Three of them left.

Aaron trotted inside the building to see Gischala's horse click-clacking up a staircase to an upper floor.

Aaron took a chance at the fact that horses would be slower on this slick pavement than humans could run.

He shouted, and he and his men dismounted to follow on foot.

They raced up the stairs.

When they got up to the third floor, they burst into a palatial assembly room.

Aaron saw Gischala out on the balcony with his comrade. The two men got off their horses and slapped their haunches.

Spooked, the horses ran at Aaron and his men, who ducked out of the way. Aaron yelled, "Slings!"

His companions pulled out their slings with a rock each just as Gischala and the other soldier stood up on the balcony ledge.

What are they doing? thought Aaron. *Are they going to jump to their death to avoid being caught?*

Aaron's men twirled their slings and released.

Their quarry jumped.

Gischala's comrade was hit twice, once in the head.

But the other rocks missed Gischala as he leapt into the air and disappeared from view.

Aaron sprinted to the balcony to see what had happened.

When he got there, he saw what Gischala had done.

Ten feet below and seven feet from the balcony was the aqueduct they had seen earlier winding its way through the city.

Gischala had jumped into the water of the aqueduct and was now rapidly floating his way back to the temple out of Aaron's reach.

The cunning badger had gotten away.

The other man was dead on the ground a floor below.

Aaron turned away and cursed to himself. This would ruin the truce that Simon had negotiated, and it would be Aaron's fault.

What would he do? What could he do? He had missed his opportunity and had endangered the entire city as a result.

He might even have reignited a civil war.

CHAPTER 53

Simon sat alone with Aaron in his war room in the safe heights of the Tower Phasael. The monk had told him everything that had happened that night in the Essene quarter: the discovery of Gischala, the chase, the escape.

Simon said, "Do not let the other men know. I'll have to meet with Gischala."

Aaron reiterated his justification. "General, he was murdering civilians for their food. Killing our own people."

"I know. But he is the general of our alliance, which is the only means of defending Jerusalem. If you had killed him, his army would have risen up against us."

"But I didn't kill him."

"Yes. And now he doesn't trust us."

It seemed to Simon that there was no good outcome. "You could have just chased him back to the temple where he belongs."

"Chase the vulture back to the carcass," Aaron muttered in response.

The monk had lost his faith. The temple had become a body of death to him.

They were interrupted by a messenger. "General Simon, a secret envoy from the Romans is here."

Secret envoy? Simon raised a quizzical eyebrow at Aaron, who appeared as surprised as he was.

Simon descended the tower into a side chamber at the bottom. He passed a guard at the door and entered, closing it behind him.

A cloaked figure looked out the small window over the night city. It turned and pulled down its hood, revealing the princess Julia Berenice, sister of Herod Agrippa.

Confusion hit Simon like a battering ram. He almost lost his balance.

"Simon." Her voice was soft, pleading.

Simon could barely contain the flood of memories that filled his mind. This was the first time he had seen Berenice in five years. This Herod, this princess of Judea, this woman he had once loved and lost. Her raven-black hair, her eyes of intensity and mystery. She was still as beautiful as he had remembered her. But her look was gaunt, lost, broken.

"Berenice."

"It's good to see you, Simon. After all this time."

She stepped toward him.

He found himself taking a slight step backward.

He didn't have to ask her how she'd gotten into the city. The known tunnels beneath the city were usually guarded. But he knew that the Herods had their own secret passages below their palace known only to themselves. Like the one used for the battle of the second wall.

He said, "It's dangerous for you to be here."

She looked into his eyes, searching for the past. "Dangerous for whom?" She stepped forward again. This time he didn't move.

"Why would Titus send you?"

"Titus does not know I am here."

"What does he know—about you?"

She looked away. "Not what you know."

"And your brother?"

"I come in secret. I loathe my brother, and I wish he would be struck dead by a Jewish arrow."

"Why are you here, Berenice?" Simon wanted to grab her, embrace her, and make love to her. He dared not bring up their past together.

"Simon, I need you to know that my brother and I opposed the starving of the city."

"Yet you preside over it."

"Titus would not listen."

Simon was not convinced. "The wily princess of the house of Herod could not get what she wanted. Now that is something to behold. What did you expect from the beast? You delivered us into his hands."

"You have no idea the Jewish lives I've saved in the campaign."

"And how many have died in the campaign?" he responded.

"I am here to help. I can show you secret stores of grain in Herod's palace underground."

This surprised him. *What is in this for her?*

She continued, "If you promise me to give half of the stores to the sick and needy."

He hardened. "My soldiers need food or we will lose this war."

"Everyone needs food."

He shook his head. "There are too many of them. There is no way we could help them all."

"The women and children did not ask for this war."

"And they didn't leave when they had the chance."

"Simon, please. Do not let the innocent die."

Simon looked away from her. He weighed his options. Half was better than nothing. He could torture her to reveal the location. He could lie to her as she had lied to him and then take it all.

No, he could not hurt her, and he would not lie to her. Even after all this time. Even after everything. Unfortunately, their problems were manifold.

He said, "Gischala will want it all for himself."

"Then don't tell him about it."

"He'll find out. And we're already on the edge of civil war. This would push us over."

She said, "Then let me appeal to him as well."

Appeal to the man who would gut her at his first opportunity? Had she learned nothing from how Gischala had betrayed her in the past? Sought to take her as his own, to dominate her?

He said resignedly, "Unfortunately, one of my men tried to assassinate Gischala. I have lost his trust."

"We must try, Simon. The lives of every single person in Jerusalem is at stake. They are dying by the hundreds every day."

He hated that she was right. And he would hate himself if he brought her into this mess only to see her killed by the hand of his enemy. But he could see she needed this redemption as much as he did.

He said, "Take me to the grain, and I'll take you to Gischala."

CHAPTER 54

Gischala looked down upon the Romans from the Antonia's wall. The fortress base was on a forty-foot incline, so Titus was building another earthworks ramp up to the gate. The newly rebuilt ram Victor stood in the distance, ready for deployment.

A messenger arrived to alert Gischala to visitors at the Huldah Gates of the temple.

When Gischala arrived at the gates, he found Simon and Berenice surrounded by thirty soldiers. Gischala stepped out with his own squad of thirty protecting him. He looked up at Simcha, the six-foot-tall mass of muscle beside Simon. He muttered, "You again."

Gischala turned to Berenice. "You I never would have imagined." He looked at Simon, "And you are a man of many surprises. And betrayals. Where is your young assassin, or are you planning on using this Goliath?" He gestured to Simcha.

Simon said, "That was not my order."

"Your man tried to kill me, Simon."

"Without my approval. And what were you doing in the Upper City?"

Gischala hesitated. He decided to tell the truth. "Scouting for food."

"Killing civilians for food," Simon countered.

Gischala leaned in with an air of condescension. "And from whom are you drawing the food for your troops to save the city, General?"

Simon said, "It appears we have a situation of extreme actions under strained circumstances on both sides."

"It appears we do," agreed Gischala. Their agreement was implicit. They could not blame each other because they were both guilty.

Simon changed the subject. "The princess has intelligence that will benefit us."

Gischala considered the offer. He said, "Leave your guards, especially this one." He gestured again to Simcha. "And your weapons."

Simon countered, "My guards, but not my weapons."

Gischala smiled. He could still defeat Simon in a match. He would welcome it. "Granted. How is that shoulder wound of yours, Simon?"

Simon responded, "Fully healed."

"Good. That keeps you at your peak of skill and strength."

He was goading his competitor. Hinting that he needed no handicap to destroy Simon. And Simon appeared to have caught on, welcoming the challenge. Perhaps they might have their long-awaited showdown after all.

But now was not the time. Gischala said, "You know this temple as well as anyone. You pick the location."

"The Hall of Hewn Stones," said Simon. "And I bring one messenger of my own."

Gischala glanced at Simcha. "Just not him."

• • • • •

Gischala led Simon, Berenice, and a strong, long-haired warrior named Uriah down into the Hall of Hewn Stones. Simon left Uriah outside the door but within audible range. If Gischala pulled anything on Simon, Uriah was to flee back to his headquarters to launch retribution.

The hall had not been used by the Sanhedrin for many months since Gischala had taken the temple from Eleazar. Gischala chose the head chair of the sanhedrin as his throne to look down upon his two visitors.

Simon got to the point. "Gischala, the Antonia is the gate to the temple and city. Titus is aiming for the heart of Jerusalem. And you are all alone."

Gischala said, "And when I have turned my back to you to engage Titus, is that when you plan to assassinate me?" He saw Simon sigh with closed eyes. Gischala added, "You have the gall to plead for unity. And you bring Titus's whore no less. Or is she playing you both?"

Berenice was not intimidated. "You cannot win. Titus will not harm the temple unless he is forced to. And that is precisely what you are doing—forcing his hand."

Gischala mocked, "*This* is the 'intelligence' you promised?"

Simon looked at Berenice. She swallowed and spoke. "I can offer you secret stores of grain from the Herodian palace if you promise me that the civilians will receive half of the food."

Gischala raised his brow in surprise. He smirked. "Why does it not surprise me that the Herod aristocracy has withheld yet more from the city?"

Berenice remained silent, but her face went flush with shame.

Gischala considered the offer. Half to the populace, half to the army. That would mean his soldiers would not receive the amount they really needed to feed their strength and defend the temple. The Herodian palace was strongly in the hands of Simon, so Gischala could not simply take it away from them. And if he agreed, it would be a concession of weakness.

Gischala had the upper hand. He was not going to give that away.

He withdrew a sacrificial dagger from his belt. He saw Simon flinch, ready to defend himself and Berenice. Gischala smiled. "This is the high priest's sacrificial dagger." He spun it around in his hand, fingering the tip. "They say that when Messiah comes, he will brandish it as a weapon against his enemies."

He jammed the dagger into the wood of the armrest of the chair. He saw Berenice cringe with fear. "Without Messiah, all this is a lost cause. An empty symbol. And the temple, a carcass of a dead religion."

Gischala stood up, leaving the dagger in the arm of the chair. "And that is the difference between us." He walked right up to Simon, daring him. "I have never been under the delusion that I could stop the Romans with human force."

Simon looked confused. "You *want* Titus to attack the temple?"

Gischala grinned. "Of course." He saw Berenice's horrified look. "That is why I burned the city's food supplies. That is why I attacked your forces. And that is why I had one of my own most trusted men guide the invading legionaries into the city from the tunnels the Herods revealed to Titus."

He held up a red cloth, exactly like those Simon had discovered were being used to guide Tiberius's men through the streets for sabotage.

"I did not reveal the tunnel to Titus," Berenice protested.

Gischala replied, "But your brother did. Herod."

Simon could not believe what he was hearing. So all this time, as he'd applauded himself for catching the mole, it had been Gischala who was traitor to the city!

Berenice's beautiful eyes blazed with fury at Gischala. "You betrayed your own people."

The general smiled mockingly. "Not as you have, Herod. You see, it is only when the invading infidels attempt to attack the holy temple that God himself will intervene. It is only then that his supernatural power will flow from heaven into the body of his anointed one, his promised deliverer, Messiah."

Turning back, Gischala pulled the blade out of the arm and held it like a talisman of power.

Berenice gasped, "Oh my God."

Simon said it clearly, "You think *you* are Messiah."

Gischala responded, "I will not unite with you again, Simon. I will not accept the food that will only prolong our misery. That would eliminate my chances of supernatural victory. Instead, I am going to imprison you." He sat on his throne again and used his fingers to whistle loudly.

Simon reached for his sword.

Thirty soldiers burst into the hall with weapons drawn and surrounded them.

Simon yelled to his messenger, "Uriah!" It was a call of warning.

Two Zealots dragged in the warrior's body by his long hair, leaving a trail of blood on the pavement.

"You mean *that* Uriah?" questioned Gischala.

They dropped the warrior at Simon's feet. Poor Uriah had his throat cut.

The Zealots grabbed Simon and Berenice, disarming the warrior.

Gischala strode up to his captives. "The Day of Atonement is coming. The day when the high priest enters the Holy of Holies—the very presence of God. A day of cleansing—and sacrifice."

Simon and Berenice watched him painfully.

"Oh, I have big plans for that day. All Israel will see the glory of the Lord in his Messiah as he triumphs over the Sons of Darkness."

Simon said, "You are a Son of Darkness."

Gischala ignored the gibe, staring back at Simon. "And the first order of my new kingdom will be to execute you before the masses. Along with your Cleopatra whore. Fitting irony, is it not? You two together at last. In death."

He commanded the guards, "Imprison them."

CHAPTER 55

A squad of thirty soldiers ushered Simon and Berenice into the temple mount's dungeon. Gischala was not about to grant his enemy a shred of opportunity to escape.

They were pushed into the closest cell near the iron door that guarded the prison chambers. The other cells were filled with hundreds of criminals, bandits, and Gischala's political prisoners.

The cell was twelve-foot square of damp and dark thick stone walls without the smallest slit of a window. It made Simon feel like they were in Sheol. This would be particularly difficult for Berenice, coming from her privileged life of comfort and luxury. He wanted to hold her, tell her everything would be all right.

But he knew it would not be.

She spoke first. "Simon, I am so sorry."

He could see she wanted him to say something. He said nothing.

She glanced around them, shivering, and then broke down weeping. She dropped to her knees on the ground in deep despairing sobs.

Simon knew her. Knew she was a master of emotional theater, that she could manufacture tears at a moment's notice. He had seen her do it years ago. But this, he knew, was real.

He thought, *What difference does it make? We're going to die anyway.*

Simon moved to Berenice and knelt down beside her, embraced her. He felt her tremble. He held her strongly until she stopped.

Then she said with a shaky voice, "I only wanted to help the people. To atone for what I have done."

"God alone can atone for our sins." Simon spoke without emotion. He spoke the truth.

"My sin is great," she whispered.

"So is mine."

She pulled away from him to look into his eyes as if to ask, *Is all hope lost?*

His return look said clearly, *It is.*

He felt her shivering again. "You are cold." He grabbed her closer, trying to share body warmth. He rubbed her bare arms.

Berenice said, "All my life I have known plotting and calculating wealth and privilege. You were the one true thing I ever really had. And that is why I never really had you."

Simon stayed silent.

"You are a righteous man, Simon."

He shook his head. "I am not the same man you once knew. I am no righteous man. I have done things..." he paused in shame.

"So have I," she replied.

"May God have mercy on our souls," he whispered.

She snuggled her head deeper into his chest. It was something he had never experienced the entire time that they had been lovers. True surrender.

She wished out loud, "If this were a different world. If we had different lives."

"We only have one life, princess. What we do with it is a measure of who we are. Not wishful thoughts."

In the past, when they'd been together and he had scolded her like this, she'd reacted with pride or condescension. But not now. Now she listened.

Simon pulled away from her and reached into his belt. "I have something for you."

He pulled out the small braid of hair in a locket she had given him in her palace before the revolt. He held it out to her.

Her eyes went wide with surprise. "You've kept this all these years?"

Now she really knew how he had felt. How he had loved her. Now she really knew everything she had lost.

Slowly, Berenice reached up with sad eyes and received the locket. He was giving it back to her. He was giving up their past.

He *was* a different man. This was a different life. And they could never be together again.

She clutched the locket to her heart, holding back a torrent of emotion. She said, "You do not deserve this prison with me."

He smiled at her. "I have never been more free."

He finally saw her as she truly was. A desperate, broken woman surviving in a world of power and corruption. She was a victim, but she was also culpable for what she had done. And she was facing her own guilt.

He could not judge her anymore. He could only pity her.

God will repay each person according to what they have done.

CHAPTER 56

Aaron put on his light leather armor and strapped his gladius blade to his side. He stood in Simon's war room in the Tower Phasael, looking out onto the temple in the distance. His eyes felt like those of a hawk, determined, ready to pounce.

"Brother Aaron, you asked for me?" Levi, Aaron's lieutenant and fiercest Essene warrior, stood in the doorway. He was seventeen, lean, with sandy, cropped hair and a no-nonsense temperament.

Aaron waved impatiently. "Come in, Levi."

Levi moved hesitantly. "Is something wrong?"

"Simon has been gone three days. I'm going to find him and bring our general back."

Levi looked troubled. "Sir, the Romans have completed their new rampart up to the Antonia. They'll be breaking through the wall soon."

"Then I had better hurry."

"But what if you are captured?"

"Then that leaves you to lead the Essenes, Lieutenant. Simon's captain will be here shortly. He will be in charge of the city forces."

"Sir, are you going to try to conduct a prison break in the bowels of Gischala's lair all by yourself?"

"Of course not," said Aaron. "I'm bringing an army." He gestured behind Levi, who turned to see the massive Simcha standing in the door with a toothy grin—ready for orders.

· · · · ·

Apollyon arrived with Marduk on Storm Demon behind the Roman lines in the unseen realm. They watched as the Romans finished preparing their huge battering ram for its approach to the Antonia.

Apollyon saw Azazel, Ares, and Zeus waiting for him at the front line with a fourth deity previously absent: Semyaza.

The chariot rolled to a stop near the gods, and Apollyon hopped off. Marduk followed him like a shadow.

"I see you heard my call," said Apollyon.

"Yes, Master," said Semyaza dutifully.

Apollyon carefully scanned Azazel's face, looking for any hint of collusion between the two. He saw none. Apollyon could not help but consider the dangerous possibility of these two ancient ones conspiring to overthrow him and steal his temple. But he had to take the risk. He needed all the help he could get.

Azazel glanced around subtly and said, "My lord, you mentioned before you left that you had one last measure."

Apollyon grinned with satisfaction. "I did."

The Watchers looked at one another with curious faces.

"But we are not at our last objective." His voice became insistent. "So do your job and take down that fortress."

The gods obeyed and followed the Romans rolling Victor up the rampart to the Antonia.

This time they were approaching the wall instead of the gates. The Antonia was a Roman construction, so Titus knew how well their defenses were constructed. The gates were often fortified to absorb battering with their wooden structures, buttresses, and armor. Stone walls however, were unyielding and therefore crumbled upon impact with the relentless iron head of battering rams.

The Jews launched hundreds of fiery arrows at the ram. But the Romans had draped wet animal skins upon it, so the flames just died out instead of catching fire.

A squad of fifty Jewish soldiers on horseback sallied out and attacked the Romans just as the ram came within contact distance of the wall. They killed many of the legionaries but Roman reinforcements, who replaced their dead comrades, quickly repelled them.

Eventually the ram's battering commenced.

The Jews' tactics only delayed the inevitable. Victor began to strike away at the stone with its hammering head. The wall of the fortress rattled with each hit.

The gods were right beside Victor in the unseen realm, pounding away at the heavenly barrier.

•••••

In the outer court of the temple mount, thousands of civilians cringed in fear at the sound of the pounding ram. Citizen supporters of the Zealot cause had been called by Gischala to the temple for a sacred ceremony.

Gischala stood on the temple steps, draped once again in his purple cape and crown. He raised his hands with assurance.

"Fear not, O children of Israel! O people of Jerusalem! What you hear is the sound of your salvation drawing near!"

A thousand soldiers at the front of the crowd applauded, bringing some calm to the rest of the masses.

A bevy of three priests came out from the gate and stood before Gischala. He bowed to the ground on one knee and took off his crown. One of the priests held up a large vial he had been carrying and poured oil onto Gischala's head.

Some in the crowd cheered. They knew what the priest was doing.

Gischala stood, wiping away the oil and replacing the crown on his head. He raised his hands high and shouted to the masses, "My people, my people! The Spirit of the Lord God is upon me because Yahweh has anointed me to bring good news to the poor. He has sent me to proclaim liberty to the captives and the opening of prison to those who are bound. To proclaim the year of the Lord's favor!"[1]

He raised his hands, and a line of dozens of men in tattered clothes exited the gates behind him to be led out into the crowd. He recognized the men as criminals and bandits who had been held in the prison cells below. The political prisoners had already been executed.

As he had anticipated, the crowd received the liberated captives with cheers. Some shouted out, "Messiah has come!" Others called, "Rescue us, O Lord!"

CHAPTER 57

Aaron held a torch before him as he led Simcha through the maze of underground passages. Simcha had to constantly duck down to keep his head from hitting the wooden beams buttressing the rocky ceiling.

Above them could be heard Victor's distant pounding upon the walls of the Antonia. They were getting near to their target.

They came upon a small cave-in with debris and a broken wooden beam. Climbing over the rubble, they found the secret entrance into the temple dungeon stairwell.

Aaron doused his light, and they descended cautiously into the belly of the beast.

When they reached the bottom, Aaron heard the sound of guards and held Simcha back. He peeked around the corner.

About fifty feet ahead, four guards stood before the door to the dungeon area. Aaron put up four fingers to Simcha, who smiled.

He nudged Aaron and gestured to wait. Then he slipped back up the stairwell, leaving Aaron wondering.

The Essene's curiosity was satisfied when Simcha returned minutes later carrying a broken timber from the ceiling of the passage. It was as tall as a man and looked to be a hundred pounds or more. Simcha held it with ease as he walked past Aaron into the hallway.

Aaron watched the big, brawny warrior run down the hallway toward the guards, holding the timber at his chest like a barbell.

At the last moment, Simcha gave a guttural yell to distract his victims. They jerked with surprise to see him barreling down on them. For just that moment, they froze.

He launched the timber. It flew ten feet and hit the soldiers square in the chests. All four of them fell to the ground like blades of wheat before a scythe.

Within seconds, Aaron was upon them, standing beside Simcha, who looked down at the unconscious guards.

The huge warrior said with disappointment, "That was too easy."

"What, do you want it to be difficult?" Aaron demanded.

"I expected a little more excitement."

"Sorry to spoil your fun." Aaron grabbed the keys from the head guard and opened the dungeon door.

They entered and immediately found Simon and Berenice asleep in their cell, holding one another.

As Aaron opened the cell door, the two prisoners awakened.

Simon rubbed his eyes and said, "I was beginning to think you forgot about us."

Aaron smiled. "Patience, General, patience."

Simon followed Aaron out of the prison hallway. He ordered Simcha, "Protect the princess."

The big warrior smiled and gently waved for Berenice to follow him. She looked up at him, a bit fearful but relieved.

Just outside the hall, Aaron noticed one of the guards stirring. He drew his blade and lifted it over the soldier to finish him off.

But Simon's hand stayed him. "Aaron, that's not necessary."

"Not necessary?" Aaron complained. "They are the enemy."

"Rome is the enemy."

Aaron dropped his sword to his side. Simon had changed. Everything had changed. He knew this world was never going to be the same.

Simon and Aaron each grabbed one of the torches on the prison wall. They raced back up the stairs and entered the secret tunnels.

The faint sound of pounding above them drew Simon's attention.

"Where exactly is the ram?"

Aaron answered, "At the Antonia's north wall." He pointed down one of the passageways. "That way."

"Both of you, take the princess to safety," said Simon. "I have a task to perform."

Aaron scolded him, "General, you're going alone again?"

"I'll be okay. Meet me at the inner temple with your squad of Essenes. We're going to do some housecleaning."

Aaron hesitated, then shrugged. "Okay."

As Aaron and Simcha started down the tunnel with Berenice, Simon took off in the opposite direction.

·····

Up on the temple mount, Gischala continued announcing messianic allusions to his crowd of trusting followers. "My people, the Jubilee of Jubilees has arrived! Those who have faith, make your way to the antechambers behind the temple. From there you will await your deliverance. The Day of Atonement is at hand!"

People applauded. The distant pounding of the ram had become less noticeable to everyone focused on Gischala's theatrics.

His guards guided the people to the cloistered colonnades behind the temple. Six thousand civilians—men, women, and children—were shepherded to the antechambers to wait obediently. Many of them bowed or knelt in prayer with excited anticipation of the coming of the Lord.

This was it. This was the visitation Yahweh had promised them through the prophets.[1] There had not been a legitimate prophet of God since Malachi four hundred years ago. Specifically, they had been waiting four hundred and ninety years—seventy weeks of years—since their exile in Babylon for the anointed prince who would finish the transgression, put an end to sin, atone for iniquity, bring in everlasting righteousness, seal both vision and prophecy, and anoint the Most Holy One.[2]

After the believers were safely in the antechambers, Gischala called together his hundred most devoted soldiers and said to them, "Follow me."

He led them into the temple.

• • • • •

Simon traveled through the tunnels, following the sounds of the battering ram above. He arrived at a spot where he could hear the pounding directly above him. He looked up and saw some dirt falling from the ceiling with each hit.

He was approximately beneath the ram at the wall of the Antonia.

He raised his torch overhead to see the trestles of wooden beams used to brace the ceilings. They ran along the tunnels like a rib cage every ten feet or so.

Simon placed his torch to the first beam until it started to burn. Then he stepped to the next and lit it on fire.

He moved along several crisscrossing tunnels, lighting all the crossbeams on fire just to make sure he would hit his target.

The flames began to fill the tunnel with smoke. Simon covered his mouth, coughing. He would have to leave soon or be overwhelmed by it.

• • • • •

248

The Romans pounded away against the wall of the Antonia with their battering ram.

Boom. Boom. Boom.

Stone crumbled beneath Victor's relentless iron head. The wall was slowly disintegrating with each hit. The bronze roof of the ram protected the Roman soldiers from the missiles above.

Boom. Boom. Boom.

The Jews could engage in no more sallies as the Romans had created a perimeter of forces around the ram.

But the rebels' tactics were not exhausted.

High above Victor, ropes hoisted down a series of large sacks full of chaff to cover the wall. They were larger than the ram's head, and designed for just this kind of attack.

The sacks hung between Victor and the wall. When the iron head hit, the sacks worked like pillows, absorbing the force and softening the blows.[3]

One of the Jews on the wall joked to his comrade, "It's like sex with my wife. She's rarely willing!"

The Jewish soldiers around him laughed. Another one shouted, "Are you Romans tired of all your boys? Come to poke a hole in our wall?"

More laughs were followed by more taunts shouted down at their attackers.

The ram's impact was deadened. But it kept pounding at the cushions.

CHAPTER 58

Simon snuffed out his torch as he approached the secret entrance into the inner temple from the tunnels below. He came out in one of the chambers of the Court of Priests that surrounded the Holy Place. Because of the political turmoil over the past three years, only a handful of priests were still serving in the temple. At this moment, their living quarters were empty.

They must have been called for service, thought Simon. *But Gischala has stopped the daily sacrifices, so what purpose could it be?*

Slipping out of the colonnade, Simon entered the Holy Place through the priest's entrance in the rear. He moved through the side chambers where priestly vestments were stored in lockers for changing.

Once inside the Holy Place, Simon hid behind one of the side curtains behind the columns looking into the room. What he was doing would have been unthinkable during normal times. Only priests were allowed to enter the Holy Place to perform their duties. The presence of anyone else would be considered a profanity of sacred space. But these were not normal times. War had changed everything. And John of Gischala himself had already profaned the temple with the presence of his soldiers and the blood of battle.

But what Simon was watching now was an abomination.

From his hiding place, he saw Gischala with a group of priests and a hundred loyal soldiers watching from the sides. Gischala was wearing the garments of the high priest! Gischala was not a priest, and he was not a Levite. But he had become so deluded by his fanatical beliefs that he thought he was Messiah, both priest and king.

Gischala had exchanged his royal crown and costume for a priestly one. The blue robe with little bells at the bottom jingled with Gischala's every move. He wore the holy ephod, an apron embroidered with blue, purple, scarlet, and gold. The breastplate of judgment was embedded with twelve gems that represented the twelve tribes of Israel. But the most disgusting profanity of all was the holy miter on his head: a turban featuring a golden plate on his forehead engraved with the words "Holy unto Yahweh."

It should say, "Harlot of Babylon," since the entire priesthood had become corrupted and used in service of an abomination. That had been the accusation of the Two Witnesses, and now Simon understood why.

Gischala passed by the golden lampstand and table of shewbread to light the golden altar of incense on fire. Its smoke filled the room with holy vapors.

Simon had thought that the priests would have removed the holy instruments and treasures of the temple to protect them. But Gischala had evidently kept them to engage in this ritual of corruption, this liturgy of abomination.

Simon decided that he would try to save as many of the holy instruments as he could. He would hide them in the tunnels before the Romans arrived. But how could he get them with all these soldiers and priests in the way?

• • • • •

The Jews had been successful using the sacks full of chaff to soften Victor's blows against the walls of the Antonia. But the sacks were starting to fall apart beneath the repeated pummeling.

The Romans now brought long poles with blades attached to their ends. They extended the poles from within the housing of the ram and used them to cut the ropes that held the cushions in place. The sacks fell to the ground, leaving the wall exposed for Victor to return to his unrelenting barrage.[1]

Boom. Boom. Boom.

They were halfway through the wall now. With each strike, the stone edifice shuddered and chunks of rock fell to the ground.

Boom. Boom. Boom.

• • • • •

In the Holy Place, Simon saw a messenger arrive and speak to Gischala. "My lord, the Romans have almost penetrated the Antonia. When they break through, it will not be long before they breach the temple mount."

"Excellent," said Gischala. "We don't want to make it too difficult for them."

• • • • •

Flames filled the tunnels beneath the Antonia like a furnace of fire.

The flames had eaten up the wooden beams and trestles as fuel. Finally, the timber could no longer hold the weight of rock above. The beams collapsed into charred embers that started a rolling cave-in of the ceiling.

Simon's arson had its planned effect.

• • • • •

Above the tunnels, Victor battered away at the Antonia. But before it could break through the wall, the ground beneath it began to crumble. The Romans could not sense the earth's movements because their battering ram created its own tremors.

So they didn't know what hit them when the ground beneath them collapsed. The ram sunk into the earth like quicksand, completely disabling it. Black smoke billowed out of the ground, suffocating the Romans. The fires below now consumed the ram's wooden structure within its angry flames.[2]

Jews on the walls cheered. God had delivered them once again.

Or so they thought until the collapsing tunnels continued their cascading effect on the ground all around them. One of those tunnels caved in beneath the very wall that had been attacked, finishing the destruction that Victor had begun.

The entire weakened barrier of stone fell to the ground in a pile of rubble. Jewish soldiers on top fell to their deaths, crushed by the debris.

When the smoke and dust cleared, the Romans could see their access into the fortress.

And they took it.

In the unseen realm, Apollyon shouted a war cry from his chariot, and the gods pushed their way in. Their next-to-last obstacle was the outer temple gate. They were so close he could almost taste the blood.

He looked up above to see the heavens swirling again. Yes, he was so close. It was time to call in the reinforcements.

He lifted his war horn and blew.

CHAPTER 59

Alexander had fallen asleep from exhaustion in the hippodrome hospital. He had performed so many surgeries, he had seen so much pain, so much blood, that he had lost the capacity to even feel anymore. It had brought to his mind the imagery in the Apocalypse of blood moons, blood rivers, and blood seas. Everywhere, blood.

And once again, he was dreaming of that imagery that haunted his spirit. Or was this a vision? It seemed as real to him as it must have been to the apostle John when he received the revelation on Patmos. Alexander could only conclude that God was allowing him another glimpse into the heavenly realm that Cassandra had been able to see as a sensitive in the earthly realm.

Alexander stood beside a massive winepress outside Jerusalem. It looked as large as the Roman camp on Mount Scopus. He saw the angel use a sickle to gather the clusters of the vine, a common symbol of Israel. He saw the grapes thrown into the winepress of the wrath of God to be trodden. He saw the wine pouring out of the channel onto the dirt.

Then he noticed it was not wine, but rather blood—the blood of those who dwelt upon the Land.[1]

And then the walls of the winepress exploded outward, and blood poured out like a tide across the landscape.

It caught Alexander and carried him in a wave as high as a horse's bridle. The blood spread out over the entire length of the land of Israel, 1600 stadia long, two hundred miles. It was the harvest of judgment that had begun with Vespasian's invasion and was now ending with Titus's siege.[2]

Suddenly, Alexander found himself back in Jerusalem at the empty tomb of Joseph of Arimathea—and the blood was gone.

He looked up into the sky and saw the clouds of heaven swirling like the beginning of a tornado in a wind storm. The wind whipped his face, but it felt cool and refreshing.

He heard the voice of a great multitude. It sounded like the roar of many waters, like peals of thunder that resounded through his body.

"Hallelujah! For the Lord our God the Almighty reigns.

Let us rejoice and exult and give him the glory,
for the marriage of the Lamb has come,
and his Bride has made herself ready.

Apocalypse 19:6-8

Alexander filled with hope and joy at the beauty of the ekklesia, the Bride of Christ, marrying her beloved and receiving the kingdom. The marriage feast was upon them, a feast that apostate Israel had rejected.

Filled with dread and horror, he remembered the messianic marriage had long been described in connection with war. It was a mysterious, glorious event that was also linked to the destruction of the king's enemies. The *parousia* of Jesus would involve both deliverance and destruction. Deliverance of his Remnant and destruction of apostates. The marriage of the new virgin bride was preceded by the execution of the harlot wife.[3]

Then the heavens opened, and Alexander saw the glorious vision that up until now he had only read about in the Apocalypse. He felt his entire body paralyzed with awe. He could not utter a word or even blink his eyes; the holiness was too overwhelming.

In the unseen realm, Jesus Christ came riding on a white horse in the clouds of heaven, crowned as king and leading an army of his saints behind him. They were dressed in fine linen, white and pure—his Tribulation martyrs.[4] But they did not battle, for their Lord would do so on their behalf.

He had eyes like a flame of fire, and his robe was dipped in the blood of his enemies.[5] The word of judgment against Israel that Jesus had pronounced on the Mount of Olives during his ministry was like a sword of judgment coming from his mouth in this vision.[6] Jesus was the one who was treading the winepress of the fury of the wrath of God the Almighty, and on his thigh was written the name "King of kings and Lord of lords."[7]

Enoch, the seventh from Adam, prophesied, saying, "Behold, the Lord comes with ten thousands of his holy ones, to execute judgment on all and to convict all the ungodly of all their deeds."

Jude 14-15

As the apostle had told him, this *parousia* was not a singular moment in time but rather a symbolic picture of Christ's historical judgment upon the Land, upon Jerusalem, and upon Israel after the flesh.[8] Messiah had been treading this winepress upon the Jews for the last three-and-a-half years, and the marriage supper was about to commence.

The Scriptures depicted the establishment of the old covenant under Moses symbolically as a feast on Leviathan's flesh in the wilderness of Sinai. Chaos had been overcome with covenant.

You [Yahweh] divided the sea by your might;
you broke the heads of the sea monsters on the waters.
You crushed the heads of Leviathan;
you gave him as food for the creatures of the wilderness.

Psalm 74:13–14

In a similar way, the Apocalypse depicted the establishment of the new covenant under Christ with birds feasting on the flesh of his enemies of chaos, their dead bodies unburied and accursed.

"Come, gather for the great supper of God, to eat the flesh of kings,
the flesh of captains, the flesh of mighty men, the flesh of horses and
their riders, and the flesh of all men, both free and slave, both small
and great, and all the birds were gorged on their flesh."

Apocalypse 19:17-18

Alexander had the image in his mind of Jewish corpses piled outside the walls of the city and a sense of urgency upon his soul. The harvest was at an end. The great supper of God was at hand. Jesus was finishing his judgment upon Jerusalem. But first, he had an appointment with a certain fleeing, twisting serpent.

Suddenly, Alexander found himself underwater, somewhere off the coast of Caesarea Maritima. But he could breathe, so he was still in his vision. A chill went down his spine as he saw a sinister shadow emerge from the depths. It grew larger as it approached him and he could see what it was. Leviathan, the seven-headed sea dragon, each of them, full of fury and rage. It was the size of several long ships in length.

The great sea monster moved its two tails with strong muscular waves as it glided effortlessly through the dark blue waters. Its presence always accompanied chaos or destruction. It fed off it as life-giving strength, and it was powerful right now with the chaos that tore apart the Holy Land.

Alexander could see fire in its throats, it's back racked with impenetrable scales like shields, it's belly like potsherds. This monster of chaos had seen much in its history on earth. It was there at creation when Yahweh separated the primeval waters of chaos to bring forth the land. It's abode was the Abyss that surrounded the firmament and lead into Hades. It was at the Great Flood, as well as the parting of Yam Suph. It rode the seas for Queen Jezebel of Tyre. It ruled the raging waves and the Gentile nations to conquer and wreak devastation in history over Yahweh's people. It had faced Jesus once in the storm and had been humbled, but it was not about to do so again. It was ready now with the surging power of chaos in its members as Rome scorched the land into tohu wa bohu. Wilderness and sea were united in their vast primeval void.

But then Alexander saw a single star fall from the sky. The Bright and Morning Star. It burned even brighter upon entry to the sky. And it landed in the sea with a large splash of waves. Alexander felt himself pushed back in the water by the concussion.

Then he saw it was Jesus carrying his mighty sword in his hand and landing right on the back of the gargantuan dragon. All the heads turned and screamed in terror at the invader in his white robe grabbing onto the back. The water muffled their noise with bubbles. Jesus raised his long sword and plunged it into the back of the creature all the way to the hilt.

The dragon stiffened first, its muscles frozen. Then it convulsed. It's heads shook out of control, as if lost in rage, but lost to the pain. And then they drooped in unconsciousness. Its heart had been split through with the supernatural force of the Son of Man's blade.

And then more stars hit the water around the inert body of Leviathan. Multiple Shining Ones.

And Alexander found himself now in the dry desert of Dudayin in his vision. The giant dragon was a dead stinking carcass dragged onto the ground, its seven heads splayed out in death. It had already been cut into pieces by the sword of Yahweh. Thousands of birds of the air and beasts of the field were landing upon it and feasting. It's long serpentine coils draped with rotting flesh. He knew what this was. This was the eschatological promise of Isaiah.

> In that day Yahweh with his hard and great and strong sword will punish Leviathan the fleeing serpent, Leviathan the twisting serpent, and he will slay the dragon that is in the sea...In days to come Jacob shall take root, Israel shall blossom and put forth shoots and fill the whole world with fruit... Therefore by this the guilt of Jacob will be atoned for, and this will be the full fruit of the removal of his sin.

Isaiah 27:1, 6, 9

The New Covenant Kingdom overcame the dragon of chaos and sin with new order and atonement.

Alexander awoke with a shock out of his desert vision to find himself back in the city of Jerusalem, his prison of punishment on earth. He had to get back to reality. The Romans would soon take the temple and from there invade the Lower City—where the hippodrome resided.

I have to move the hospital behind the walls of the Upper City. I have to get everyone to the theater for safety.

There were just over a thousand sick or wounded who were still alive. And Alexander only had a hundred and fifty volunteers. Moving them all would take multiple trips across the valley. And they would hardly fit into the theater's area. It was about a third the size of the hippodrome.

It would also only delay the inevitable. The Romans would eventually take the Upper City as well.

But he couldn't leave his patients when there was still a place to run. He had to move everyone now.

CHAPTER 60

The Jews were not prepared when the Romans breached the Antonia's wall. They froze with indecision until the first legionaries became visible, climbing the rubble to invade the fortress, then bolted for the temple.

By the time the Jews had retreated to the temple's gate, the Romans were already at their heels. The defenders could not successfully lock the gate, so they found themselves in a match of human strength as hundreds of them joined together to push the door closed while hundreds of Romans joined their comrades to push the door open.

Other Romans brought ladders to climb the attached wall of the temple. Jews lit the portico roof on fire to repel their attackers. Legionaries scrambled back down their ladders to safety, waiting for the flames to burn out.

Down by the gate, the massive Simcha made his way through the mass of fellow soldiers to the front, placing his hands on the very wood of the gates. The opening between the gates was the width of a man's shoulders. Roman and Jew yelled and cursed each other through that gap, but the gates did not give one way or the other.

In the unseen realm, dozens of heavenly creatures from the four winds of the earth began to arrive at the city of Jerusalem. This was the final army of throne guardians that Apollyon had called for at Hermon.

The first to arrive were the Assyrian lamassu, giant hybrid creatures with the winged bodies of bulls and lions but the humanoid heads of kingly men. These creatures were among the most ancient, going back to Sumer, and the largest as they often guarded city gates and palace entrances. They were at least fifteen feet tall, and their roar could be heard throughout the spiritual realm.

Next came the mushussu from Mesopotamia, infamous for guarding the gates of Babylon. These mutant dragon monstrosities were frightening with their long necks and reptilian heads, birdlike talons for hind legs, and lion forelegs. If their teeth, talons, or claws did not rip their enemy apart, their tails with the head of a venomous snake could kill them with lethal poison. Though they did not roar like the lamassu, mushussu were just as terrifying and ruthless.

Third came the sphinxes from Egypt, also chimeric creatures with powerful lionlike bodies and the heads of Pharaoh-like humans. Some had wings, but all were known for guarding entrances to tombs and temples with occult magic and cunning intelligence.

The last to arrive had come the farthest—the griffins of Greece. Known for protecting royal treasures, these divine guardians were considered the kings of creatures. They had bodies of lions and the wings, talons, and heads of eagles. Together, this army of hundreds of abominable throne guardians could wipe out legions of heavenly host. Apollyon was not taking any chances to achieve complete and total desolation.

As they all descended upon the city, Apollyon met them at the gate of the Antonia with Marduk, Azazel, Semyaza, Ares, and Zeus. The time had arrived to storm the temple.

In the earthly realm, Romans and Jews continued to fight for control of the temple gate as the portico burned overhead, ready to engulf them all in an avalanche of burning fury.

Simcha had one hand on each door with a hundred men behind him pushing forward against the legionaries on the other side. The gate began to close. Simcha was barely holding on, giving every ounce of strength in his Samson-like body to keep the Romans from breaking through.

Titus and Tiberius entered the newly-opened Antonia gate on horseback, leading a cohort of cavalry. Tiberius saw the contest of brawn between the two forces. He saw the gap closing. It was now only as wide as Simcha's head.

Tiberius gestured to three accompanying archers on horseback. They launched missiles through the slim opening of the gates.

All three hit their target with precision in the torso of the Jewish mighty man. But he merely faltered a moment before returning to holding the doors! The arrows seemed a minor inconvenience.

Simcha bellowed a war cry that surely frightened the opposing Romans.

Titus and Tiberius shared a glance of surprise—and respect for their fearsome nemesis.

Tiberius pulled out a javelin and prepared to launch it. But Titus held his arm and took the javelin, shifting its weighted balance in his hand.

He hurled it at the mighty warrior.

It struck Simcha in the chest.

Like Samson betrayed, his strength left his body.

The men behind him fell back as the door burst open to the legionaries.

The outer temple had been breached.

Titus raised his sword and screamed to his men to push through.

The Romans flooded in, their swords, battle axes, and arrows clashing with the Jewish defenders.

The once mighty Simcha was crushed beneath the feet of the warrior mob.

On the other side of the outer Court of Gentiles, thousands of civilians and hundreds of soldiers panicked and stampeded for the Huldah Gates to escape the temple mount. The swarming masses trampled to death the older and weaker people in the crowd.

In the unseen realm, Apollyon's throne guardians bounded through the gates with the Romans in attack formation. They were ready to face the worst. Apollyon had expected Yahweh's throne guardians to meet them head on.

But the court was empty of heavenly host.

No seraphim, cherubim, or ophanim. That struck him with surprise. The army of Yahweh's guardians was too big to fit in the inner temple, so they would have to be in the outer court protecting the inner temple building.

But they weren't.

Then again, the Witnesses were dead. So what was left to protect? The temple was his by covenantal right.

Apollyon wasn't going to waste the opportunity. He snapped the reins of his hellions and charged for the inner temple with Marduk aboard the chariot.

Azazel and the others followed on foot through the gauntlet created by the throne guardians.

Apollyon slid Storm Demon to a stop in front of the temple. He and Marduk bounded up the stairs with Azazel and Semyaza close behind. They had already violated the outer temple's sacred space. The final spiritual rape would be easy.

Apollyon threw Chaser, Ba'al's javelin, to Azazel and withdrew the storm god's war hammer Driver off his back. One mighty swing and the spiritual gates broke open wide with a resounding earthquake in both heaven and earth.

In the midst of the melee, Apollyon hadn't noticed that Zeus and Ares were no longer behind them.

The three Watchers stepped into the Women's Court. But before Semyaza could make it in, the gates suddenly slammed shut as if by Yahweh's own hand. Semyaza was locked outside.

The three Watchers turned back. Azazel looked out the gate window and gasped. "My lord, the outer court is filled with heavenly host. They are engaging your throne guardians."

"What?" complained Apollyon. He'd been sure there was nothing left to defend. He yanked Azazel aside and looked into the outer court.

The Watcher was right. Apollyon's titans were clashing with Yahweh's. Griffins, sphinxes, lamassu, and mushussu versus seraphim, cherubim, and ophanim.

Seraphim were serpentine divinities with six powerful wings that were used as mighty shields and weapons. In Yahweh's throne room, the wings protected the seraphim from God's glory in his presence, so their power was devastating against their enemies.[1]

Cherubim were ugly monstrosities to Apollyon—humanoid in shape but with bronze legs like a bull, four faces, and four wings. The cherubim were accompanied by the ophanim, divine flames with eyes all around. Like the wheels of Ezekiel's vision, these creatures moved every which way in circular motion as though they were whirling swords. Eden was protected by paired sentinels like these.[2]

A divine battle of throne guardians had been launched by Yahweh for the obvious purpose of removing Apollyon's protection. But again, why? He was already in the temple.

When the Watcher turned back to the inner court, he saw the reason why. Seven archangels stood on the top of the steps of the Nicanor Gate glaring down at them. They had Ares and Zeus bound beside them in chains.

Apollyon saw Zeus grinning with hatred at his master.

"So you were the traitor after all," said Apollyon to the Greek king of the gods. Evidently, he had betrayed Apollyon to help the archangels spring this trap. After all Apollyon's paranoia of mutiny by the others, it had never crossed his mind that it would be the once-obese Greek buffoon who would stab him in the back.

"I have to thank you," said Zeus. "It was your mocking of me and utter humiliation of my dignity at the very start of this war that caused me to become disciplined, lose some weight, and plan my ultimate revenge."

Apollyon said, "There is no forgiveness for you, fool. You'll still end up in the Lake of Fire."

Zeus kept grinning. "But I will have the satisfaction of having thwarted you. And that is enough."

Apollyon, Marduk, and Azazel drew their weapons.

Michael announced, "You fulfilled your purpose, Angel of the Abyss. Now it is time for your banishment."

So that was why the angels had sprung this trap. Inside the temple was a shaft that led to the Abyss, and Apollyon had previously stolen the key to it. These godlickers wanted to bind him there.

Apollyon spit out, "You want the key back, archangel? Come and get it."

The archangels pushed their captives into a side chamber and prepared to fight.

CHAPTER 61

Inside the Holy Place, John of Gischala led his hundred loyal body guards through the stairway up to the temple's roof. Simon knew what his nemesis was doing. He was going to await the supposed visitation of Yahweh to miraculously rescue them.

But that was never going to happen. The madman was leading his followers to their deaths.

Simon ripped down one of the side curtains and laid it out on the floor to start bagging up some of the holy utensils. Maybe he could save some of them before the beast Titus pillaged the house of God.

• • • • •

Gischala stood with his loyal followers on the roof of the temple. The golden-horned edges of the rim glimmered in the sun like a crown of gold around them.

"Pray for the Lord's deliverance," Gischala addressed them all. "I have one last task below to ensure his arrival."

He left them praying and returned to the stairwell. Making his way down to the priest's chambers, he grabbed a torch.

He then proceeded to light on fire any wood that he could find in the building.

• • • • •

In the Court of Gentiles, Titus led his cavalry to plow through the Jewish defenses. They hacked and trampled their way toward the inner temple structure.

Thousands of legionaries and Zealots faced off with sword and shield. The stone pavement at their feet became soaked with blood.

The discipline and order of the Roman legions was well practiced and pushed the less orderly Jewish forces back.

But the Jews were fighting for their survival and their religion. The Romans were defiling their most holy space, the very house of God. The defenders held the line with their zeal and passion.

But the bodies began to pile up.

263

Unseen and unheard by the humans, the spiritual battle around them also raged. Throne guardians collided with each other in a fierce battle of wings, talons, claws, and fangs. The roar of lamassu and the screeching of griffins filled the air.

The front line of lamassu and sphinxes clashed with cherubim. The pagan leonine creatures launched at their holy enemies with feral savagery. The cherubim wrestled with them like Samsons with lions.

Mushussu assaulted ophanim with dragon power and writhing serpent tails.

Up above, griffins and seraphim engaged in aerial combat. The seven-fold advantage of seraphim wings was countered by the agility and speed of the griffins. But even more so, lions were the king of animals, and eagles were expert serpent hunters. Griffins were a divine hybrid of both.

• • • • •

In the Court of Women, the Watchers and angels faced off against each other. It would have been a simple task for seven archangels to subdue three Watchers, but the gods had weapons that levelled the odds. Apollyon swung Driver, the mighty war hammer of Ba'al that crushed everything in its wake. Azazel had Chaser, Ba'al's javelin of lightning. Marduk carried the weapons he'd used to take down the titanic dragon Tiamat: his bow, his mace, his battle net of the four winds, and his mighty cleaver with which he split the heavens and earth.[1]

Azazel held Chaser in the air. A bolt of lightning fired from the heavens and filled him with power. The heavenly skies above matched the earthly turmoil below with a swirling ferocity.

Apollyon taunted his adversaries, "So, here we are again, angels. Though I recall, it did not go well for Gabriel last time." At the beginning of the revolt, the angels had tried to ambush Apollyon in the temple, but he had managed to crush Gabriel with Driver. That was when he had stolen the key to the Abyss from the foundation stone in the Holy of Holies. It was the worst injury Gabriel had ever experienced.

Gabriel unfurled his whip-sword Rahab, ten feet of flexible heavenly metal that could cut through anything. He said, "This time, serpent, you're the one going down."

"Into the Abyss," added Uriel, who drew his two swords and swirled them through the air with lethal expertise.

The other archangels drew their swords as well, and Michael gave a war cry that resounded through the unseen realm. The angels leapt down the stairs to meet the Watchers weapon-for-weapon.

•••••

Inside the Holy Place, Simon tried to gather as many priestly instruments as he could. The menorah was too large, but he planned to draw up the utensils in the curtain and maybe drag the censers and table of shewbread out one at a time.

"There you are, Simon bar Giora. Pilfering my house."

The voice drew his attention to the side chamber where Gischala stood with flaming torch in his hand, still wearing the garments of the high priest.

Simon retorted, "This is not your temple."

Gischala pulled off his miter and set it down. He pulled off the ephod and breastplate. Then he drew his weapon. "I hope you've gotten better with a sword since we last faced off. Or else you're in trouble."

When Simon and Gischala had been in the temple guard together years ago, Gischala had been a superior fighter. In fact, he had taught Simon some of his own technique. But Simon had lived a hard life of survival in the wilderness for the past six years. He drew his sword and inched cautiously toward his opponent.

Gischala touched the torch to the curtains and made his way to the veil of the Holy of Holies.

Simon demanded, "You would burn the holy temple of God?"

"Only to hasten the coming of Yahweh to Zion to save us." Gischala looked at the temple treasures Simon had been trying to gather together. "I must say, Simon, it is good to see you believe in something again. Or are you just a petty thief?"

Simon froze with shock as Gischala lit the veil on fire as well. The flame climbed the beautiful blue tapestry, consuming the images of cherubim and stars in its raging fury.

"You are possessed by a demon," said Simon.

"Or the Spirit of the Lord," said Gischala. "It depends on which side you are standing."

Simon gritted his teeth in preparation for battle. "I stand on the side of the temple."

"Well, I suppose that means you won't be joining me." Gischala threw the torch to the other side of the chamber. It struck the side curtains there, which caught aflame.

Distracted by the move, Simon wasn't prepared for Gischala's attack.

• • • • •

Outside in the Court of Gentiles, Titus's unit of horsemen met a cohort of Jews guarding the Beautiful Gate that led to the inner temple. Roman cavalry was usually an unstoppable force against infantry, but these Jews were like heavenly throne guardians protecting their most sacred house with everything in them and more.

The defenders also cleverly used captured Roman shields to arrange a testudo formation. The Romans were forced to fight against their own battle tactic, only to discover why it worked so effectively.

In the unseen realm, Yahweh's heavenly host began to overcome Apollyon's spiritual forces. Griffins could not break through the powerful shielding of seraphim wings, which were also used to cut through the wings and bodies of their pagan enemies. Their holiness was impenetrable and razor-sharp. The Greek hybrids fell from the sky like swatted flies.

On the ground, ophanim cut off the serpent tails and dragon heads of the mushussu. Their reptilian enemies could not keep up with the superior agility of ophanim on the battlefield. They were like wheels within wheels, capable of moving in any direction with instant speed and power. Long dragon necks presented easy targets for the whirling swords of flame.

Cherubs wrestled sphinxes and lamassu, breaking their necks and using their swords with deadly accuracy on their hybrid feline opponents.

What had begun as a contest of throne guardians had descended into a bloodbath of holy victory for Yahweh.

It had been Apollyon's gamble, and he was losing the bet. His guardians would no longer be guarding him.

• • • • •

Inside the Court of Women, Michael, Raphael, and Gabriel faced off against Apollyon. Uriel and Remiel fought Marduk while Saraqel and Raguel took on Azazel.

Apollyon pummeled the ground with his war hammer. This set off a massive earthquake in the spiritual realm that caused the foundation of the inner temple to shake, throwing the angels to the ground.

Marduk released a stream of arrows at Uriel and Remiel with supernatural speed. The angels used their swords like windmill blades to block the missiles from hitting their targets.

Azazel was the first to take down his enemies. His lightning javelin launched a blast of energy at Saraqel and Raguel that they could not withstand. They crashed into the pillars of the portico, and the roof collapsed, burying them in the rubble.

· · · · ·

In the Holy Place, Simon exchanged sword blows with Gischala. Around them, the curtains burned like funeral pyres. Flames traveled upward, catching the ceiling beams on fire. The temple structure was marble and stone, but there was enough wood in the building for the arson to do devastating damage. And to kill them both in a furnace of fire.

Simon was stronger than Gischala, but he had been weakened by several days in prison with little food and water. He felt his strength lessening with each jarring hit.

Gischala pushed him back up against a pillar. "You cannot kill me, Simon."

Rather than respond to his messianic delusion, Simon focused on one last burst of energy against Gischala.

He swung with every ounce of strength in his body. His sword hit Gischala's with clang after clang. Gischala moved backward, countering and parrying.

But then Simon's strength ran out.

· · · · ·

Outside in the Court of Gentiles, the few surviving throne guardians of Apollyon fled the battlefield to return to the four corners of their origins. Seraphim, cherubim, and ophanim finished mopping up their adversaries. They beheaded the wounded griffins, sphinxes, lamassu, and mushussu. The blood of divine creatures mixed with that of humans in this cosmic war of mountains, the battleground of Armageddon.

The heavenly host then left the temple mount, their strategic objective completed. Apollyon had no guardians left to protect him.

267

CHAPTER 62

Titus and his Roman forces shattered the ranks of their Jewish combatants at the temple entrance. A line of fifty legionaries pushed open the Beautiful Gate, and Titus entered with his horsemen.

There were a hundred Jewish guards in the temple area, but they were quickly dispatched or ran away at the confrontation.

The Romans had become an unstoppable tidal wave of force that continued to roll through the Nicanor Gate into the Court of Priests and up to the entrance of the very temple itself.

They brought a large log carried by fifty soldiers and began to hammer the huge doors.

•••••

Inside the Court of Women, Apollyon and his Watchers pushed the archangels up into the Court of Priests. The heavens above them were black with violent turbulence. Lightning and thunder charged Azazel's mighty javelin.

Marduk swung his battle net and threw it upon Uriel as its winds whipped around him with fury. But the angel had seen it coming and had performed his signature move. With swords out, one on each side, he spun in a tight circle like his own tornado. The whirlwind of blades cut the net into pieces at Uriel's feet. When he came to a stop, he steadied himself, steely glare forward and swords ready for more.

Marduk pulled out his massive cleaver.

But the Babylonian deity had so focused on Uriel that he had lost sight of the other angel, Remiel, who was now on the monster's back, arms around his muscle-thick neck. Marduk ignored the gadfly as if he was a minor annoyance and swung his cleaver at Uriel.

Michael and Gabriel battled Apollyon and Azazel as Raphael tried to free his brother angels from the ruins.

Apollyon swung Driver at Michael, but the angel dodged each strike. If that warhead connected with angelic flesh, it would pulverize him like clay.

Michael dove out of the way, and the war hammer hit the huge altar behind them. The stone structure exploded into a thousand rocks and pieces.

Gabriel cracked Rahab at Azazel, backing him up against the bronze sea. The Watcher raised his javelin to receive a new surge of power from above.

But as the flash of lightning charged the weapon with flaming fire, Gabriel's whip-sword wrapped around Azazel's arm and sliced it from his body. The Watcher screamed in agony as his arm fell to the ground. The javelin rolled away from him on the pavement.

Raphael came out of nowhere and tackled Azazel. The archangel had freed Saraqel and Raguel.

• • • • •

Inside the Holy Place, Simon felt the pounding on the temple entrance as if it were battering his own soul.

Pounding. Pounding. Pounding.

Gischala yelled, "That's Titus at the door. Your time is up, Simon."

Gischala pushed him up against the pillar again. But this time Simon had no energy left to counter. He had been pushed to his limit and had exhausted his strength. He had one strategic move left. Gischala had taught it to him years ago, but Simon was counting on his opponent's lack of memory.

Simon turned his sword in on the handle of Gischala's and made a circular spinning move that caught the blade, yanking it out of Gischala's hands and away from him into the air. It clattered on the pavement yards away.

Gischala stood stunned, Simon's blade to his throat.

The wild-eyed Galilean grinned, his delusion unaltered. "I regret teaching you that move."

Simon said, "You'll have more to regret before God this day."

Gischala raised his eyebrows. "And you?"

The accusation reverberated through Simon like the pounding on the door behind them.

"Behold, the abomination of desolation!" Gischala proclaimed.

At that moment, the door to the temple cracked beneath the weight of the battering ram. The sound drew Simon's attention to the entrance, where he saw

Titus Caesar march in surrounded by a company of legionaries. The Roman general stood tall like a god, the daylight shining behind him like Apollo in the rays of the sun.

When Simon turned back, Gischala was gone.

• • • • •

In the Court of Priests, Azazel was bound by Raphael and Gabriel.

Marduk swung his cleaver at Uriel, demolishing everything he hit. The bronze sea was cleft in two like the heavens and earth, and its water poured out like a flood upon the land.

But Marduk had not been paying attention to the angel on his back, whose unbreakable grasp around the Watcher's neck slowly cut off his air. Marduk suddenly collapsed into unconsciousness, a worthless heap of brawn and muscle.

Apollyon swung wide with Driver at Michael and Raphael. He shattered the stone altar into pieces, smashed the slaughter tables into splinters, and destroyed a dozen colonnades in the court, collapsing them into piles of rubble. But now he stood alone, surrounded by seven archangels.

"It's over, Apollyon," said Michael.

The Angel of the Abyss was heaving for breath. He had expended every ounce of hatred for these godlickers and demolished half the temple complex in the process. He was exhausted. But he felt invigorated.

"No, it's not."

He raised his war hammer once again. He was determined to go down swinging.

• • • • •

Inside the Holy Place, legionaries quickly surrounded Simon, forcing him to drop his sword to the floor.

Titus walked around the antechamber. He spied the priestly instruments bundled for extraction. He saw the menorah, the censers, the burning curtains. He looked above at the rafters on fire.

He walked over to the veil just as half of it fell to the ground in charred smoking cinders.

The Holy of Holies was laid bare.

Titus walked over to it and peered in. It was empty, long ago deprived of its guardian cherubim and holy ark.

The Roman general walked up to Simon with recognition in his eyes. "Simon bar Giora."

Simon glared silently in the eyes of his nemesis.

Titus looked back at the room around them. "You know, I must admit, part of me did anticipate some kind of..." He waved his hands. "Oh, I don't know. Something. Maybe bolts of lightning from heaven."

The Roman general opened his arms wide with a wrinkle of disappointment on his brow. "But there is nothing here. Nothing but a large, empty chamber. Where is this god of yours, this rock in whom you trust?"

Simon glared at him silently, refusing to answer.

Titus stepped close. Within inches. He was daring Simon.

He whispered to him, "You, however, are one formidable adversary."

Titus smirked and turned his back, walking to the center of the room. "I commend you on your defense of the city. You and this madman, Gischala."

He turned back to face Simon. "Where is he?"

Simon stayed silent. *Let him find out for himself.*

Titus took off his helmet and handed it to a legionary. He unclasped his cape and shed his armor, handing it to another soldier.

What was he doing? Everyone around him looked confused. Everyone but Simon, who knew exactly what Titus was doing.

The Roman crossed his arms and said, "So you and I have someone very intimate in common."

Simon thought it. *Berenice.*

"And I have to admit, I am a bit envious of you. Of what you had." Titus considered his words carefully. "Of what you still have."

Simon was still the possessor of Berenice's heart.

A small piece of burning wood fell from the ceiling onto the floor in an explosion of sparks and cinders.

Simon looked above. The ceiling was going to collapse soon. Titus appeared to not even care.

The Roman general concluded, "Do not consider this my desire for revenge. Think of it rather as a gesture of respect. To allow *you* the opportunity for revenge."

He commanded his soldiers, "Let him pick up his sword."

A bold soldier protested, "But, Caesar..."

"I said let him pick up his sword. And do not molest him."

Simon saw his sword on the ground atop some debris. He placed his foot beneath the blade and kicked upward. The sword launched into the air, and he caught the handle firmly. He felt a surge of energy fill him. He was renewed. He was ready to kill the prince of abomination.

· · · · ·

In the Court of Priests, Apollyon swung Driver just as Remiel tried to jump him. The head hit Remiel square in the chest, crushing him and launching the angel into Saraqel. The two flew into a wall with such force that it collapsed upon them. They were buried in stone like the two others had been.

Uriel and Gabriel looked at each other with secret agreement.

Uriel stepped out of the circle toward Apollyon and shouted, "Enough! You belly-crawling, dirt-eating coward!"

The Watcher swung his hammer down upon Uriel, who crossed his swords over his head to catch the weapon's shaft before the head could hit him.

Both warrior's muscles shook with the strain of contested power.

Rahab then snapped through the air and cut the handle of the hammer in half, separating it from the hands of Apollyon, who now stood without protection against five angry archangels.

Raphael tossed a chain over to Michael. Catching it, Michael wrapped it in his fists. He said to Apollyon, "Get ready for a binding."

· · · · ·

Inside the Holy Place, Simon and Titus circled one another with their weapons ready. The legionaries surrounded them like a fence. More burning embers fell to the floor, barely missing them with flaming debris.

But just as the two warriors were about to engage, shadows came out from behind the colonnades all around them—behind the legionaries.

Before any of them knew what was happening, arrows released from bows, knives, and swords slit the throats and the hearts of the soldiers in the circle.

They fell to the ground dead. All of them.

Behind every Roman corpse now stood an Essene warrior with bow or blade in hand. Those weapons were now pointed at Titus Caesar, standing vulnerable in the open.

He dropped his sword to the ground in surrender.

The leader of the Essenes stepped forward: Aaron ben Hyam.

Simon smiled. "You know, I actually forgot you were coming."

Aaron smiled in return. "So did I until I realized you would get all the glory."

"Lower your weapons," Simon ordered the Essenes. They obeyed. Aaron watched him curiously.

Simon turned back to Titus and approached him slowly, holding his sword tightly in his hand and pointed at the Roman's throat.

Titus stared back defiantly. The end had turned in Simon's favor. And all the weight of history came upon this one single moment in time.

They glared silently at each other.

Then Simon said, "Go."

Titus looked confused. As if he had expected to die.

Simon spoke with a voice of calm, "And when you are emperor over my people, remember this day."[1]

Titus hesitated as if he were going to respond. Instead he turned and walked quickly back out the entrance of the Holy Place.

A large burning rafter hit the floor near Simon. He felt the flush of hot air and sparks hit him.

"Simon," barked Aaron. "We must get out of here."

But Simon was resolved. He said, "Take the tunnels. There is still time to escape."

Aaron was about to protest, but as he looked into Simon's eyes, he changed his mind. Simon knew what he had to do.

Aaron turned and commanded his men, "Let's go, quickly."

They ran for the tunnel exits in the side chambers.

Michael dragged Apollyon into the Holy Place, bound in the special chain they had forged for this purpose.

Uriel and Gabriel followed, dragging Marduk and Azazel behind them.

Saraqel and Raguel carried the crushed Remiel, all three of them seriously wounded.

They plowed through burning timbers from the roof above.

They dragged their captives up into the Holy of Holies.

The archangels stood around the Foundation Stone at the center of the most holy place.

Uriel rifled through Apollyon's tunic and found what he was looking for. He tossed it to Michael, who caught it and smiled.

As he held the ring seal of Solomon, the prince of Israel said to Apollyon, "Do you really think you stole the key to the Abyss? You fool. It was given to you."

When Apollyon first absconded with the seal years ago, he had used it to open the Abyss and let out the locust demons of hell along with the ancient ones bound at the Flood. His pride had blinded him to the realization that Yahweh had allowed such evil for his own purposes. That it was all part of the secret providential decrees of God.[2]

Michael used the signet ring to remove the foundation stone and open the shaft of the Abyss.

Gabriel and Uriel held the other two Watchers firmly.

Apollyon struggled with his chains, but he was not going anywhere.

Michael said, "Apollyon, you ancient serpent, I consign you to the Abyss. You will no longer be able to deceive the nations. Gospel messengers will continue to go out, and they will draw his elect from the four winds, from one end of heaven to the other. From every tribe and people and language and nation. But you shall be bound in your prison for a thousand years, for he must reign until he has put all enemies under his feet."

"What about them?" Apollyon complained, desperately gesturing at the other Watchers.

Uriel said, "It's the Lake of Fire for these two beasts."

Now it was Marduk and Azazel's turn to squirm with panic. The bindings held them tight.

"Wait a second," barked Apollyon.

But before he could register his complaint, he was cast into the Abyss and the Foundation Stone was sealed over the pit.

· · · · ·

When Titus left the Holy Place, he was received by Tiberius and a cohort of legionaries that had been waiting for him in the inner court.

Titus got up on his horse as Tiberius drew near.

"What happened to the others, General?"

"They didn't make it."

"Thank the gods you survived," said Tiberius.

Titus looked up at the temple. His second-in-command followed his gaze.

Flames licked the building out of every window now.

They saw Gischala high above on the roof with his arms out, surrounded by a crowd of soldiers.

"What is that moron doing?" asked Tiberius.

"He's calling upon his god," said Titus. "But he doesn't realize that his god is on our side."[3]

Tiberius told him, "Well, some legionaries torched the portico behind the temple as well. The rooms were filled with fanatics waiting for the same deliverance."

Then they saw a figure exit from between the two large pillars of the temple entrance.

It was Simon. He had no sword, and his hands were raised in surrender.[4]

Titus yelled to his troops, "Do not kill that man! He is the general of the Jewish forces."

Tiberius gave Titus a look of surprise.

Titus turned to his prefect. "Tiberius. Treat him with respect."

"Yes, General." Tiberius went to supervise the taking of the prisoner.

An officer asked Titus, "General, shall we put out the fire?"

"No," said Titus, looking up at Gischala. "Let it burn."

CHAPTER 63

The Romans had secured the temple mount. The last of the Jewish forces had fled into the Lower and Upper Cities. Josephus led Agrippa into the Court of the Gentiles on their horses, dreading what he would find.

All around them, the pavement was littered with the corpses of Jewish soldiers. Thousands of them. The bodies had been pushed into piles to allow a pathway for the Romans and their allies. The dead legionaries had been separated from them.

The two Jewish leaders arrived outside the inner temple where Titus, Tiberius, and several other leaders watched as the flames consumed the holy house of God.

Josephus felt like vomiting. But he dared not show the smallest sign of Jewish sympathy at this moment for he needed to maintain the trust of Titus.

He looked down to see Simon bar Giora, draped in chains, being pulled along on foot behind a horse. Obviously being taken into captivity.

As Simon passed him, Josephus caught his eye. A chill went through him. He knew the horrible destiny that awaited his fellow Jew—the Roman Triumph. He would be shipped to Rome with other captive leaders and dragged through the streets before a mocking crowd of Romans, who would pelt him with stones and rotten food. After a sacrifice to the gods, the captives would then all be executed for the glory of Caesar and Rome.

Josephus saw the anger in Simon's eyes, the righteous indignation of a hero who had fought to the very end on behalf of his nation, his people, and his religion. The look triggered a sudden guilt in Josephus's soul. He felt as if he were a traitor. Or worse, a coward. That he had done what he had to do only to stay alive above all else. Above his nation, his people, and his religion.

Josephus shook his head to himself. No. He was a captive, not a deserter. He had tried to save his people. He had pleaded with them. He had offered them the mercy of Caesar. But they had refused. If Vespasian was God's anointed one, then Josephus was doing the right thing. Surely he had done the right thing.

He decided he would tell the story of this horrible war for future generations. To leave a lasting legacy that would justify his survival and remedy the gnawing guilt in his conscience.

Titus saw the two of them as they arrived. The general gestured to the golden roof of the Holy Place. Josephus saw the flames rising from below with clouds of black smoke pulsing upward. He saw a crowd of people with their hands raised to heaven, praying for deliverance. He thought he recognized their leader, though at this distance he could not be sure.

"Is that...?" he asked.

"John of Gischala," Titus confirmed. "Apparently, he still disagrees with you over whose side your god is on."

Josephus saw that Gischala was dressed in the garments of the high priest— blue robe, ephod, and miter. It all became clear to him. Gischala saw himself as the Messiah. He believed he was leading his people to wait for Yahweh's return to Zion to rescue them and destroy the Romans.

What delusions we have all suffered.

Josephus then saw that the portico of the courtyard behind the temple was also on fire. Several people came running out of the burning structures, engulfed in flames and screaming in agony until they collapsed and died on the pavement.

Seeing Josephus's revulsion, Titus explained, "My soldiers set the porticos on fire. It turns out that some six thousand or so of Gischala's followers were waiting in the chambers for their deliverance."

"Six thousand?" Josephus asked with cracking voice. He closed his eyes at the thought of the holocaust. So many dead.[2]

Titus added, "I must say, you Jews display a kind of masochistic lunacy in your suffering. It's almost as if you welcome the pain as a pleasure to endure." He thought for a second, then added, "Present company of collaborators excluded, of course."

Josephus felt stung by the remark. It burrowed its way deeply into his liver like a diseased worm.

Collaborator.

He looked over and saw Agrippa smiling with amusement.

Soulless was the word he thought of for Herod.

The sound of breaking timbers echoed throughout the courtyard and drew everyone's attention just in time to see the roof of the holy temple collapse beneath the feet of Gischala and his followers.[3]

They were swallowed up in an explosion of flames and surging smoke as if from the fires of Gehenna itself.

Josephus fought the urge to burst into weeping. *So many dead.* So *many dead.*

He noticed Titus watching him. He realized he had tears rolling down his cheeks.

Titus assured him, "If you didn't cry at the desolation of your holy temple, I would think you weren't human."

They both glanced at Herod. He wasn't crying. He glanced away in shame.

Josephus stared unblinkingly into the flames and spoke, "God had for certain long ago doomed this holy house to the fire. That fatal day has come at the end of the ages on the same exact day as the first temple was burnt by the king of Babylon."[4]

They stood in silent awe as black billowing plumes filled the sky and darkened the sun.

CHAPTER 64

Alexander oversaw the transfer of the last of the patients from the hippodrome hospital into the theater in the Upper City. They were the most sickly and wounded of all the victims of war, three hundred of them, who could not travel without aid. The Christian assistants paired up with those who were strong enough to help for a total of several hundred volunteers. They carried beds and pallets of the infirm up the steep valley walkways behind the walls of the Upper City.

It had taken them six hours to move everyone and another four to move the food, tents, tools, and instruments used in the hospital. Everyone who could do so made several trips.

Alexander entered the large semi-circular theater that sat safely behind the Upper City wall. The proscenium stage had been broken down, providing more room to be filled with beds and pallets virtually on top of one another. The sounds of patients moaning in pain seemed to echo loudly because of the acoustic structure of the theater.

The orchestral pit was overflowing with bedded patients as well. The first level of seats was filled with those who could sit or lie across the benches.

There was barely enough room for them all. But they had no other choice. The Romans had captured the temple mount and were preparing to raid the Lower City where the hippodrome was. They could not afford to gamble on the mercy of Titus.

Alexander was not sure what had happened to most of the refugees who had deserted the city into the arms of Rome. But word had spread that the Roman soldiers cut open the bellies of thousands of Jews to obtain the gold and silver coins the Jews had swallowed. The doctor figured that the Romans would not bother caring for the wounded. They would be considered a burden and most likely be slaughtered en masse. Alexander had to do everything he could to protect those under his care.

But this was the last refuge. There were no more walls to hide behind, nowhere else to run. He had done everything he could to help the innocents in this war. Now he had to find a way out for the Christians.

He remembered back several years ago when he, Cassandra, and Severus had persuaded the Christians to leave Jerusalem after Cestius Gallus first surrounded the city. It had been the fulfillment of Jesus's warning, and the elect had finally heeded his advice to flee to the mountains.

But Alexander had returned to the doomed city because he wanted to care for the suffering and share the Gospel. God always offered salvation even in the midst of judgment. And Alexander wanted to be a vessel of that redemption. Many had been saved. Of those still remaining with Alexander as his assistants, the numbers were about a hundred and fifty. One hundred and fifty of God's elect. It was time to get them out. But how?

"Doctor Maccabaeus."

Alexander turned to see Aaron and his squad of forty Essene warriors at the entrance of the theater.

"How can I help you?" he asked.

"On the contrary," countered the monk. "How can we help you?"

"What do you mean? Are you not needed in battle?"

"Doctor, the war is lost. The temple is occupied, John of Gischala is dead, Simon bar Giora captured. It is only a matter of days before Rome burns the rest of the city to the ground."

Alexander felt a sinking in the pit of his stomach. Aaron spoke with solemn resignation. "There will be no mercy."

Alexander's mind spun, trying to figure out a new plan.

Then Aaron said, "We will help you get these people to safety."

"How? The only possible way is to hide out in the tunnels below Jerusalem and pray that the Romans do not find them."

"Exactly," said Aaron.

"But the only tunnel I knew of was in the Lower City."

Aaron smiled. "You are now in the Essene quarter. I know a secret tunnel in one of our old synagogues. It's not far from here. You can hide there as long as you need until the Romans leave."

"Won't Titus occupy the city?"

Aaron remained sober. "There will be nothing left to occupy. Whoever the Romans don't kill, they'll enslave, then leave."

"All right. Show me this secret passage."

"I have one caveat," said the Essene. "The tunnel is small and tight. You will not be able to bring any beds down there for those most in need of medical attention. And we must maintain stealth."

Alexander felt dread wash over him as he considered the implication. They would have to leave behind anyone who was too sick or wounded to carry themselves—and to do so quietly.

The monk said to him as if reading his thoughts, "Doctor, you have done everything you can do for these people. There is nothing more you can do."

Still, Alexander's thoughts searched for a way, any way to protect the hundreds who would be left behind to face the sword of Rome.

He muttered, "I haven't given my life."

Aaron said, "It wouldn't save them if you did. But you can still save some."

The monk was right. It had been Alexander's driving goal this entire war: *to save some*, any whom he could rescue from the flames. He knew he couldn't save them all. But for the first time he was facing the hard decision that until now he had been able to put off—the reality of finally leaving the city. Leaving those in need.

CHAPTER 65

Abomination of Desolation

The temple mount had burned out. The porticos around the court of Gentiles were smoldering ruins. Legionaries were removing dead bodies and mopping up blood from the pavement. The Roman army now occupied the temple mount in preparation for taking the rest of Jerusalem.

But Titus had an important task to do. A symbolic task. In war, symbolism was everything. Symbolic behaviors struck fear into the heart of the enemy and energized the bloodlust of one's own troops.

Titus had thought this one through. He had remembered the words of the crazy Jewish apocalypse confiscated from the Christians as well as the sacred prophecies of the Jews in Babylon about which Josephus had told him.

Titus had decided to do the very things that these religious fanatics feared most. Which was why he'd chosen not to bring Josephus or the Herods with him today. He didn't want to dishearten them, seeing that they were going to be his liaisons in the aftermath.

He marched into the ruins of the inner temple escorted by a company of soldiers leading a tethered bull and a very specific captive. Legionaries were still carrying out chests and pallets of silver, gold, and other valuables hidden in chambers beneath the temple. The plunder, split as booty among the soldiers, was so great it was sure to bring the price of rare metals down throughout the empire.

Tiberius met Titus at the steps of the Holy Place. He saluted. "Caesar, the temple has been cleaned out of the debris as you requested."

Titus looked up at the marble structural remains, blackened by soot. The golden roof had melted with the intense heat of the flames, the molten precious metal seeping into the cracks and joints between the stones.[1]

Tiberius added, "We found some priests hiding in chambers around and beneath the structure." He gestured to his left. Titus saw thirty Jews with priestly garb in bonds, beaten bloody, and ragged.

"Excellent work," said Titus. "Did you find a Torah scroll?"

282

Tiberius reached out his hand to a soldier, who handed him a holy scroll wrapped in blue cloth, its two golden handles sticking out on both sides.

Titus smiled, then ordered, "Bring the priests over here."

Tiberius alerted the guards and waved them over. The priests had also chains on their feet, so that they had to hop with small steps like hobbled beasts.

They lined up before Titus, and he looked out over them. He thought what he might say to them, then simply pronounced, "I have killed the god of Israel."

Titus gestured to his standard bearers to set up the Roman standards from each of the legions around the stone altar that stood to one side of a large bronze laver.

Some of the priests began to weep. The standards, or ensigns, were the banners of each legion attached to large staffs. Each was a different color designating the regiment's number. They were emblazoned with the symbolic image of the legion as well as an image of Caesar. The soldiers considered the standard to be a holy representation of the emperor and, therefore, defended it to the death. The Jews considered them idols. So bringing them into the temple was a blasphemous sacrilege.[2]

This was only the beginning of blasphemies that Titus had planned for today.

Soldiers led the tethered bull they had brought up the ramp to the top of the stone altar and tied it down. One of them announced with a loud voice, "We sacrifice this bull to the glory of our savior and god, Caesar!"

One of the other soldiers took a large machete he had confiscated from the temple slaughterhouse and brought it down upon the neck of the beast, nearly severing its head. It made a sickening death squeal and fell to the floor of the altar. Its blood poured out and into the drains at the edge of the altar.

Titus turned to the soldiers guarding the priests and commanded, "Bring them in."

He entered the Holy Place.

The interior stank of smoke and charred wood that had been pushed to the sides of the chamber. They had even swept the floor for Titus. Excellent.

He walked up to the Holy of Holies, now, a bare small stage without a curtain. He ordered the soldiers, "Line up the priests for the show."

They obeyed, and the fearful Jews looked at one another, wondering what abomination he had planned.

"Bring me the harlot."

One of the soldiers brought forth a Jewish captive they had brought along. Titus had deliberately chosen a harlot to match the symbolic language of the Apocalypse.

She ascended the steps and met Titus at the top.

"Tiberius," he called out.

Tiberius walked up the stairs with the Torah scroll. Titus gestured to the floor. The Prefect placed the scroll on the floor and unrolled it like a carpet.

The Jewish priests gasped at the horror of placing the holy Scripture on the ground.

Oh, I'm just getting started, thought Titus with a smile.

He turned to the harlot and said, "Take off your clothes and lie on the scroll." She dutifully obeyed. Titus then removed his undergarment beneath his battle skirt and proceeded to fornicate with the harlot on top of the scroll in the Holy of Holies.

The priests wept. Some fainted.

All was lost.[3]

After he had finished his abominable symbolic deed, he handed the woman to Tiberius. "Burn her on a pyre."

The woman whimpered and squirmed hopelessly in Tiberius's grip. He stiffened in obedience. "Yes, Caesar."

But Titus was not done. "And execute all the priests where they stand."

The Jews trembled with shock.

One of them cried out, "Mercy, Caesar! Mercy!"

Titus turned to the audacious priest and announced, "The time for pardon is over. You deserve to perish with your holy house."

He marched past the soldiers and their captives as they all drew swords and hacked the Jews to death.[4]

He muttered to himself, "Ask your god for mercy."

CHAPTER 66

Alexander had not managed any sleep. The sounds of war outside the Upper City wall kept him awake, and nightmares of atrocities woke him if he did close his eyes. The Romans had invaded the Lower City and enslaved thousands more Jews. They had also slaughtered the weak and elderly, just as Alexander had expected.

He stood on the wall of the Upper City looking down upon the field of slaughter. Bodies were stacked in the streets like cordwood. The Romans were demolishing all the buildings and burning everything to the ground. The rest of the legionaries were now completing their earthworks ramp to take their final objective: the Upper City, where the last of the Jewish soldiers and refugees had fled.

One of those Jewish soldiers next to Alexander said, "You'd better return to your loved ones and say your prayers. We are all going to die. Or be enslaved. I can't honestly say one is better than the other."

Alexander left the city wall to return to the theater.

On his walk back, the words of Aaron haunted him. *You can still save some.*

The Essene knew what he was talking about. His was the sole surviving group from Qumran after that community had been wiped out. The Christians would have suffered the same fate had they not left Jerusalem over three years ago.

Alexander had to focus not on those he could not save, but on those he could, those few innocents well enough to escape and the last of the Christians in the city.

When Alexander arrived at the theater, he called together all the Christian assistants to gather around the patients for his announcement.

"The Romans are at the walls of the Upper City. They will breach it shortly, and they will burn this city to the ground. I've seen it with my own eyes in the Lower City. I will not give you false hope. None of you are safe. They will most likely kill us all."

The crowd burst out in frightened chatter. Some wept.

"But there is hope for some. The Essene warrior has shown me a secret entrance to a tunnel beneath the city."[1]

Now the chatter became a buzz of excitement.

Someone shouted out, "Can we carry the beds there?"

Alexander hesitated. He didn't want to say what he said next. "No. The entrance is not large enough to accommodate beds, and we must be inconspicuous. So only those who can walk of their own accord will be able to go."

Horrified gasps and cries for the Lord broke out.

"Please, quiet down!" When they did, he continued. "Because the Romans have surrounded the city, we cannot leave the tunnel. We must hide out down there until they leave. With our lack of food, we still don't stand much of a chance."

Someone shouted out, "You are leaving us to die!"

Another yelled, "It's not fair!"

The crowd became riled. Patients argued amongst themselves. Alexander's heart dropped. He didn't want to leave any of them. But if the able didn't leave, then they would all die.

If he could only save some...

A whistle penetrated the cacophony. Everyone settled down when they saw who it was. A young, ten-year-old boy, dark-skinned, wavy black hair. Alexander recognized him as Samuel, the son of the father Alexander had saved months ago with a tracheotomy and a skull drill. The doctor was sure the father wouldn't last two days with his wounds, but he did. And he was still alive today.

The boy helped his father to stand and kept him from falling. The man still had a head bandage and his voice was not strong, having only partially healed from the tracheotomy. It had the effect of piquing everyone's attention.

"Without this man and those who helped him, most of us would be dead already. I would be dead. They have sacrificed everything to help us. But the time has come when there is nothing more that can be done. How dare you try to pull down with you those who have protected you as long as they could. Now is their opportunity. And I for one will not betray them. God bless you, Alexander Maccabeus, and all the Christians who have helped us. May the Lord bless you and keep you. May his face shine upon you and protect you."

The silence of the crowd penetrated Alexander. He could see the remorse in the eyes of those closest to him. He could feel their shame. And he knew that this man had just saved the lives of those who still had a chance.

But the father still wasn't done. He raised a rag that was wrapped around something. He said, "You will need food and water to survive in the tunnels. Here is a piece of bread that I have saved for a moment like this. I want you to have it."

Alexander could not speak. His eyes filled with tears.

Then the silence was broken by another voice coming from a pallet. An elderly woman with a broken leg. She raised a piece of vegetable in her hand. "I want to donate my food as well. Thank you, Alexander Maccabaeus. You did everything you could."

All over the theater, feeble and wounded patients reached under their pillows and mattresses, pulling out scraps of food they had hoarded away from the scant rations they'd been provided, raising them in the air as food offerings.

"Me too," came a voice.

Another, "Thank you, Alexander!"

And another, "God bless Alexander, and God bless the Christians."

Alexander could not stop the tears. Neither could the other Christians who had served by his side. This was the hardest thing they had ever done in more than three years of war. And now it was as if all they had given was being given back to them.

It didn't make the loss any easier.

The rest of the day was spent with much crying and saying goodbyes. Alexander spent as much of it as he could spare from preparations away from everyone in his small area, praying and worshipping the Alpha and Omega, apart from whose will not a single sparrow fell to the ground.

So many sparrows.

Those words of his wife Cassandra filled Alexander's heart with deep sorrow and pain. He missed her so. But he would see her again one day. Hope was all he had left.

When the time had come, Alexander gathered those who were able to care for themselves, about a thousand of them. They would move through the back alleys under cloak of night in groups of twenty or so to avoid detection. Every person carried water skins and whatever scraps and crumbs of food they had left along with what had been given to them.

They might end up being starved out after all.

Alexander led the first group to show them where the tunnel entrance was. He moved swiftly through the Essene quarter to the place which Aaron had shown him earlier. His twenty followers moved noiselessly like phantoms in the dark. The entrance was hidden in an Essene synagogue that had been destroyed by the catapults. This was a good thing, because the Romans would be less likely to search through rubble looking for such escape routes.

He found the building, half the walls still standing, the other half piles of debris. He led them up to the corner of a stone wall and gestured to a large boulder.

Two men moved it aside, and the group descended into a secret passageway. Aaron had told the truth—it was indeed a small opening. As undernourished and scrawny as the group now was, they had no difficulty squeezing through. But a large, well-fed man would find it a tight squeeze, and it would certainly be impossible to maneuver beds or even pallets through the tunnel's low, narrow expanse.

Alexander used a small lamp they had carried along to light a series of other lamps and some torches in the passageway. Following Aaron's meticulous directions, he made some turns until he arrived at a larger hallway with several conjoining tunnels.

"You can comfortably fit a couple hundred or so down each of these passages," he told his companions. "That should do it."

With a few others, he made his way back to the theater to organize the rest of the groups of refugees for the exodus.

CHAPTER 67

September 26, AD 70
45 Days after the cessation of sacrifice

*And from the time that the regular burnt offering is taken away
and the abomination that makes desolate is set up, there shall be
1,290 days. Blessed is he who waits and arrives at the 1,335 days
[45 days later].*

Daniel 12:11–12

Upon completion of the earthworks ramp, the Romans had battered their way into the Upper City, pushing the remaining rebels back into Herod's palace, where they too were eventually overtaken.

On this day of September 26 in the second year of Vespasian's reign, Titus had conquered Jerusalem. The war was over.[1]

But not so his dealings with the Jews.

Titus had moved his headquarters into the temple complex. He convened a council of advisors in his war tent to discuss what to do with the holy temple.

"Destroy it," said Tiberius. "These hard-nosed Jews will simply not learn their lesson unless you take everything from them. Leave one stone standing, and they'll cling to that tiny piece until they can rebel again."

Josephus sat beside Agrippa and Berenice, listening intently to the arguments, forming his response.

Another tribune spoke up. "We've lost too many legionaries because of their fanatical devotion to this unholy house. You may lose the respect of your troops if you don't allow them satisfaction of total destruction."

"On the other hand," said another tribune, "the temple is an extraordinary work of human achievement. If preserved, it might furnish evidence of Roman moderation. If destroyed, it could serve a perpetual proof of Roman cruelty."

"Nonsense," barked Tiberius. "Roman moderation has been proven with every city in this Land that was permitted to surrender. Allowing the temple to stand is not 'moderation'; it is weakness."

The other dozen-plus leaders quietly deferred to Tiberius.

Titus turned to Josephus. "And what do my Jewish collaborators say?"

Josephus glanced at the Herods. Agrippa spoke first. "If you leave the temple intact, I can ensure you a generation of a loyal and submissive priesthood."

Titus raised his brow. That could be beneficial.

Josephus stepped in. "If you tear it down, you will only fuel rebellion in their hearts. They will obey on the outside, but inside they will never be loyal."

Titus replied, "Unlike you, Josephus?"

Josephus felt humiliated. But he bit his tongue and said humbly, "Yes, my lord Caesar, unlike me. I am your servant."

Titus considered the advice that he had been given. He began to think out loud. "This temple is the heart and soul of the two religions that have caused the most trouble for the empire. Overthrowing the temple would thoroughly subvert both Judaism and Christianity."[2]

Josephus protested, "Caesar, forgive my interruption, but Jews and Christians are completely contrary to one another. Christians reject the temple. They would revel in its desolation. You might even empower them. Remember the Great Fire of Rome."

The Herods mumbled in agreement. Titus looked unconvinced. Josephus knew the Roman general had his doubts about whether the Christians had really started the fire even though the Pharisee had convinced Nero that they had.

"Nevertheless, you both sprang from the same root," Titus said. "And if the root is destroyed, the offshoots would perish as well."

Berenice spoke up. "Caesar, if I may?"

He nodded to her.

She said, "Our people have already suffered so much. Yet they will still be obedient if you do not make the humiliation absolute. The people will respond more favorably to a marriage than a funeral."

Josephus knew that she was speaking more of her own future with Titus than that of her so-called people. *Edomite.*

Titus considered the advice. As his contemplation dragged on, an awkward silence fell over the council. Someone cleared their throat. Another coughed.

Finally, Titus gave his pronouncement to Tiberius. "Tear it to the ground. Do not leave one stone upon another."[3]

Tiberius stood to attention. "Yes, my lord Caesar."

Titus turned to the other tribunes and added, "Then burn down this city, kill everyone who resists, and enslave the rest."

Tiberius saluted and left the war tent, followed by the rest of the commanders to prepare for their final assault.

Josephus glanced at the Herods. Berenice was holding back tears, and Agrippa looked pale.

For his own part, Josephus felt a total failure. He had sought to convince the Jews to surrender and avoid this very thing. They had branded him a traitor. He'd sought to persuade Titus to refrain from total desolation, but he had been ignored and relegated to a "court prophet" promoting Flavian imperial ambitions.

Had he sold his soul to gain the world—only to lose everything?

Certainly, his people had lost everything.

The heavens and earth shook, the sky rolled up like a scroll, and the constellations went dark. With the destruction of the temple, the end of days had arrived, the whole cosmos destroyed. The power of the holy people was shattered forever.[4]

> Then I saw a new heaven and a new earth, for the first heaven and the first earth had passed away, and the sea was no more. And I saw the holy city, new Jerusalem, coming down out of heaven from God, prepared as a bride adorned for her husband. And I heard a loud voice from the throne saying, "Behold, the dwelling place of God is with man. He will dwell with them, and they will be his people, and God himself will be with them as their God. He will wipe away every tear from their eyes, and death shall be no more, neither shall there be mourning, nor crying, nor pain anymore, for the former things have passed away." And he who was seated on the throne said, "Behold, I am making all things new." Also he said, "Write this down, for these words are trustworthy and true."
>
> Apocalypse 21:1–5

CHAPTER 68

Alexander had lost track of how many days they had been down in the darkness of these secret tunnels beneath the city. What little food they had was gone. Some had already died of starvation.

The hiding Jews had sent a few scouts out of the tunnels, only to discover that the Roman blockade was still up. They could not leave their hiding place without being discovered. They could hear the distant sounds and feel the rumblings of the destruction of the city just above them. They tried to pass the time by telling stories and giving sermons of hope.

Alexander didn't want to feed the delusion that they would all escape their dilemma by God's hand. Yes, sometimes God did deliver his people as he had done at the Red Sea or with the Christians at Pella. But not always and not everyone.

Faithful believers had suffered and died before the exodus from Egypt. Righteous men of God had died in the holy wars of Joshua's conquest as had many of the righteous in the Babylonian exile. God had preserved his Remnant as a whole through those trying times, but some had not made it. The heavenly Father did not owe anyone their life. But he did promise the resurrection that would put all things to rights in the end. And that is what Alexander spoke of, the true hope of the resurrection.

Presently, he had been explaining how Jesus fulfilled the Feasts of Israel. The fifth of seven, the Feast of Trumpets, was supposed to occur on the first of this very month. But with the capture of the temple, it had not been celebrated, which was fitting because the Feast of Trumpets was being fulfilled in the destruction of Jerusalem.

Because it was the only feast that began on the first day of the month, it was the only one where the moon was nothing but a sliver in darkness. The start of the feast was therefore determined by two witnesses sighting the new moon and reporting to the Sanhedrin. Because of weather and other difficulties, it was not always easy or precise in the timing, so the beginning of the feast was not known with certainty until the witnesses arrived. This left the people in a continual state of alertness. Thus the well-known phrase, "No man knows the day or the hour" when the feast would begin.[1]

Jesus had used this same phrase of his *parousia*, his coming on the clouds. It had been like a thief in the night.

> But concerning that day and hour no one knows, not even the angels of heaven, nor the Son, but the Father only... Therefore, stay awake, for you do not know on what day your Lord is coming. But know this, that if the master of the house had known in what part of the night the thief was coming, he would have stayed awake and would not have let his house be broken into. Therefore you also must be ready, for the Son of Man is coming at an hour you do not expect.[2]

The prophet Joel had predicted the Day of the Lord when Yahweh would pour out his wrath upon Israel. He had written, "Blow a trumpet in Zion, and sound an alarm on My holy mountain! Let all the inhabitants of the land tremble, for the day of the Lord is coming. Surely it is near."[3]

On the Day of Pentecost forty years ago, the apostle Peter had said that Joel's Day of the Lord was at hand. The Holy Spirit was being poured out upon all flesh. The new covenant had been inaugurated. The cosmic order was already changing.[4]

Zephaniah had foretold what Alexander and the Jews of Jerusalem had been experiencing these past five months.

> Near is the great day of the Lord, Near and coming very quickly; listen, the day of the LORD! In it the warrior cries out bitterly. A day of wrath is that day, a day of trouble and distress, a day of destruction and desolation, a day of darkness and gloom, a day of clouds and thick darkness, a day of trumpet and battle cry against the fortified cities and the high corner towers.
>
> *Zephaniah 1:14–16*

The day and the hour had arrived. With the fall of this great city, the Feast of Trumpets was fulfilled. Now Jesus would send out his messengers—Christian believers—and would use the Gospel to gather his elect from the four winds into his kingdom, a mountain that would grow to fill the earth in God's time.

Alexander had been explaining all this to the hundreds of refugees surrounding him in the tunnel beneath the sounds of the city being destroyed above them: Jerusalem's Day of the Lord.

They tried to concentrate, but he could tell with every jerk or cringe at every concussive sound from above that they were barely holding their fears at bay.

Nevertheless, the Holy Spirit had fallen upon them, and many Jews had surrendered to Jesus as their Messiah. Some no doubt did so with the hope that God would reward them by rescuing them out of this trap. But most of them were genuine in their reception. They had come to realize that Jesus was the end goal of Torah. That all the promises of God were fulfilled in Jesus as Messiah. That the end of sacrifice and offering had arrived. That vision and prophecy had been sealed up. Even at this last hour, God was redeeming souls.[5]

You can still save some.

The sound of screaming echoed through the tunnels, interrupting Alexander's sermon. Everyone's attention was drawn to the other passageways filled with refugees. The screams increased, followed by shouting and a stampede of people running toward them.

Alexander asked, "What's happening?"

One of the fleeing refugees yelled out, "Romans! We've been discovered!"

The Romans had found the tunnels.

Everyone around Alexander panicked. Shrieks were followed by an attempt to scatter. It was like a bunch of frightened sheep caught in a maze trampling over one another to escape their predators.

Alexander looked down the passageway they were in toward the far end. Torches emerged into view, the light glinting off drawn swords and the frightful, red, full body shields of Rome.

They were trapped. Wedged in. On one side, their fellow patients pushed toward them like a mob. On the other side, a company of legionaries descended upon them like a lion.

A burly man named Obadiah stood in front of Alexander. "Stay behind me, doctor." He had been one of the medical assistants saved through the Gospel.

But it was useless. There was no defense left and no deliverance.

The Romans thrust their javelins into the outliers, then when they were in close, they lowered their shields and began hacking away at their unarmed victims: men, women, and children. No one was spared. No one was taken captive.[6]

Alexander was pushed up against the tunnel wall, crushed by the hundreds of crying, screaming people trying to get away with nowhere to go. Swords and javelins were thrusted and jabbed into bodies. People fell to the ground in piles.

Obadiah tried to cover Alexander, but in the end he could not do it. Alexander felt the large man smash him against the wall, followed by the sharp pain of a javelin entering his side.

He fell down beneath the big man and several others. He couldn't move.

Alexander felt his life bleeding out of him. The last thought that went through his mind was that Christ had been pierced in his side. And what an honor it was…

And then he thought no more.

CHAPTER 69

The Divine Council

Alexander felt himself floating into the sky as the seventh and final trumpet of judgment sounded upon the Land. He looked below him to see the corpses of his fellow refugees in the tunnels beneath the city. His heart became heavy with sorrow. The Romans cut through the Jewish residents like demon-possessed madmen.[1]

Alexander saw the city burning and destroyed, tens of thousands of people dead in the streets and valleys—citizens, soldiers, and rulers. Birds of prey consumed the flesh of the dead, reminding Alexander of the words of the Apocalypse.

> *Then I saw an angel standing in the sun, and with a loud voice he called to all the birds that fly directly overhead, "Come, gather for the great supper of God, to eat the flesh of kings, the flesh of captains, the flesh of mighty men, and the flesh of all men, both free and slave, both small and great".*
>
> *Apocalypse 19:17–18*

Alexander was high enough now to see the temple mount, its holy house vanished, desolate. Daniel had foretold it. Jesus had foretold it. The Two Witnesses had foretold it. The temple had been given over to the nations of Rome and trampled beneath the feet of the iron beast for 42 months. Not one of its stones were left upon another. The great city of Jerusalem had become Babylon the great and had been thrown down with violence. The voice of the bridegroom and bride would be heard in her no more.

> *"Alas! Alas! You great city, you mighty city, Babylon! For in a single hour your judgment has come."*
>
> *Apocalypse 18:10*

From his lofty height of observation, Alexander could only conclude one thing: he was dead and was about to face his Creator.

But he felt peace in his whole being. He knew the blood of Christ covered him like the blood of the Passover Lamb. Messiah's death had brought about the new exodus like the Unleavened Bread, and his resurrection had been the first fruits of the resurrection to come. He had begun his new covenant ekklesia on the Feast of Pentecost, and the Feast of Trumpets had been fulfilled in the destruction of the temple. The Day of the Lord had come when the Jews had not expected it would.

Now the Day of Atonement was fulfilled in Christ. The sixth of seven feasts, the Day of Atonement was supposed to have occurred in this same month of September. It was a solemn day of fasting and sacrifice. It included the scapegoat rite where the sins of the people were placed upon two goats, one for Yahweh that was sacrificed and one for the wilderness of Azazel that would wander into oblivion.[2]

This was the one and only day of the year that the high priest was allowed to enter into the Holy of Holies and stand before the presence of God, who stood between the cherubim on the mercy seat. There the high priest would offer atonement for the priesthood, the people, and the Holy Place as well. Atonement was completed after the high priest came out of the Holy Place, sending the sins of the people into the wilderness.

This solemn and holy day had been fulfilled in Jesus Christ as our scapegoat, but also as our high priest who had entered into the true Holy Place in heaven and offered his once-for-all sacrifice.[3] But the way into that heavenly Holy of Holies would not be made open until the earthly Holy Place was destroyed.[4]

That destruction was now complete.

Alexander saw Jesus exiting the Holy Place of heaven, opening that Holy of Holies forever.[5] The transgression of Israel had been put to an end and finished, atoned for. Jesus had been anointed the Most Holy, securing everlasting righteousness.[6]

The ark of the covenant was supposed to have been inside the earthly Holy of Holies, but it had been destroyed during the Babylonian exile hundreds of years ago. It was the footstool of Yahweh's throne where his presence resided, and yet it had never been returned to its rightful location in the temple—until now.[7]

As heaven opened, Alexander could see the new ark of the covenant surrounded by heavenly host in the temple above the waters. Flashes of lightning, peals of thunder, and even earthquakes and heavy hail accompanied this vision of holy beauty.[8]

He remembered this part of John's Apocalypse as well as Daniel's night visions.[9] He had read them both often. But this couldn't be another dream because he was dead. This must be the real thing.

He then realized that the ark was indeed a footstool before a throne of fiery flames with wheels of burning fire. Cherubim supported the throne with their strange hybrid bodies and their multiple wings. Alexander was in the very throne room of Yahweh.[10]

He saw martyrs sitting on thrones surrounded by ten thousand times ten thousand heavenly host. He knew these martyrs represented the Christians who had been killed during the Great Tribulation. They had been slaughtered because they would not worship the Beast or take his mark. John's Apocalypse had been written to comfort these blessed and holy ones with the assurance that they would sit in judgment over their persecutors. That they would reign with Christ for a millennium, a symbolically long future. Alexander was watching the vindication of the martyrs for which Jesus himself had called a generation ago. The cry of their souls beneath the altar had finally been answered.[11]

> *Then I saw the souls of those who had been beheaded for the testimony of Jesus and for the word of God, and those who had not worshiped the beast or its image and had not received its mark on their foreheads or their hands. They came to life and reigned with Christ for a thousand years. The rest of the dead did not come to life until the thousand years were ended. This is the first resurrection. Blessed and holy is the one who shares in the first resurrection! Over such the second death has no power, but they will be priests of God and of Christ, and they will reign with him for a thousand years.*
>
> *Apocalypse 20:4–6[12]*

Alexander heard the voice of living creatures call out, "Holy, holy, holy is the Lord God Almighty, who was and is and is to come!"

Then he saw the Ancient of Days take a seat on his throne before a sea of glass like crystal. Alexander felt his entire body stiffen with paralysis. His soul was filled with both terror and joy. The brightness of Yahweh's glory penetrated him. He could barely look upon the presence of the Lord.

His clothing was white as snow, his hair like pure wool. A stream of fire issued forth from the throne into the crystal sea. Those on their thrones then cast their crowns before the throne, and they proclaimed, "Worthy are you, our Lord and God, to receive glory and honor and power, for you created all things, and by your will they existed and were created."

Alexander knew what this was. The prophet Daniel had written of it. The court was sitting in judgment. The books were opened.

He looked over to see Jesus, the Son of Man, coming with the clouds of heaven. Jesus came up to the Ancient of Days and was presented before him: *Parousia.*[13]

The Ancient of Days then announced to his Son, "To you is given dominion and glory and a kingdom, that all peoples should serve you. Your dominion is an everlasting dominion, which shall not pass away, and your kingdom one that shall not be destroyed."

A voice called out, "The dominion of the iron beast of Rome and its Little Horn has been taken away. It will be consumed and destroyed to the end."[14]

The Little Horn had been prophesied by Daniel in his vision to be one of ten horns of the trampling iron beast of Rome. Those horns represented ten kings. The Little Horn was Nero Caesar.

> *And behold, there came up among them another horn, a little one, before which three of the first horns were plucked up by the roots. He shall put down three kings. And behold, in this horn were eyes like the eyes of a man, and a mouth speaking boastful things. He shall speak words against the Most High, and shall think to change the times and the law. As I looked, this horn made war with the saints and prevailed over them. They were given into his hand for a time, times, and half a time [3-1/2 years]. But his dominion shall be taken away, to be consumed and destroyed to the end. For the Ancient of Days came, and judgment was given for the saints of the Most High, and the time came when the saints possessed the kingdom.*
>
> *Daniel 7:8, 21-22, 24–26*

Daniel had foreseen three Caesars violently uprooted before Nero: the three horns of Tiberius, Caligula, and Claudius. All three had been assassinated, which cleared the way for ascendancy of the last of the Julio-Claudian line of Caesars, the Little Horn.[15]

Nero had blasphemed Yahweh with high and mighty words. He had made war on the Christians, prevailing over them for three-and-a-half years. He had sought to change the times and laws as a god until his dominion was taken away from him. All foretold by Daniel.

But the apocalyptic cosmos was not only about human monsters. Behind earthly rulers were spiritual rulers or principalities. The Watcher Azazel had been brought up from the Abyss to become the principality behind the Roman Beast in Palestine. Azazel had been captured and thrown into the Lake of Fire, ending the spiritual Beast's reign of terror, while its earthly counterpart kingdoms would be prolonged for a season and a time.[16]

Alexander was shaken out of his thoughts by the next sight. He looked down and saw the whole of the Land of Israel laid out below him like a cemetery of the dead. It was the symbolic vision of Daniel's time of the end. Alexander saw many of those sleeping in the dust of the Land rise up to be judged for what they had done during the Great Tribulation. The judgment upon apostate Israel had reduced the Land and people to a graveyard of old covenant death. Those who had rejected Messiah's visitation arose from the dust to be judged by their victims, the martyrs. Those who had embraced Messiah rose to become the new covenant body of Israel, shining like the stars. The Israel of faith had resurrected out of the corpse of the Israel of flesh.[17]

Jesus had called it the Regeneration.[18] It was the spiritual metaphor that foreshadowed the resurrection of the great white throne judgment that would one day occur at the end of the millennium. At that time, the sea would give up its dead, and Death and Hades would give up their dead. And if anyone's name was not written in the book of life, they would be thrown into the Lake of Fire.[19]

The voices of those on the thrones rang out, "The kingdom and the dominion and the greatness of the kingdoms under the whole heaven is given to the people of the saints of the Most High. His kingdom shall be an everlasting kingdom, and all dominions shall serve and obey him."

The true saints of the Most High were the Christians, both Jew and Gentile believers in Jesus Christ. They would live out his spiritual kingdom on earth as Jesus reigned from his heavenly throne.

Alexander suddenly noticed that he was the only human experiencing this apart from the martyrs on their thrones. Where were the great cloud of witnesses? All those Christians who had gone before him.

Jesus looked at Alexander from his throne as if he had heard his question clearly. Again, the shining brightness caused Alexander to close his eyes.

He heard the Son of Man's response in his head. "You are not dead."

Alexander thought, *This must be my resurrection.* He remembered the words of Jesus,

> "Whoever believes in me, though he die, yet shall he live, and everyone who lives and believes in me shall never die."
>
> *John 11:25-26*

He closed his eyes and felt himself pulled away from the throne room of God.

CHAPTER 70

Qumran

Aaron and his company of thirty surviving Essene warriors had escaped from the tunnels beneath the city. Unlike the large groups of civilians hiding there, Aaron's squad was small and able to move with stealth, killing a group of Roman guards on the perimeter wall before making their way to freedom.

Now Aaron and his comrades walked through the ruins of their once beloved community on the shores of the Dead Sea. They were like parents looking for the remains of their children in the aftermath.

Aaron was searching for something very specific. And he found it in the scriptorium. Though most everything had been pillaged or burned, marauders had taken no interest in scrolls and scribal materials. This resounded to Aaron's benefit as he picked up a piece of flexible copper sheet metal and a small chisel.

The majority of their manuscripts were on parchment or papyrus. But the Essenes occasionally hammered out strips of copper to provide longer lasting materials for the future.

Aaron took the copper sheet and began to etch words into it with the chisel.

In the ruin which is in the valley of Acor under the steps leading to the East, sixty feet: a chest of silver and its vessels with a weight of seventeen talents.[1]

He paused to think of another location, then began engraving the next on the list: one hundred gold ingots in a cistern of a courtyard.

After a short time, some of his men joined him in the scriptorium. One of them, Levi, read what Aaron was engraving and asked, "What are you doing, Aaron?"

"I'm writing a list of buried treasures from the temple."

Levi twisted his brow and said, "But it's not true. We were all there with you. The treasures were not saved. They were burned up in the fire or taken as booty by Titus."

"I know." Aaron continued to chisel away the next location and treasure.

"Then why are you doing it? Why do you lie to posterity?"

Aaron stopped and looked up at his inquisitor, then at the others around him waiting for an answer.

"Because they need hope."

"Hope?" repeated Levi. "Our community has been destroyed, our prophecies proven false. Our religion is a fraud. The temple is no more, and the covenant is broken. There is nothing left to hope for."

"That is where you are wrong, my brother. People are obstinate. Many will continue to believe, no matter what has happened this day. And who are we to take that away from them?"

Levi was obstinate. "What about the truth?"

Aaron chortled. "Truth. What is truth." He said it more as a statement than a question.

Levi narrowed his eyes. "Are you telling us that we should believe in something even if it is not true?"

"I am saying that there is nothing more horrible in this life than having nothing to believe in. Can you face that void, Levi? Can you live without hope or meaning or purpose?"

Levi and the others stood silent.

"Well, I cannot. And I cannot imagine the hell that will be unleashed when the whole world looks into the Abyss and the Abyss looks back into us."

Levi looked for support from his other brothers. Aaron stared at him, daring him to do so.

Levi said, "The brothers and I have counseled. We want to go to Masada. It's safe there. We can wait for the Romans to leave, then start over."

Aaron returned to his engraving. "Then go. I release you from my command. And I thank you for your service to the cause."

Levi nodded to the others. One by one, they left the scriptorium.

Aaron stopped for a moment, his eyes still on the copper sheet, unwilling to see who, if any, would stay.

He wiped away a tear that had fallen on the copper and continued to engrave his false hope into history.[2]

303

CHAPTER 71

Pella

Cassandra sat alone, praying, on a rock overlooking the valley of Pella. The Hasmonean fortress still stood on the tall hill across the valley. From this very spot, she had watched the cult of a thousand Ebionites lead their wagons and mules out of Pella on their way back to Jerusalem. The cancer had been cut from the body. The Congregation of the Lord was on its journey toward healing.

She often spent time out here by herself, crying out to the Father. She had heard the news that the Romans had slaughtered most of the inhabitants of the city and enslaved the rest in Rome. The odds were not good for Alexander.

She had lost her husband, either to glory or to suffering. But in either case, she had lost him. She sought to keep a positive view of the future. But she could not let him go without knowing. Without being able to say goodbye. It was living torture.

"Forgive me, Lord," she prayed. "You give, and you take away. Blessed be your name. Watch over my children and give them the abiding joy that I should have. Especially Rachel."

Her attention was taken by the arrival of a couple dozen travelers in the valley coming up the pathway to the city.

Her immediate response was fear. She was alone out here. Strangers could not be trusted even this close to the city.

But they weren't riding horses. Bandits almost always rode horses.

As they came closer, Cassandra could see they were not well. Some were limping. Others had bandages around their arms or chests.

Survivors of a battle.

But they had no weapons, and they didn't look like soldiers. Several of them were women and children.

Then she focused in on the man in the lead. He had a bandage around his torso. And his walk was familiar.

The way he carried his tall frame. The way he helped others instead of himself.

"Dear Jesus," she blurted out. "Alexander?"

She got off her rock and began hurrying down the path toward the visitors, dazed, still not believing her eyes.

"Alexander?" she kept asking. "Alexander?"

When she was within fifty yards, she saw his face clearly. At that moment his head turned to see the woman hurrying down the path. He froze, seemingly stunned, a hand holding his side.

"Alexander!" This time she almost fainted.

He moved at last. Away from his fellow travelers and toward Cassandra. He couldn't move quickly, one hand still clutching his side.

But she could.

She could run.

"Alexander!" she shouted, charging him with her arms out.

"Cassandra!" he yelled back, quickening his awkward limp.

When they met, she didn't hesitate, wrapping her arms around him and squeezing for all her life.

He grunted with pain and almost fell backward.

She kept repeating, "I thought you were dead, I thought you were dead."

They pulled apart to look at each other. He had a full beard, his hair wild and dirty. But his eyes were like glittering stars of happiness.

"So did I," he said. "Until I realized I wasn't."

They laughed together. Cassandra had no idea what that meant, but she laughed. They kissed each other like a couple of young lovers.

When they stopped to catch their breath, she asked, "What happened? How did you survive?"

Alexander smiled. "By God's grace alone." She could see his eyes were wet with tears.

The others met them now. Surviving residents of Jerusalem. He introduced each of them to Cassandra.

He told her, "Hundreds of us were hiding in the tunnels beneath the city. The Romans found us and slaughtered us like lambs." He held his wound and smiled. "But there were so many of us, they didn't wait around to make sure we were all dead."

His brightness dimmed. "I had been protected by a brother in the Lord whose body shielded me from a wound that could have been fatal."

Someone in the group spoke out, "If it were not for your husband, we wouldn't be here."

She looked him in the eye. "I have so much to tell you."

"And I, you."

She held him up as they made their way into the city.

"How are the children?" he asked.

"Noah has become quite a young man—and warrior. Samuel is two years old. He's walking now."

Alexander began to tear up.

She reluctantly added, "And I think he sees angels."

Alexander looked at her, surprised. She nodded. She wasn't joking. He smiled with joy. "Thank God he's not like his father."

They walked on.

But he stopped her. "You didn't mention Rachel. How is Rachel?" He looked like he didn't want to hear her answer.

Cassandra's look was grave. "You are about to lose your daughter."

"What do you mean? Is she sick?"

"Yes." She said. But then she beamed into a grin. "She is sick in love." Her voice cracked. "And you made it just in time to give away your daughter in marriage."

He was stunned. "She's getting married?"

Cassandra hadn't known his eyes could open any wider. Turning to his companions, he exclaimed, "My daughter is getting married!" He stopped and turned back to Cassandra. "Wait a second. To whom?"

She smiled. "He's a fine young man named Jonathan. Don't worry, you'll meet him soon."

He turned back to his companions, and they congratulated him. For a single moment in time, the entire band of wounded appeared to be completely unaware of their pain as they focused on the joy of this man who had given everything for them.

After they had congratulated him, Alexander seemed to limp even faster toward home.

She heard him muttering, "I do not deserve such happiness. Thank you, Lord Jesus, thank you." He turned to Cassandra and said, "I have been away for too long."

"So have I," she responded. "So have I."

CHAPTER 72

The wedding reminded Alexander of his own wedding to Cassandra just a few years ago. The joy, the celebration, the hope. Samuel had been sitting on his lap, but the child soon squirmed his way off, and Noah had to take him.

Okay, thought Alexander. *He doesn't know me yet*. It would take some time for a child of two to warm up to a father he had never known. Even Noah and Rachel had not had the time to get to know their adopted father. Alexander would be patient. He had time. He finally had time.

When Alexander had first met Samuel, he could not help but cry with joy, which had frightened the little lad. Alexander had cried a lot with his new family.

Rachel had turned pale at his appearance as though seeing a ghost, swaying as though she might faint. But Jonathan had immediately stepped forward to offer support, which made Alexander immediately like the young man. And some time spent with him assured Alexander that Jonathan would be a fine husband for Rachel.

Noah had at first stayed away from Alexander, avoiding his touch. The feeling of abandonment ran deep in his life. Alexander didn't blame him. But Noah soon got over it and had much to tell Alexander about all he had learned from Michael and the Kharabu.

Now here they were at the wedding feast dancing, eating, drinking, and celebrating a new life for a future Christian family. The ceremony had been touching but triggered many thoughts in Alexander's mind. As he watched Rachel travel the streets with her wedding party in her beautiful dress and ornaments, his heart filled with gladness at the chance to see her so happy and to gain a new son-in-law.

It made him think of Jesus's parables of the kingdom's wedding feast. The five virgins who didn't have the oil of the endurance of faith to meet Messiah when he came were shut out of the kingdom. But five had rejoiced in the day.[1] Similarly, the apostate Jews who had rejected the offer of Messiah were not allowed into the wedding feast of the Lamb. Their city had been destroyed and the celebration offered to others. Those without the wedding garments of faith had been cast into outer darkness with weeping and gnashing of teeth. For many are called, but few are chosen.[2]

It was the sad irony of the kingdom of God that the marriage feast of the Lamb included both the joy of redemption and the suffering of war. Both deliverance and judgment. Their nation had just gone through the most devastating event in her history. Many of their friends and family had perished in the war with Rome. But now the Remnant were here rejoicing with a feast of hope for the future.

Alexander got up at the appropriate moment and gave a toast to the bride and bridegroom. He saw the happiness on Rachel's and Jonathan's faces. And Cassandra's. He lifted his chalice to the couple.

"Rachel and Jonathan. May you have many years of happiness and many children to keep you from becoming too selfish!"

Everyone laughed and drank.

He continued, "As you know, my family had suffered separation these past few years because of the will of God. I thank those of you who helped my wife and children until I returned." He looked at Rachel. "Rachel, I have missed you." She was already crying. "I have missed your coming of age, your discovery of love. But I thank God I did not miss your wedding."

Several friends shouted out, "Amen! Amen!"

He looked at the handsome young bridegroom. "And Jonathan, just as the Father watches over the bride of Christ, so I too stand watching over you—with a gladius in my hand."

Alexander waited for the laughs to subside before turning serious again.

"I wanted to take a moment to remind us of another marriage feast of which we Christians all partake. The wedding feast of the Lamb. During the days of Moses, our people wandered in the wilderness for forty years while Yahweh destroyed that adulterous generation so that the Remnant would inherit the Promised Land. And when they did, Yahweh gave them the Feast of Tabernacles to commemorate that he was with them in that time of suffering, of endurance, and of ultimate victory."[3]

Voices of agreement peppered the crowd.

"So too, the Bride of Christ has had our forty years of wilderness from the ministry of Jesus until now, when the adulterous generation was destroyed. So, too, do we enter into our inheritance of the kingdom of God because Jesus fulfills the Feast of Tabernacles. He is God dwelling with us and in us as his tabernacle.

Jesus the Messiah is our temple. He is our Jerusalem, our Mount Zion. Jesus is our Promised Land. And he is our bridegroom of marriage."[4]

The sound of the crowd cheering gave Alexander deep joy as he looked at Cassandra, her look beaming with pride at her husband. She held his hand and squeezed it lovingly.

Rachel came out from her table with Jonathan to hug and kiss Alexander and Cassandra.

Alexander looked over his family and thought of the symbol of a spiritual tree. The seed of little Samuel watched over by young warrior Noah. The growing branch of Rachel and Jonathan. And Cassandra, his devoted, loyal, and godly wife. They were all grafted onto Jesus, the root of Israel.

> *"I, Jesus, have sent my angel to testify to you about these things for the churches. I am the root and the descendant of David, the bright morning star." The Spirit and the Bride say, "Come." And let the one who hears say, "Come." And let the one who is thirsty come; let the one who desires take the water of life without price."*
>
> *Apocalypse 22:16–17*

EPILOGUE

The Jewish historian Josephus wrote that over one million Jews perished in the siege of Jerusalem. Ninety-nine thousand were made slaves and used in the Roman arena for sport. He concluded with prophetic hyperbole, "The multitude of those that therein perished exceeded all the destructions that either men or God ever brought upon the world."[1]

After the destruction of Jerusalem and the holy temple, a thousand Zealot rebels and their families fled to the fortress of Masada near the Dead Sea, only to find themselves again under siege by the Romans. All thousand Jews committed suicide rather than submit to Caesar.[2]

Simon bar Giora was brought back to the eternal city of Rome, paraded through the streets in a triumphal procession, and then hanged.[3]

The Roman triumph included the wealth of Jerusalem and holy instruments of the temple such as the golden menorah lampstand.[4]

Vespasian ruled as emperor for ten years until his death in AD 79. He helped rebuild Rome and established a new family dynasty that replaced the Julio-Claudian line.[5]

Titus led the triumphal procession in Rome for his victory in the Judean campaign and siege of Jerusalem. He became emperor at his father's death in AD 79.[6]

Berenice accompanied Titus to Rome with the intention of marrying him and becoming empress. But the Roman people rejected her, so Titus discarded her and she faded into obscurity.[7]

Herod Agrippa II received more territory from Caesar for his loyalty during the Judean campaign. He died, the last prince of the house of Herod.[8]

Josephus became a client historian for Vespasian. He would write the only existing detailed history of the Revolt of the Jews. He was branded a traitor by many of his countrymen.[9]

Yohanan ben Zakkai and his school at Yavneh created a new version of Judaism based on rabbinic writings in order to accommodate the lack of a temple. Judaism was no longer Torah-based.[10]

The Dead Sea community of Qumran disappeared into the mists of history until 1948 when some of its ancient scrolls were discovered in secret caves. Amongst them was a mysterious copper scroll containing a list of hidden treasures.[11]

Not one stone of the earthly temple in Jerusalem was left upon another. It has never been rebuilt.[12] The Messianic temple had arrived.[13]

Christianity overcame its humble and persecuted beginnings to eventually destroy the rule and authority of ancient Rome. The stone cut without hands had brought down the mighty empire with a kingdom that would never be destroyed, a mountain that would grow to fill the whole earth.[14]

Then comes the end, when Christ delivers the kingdom to God the Father after destroying every rule and every authority and power. For he must reign until he has put all his enemies under his feet.

1 Corinthians 15:24–26

Then I saw a great white throne and him who was seated on it. From his presence earth and sky fled away, and no place was found for them. And I saw the dead, great and small, standing before the throne, and books were opened. Then another book was opened, which is the book of life. And the dead were judged by what was written in the books, according to what they had done. And the sea gave up the dead who were in it, Death and Hades gave up the dead who were in them, and they were judged, each one of them, according to what they had done. Then Death and Hades were thrown into the lake of fire.

Apocalypse 20:11–14

• • • • •

If you liked this book, then please help me out by writing a positive review of it wherever you purchased it. That is one of the best ways to say thank you to me as an author. It really does help my sales and status. Thanks! – *Brian Godawa*

More Books by Brian Godawa

See www.Godawa.com for more information on other books by Brian Godawa. Check out his other series below:

Chronicles of the Nephilim

Chronicles of the Nephilim is a saga that charts the rise and fall of the Nephilim giants of Genesis 6 and their place in the evil plans of the fallen angelic Sons of God called, "The Watchers." The story starts in the days of Enoch and continues on through the Bible until the arrival of the Messiah, Jesus. The prelude to Chronicles of the Apocalypse. ChroniclesOfTheNephilim.com

Chronicles of the Watchers

Chronicles of the Watchers is a series that charts the influence of spiritual principalities and powers over the course of human history. The kingdoms of man in service to the gods of the nations at war. Completely based on ancient historical and mythological research. ChroniclesOfTheWatchers.com

• • • • •

Biblical & Historical Research

For additional free biblical and historical scholarly research related to this novel and series, go to Godawa.com > Chronicles of the Apocalypse > *Scholarly Research.*

BIBLIOGRAPHY OF BOOKS ON BIBLE PROPHECY THAT INFLUENCED AUTHOR BRIAN GODAWA

For additional biblical and historical research related to this series, go to www.ChroniclesoftheApocalypse.com and Click on Scholarly Research.

John L. Bray, *Matthew 24 Fulfilled*, (American Vision; 5th Edition, 2009).

David Chilton, *The Days of Vengeance: An Exposition of the Book of Revelation*, (Dominion Press; 1st Edition, 2006).

Gary DeMar, *10 Popular Prophecy Myths Exposed: The Last Days Might Not Be as Near as You Think*, (American Vision, 2010).

– *Last Days Madness: Obsession of the Modern Church* Wolgemuth & Hyatt Pub; 4th Revised edition (September 1999).

– *Left Behind: Separating Fact From Fiction*, (American Vision; First edition, 2010).

– *Why the End of the World is Not in Your Future: Identifying the Gog-Magog Alliance*, (American Vision; First edition, 2010)

Kenneth L. Gentry, Jr., *The Beast of Revelation*, (American Vision, 2002).

– *Before Jerusalem Fell: Dating the Book of Revelation*, (Victorious Hope Publishing, 2010)

– *The Book of Revelation Made Easy: You Can Understand Bible Prophecy*, American Vision (December 31, 2009).

– *The Divorce of Israel: A Redemptive-Historical Interpretation of Revelation Vol. 1 & 2*, (Liberty Alliance, 2016).

– *Navigating the Book of Revelation: Special Studies on Important Issues*, (GoodBirth Ministries, 2011).

– *The Olivet Discourse Made Easy*, (Apologetics Group. 2010)

– *Perilous Times: A Study in Eschatological Evil*, (Covenant Media Press, 1999).

Kenneth L. Gentry Jr., and Thomas Ice, *The Great Tribulation: Past or Future?: Two Evangelicals Debate the Question*, (Kregel Academic & Professional, 1999).

John H. Gerstner, *Wrongly Dividing the Word of Truth: A Critique of Dispensationalism 3rd Edition* (Nicene Council, 2009).

Hank Hanegraaff, *The Apocalypse Code: Find out What the Bible Really Says About the End Times and Why It Matters Today,* (Thomas Nelson, 2010).

George Peter Holford, *The Destruction of Jerusalem: An Absolute and Irresistible Proof of the Divine Origin of Christianity*, (Covenant Media Press; 6th American edition, 2001).

Peter J. Leithart, *The Promise of His Appearing: An Exposition of Second Peter* (Canon Press, 2004).

Keith A. Mathison, *Dispensationalism: Rightly Dividing the People of God?* (P & R Publishing, 1995).

Philip Mauro, *The Seventy Weeks and the Great Tribulation: A Study of the Last Two Visions of Daniel and the Olivet Discourse of the Lord Jesus Christ* (Hamilton Brothers, 1922).

R.C. Sproul, *The Last Days According to Jesus: When Did Jesus Say He Would Return? 2nd Edition,* (Baker Pub Group, 1998).

If You Like This Novel
Get This Free eBook
Limited Time Offer

FREE

The Research Notes behind the Novel Series
Chronicles of the Apocalypse

By Brian Godawa. Over one hundred pages of Biblical and historical sources, with citations, addressing each verse in Matthew 24.

Download
Free eBook

https://godawa.com/matthew-24/

Get the Theology behind
This Novel Series

The Biblical Theology behind
Chronicles of the Apocalypse

By Brian Godawa

Brian Godawa reveals the Biblical and historical basis for the Last Days presented in the novel series *Chronicles of the Apocalypse*. Godawa unveils the biblical meaning of many End Times notions like the Last Days, cosmic catastrophes, the Abomination of Desolation, the antichrist, the Great Tribulation, and more!

Available in eBook, Paperback & Audiobook

https://godawa.com/get-end-times/

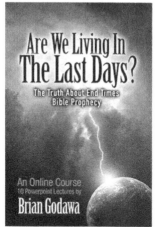

317

GET MORE BIBLICAL IMAGINATION

Get More
Biblical Imagination

Sign up Online For The Godawa Chronicles

www.Godawa.com

Insider information on the novels of Brian Godawa
Special Discounts, New Releases,
Bible Mysteries!

We won't spam you.

CHRONICLES OF THE NEPHILIM

The Prequel Series to Chronicles of the Apocalypse.
Nephilim Giants, Watchers, Cosmic War.

www.Godawa.com

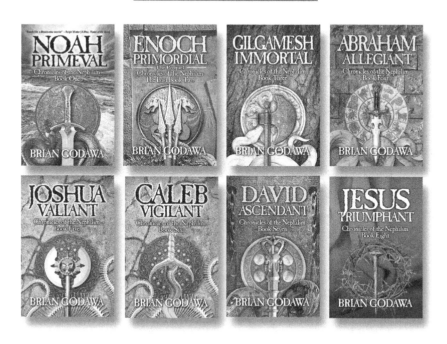

CHRONICLES OF THE WATCHERS

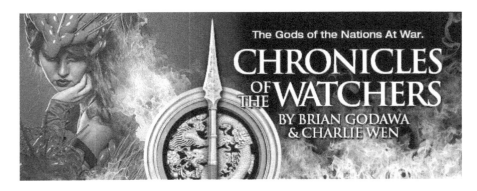

A Series About the Watchers in History.
Action, Romance, Gods, Monsters & Men.

The first novel is *Jezebel: Harlot Queen of Israel.*

www.Godawa.com

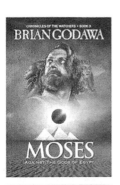
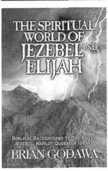
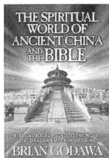
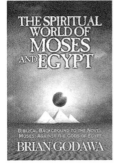

ABOUT THE AUTHOR

Brian Godawa is the screenwriter for the award-winning feature film, *To End All Wars*, starring Kiefer Sutherland. It was awarded the Commander in Chief Medal of Service, Honor and Pride by the Veterans of Foreign Wars, won the first Heartland Film Festival by storm, and showcased the Cannes Film Festival Cinema for Peace.

He previously adapted to film the best-selling supernatural thriller novel *The Visitation* by author Frank Peretti for Ralph Winter (*X-Men, Wolverine*), and wrote and directed *Wall of Separation*, a PBS documentary, and *Lines That Divide*, a documentary on stem cell research.

Mr. Godawa's scripts have won multiple awards in respected screenplay competitions, and his articles on movies and philosophy have been published around the world. He has traveled around the United States teaching on movies, worldviews, and culture to colleges, churches and community groups.

His popular book *Hollywood Worldviews: Watching Films with Wisdom and Discernment* (InterVarsity Press) is used as a textbook in schools around the country. In the Top 10 of Biblical Fiction on Amazon, his first novel series, *Chronicles of the Nephilim*, is an imaginative retelling of Biblical stories of the Nephilim giants, the secret plan of the fallen Watchers, and the War of the Seed of the Serpent with the Seed of Eve. The sequel series, *Chronicles of the Apocalypse*, tells the story of the apostle John's book of Revelation, and *Chronicles of the Watchers* recounts true history through the Watcher paradigm.

Find out more about his other books, lecture tapes and DVDs for sale at his website, www.godawa.com.

End Notes for Judgment: Wrath of the Lamb

[1] With the death of Nero, the "death" of the Julio-Claudian line spelled the death of the empire. But Vespasian would save it. This matches with Revelations' notion that one head of the Beast dies with a mortal wound, but is miraculously healed. The empire was "healed" with Vespasian.

> Revelation 13:3
> One of its heads seemed to have a mortal wound, but its mortal wound was healed, and the whole earth marveled as they followed the beast.

"The upheaval caused by the death of Nero, Rome's head (the beast specifically considered), would strike both the subjects and the enemies of the vast empire as being the very death throes of the empire itself (the beast generically considered)...

But then the unthinkable occurred, the fatally-struck beast arose – his fatal wound was healed (13:3a). This pictures the surprising resurgence of the dying empire by Vespasian's coming to power. Suetonius (Vesp. 1) writes: "The empire, which for a long time had been unsettled and, as it were, drifting through the usurpation and violent death of three emperors, was at last taken in hand and given stability by the Flavian family."

Kenneth L. Gentry, Jr., The Divorce of Israel: A Redemptive-Historical Interpretation of Revelation Vol. 2 (Dallas, GA: Tolle Lege Press, 2016), 205-208..

[2] The seventh king would reign a short while: This series has explained that Nero is the sixth king of Revelation 17:10. He was the king that "is" at the time of John's writing. But the king after him would only reign a short while. That king as Galba, who was Caesar for only a short six months.

> Revelation 17:9–10
> [9] This calls for a mind with wisdom: the seven heads are seven mountains on which the woman is seated; [10] they are also seven kings, five of whom have fallen, one is, the other has not yet come, and when he does come he must remain only a little while.

[3] Prophecy of a "ruler from the east" or "from Judea": "But now, what did most elevate them [the Jews] in undertaking this war was an ambiguous oracle that was found in their sacred writings, how, "about that time, one from their country should become governor of the habitable earth." The Jews took this prediction to belong to themselves in particular; and many of their wise men were thereby deceived in their determination. Now, this oracle certainly denoted the government of Vespasian, who was appointed emperor in Judea." Flavius Josephus, The Wars of the Jews, 6.5.4.

[Some understand that this meant Herod, others the crucified wonder-worker Jesus, others again Vespasian.] Slavonic addition, Loeb, vol. 2, p. 658.

"The majority were convinced that the ancient scriptures of their priests alluded to the present as the very time when the Orient would triumph and from Judaea would go forth men destined to rule the world. This mysterious prophecy really referred to Vespasian and Titus, but the common people, true to the selfish ambitions of mankind, thought that this exalted destiny was reserved for them, and not even their calamities opened their eyes to the truth." Tacitus, The Histories, 5.13.

"It may be that mysterious prophecies were already circulating, and that portents and oracles promised Vespasian and his sons the purple; but it was only after the rise of the Flavians that we Romans believed in such stories." Tacitus, The Histories, 1. 10.

"An ancient superstition was current in the East, that out of Judea would come the rulers of the world. This prediction, as it later proved, referred to the two Roman Emperors, Vespasian and his son Titus; but the rebellious Jews, who read it as referring to themselves, murdered their Procurator, routed the Governor-general of Syria when he came down to restore order, and captured an Eagle." Suetonius, Lives of the Twelve Caesars, Vespasian, 4.

These passages were drawn from a chart by C.N. Carrington on his article, "The Favian Testament" that details the oracles surrounding Vespasian as "the ruler" and their interpretations at the time. http://carrington-

[4] Vespasian secures the grain of Egypt:

Flavius Josephus, *The Wars of the Jews* 4.10.5, §605
"5. (605) So upon the exhortations of Mucianus and the other commanders, that he would accept of the empire, and upon that of the rest of the army, who cried out that they were willing to be led against all his opposers, he was in the first place intent upon gaining the dominion over Alexandria, as knowing that Egypt was of the greatest consequence, in order to obtain the entire government, because of its supplying corn [to Rome]; (606) which corn, if he could be master of, he hoped to dethrone Vitellus, supposing he should aim to keep the empire by force (for he would not be able to support himself, if the multitude at Rome should once be in want of food); and because he was desirous to join the two legions that were at Alexandria to the other legions that were with him."

Flavius Josephus and William Whiston, *The Works of Josephus: Complete and Unabridged* (Peabody: Hendrickson, 1987), 693.

Nero dying is the Beast's head mortally wounded because the entire history of the Julio-Claudian line was dead. But the Flavians starting a new dynasty revived the Beast of Rome:

Revelation 13:3
One of its heads seemed to have a mortal wound, but its mortal wound was healed, and the whole earth marveled as they followed the beast.

[5] Ten horns as ten client kings of Rome:

Revelation 17:12–17
[12] And the ten horns that you saw are ten kings who have not yet received royal power, but they are to receive authority as kings for one hour, together with the beast. [13] These are of one mind, and they hand over their power and authority to the beast. [14] They will make war on the Lamb, and the Lamb will conquer them, for he is Lord of lords and King of kings, and those with him are called and chosen and faithful." [15] And the angel said to me, "The waters that you saw, where the prostitute is seated, are peoples and multitudes and nations and languages. [16] And the ten horns that you saw, they and the beast will hate the prostitute. They will make her desolate and naked, and devour her flesh and burn her up with fire, [17] for God has put it into their hearts to carry out his purpose by being of one mind and handing over their royal power to the beast, until the words of God are fulfilled.

"Though provincial governors are quite possibly in view, I am inclined, however, to see them as does Aune (951): "Here the ten kings represent Roman client kings." Rome's system of client kingship was such that kings (including even ethnarchs, tetrarchs, etc.) were appointed by Roman authorities from within various localities. They were responsible for keeping the peace, assisting Rome with defense, and ensuring the flow of tribute money to Rome. They would provide soldiers "as part of tribute, or through friendships and alliances" (Gilliver 2001: 24). During Nero's rule "the client system of the East [including Judea] was then revealed at its most efficient" (Luttwak 1976: 112)...

"Archelaus himself recognized that "the power of disposing of it [his kingdom rule] belonged to Caesar, who could either give it to him or not, as he pleased" (Ant. 17:11:2 §312). Their rule was tenuous, so that John could say "they receive authority"; that authority was "with the beast"; and it was for "one hour."

"Client kings, such as the Antiochus, Agrippa, Sohemus, Malchus, and Alexander provided auxiliary forces for Rome during the Jewish War (J.W. 2:18:9 §499–501; 3:4:2 §68; 5:1:6 §45) (cf. Aune 951; Stuart 2:327). Dio Cassius (65:4:3) mentions that the Roman siege of Jerusalem included "many slingers and bows that had been sent by some of the barbarian kings." In fact, "a Roman army on campaign always included a complement of allies.... Rome relied very heavily on others for her cavalry forces" in that "such troops might have local knowledge of topography and the enemy, and could provide specialist fighting techniques appropriate to the situation" (Gillver 2001: 22; cp. Grant 1974: 77). The auxiliary forces in the empire after Augustus comprised about half of Rome's military might (cf. Luttwak 1976: 16; cf. Tac., Ann. 4:5)." Kenneth L. Gentry, Jr., *The Divorce of Israel: A Redemptive-Historical Interpretation of Revelation Vol. 2* (Dallas, GA: Tolle Lege Press, 2016), 474-475.

The Ten Client Kings Named: We do not know them all, but Wellesley lists 8 of them (assuming Berenice is not counted as a king). Malchus of Nabatea makes the 9th (*Wars of the Jews* 3.4.2), and Tiberius Alexander, governor of Egypt makes 10 (*Wars of the Jews* 4.10.6): "Mucianus, governor of Syria; Sohaemus of Emesa, Antiochus IV, ruler of Comagene, King Agrippa, sheikh of Anjar and Golan; Berenice, widow of Herod of Anjar. "We are not surprised to learn that the governors of all the provinces of Asia Minor, through disposing of no legionary garrisons, had promised such support in supplies, facilities and auxiliary forces as they could give and Vespasian might require. Among them were the proconsul of Asia, Gaius Fonteius Agrippa, and the legate of Galatia-with-Pamphylia, Lucius Nonius Calpurnius Asprenas. Both In addition, there was Cappadocia, still a procuratorial province governed by a knight without the legionary garrison which Vespasian himself was to give it; its governor in 69 is unknown, and equally unknown is the governor of Pontus, added to Bithynia five years before." Kenneth Wellesley, *Year of the Four Emperors* (Taylor and Francis, 2014) 123-124.

"According to David S. Clark,

"These ten horns were ten kings, not kings sitting on the throne of Rome, as I understand, but those kings and countries subjected by Rome, and which made the empire great. We know that Rome embraced at that time the countries of Europe that bordered on the Mediterranean Sea, and the northern part of Africa and considerable territory in Asia, and also in central Europe. Rome had conquered the world.

Adams writes that,

"the ten horns may represent the provincial governors and their provinces which at first gave support to Rome (vv. 12, 13), and in turn received their authority from her. They persecute Christians in carrying out her interdicts against them (v. 14). But in the end, it is these provinces which turned upon and destroyed Rome (v. 16).

According to Russell,

"on the whole, we conclude that this symbol signifies the auxiliary princes and chiefs who were allies of Rome and received commands in the Roman army during the Jewish war. We know from Tacitus and Josephus that several kings of neighboring nations followed Vespasian and Titus to the war.... It is not incumbent to produce the exact number of ten, which, like seven, appears to be a mystic or symbolic number.

Chilton writes:

"Rome actually had ten imperial provinces, and some have read this as a reference to them. It is not necessary, however, to attempt a precise definition of these ten subject kings; the symbol simply represents [quoting Terry] "the totality of those allied or subject kings who aided Rome in her wars both on Judaism and Christianity."

Steve Gregg, *Revelation, Four Views: A Parallel Commentary* (Nashville, TN: T. Nelson Publishers, 1997), 414–416.

[6] Titus as Caesar:

It is important to understand Revelation by realizing that there are several representatives of the Beast of Rome. Though Vespasian becomes the new Caesar, Titus carries his title and represents Caesar's very authority where he is. This explains why historically the prophecies about the Beast in Revelation are fluid in their application.

Cassius Dio, *Roman History* 65.1.1
"Such was the course of these events; and following them Vespasian was declared emperor by the senate also, and Titus and Domitian were given the title of Caesars. The consular office was assumed by Vespasian and Titus while the former was in Egypt and the latter in Palestine."

http://penelope.uchicago.edu/Thayer/E/Roman/Texts/Cassius_Dio/65*.html

Upon Vespasian's ascent to Caesar, he gave the title of Caesar to Titus: "There also had to be consulships for Vespasian and Titus, and a praetorship with imperium equal to a consul's for Domitian. The young men were each honoured with the designation 'Caesar.'" Barbara Levick, *Vespasian* (New York: Rutledge, 1999) 79.

"Vespasian bestowed the title of Caesar on Titus in AD 69. Roman historian Mary Smallwood writes the

324

following on this. 'The title 'Caesar' was conferred on both Vespasian's sons [Titus and Domitian] when he became emperor.[From this point on in The Jewish War] Josephus frequently refers to Titus simply as 'Caesar.'" (e.g., 'the men on the the the wall hurled insults at Caesar himself and at his father.' The Jewish War, 5.11.2)" Duncan MacKenzie, Ph.D. *The Antichrist and the Second Coming: A Preterist Examination Vol 2: The Book of Revelation* (Xulon Press, 2012) 157.

Titus was called Caesar by Josephus:

Flavius Josephus, *The Wars of the Jews* 5.2.2, §63
[during the siege of Jerusalem] The enemy indeed made a great shout at the boldness of Caesar [Titus], and exhorted one another to rush upon him..."

Flavius Josephus and William Whiston, *The Works of Josephus: Complete and Unabridged* (Peabody: Hendrickson, 1987), 700.

Flavius Josephus, *The Wars of the Jews* 3.8.9, §401
[Josephus describing his dream] "Thou, O Vespasian, art Caesar and emperor, thou, and this thy son."

Flavius Josephus and William Whiston, *The Works of Josephus: Complete and Unabridged* (Peabody: Hendrickson, 1987), 657.

[7] Three-fold division of Jerusalem:

Revelation 16:19
[19] The great city was split into three parts, and the cities of the nations fell, and God remembered Babylon the great, to make her drain the cup of the wine of the fury of his wrath.

"Revelation speaks of a three-fold division in the city (16:19). We learn from Josephus (J.W. 5:1:4 §21) that "there were three treacherous factions in the city, the one parted from the other. Eleazar and his party, that kept the sacred firstfruits, came against John in their cups. Those that were with John plundered the populace, and went out with zeal against Simon. This Simon had his supply of provisions from the city, in oppositions to the seditious" (cp. Witherington 2001b: 359; Buchanan 119, 431, 530). This division was significant enough that even the Roman historian Tacitus mentions that "there were three generals, three armies" fighting inside Jerusalem (Hist 5:12:3). In fact, Josephus (J.W. 5:1:1 §3) sees this as "the beginning of the city's destruction." The problem of factionalism which eventually led to the three-fold division in Jerusalem."

Kenneth L. Gentry, Jr., *The Divorce of Israel: A Redemptive-Historical Interpretation of Revelation Vol. 2* (Dallas, GA: Tolle Lege Press, 2016), 376-378.

"First, as a practical matter it seems virtually impossible that a quake could literally divide a city into three parts. Actual earthquakes do not divide cities, they desolate them by toppling buildings (Jer 51:29; Eze 38:19-20; Nah 1:5-6; Ac 16:26). Besides, this quake occurring in Jerusalem is called "a great earthquake, such as there had not been since man came upon the earth, so great an earthquake was it, and so mighty" (16:18b). Surely if literal (or even hyperbolical), this would not merely divide the city into three different parts. Interestingly, Josephus records an earthquake during Herod's reign using similar hyperbolic language, and it certainly does not merely divide the city: "Then it was also that there was an earthquake in Judea, such a one as had not happened at any other time, and which earthquake brought a great destruction upon the cattle in that country. About ten thousand men also perished by the fall of houses" (Ant 15:5:2 §121–22; cp. J.W. 1:20:3 §370).

"Second, as a literary matter we note that every island and mountain disappears, which cannot be literal (see discussion below). The islands are even personified as fleeing away (ephugen), not collapsing into the sea (cf. Ps 46:2). All of them. And if all mountains disappeared, Jerusalem would have been absolutely devastated (not divided) because it was built on a mountain: "The city was built upon two hills, which are opposite to one another, and have a valley to divide them asunder; at which valley the corresponding rows of houses on both hills end" (J.W. 5:4:1 §136).

"Third, we find the fuller description of Babylon's fall in Revelation 17–18, and "since the fall of Babylon takes place already in 16.19, it appears that Revelation 17:1–18.24 serves as a parenthetical expansion to describe and explain the Babylon theme in more detail"

[1] **Apollyon as Satan:** "This angel is named only here in Revelation [9:11 as Apollyon], and elsewhere in the OT and early Jewish literature is mentioned only in 4Q280 10 ii 7:"[Cursed be you Angel of the Pit, and Spirit of Abaddon" (Kobelski, Melchizedek, 43–44). While in 4Q280 and related texts these two titles are alternate ways of describing Belial, in Revelation it is not at all clear that the angel of the abyss is a designation for Satan, for he is carefully named elsewhere with a selection of aliases in two different contexts (12:9; 20:2), and neither Abaddon nor the angel of the abyss is mentioned again. The fact that ἄγγελον is articular here, however, suggests that the author expected the readers to be familiar with this figure, i.e., that the angel of the abyss is none other than Satan-Belial." David E. Aune, *Revelation 6–16, vol. 52B, Word Biblical Commentary* (Dallas: Word, Incorporated, 1998), 534.

"The "Destroyer" in Rev. 9:11 is either the devil himself or an evil representative of the devil; either alternative receives confirmation from Jewish exegetical tradition on Exodus (see below). Rev. 12:3–4 and 13:1ff. are compatible with this conclusion, since there the devil and the Beast respectively are pictured wearing royal diadems and leading evil forces. This is also in line with the same conclusion already reached about the angel's identification in 9:1." G. K. Beale, *The Book of Revelation: A Commentary on the Greek Text, New International Greek Testament Commentary* (Grand Rapids, MI; Carlisle, Cumbria: W.B. Eerdmans; Paternoster Press, 1999), 503.

"The title "angel of the abyss" is not found anywhere else in antiquity except in 2Q280. The demons this trumpet unleashes upon Jerusalem are under the dominion of a king whose name in Hebrew is Abaddon, and in the Greek he has the name Apollyon (9:11b). …The following evidence suggests to me that this "king" is Satan: (1) John describes him both as a "king" as well as "the angel of the abyss" (from which come the demons; 9:1–3). In Scripture, Satan functions as an evil ruler of great power in the fallen world (Mt 4:8; Jn 12:31; 14:30; 16:11; 1Jo 5:19), and even as the ruler of demons (Mt 9:34; 12:24–27; Lk 10:17–18; Eph 2:2; cp. Jub. 11:15; 17:16; 18:9, 12; 48:2–15). In fact, the Bible calls fallen angels (demons) "his angels" (Mt 25:41; Rev 12:9). Later in Revelation, we see Satan appearing as a dragon with diadems, showing his kingship (12:3).

"(2) John refers to him as "the angel of the abyss [ton aggelon tēs abussou]," where the definite article suggests this angel is well-known. Satan is certainly a well-known figure in Scripture and in first-century Judaism. John even mentions him in Revelation four times before now (2:9, 13, 24; 3:9). (3) The symbolic names given to him, "Apollyon" and "Abaddon" (9:11b), both mean "destroyer," which fits Satan's character and work (1Co 5:5; Eph 6:11; Heb 2:14; 1Pe 5:8). This is true even in Revelation where he seeks to destroy Jesus at his birth (12:3–4) and then his saints (12:12–13, 17). Indeed, the name "Satan" means "adversary" which comports with the concept of "destroyer" – since he seeks a legal means to destroy God's people (e.g., 2:9–10). So once again we see Satan's work among the Christ-denying Jews, as per Christ's declaration that their father is the devil (Jn 8:44) and that they are a "synagogue of Satan" (Rev 2:9; 3:9). They are now receiving their just desserts: Satan sends his demon army to sorely afflict them.

"John's Greek abbadōn is a transliteration of the Hebrew ʾbaddōn, which appears in the Old Testament only in the Wisdom literature (Job 26:6; 28:22; 31:12; Ps 88:11; Pr 15:11; 27:20). It also appears four times in the DSS (NIDOTTE 1:226). It means "destruction" and in the LXX is always translated by apōleia ("destruction, annihilation), except in Job 31:12 which translates it apolluein. In Job 31:12 it is the place of destruction, whereas elsewhere it parallels Sheol (Job 26:6; Pr 15:11; 27:20), death (Job 28:22), or the grave (Ps 88:11), and is thus strongly associated with death. The word "Apollyon" is apolluōn in the Greek: it is the present participle of apollumi, which means to "destroy." Like the Hebrew ʾbaddōn it is often used to refer to killing (Mt 2:13; 12:114; 27:20; Mk 3:6; 9:41; 11:18; Lk 11:51; 12:33; 15:17; 17:27; 19:47). Satan himself virtually personifies death in Heb 2:14b: "who had the power of death, that is, the devil" (cp. 1Co 5:5).

"In addition to the designation "Apollyon" referring to Satan as the "destroyer," the term has an "etymological connection" with the name of Apollo the sun god and may therefore allude to him (Smalley 234; cp. Caird 120; Sweet 170; TDNT 1:397; Beagley 54; Ford 152; Morris 128; Lupieri 163; M. Wilson 2002: 305; Boxall 145; Osborne 374). If so, Apollo would serve as a link to the Roman emperor Nero who held Apollo as his patron deity. Suetonius notes that Nero drove a chariot in the games (Nero 24:2) mimicking Apollo. Nero "was acclaimed as the equal of Apollo in music and of the Sun in driving a chariot" (Nero 53)." Kenneth L. Gentry, Jr., *The Divorce of Israel: A Redemptive-Historical Interpretation of Revelation Vol. 1* (Dallas, GA: Tolle Lege

Press, 2016), 750-752.

2 Apollyon is referring to Jesus' prophecy:

Matthew 23:34–24:2
34 Therefore I send you prophets and wise men and scribes, some of whom you will kill and crucify, and some you will flog in your synagogues and persecute from town to town, 35 so that on you may come all the righteous blood shed on earth, from the blood of righteous Abel to the blood of Zechariah the son of Barachiah, whom you murdered between the sanctuary and the altar. 36 Truly, I say to you, all these things will come upon this generation. 37 "O Jerusalem, Jerusalem, the city that kills the prophets and stones those who are sent to it! How often would I have gathered your children together as a hen gathers her brood under her wings, and you were not willing! 38 See, your house is left to you desolate... 1 Jesus left the temple and was going away, when his disciples came to point out to him the buildings of the temple. 2 But he answered them, "You see all these, do you not? Truly, I say to you, there will not be left here one stone upon another that will not be thrown down."

3 **The rebellion of the angels led by Azazel and Semyaza**: 1 Enoch 9:7-9; 10:4-13. Their story is fictionalized in the novel, *Enoch Primordial*, book 2 of *Chronicles of the Nephilim* (Embedded Pictures Publishing, 2014)

Watchers cast into Tartarus: Jude 12-16: 2 Peter 2:4-11, 17; Genesis 6:1-4. 1 Enoch 1-16 (Book of the Watchers) is an extended amplification of the Genesis 6 passage. My novel series *Chronicles of the Nephilim* recounts the story of the Fall of the Watchers in *Enoch Primordial* and *Noah Primeval*.

4 Apollyon's connection to the locust demons:

Revelation 9:1–11
1 And the fifth angel blew his trumpet, and I saw a star fallen from heaven to earth, and he was given the key to the shaft of the bottomless pit. 2 He opened the shaft of the bottomless pit, and from the shaft rose smoke like the smoke of a great furnace, and the sun and the air were darkened with the smoke from the shaft. 3 Then from the smoke came locusts on the earth, and they were given power like the power of scorpions of the earth. 4 They were told not to harm the grass of the earth or any green plant or any tree, but only those people who do not have the seal of God on their foreheads. 5 They were allowed to torment them for five months, but not to kill them, and their torment was like the torment of a scorpion when it stings someone. 6 And in those days people will seek death and will not find it. They will long to die, but death will flee from them. 7 In appearance the locusts were like horses prepared for battle: on their heads were what looked like crowns of gold; their faces were like human faces, 8 their hair like women's hair, and their teeth like lions' teeth; 9 they had breastplates like breastplates of iron, and the noise of their wings was like the noise of many chariots with horses rushing into battle. 10 They have tails and stings like scorpions, and their power to hurt people for five months is in their tails. 11 They have as king over them the angel of the bottomless pit. His name in Hebrew is Abaddon, and in Greek he is called Apollyon.

5 **The gathering of remnant Israel back to the land prophesied in the Old Testament**: "Ezekiel 36:24 I will take you from the nations and gather you from all the countries and bring you into your own land.

Amos 9:9–15 9 "For behold, I will command, and shake the house of Israel among all the nations as one shakes with a sieve...14 I will restore the fortunes of my people Israel, and they shall rebuild the ruined cities and inhabit them;...15 I will plant them on their land, and they shall never again be uprooted.

Micah 2:12 I will surely assemble all of you, O Jacob; I will gather the remnant of Israel; I will set them together like sheep in a fold.

"Isaiah 11:10–12 In that day the Lord will extend his hand yet a second time to recover the remnant that remains of his people, from Assyria, from Egypt, from Pathros, from Cush, from Elam, from Shinar, from Hamath, and from the coastlands of the sea. 12 He will raise a signal for the nations and will assemble the banished of Israel, and gather the dispersed of Judah from the four corners of the earth.

Remnant theology is that only the true believers WITHIN Israel are the true Israel: Romans 11:1–6 [1] I ask, then, has God rejected his people? By no means! For I myself am an Israelite, a descendant of Abraham, a member of the tribe of Benjamin. [2] God has not rejected his people whom he foreknew. Do you not know what the Scripture says of Elijah, how he appeals to God against Israel? [3] "Lord, they have killed your prophets, they have demolished your altars, and I alone am left, and they seek my life." [4] But what is God's reply to him? "I have kept for myself seven thousand men who have not bowed the knee to Baal." [5] So too at the present time there is a remnant, chosen by grace. [6] But if it is by grace, it is no longer on the basis of works; otherwise grace would no longer be grace.

Jesus is coming to judge the Jews of the first century because they killed him. He will then give the kingdom to another "people" a new congregation of the Lord: Matthew 21:33-44

Also: Luke 19:11, 27 As they heard these things, he proceeded to tell a parable, because he was near to Jerusalem, and because they supposed that the kingdom of God was to appear immediately…But as for these enemies of mine, who did not want me to reign over them, bring them here and slaughter them before me.' " (parable about Israel not prepared for God's arrival in Messiah)

Also: Matthew 22:2–7 "The kingdom of heaven may be compared to a king who gave a wedding feast for his son, [3] and sent his servants to call those who were invited to the wedding feast, but they would not come…[5] But they paid no attention and went off, one to his farm, another to his business, [6] while the rest seized his servants, treated them shamefully, and killed them. [7] The king was angry, and he sent his troops and destroyed those murderers and burned their city.

Gentiles who were not God's people are now God's people: Romans 9:23–26 [23] in order to make known the riches of his glory for vessels of mercy, which he has prepared beforehand for glory – [24] even us whom he has called, not from the Jews only but also from the Gentiles? [25] As indeed he says in Hosea, "Those who were not my people I will call 'my people,' and her who was not beloved I will call 'beloved.' " [26] "And in the very place where it was said to them, 'You are not my people,' there they will be called 'sons of the living God.' "

The gathering of Christians, before or after the parousia (judgment-coming of Christ on Jerusalem), is the promised restoration of the twelve tribes of Israel, that is, the remnant of true Israel: "The author's insistence on an equal number (12,000) from each of twelve tribes indicates his interest in the eschatological restoration of the the the twelve-tribe nation of Israel (Luke 22:30; 24:21; Acts 1:6; see Geyser, NTS 28 [1982] 389). The eschatology of the late OT and early Jewish periods emphasized the hope of the restoration of Israel (Deut 30:3–5; Isa 11:11–16; 27:12–13; 49:5–6; 54:7–10; Jer 31:7–14; Ezek 37:15–23; Hos 11:10–11; Pss 106:47; 147:2; Bar 5:5–9; 2 Macc 2:7; Sir 36:11; Tob 13:13; 1 Enoch 57; 90:33; 4 Ezra 13:12–13, 39–47; 2 Apoc. Bar. 78:5–7; T. Jos. 19:4; Pss. Sol. 11:2–7; 17:26; Shemoneh Esreh 10; m. Sanh. 10:3; Matt 19:28). In m. Sanh. 10:3 the opinions that the ten tribes will not return and that they will return are juxtaposed. This motif of the restoration of Israel was transmuted in early Christianity into the gathering of the elect from the four winds at the Parousia (Mark 13:27 = Matt 24:31; 1 Thess 4:16–17; 2 Thess 2:1)." David E. Aune, *Revelation 6–16, vol. 52B, Word Biblical Commentary* (Dallas: Word, Incorporated, 1998), 436.

The gathering of Israel or "return from exile" is fulfilled in the New Covenant: This is a complex theological issue. The single best source for understanding this principle is probably N. T. Wright, *The New Testament and the People of God, Christian Origins and the Question of God* (London: Society for Promoting Christian Knowledge, 1992).

But one example can show how the language of the gathering into the land is a reference not to a modern geopolitical nation-state and physical land, but rather a metaphorical image of God drawing both Jew and Gentile from all over the earth.

> Eze 36:24–28 I will take you from the nations and gather you from all the countries and bring you into your own land. 25 I will sprinkle clean water on you, and you shall be clean from all your uncleannesses, and from all your idols I will cleanse you. 26 And I will give you a new heart, and a new spirit I will put within you. And I will remove the heart of stone from your flesh and give you a heart of flesh. 27 And I will put my Spirit within you, and cause you to walk in my statutes and be careful to obey my rules. 28 You shall dwell in the land that I gave to your fathers, and you shall be my people, and I will be your God.

The language in this passage is all related to the new covenant. Notice the elements of the promise in Ezekiel

36: 1) sprinkle clean water on you (the sprinkled water of our clean conscience in the new covenant Hebrews 10:22); 2) I will give you a new heart of flesh and new spirit (the new heart and spirit of the new covenant Romans 2:28-29; Hebrews 10:22); 3) I will put my Spirit within you (The new covenant Holy Spirit is in us 2Corinthians 1:22; Ephesisan 1:13); 4) Cause you to walk in my statutes (This Scripture is fulfilled in the new covenant Hebrews 8:10; 10:15-18) 5) Take you from the nations and bring you into your own land (Acts 2). This last promise has transformed from the literal land of Israel into all the earth because when Messiah came, the whole earth became his inheritance, not merely the single plot of land on the coast of the Mediterranean Sea. Jesus is our "inheritance," he is the Promised Land. For a more in depth examination of this notion, see Brian Godawa, *Israel in Bible Prophecy: The New Testament Fulfillment of the Promise to Abraham* (Embedded Pictures Publishing, 2017).

CHAPTER 2

[1] The omens surrounding Vespasian's rise to power, including messianic pretensions:

Suetonius, *The Twelve Caesars, Vespasian* 5.6-7
"one of his high-born prisoners, Josephus by name, as he was being put in chains, declared most confidently that he would soon be released by the same man, who would then, however, be emperor. Omens were also reported from Rome: Nero in his latter days was admonished in a dream to take the sacred chariot of Jupiter Optimus Maximus from its shrine to the house of Vespasian and from there to the Circus. Not long after this, too, when Galba was on his way to the elections which gave him his second consulship, a statue of the Deified Julius of its own accord turned towards the East; and on the field of Betriacum, before the battle began, two eagles fought in the sight of all, and when one was vanquished, a third came from the direction of the rising sun and drove off the victor."
http://penelope.uchicago.edu/Thayer/E/Roman/Texts/Suetonius/12Caesars/Vespasian*.html

Dio Cassius, *Histories* 65.1.1-4
"Such was the course of these events; and following them Vespasian was declared emperor by the senate also, and Titus and Domitian were given the title of Caesars. The consular office was assumed by Vespasian and Titus while the former was in Egypt and the latter in Palestine. Now portents and dreams had come to Vespasian pointing to the sovereignty long beforehand. Thus, as he was eating dinner on his country estate, where most of his time was spent, an ox approached him, knelt down and placed his head beneath his feet. On another occasion, when he was also eating, a dog dropped a human hand under the table. And a conspicuous cypress tree, which had been uprooted and overthrown by a violent wind, stood upright again on the following day by its own power and continued to flourish. From a dream he learned that when Nero Caesar should lose a tooth, he himself should be emperor. This prophecy about the tooth became a reality on the following day; and Nero himself in his dreams once thought that he had brought the car of Jupiter to Vespasian's house. These portents needed interpretation; but not so the saying of a Jew named Josephus: he, having earlier been captured p261 Vespasian and imprisoned, laughed and said: "You may imprison me now, but a year from now, when you have become emperor, you will release me."

Dio Cassius, *Histories* 65.8.1
"Following Vespasian's entry into Alexandria the Nile overflowed, having in one day risen a palm higher than usual; such an occurrence, it was said, had only taken place only once before. Vespasian himself healed two persons, one having a withered hand, the other being blind, who had come to him because of a vision seen in dreams; he cured the one by stepping on his hand and the other by spitting upon his eyes."
http://penelope.uchicago.edu/Thayer/E/Roman/Texts/Cassius_Dio/65*.html

[2] **Prophecy of a "ruler from the east" or "from Judea":** "But now, what did most elevate them [the Jews] in undertaking this war was an ambiguous oracle that was found in their sacred writings, how, "about that time, one from their country should become governor of the habitable earth." The Jews took this prediction to belong to themselves in particular; and many of their wise men were thereby deceived in their determination. Now, this oracle certainly denoted the government of Vespasian, who was appointed emperor in Judea." Flavius Josephus, *The Wars of the Jews*, 6.5.4.

[Some understand that this meant Herod, others the crucified wonder-worker Jesus, others again Vespasian.] *Slavonic addition, Loeb*, vol. 2, p. 658.

"The majority were convinced that the ancient scriptures of their priests alluded to the present as the very time when the Orient would triumph and from Judaea would go forth men destined to rule the world. This

329

mysterious prophecy really referred to Vespasian and Titus, but the common people, true to the selfish ambitions of mankind, thought that this exalted destiny was reserved for them, and not even their calamities opened their eyes to the truth." Tacitus, *The Histories*, 5.13.

"It may be that mysterious prophecies were already circulating, and that portents and oracles promised Vespasian and his sons the purple; but it was only after the rise of the Flavians that we Romans believed in such stories." Tacitus, *The Histories*, 1. 10.

"An ancient superstition was current in the East, that out of Judea would come the rulers of the world. This prediction, as it later proved, referred to the two Roman Emperors, Vespasian and his son Titus; but the rebellious Jews, who read it as referring to themselves, murdered their Procurator, routed the Governor-general of Syria when he came down to restore order, and captured an Eagle." Suetonius, *Lives of the Twelve Caesars, Vespasian*, 4.

These passages were drawn from a chart by C.N. Carrington on his article, "The Flavian Testament" that details the oracles surrounding Vespasian as "the ruler" and their interpretations at the time. http://carrington-arts.com/cliff/FlavSyn.htm

[3] Josephus on Vespasian as messiah:

Flavius Josephus, *The Wars of the Jews* 6.5.4 §312-313
"But now, what did most elevate them in undertaking this war, was an ambiguous oracle that was also found in their sacred writings, how, "about that time, one from their country should become governor of the habitable earth." (313) The Jews took this prediction to belong to themselves in particular and many of the wise men were thereby deceived in their determination. Now, this oracle certainly denoted the government of Vespasian, who was appointed emperor in Judea." Flavius Josephus and William Whiston, *The Works of Josephus: Complete and Unabridged* (Peabody: Hendrickson, 1987), 743.

Josephus upon being captured by Vespasian:

Flavius Josephus, *The Wars of the Jews* 3.8.9 §400-404
"[Josephus to Vespasian]: "Thou, O Vespasian, thinkest no more than that thou hast taken Josephus himself captive; but I come to thee as a messenger of greater tidings; for had not I been sent by God to thee, I knew what was the laws of the Jews in this case, and how it becomes generals to die. (401) Dost thou send me to Nero! For why? Are Nero's successors till they come to thee still alive? Thou, O Vespasian, art Caesar and emperor, thou, and this thy son. (402) Bind me now still faster, and keep me for thyself, for thou, O Caesar, art not only lord over me, but over the land and the sea, and all mankind; and certainly I deserve to be kept in closer custody than I am now in, in order to be punished, if I rashly affirm anything of God." (403) When he had said this, Vespasian at present did not believe him, but supposed that Josephus said this as a cunning trick, in order to his own preservation; (404) but in a little time he was convinced, and believed what he said to be true, God himself erecting his expectations, so as to think of obtaining the empire, and by other signs foreshowing his advancement." Flavius Josephus and William Whiston, *The Works of Josephus: Complete and Unabridged* (Peabody: Hendrickson, 1987), 657.

Suetonius on Vesapasian's awakening of imperial desires based on omens that followed him:

Suetonius, *Lives of the Caesars, Vespasian* 4:5, 5
"There had spread over all the Orient an old and established belief, that it was fated at that time for men coming from Judaea to rule the world. This prediction, referring to the emperor of Rome, as afterwards appeared from the event, the people of Judaea took to themselves; accordingly they revolted and after killing their governor, they routed the consular ruler of Syria as well, when he came to the rescue, and took one of his eagles...While Otho and Vitellius were fighting for the throne after the death of Nero and Galba, he began to cherish the hope of imperial dignity, which he had long since conceived because of the following portents...." [Suetonius then describes multiple ones including the consultation of the oracle at Carmel in Judea.) http://penelope.uchicago.edu/Thayer/E/Roman/Texts/Suetonius/12Caesars/Vespasian*.html

[4] The god Serapis of Egypt revealed himself to Vespasian in Egypt around the winter of AD 69.

"Sarapis made himself known to the Flavians during the pivotal time when they were in Alexandria securing the precious things of Egypt (Dan. 11:42-43) to help them finance their takeover of the Roman Empire. This was in the late winter of AD 69-70, around the time that Vespasian was proclaimed emperor and Titus was getting ready to re-invade the Holy Land (vv. 44-45) to finish his destruction of the Jews."

McKenzie PhD, Duncan W.. *The Antichrist and the Second Coming: A Preterist Examination Volume I* (K-Locations 3195-3198). Xulon Press. K-Edition.

Basilides the oracle alleged miraculous visit to Vespasian:

"These events gave Vespasian a deeper desire to visit the sanctuary of the god to consult him with regard to his imperial fortune: he ordered all to be excluded from the temple. Then after he had entered the temple and was absorbed in contemplation of the god, he saw behind him one of the leading men of Egypt, named Basilides, who he knew was detained by sickness in a place many days' journey distant from Alexandria. He asked the priests whether Basilides had entered the temple that day; he questioned the passers-by whether he had been seen in the city; finally, he sent some cavalry and found that at that moment he had been eighty miles away: then he concluded that this was a supernatural vision and drew a prophecy from the name Basilides. http://penelope.uchicago.edu/Thayer/E/Roman/Texts/Tacitus/Histories/4D*.html

[5] Alleged miracles of healing by Vespasian:

Tacitus *Histories* 4.81-82
"During the months while Vespasian was waiting at Alexandria for the regular season of the summer winds and a settled sea, many marvels continued to mark the favour of heaven and a certain partiality of the gods toward him. One of the common people of Alexandria, well known for his loss of sight, threw himself before Vespasian's knees, praying him with groans to cure his blindness, being so directed by the god Serapis, whom this most superstitious of nations worships before all others; and he besought the emperor to deign to moisten his cheeks and eyes with his spittle. Another, whose hand was useless, prompted by the same god, begged Caesar to step and trample on it. Vespasian at first ridiculed these appeals and treated them with scorn; then...

"So Vespasian, believing that his good fortune was capable of anything and that nothing was any longer incredible, with a smiling countenance, and amid intense excitement on the part of the bystanders, did as he was asked to do. The hand was instantly restored to use, and the day again shone for the blind man. Both facts are told by eye-witnesses even now when falsehood brings no reward....
http://penelope.uchicago.edu/Thayer/E/Roman/Texts/Tacitus/Histories/4D*.html

Suetonius tells the same story as Tacitus. But he has Vespasian visiting the temple of Serapis first before the "miracle healings."

Suetonius, *Vespasian* 7.1
"Therefore beginning a civil war and sending ahead generals with troops to Italy, he crossed meanwhile to Alexandria, to take possession of the key to Egypt. There he dismissed all his attendants and entered the temple of Serapis alone, to consult the auspices as to the duration of his power. And when after many propitiatory offerings to the god he at length turned about, it seemed to him that his freedman Basilides offered him sacred boughs, garlands, and loaves, as is the custom there; and yet he knew well that no one had let him in, and that for some time he had been hardly able to walk by reason of rheumatism, and was besides far away. And immediately letters came with the news that Vitellius had been routed at Cremona and the emperor himself slain at Rome.

"Vespasian as yet lacked prestige and a certain divinity, so to speak, since he was an unexpected and still new-made emperor; but these also were given him. A man of the people who was blind, and another who was lame, came to him together as he sat on the tribunal, begging for the help for their disorders which Serapis had promised in a dream; for the god declared that Vespasian would restore the eyes, if he would spit upon them, and give strength to the leg, if he would deign to touch it with his heel. Though he had hardly any faith that this could possibly succeed, and therefore shrank even from making the attempt, he was at last prevailed upon by his friends and tried both things in public before a large crowd; and with success."
http://penelope.uchicago.edu/Thayer/E/Roman/Texts/Suetonius/12Caesars/Vespasian*.html

Vespasian's acceptance as Caesar by the Egyptians:

"The implications of the episodes turn out the same: Vespasian was the legitimate King of Egypt, and one favoured by and intimately associated with Serapis. At some time during his stay, possibly immediately after his arrival, or perhaps after he had attended a performance in the Hippodrome and after the miracles, Vespasian was saluted by his Prefect in terms that included not only 'Caesar the god', but 'son of Ammon', that is, of Re, a title of Pharaohs and Ptolemies in their capacity as kings. In the temple, he was King, and received the garlands due to one, and the boughs of a victor. The disabled men he cured were directed to him by Serapis in a dream, and the miracles were fit for Serapis himself, whose mediator he was, one involving precisely the part of Vespasian's body that was venerated for its powers in the deity.

"All classes in a difficult city alien to Vespasian were being won over. The vision legitimated him as the protégé of a deity once of particular importance to upper-class Greeks, while the miracles had an instant effect on a mixed crowd like the audience assembled for Ti. Julius Alexander's speech. Those who delivered the loyalty of the Alexandrians also benefited. The priests of Serapis, who vouched for the fact that Vespasian was alone in the temple, earned at least as much gratitude as those of Paphos and Carmel, while Serapis and the Fortune of Alexandria rose in status as protectors of the Emperor. Indeed, Alexandrian priests might well have been concerned to rival the hold that Mt Carmel had gained...

"With Rome under Flavian occupation the senate met on 21 December, the day after Vitellius died, to legalize Vespasian's position."

Barbara Levick, *Vespasian* (New York: Rutledge, 1999) 69, 79.

[1] **The Christian flight to Pella**: This was depicted in the second Chronicle of the Apocalypse, *Remnant: Rescue of the Elect.*

> Luke 21:20–24
> [20] "But when you see Jerusalem surrounded by armies, then know that its desolation has come near. [21] Then let those who are in Judea flee to the mountains, and let those who are inside the city depart, and let not those who are out in the country enter it, [22] for these are days of vengeance, to fulfill all that is written. [23] Alas for women who are pregnant and for those who are nursing infants in those days! For there will be great distress upon the earth and wrath against this people. [24] They will fall by the edge of the sword and be led captive among all nations, and Jerusalem will be trampled underfoot by the Gentiles, until the times of the Gentiles are fulfilled.

"Two important fourth-century sources relate the tradition that the disciples heeded the warnings of Jesus and fled to the Transjordanian town of Pella from Jerusalem before it fell.

Eusebius (H.E. 3.5.3) relates:

> On the other hand, the people of the church in Jerusalem were commanded by an oracle given by revelation before the war to those in the city who were worthy of it to depart and dwell in one of the cities of Perea which they called Pella.

According to Epiphanius (De mens, et pond. [*Treatise on Weights and Measures*] 15):

> When the city (Jerusalem) was about to be taken by the Romans, it was revealed to all the disciples by an angel of God that they should remove from the city, as it was going to be completely destroyed. They sojourned as emigrants in Pella...in TransJordania. And this city is said to be of the Decapolis.38

According to Epiphanius (Haer. 29.7.7f. and 30.2.7):

> "This heresy of the Nazoraeans exists in Beroea in the neighbourhood of Coele Syria and the Decapolis in the region of Pella and in Basanitis in the so-called Kokaba, Chochabe in Hebrew. For from there it took its beginnings after the exodus from Jerusalem when all the disciples went to live in Pella because Christ had told them to leave Jerusalem and to go away since it would undergo a siege After all those who believed in Christ had generally come to live in Perea, in a city called Pella of the Decapolis of which it is written in the Gospel and which is situated in the neighbourhood of the region of Batanaea and Basanitis.

"Some scholars believe that Epiphanius and Eusebius derived their accounts from Hegesippus, a second-century source. But an even more probable source was Aristo, an apologist from Pella, who wrote in the mid-second century."

"Pella was a Gentile city of the Decapolis. The choice of Pella as a place of refuge may have been influenced by a Gentile church in the city. Sowers suggests, "The antipathy of that city toward political revolt against Rome made the city a logical choice for the Jerusalem Church, seeking a haven from rebellious territory, to settle in." Brandon has exaggerated the damage which might have been done to Pella by the Jewish and Roman attacks on it. Gray notes, "Careful examination of the evidence shows that Pella was not the complete ruin that has been suggested; in fact, compared with other Palestinian towns, it fared quite well during the war/'48 She states, "We may say, in conclusion, that there is nothing incredible in a settlement of members of the Jerusalem Church in Pella, at least in part, between the years A.D. 66-8."

"Indeed, it became a commonplace motif among the church fathers to allege that the destruction of Jerusalem and its temple was God's punishment upon the Jews for the death of Christ. This judgment was first expressed by Justin Martyr (1 Apol. 47). Eusebius (H.E. 3.5.3), after reporting the flight of the Christians to Pella, expresses his opinion as follows:

"To it those who believed on Christ migrated from Jerusalem, that when holy men had altogether deserted the royal capital of the Jews and the whole land of Judaea the judgment of God might at last overtake them for all their crimes against the Christ and his Apostles, and all that generation of the wicked be utterly blotted out from among men.

"This same motif was to be repeated by Hilary, Jerome, Sulpicius Severus, and Augustine. To be sure, this is a theological reflection, but it is surely more probable that it was founded on the historical reality of the Pella tradition." Edwin M. Yamauchi, "Christians and the Jewish revolts against Rome," *Fides et historia*, 23 no 2 Sum 1991, p 18, 20, 22.

This passage from the Pseudo-Clementines affirms the belief that Christians fled to Pella because they believed the destruction of Jerusalem was the proof that Jesus was Messiah:

Pseudo-Clement of Rome, *Recognitions of Clement*, 1.37 (2nd or 4th century AD)
"In addition to these things, he also appointed a place [Pella] in which alone it should be lawful to them to sacrifice to God...This place [Jerusalem], which seemed chosen for a time, often harassed as it had been by hostile invasions and plunderings, was at last to be wholly destroyed. And in order to impress this upon them, even before the coming of the true Prophet [Jesus], who was to reject at once the sacrifices and the place, it was often plundered by enemies and burnt with fire, and the people carried into captivity among foreign nations, and then brought back when they betook themselves to the mercy of God; that by these things they might be taught that a people who offer sacrifices are driven away and delivered up into the hands of the enemy, but they who do mercy and righteousness are without sacrifices freed from captivity, and restored to their native land."

Pseudo-Clement of Rome, "Recognitions of Clement," in Fathers of the Third and Fourth Centuries: The Twelve Patriarchs, Excerpts and Epistles, the Clementina, Apocrypha, Decretals, Memoirs of Edessa and Syriac Documents, Remains of the First Ages, ed. Alexander Roberts, James Donaldson, and A. Cleveland Coxe, trans. M. B. Riddle, vol. 8, The Ante-Nicene Fathers (Buffalo, NY: Christian Literature Company, 1886), 87.

Exactly when did the Christians flee Jerusalem?: "We might surmise that once Jerusalem had been surrounded, it was already too late to flee. But the city was surrounded on several occasions before Titus's final circumvallation. For instance, before the Jewish revolt became a full-scale war, Cestius Gallus surrounded the city, only to suddenly cease operations and leave. Josephus notes that he surrounded the city "on all sides" (Gk.: pantothen), allowing him to besiege her walls for five days (J.W. 2:19:5 §535). At that time "many of the most eminent of the Jews swam away from the city, as from a ship when it was going to sink" (J.W. 2:20:1 §556). Perhaps the Christians escaped at this time also. Later in AD 68, generals Vespasian and Titus "had fortified all the places round about Jerusalem. . . encompassing the city round about on all sides" (Josephus, J.W. 4:9:1§486). But when Vespasian and Titus were "informed that Nero was dead" (4:9:2 §491), they "did not go on with their expedition against the Jews" (4:9:2 §497; cp. 4:10:2 §590) until after Vespasian became emperor in AD 69 (4:11:5 §567). This would have been the last reasonable opportunity for escape from Jerusalem because eventually Titus built "a wall round about the whole city" (J.W. 5:12:1 §499). With this action he largely sealed off Jerusalem, for he had "encompassed the city with this wall, and put garrisons into proper places" (J.W. 5:12:2 §510).Though even then Jews could escape, as Titus recognized (J.W. 5:12:1 §496)." Kenneth L. Gentry, Jr., *The Divorce of Israel: A Redemptive-Historical Interpretation of Revelation Vol. 2* (Dallas, GA: Tolle Lege Press, 2016), 515-516.

Josephus on the flight of Jews after Cestius left: "After this calamity had befallen Cestius, many of the most eminent of the Jews swam away from the city, as from a ship when it was going to sink." (*Wars* 2.20.1

556).

Josephus on Pella being devastated before Christians fled to it: "Upon which stroke that the Jews received at Caesarea, the whole nation was greatly enraged; so they divided themselves into several parties, and laid waste the villages of the Syrians, and their neighboring cities, Philadelphia, and Sebonitis, and Gerasa, and <u>Pella</u>, and Scythopolis." (*Wars* 2.458)

[2] **Cassandra quotes from:** Revelation 12:13-17.

[3] **Cassandra quotes from:** Revelation 12:14.

[4] **Cassandra quotes from:** Revelation 12:15–17.

[5] The Ebionites:

"The church fathers Eusebius and Epiphanius said that before Jerusalem was destroyed in A.D. 70, Christians fled from the city to the town of Pella in Transjordan. Some scholars suggest that the Pseudo-Clementine Recognitions and Luke 21:20-22 implicitly refer to the same event. The tradition about the flight to Pella is an important piece in the puzzle of Christian origins and early expansion...

"Initially, the Ebionites were held in a respectable light. The term Ebionim, meaning poor (plural form), was later changed to Ebionite. It had been an honorable term but as the split grew wider and time passed, the name began to carry very negative connotations.

Eusebius reports in his chapter entitled: "The Heresy of the Ebionites:

"The spirit of wickedness, however, being unable to shake some in their love of Christ, and yet finding them susceptible of his impressions in other respects, brought them over to his purposes. These are properly called Ebionites by the ancients, as those who cherished low and mean opinions of Christ. For they consider him a plain and common man, and justified only by his advances in virtue, and that he was born of the Virgin Mary, by natural generation.

Randall A. Weiss, *Jewish Sects of the New Testament Era* (Cedar Hill, TX: Cross Talk, 1994).

"A form of the Pella tradition appears again in the late fourth century, in two works by Epiphanius, who spent much of his life in Palestine, near Eleutheropolis, until becoming bishop on Cyprus in a.D. 367. His first reference to the Pella tradition appears in his Panarion 29.7.7-8:6 7.

Ebionites were linked to the Nazoreans, and sometimes considered synonymous:

"This heresy of the Nazoraeans exists in Beroea around Coele Syria, and in the Decapolis around the area of Pella, and in Basanitis in the so-called Kokabe (but the so-called Chochabe in Hebrew). 8. For from there it originated after the migration from Jerusalem, after all the disciples had settled in Pella, because Christ had told them to leave Jerusalem and to depart, since it was about to suffer siege; and for this reason, after settling in Perea, they were living there, as I said. There the Nazoraean heresy had its beginning.

"A second reference to the Pella flight occurs in the Panarion 30.2.7 in a discussion of the Ebionites: [The Ebionites] originated after the capture of Jerusalem. For at that time all who believed in Christ had settled predominantly in Perea, in a certain city called Pella of the Decapolis, of which it is written in the gospel [that it is near] the region of Batanaea and Basanitis. At that time, after having and while they were living there, from this [place] region Ebion's."...

"that Epiphanius saw the refugees from Jerusalem as orthodox Christians who later fell prey to heresy. could hold such a position because he, like Eusebius, assumed that the group that went to Pella included no apostles, whom he considered to be the guardians of orthodoxy. The fugitives to Pella included "all the disciples" (Pan. 29.7.8), which meant "all who believed in Christ" (30.2.7). They were "the disciples of the apostles" rather than the apostles themselves...

"The Ebionites claimed that their name, meaning "the poor," derived from a time when they sold their longings and laid the money at the feet of the apostles (Pan. 30.17.2). Epiphanius denied this, insisting that their identity derived from Ebion, their founder. The Ebionites had noncanonical books bearing the names of apostles (30.23. 1-2). Epiphanius attacked these writings by telling a story to show that the apostle John knew

334

of Ebion and considered him heretical. He concluded: "It is clear to everyone that the apostles disowned the faith of Ebion and considered it foreign to the character of their own preaching" (30.24.7)…

Craig Koester, "The Origin and Significance of the Flight to Pella Tradition," *The Catholic Biblical Quarterly*, Vol. 51, No. 1 (January, 1989), 92-93, 96.

[6] Cassandra is referring to Jude:

> Jude 3–4, 17-19
> [3] Beloved, although I was very eager to write to you about our common salvation, I found it necessary to write appealing to you to contend for the faith that was once for all delivered to the saints. [4] For certain people have crept in unnoticed who long ago were designated for this condemnation, ungodly people, who pervert the grace of our God into sensuality and deny our only Master and Lord, Jesus Christ…[17] But you must remember, beloved, the predictions of the apostles of our Lord Jesus Christ. [18] They said to you, "In the last time there will be scoffers, following their own ungodly passions." [19] It is these who cause divisions, worldly people, devoid of the Spirit.

CHAPTER 4

[1] The thief coming upon that generation:

> Matthew 24:34, 43-44
> [34] Truly, I say to you, this generation will not pass away until all these things take place…[43] But know this, that if the master of the house had known in what part of the night the thief was coming, he would have stayed awake and would not have let his house be broken into. [44] Therefore you also must be ready, for the Son of Man is coming at an hour you do not expect.

[2] **Alexander is here referring to**: 2Peter 3. The following is from Brian Godawa, "Appendix: The Day of the Lord in 2Peter" in *End Times Bible Prophecy: It's Not What They Told You* (Los Angeles, CA: Embedded Pictures Publishing, 2017) 165-168.

> 2 Peter 3:3–13
> [3] knowing this first of all, that scoffers will come in the last days with scoffing, following their own sinful desires. [4] They will say, "Where is the promise of his coming? For ever since the fathers fell asleep, all things are continuing as they were from the beginning of creation." [5] For they deliberately overlook this fact, that the heavens existed long ago, and the earth was formed out of water and through water by the word of God, [6] and that by means of these the world that then existed was deluged with water and perished. [7] But by the same word the heavens and earth that now exist are stored up for fire, being kept until the day of judgment and destruction of the ungodly.
>
> [8] But do not overlook this one fact, beloved, that with the Lord one day is as a thousand years, and a thousand years as one day. [9] The Lord is not slow to fulfill his promise as some count slowness, but is patient toward you, not wishing that any should perish, but that all should reach repentance. [10] But the day of the Lord will come like a thief, and then the heavens will pass away with a roar, and the heavenly bodies will be burned up and dissolved, and the earth and the works that are done on it will be exposed.
>
> [11] Since all these things are thus to be dissolved, what sort of people ought you to be in lives of holiness and godliness, [12] waiting for and hastening the coming of the day of God, because of which the heavens will be set on fire and dissolved, and the heavenly bodies will melt as they burn! [13] But according to his promise we are waiting for new heavens and a new earth in which righteousness dwells

The interpretation I have presented in this book is no doubt earth shattering for some eschatological paradigms about the end times. Such radical departures from the futurist's perceived wisdom always begs plenty of questions about other passages and concepts taken for granted by the futurist interpretation.

One passage is the apparently clear description in 2 Peter about the day of the Lord and the passing away of the heavens and the earth that are replaced by a new heavens and earth. Isn't that unambiguous language to be taken literally? Well, actually, no. As a matter of fact, orthodox believers have wide-ranging interpretations of this passage, so it is a controversial one to begin with.

We must remember our dictum to seek to understand the text within its ancient Jewish setting steeped in Old Testament imagery and symbols. I believe when we do this, we will have to conclude that the decreation of the heavens and earth is covenantal mythopoeia, not literal, physical, scientific observation. Peter wrote figuratively about the final ending of the old covenant, with God's judgment on Israel for rejecting Messiah and the final establishment of his new covenant as a new world order, or, in their case, a "new heavens and new earth."

In the beginning of chapter 3, Peter compared the scoffers of his day and their impending judgment with the scoffers of Noah's day before their judgment. The judgment was near; and, what's more, these scoffers were in the last days, which we have already seen were considered the last days of the old covenant that the New Testament writers were living in. Those last days would be climaxed by judgment. But what kind of judgment?

Peter referenced the creation of the heavens and earth (red flag about covenants!) and then the destruction of that previous world by water. Scholars have indicated how the flood of Noah was described using terms similar to Genesis 1, as if God was "decreating" the earth because of sin, in order to start over with a new Noahic covenant. The ark floated over the chaotic "face of the waters" (Gen 7:17), just as God's spirit had hovered over the chaotic face of the waters before creation (Gen 1:2). The dry land receded from the waters (8:3), just as it had been separated in creation (1:9). God gave the command to Noah to be fruitful and multiply and fill the earth (9:1), just as he had given it to Adam and Eve (1:28). So the covenantal connections are loud and clear.

As already noted, the day of the Lord is always used in the Bible for a localized judgment upon a people, which, by way of reminder, Jesus had already prophesied was coming upon Jerusalem to the very generation he spoke to (Matt. 23:36-24:2). But what makes some interpreters think this is the final judgment of the universe is the very bad translation of the Greek word stoicheion as "elements" in some English texts. This makes modern readers think of the periodic table of elements as being the most foundational building blocks of the universe. They conclude that the Bible must be talking about the actual elements of helium, hydrogen, deuterium, and others being burned up and melted!

But this is not what the Greek word means. Though some Greek thinkers believed in the existence of atoms, the common understanding was that there were four basic elements – earth, water, wind, and fire. Though someone may conjecture that these could still be considered physical elements that could be destroyed, a simple look at the usage of stoicheion throughout the New Testament shows that the Hebrew usage had nothing to do with Greek primitive scientific notions.

In every place that stoicheion shows up in the New Testament it refers to elementary principles of a worldview, sometimes a godless worldview (Col 2:8), but, more often, the elementary principles of the old covenant law described as a "cosmos" (Gal 4:3, 9; Col 2:20; Heb 5:12).

Remember how the cosmic language of creating heavens and earth was used to describe the cosmic significance of God establishing a covenant? And remember how in the Old Testament, the destruction of covenants, nations, and peoples was described in decreation terms as the collapsing of the universe?

That is the case in these passages as well, with the term "cosmos" being used metaphorically for the "universe" of God's covenantal order as embodied in the old covenant laws of Jewish separation: circumcision, dietary restrictions, and sabbaths. Paul was telling his readers that the stoicheion of the old covenant cosmos were no longer over them because the people of God were under new stoicheion, the elementary principles of faith (Gal 4:1-11).

Peter meant the same thing. When he said that the heavens will pass away and the stoicheion will be burned up, he was claiming that when the temple in Jerusalem is destroyed, it will be the final passing away of the old covenant cosmos. This would include all the elementary principles tied to that physical sacramental structure – the laws that once separated Jew and Gentile. The new cosmos would be one in which both Jew and Gentile "by God's power are being guarded through faith for a salvation ready to be revealed in the last time" (1 Pet 1:5).

As Gary DeMar concluded, "The New Covenant replaces the Old Covenant with new leaders, a new priesthood, new sacraments, a new sacrifice, a new tabernacle (John 1:14), and a new temple (John 2:19; 1 Cor. 3:16; Eph. 2:21). In essence, a new heaven and earth." Eminent Greek scholar John Lightfoot agreed, "The destruction of Jerusalem and the whole Jewish state is described as if the whole frame of this world were to be dissolved." Kenneth Gentry adds, "'The temple was more than a building and more than the home of the sacrificial cult. It was the sacred center of the cosmos, the place where heaven and earth meet.' Thus, the collapse of the temple becomes a picture of the end of Israel's world, her covenantal universe."

The new heavens and new earth in which righteousness dwells that Peter was waiting for was the new covenant cosmos of righteousness by faith inaugurated by Christ's death and resurrection. That new covenant inauguration and implementation was not merely an abstract claim of contractual change, it was physically verified with the destruction of the old covenant emblem, the temple, that finalized the dissolution of the old covenant itself.

Matt. 23:36-38
"O Jerusalem, Jerusalem, the city that kills the prophets and stones those who are sent to it! How often would I have gathered your children together as a hen gathers her brood under her wings, and you would not! See, your house [temple] is left to you desolate. Truly, I say to you, all these things will come upon this generation..

[3] **Elihu refers to**: Christ is the final goal ("telos") of the law.

Romans 10:4
[4] For Christ is the end [final goal] of the law for righteousness to everyone who believes.

Galatians 3:23–25
[23] Now before faith came, we were held captive under the law, imprisoned until the coming faith would be revealed. [24] So then, the law was our guardian until Christ came, in order that we might be justified by faith. [25] But now that faith has come, we are no longer under a guardian,

[4] Elihu is quoting from: Hebrews 8-10

Hebrews 8:5
[5] They serve a copy and shadow of the heavenly things. For when Moses was about to erect the tent, he was instructed by God, saying, "See that you make everything according to the pattern that was shown you on the mountain."

Hebrews 10:1
[1] For since the law has but a shadow of the good things to come instead of the true form of these realities, it can never, by the same sacrifices that are continually offered every year, make perfect those who draw near.

See also:

1 Peter 1:18–19
[18] knowing that you were ransomed from the futile ways inherited from your forefathers, not with perishable things such as silver or gold, [19] but with the precious blood of Christ, like that of a lamb without blemish or spot.

1 Corinthians 5:7–8
[7] Cleanse out the old leaven that you may be a new lump, as you really are unleavened. For Christ, our Passover lamb, has been sacrificed. [8] Let us therefore celebrate the festival, not with the old leaven, the leaven of malice and evil, but with the unleavened bread of sincerity and truth.

[5] **Elihu quotes from**: Isaiah 53:1-12.

[6] **Jesus fulfilled all the Jewish feasts**: Special thanks to David Curtis of Berean Bible Church for his teaching on this topic. You can get his free teachings on these at:
http://www.bereanbiblechurch.org/studies/leviticus.php

CHAPTER 7

[1] Thelonius is referring to:

Revelation 17:17
[17] for God has put it into their hearts to carry out his purpose by being of one mind and handing over their royal power to the beast, until the words of God are fulfilled.

God providentially uses pagan armies to accomplish his will: Isa 10:5-7, 25-27; 44:27–45:7; Hab 1:6-11; Jer 51:11, 28. Note especially that though God calls Nebuchadnezzar "My Servant" (Jer 25:9), he nevertheless destroys his kingdom (Jer 25:12).

God's providential control of the pagan destruction of Jerusalem and the temple: "Revelation emphasizes the divine governance over and again: Its very theme shows Christ's vengeance against Israel (1:7; 6:16; 19:2). The first vision in the opening of the judgment material shows God on his throne above the history that he controls (4:1ff) and through which he avenges himself (6:10-11, 16-17; 11:8; 14:19; 15:1,7; 16:1, 7, 19; 19:2, 15). His throne is repeatedly emphasized throughout the drama (1:4; 3:21; 4:2-10; 15:1, 6, 11, 13; 6:16; 7:9, 10-11, 15, 17; 14:3; 16:17; 20:11; 21:5; 22:1, 3). We see this also in the abundant use of divine passives (e.g., 6:2, 4, 8; 9:1, 3; 13:7) and judgments falling from heaven upon men (8:2, 5, 7; 9:1; 12:9, 12; 16:1-2, 8). This reminds us of an earlier reference to Israel and Rome in Acts 4:27-28: "For truly in this city there were gathered together against Your holy servant Jesus, whom You anointed, both Herod and Pontius Pilate, along with the Gentiles and the peoples of Israel, to do whatever Your hand and Your purpose predestined to occur." Kenneth L. Gentry, Jr., *The Divorce of Israel: A Redemptive-Historical Interpretation of Revelation Vol. 2* (Dallas, GA: Tolle Lege Press, 2016), 486.

In each of these cases, God used a different nation or people as his tool to perform the judgment. In other words, the pagan people carried out God's will; they represented him spiritually.

Notice in these Old Testament passages how God describes the pagan nations' actions as his own actions:

Isaiah 10:5–6
[5] Woe to Assyria, the rod of my anger; the staff in their hands is my fury! [6] Against a godless nation I send him, and against the people of my wrath I command him, to take spoil and seize plunder, and to tread them down like the mire of the streets.

Isaiah 10:15
[15] Shall the axe boast over him who hews with it, or the saw magnify itself against him who wields it? As if a rod should wield him who lifts it, or as if a staff should lift him who is not wood!

Isaiah 45:1–2
[1] Thus says the LORD to his anointed, to Cyrus, whose right hand I have grasped, to subdue nations before him and to loose the belts of kings, to open doors before him that gates may not be closed: [2] "I will go before you and level the exalted places, I will break in pieces the doors of bronze and cut through the bars of iron,

God uses Nebuchadnezzar as his tool to judge Egypt

Ezekiel 30:24–26
[24] And I will strengthen the arms of the king of Babylon and put my sword in his hand, but I will break the arms of Pharaoh, and he will groan before him like a man mortally wounded. [25] I will strengthen the arms of the king of Babylon, but the arms of Pharaoh shall fall. Then they shall know that I am the LORD, when I put my sword into the hand of the king of Babylon and he stretches it out against the land of Egypt. [26] And I will scatter the Egyptians among the nations and disperse them throughout the countries. Then they will know that I am the LORD."

God uses the Medes to destroy Babylon in 539 BC

Isa. 13:1
The oracle concerning Babylon ...The LORD of hosts is mustering the army for battle. 5 They are coming from a far country, From the farthest heavens, The LORD and His instruments of indignation, To destroy the whole earth. ...11 Thus I will punish the world for its evil..17 Behold, I am going to stir up the Medes against them..

God used Babylonians to perform his judgment destroying the first temple 587 BC

Jeremiah 4:12–27
Now it is I who speak in judgment upon them." [13] Behold, he comes up like clouds; his chariots like the whirlwind; his horses are swifter than eagles... Warn the nations that he is coming; announce to Jerusalem, "Besiegers come from a distant land; they shout against the cities of Judah...[27] For thus says the LORD, "The whole land shall be a desolation; yet I will not make a full end.

God used Babylon to judge Edom And The Nations surrounding them. (fulfilled in the Babylonian Invasion of Judah 587-586 BC -- Jer. 25, Ezek. 35, Obad 15, Mal 1:2

Isaiah 34:2–6
[2] For the LORD is enraged against all the nations, and furious against all their host; he has devoted them to destruction, has given them over for slaughter. [3] ...[5] For my sword has drunk its fill in the heavens; behold, it descends for judgment upon Edom, upon the people I have devoted to destruction. [6] The LORD has a sword; it is sated with blood; it is gorged with fat, ... For the LORD has a sacrifice in Bozrah, a great slaughter in the land of Edom.

God uses Babylon to judge Assyria and Israel

Habakkuk 1:5–6 [5] "Look among the nations, and see; wonder and be astounded. For I am doing a work in your days that you would not believe if told. [6] For behold, I am raising up the Chaldeans, that bitter and hasty nation, who march through the breadth of the earth, to seize dwellings not their own.

Then God judges Babylon

Habakkuk 2:16
[16] You will have your fill of shame instead of glory. Drink, yourself, and show your uncircumcision! The cup in the LORD's right hand will come around to you, and utter shame will come upon your glory!

The Destruction of Samaria and the exile of 10 northern tribes by Assyria, 8th century BC

Micah 1:3–7 [3] For behold, the LORD is coming out of his place, and will come down and tread upon the high places of the earth. [4] And the mountains will melt under him, and the valleys will split open, like wax before the fire, like waters poured down a steep place. [5] All this is for the transgression of Jacob and for the sins of the house of Israel. What is the transgression of Jacob? Is it not Samaria? And what is the high place of Judah? Is it not Jerusalem? [6] Therefore I will make Samaria a heap in the open country.

Against Assyria (fulfilled: 701 BC against Sennacherib Isa. 37:36)

Isaiah 30:25–28
on the day of the great slaughter, when the towers fall. [27] Behold, the name of the LORD comes from afar, burning with his anger, and in thick rising smoke; his lips are full of fury, and his tongue is like a devouring fire; [28] his breath is like an overflowing stream that reaches up to the neck; to sift the nations with the sieve of destruction, and to place on the jaws of the peoples a bridle that leads astray.

Revelation 17:16–17 [16] And the ten horns that you saw, they and the beast will hate the prostitute. They will make her desolate and naked, and devour her flesh and burn her up with fire, [17] for God has put it into their hearts to carry out his purpose by being of one mind and handing over their royal power to the beast, until the words of God are fulfilled.

Examples throughout Revelation of God "allowing" or "giving power" to the wicked: Revelation 6:2, 4, 8; 9:1, 3; 13:5, 7, 14–15; 16:8.

[2] God has gone over to the Romans, and using them as his means to judge Israel:

Flavius Josephus, *The Wars of the Jews* 3.8.3 §354
(354) and [Josephus] said [to God], – "Since it pleaseth thee, who hast created the Jewish nation, to depress

the same, and since all their good fortune is gone over to the Romans..."

Flavius Josephus and William Whiston, *The Works of Josephus: Complete and Unabridged* (Peabody: Hendrickson, 1987), 655.

Flavius Josephus, *The Wars of the Jews* 6.2.1 §110
"(110) And are not both the city and the entire temple now full of the dead bodies of your countrymen? It is God therefore, it is God himself who is bringing on this fire, to purge that city and temple by means of the Romans, and is going to pluck up this city, which is full of your pollutions."

Flavius Josephus and William Whiston, *The Works of Josephus: Complete and Unabridged* (Peabody: Hendrickson, 1987), 732.

Flavius Josephus, *The Wars of the Jews* 6.5.4, §311-313
"while at the same time they had it written in their sacred oracles, – "That then should their city be taken, as well as their holy house, when once their temple should become foursquare." (312) But now, what did most elevate them in undertaking this war, was an ambiguous oracle that was also found in their sacred writings, how, "about that time, one from their country should become governor of the habitable earth." (313) The Jews took this prediction to belong to themselves in particular and many of the wise men were thereby deceived in their determination. Now, this oracle certainly denoted the government of Vespasian, who was appointed emperor in Judea."

Josephus even puts his own beliefs about God being with the Romans into the mouth of Titus:

Flavius Josephus, *The Wars of the Jews* 6.9.1, §411
"[Titus] expressed himself after the manner following: – "We have certainly had God for our assistant in this war, and it was no other than God who ejected the Jews out of these fortifications; for what could the hands of men, or any machines, do towards overthrowing these towers!"

[3] Joseph's interpretation of Daniel's prophecy applied to Vespasian:

Flavius Josephus, *The Wars of the Jews* 6.5.4, §312-313
"(312) But now, what did most elevate them in undertaking this war, was an ambiguous oracle that was also found in their sacred writings, how, "about that time, one from their country should become governor of the habitable earth." (313) The Jews took this prediction to belong to themselves in particular and many of the wise men were thereby deceived in their determination. Now, this oracle certainly denoted the government of Vespasian, who was appointed emperor in Judea."

Flavius Josephus and William Whiston, *The Works of Josephus: Complete and Unabridged* (Peabody: Hendrickson, 1987), 743.

CHAPTER 8

[1] The taurobolium:

From: Prudentius, Peristephanon, Carmen X, 1011-50: Translation and notes by C. K. Barrett, The New Testament Background (London, SPCK 1956), pp. 96-7.

https://www.roger-pearse.com/weblog/2009/04/28/the-taurobolium/

"The high priest who is to be consecrated is brought down under ground in a pit dug deep, marvellously adorned with a fillet, binding his festive temples with chaplets, his hair combed back under a golden crown, and wearing a silken toga caught up with Gabine girding.

"Over this they make a wooden floor with wide spaces, woven of planks with an open mesh; they then divide or bore the area and repeatedly pierce the wood with a pointed tool that it may appear full of small holes.

"Hither a huge bull, fierce and shaggy in appearance, is led, bound with flowery garlands about its flanks, and with its horns sheathed; Yea, the forehead of the victim sparkles with gold, and the flash of metal plates colours its hair.

"Here, as is ordained, the beast is to be slain, and they pierce its breast with a sacred spear; the gaping wound emits a wave of hot blood, and the smoking river flows into the woven structure beneath it and surges

340

wide.

"Then by the many paths of the thousand openings in the lattice the falling shower rains down a foul dew, which the priest buried within catches, putting his shameful head under all the drops, defiled both in his clothing and in all his body.

"Yea, he throws back his face, he puts his cheeks in the way of the blood, he puts under it his ears and lips, he interposes his nostrils, he washes his very eyes with the fluid, nor does he even spare his throat but moistens his tongue, until he actually drinks the dark gore.

"Afterwards, the flamens draw the corpse, stiffening now that the blood has gone forth, off the lattice, and the pontiff, horrible in appearance, comes forth, and shows his wet head, his beard heavy with blood, his dripping fillets and sodden garments.

"This man, defiled with such contagions and foul with the gore of the recent sacrifice, all hail and worship at a distance, because profane blood and a dead ox have washed him while concealed in a filthy cave."

[2] Prohibition of drinking blood for Jews:

Leviticus 17:13–14
[13] "Any one also of the people of Israel, or of the strangers who sojourn among them, who takes in hunting any beast or bird that may be eaten shall pour out its blood and cover it with earth. [14] For the life of every creature is its blood: its blood is its life. Therefore I have said to the people of Israel, You shall not eat the blood of any creature, for the life of every creature is its blood. Whoever eats it shall be cut off.

[3] Titus's hatred of the Christians:

"Feuillet states that "the Jewish war and the destruction of Jerusalem… are of tremendous importance because they mark the definitive independence of the Christian religion from that of Israel, thereby preparing the way for the advance of the Church among the pagans of the Gentile world." It is likely, however, that Titus actually intended the opposite effect: to destroy Christianity in the process. Since apostolic Christianity was so tied up with Israel and the temple, Titus apparently hoped to crush both Judaism and Christianity with the destruction of the temple. According to Sulpicius Severus (ca. AD 400), whose "authority is undoubtedly Tacitus," we learn that "Titus is said, after calling a council, to have first deliberated whether he should destroy the temple, a structure of such extraordinary work. For it seemed good to some that a sacred edifice, distinguished above all human achievements, ought not to be destroyed…But on the opposite side, others and Titus himself thought that the temple ought specially to be overthrown in order that the religion of the Jews and of the Christians might more thoroughly be subverted; for that these religions, although contrary to each other, had nevertheless proceeded from the same authors; that the Christians had sprung up from among the Jews; and that, if the root were extirpated, the offshoot would speedily perish" (Severus 2:30). Tommaso Leoni notes that "very few have doubts… that the version of the Christian chronographer [Severus] should be preferred" over Josephus' account, which states that Titus tried to prevent the burning of the temple (Jos., J.W. 6:4:3 §236–43).44 J. Barclay (1996: 353) argues that "this notorious feature of Josephus' account is certainly 'economical with the truth' and possibly a complete fabrication." Kenneth L. Gentry, Jr., *The Divorce of Israel: A Redemptive-Historical Interpretation of Revelation Vol. 2* (Dallas, GA: Tolle Lege Press, 2016), 57-58.

CHAPTER 10

[1] Symeon and the Ebionites:

"Simon [spelled in other manuscripts as Symeon] led the Ebionite believers across the Jordan to Pella. This same Simon led them back to Jerusalem after the war. By this time, the Jewish Christians were viewed as traitors by the rest of the Jews. They weren't allowed synagogue membership and they were actually excommunicated. There is a dramatic perspective on this Pella tradition which contends that these Ebionite refugees establish the link to early Christianity.

Randall A. Weiss, *Jewish Sects of the New Testament Era* (Cedar Hill, TX: Cross Talk, 1994).

The texts of the Ebionites:

"Modern research has generally differentiated between an Aramaic Gospel of the Nazoreans and a Greek Gospel of the Ebionites. Both originated in the first half of the second century, are inclined to paraphrase like the Targums, and are greatly dependent upon the canonical Matthew, which probably derived from Jewish Christian circles in the Great Church...

"specific tendencies of heretical Ebionitism (vegetarianism, hostility toward the sacrificial cult, opposition to Paul, etc.) are reflected in these fragments...

"It seems to me that an Ebionite "Acts of the Apostles" underlies this outline of the development of the history of salvation. According to Epiphanius, one chapter of this Ebionite "Acts" may have been called "The Ascents of James". For the Ebionite self-consciousness and their particular view of history the Ebionite "Acts" was of fundamental significance. The texts claim to be documents deriving from the physical descendants of Jewish Christians belonging to the original church in Jerusalem..."

Hans-Joachim Schoeps, trans., Douglas R.A. Hare, *Jewish Christianity: Factional Disputes in the Early Church* (Philadelphia: Fortress Press, 1969), 14, 16-17.

Gospel of the Ebionites:

Epiphanius writing about the Gospel of the Ebionites: "And on this account they say that Jesus was begotten of the seed of a man, and was chosen; and so by the choice of God he was called the Son of God from the Christ that came into him from above in the likeness of a dove. And they deny that he was begotten of God the Father, but say that he was created, as one of the archangels, yet greater, and that he is Lord of angels and of all things made by the Almighty, and that he came and taught, as the Gospel (so called) current among them contains, that, 'I came to destroy the sacrifices, and if ye cease not from sacrificing, the wrath of God will not cease from you'."

Montague Rhodes James, ed., The Apocryphal New Testament: Being the Apocryphal Gospels, Acts, Epistles, and Apocalypses (Oxford: Clarendon Press, 1924), 10.

"The matter of these Judaic-Christian gospels, namely, the Gospel of the Ebionites, the Gospel of the Hebrews, and the Gospel of the Nazoraeans has been called the most irritating problem in the NT Apocrypha.

Confusion stems from the fact that the title "Gospel of the Ebionites" is never used by the Fathers. Rather, it is the creation of modern scholarship to reference a specific source cited by Epiphanius. He quotes from "The gospel which is called with them (viz. the Ebionites) according to Matthew which is not complete but falsified and distorted, they call it the Hebrew Gospel ..." (Haer. 30.13.1). He further states that the Ebionites "also accept the gospel according to Matthew. For they too use only this like the followers of Cerinthus and Merinthus..."

William L. Petersen, "Ebionites, Gospel of the," ed. David Noel Freedman, *The Anchor Yale Bible Dictionary* (New York: Doubleday, 1992), 261–262.

[2] Ebionite denial of Christ's deity:

Eusebius reports in his chapter entitled: "The Heresy of the Ebionites."

Eusebius of Caesaria, *Church History* 3.27.1-2
"The spirit of wickedness, however, being unable to shake some in their love of Christ, and yet finding them susceptible of his impressions in other respects, brought them over to his purposes. These are properly called Ebionites by the ancients, as those who cherished low and mean opinions of Christ. For they consider him a plain and common man, and justified only by his advances in virtue, and that he was born of the Virgin Mary, by natural generation."

Randall A. Weiss, *Jewish Sects of the New Testament Era* (Cedar Hill, TX: Cross Talk, 1994).

"Epiphanius writing about the Gospel of the Ebionites: "And on this account they say that Jesus was begotten of the seed of a man, and was chosen; and so by the choice of God he was called the Son of God from the Christ that came into him from above in the likeness of a dove. And they deny that he was begotten of God the Father, but say that he was created, as one of the archangels, yet greater, and that he is Lord of angels and of all things made by the Almighty, and that he came and taught, as the Gospel (so called) current among them contains, that, 'I came to destroy the sacrifices, and if ye cease not from sacrificing, the wrath of God will not cease from you'."

Montague Rhodes James, ed., The Apocryphal New Testament: Being the Apocryphal Gospels, Acts, Epistles, and Apocalypses (Oxford: Clarendon Press, 1924), 10.

"The Person of Christ. As the Righteous One (saddiq), the only man who has completely fulfilled the law, Jesus has been appointed to be the Christ (Hippolytus, Origen, Epiphanius). "Had another likewise fulfilled the precepts of the law, he too would have become Christ, for by like deeds other Christs (Christoi) could occur," reports Hippolytus concerning their faith (Philosophumena 7.34.1 f.).

"Jesus, moreover, fulfilled the law as man, not as Son of God but as Son of man. He was consecrated for Messiahship and endowed with the power of God not through real preexistence but through the act of adoption which was announced in Psalm 2:7 and which occurred at the time of his baptism, i.e., through the Holy Spirit present in the water of the baptismal bath. This "adoptionism" – in Recognitions 1.48 it is said that Jesus is he qui in aquis baptismi filius a deo appellatus est ("who in the waters of baptism was called Son by God")."

Hans-Joachim Schoeps, trans., Douglas R.A. Hare, Jewish Christianity: Factional Disputes in the Early Church (Philadelphia: Fortress Press, 1969), 61.

CHAPTER 12

[1] The Feast of Unleavened Bread:

Leviticus 23:6–8
[6] And on the fifteenth day of the same month is the Feast of Unleavened Bread to the LORD; for seven days you shall eat unleavened bread. [7] On the first day you shall have a holy convocation; you shall not do any ordinary work. [8] But you shall present a food offering to the LORD for seven days. On the seventh day is a holy convocation; you shall not do any ordinary work."

[2] Gischala's capture of the inner temple from Eleazar:

Flavius Josephus, The Wars of the Jews 5.3.2, §98-105
"On the feast of unleavened bread, which was come, it being the fourteenth day of the month Xanthicus [Nisan], when it is believed the Jews were first freed from the Egyptians, Eleazar and his party opened the gates of this [inmost court of the] temple, and admitted such of the people as were desirous to worship God into it. (100) But John made use of this festival as a cloak for his treacherous designs, and armed the most inconsiderable of his own party, the greater part of whom were not purified, with weapons concealed under their garments, and sent them with great zeal into the temple, in order to seize upon it; which armed men, when they were gotten in, threw their garments away, and presently appeared in their armor. (101) Upon which there was a very great disorder and disturbance about the holy house; while the people who had no concern in the sedition, supposed that this assault was made against all without distinction, as the zealots thought it was made against themselves only. (102) So these left off guarding the gates any longer, and leaped down from their battlements before they came to an engagement, and fled away into the subterranean caverns of the temple; while the people that stood trembling at the altar, and about the holy house, were rolled on heaps together, and trampled upon, and were beaten both with wooden and with iron weapons without mercy. (103) Such also, as had differences with others, slew many persons that were quiet, out of their own private enmity and hatred, as if they were opposite to the seditious; and all those that had formerly offended any of these plotters, were now known, and were now led away to the slaughter; (104) and, when they had done abundance of horrid mischief to the guiltless, they granted a truce to the guilty, and let those go off that came out of the caverns. These followers of John also did now seize upon this inner temple, and upon all the warlike engines therein, and then ventured to oppose Simon. (105) And thus that sedition, which had been divided into three factions, was now reduced to two."

Flavius Josephus and William Whiston, The Works of Josephus: Complete and Unabridged (Peabody: Hendrickson, 1987), 701–702.

CHAPTER 13

343

[1] Azazel:

In Leviticus 16, we read of the sacrificial offering on the Day of Atonement. Among other sacrifices, the high priest would take two goats for atonement of the people. One, he would kill as blood sacrifice on the altar, and the other, he would transfer the sins of the people onto the goat by confession and the laying on of his hands. This action of transferring the bloodguilt onto the "other" is where we got the concept of "scapegoat."

But that is not the most fascinating piece of this puzzle. For in verses 8–10 and 26, the priest is told to send the goat "away into the wilderness to Azazel" (v. 10)! You read that right: Azazel.

> Leviticus 16:7-10
> Then he shall take the two goats and set them before the Lord at the entrance of the Tent of Meeting. And Aaron shall cast lots over the two goats, one lot for the Lord and the other lot for Azazel.And Aaron shall present the goat on which the lot fell for the Lord and use it as a sin offering, but the goat on which the lot fell for Azazel shall be presented alive before the Lord to make atonement over it, that it may be sent away into the wilderness to Azazel.

The name Azazel is not explained anywhere in the Old Testament, but we've heard that name before in the book of 1Enoch. Azazel was one of the lead Watchers who led the rebellion of 200 Watchers to mate with the daughters of men. And that Watcher was considered bound in the desert of Dudael.

The natural question arises whether this is the same sacrifice to goat demons that Yahweh condemns in the very Leviticus and Isaiah passages we already looked at. But a closer look dispels such concerns.

The first goat was "for Yahweh" and the second "for Azazel" (v. 8). But whereas the first goat was a sacrifice, the second was not. As commentator Jacob Milgrom claims, "In pre-Israelite practice [Azazel] was surely a true demon, perhaps a satyr, who ruled in the wilderness – in the Priestly ritual he is no longer a personality but just a name, designating the place to which impurities and sins are banished."

Milgrom then explains that in the ancient world, purgation and elimination rites went together. The sending out of the scapegoat to Azazel in the wilderness was a way of banishing evil to its place of origin which was described as the netherworld of chaos, where its malevolent powers could no longer do harm to the sender. This wilderness of "tohu and wabohu" or emptiness and wasteland was precisely the chaos that Yahweh pushed back to establish his covenantal order of the heavens and earth, so it was where all demonic entities were considered to reside.

So Azazel could very well have been considered the father or leader of the goat demons.

Brian Godawa, When Giants Were Upon the Earth: The Watchers, the Nephilim, and the Biblical Cosmic War of the Seed (Los Angeles, CA: Embedded Pictures Publishing, 2014), 218-219.

[2] Ten thousand times ten thousand of his holy ones: The heavenly host of God's throne.

> **Daniel 7:10** (The throne of the Ancient of Days in heaven)
> [10] A stream of fire issued and came out from before him; a thousand thousands served him, and **ten thousand times ten thousand** stood before him; the court sat in judgment, and the books were opened.

> **Enoch 1:9**
> Behold, he will arrive with **ten million [ten thousand times ten thousand]** of the holy ones in order to execute judgment upon all. He will destroy the wicked ones and censure all flesh on account of everything that they have done, that which the sinners and the wicked ones committed against him.

> **Deuteronomy 33:2–3**
> [2] He said, "The LORD came from Sinai and dawned from Seir upon us; he shone forth from Mount Paran; he came from the **ten thousands of holy ones**, with flaming fire at his right hand. [3] Yes, he loved his people, all **his holy ones** were in his hand; so they followed in your steps, receiving direction from you,

> **Deuteronomy 33:2–3 (LXX)**
> The Lord is come from Sinai, and has appeared from Seir to us, and has hasted out of the mount of Pharan, with the ten thousands of Cades; on his right hand *were* his angels with him. [3] And he

spared his people, and all his sanctified ones *are* under thy hands; and they are under thee; and he received of his words [4] the law which Moses charged us[2]

Psalm 68:17 (Context: Spiritual cosmic mountain comparison of Bashan with Sinai)
[17] The chariots of God are twice ten thousand, thousands upon thousands; the Lord is among them; Sinai is now in the sanctuary.

Hebrews 2:2
For since the message **declared by angels** proved to be reliable, and every transgression or disobedience received a just retribution,

Jude 14–15
Enoch...prophesied, saying, "Behold, the Lord came with many thousands of His holy ones, to execute judgment upon all, and to convict all the ungodly of all their ungodly deeds which they have done in an ungodly way, and of all the harsh things which ungodly sinners have spoken against Him."

[3] This description of the demonic hordes comes from: Revelation 9:7-19.

[4] **Foes of Israel coming from the Euphrates river and the north**: "That they have been held at "the great river Euphrates" evokes the OT prophecy of an army from beyond the Euphrates (from "the north") whom God will bring to judge sinful Israel (Isa. 5:26–29; 7:20; 8:7–8; 14:29–31; Jer. 1:14–15; 4:6–13; 6:1, 22; 10:22; 13:20; Ezek. 38:6, 15; 39:2; Joel 2:1–11, 20–25) and other ungodly nations around Israel (Isa. 14:31; Jer. 25:9, 26; 46–47; 50:41–42; Ezek. 26:7–11; cf. Assumption of Moses 3:1)."

G. K. Beale, The Book of Revelation: A Commentary on the Greek Text, New International Greek Testament Commentary (Grand Rapids, MI; Carlisle, Cumbria: W.B. Eerdmans; Paternoster Press, 1999), 506.

"Not only is the Euphrates Israel's ideal northern border, but it is also the extent of the power of Israel's two most powerful kings, David (2Sa 8:3; 1Ch 18:3) and Solomon (2Ch 9:26). Because it is an important marker of the northern border of Israel, Beale (506) notes that in the Old Testament the Euphrates long serves as an apocalyptic image of God's threatened judgment upon his covenant people by means of invading forces (Isa 7:20; 8:7–8; 27:12; Jer 1:14–15; 6:1, 22; 10:22; 13:20; Eze 38:6, 15; 39:2; Joel 2:20-25). This is because historically "from the River Euphrates had come Sennacherib and Nebuchadnezzar, destroyers of Samaria and Jerusalem; by now the Euphrates has become a mere symbol for the quarter from which judgment is to come on Jerusalem" (Carrington 165)."

Kenneth L. Gentry, Jr., The Divorce of Israel: A Redemptive-Historical Interpretation of Revelation Vol. 1 (Dallas, GA: Tolle Lege Press, 2016), 758-759.

"The Bible often uses north as a designation for a geographical area that includes the north as well as the northeast. For example, Babylon was mostly east of Israel, but Jeremiah 4:6 warns that the disaster that came upon Judah would arrive "from the north," a reference to Babylon (Jer. 1:13–15; 3:18; 6:1, 22; 10:22; Zech. 2:6–7). Notice that "all the families of the kingdoms of the north will break forth on all the inhabitants of the land" (Jer. 1:15). Charles Dyer, who teaches that Ezekiel 38 and 39 are describing a future battle,5 makes the point that "from the north land" and "remote parts of the earth" (Jer. 6:22) are "an apt description of the Babylonians (cf. Hab. 1:6–11)"6 and their invasion of Israel in the sixth century B.C. If Babylon is said to invade Israel from the north when it is actually mostly east of Israel, and north is the "remote parts of the earth,"7 then "far north" can have a similar meaning in Ezekiel (38:6, 15; 39:2).

"The same is also the case when Israel was overrun by the Assyrians (Zeph. 2:13) and Persians (Isa. 41:25; Jer. 50:3). Consider this description of a northern invasion that was on the prophetic horizon, a battle fought with bows and arrows and javelins: "Behold, a people is coming from the north, and a great nation and many kings will be aroused from the remote parts of the earth" (Jer. 50:41). The "remote parts of the earth" seems like a description far beyond the then-known world, but it wasn't. Jeremiah was describing the judgment of Babylon (50:42). Is the Bible mistaken? Not at all. The language is typical of prophetic/poetry passages, and it's no different from the way Ezekiel uses the "remote parts of the north." As Timothy Daily concludes, "From the perspective of the Holy Land, the invaders came down from the north, even if their place of origin was actually to the east. Ezekiel is giving the direction of the invasion, not the place of the invader's origin."

"Archeologist Barry Beitzel confirms this analysis when he states that "the Bible's use of the expression 'north' denotes the direction from which a foe would normally approach and not the location of its homeland." 9 The

345

same holds true for any invading army that was north and east of Israel. They, too, would have to bring a land army into Israel from the north since the Mediterranean Sea is directly west of Israel. Tanner concludes: "'North' refers not so much to the precise geographical direction from Israel, but rather to the direction of advance and attack upon Israel (armies came against Israel from the north). This is how Jeremiah viewed Babylonia, though Babylonia was technically to the east."

Gary DeMar, *The Gog and Magog End-Time Alliance*, (Powder Springs, GA: American Vision Inc., 2016), 90-91.

CHAPTER 14

[1] The haste of leaving Egypt:

Exodus 12:33–34
[33] The Egyptians were urgent with the people to send them out of the land in haste. For they said, "We shall all be dead." [34] So the people took their dough before it was leavened, their kneading bowls being bound up in their cloaks on their shoulders.

[2] This is quoted from: Psalm 74:13–17

[3] Covenant described as Creation:

From Brian Godawa, *End Times Bible Prophecy: It's Not What They Told You* (Los Angeles, CA: Embedded Pictures Publishing, 2017), 45-46.

When God created the heavens and the earth in Genesis 1, he was creating order out of the chaos of Genesis 1:2, the formlessness and emptiness of creation. Part of that created order was the sun, moon, and stars. They were to separate light and dark and be for signs and seasons (1:14-15). In ancient Near Eastern religions, people pictured the gods fighting the sea (a symbol of chaos) as an expression of their rule and power to illustrate their creation of order out of chaos. The Hebrew scriptures do the same thing, only in a way that says Yahweh is the true God. He is the one who created his covenant order within the chaos of the world.

Psalm 74 is a good example of this creation and covenant motif out of the chaos of the sea. Read this passage and notice how God had power over the chaos of the sea when he established his covenant through Moses. But then read on and you will see the language of creation connected to that covenant.

Psalm 74:13–17
You divided the sea by your might; you broke the heads of the sea monsters on the waters. [14] You crushed the heads of Leviathan; you gave him as food for the creatures of the wilderness. [15] You split open springs and brooks; you dried up ever-flowing streams. [16] Yours is the day, yours also the night; <u>you have established the heavenly lights and the sun.</u> [17] You have fixed all the boundaries of the earth.

The creation language of the sun, moon, and stars separating day and night is part of God fixing or establishing the boundaries of the earth. God's covenant with Israel is described in the language of creation of the universe. It is poetic metaphor, an image that stands for something else.

Isaiah also wrote about the Mosaic covenant beginning when God conquered the chaos of the Red Sea. Creating God's people, Zion, is expressed in terms of Genesis 1, establishing the heavens and earth.

Isaiah 51:15–16
I am the LORD your God, who stirs up the sea so that its waves roar – the LORD of hosts is his name. [16] And I have put my words in your mouth and covered you in the shadow of my hand, <u>establishing the heavens and laying the foundations of the earth</u>, and saying to Zion, "You are my people."

So we see that God described his covenantal relationship in the cosmic terms of creation, including the sun, moon, and stars. He created order out of chaos with his covenantal rule. Creating his covenantal order with his people was spiritually likened to the creation of the heavens and the earth.

[4] Temple destruction as decreation/return to chaos:

"In a passage filled with striking imagery, the judgment that is to fall on Judah takes on the aspect of a cosmic conflagration. Jeremiah experiences a dramatic glimpse into the outpouring of divine anger upon Judah. The earth and the heavens (v. 23), the mountains and the hills (v. 24), humanity and the birds (v. 25), the fields and the cities (v. 26), all were to feel the weight of Yahweh's wrath. To a degree the language is Oriental hyperbole, but Jeremiah uses imagery and phraseology which his predecessors used in their references to the divine judgment (cf. Isa. 2:12ff.; Hos. 4:3). The range of disturbance was thus so great that it seemed to represent a return to primeval chaos. Little wonder that Jeremiah was filled with anguish and amazement. None of the other contemporary prophets spoke of the coming doom in such powerful terms.

"23 Jeremiah made use of a phrase known from Gen. 1:2 tōhû wāḇōhû, "without form and void" (AV), that is, primeval chaos, the formless void that existed before God began to work on the newly created earth. The picture is of a reversal of the story of Gen. 1. Men, beasts, plants have all gone, the mountains reeled, the hills rocked to and fro, light vanished from the heavens, farm lands reverted to desert, towns were levelled to the ground. It was as if the earth had been "uncreated" and reverted to its erstwhile primeval chaos. Order seemed to return to confusion. Imagery something like this, referring to the Day of the Lord, is known elsewhere in the prophets (cf. Joel 2:1–11; Amos 8:9–10; Nah. 1:2–8; Zeph. 1:2–3)."

J. A. Thompson, *The Book of Jeremiah, The New International Commentary on the Old Testament* (Grand Rapids, MI: Wm. B. Eerdmans Publishing Co., 1980), 229–230.

[5] Unleavened Bread fulfillment:

"Unleavened bread (matzah) is a symbol of Passover. Leaven represents sin (Luke 12:1; 1 Cor. 5:7–8). Matzah stands for "without sin" and is a picture of Jesus, the only human without sin. Jesus said that the "bread of God is he who comes down from heaven and gives life to the world" and that he (Jesus) is the "bread of life," the "bread that came down from heaven," "the living bread" which a person may eat and not die (John 6:32, 35, 41, 48). While leaven is a symbol of sin, the Messiah is "unleavened" or sinless. He conquers the grave with his resurrection because he is not a sinner under the curse of death. Jesus was scourged and pierced at his crucifixion. As the prophet Isaiah proclaims, "By his stripes we are healed" (Isa. 53:5 KJV). All of the festivals instituted by God, including Passover and Unleavened Bread, are "shadows of things to come" (Col. 2:17).

Feasts and Holidays of the Bible (Rose Publishing, 2004, 2013), 7.

[6] Hebrews 2:5-6.

[7] New heavens and earth of Isaiah 65:

"Isaiah 65:17–25. In that glorious scene Isaiah presents a dramatic image of the gospel economy's historical impact. This economy will develop through "a multi-stage process that culminates at the final judgment."98 This redemptive economy will gradually transform the world ethically and spiritually, so that it appears as a "new heavens and a new earth" of which "the former shall not be remembered or come to mind" (Isa 65:17).

"Isaiah's vision is the background of Paul's statement in 2 Corinthians 5:17, which refers to contemporary spiritual realities: "Therefore, if anyone is in Christ, he is a new creation; old things have passed away; behold, all things have become new."99 According to New Testament theology, the Second Adam, Christ, stands at the head of a new creation (Ro 5:14; 1Co 15:22, 45).

"Calvin views Isaiah 65:17–25 as a new covenant blessing that results from a change in covenantal administration:

> By these metaphors he promises a remarkable change of affairs; as if God had said that he has
> both the inclination and the power not only to restore his Church, but to restore it in such a manner
> that it shall appear to gain new life and to dwell in a new world. These are exaggerated modes of
> expression; but the greatness of such a blessing, which was to be manifested at the coming of
> Christ, could not be described in any other way. Nor does he mean only the first coming, but the
> whole reign, which must be extended as far as to the last coming.

"The transformational effect of the gospel kingdom is such that those who are newly born of its power101 are thereby constituted new creatures: "in Christ Jesus neither circumcision nor uncircumcision avails anything, but a new creation" (Gal 6:15). The transforming power of the gospel creates a "new man" of two warring factions, Jew and Gentile (Eph 2:15–18). Gospel-transformed new creatures are to lay aside the old self and take on the new (Eph 4:22–23), which is "created according to God, in righteousness and true holiness" (Eph 4:24; cf. Col 3:9–11). This is because they are "His workmanship, created in Christ Jesus for good works, which God prepared beforehand that we should walk in them" (Eph 2:10).

"This glorious conception involves both a re-created "Jerusalem" and "people" (Isa 65:18–19). Interestingly, in Galatians 6 Paul speaks of the new creation in the context of a transformed "Israel of God" existing in his day: "For in Christ Jesus neither circumcision nor uncircumcision avails anything, but a new creation. and as many as walk according to this rule, peace and mercy be upon them, even upon the Israel of God" (Gal 6:15–16; cf. Ro 2:28–29). In that same epistle, he urges a commitment to the "Jerusalem above" (the heavenly Jerusalem, Heb 12:22) rather than to the cast out Jerusalem that now is (the historical capital city of Israel, Gal 4:25–26).

"The heavenly Jerusalem is the bride of Christ that comes down from God to replace the earthly Jerusalem (Rev 21:2–5) in the first century (Rev 1:1, 3; 22:6, 10). With the shaking and destruction of the old Jerusalem in AD 70, the heavenly (re-created) Jerusalem replaces her: His "voice then shook the earth; but now He has promised, saying, 'Yet once more I shake not only the earth, but also heaven.' Now this, 'Yet once more,' indicates the removal of those things that are being shaken, as of things that are made [i.e., the Levitical ritual system102], that the things which cannot be shaken may remain. Therefore, since we are receiving a kingdom which cannot be shaken, let us have grace, by which we may serve God acceptably with reverence and godly fear" (Heb 12:26–28; cp. 8:13)."

Kenneth Gentry, *He Shall Have Dominion: A Postmillennial Eschatology* (Apologetics Group Media, 1992, 1997, 1999, 2009), 406-408..

[8] The New Covenant Church is the New Jerusalem. And the old covenant is about to be "shaken" or removed:

Hebrews 12:22–28
22 But you have come to Mount Zion and to the city of the living God, the heavenly Jerusalem, and to innumerable angels in festal gathering, 23 and to the assembly of the firstborn who are enrolled in heaven, and to God, the judge of all, and to the spirits of the righteous made perfect, 24 and to Jesus, the mediator of a new covenant, and to the sprinkled blood that speaks a better word than the blood of Abel. 25 See that you do not refuse him who is speaking. For if they did not escape when they refused him who warned them on earth, much less will we escape if we reject him who warns from heaven. 26 At that time his voice shook the earth, but now he has promised, "Yet once more I will shake not only the earth but also the heavens." 27 This phrase, "Yet once more," indicates the removal of things that are shaken – that is, things that have been made – in order that the things that cannot be shaken may remain. 28 Therefore let us be grateful for receiving a kingdom that cannot be shaken…

The bride of Christ is the New Jerusalem:

Revelation 21:1–2; 9-10
1 Then I saw a new heaven and a new earth, for the first heaven and the first earth had passed away, and the sea was no more. 2 And I saw the holy city, new Jerusalem, coming down out of heaven from God, prepared as a bride adorned for her husband.

9 Then came one of the seven angels who had the seven bowls full of the seven last plagues and spoke to me, saying, "Come, I will show you the Bride, the wife of the Lamb." 10 And he carried me away in the Spirit to a great, high mountain, and showed me the holy city Jerusalem coming down out of heaven from God…

The new covenant makes the old covenant obsolete when the temple is destroyed:

Hebrews 8:13
13 In speaking of a new covenant, he makes the first one obsolete. And what is becoming obsolete and growing old is ready to vanish away. [the temple had not yet been destroyed when this was first written]

[9] **Boaz refers to**: Romans 16:20.

[10] **Boaz quotes from**: Ephesianns 6:12.

[11] John 6:32–35.

[12] The fortress at Pella:

"South of the main mound of Pella, across the deeply carved Wadi Jirm, is the steep, largely natural hill called Tell el-Husn (Arabic for fortress). On the northern slopes of the hillside of Tell el-Husn is a stretch of beautifully constructed limestone fortification wall. This wall probably once ringed the summit of the hill. Basil Hennessy's codirector and Hellenistic pottery ceramicist, Tony McNicoll, dated some of the material linked to the wall to the Herodian and early Roman Imperial age. Several coins support this dating…

"As already noted, traces of a near-impregnable Husn fortress have survived. We can assume Pella's citizens continued to occupy the Husn summit in the years after the Hasmonean sack by Alexander Jannaeus."

Stephen Bourke, "The Christian Flight to Pella: True or Tale?" *Biblical Archeology Review* Vol 39 No 3

http://earlywritings.com/forum/viewtopic.php?t=2742

[13] The caves of Pella:

"The last hope for those seeking remains of early Christians at ancient Pella seemingly rests in a cave complex just a short distance from the main mound. Although the caves have not been fully surveyed or excavated due to health risks, several of them were outfitted as residences in antiquity and may have served as ideal living spaces or hideouts for fleeing Christians."

"Excavating Ancient Pella, Jordan: Archaeology investigates the Jerusalem Christians' escape to Pella," Biblical Archaeology Society Staff, 12/23/2017, Bible History Daily Online.
https://www.biblicalarchaeology.org/daily/biblical-sites-places/biblical-archaeology-sites/excavating-ancient-pella-jordan/

"This brings us back to "Schumacher's Caves," the caves that Gottlieb Schumacher explored at the end of the 19th century, which he thought might have been occupied by the Christians who supposedly fled to Pella in 70 A.D. These caves were cut into the sharply rising north face of the Wadi Jirm some 1,600 feet southwest of the main mound, and nearly a mile from the Civic Complex at the head of the Wadi Jirm…

"These caves, apparently unknown to Schumacher (or to his successor Richmond), were partly natural, and partly hewn, and consisted of a series of large, roughly rounded chambers between 10 by 10 feet and 15 by 15 feet, connected together by narrow passageways…

"As strings of connected rooms, these complexes penetrated deep under the rock escarpment, forming a series of hewn and columned rooms, well provisioned with lamp niches and sleeping benches. Airflow and light were ensured by wide porch-like galleries that opened onto the sheer north face of the wadi, completely inaccessible from the wadi bottom some 125 feet below. Entranceways into these caves were small, concealed and easily defended."

http://earlywritings.com/forum/viewtopic.php?t=2742

[14] **The whip-sword Rahab and its story**: Uriel actually got the sword from Jesus. This weapon has a long fictional history that is told through the entire *Chronicles of the Nephilim* series ending with *Jesus Triumphant*.

[15] **These stories are all found in the prior series**: *Chronicles of the Nephilim* by Brian Godawa.

[1] **Elihu quotes from**: Revelation 18:2-3 and 18:9.

Jerusalem as a dwelling place of demons:

"During the Jewish War, Jerusalem (and the Land) became very much a "dwelling place of demons" in that she "became infested with demoniacal exhibitions of wickedness" (Terry 437). We may discern this from Josephus's lament that "neither did any other city ever suffer such miseries, nor did any age ever breed a generation more fruitful in wickedness that this was, from the beginning of the world" (J.W. 5:10:5 §442). He writes that "the madness of the rebellious did also increase together with their famine, and both those miseries were every day inflamed more and more" (J.W. 5:10:2 §424). "And indeed that was a time most fertile in all manner of wicked practices, insomuch that no kind of evil deeds were then left undone; nor could any one so much as devise any bad thing that was new, so deeply were they all infected, and strove with one another in their single capacity, and in their communities, who should run the greatest lengths in impiety

349

towards God, and in unjust actions towards their neighbors; the men of power oppressing the multitude, and the multitude earnestly laboring to destroy the men of power. The one part were desirous of tyrannizing over others, and the rest of offering violence to others, and of plundering such as were richer than themselves. They were the Sicarii who first began these transgressions, and first became barbarous towards those allied to them, and left no words of reproach unsaid, and no works of perdition untried, in order to destroy those whom their contrivances affected" (J.W. 7:8:1 §259–62). He states that John of Gischala "filled his entire country with ten thousand instances of wickedness, such as a man who was already hardened sufficiently in his impiety towards God would naturally do" (J.W. 7:8:1 §263)."

Kenneth L. Gentry, Jr., The Divorce of Israel: A Redemptive-Historical Interpretation of Revelation Vol. 2 (Dallas, GA: Tolle Lege Press, 2016), 494.

² "The wine of the passion of her immorality":

"By the "wine of the passion [thumos] of her immorality" (18:3), John appears to be symbolically portraying the widespread Jewish passion for stirring up the nations (ta ethnē, "Gentiles," 18:3a) against Christians (see discussion of the Jewish role in the Neronic persecution at 13:7b).17 This repeats the idea found in 17:1-2 (drunkenness + immorality) where we hear of the "judgment" (krima) of the Babylonian harlot who "sits on many waters," which waters represent "peoples and multitudes and nations [ethnē] and tongues" (17:15). There Babylon-Jerusalem is drunk on the blood of the saints (17:6)."

Kenneth L. Gentry, Jr., The Divorce of Israel: A Redemptive-Historical Interpretation of Revelation Vol. 2 (Dallas, GA: Tolle Lege Press, 2016), 503.

Jewish leaders influenced Nero to persecute Christians:

In Tyrant: Rise of the Beast, I argue that high placed Jews like Josephus and Poppea most likely inspired Nero to blame the Great Fire of Rome on the Christians in order to save their own people.

Josephus was in Rome during the Great Fire:

Flavius Josephus, The Life of Flavius Josephus, 13-16. Flavius Josephus, The Antiquities of the Jews, 20.195.

Tigellinus, Poppaea, Aliturius and Josephus are all considered possible candidates of influencing Nero to blame the Christians for the Great Fire: Leon Hardy Canfield, The Early Persecutions of the Christians (New York, Columbia, 1913), 69.

The Jews diverting Nero away from them to the Christians:

Regarding Nero's search for scapegoats on which to blame the Roman fires of July, AD 64 (Tac., Ann. 15:41), Gibbon sees the Jews behind Nero's choice of Christians. He notes that the Jews "possessed very powerful advocates in the palace, and even in the heart of the tyrant: his wife and mistress, the beautiful Poppaea, and a favourite player of the race of Abraham." These two suggest to Nero "the new and pernicious sect of Galileans," the Christians…

Clement (1 Clem 6:5) claims that the Neronic persecution was prompted "through envy [dia zēlos pathontes]," which many scholars believe refers to the Jews…

(2) Suetonius (Claud. 25:4; cp. Dio 60:66:6) shows that the Jews were expelled from Rome under Claudius around AD 50 for causing riots in their confrontations with Christians (cp. Ac 18:2; 24:5). The Romans disliked the Jews (Jos., Ap 2:66-92) even declaring that "the Jews regard as profane all that we hold sacred; on the other hand, they permit all that we abhor" (Tac., Hist 5:4). Tacitus (Hist. 5:5) adds that "the other customs of the Jews are base and abominable, and owe their persistence to their depravity" and that toward the non-Jewish "they feel only hate and enmity." Romans saw the Jews as troublemakers frequently stirring riots in Rome. Such conduct caused the Romans to expel them from Rome on several occasions (Suet., Tib. 36; Tac. Ann. 2:85; Jos. Ant. 18:3:5 §81). The Jews could rightly fear that blame for the AD 64 fires in Rome might fall upon them and would therefore be motivated to deflect attention to the Christians…

Schaff (HCC 1:383) comments that "it is not unlikely that in this (as in all previous persecutions, and often afterwards) the fanatical Jews, enraged by the rapid progress of Christianity, and anxious to avert suspicion from themselves, stirred up the people against the hated Galileans." Kenneth L. Gentry, Jr., The Divorce of Israel: A Redemptive-Historical Interpretation of Revelation Vol. 2 (Dallas, GA: Tolle Lege Press, 2016), 220-

223.

[3] **Moshe quotes from:** Revelation 18:10-11.

[4] The merchant goods listed here:

This list of merchandise parallels Ezekiel 27:12-24 list of Tyre's merchandise in her judgment.

Even better, with the merchandise of the first temple aided by Tyre: 2 Chronicles 2:11-14

"This list follows Ezek 27. Not exactly, but very close. It is Solomon who is the Israelite most associated in the Old Testament with Tyrian trade (the subject of Ezek. 27.12-24), and what was it, according to 1 Kings 5, that Hiram of Tyre provided Solomon with? Materials for the building of the Jerusalem temple!"

The Temple only accepted the currency of Tyre, and ironically, the Tyrian coinage had an image of Melkart on it, which made it idolatrous used in the temple!:

"There is also evidence of commerce with Tyre in the frequent equivalents drawn between the Jerusalem money and the Tyrian (p. 33). According to T. Ket. xiii.3, and elsewhere, the Jerusalem standard of currency was the same as the Tyrian. The prevalence of the Tyrian standard is explained not only by the brisk trade which went on, but also because in the Temple only Tyrian currency was allowed."

Joachim Jeremias, *Jerusalem in the time of Jesus*, (Christian Book Distributors, 2014), 36.

[5] **A condensation of** Revelation 18:20-24.

[6] **Jerusalem's covenantal glory:** "The angel now identifies the Harlot as the Great City, which, as we have seen, St. John uses as a term for Jerusalem, where the Lord was crucified (11 :8; 16: 19). Moreover, says the angel, this City has a Kingdom over all the kings of the earth. It is perhaps this verse, more than any other, which has confused expositors into supposing, against all other evidence, that the Harlot is Rome. If the City is Jerusalem, how can she be said to wield this kind of worldwide political power? The answer is that Revelation is not a book about politics; it is a book about the Covenant. Jerusalem did reign over the nations. She did possess a Kingdom which was above all the kingdoms of the world. She had a covenantal priority over the kingdoms of the earth. Israel was a Kingdom of priests (Ex. 19:6), exercising a priestly ministry of guardianship, instruction, and intercession on behalf of the nations of the world. When Israel was faithful to God, offering up sacrifices for the nations, the world was at peace; when Israel broke the Covenant, the world was in turmoil. The Gentile nations recognized this (1 Kings 10:24; Ezra 1; 4-7; cf. Rom. 2:17-24).26 Yet, perversely, they would seek to seduce Israel to commit whoredom against the Covenant – and when she did, they would turn on her and destroy her. That pattern was repeated several times over until Israel's final excommunication in A.D. 70, when Jerusalem was destroyed. The desolation of the Harlot was God's final sign that the Kingdom had been transferred to His new people, the Church (Matt. 21:43; 1 Pet. 2:9; Rev. 11:19; 15:5; 21:3). The Kingdom over the kingdoms will never again be possessed by national Israel." David Chilton, *The Days of Vengeance: An Exposition of the Book of Revelation* (Texas: Dominion Press, 1987, 1990) 442-443.

[7] The blood of the prophets upon the first century generation:

> Matthew 23:35–36
> [35] so that on you may come all the righteous blood shed on earth, from the blood of righteous Abel to the blood of Zechariah the son of Barachiah, whom you murdered between the sanctuary and the altar. [36] Truly, I say to you, all these things will come upon this generation.

CHAPTER 18

[1] **This past encounter between Uriel and Molech during the days of Messiah:** This is a fictional event that occurs in the novel Jesus Triumphant, book 8 of Chronicles of the Nephilim by Brian Godawa. You're just going to have to buy it to find out.

[2] **Cherubim hair as binding the angels:** The concept is entirely fictional. But it is based on some mythopoeic research. "Through the entire Chronicles of the Nephilim series, I have used a concept called "binding" of angels, demons, and Watchers. This binding is accomplished through imprisonment in the earth or Tartarus.

351

"This binding notion originates theologically from the binding of Satan in the ministry of Christ as noted above in Matthew 12, as well as the binding of angels in "chains of gloomy darkness" in Tartarus in Jude 6 and 2 Peter 2:4. And these New Testament Scriptures are paraphrases of the Enochian narrative of the antediluvian Watchers who at the Flood were "bound" "for seventy generations underneath the rocks of the ground until the day of their judgment" (1 Enoch 10:12).

"The idea of binding spirits is a common one in ancient religion and magic. Michael Fishbane notes that in the ancient Near East, incantations and spells were used by sorcerers and enchanters to bind people and spirits in spiritual "traps, pits, snares, and nets," using venomous curses from their lips like serpents. In response to some of these verbal sorceries, the Psalmist himself calls upon Yahweh in similar utterances to reverse the spells upon his enemies that they would be trapped, ensnared and bound by their own magical devices (Psalm 140; 64; 57:4-6). Exorcists of the first century used incantations to cast out demons in Jesus' name (Acts 16:18), the same incantation used by Demons against Jesus before being cast out (Mk 1:27).

"Ezekiel 13:18 refers to a specific form of hunting and binding spirits in a practice of women "who sew magic bands upon all wrists...in the hunt for souls!" I reversed this pagan version of using magical armbands by creating a heavenly version of the archangels with armbands of indestructible Cherubim hair for their hunting and binding of evil spirits. The hair is wrapped as bands around the arms of archangels and used like a rope to bind the Watchers' hands and feet." Brian Godawa, *When Giants Were Upon the Earth: The Watchers, the Nephilim, and the Biblical Cosmic War of the Seed* (Embedded Pictures, 2014), 285-286.

For the story of the angels being bound at the Flood, see: Brian Godawa, *Noah Primeval* (Los Angeles, CA: Embedded Pictures Publishing, 2011).

[3] **Watchers weakened by water**: This is creative license that is based on theological possibilities. Jesus speaks of demons traveling over waterless places when cast out of humans.

Matthew 12:43
When the unclean spirit has gone out of a person, it passes through waterless places seeking rest, but finds none.

Most commentaries have no idea what this means. But there is connection between demons and the desert that suggest that the desert is a metaphor for chaos in contrast with the orderliness of his Promised Land of milk and honey. Thus, the desert is the habitation of demons without human hosts.

The notion of Azazel in the Leviticus law of scapegoating carries this meaning. In Leviticus 16, the high priest Aaron is instructed in sin offerings for the people of Israel. One of those offerings is to be a scapegoat.

Leviticus 16:7–10
Then he shall take the two goats and set them before the LORD at the entrance of the tent of meeting. And Aaron shall cast lots over the two goats, one lot for the LORD and the other lot for Azazel. And Aaron shall present the goat on which the lot fell for the LORD and use it as a sin offering, but the goat on which the lot fell for Azazel shall be presented alive before the LORD to make atonement over it, that it may be sent away into the wilderness to Azazel.

The name Azazel is not explained anywhere in the Old Testament, but we've heard that name before in the book of 1Enoch. Azazel was one of the lead Watchers who led the rebellion of 200 Watchers to mate with the daughters of men. And that Watcher was considered bound in the desert of Dudael.

The natural question arises whether this is the same sacrifice to goat demons that Yahweh condemns in the very Leviticus and Isaiah passages we already looked at. But a closer look dispels such concerns.

The first goat was "for Yahweh" and the second "for Azazel" (v. 8). But whereas the first goat was a sacrifice, the second was not. As commentator Jacob Milgrom claims, "In pre-Israelite practice [Azazel] was surely a true demon, perhaps a satyr, who ruled in the wilderness – in the Priestly ritual he is no longer a personality but just a name, designating the place to which impurities and sins are banished."

Milgrom then explains that in the ancient world, purgation and elimination rites went together. The sending out of the scapegoat to Azazel in the wilderness was a way of banishing evil to its place of origin which was described as the netherworld of chaos, where its malevolent powers could no longer do harm to the sender. This wilderness of "tohu and wabohu" or emptiness and wasteland was precisely the chaos that Yahweh pushed back to establish his covenantal order of the heavens and earth, so it was where all demonic entities were considered to reside.

From this connection of demons with desert and "waterless" places, I speculated that maybe demons were afraid of water in light of their desert habitations. And since the Enochian interpretation of demons defines them as spirits of the dead Nephilim, and since the Nephilim were destroyed in the Flood, along with the binding of the Watchers into the earth, then I added speculation that water might have made it easier for the angels to bind the Watchers into the earth during the Flood. Again, this is purely creative theological speculation that seeks to give meaning to the text by using the imagination.

I think the important point is that I didn't make it up out of whole cloth, but rather stitched together pieces of the Scriptural tapestry.

CHAPTER 21

[1] Mount Hermon is the Mountain of Bashan, the spiritual opponent of Yahweh in the Bible:

In Matthew 16:13-20 is the famous story of Peter's confession of Jesus as the Christ, who then responds, "I tell you, you are Peter, and on this rock I will build my church, and the gates of hell [Hades] shall not prevail against it" (v. 18). Shortly after, Jesus leads them up to a high mountain where he is transfigured.

In order to understand the spiritual reality of what is going on in this polemical sequence and its relevance to the cosmic War of the Seed, we must first understand where it is going on.

Verse 13 says that Peter's confession takes place in the district of Caesarea Philippi. This city was in the heart of Bashan on a rocky terrace in the foothills of Mount Hermon. This was the celebrated location of the grotto of Banias or Panias, where the satyr goat god Pan was worshipped and from where the mouth of the Jordan river flowed. This very location was what was known as the "gates of Hades," the underworld abode of dead souls.

The Jewish historian Josephus wrote of this sacred grotto during his time, "a dark cave opens itself; within which there is a horrible precipice, that descends abruptly to a vast depth; it contains a mighty quantity of water, which is immovable; and when anybody lets down anything to measure the depth of the earth beneath the water, no length of cord is sufficient to reach it."

As scholar Judd Burton points out, this is a kind of ground zero for the gods against whom Jesus was fighting his cosmic spiritual war. Mount Hermon was the location where the Watchers came to earth, led their rebellion and miscegenation, which birthed the Nephilim (1 Enoch 13:7-10). It was their headquarters, in Bashan, the place of the Serpent, where Azazel may have been worshipped before Pan as a desert goat idol.

When Jesus speaks of building his church upon a rock, it is as much a polemical contrast with the pagan city upon the rock, as it may have been a word play off of Peter's name, meaning "stone." In the ancient world, mountains were not only a gateway between heaven, earth, and the underworld, but also the habitations of the gods that represented their heavenly power and authority. The mountain before them, Hermon, was considered the heavenly habitation of Canaanite gods as well as the very Watchers before whose gates of Hades Jesus now stood. The polemics become clearer when one realizes that gates are not offensive weapons, but defensive means. Christ's kingship is storming the very gates of Hades/Sheol in the heart of darkness and he will build his cosmic holy mountain upon its ruins.

But the battle is only beginning. Because the very next incident that occurs is the transfiguration (Matt. 17:1-13). The text says that Jesus led three disciples up a high mountain. But it doesn't say which mountain. Though tradition has often concluded it was Mount Tabor, a more likely candidate is Mount Hermon itself. The reasons are because Tabor is not a high mountain at only 1800 feet compared to Hermon's 9000 feet height, and Tabor was a well traveled location which would not allow Jesus to be alone with his disciples (17:1).

Then the text says, that Jesus "was transfigured before them, and his face shone like the sun, and his clothes became white as light. And behold, there appeared to them Moses and Elijah, talking with him" (Matthew 17:2–3). When Peter offers to put up three tabernacles for each of his heroes, he hears a voice from the cloud say, "This is my beloved Son with whom I am well pleased, listen to him" (vs. 4-5). The theological point of this being that Moses and Elijah are the representatives of the Old Covenant, summed up as the Law (Moses) and the Prophets (Elijah), but Jesus is the anointed King (Messiah) that both Law and Prophets pointed toward.

So God is anointing Jesus and transferring all covenantal authority to him as God's own Son. And for what purpose? To become king upon the new cosmic mountain that God was establishing: Mount Zion in the city of God. In the Mosaic Covenant, Mount Sinai was considered the cosmic mountain of God where God had his assembly of divine holy ones (Deut. 33:2-3). But now, as pronounced by the prophets, that mountain was being transferred out of the wilderness wandering into a new home in the Promised Land as Mount Zion (ultimately in Jerusalem). And that new mountain was the displacement and replacement of the previous divine occupants of Mount Hermon. Of course, just like David the messianic type, Jesus was anointed as king, but there would be a delay of time before he would take that rightful throne because he had some Goliaths yet to conquer (1 Sam. 16:13; 2 Sam. 5:3).

Take a look at this Psalm and see how the language of cosmic war against the anointed Messiah is portrayed as a victory of God establishing his new cosmic mountain. We see a repeat of the language of Jesus' transfiguration at Hermon.

Psalm 2:1–8 (NASB95)
1 Why are the nations in an uproar And the peoples devising a vain thing? 2 The kings of the earth take their stand And the rulers [heavenly as well?] take counsel together Against the LORD and against His Anointed [Messiah], saying, 3 "Let us tear their fetters apart And cast away their cords from us!" 4 He who sits in the heavens laughs, The Lord scoffs at them. 5 Then He will speak to them in His anger And terrify them in His fury, saying, 6 "But as for Me, I have installed My King Upon Zion, My holy mountain." 7 "I will surely tell of the decree of the LORD: He said to Me, 'You are My Son, Today I have begotten You. 8 'Ask of Me, and I will surely give the nations as Your inheritance, And the very ends of the earth as Your possession.

Like Moses' transfiguration in Exodus 34:29, Jesus' body was transformed by his anointing to shine with the glory of those who surround God's throne (Dan. 10:6; Ezek 1:14-16, 21ff.; 10:9). But that description is no where near the ending of this spiritual parade of triumph being previewed in God's Word. One last passage illustrates the conquering change of ownership of the cosmic mountain in Bashan. Notice the ironic language used of Bashan as God's mountain, and the spiritual warfare imagery of its replacement.

Psalm 68:15–22
15 O mountain of God, mountain of Bashan; O many-peaked mountain, mountain of Bashan! 16 Why do you look with hatred, O many-peaked mountain, at the mount that God desired for his abode, yes, where the LORD will dwell forever? 17 The chariots of God are twice ten thousand, thousands upon thousands; the Lord is among them; Sinai is now in the sanctuary. 18 You ascended on high, leading a host of captives in your train and receiving gifts among men, even among the rebellious, that the LORD God may dwell there… 21 But God will strike the heads of his enemies, the hairy crown of him who walks in his guilty ways. 22 The Lord said, "I will bring them back from Bashan, I will bring them back from the depths of the sea.

In this Psalm, God takes ownership of Bashan with his heavenly host of warriors, but then replaces it and refers to Sinai (soon to be Zion). It is not that God is making Bashan his mountain literally, but conquering its divinities and theologically replacing it with his new cosmic mountain elsewhere. In verse 18 we see a foreshadowing of Christ's own victorious heavenly ascension, where he leads captives in triumphal procession and receives tribute from them as spoils of war (v. 18). He will own and live where once the rebellious ruled (v. 18). He strikes the "hairy crown" (seir) of the people of that area (v. 21), the descendants of the cursed hairy Esau/Seir, who worshipped the goat demons (as depicted in Joshua Valiant and Caleb Vigilant). He will bring them all out from the sea of chaos, that wilderness where Leviathan symbolically reigns.

This is taken from: Brian Godawa, When Giants Were Upon the Earth: The Watchers, the Nephilim, and the Biblical Cosmic War of the Seed (Los Angeles, CA: Embedded Pictures Publishing, 2014), 292-295.

2 The high mountain as Mount Zion:

Perhaps there is a dual image going on here, much like the seven heads of the dragon in Revelation 17 represent both the mountains of Rome and the Caesars who ruled it. Here is the passage where Mount Bashan is shown in antagonist toward Zion as cosmic mountains:

Psalm 68:15–16
[15] O mountain of God, mountain of Bashan; O many-peaked mountain, mountain of Bashan! [16] Why do you look with hatred, O many-peaked mountain, at the mount that God desired for his abode, yes, where the LORD will dwell forever?

Here is the spiritual Mount Zion described as the highest of mountains:

Isaiah 2:2
[2] It shall come to pass in the latter days that the mountain of the house of the LORD shall be established as the highest of the mountains, and shall be lifted up above the hills; and all the nations shall flow to it,

"The mountain John sees in his vision is probably Mount Zion, the location of the Lamb and his followers (14:1; cp. Ps 2:6), because it is associated with the heavenly Jerusalem in Scripture (Heb 12:22) just as historical Zion was related to historical Jerusalem.238 Zion is the center of the messianic kingdom (Corsini 394). In that God makes his residence there to dwell among men (21:3), this reflects Zechariah 8:3: "Thus says the Lord, 'I will return to Zion and will dwell in the midst of Jerusalem. Then Jerusalem will be called the City of Truth, and the mountain of the Lord of hosts will be called the Holy Mountain.'" There they "will be My people and I will be their God" (Zec 8:8; cp. Rev 21:3)."

Kenneth L. Gentry, Jr., The Divorce of Israel: A Redemptive-Historical Interpretation of Revelation Vol. 2 (Dallas, GA: Tolle Lege Press, 2016), 772.

[3] Revelation 21:3-6.

[4] The New Covenant as new creation:

"As stated above the new creation begins flowing into and impacting history in the first century long before the consummate order. Once again John picks up on Old Testament imagery. Let us compare John's statement with Isaiah's Old Testament prophecy to see that Isaiah is the evident source of his description:

Isaiah 65:17 – 19
For behold, I create new heavens and a new earth; and the former things shall not be remembered or come to mind. But be glad and rejoice forever in what I create; For behold, I create Jerusalem for rejoicing, and her people for gladness. I will also rejoice in Jerusalem, and be glad in My people; and there will no longer be heard in her the voice of weeping and the sound of crying.

Revelation 21:1-4
And I saw a new heaven and a new earth; for the first heaven and the first earth passed away, and there is no longer any sea…. And He shall wipe away every tear from their eyes; and there shall no longer be any death; there shall no longer be any mourning, or crying, or pain; the first things have passed away.

"Given John's predilection for Old Testament source material, I find it impossible to deny that these very similar statements refer to the same phenomenon.

"A first look at either passage inclines the reader to surmise that the writer is speaking of the eternal, perfected, consummate order. However, looks are deceiving – for no orthodox Christian believes that in the eternal order anyone will give birth to children, experience sin, grow old, die, and endure the curse. Yet Isaiah's very next verse reads:

No longer will there be in it an infant who lives but a few days, or an old man who does not live out his days; for the youth will die at the age of one hundred and the one who does not reach the age of one hundred shall be thought accursed." (Isa. 65:20)

"How shall we understand Isaiah's poetic description of the new creation? Isaiah is prophesying the coming of Christ's new covenant kingdom, the gospel era, the church age. John is expanding on that theme. After all, Paul himself likens salvation to a new creation – even using Isaiah's language:

Therefore if any man is in Christ, he is a new creature; the old things passed away; behold, new things have come (2 Cor. 5:17).

But may it never be that I should boast, except in the cross of our Lord Jesus Christ, through which the world has been crucified to me, and I to the world. For neither is circumcision anything, nor uncircumcision, but a new creation (Gal. 6:14-15).

"Paul's declaring "old things passed away; behold, new things have come" also matches closely with God's statement in Revelation 21:1, 5: And I saw a new heaven and a new earth; for the first heaven and the first earth passed away, and there is no longer any sea…. And He who sits on the throne said, "Behold, I am making all things new.""

The New Bride Described

"If this new bride represents the church, what does all of this bold, dramatic imagery mean? Given the dramatic character of the Revelation, John speaks of the church in elevated and ideal terms because of her redemptive standing with God. John presents her glorious and secure repose based on her prophetic promises. Though the church in John's time was under unrelenting assault, John sees through the "fog of war" and visualizes her as she stands before God, virtually merging the heavenly and the earthly phases of the church. The picture he presents is not only symbolic but also protensive: He looks at the end results of the present redemptive reality."

Kenneth L. Gentry, Jr., *The Book of Revelation Made Easy: You Can Understand Bible Prophecy* (Powder Springs, GA: American Vision Press, 2008), 115-116.

[5] The body of Christ is the new temple of God's presence:

"Though God established his holy Temple as the centerpiece of worship for his old covenant people, with the coming of the new covenant he dis-establishes the external Temple system. The bride-church is the tabernacle-temple of God (Rev. 21:3) because God dwells within her and no literal temple is needed (Rev. 21:22; cp. Eph 2:19–22; 1 Cor. 3:16; 6:19; 2 Cor. 6:16; 1 Pet. 2:5, 9). The old Jerusalem with its physical Temple "made with hands" is passing away as the new Jerusalem temple without the Temple supplants it (Heb. 8:13; 9:11, 24; 12:18–28). This is finalized in A.D. 70."

Kenneth L. Gentry, Jr., *The Book of Revelation Made Easy: You Can Understand Bible Prophecy* (Powder Springs, GA: American Vision Press, 2008), 118.

2 Corinthians 6:16
[16] For we are the temple of the living God; as God said, "I will make my dwelling among them and walk among them, and I will be their God, and they shall be my people.

1 Peter 2:4–7
[4] As you come to him, a living stone rejected by men but in the sight of God chosen and precious, [5] you yourselves like living stones are being built up as a spiritual house, to be a holy priesthood, to offer spiritual sacrifices acceptable to God through Jesus Christ. [6] For it stands in Scripture: "Behold, I am laying in Zion a stone, a cornerstone chosen and precious, and whoever believes in him will not be put to shame." [7] So the honor is for you who believe, but for those who do not believe, "The stone that the builders rejected has become the cornerstone,"

Ephesians 2:19–22
[19] So then you are no longer strangers and aliens, but you are fellow citizens with the saints and members of the household of God, [20] built on the foundation of the apostles and prophets, Christ Jesus himself being the cornerstone, [21] in whom the whole structure, being joined together, grows into a holy temple in the Lord. [22] In him you also are being built together into a dwelling place for God by the Spirit.

[6] Alexander is quoting: Daniel 7:14.

[7] 12,000 stadia, the dimensions of the Roman empire:

"In 21:16 we learn that the city appears as a cube of 12,000 stadia on each side. This also suggests a first-century setting for the new Jerusalem. Mulholland (1996:122) writes: "The vision has a practical purpose in the dimensions of the city. If one takes a map of the Mediterranean area and draws a square of 1,400 miles [his value for the Greek measure; others compute it as almost 1,500 miles] to the scale of the map, then

356

places the center of the square on Patmos, the western edge of the square extends to Rome, the eastern edge to Jerusalem, and northern and southern edges approximate the northern and southern boundaries of the Roman Empire in the first century. At the time of John's revelation, whether it took place in the 60s or the 90s, all the Christian communities known to exist were located within those boundaries.""

Kenneth L. Gentry, Jr., The Divorce of Israel: A Redemptive-Historical Interpretation of Revelation Vol. 2 (Dallas, GA: Tolle Lege Press, 2016), 726.

[8] Twelve tribes on the gates and twelve apostles on the foundation:

"And the wall of the city had twelve foundation stones, and on them were the twelve names of the twelve apostles of the Lamb (21:14). We might have expected John to place "the twelve tribes of the sons of Israel" as the "twelve foundation stones" of the city, since Israel historically preceded, anticipated, and gave way to new covenant Christianity (cp. Ge 12:3; Jn 4:22c; Ac 1:8; Ro 11:17–21). However, Revelation dramatically presents Israel's then current judgment and collapse which required a "new" Jerusalem (21:2) upon new, more secure foundations. After all, Abraham "was looking for the city which has foundations, whose architect and builder is God" (Heb 11:10; cp. Heb 12:28). Nevertheless, the "juxtaposition of the twelve tribes and the twelve apostles shows the unity of ancient Israel and the NT church""

Kenneth L. Gentry, Jr., The Divorce of Israel: A Redemptive-Historical Interpretation of Revelation Vol. 2 (Dallas, GA: Tolle Lege Press, 2016), 783.

The jewels on the foundation represent the 12 jewels of the high priest's breastplate that represent the 12 tribes, now fulfilled in the new 12 apostles:

Revelation 21:19–20
[19] The foundations of the wall of the city were adorned with every kind of jewel. The first was jasper, the second sapphire, the third agate, the fourth emerald, [20] the fifth onyx, the sixth carnelian, the seventh chrysolite, the eighth beryl, the ninth topaz, the tenth chrysoprase, the eleventh jacinth, the twelfth amethyst.

Exodus 28:17–21
[17] You shall set in it four rows of stones. A row of sardius, topaz, and carbuncle shall be the first row; [18] and the second row an emerald, a sapphire, and a diamond; [19] and the third row a jacinth, an agate, and an amethyst; [20] and the fourth row a beryl, an onyx, and a jasper. They shall be set in gold filigree. [21] There shall be twelve stones with their names according to the names of the sons of Israel. They shall be like signets, each engraved with its name, for the twelve tribes.

[9] Rivers of living waters: Revelation 22:1.

"But this image of the "river of the water of life" probably "reaches even farther back" to the original river in Eden (Beale and Carson 2007:1153). Indeed, "few doubt that Ezekiel's vision of a life-giving stream has been influenced at least in part, by Gen. 2:10–14, which portrays paradise as a garden, rendered fruitful by a river flowing out of Eden"…

"In the New Testament the concept of "living water" is distinctively Johannine (Jn 4:10–11, 14; 7:38) and pictures the Holy Spirit cleansing and giving eternal life (cf. Isa 44:3; Eze 36:25–27; Tit 3:5)."

Kenneth L. Gentry, Jr., The Divorce of Israel: A Redemptive-Historical Interpretation of Revelation Vol. 2 (Dallas, GA: Tolle Lege Press, 2016), 805.

John 4:10–11
10 Jesus answered her, "If you knew the gift of God, and who it is that is saying to you, 'Give me a drink,' you would have asked him, and he would have given you living water." 11 The woman said to him, "Sir, you have nothing to draw water with, and the well is deep. Where do you get that living water?

John 4:14
14 but whoever drinks of the water that I will give him will never be thirsty again. The water that I will give him will become in him a spring of water welling up to eternal life."

John 7:38
"Whoever believes in me, as the Scripture has said, 'Out of his heart will flow rivers of living

water."

Titus 3:5
[5] he saved us, not because of works done by us in righteousness, but according to his own mercy, by the washing of regeneration and renewal of the Holy Spirit,

[10] **From**: Revelation 22:2

[11] "Tree" as tree in the Garden of Eden and the "tree" of Christ's crucifixion:

"John probably chose this [Greek word for "tree"] for two reasons: First, this is the word the LXX employs in referring to Eden's tree of life (Ge 2:9; 3:22). Thus it strengthens his association with Eden. Second, and just as importantly, in the New Testament this word frequently refers to Christ's cross: Acts 5:30; 10:39; 13:29; Galatians 3:13; 1 Peter 2:24; cp. Deuteronomy 21:22. Thus, the tree of life ultimately reflects the cross-work of the Lamb, his redemptive labor which is so important in Revelation (22:1; cp. 5:6, 12; 7:9–10, 14, 17; 12:11; 14:4c; 15:3; 17:14; 19:7, 9)."

Kenneth L. Gentry, Jr., *The Divorce of Israel: A Redemptive-Historical Interpretation of Revelation* Vol. 2 (Dallas, GA: Tolle Lege Press, 2016), 808.

[12] **From**: Revelation 22:3.

[13] **From**: Revelation 21:22.

[14] Believers as the new covenant temple of God:

Ephesians 2:19–22
[19] So then you are no longer strangers and aliens, but you are fellow citizens with the saints and members of the household of God, [20] built on the foundation of the apostles and prophets, Christ Jesus himself being the cornerstone, [21] in whom the whole structure, being joined together, grows into a holy temple in the Lord. [22] In him you also are being built together into a dwelling place for God by the Spirit.

1 Peter 2:4–5
[4] As you come to him, a living stone rejected by men but in the sight of God chosen and precious, [5] you yourselves like living stones are being built up as a spiritual house, to be a holy priesthood, to offer spiritual sacrifices acceptable to God through Jesus Christ.

CHAPTER 22

[1] Marduk's four war horses:

Marduk did have four horses but they did not have the colors of the four horses of the Apocalypse. I made that creative license choice, not to claim a literal correspondence, but only a literary reflection.

Enuma Elish Tablet IV:50-54:
He mounted the terrible chariot, the unopposable Storm Demon,
He hitched to it the four–steed team, he tied them at his side:
"Slaughterer," "Merciless," "Overwhelmer," "Soaring."
Their lips are curled back, their teeth bear venom,
They know not fatigue, they are trained to trample down.

William W. Hallo and K. Lawson Younger, *The Context of Scripture* (Leiden; New York: Brill, 1997–), 397.

A different translation of their names:

He mounted the storm-chariot irresistible [and] terrifying.
He harnessed (and) yoked to it a team-of-four,
The Killer, the Relentless, the Trampler, the Swift.

James Bennett Pritchard, ed., *The Ancient Near Eastern Texts Relating to the Old Testament* , 3rd ed. with Supplement (Princeton: Princeton University Press, 1969), 66.

CHAPTER 23

¹ **Gischala is quoting from:** Zechariah 9:10-12; 3:8; 6:12.

² **Jacob is quoting** Zechariah 6:12-15.

Zechariah 6:12–15
¹² And say to him, 'Thus says the LORD of hosts, "Behold, the man whose name is the Branch: for he shall branch out from his place, and he shall build the temple of the LORD. ¹³ It is he who shall build the temple of the LORD and shall bear royal honor, and shall sit and rule on his throne. And there shall be a priest on his throne, and the counsel of peace shall be between them both." ' ¹⁴ And the crown shall be in the temple of the LORD as a reminder to Helem, Tobijah, Jedaiah, and Hen the son of Zephaniah. ¹⁵ "And those who are far off shall come and help to build the temple of the LORD. And you shall know that the LORD of hosts has sent me to you. And this shall come to pass, if you will diligently obey the voice of the LORD your God."

³ Spiritual temple with living stones:

1 Peter 2:4–5
⁴ As you come to him, a living stone rejected by men but in the sight of God chosen and precious, ⁵ you yourselves like living stones are being built up as a spiritual house, to be a holy priesthood, to offer spiritual sacrifices acceptable to God through Jesus Christ.

The Prophet like Moses:

Deuteronomy 18:18–19
¹⁸ I will raise up for them a prophet like you from among their brothers. And I will put my words in his mouth, and he shall speak to them all that I command him. ¹⁹ And whoever will not listen to my words that he shall speak in my name, I myself will require it of him.

For a detailed explanation of how Jesus fulfills this prophecy of being like Moses, see: "Islam's Objection To Jesus Being The Prophet Of Deut. 18:15" Let Us Reason Ministries, 2009, online.
http://www.letusreason.org/islam2.htm

⁴ Gischala quotes from:

Zechariah 10:9–10
⁹ Though I scattered them among the nations, yet in far countries they shall remember me, and with their children they shall live and return. ¹⁰ I will bring them home from the land of Egypt, and gather them from Assyria, and I will bring them to the land of Gilead and to Lebanon, till there is no room for them.

⁵ The protected Remnant in Zechariah:

Zechariah 8:6–8
⁶ Thus says the LORD of hosts: If it is marvelous in the sight of the **remnant** of this people in those days, should it also be marvelous in my sight, declares the LORD of hosts? ⁷ Thus says the LORD of hosts: Behold, I will save my people from the east country and from the west country, ⁸ and I will bring them to dwell in the midst of Jerusalem. And they shall be my people, and I will be their God, in faithfulness and in righteousness."

"And they shall be my people and I will be their God" is defined by Paul as being fulfilled in the new covenant Gospel (2Cor 6:16; Heb 8:8-13).

Zechariah 8:11–12
¹¹ But now I will not deal with the **remnant** of this people as in the former days, declares the LORD of hosts. ¹² For there shall be a sowing of peace. The vine shall give its fruit, and the ground shall give its produce, and the heavens shall give their dew. And I will cause the remnant of this people to possess all these things.

Zechariah 9:7–8
⁷ I will take away its blood from its mouth, and its abominations from between its teeth; it too shall

be a **remnant** for our God; it shall be like a clan in Judah, and Ekron shall be like the Jebusites. [8] Then I will encamp at my house as a guard, so that none shall march to and fro; no oppressor shall again march over them, for now I see with my own eyes.

The gathering and restoration of Israel:

The following is from Brian Godawa, *Israel in Bible Prophecy: The New Testament Fulfillment of the Promise to Abraham*, (Los Angeles, Embedded Pictures Publishing, 2017), 59-61.

In Acts 2, we read about the first explosion of the Gospel with the first baptism of the Holy Spirit. It was the thing that Jesus had told them to wait for, which would launch them into all the world with the Good News (Acts 1:4). Pentecost would be the historical inauguration of the heavenly New Covenant achieved by the death, resurrection and ascension of Christ. It would be the pouring out of God's Spirit upon his people (Isa 32:12-19; 44:5; Ezek 36:25-28; 37:14).

The disciples asked Jesus if this was the time of the restoration of Israel (1:6), the very thing we have been discussing in this work. Jesus told them that the restoration of Israel would begin occurring when the Holy Spirit came upon them, but they were not to worry themselves with the timing (1:8).

And what was the restoration, but the pouring out of God's Spirit and the regathering of Jews from all over the known earth in a spiritual metaphorical resurrection? (Ezek 37). So when the disciples were baptized with the Spirit at Pentecost and began to speak in foreign tongues, that was the fulfillment of God's pouring out of his Spirit. Pouring is a form of baptizing (Heb 9:10, 13, 19, 21). But it was also the beginning of the regathering of Jews because "there were dwelling in Jerusalem Jews, devout men from every nation under heaven" (Acts 2:5). The list of nations that are described (Acts 2:9-11) just happens to be a representative sampling of the seventy nations of Genesis 10. To the ancient Jew, those seventy were "all the nations" to which the Jews were scattered (Amos 9:9). According to the apostle Luke, Pentecost of AD 30 was transformed into the beginning of the gathering of Jews from all the nations.

And that gathering of Jews included the Gentiles. It was a gathering of two bodies into one that was occurring all throughout the book of Acts. Notice these passages that say that the evangelism of Acts is the very fulfillment of the promise to gather the Gentiles with the Jews as his people:

Acts 15:13–19
[13] After they finished speaking, James replied, "Brothers, listen to me. [14] Simeon has related how God first visited the Gentiles, to take from them a people for his name. [15] And with this the words of the prophets agree, just as it is written.

Acts 26:23
[Paul:] [23] that the Christ must suffer and that, by being the first to rise from the dead, he would proclaim light both to our people and to the Gentiles."

The "ingathering" was based upon the unity of belief in Jesus as Messiah. Isaiah had prophesied that when Messiah first came (the branch of Jesse), *in that very day*, the Lord would "recover the remnant that remains of his people," from all the nations. "In that day," the root of Jesse would be "raised (resurrected) as a signal for the nations," and would "assemble the banished of Israel and gather the dispersed of Judah from the four corners of the earth" (Isa 11:1-2, 10-12). According to the prophecy, the gathering of the remnant and the Gentiles would occur at the *first coming* of Messiah, when Jesus was resurrected, not the second coming. *In that day* of Messiah's arrival and resurrection (his raising as a signal), he would draw both the remnant of Israel as well as Gentile believers. This will not start in our future, it already started in the book of Acts! Paul likened that raising of the signal to Christ's resurrection, and confirmed this Isaianic promise as already being fulfilled *during his ministry*:

Romans 15:8–9, 12
[8] For I tell you that Christ became a servant to the circumcised to show God's truthfulness, in order to confirm the promises given to the patriarchs, [9] and in order that the Gentiles might glorify God for his mercy...[12] And again Isaiah says, "The root of Jesse will come, even he who arises to rule the Gentiles; in him will the Gentiles hope.

What were the promises given to the patriarchs that Paul says were confirmed ("verified") in Christ's resurrection? All of them, including the regathering (Acts 3:24; 32; 15:13-15; 24:24; 26:6). In fact, most of the prophecies about the regathering of Israel almost always add the inclusion of Gentiles as a simultaneous event (See more below). But the point is that the book of Romans says explicitly that the Isaianic prophecy about the gathering of the remnant along with the Gentiles was already being fulfilled *in his own day*. This is not an eschatological system demanding something must be fulfilled in the future, this is the New Testament itself saying the prophecy was fulfilled in the first century, *in that day*.

One of the ways that Dispensationalists seek to deny the fulfillment of the regathering is to suggest that the inclusion of the Gentiles has been fulfilled in Christ, but the gathering of Israel has not yet been fulfilled. They argue that "confirmation" of promises to the patriarchs is not the same as "fulfillment." God only verified the promises to Israel, not fulfilled them. They see this split because they do not see an earthly nation called Israel regathered into the land in the way that they expect it to be. But their problem is that, as we have seen, the gathering of the Jews was simultaneous with the gathering of the Gentiles. If we return to Acts 2, the holy Scripture says again that both the gathering *and* Gentile inclusion were being fulfilled *in their day*.

⁶ **Gischala quotes from**: Zechariah 14:2, 5.

⁷ **Gischala is quoting from**: Zechariah 13:8; 14:1-5.

⁸ Alexander is remembering:

> Micah 1:3–5
> ³ For behold, the LORD is coming out of his place, and will come down and tread upon the high places of the earth. ⁴ And the mountains will melt under him, and the valleys will split open, like wax before the fire, like waters poured down a steep place. ⁵ All this is for the transgression of Jacob and for the sins of the house of Israel. What is the transgression of Jacob? Is it not Samaria? And what is the high place of Judah? Is it not Jerusalem?

God judging his tools of judgment, and God striking the earth:

> Then the LORD will go forth and fight against those nations, as when He fights on a day of battle (14:3).

"After using Rome as His rod to smite Jerusalem, God turns on Rome in judgment. Once again, Assyria is the model: "I send it against a godless nation and commission it against the people of My fury to capture booty and to seize plunder, and to trample them down like mud in the streets . . . . So it will be that when the Lord has completed all His work on Mount Zion and on Jerusalem, He will say, 'I will punish the fruit of the arrogant heart of the king of Assyria and the pomp of his haughtiness'" (Isa. 10:5-6, 12-13). "It is significant that the decline of the Roman Empire dates from the fall of Jerusalem."4 Thomas Scott concurs: "It is also observable, that the Romans after having been thus made the executioners of divine vengeance on the Jewish nation, never prospered as they had done before; but the Lord evidently fought against them, and all the nations which composed their overgrown empire; till at last it was subverted, and their fairest cities and provinces were ravaged by barbarous invaders."

> And in that day His feet will stand on the Mount of Olives, which is in front of Jerusalem on the east; and the Mount of Olives will be split in its middle from east to west by a very large valley, so that half of the mountain will move toward the north and the other half toward the south (Zech. 14:4).

"It is this passage that dispensationalists use to support their view that Jesus will touch down on planet earth and set up His millennial kingdom. Numerous times in the Bible we read of Jehovah "coming down" to meet with His people. In most instances His coming is one of judgment; in no case was He physically present. Notice how many times God's coming is associated with mountains.

> "And the LORD came down to see the city and the tower which the sons of men had built. . . . Come, let Us go down and there confuse their language, that they may not understand one another's speech" (Gen. 11:5, 7).

> "So I have come down to deliver them from the power of the Egyptians, and to bring them up from that land to a good and spacious land, to a land flowing with milk and honey. . . (Ex. 3:8).

> "Then Thou didst come down on Mount Sinai, and didst speak with them from heaven. . . (Neh. 9:13a).

> "Bow Thy heavens, O LORD, and come down; touch the mountains, that they may smoke" (Psalm

144:5).

"For thus says the LORD to me, 'As the lion or the young lion growls over his prey, against which a band of shepherds is called out, will not be terrified at their voice, nor disturbed at their noise, so will the LORD of hosts come down to wage war on Mount Zion and on its hill'" (Isa. 31:4).

"Oh, that Thou wouldst rend the heavens and come down, that the mountains might quake at Thy presence-" (Isa. 64:1).

"When Thou didst awesome things which we did not expect, Thou didst come down, the mountains quaked at Thy presence" (Isa. 64:3).

"In Micah 1:3 we are told that God "is coming forth from His place" to "come down and tread on the high places of the earth." How is this descriptive language different from the Lord standing on the Mount of Olives with the result that it will split? Micah says "the mountains will melt under Him, and the valleys will be split, like wax before the fire, like water poured down a steep place" (1:4). "It was not uncommon for prophets to use figurative expressions about the Lord 'coming' down, mountains trembling, being scattered, and hills bowing (Hab. 3:6, 10); mountains flowing down at his presence (Isaiah 64:1, 3); or mountains and hills singing and the trees clapping their hands (Isaiah 55:12)."6

"What is the Bible trying to teach us with this descriptive language of the Mount of Olives "split in its middle"? The earliest Christian writers applied Zechariah 14:4 to the work of Christ in His day. Tertullian (A.D. 145-220) wrote: "'But at night He went out to the Mount of Olives.' For thus had Zechariah pointed out: 'And His feet shall stand in that day on the Mount of Olives' [Zech. xiv. 4]."7 Tertullian was alluding to the fact that the Olivet prophecy set the stage for the judgment-coming of Christ that would once for all break down the Jewish/Gentile division. Matthew Henry explains the theology behind the prophecy:

"The partition-wall between Jew and Gentiles shall be taken away. The mountains about Jerusalem, and particularly this, signified it to be an enclosure, and that it stood in the way of those who would approach to it. Between the Gentiles and Jerusalem this mountain of Bether, of division, stood, Cant. ii. 17. But by the destruction of Jerusalem this mountain shall be made to cleave in the midst, and so the Jewish pale shall be taken down, and the church laid in common with the Gentiles, who were made one with the Jews by the breaking down of this middle wall of partition, Eph. ii. 14.8"

Gary DeMar, "Zechariah 14 and the Coming of Christ," The Preterist Archive online. https://www.preteristarchive.com/Modern/2001_demar_zechariah-14.html

9 John's thematic verse in Revelation is a quote from Zechariah 12:10-12:

Revelation 1:7
7 Behold, he is coming with the clouds, and every eye will see him, even those who pierced him, and all tribes of the earth will wail on account of him. Even so. Amen.

10 **Alexander quotes from**: Zechariah 12:10 and 8:12.

11 **Alexander quotes from**: Zechariah 14:8, 11.

Living water of Zechariah is the Holy Spirit of the New Covenant:

John 4:10, 13-14
10 Jesus answered her, "If you knew the gift of God, and who it is that is saying to you, 'Give me a drink,' you would have asked him, and he would have given you living water."...
13 Jesus said to her, "Everyone who drinks of this water will be thirsty again, 14 but whoever drinks of the water that I will give him will never be thirsty again. The water that I will give him will become in him a spring of water welling up to eternal life."

John 7:37–39
37 On the last day of the feast, the great day, Jesus stood up and cried out, "If anyone thirsts, let him come to me and drink. 38 Whoever believes in me, as the Scripture has said, 'Out of his heart will flow rivers of living water.' " 39 Now this he said about the Spirit, whom those who believed in him were to receive, for as yet the Spirit had not been given, because Jesus was not yet glorified.

The shaking of heavens and earth was the change of covenants. The writer of Hebrews explains that the old covenant was about to end and the new covenant would remain with the destruction of the temple in AD 70.

Hebrews 12:26–28
[26] At that time his voice shook the earth, but now he has promised, "Yet once more I will shake not only the earth but also the heavens." [27] This phrase, "Yet once more," indicates the removal of things that are shaken – that is, things that have been made – in order that the things that cannot be shaken may remain. [28] Therefore let us be grateful for receiving a kingdom that cannot be shaken...

Hebrews 9:8 (NKJV)
[8] the Holy Spirit indicating this, that the way into the Holiest of All was not yet made manifest while the first tabernacle was still standing.

[12] Elijah's Day of the Lord included both salvation and judgment:

Malachi 3:1–5
[1] "Behold, I send my messenger, and he will prepare the way before me. And the Lord whom you seek will suddenly come to his temple; and the messenger of the covenant in whom you delight, behold, he is coming, says the LORD of hosts. [2] But who can endure the day of his coming, and who can stand when he appears? ... [5] "Then I will draw near to you for judgment.

Malachi 4:5–6
[5] "Behold, I will send you Elijah the prophet before the great and awesome day of the LORD comes. [6] And he will turn the hearts of fathers to their children and the hearts of children to their fathers, lest I come and strike the land with a decree of utter destruction."

Elijah was fulfilled in John the Baptist who also declared the coming wrath of AD 70 upon Jerusalem:

Matthew 3:1–12
[1] In those days John the Baptist came preaching in the wilderness of Judea, [2] "Repent, for the kingdom of heaven is at hand." [3] For this is he who was spoken of by the prophet Isaiah when he said, "The voice of one crying in the wilderness: 'Prepare the way of the Lord; make his paths straight.' "... he said to them, "You brood of vipers! Who warned you to flee from the wrath to come? [8] Bear fruit in keeping with repentance. [9] And do not presume to say to yourselves, 'We have Abraham as our father,' for I tell you, God is able from these stones to raise up children for Abraham. [10] Even now the axe is laid to the root of the trees. Every tree therefore that does not bear good fruit is cut down and thrown into the fire. [11] "I baptize you with water for repentance, but he who is coming after me is mightier than I, whose sandals I am not worthy to carry. He will baptize you with the Holy Spirit and fire. [12] His winnowing fork is in his hand, and he will clear his threshing floor and gather his wheat into the barn, but the chaff he will burn with unquenchable fire."

[13] Isaiah's prophecy of Messiah coming to bring Jubilee cleansing also included judgment:

Isaiah 61:1–2
[1] The Spirit of the Lord GOD is upon me, because the LORD has anointed me to bring good news to the poor; he has sent me to bind up the brokenhearted, to proclaim liberty to the captives, and the opening of the prison to those who are bound; [2] to proclaim the year of the LORD's favor, and the day of vengeance of our God; to comfort all who mourn;

Jesus claimed to fulfill the first half of Isaiah's prophecy in his ministry, and then later, proclaimed the "day of vengeance" would be fulfilled in AD 70:

Luke 4:18–21
[18] "The Spirit of the Lord is upon me, because he has anointed me to proclaim good news to the poor. He has sent me to proclaim liberty to the captives and recovering of sight to the blind, to set at liberty those who are oppressed, [19] to proclaim the year of the Lord's favor." [20] And he rolled up the scroll and gave it back to the attendant and sat down. And the eyes of all in the synagogue were fixed on him. [21] And he began to say to them, "Today this Scripture has been fulfilled in your hearing."

363

Luke 21:20–24

[20] "But when you see Jerusalem surrounded by armies, then know that its desolation has come near. [21] Then let those who are in Judea flee to the mountains, and let those who are inside the city depart, and let not those who are out in the country enter it, [22] for these are days of vengeance, to fulfill all that is written. [23] Alas for women who are pregnant and for those who are nursing infants in those days! For there will be great distress upon the earth and wrath against this people. [24] They will fall by the edge of the sword and be led captive among all nations, and Jerusalem will be trampled underfoot by the Gentiles, until the times of the Gentiles are fulfilled.

[14] Mercy and justice united in Christ:

Psalm 85:9–10
[9] Surely his salvation is near to those who fear him, that glory may dwell in our land. [10] Steadfast love and faithfulness meet; righteousness and peace kiss each other.

CHAPTER 24

[1] Christ as first fruits of resurrection:

1 Corinthians 15:20–26
[20] But in fact Christ has been raised from the dead, the firstfruits of those who have fallen asleep. [21] For as by a man came death, by a man has come also the resurrection of the dead. [22] For as in Adam all die, so also in Christ shall all be made alive. [23] But each in his own order: Christ the firstfruits, then at his coming those who belong to Christ. [24] Then comes the end, when he delivers the kingdom to God the Father after destroying every rule and every authority and power. [25] For he must reign until he has put all his enemies under his feet. [26] The last enemy to be destroyed is death.

[2] Elihu quotes from: Daniel 12:2.

[3] Daniel's resurrection as typological:

"The resurrection of verse 2 seems to connect to the evangelistic and teaching ministry spoken of in verse 3; thus, it is some kind of historical resurrection that is spoken of, a resurrectional event in this world, in our history.

"The solution to our difficulty is found in Ezekiel 37. There the prophet is told to prophesy to the dead bones of the idolaters scattered all over the mountains of Israel (see Ezekiel 6:5). Ezekiel prophesies and the bones come to life again. This is explained in Ezekiel 37:11 as the national resurrection of Israel after the captivity. The language used by God is very "literal sounding," to wit: "I will open your graves and cause you to come up out of your graves" (vv. 12–13). Yet, this graphic language refers to the spiritual resurrection of the nation.

"Now clearly, the resurrection of the whole nation does not mean the salvation of each individual. Thus, Daniel 12:2 tells us that in the days of Jesus the nation will undergo a last spiritual resurrection, but some will not persevere and their resurrection will only be unto destruction. The Parable of the Soils fits here (Matthew 13:3–23): three different kinds of people come to life, but only one of the three kinds is awakened to persevering, everlasting life.

"During His ministry, Jesus raised the nation back to life. He healed the sick, cleansed the unclean, brought dead people back to life, restored the Law, entered the Temple as King, etc. Then, as always, the restored people fell into sin, and crucified Him.

"Thus, a resurrection of Israel is in view. The wicked are raised, but do not profit from it, and are destroyed. The saints experience a great distress, and live with God forever and ever."

James B. Jordan, *The Handwriting on the Wall: A Commentary on the Book of Daniel* (Powder Springs, GA: American Vision, 2007), 618–619.

"Many of them that sleep in the dust of the earth shall awake – This refers primarily to the Gospel being preached. Many who sleep in the dust, both Jews and Gentiles, shall be awakened by the preaching of the Gospel out of their heathenism. It has a secondary application to a future resurrection when the multitude that sleep in the dust shall awake; many shall arise to life, and many to shame.

364

"Is this referring to the First Resurrection in which we receive eternal life through regeneration?

"Or does it refer to the Final Resurrection that will occur at the Second Coming of Jesus when we will be raised as spiritual bodies and glorified with Christ?

"This is one of the verses in Daniel that creates a lot questions from a preterist perspective. In the context of the following verses, I believe it refers to awakening of God's chosen people at the preaching of the Gospel. However, like other apocalyptic passages in the Bible, there is also a "telescoping" aspect of this imagery. The Final Resurrection is projected onto the historical events of the first century. We see in the dawning light of the Gospel during the first century a prefiguring of the final glorious state of the kingdom of God at the Second Coming of Christ and the Resurrection of the saints.

> Daniel 12:3 – And they that be wise shall shine as the brightness of the firmament; and they that turn many to righteousness as the stars for ever and ever.

"They that be wise shall shine – Just as the kingdom of God is in the here and now, but won't be revealed in all its glory until Christ returns, so the born-again believers in Jesus Christ are seated in heavenly places reigning with Christ in the present (Ephesians 2:4-7). This began to be made manifest when Jesus first began to preach the kingdom of God...

"There are two aspects of our resurrection just as there are two aspects of Christ's coming in the glory of His kingdom. We are even now raised with Christ and seated with Him. Spiritual death has been defeated."

Jay Rogers, In the Days of These Kings: The Book of Daniel in Preterist Perspective (Clermont, FL, Media House Intl., 2017) 477-478.

[4] Moshe quotes from:

> Isaiah 11:10–11
> [10] In that day the root of Jesse, who shall stand as a signal for the peoples – of him shall the nations inquire, and his resting place shall be glorious. [11] In that day the Lord will extend his hand yet a second time to **recover the remnant that remains of his people...**

Paul shows that this is fulfilled in Christ in Romans 15:8-12.

CHAPTER 26

[1] **This incident is drawn from two incidents that I blended into one:** Flavius Josephus, *The Wars of the Jews* 5.2.1-2, §47-66 and *The Wars of the Jews* 5.3.3, §109-119.

[2] The king shall do as he wills:

> Daniel 11:36
> [36] "And the king shall do as he wills. He shall exalt himself and magnify himself above every god, and shall speak astonishing things against the God of gods. He shall prosper till the indignation is accomplished; for what is decreed shall be done.

Duncan McKenzie makes a good argument that Titus is the king of Daniel 11:36. Jay Rogers argues that it is the line of Caesars beginning with Julius, and Philip Mauro argues for Herod the Great. But there is certainly a consistency of this tyrannical will between all tyrants in Daniel, indeed in Scripture.

Other kings who "did as he wills" were:

1) Cyrus the Great: Dan 8:4
2) Alexander the Great Dan 11:3
3) Antiochus III the Great: Dan 11:16
4) Ptolemy VI Philometer: Dan 11:28
5) Dan 11:36: Julius and Caesars, or Titus or Herod the Great

"Exegetical necessity requires that 11:36-45 be applied to someone other than Antiochus IV. The context indicates that the ruler now in view will live in the last days, immediately prior to the coming of the Lord. Verse 40 reveals that this king's activities will take place "at the time of the end" (cf. 10:14), and the "time of distress" mentioned in 12:1 is best understood as the same "distress" (the tribulation) predicted by Jesus Christ in Matt

24:21 as occurring immediately before his second advent (Matt 24:29-31; cf. Rev 7:14). But the clearest indication that this "king" will live in the latter days is that the resurrection of the saints will take place immediately after God delivers his people from this evil individual's power (cf. 12:2). Of course, the resurrection is an eschatological event. Finally, vv. 36-39 seem to introduce this king as if for the first time."

McKenzie PhD, Duncan W., *The Antichrist and the Second Coming: A Preterist Examination Volume I* (Kindle Locations 2896-2903). Xulon Press. Kindle Edition.

[3] **This incident with Titus is adapted from Josephus**: Flavius Josephus, *The Wars of the Jews* 5.2.1-2, §52-66.

CHAPTER 27

[1] Treatment of snake bites in the ancient world:

Adrienne Mayor, "Treating Snake Bite in Antiquity," Wonders and Marvels online: http://www.wondersandmarvels.com/2012/08/treating-snake-bite-in-antiquity.html

[2] **Opium poppy seeds as anesthesia**: Roman Medicine http://www.crystalinks.com/romemedicine.html

[3] The visitation of Yahweh and judgment:

> Luke 19:43–44
> [43] For the days will come upon you, when your enemies will set up a barricade around you and surround you and hem you in on every side [44] and tear you down to the ground, you and your children within you. And they will not leave one stone upon another in you, because you did not know the time of your visitation."

CHAPTER 28

[1] **Cassandra is quoting**: Matthew 24:40–41.

Some Christians mistake this verse as an oblique reference to a "rapture" of Christians being taken away FROM judgment. But the phrase is taken from the Flood and the Babylonian exile where those who were taken away were judged and/or sold into captivity. That is not a rapture away from judgment, but a deliverance INTO judgment.

Here is a verse about the Babylonian exile:

> Jeremiah 6:11–12
> [11] Therefore I am full of the wrath of the LORD; I am weary of holding it in. "Pour it out upon the children in the street, and upon the gatherings of young men, also; both husband and wife <u>shall be taken</u>, the elderly and the very aged. [12] Their houses <u>shall be turned over to others</u>, their fields and wives together, for <u>I will stretch out my hand against the inhabitants of the land</u> [of Israel]," declares the LORD.

Here is a verse from Josephus about the AD 70 destruction of Jerusalem that is similar:

> Josephus, *Wars of the Jews*, 6:8:2 (6.384-386)
> [The Romans] <u>left only the populace</u> [of Jerusalem], and <u>sold the rest of the multitude</u>, with their wives and children, and every one of them at a very low price... (386) and indeed the number of those that were sold was immense; but of the populace above <u>forty thousand were saved, whom Caesar let go whither every one of them pleased</u>.

[2] The Parousia "coming" of Christ in the Thessalonian letters: Gary DeMar writes:

"Is "the coming of our Lord Jesus Christ" a reference to the Second Coming, that is, an event that is still in our future, or is it a coming in judgment upon first-century Jerusalem that would be the event to bring the "last days" to a close (2 Thess. 2:1)?[7] The word translated "coming" in verse 1 is the Greek word parousia, best translated as "presence" in other contexts (2 Cor. 10:10; Phil. 2:12). "The term itself does not mean 'return' or 'second' coming; it simply means 'arrival' or 'presence.'

"Translating parousia as "coming" is not at all improper, however, since the Bible's use of "coming" does not always mean bodily presence, as so many Old and New Testament passages make clear. In addition, we know that the Bible clearly states that "the coming [parousia] of the Lord" was said to be "at hand," that is, "near" to Christians living prior to the destruction of Jerusalem in A.D. 70 (James 5:8). How could James have told his readers to "be patient ... until the "coming of the Lord" if the Lord's coming was not "near" for them? James bases his call for patience upon the fact that the Lord's coming was near, near for those who first read his letter. "James clearly believed, as others of his time did, that the Coming of Christ was imminent. Since, then, there is not long to wait, his plea for patience is greatly reinforced."[10]

"God's presence was a sign of blessing because of Israel's special covenantal status (Isa. 55:3; Jer. 1:19). God's departure was a sign of judgment. For the nations, God's presence was a sign of judgment because of their wickedness. Because of Israel's abominations, God's presence left the temple (Ezek. 5–11). Israel was then treated like the nations and would hide from and lament His presence in the future. In similar fashion, because of Israel's rejection of the Messiah and the persecution of His church, Christ's bride, God would make His presence known to Israel in the form of judgment. God rejected His once-covenanted people and their temple of stone because of the nation's rejection of the promised Son of Man (Matt. 23:38; 24:1). Like Ezekiel (Ezek. 8), Jesus inspected the temple, found it filled with abominations (Matt. 21:12–13), and left it desolate (23:38). He returned in A.D. 70 to inspect the temple for a final time and found it full of abominations. His presence now abides with a new people of God constructed as a "spiritual house," the true temple of God (1 Peter 2:4–10; cf. 2 Cor. 6:14–18). In effect, Christ's parousia in 2 Thessalonians 2:1 is the fulfillment of the promise that the presence of Christ will reside with the true Israel forever (Rom. 2:28–29; 9:6; 10:12; Gal. 6:15–16; Phil. 3:3; Col. 3:11; Heb. 8:8, 10). Remember, during His earthly ministry Jesus "came out from the temple" (Matt. 24:1), foretold its destruction (24:15–34), and returned in A.D. 70 to destroy it (22:7).

"There is no doubt that Jesus' "coming" in 2 Thessalonians 2:1 should be attributed to the first century since the time indicators ("has come," "now," "already") leave no room in this passage for a coming in the distant future (e.g., Matt. 16:27–28; 24:29–31; 26:64; Heb. 10:37; James 5:7–8; Rev. 2:5, 16; 3:11). Jesus' coming in A.D. 70 was a coming in judgment upon an apostate nation."

Gary DeMar, *Last Days Madness: Obsession of the Modern Church* (Powder Springs, American Vision, 1999), 274-277.

"The word 'parousia' is itself misleading, anyway, since it merely means 'presence'; Paul can use it of his being present with a church, and nobody supposes that he imagined he would make his appearance flying downwards on a cloud. The motif of delay ('how long, O Lord, how long?'69) was already well established in Judaism, and is hardly a Christian innovation, as is often imagined. The usual scholarly construct, in which the early church waited for Jesus' return, lived only for that future and without thought for anything past (such as memories of Jesus himself), only to be grievously disappointed and to take up history-writing as a displacement activity, a failure of nerve – this picture is without historical basis. The church expected certain events to happen within a generation, and happen they did."

N. T. Wright, *The New Testament and the People of God, Christian Origins and the Question of God* (London: Society for Promoting Christian Knowledge, 1992), 462–463.

[3] The end of all things was not the end of all physical things or all earthly history. It was the end of all things related to the old covenant.

The end of all things is at hand in the first century, not thousands of years from then:

> 1Pet. 4:7
> The end of all things is at hand; therefore, be of sound judgment and sober spirit for the purpose of prayer.

Last days were in the first century, not thousands of years from then:

> Hebr. 1:1
> God, after He spoke long ago to the fathers in the prophets in many portions and in many ways, 2 in these last days has spoken to us in His Son,...

> Hebrews 9:26
> but now once at the consummation of the ages He has been manifested to put away sin by the

sacrifice of Himself.

1Cor 10:11
Now these things happened to them as an example, and they were written <u>for our instruction, upon whom the ends of the ages have come.</u>

1Peter 1:5, 10, 20
by God's power [you] are being guarded through faith for <u>a salvation ready to be revealed</u> in <u>the last time</u>... ¹⁰ Concerning this salvation, the prophets who prophesied about the grace that was to be yours searched and inquired carefully...For [Jesus] was foreknown before the foundation of the world, but has appeared <u>in these last times</u> for the sake of you

1John 2:18
Children, <u>it is the last hour</u>; and just as you heard that antichrist is coming, even now many antichrists have arisen; from this we know that <u>it is the last hour.</u>

1John 4:3
and every spirit that does not confess Jesus is not from God; and this is the spirit of the <u>antichrist, of which you have heard that it is coming, and now it is already in the world.</u>

Other ancient writers used this terminology of their own world as well.

Tacitus, *The Histories* 1.2
The history on which I am entering is that of a period rich in disasters, terrible with battles, torn by civil struggles, horrible even in peace. Four emperors fell by the sword;6 there were three civil wars, more foreign wars, and often both at the same time... Moreover, Italy was distressed by <u>disasters unknown before or returning after the lapse of ages.</u>

End of the Ages:

The following is from Brian Godawa, *End Times Bible Prophecy: It's Not What They Told You* (Los Angeles, CA: Embedded Pictures Publishing, 2017), 78-80.

"The notion of the present age and the messianic age to come was prevalent in Jewish understanding and in the New Testament as well. Paul wrote of the Christians living in "this age" (1 Cor 3:18), "this present evil age" (Gal 1:4) that had evil spiritual rulers of this age (1 Cor 2:8; 2 Cor 4:4); but there was the messianic "age to come" (Eph 1:21, Heb 6:4). When Messiah came, he would usher in a new covenant, a new age of spiritual transformation in the world.

"Well, of course, Messiah had come. That "age to come" was not a reference to a second coming of Jesus, but his first coming, bringing the kingdom of God (the kingdom age to come), a kingdom that was both now and not yet. It was inaugurated but not consummated.

"This "age to come" was the new covenant age. Paul wrote elsewhere that the gospel (the new covenant) was "hidden for ages, <u>but now revealed</u> to his saints (Col 1:26). In 1 Corinthians 10:11, he wrote that the old covenant events occurred as an example "for our instruction <u>upon whom the end of the ages has come.</u>" Did you catch that? The temple had not yet been destroyed, and Paul was saying that his generation was at the end of the ages! He said that it *had come* upon that first century of believers. The end of the age is not a future event that hasn't happened yet; it occurred in the first century with the coming of the new covenant, confirmed in the destruction of the temple. But Paul isn't the only one who wrote that in the New Testament.

"Hebrews 9:26 says that Jesus suffered on the cross, "once for all <u>at the end of the ages</u> to put away sin by the sacrifice of himself." The end of the ages is not the end of history or the end of the world as we understand it. The end of the ages had already occurred at the time of the crucifixion of Christ. The end of the ages was the end of the old covenant era and the beginning of the new covenant in Christ's blood!

"But get this: that same writer of Hebrews talked about the new covenant in Christ being superior to the old covenant in Hebrews 8. He quoted Jeremiah confirming that the prophets predicted the arrival of the new covenant age. And then he said, "In speaking of a new covenant, he makes the first one obsolete. And what is becoming obsolete and growing old is ready to vanish away" (8:13).

"What was growing old and ready to vanish at that time?

368

"It blew my theology when I realized that he was talking about the destruction of the temple as the final culmination of the new covenant replacement of the old covenant! He was writing in the time period after Christ's death and resurrection and right before the temple had been destroyed. So the new covenant had been established in Christ's blood, but it was not consummated with historical finality. Like Paul, the writer believed they were at the end of the ages. The new covenant would make the old covenant obsolete. But take a closer look at the language he used. He said that the old is "becoming obsolete and is ready to vanish away," as if the old covenant had not vanished yet. It was only in the process of *becoming* obsolete. "Becoming," not "had become," and not "would become" thousands of years in the future. What could that mean?

"Well, the writer was writing within the generation that Jesus said would see the destruction of the temple. The temple had not yet been destroyed. Hebrews 8 says that they were in a time period of change between covenants and that change had not yet been fully or historically consummated. That first century generation was in the transition period between ages or covenants. So, what would be the event that would embody the theological claim that the old covenant was obsolete and the new covenant had replaced it? The destruction of the symbol of the old covenant, the temple! The old covenant would not be obsolete until its symbolic incarnation, the temple, was made desolate."

[4] Wrath come upon the first century Jews described as "utmost" or "forever" or "Completely":

1 Thessalonians 2:14–16 (NASB95)
[14] For you, brethren, became imitators of the churches of God in Christ Jesus that are in Judea, for you also endured the same sufferings at the hands of your own countrymen, even as they *did* from the Jews, [15] who both killed the Lord Jesus and the prophets, and drove us out. They are not pleasing to God, but hostile to all men, [16] hindering us from speaking to the Gentiles so that they may be saved; with the result that they always fill up the measure of their sins. But wrath has come upon them to the utmost. (NOTES ON THE TEXT in LOGOS Bible Software: or "forever," "completely")

[5] The first century Jews filled up the measure of their sins just like the Amorites:

1 Thessalonians 2:14–16 (NASB95)
[14] For you, brethren, became imitators of the churches of God in Christ Jesus that are in Judea, for you also endured the same sufferings at the hands of your own countrymen, even as they *did* from the Jews, [15] who both killed the Lord Jesus and the prophets, and drove us out. They are not pleasing to God, but hostile to all men, [16] hindering us from speaking to the Gentiles so that they may be saved; with the result that they always fill up the measure of their sins. But wrath has come upon them to the utmost.

Matthew 23:29–32
[29] "Woe to you, scribes and Pharisees, hypocrites! For you build the tombs of the prophets and decorate the monuments of the righteous, [30] saying, 'If we had lived in the days of our fathers, we would not have taken part with them in shedding the blood of the prophets.' [31] Thus you witness against yourselves that you are sons of those who murdered the prophets. [32] Fill up, then, the measure of your fathers.

Genesis 15:16
[16] And they shall come back here in the fourth generation, for the iniquity of the Amorites is not yet complete."

[6] Daniel 7 and the coming of the Son of Man up to the Ancient of Days:

"There is a third cloud motif in Scripture. The reference is found in Daniel 7:13–14, the passage that Jesus quotes in Matthew 24:30. Notice that the coming of the Son of Man in Daniel 7 is not down but up! The Son of Man, Jesus, comes up "with the clouds of heaven" to "the Ancient of Days and was presented before Him."

"In Daniel's vision, coming on the clouds means that the Son of Man was coming onstage, into the scene. It is not a coming toward Daniel or toward earth, but a coming seen from the standpoint of God, since Daniel uses three verbs that all indicate this: "coming … approached … was led to" the Ancient of Days. This is no picture of the Second Coming, because the Son of man is going the wrong way for that. His face is turned, not toward earth, but toward God. His goal is not to receive His saints, but to receive His kingdom (Cf. 1 Peter 3:22; Luke 19:12; Acts 2:32–36; 3:22; 5:31; Col. 3:1; Rev. 3:21.).

"Jesus had Daniel 7 in mind as He described His enthronement: "The key verse in Daniel 7:13 that predicts the triumph of the Son of Man represents Him as coming into the presence of the Ancient of Days 'with the clouds of heaven,' a phrase that is repeated in Matthew 26:64; Mark 14:62; Revelation 14:14. Clouds are much more closely associated with the glory and throne of God than they are connected with the earth."

Being familiar with the Hebrew Scriptures, Jesus' disciples understood the context of His words and grasped their meaning. Jesus spoke against the backdrop of the Old Testament.

"Our discussion of the meaning of Daniel 7:13 in its Old Testament context led us to the conclusion that its keynote is one of vindication and exaltation to an everlasting dominion, and that the "coming" of verse 13 was a coming to God [the Ancient of Days] to receive power, not a "descent" to earth. When we studied Jesus' use of these verses, we found that in every case this same theme was the point of the allusion, and, in particular, that nowhere (unless here) was verse 13 [in Dan. 7] interpreted of his coming to earth at the Parousia. In particular, the reference to Mark 14:62, where the wording is clearly parallel to that in the present verse [Mark 13:26], was to Jesus' imminent vindication and power, with a secondary reference to a manifestation of that power in the near future. Thus, the expectation that Jesus would in fact use Daniel 7:13 in the sense in which it was written is amply confirmed by his actual allusions. He saw in that verse a prediction of his imminent exaltation to an authority which supersedes that of the earthly powers which have set themselves against God.... Jesus is using Daniel 7:13 as a prediction of that authority which he exercised when in AD 70 the Jewish nation and its leaders, who had condemned him, were overthrown, and Jesus was vindicated as the recipient of all power from the Ancient of Days.

"At His trial, Jesus told Caiaphas the high priest and the Sanhedrin that they would see "the Son of Man sitting at the right hand of power and coming on the clouds of heaven" (Matt. 26:64). When would this take place? "The phrase … 'from now on' means exactly what it says …, and refers not to some distant event but to the imminent vindication of Jesus which will shortly be obvious to those who have sat in judgement over him." What did they "see"? Certainly not an event that was thousands of years in the future. N.T. Wright comments:

"Jesus is not, then, suggesting that Caiaphas will witness the end of the space-time order. Nor will he look out of the window one day and observe a human figure flying downwards on a cloud. It is absurd to imagine either Jesus, or Mark, or anyone in between, supposing the words to mean that. Caiaphas will witness the strange events which follow Jesus' crucifixion: the rise of a group of disciples claiming that he has been raised from the dead, and the events which accelerate towards the final clash with Rome, in which, judged according to the time-honoured test, Jesus will be vindicated as a true prophet. In and through it all, Caiaphas will witness events which show that Jesus was not, after all, mistaken in his claim, hitherto implicit, now at last explicit: he is the Messiah, the anointed one, the true representative of the people of Israel, the one in and through whom the covenant God is acting to set up his kingdom.

"At His ascension, Jesus had come up to the Ancient of Days "with the clouds of heaven" to receive the kingdom from His Father (Mark 16:19; Acts 1:9). Jesus' reception of the kingdom gave Him possession so that He could do with it as He pleased. He had earlier stated that the kingdom would be "taken away from" those who rejected Him and would "be given to a nation producing the fruit of it" (Matt. 21:43). The church – made up initially of believing Jews and later of believing Gentiles – is described by Peter as a "holy nation" (1 Peter 2:9). It is this "nation" that is in possession of the kingdom by right of transfer. This covenant transfer is confirmed for us at the stoning of Stephen (Acts 7:54–56). Stephen's murderers objected to being called "stiff-necked and uncircumcised in heart and ears" (7:51). His words of condemnation had put them outside the covenant community because they, too, persecuted and killed the prophets by publicly denouncing the gospel message (7:52).

"So Stephen saw Him, before his death by stoning (Acts 7:56), and thus prophesied judgment on his murderers, at the very moment when he prayed for their forgiveness. The priesthood stood on trial that day, although the execution of their sentence was yet to come, on that awful day in AD 70 when the priests were cut down at the altar as they steadily continued their sacrifices.

"The church was persecuted by Jewish opposition for forty years after Jesus' death, once again confirming what Jesus had prophesied. With the destruction of Jerusalem in A.D. 70, the truth was comprehended by the tribes of Israel (Rev. 1:7). The generation that Jesus said would not pass away until all these things came to pass finally came to understand the implications of their rebellion: Jesus is the one who was given

"[D]ominion, Glory and a kingdom, that all the peoples, nations, and men of every language might serve Him" (Dan. 7:14). They were not to look for another (Matt. 24:26)."

Gary DeMar, Last Days Madness: Obsession of the Modern Church, Fourth revised edition (Powder Springs, GA: American Vision, 1999), 161–164.

[7] **The Times of the Gentiles**: They end in the first century with the destruction of the temple. They began with Daniel's prophecy of the four Gentile kingdoms that started with Babyon and ended with ancient Rome.

> Luke 21:20–24
> [20] "But when you see Jerusalem surrounded by armies, then know that its desolation has come near. [21] Then let those who are in Judea flee to the mountains, and let those who are inside the city depart, and let not those who are out in the country enter it, [22] for these are days of vengeance, to fulfill all that is written. [23] Alas for women who are pregnant and for those who are nursing infants in those days! For there will be great distress upon the earth and wrath against this people. [24] They will fall by the edge of the sword and be led captive among all nations, and Jerusalem will be trampled underfoot by the Gentiles, until the times of the Gentiles are fulfilled.

[8] **This is from**: Isaiah 2:2–4.

[9] The Gospel had reached the "whole world," "all the nations" through "all creation," the "whole cosmos" and "all the earth":

> Colossians 1:5–6
> … the gospel, 6 which has come to you, as indeed in the whole world it is bearing fruit and increasing…

The Gospel had reached the "whole world":

> Romans 1:8
> because your faith is being proclaimed throughout the whole world.

Same Greek word for "whole world" (Oikoumene) in Matthew 24:14 is used in these passages to means the Roman Empire:

> Luke 2:1 Now it came about in those days that a decree went out from Caesar Augustus, that a census be taken of all the world [Roman empire].

> Acts 11:28
> 28 And one of them named Agabus stood up and foretold by the Spirit that there would be a great famine over all the world [Roman empire](this took place in the days of Claudius).

> Acts 24:5
> "[Paul] stirs up riots among all the Jews throughout the world [Roman empire]."

The Gospel had reached "all the nations":

> Matthew 28:19
> 19 Go therefore and make disciples of all nations, baptizing them in the name of the Father and of the Son and of the Holy Spirit,

> 1 Timothy 3:16
> 16 Great indeed, we confess, is the mystery of godliness: He was manifested in the flesh, vindicated by the Spirit, seen by angels, proclaimed among the nations (ethne), believed on in the world, taken up in glory.

> Romans 16:25–26
> 25 Now to him who is able to strengthen you according to my gospel and the preaching of Jesus Christ, according to the revelation of the mystery that was kept secret for long ages 26 but has now been disclosed and through the prophetic writings has been made known to all nations (ethne)

> 2 Timothy 4:17
> 17 But the Lord stood by me and strengthened me, so that through me the message might be fully

proclaimed and all the Gentiles (ethne) might hear it. So I was rescued from the lion's mouth.

The Gospel had been preached through all "creation":

Mark 16:15
15 And he said to them, "Go into all the world and proclaim the gospel to the whole creation.

Colossians 1:23
23 if indeed you continue in the faith, stable and steadfast, not shifting from the hope of the gospel that you heard, which has been proclaimed in all creation (ktizo) under heaven, and of which I, Paul, became a minister.

The Gospel had reached the whole "cosmos":

John 17:18
18 As you sent me into the world, so I have sent them into the world (cosmos).

Romans 1:8
8 First, I thank my God through Jesus Christ for all of you, because your faith is proclaimed in all the world (cosmos).

The Gospel had reached "all the earth":

Acts 1:8
8 But you will receive power when the Holy Spirit has come upon you, and you will be my witnesses in Jerusalem and in all Judea and Samaria, and to the end of the earth (ge)."

Romans 10:17–18
So faith comes from hearing, and hearing through the word of Christ. 18 But I ask, have they not heard? Indeed they have, for "Their voice has gone out to all the earth (ge), and their words to the ends of the world."

[10] **Cassandra is drawing from**: The Greek of Ephesians 2:8 incorporates the entire process of grace, faith and salvation as gift-given.

Ephesians 2:8
For by grace you have been saved through faith. And this is not your own doing; it is the gift of God.

CHAPTER 29

[1] **This story is taken from**: Flavius Josephus, *The Wars of the Jews* 5.3.3, §109-119.

[2] **This scene is taken from**: Flavius Josephus, *The Wars of the Jews* 5.3.4-5, §120-128.

CHAPTER 30

[1] Jacob is referring to:

Hebrews 6:4–8
4 For it is impossible, in the case of those who have once been enlightened, who have tasted the heavenly gift, and have shared in the Holy Spirit, 5 and have tasted the goodness of the word of God and the powers of the age to come, 6 and then have fallen away, to restore them again to repentance, since they are crucifying once again the Son of God to their own harm and holding him up to contempt. 7 For land that has drunk the rain that often falls on it, and produces a crop useful to those for whose sake it is cultivated, receives a blessing from God. 8 But if it bears thorns and thistles, it is worthless and near to being cursed, and its end is to be burned.

[2] Matthew 25:44–46.

[3] Mark 8:36.

[1] Jesus is seated right now at the right hand of God in heaven reigning over all things:

> Ephesians 1:19–23
> [20] that he worked in Christ when he raised him from the dead and seated him at his right hand in the heavenly places, [21] far above all rule and authority and power and dominion, and above every name that is named, not only in this age but also in the one to come. [22] And he put all things under his feet and gave him as head over all things to the church, [23] which is his body, the fullness of him who fills all in all.

> 1 Peter 3:21–22
> [21] Jesus Christ, [22] who has gone into heaven and is at the right hand of God, with angels, authorities, and powers having been subjected to him.

> 1 Corinthians 15:24–27
> [24] Then comes the end, when he delivers the kingdom to God the Father after destroying every rule and every authority and power. [25] For he must reign until he has put all his enemies under his feet. [26] The last enemy to be destroyed is death. [27] For "God has put all things in subjection under his feet."

> Hebrews 2:7–8
> [7] You made him for a little while lower than the angels; you have crowned him with glory and honor, [8] putting everything in subjection under his feet." Now in putting everything in subjection to him, he left nothing outside his control. At present, we do not yet see everything in subjection to him.

The thousand year reign of Christ: Revelation 20:1-5.

The smallest of seeds to the largest of trees: Matthew 13:31-32

[2] Cassandra is quoting from:

> Genesis 50:20
> [20] As for you, you meant evil against me, but God meant it for good, to bring it about that many people should be kept alive, as they are today.

CHAPTER 32

[1] The white stones of the catapults:

Flavius Josephus, *The Wars of the Jews* 5.6.3, §270-272
"Now, the stones that were cast were of the weight of a talent, and were carried two furlongs and farther. The blow they gave was no way to be sustained, not only by those that stood first in the way, but by those that were beyond them for a great space. (271) As for the Jews, they at first watched the coming of the stone, for it was of a white color, and could therefore not only be perceived by the great noise it made, but could be seen also before it came by its brightness; (272) accordingly the watchmen that sat upon the towers gave them notice when the engine was let go, and the stone came from it, and cried out aloud in their own country language, "THE SON COMETH:"

Flavius Josephus and William Whiston, *The Works of Josephus: Complete and Unabridged* (Peabody: Hendrickson, 1987), 710.

[2] **The shekinah glory leaving the temple**: Biblically, the shekinah had left Israel in Ezekiel's day, along with the ark. However, it is an interesting footnote of history that the following legends support the idea of the shekinah leaving right before the destruction of Jerusalem in AD 70:

"Rabbi Jonathan (a few years after the fall of Jerusalem in A.D.70) reported that the Shekinah glory of God left the inner Temple in A.D.66. For three-and-a-half years, he said the Shekinah...

"abode on the Mount of Olives hoping that Israel would repent, but they did not; while a Bet Kol [a supernatural voice from heaven] issued forth announcing, Return, O backsliding children [Jeremiah 3:14]. Return unto Me, and I will return unto you [Malachi 3:7], when they did not repent, it said, I will return to my place [Hosea 5: 15]" (Midrash Rabbah, Lamentations 2:11).

Early Jewish Christians in Jerusalem would have known about this event mentioned by Rabbi Jonathan which both Jewish Christians and ordinary Jews reckoned as a miraculous sign concerning the holiness of the Mount of Olives. Christians in particular would no doubt have seen in this miraculous event much more significance than may meet the eye today. And indeed they did! Eusebius mentioned the importance of this removal of the Shekinah glory from the Temple mount to the Mount of Olives in his Proof of the Gospel (Bk. VI. ch.18).

"Believers in Christ congregate from all parts of the world, not as of old time because of the glory of Jerusalem, nor that they may worship in the ancient Temple at Jerusalem, but...that they may worship at the Mount of Olives opposite the city, whither the glory [the Shekinah Glory] of the Lord migrated when it left the former city."

To Eusebius, it was a sign that God had departed from the Temple on the western hill and had retreated to the Mount of Olives on the east as the new place of his divine residence. This event of the Shekinah glory leaving the Temple and abiding on the Mount of Olives became highly significant to Christians because this was the mountain where Jesus did most of his teachings in Jerusalem (and telling the Jews to repent in his day).

Ernest L. Martin, *Secrets of Golgotha (Second Edition): The Lost History of Jesus' Crucifixion (Portland OR: Associates for Scriptural Knowledge*, 1996), 167-168.
http://www.askelm.com/golgotha/Golgotha%20Chap%2000.pdf

[3] The spiritual harlotry of Israel:

"Ortlund points out regarding this harlotry theme that "what begins as Pentateuchal whispers rises later to prophetic cries and is eventually echoed in apostolic teaching." Eventually this harlotry image is especially employed by the prophets Hosea, Jeremiah, and Ezekiel who "exploit it to the fullest." Hosea develops the theme of harlotry throughout his entire book, even marrying a harlot himself to illustrate Israel's sin (Hos 1:2; 3:1–3). For instance, Hosea 2:2 reads: "Contend with your mother, contend, / For she is not my wife, and I am not her husband; / And let her put away her harlotry from her face, / And her adultery from between her breasts." Jeremiah 3:6 speaks similarly: "Then the Lord said to me in the days of Josiah the king, 'Have you seen what faithless Israel did? She went up on every high hill and under every green tree, and she was a harlot there'" (Jer 3:6). Jeremiah and Ezekiel particularly develop it "into elaborate images." The harlot metaphor is applied to Israel dozens of times in the Old Testament.18 The prophets speak of Israel's unfaithfulness through idolatry as hurtful to her husband: "Then those of you who escape will remember Me among the nations to which they will be carried captive, how I have been hurt by their adulterous hearts which turned away from Me, and by their eyes, which played the harlot after their idols" (Eze 6:9a). Consequently, "in a number of passages in the Old Testament, therefore, the 'lovers' after whom Israel went were other deities who were making a bid for her allegiance" (J. Thompson 1997: 476).

We must realize that although the charge of Israel's spiritual harlotry tends to focus on its most egregious manifestation in idolatry, it is not limited to idol worship. In the biblical view of marriage, the wife's faithfulness involves a wholesale relationship of loving obedience to her husband (Nu 5:29; Jer 31:32; Eph 5:22–23; 1Pe 3:1, 6), not just the avoidance of adulterous relations. Consequently, there are places where charges of harlotry against Israel speak of situations not involving actual, formal idolatry. For instance, when lawlessness (not idolatry) prevails in Jerusalem, the "faithful city" becomes a "harlot" (Isa 1:21–23). Here Isaiah declares that the "faithful city has become a harlot" because she was "full of justice" and "righteousness" but "now murderers." The "faithful [Heb., amen] city" is now acting like a "harlot," the most unfaithful of women."

Kenneth L. Gentry, Jr., The Divorce of Israel: A Redemptive-Historical Interpretation of Revelation Vol. 1 (Dallas, GA: Tolle Lege Press, 2016), 526-527.

Israel has become a symbolic Sodom, Egypt:

> Revelation 11:8 ...and their dead bodies will lie in the street of the great city that symbolically is called Sodom and Egypt, where their Lord was crucified.

Israel called by the name of Sodom: Isaiah 3:8–9; Jeremiah 23:14; Lamentations 4:6; Ezekiel 16:46, 48–49,

55–56; Amos 4:11; John 11:8 Matthew 10:15; 11:23–24).

Israel likened to Egypt: Amos 4:10-11.

The Great City of Babylon in Revelation 17 is Jerusalem:

Revelation 18:21–24 [21] "So will <u>Babylon the great city</u> be thrown down with violence, and will be found no more;.. [24] And in her was found the blood of prophets and of saints, and of all who have been slain on the land."

The Great City was previously introduced as the place of the crucifixion, which is Jerusalem.

Revelation 11:8 …and their dead bodies will lie in the street of <u>the great city</u> that symbolically is called <u>Sodom and Egypt</u>, where their Lord was crucified.

Jerusalem was the one guilty of the "blood of all the prophets and saints who have been slain on the land." (Rev 18:24):

Matthew 23:35–37 [35] so that on you [Jerusalem] may come all the righteous blood shed on the land…. [37] "O Jerusalem, Jerusalem, the city that kills the prophets and stones those who are sent to it!!

Old Testament prophets call Jerusalem the Great City: Jeremiah 22:8 " 'And many nations will pass by this city, and every man will say to his neighbor, "Why has the LORD dealt thus with this great city?"

Lamentations 1:1 How lonely sits the city that was full of people! How like a widow has she become, she who was great among the nations! She who was a princess among the provinces has become a slave.

Josephus calls Jerusalem a great city:

Flavius Josephus, *The Wars of the Jews*, 7.4.
"This was the end which Jerusalem came to by the madness of those that were for innovations; **a city otherwise of great magnificence**, and of mighty fame among all mankind."

Flavius Josephus, *Jewish Wars* 7:8:7 §375
"And where is now that **great city**, the metropolis of the Jewish nation, which was fortified by so many walls round about, which had so many fortresses and large towers to defend it, which could hardly contain the instruments prepared for the war, and which had so many ten thousands of men to fight for it? (376) Where is this city that was believed to have God himself inhabiting therein?"

Roman historians Tacitus and Pliny call Jerusalem a great city: "However, as I am about to describe the last days of a famous city, it seems proper for me to give some account of its origin." Tacitus, *Histories* 5.2

"Jerusalem, by far the most famous city, not of Judæa only, but of the East, and Herodium, with a celebrated town of the same name." Pliny the Elder, *The Natural History*, 15.15, ed. John Bostock (Medford, MA: Taylor and Francis, Red Lion Court, Fleet Street, 1855), 1428.

The Great City is Jerusalem. Extra biblical sources: Sibylline Oracles 5:154, 226, 413.

Babylon in Revelation 17 and 18 is Jerusalem, not Rome: "Several textual indicators suggest that John is focusing on Jerusalem rather than Rome (cp. Provan 1996: 94). (1) In this very Judaic book the language of religious defilement in 18:2 would suggest a Jewish city is in view. (2) Babylon's double punishment reflects the Old Testament prophetic witness against Jerusalem (18:6; see below). (3) The "great city" (18:10, 16, 18, 19, 21; cp. 18:2) was previously introduced as the place of the crucifixion (11:8). (4) In 18:24 the killing of the prophets by Babylon reflects a familiar sin of Jerusalem (Neh 9:26; cp. 1Ki 19:10, 14; 21:13; 2Ch 24:19, 21; 36:14-16; Isa 1:15; Jer 2:30; 25:4; 26:20-23). (5) The bowl judgments in Revelation 16 are being expanded upon in Revelation 17-18. In the latter bowls "Babylon the great" was distinguished from the cities of the nations (16:19)."Kenneth L. Gentry, Jr., *The Divorce of Israel: A Redemptive-Historical Interpretation of Revelation Vol. 2* (Dallas, GA: Tolle Lege Press, 2016), 506-507.

"It might be objected that the great city in Revelation appears too important among the nations to be identified with Jerusalem rather than Rome. However, Jerusalem was thought to be the "navel" or center of the earth (Gen R 59:5), "destined to become the metropolis of all countries" (Exod R 23:10), and the Psalms (e.g. 48:2–

3, 50:2); Lamentations (e.g. 1:1, 2:15) and Prophets (e.g. Zech 14:16–21, Isa 2:2–4, Micah 4:1–3) speak in the loftiest terms of Jerusalem's place among the nations. Rev 17:18 is probably a similar hyperbole; cf. 4QLam which describes her as "princess of all nations."

J. Massyngberde Ford, Revelation: Introduction, Translation, and Commentary, vol. 38, Anchor Yale Bible (New Haven; London: Yale University Press, 2008), 285

[4] **Mount Bashan as location of the fall of the Watchers and place of the serpent**: "Bashan was a deeply significant spiritual location to the Canaanites and the Hebrews. And as the Dictionary of Deities and Demons in the Bible puts it, Biblical geographical tradition agrees with the mythological and cultic data of the Canaanites of Ugarit that "the Bashan region, or a part of it, clearly represented 'Hell', the celestial and infernal abode of their deified dead kings," the Rephaim.

"Mount Hermon was in Bashan, and Mount Hermon was a location in the Bible that was linked to the Rephaim (Josh. 12:1-5), but was also the legendary location where the sons of God were considered to have come to earth and have sexual union with the daughters of men to produce the giant Nephilim. The non-canonical book of Enoch supports this same interpretation: "Enoch 6:6 And they were in all two hundred [sons of God]; who descended in the days of Jared on the summit of Mount Hermon, and they called it Mount Hermon, because they had sworn and bound themselves by mutual imprecations upon it." Brian Godawa, *When Giants Were Upon the Earth: The Watchers, the Nephilim, and the Biblical Cosmic War of the Seed* (Embedded Pictures, 2014), 75.

"Bashan/Bathan both also mean "serpent," so that the region of Bashan was "the place of the serpent." As we saw earlier, the divine serpent (nachash, another word so translated) became lord of the dead after his rebellion in Eden. In effect, Bashan was considered the location of (to borrow a New Testament phrase) "the gates of hell." Later Jewish writers understood these conceptual connections. Their intersection is at the heart of why books like 1 Enoch teach that demons are actually the spirits of dead Nephilim.

"Lastly, aside from Bashan being the gateway to the underworld, the region has another sinister feature identified in the Deuteronomy 3 passage: Mount Hermon. According to 1 Enoch 6:1–6, Mount Hermon was the place where the sons of God of Genesis 6 descended when they came to earth to cohabit with human women – the episode that produced the Nephilim. Joshua 12:4–5 unites all the threads: "Og king of Bashan, one of the remnant of the Rephaim, who lived at Ashtaroth and at Edrei and ruled over Mount Hermon."

"Just the name "Hermon" would have caught the attention of Israelite and Jewish readers. In Hebrew it's pronounced khermon. The noun has the same root as a verb that is of central importance in Deuteronomy 3 and the conquest narratives: kharam, "to devote to destruction." This is the distinct verb of holy war, the verb of extermination. It has deep theological meaning, a meaning explicitly connected to the giant clans God commanded Joshua and his armies to eradicate."

Michael S. Heiser, *The Unseen Realm: Recovering the Supernatural Worldview of the Bible*, First Edition (Bellingham, WA: Lexham Press, 2015), 200–201.

Mount Sinai replacing Mount Hermon through conflict: Psalm 68:15-22

Psalm 68:15–22 (ESV)
15 O mountain of God, mountain of Bashan;
O many-peaked mountain, mountain of Bashan!

16 Why do you look with hatred, O many-peaked mountain,
at the mount that God desired for his abode,
yes, where the Lord will dwell forever?

17 The chariots of God are twice ten thousand,
thousands upon thousands;
the Lord is among them; Sinai is now in the sanctuary.

18 You ascended on high,
leading a host of captives in your train
and receiving gifts among men,
even among the rebellious, that the Lord God may dwell there.

19 Blessed be the Lord,
who daily bears us up;
God is our salvation. Selah

20 Our God is a God of salvation,
and to God, the Lord, belong deliverances from death.

21 But God will strike the heads of his enemies,
the hairy crown of him who walks in his guilty ways.

22 The Lord said,
"I will bring them back from Bashan,
I will bring them back from the depths of the sea,

Installing Messiah on Mount Zion as God's cosmic mountain:

Psalm 2:6–8
6 "As for me, I have set my King
on Zion, my holy hill."

7 I will tell of the decree:
The Lord said to me, "You are my Son;
today I have begotten you.

8 Ask of me, and I will make the nations your heritage,
and the ends of the earth your possession.

Jesus builds his church upon the rock of Hermon: Matthew 16:13-20. "We've seen already that the Jewish tradition about the descent of the Watchers, the sons of God of Genesis 6:1–4, informed the writings of Peter and Jude. Now we see that the transfiguration of Jesus takes place on the same location identified by that tradition. Jesus picks Mount Hermon to reveal to Peter, James, and John exactly who he is – the embodied glory-essence of God, the divine Name made visible by incarnation. The meaning is just as transparent: I'm putting the hostile powers of the unseen world on notice. I've come to earth to take back what is mine. The kingdom of God is at hand." Michael S. Heiser, *The Unseen Realm: Recovering the Supernatural Worldview of the Bible, First Edition* (Bellingham, WA: Lexham Press, 2015), 286.

[5] Mount Zion, Jerusalem and the temple have all been spiritually fulfilled in the Body of Christ:

Hebrews 12:12–24 But you have come to Mount Zion and to the city of the living God, the heavenly Jerusalem, and to innumerable angels in festal gathering, [23] and to the assembly of the firstborn who are enrolled in heaven, and to God, the judge of all, and to the spirits of the righteous made perfect, [24] and to Jesus, the mediator of a new covenant.

Ephesians 2:19–22
[19] So then you are no longer strangers and aliens, but you are fellow citizens with the saints and members of the household of God, [20] built on the foundation of the apostles and prophets, Christ Jesus himself being the cornerstone, [21] in whom the whole structure, being joined together, grows into a holy temple in the Lord. [22] In him you also are being built together into a dwelling place for God by the Spirit.

1 Peter 2:4–5
[4] As you come to him, a living stone rejected by men but in the sight of God chosen and precious, [5] you yourselves like living stones are being built up as a spiritual house, to be a holy priesthood, to offer spiritual sacrifices acceptable to God through Jesus Christ.

[6] Drain the cup of the wine of the fury of his wrath: Revelation 16:19.

Relocation of Mount Zion and Jerusalem to the Body of Christ:

Hebrews 12:22–24
[22] But you have come to Mount Zion and to the city of the living God, the heavenly Jerusalem, and to innumerable angels in festal gathering, [23] and to the assembly of the firstborn who are enrolled in heaven, and to God, the judge of all, and to the spirits of the righteous made perfect, [24] and to

Jesus, the mediator of a new covenant.

Destruction of temple as the sign of the Son of Man in heaven and the new covenant access:

Matthew 23:35–24:2
[35] so that on you may come all the righteous blood shed on earth, from the blood of righteous Abel to the blood of Zechariah the son of Barachiah, whom you murdered between the sanctuary and the altar. [36] Truly, I say to you, all these things will come upon this generation. [37] "O Jerusalem, Jerusalem, the city that kills the prophets and stones those who are sent to it! How often would I have gathered your children together as a hen gathers her brood under her wings, and you were not willing! [38] See, your house is left to you desolate. [39] For I tell you, you will not see me again, until you say, 'Blessed is he who comes in the name of the Lord.' " [1] Jesus left the temple and was going away, when his disciples came to point out to him the buildings of the temple. [2] But he answered them, "You see all these, do you not? Truly, I say to you, there will not be left here one stone upon another that will not be thrown down."

Matthew 24:30
[30] Then will appear the sign of the Son of Man in heaven, and then all the tribes of the Land [of Israel] will mourn, and they will see the Son of Man coming on the clouds of heaven with power and great glory.

Hebrews 9:8–9 (NASB95)
[8] The Holy Spirit *is* signifying this, that the way into the holy place has not yet been disclosed while the outer tabernacle is still standing, [9] which *is* a symbol for the present time.

[7] Armageddon:

Revelation 16:13–16
[13] And I saw, coming out of the mouth of the dragon and out of the mouth of the beast and out of the mouth of the false prophet, three unclean spirits like frogs. [14] For they are demonic spirits, performing signs, who go abroad to the kings of the whole world, to assemble them for battle on the great day of God the Almighty. [15] ("Behold, I am coming like a thief! Blessed is the one who stays awake, keeping his garments on, that he may not go about naked and be seen exposed!") [16] And they assembled them at the place that in Hebrew is called Armageddon.

"The correct (Hebrew) term John uses to describe the climactic end-times battle is *harmagedon*. This spelling becomes significant when we try to discern what this Hebrew term means. The first part of the term (har) is easy. In Hebrew har means "mountain." Our term is therefore divisible into har-magedon, "Mount (of) magedon...the Hebrew phrase behind John's Greek transliteration of our mystery Hebrew term is actually h-r-m-ʾ-d. But what does that mean? If the first part (h-r) is the Hebrew word har ("mountain"), is there a har m-ʾ-d in the Hebrew Old Testament? There is – and it's stunning when considered in light of the battle of "Armageddon" and what we discussed in the previous chapter about the supernatural north and antichrist.The phrase in question exists in the Hebrew Bible as har moʿed. Incredibly, it is found in Isaiah 14:13...the phrase har moʿed was one of the terms used to describe the dwelling place of Yahweh and his divine council – the cosmic mountain...When John draws on this ancient Hebrew phrase, he is indeed pointing to a climactic battle at Jerusalem. Why? Because Jerusalem is a mountain – Mount Zion. And if Baal and the gods of other nations don't like Yahweh claiming to be Most High and claiming to run the cosmos from the heights of Zaphon/Mount Zion, they can try to do something about it."

Michael S. Heiser, The Unseen Realm: Recovering the Supernatural Worldview of the Bible, First Edition (Bellingham, WA: Lexham Press, 2015), 369-373.

"The rulers of the empire": I use this phrase because the translation "kings of the whole world" is a bad translation that gives a false picture of the original language. In Greek, the word for "whole world" is *oikoumene*, which contextually in the New Testament means the Roman empire.

The same Greek word is used in Luke 2:1: "Now it came about in those days that a decree went out from Caesar Augustus, that a census be taken of all the inhabited earth." In the New American Standard Version, the marginal note in Luke 2:1 reads "the Roman empire" (also see Acts 11:28, 24:5)."

Gary DeMar, *Last Days Madness: Obsession of the Modern Church*, Fourth revised edition (Powder Springs,

GA: American Vision, 1999), 88.

In NT thinking the Roman empire is the world (Ac 11:28; 17:6; 24:5; Col 1:6, 24). This is true among non-biblical writers, as well (Jos., J.W. 2:16:4 §361, 380, 388; 4:3:10 §78; Ap. 2:4 §8; Tac., His. 2:78).

And the Greek word for "kings" mean rulers of all kinds, not merely kings as in monarchies:

"The NT has 115 occurrences of βασιλεύς. "king" a) As in the LXX, references to the secular ruler predominate with 72 occurrences (25 in the Synoptics, 19 in Acts, 17 in Revelation, 7 in Hebrews, and 2 Cor 11:32; 1 Tim 2:2; 1 Pet 2:13, 17). b) 38 occurrences refer to Jesus (19 in the Synoptics and 16 in John, of which 26 are in the Passion narrative; Acts 17:7; Rev 17:14; 19:16)."

Horst Robert Balz and Gerhard Schneider, *Exegetical Dictionary of the New Testament* (Grand Rapids, Mich.: Eerdmans, 1990–), 206.

Spiritual war of cosmic mountains: Isaiah 14:13-15. For the fictional depiction of this spiritual war of cosmic mountains see Brian Godawa *Jesus Triumphant: Chronicles of the Nephilim Book 8* (Embedded Pictures, 2015). For an explanation of the theology behind that fiction see the appendix of that same book, pages 308-311. For the academic defense of the interpretation, see Michael S. Heiser, *The Unseen Realm: Recovering the Supernatural Worldview of the Bible, First Edition* (Bellingham, WA: Lexham Press, 2015), 288-295.

Armageddon as battle of cosmic mountains: Richard J. Clifford, *The Cosmic Mountain in Canaan and the Old Testament* (Wipf & Stock Pub, 2010).

[8] This description of the demons taken from: Revelation 9:7-10.

Ken Gentry makes a strong argument for the case that these demons are described this way in order to link them to the Roman legions that would besiege Jerusalem for 5 months in AD 69-70.

1. "**Their appearance was like horses prepared for battle**" (Rev 9:7) is a reference to the war horses of the legion.

2. "**On their heads appeared to be crowns like gold**" (9:7) Crowns are symbols of victorious march. These could be symbolic of the spiritual powers and authorities of darkness.

3. "And their faces were like the faces of men" (9:7).

"This may also imply that these demons inhabit those Jews – particularly the Idumeans, zealots, and Sicarii – within the city during the final five month siege. They lead these men to act in a bestial manner, for as Josephus writes of that period: the trapped citizens are "like a wild beast [thērion] grown mad, which, for want of food from abroad, fell now upon eating its own flesh" (J.W. 5:1:1 §4). Thus, those men operate "without mercy, and omitted no method of torment or of barbarity" (J.W. 5:1:5 §35)."

4. "These demon-locusts also had hair like the hair of women" (9:8a).

"This additional anthropomorphism may indicate the demonically-enhanced, shameful crimes committed within Jerusalem of this period. According to Paul long hair (such as women have) on men may picture that which is dishonorable: "even nature itself teaches you that if a man has long hair, it is a dishonor to him" (1Co 11:14). Or this image may even more particularly anticipate the demonic actions of John of Gischala's men:

> They also devoured what spoils they had taken, together with their blood, and indulged themselves in feminine wantonness, without any disturbance, till they were satiated therewith; while they decked their hair, and put on women's garments, and were besmeared over with ointments; and that they might appear very comely, they had paints under their eyes, and imitated not only the ornaments, but also the lusts of women, and were guilty of such intolerable uncleanness, that they invented unlawful pleasures of that sort. And thus did they roll themselves up and down the city, as in a brothel-house, and defiled it entirely with their impure actions; nay, while their faces looked like the faces of women, they killed with their right hands; and when their gait was effeminate, they presently attacked men. (J.W. 4:9:10 §561–563)

5. "Their teeth were like the teeth of lions" (9:8b)

"This not only picks up again from the Joel backdrop (Joel 1:4, 6; cf. Rev 13:2), but enhances the terror imagery. It is a proverbial image denoting the frightening and destructive power of lions (Job 4:10; Ps 7:2;

57:4; 58:6; Jer 2:30; Joel 1:6; Sir. 21:1–3; cp. 2Sa 1:23) from whom "none can deliver" (Pr 30:30; Isa 5:29; Hos 5:14)…Not only does this add to the fear John is evoking, but may indicate their insatiable appetite which is used in Scripture as a metaphor of destructive war: "Behold, a people rises like a lioness, / And as a lion it lifts itself; / It will not lie down until it devours the prey, / And drinks the blood of the slain" (Nu 23:24; cp. Job 38:39; Ps 17:12; 22:13; 104:21; Eze 19:6; Na 2:12; 1Pe 5:8)."

6. "They had breastplates like breastplates of iron" (9:9)

"This is a part of their look as "horses prepared for battle" (9:7a): fully dressed for battle in their protective plated armor."

7. "The sound of their wings was like the sound of chariots, of many horses rushing to battle" (9:9b).

"The visual image (along with its audial element) also is designed to impart fear, for in antiquity the attack of war horses and chariots was a signal of approaching devastation (1Sa 13:5; 1Ki 20:1; Isa 2:7; 5:28; Jer 6:23; 46:9; 47:3–4; 50:42; Eze 23:24; 26:7, 10; Nah 3:1–4)."

8. "They have tails like scorpions, and stings; and in their tails is their power to hurt men for five months" (9:10).

"Here in 9:10 John repeats the "five months" time frame from 9:5b which emphasizes this particular period of the Jewish War. This five-month period represents the last days of Israel's temple and the death throes of her holy city."

Kenneth L. Gentry, Jr., The Divorce of Israel: A Redemptive-Historical Interpretation of Revelation Vol. 1 (Dallas, GA: Tolle Lege Press, 2016), 742-750.

"The Roman Soldiers as the great army. Their similarity of description to the locust demons: "Foot-soldiers wear breastplate and helmet, with a sword on each side, the longer on the left while that on the right is only nine inches long. The picked troops around the general are armed with a half-pike and small shield, but most of the infantry are equipped with a javelin and a long shield, a saw, a [hod-like] basket and a pick, together with an axe, a strap and a sickle, besides enough provisions for three days – so there is not much difference between an infantry man and a packhorse. A cavalryman has a long sword at his right side and carries a lance, protected by a shield slanted to cover his horse's flank, while he also has a quiver holding three broad-bladed javelins that are not much smaller than spears. Like the foot-soldiers, he wears breastplate and helmet…

"This account needs qualification. Although they had metal helmets, legionaries wore armor made from hardened leather straps and metal studs and carried oblong leather shields that were strengthened with iron. Officers (including centurions) were distinguished by cuirasses of scale, chain, or plate armor, red horsehair crests, and colored cloaks. The sword – worn on the right side and not on the left, as Josephus says – was the gladius, a short, straight weapon with a blade two feet long and two inches wide. The javelin was the pilum, with a slender wooden shaft four and half feet long with a barbed iron head of the same length – its neck made of soft metal, which bent and hung down after piercing an enemy's shield, so as to hamper him. The stirrup had not yet been invented, and a charge by mounted troops did not have the impact it would have in later centuries."

Desmond Seward, Jerusalem's Traitor: Josephus, Masada, and the Fall of Jerusalem (Da Capo Press, 2009), Chapter 3 online: http://erenow.com/ancient/jerusalems-traitor-josephus-masada-and-the-fall-of-judea/2.html

CHAPTER 33

[1] Ancient tracheotomy:

"A fragment of the writings of Antyllus is preserved by Paulus Ægineta, [1] and shows the quality of the work done in bygone ages. It is his description of the operation of tracheotomy, and runs as follows: –

"When we proceed to perform this operation we must cut through some part of the windpipe, below the larynx, about the third or fourth ring; for to divide the whole would be dangerous. This place is commodious, because it is not covered with any flesh, and because it has no vessels situated near the divided part. Therefore, bending the head of the patient backward, so that the windpipe may come more forward to the view, we make a transverse section between two of the rings, so that in this case not the cartilage but the membrane which unites the cartilages together, is divided. If the operator be a little timid, he may first stretch the skin with a hook and divide it; then, proceeding to the windpipe, and separating the vessels, if any are in the way, he may make the incision." This operation had been proposed by Asclepiades about three hundred years before the time of Antyllus."

Elliott, James. Outlines of Greek and Roman Medicine (p. 57) K-Edition.

CHAPTER 34

[1] **This story is told in**: Flavius Josephus 5.7.1-2, *The Wars of the Jews*, §291-302. I withheld the battering rams here in order to avoid redundancy later in the story when they use the rams against the Antonia.

[2] **Fenugreek defense**: Flavius Josephus, The Wars of the Jews 3.7.29, §276-282. Although this description is used at the battle of Jotapata.

[3] **Warm welcome**: This was a popular phrase said by those who used this tactic.

CHAPTER 35

[1] The Ebionites and heresy in the early church:

"In addition to these things the same man, while recounting the events of that period, records that the Church up to that time had remained a pure and uncorrupted virgin, since, if there were any that attempted to corrupt the sound norm of the preaching of salvation, they lay until then concealed in obscure darkness.

But when the sacred college of apostles had suffered death in various forms, and the generation of those that had been deemed worthy to hear the inspired wisdom with their own ears had passed away, then the league of godless error took its rise as a result of the folly of heretical teachers, who, because none of the apostles was still living, attempted henceforth, with a bold face, to proclaim, in opposition to the preaching of the truth, the 'knowledge which is falsely so-called.'

"Therefore, they called the Church a virgin, for it was not yet corrupted by vain discourses. But Thebuthis, because he was not made bishop, began to corrupt it."

Eusebius of Caesaria, "The Church History of Eusebius," in Eusebius: Church History, Life of Constantine the Great, and Oration in Praise of Constantine, ed. Philip Schaff and Henry Wace, trans. Arthur Cushman McGiffert, vol. 1, A Select Library of the Nicene and Post-Nicene Fathers of the Christian Church, Second Series (New York: Christian Literature Company, 1890), 164, 199.

"Up to that period the Church had remained like a virgin pure and uncorrupted: for, if there were any persons who were disposed to tamper with the wholesome rule of the preaching of salvation, they still lurked in some dark place of concealment or other. But, when the sacred band of apostles had in various ways closed their lives, and that generation of men to whom it had been vouchsafed to listen to the Godlike Wisdom with their own ears had passed away, then did the confederacy of godless error take its rise through the treachery of false teachers, who, seeing that none of the apostles any longer survived, at length attempted with bare and uplifted head to oppose the preaching of the truth by preaching "knowledge falsely so called."

Hegesippus, "Fragments from His Five Books of Commentaries on the Acts of the Church," in Fathers of the Third and Fourth Centuries: The Twelve Patriarchs, Excerpts and Epistles, the Clementina, Apocrypha, Decretals, Memoirs of Edessa and Syriac Documents, Remains of the First Ages, ed. Alexander Roberts, James Donaldson, and A. Cleveland Coxe, trans. B. P. Pratten, vol. 8, The Ante-Nicene Fathers (Buffalo, NY: Christian Literature Company, 1886), 764.

The Nazoreans, a group similar to Ebionites with possible ties:

"Epiphanius is, as far as we know from historical records that have been preserved, the first writer to mention a distinct Jewish Christian sect of Nazoraeans, in chapter 29 of his Panarion. According to the Panarion, the Nazoraeans began when Jewish followers of the apostles who practiced circumcision and lived by the Torah left the "church" after the ascension. To put Epiphanius's view in modern terms, he understands the Nazoraeans to be Jewish Christians who backslid and reverted to Judaism. Epiphanius is confused by the fact that he knows of a Jewish Christian sect called Nazoraeans existing in his own day, but he also knows from the book of Acts that the earliest Christians were called by a similar name (Nazarenes): "For this group did not name themselves after Christ or with Jesus's own name, but 'Nazoraeans.' However, at that time all Christians were called Nazoraeans in the same way…"

"[H]e goes on to say that the beginnings of the Nazoraeans can be traced to a group of Christians in Transjordan who had fled Jerusalem before its capture in 70 CE…

"Epiphanius confirms what we know from other sources that these Nazoraeans lived in Pella and Kokhaba, and also adds the name of the village of Beroea, near Syria. Beroea, which is some distance from Pella and Kokhaba, is not mentioned in any other source as a dwelling for Jewish Christians, except for Jerome, who independently confirms this. Epiphanius considers the Nazoraeans to be somewhat orthodox because they believe in the resurrection of the dead and believe that Jesus is the Son of God. These are, however, things the Ebionites also accepted, though they understood the title "Son of God" in its original Jewish sense."

Jeffrey J. Bütz and James D. Tabor, The Secret Legacy of Jesus: The Judaic Teachings That Passed from James the Just to the Founding Fathers (Simon & Schuster, 2009), 335.

[2] **Boaz quotes from**: John 1:1, 14.

Logos in Greek and Hebrew understanding:

"Logos (usually translated 'Word', sometimes also 'Reason') plays a central role in Greek thought, and is frequently associated with divinity…

"The meanings of the word most relevant to the divine are 'reason' (i.e. divine thought), 'speech' (divine revelation), and 'order' (divine activity)…

"Although the Logos has a rich history in Greek thought as a philosophical principle and is often associated with the divine (whether in general or with specific deities), it is not personified as an independent deity, and is not the object of cultic worship in the form of statues or altars (in contrast to personified gods such as →Dikē, Moira, →Tychē, Heimarmenē, →Pronoia). The reason for this may be the generality and abstract nature of Logos as rational or creative principle…

"God's logos is associated with action rather than rationality (cf. also Ps 147:4, 7 [MT 15, 18]), and is in no way yet regarded as in any way independent from God himself.

"The theme is continued in the Wisdom literature. In a number of texts Sirach associates God's logos with the creation and maintainance of the creational order (39:17, 31; 43:10, 26). Logos is linked with the more prominent theme of Wisdom (Sophia), who is regarded as God's instrument in creation (Prov 8:22–31, Sir 24). In Wisdom theology a clear separation is made between God and his Wisdom: Prov 8:22 "God established me as beginning (archē) of his ways to brings about his works;" 8:30 "I was beside him bringing things together, and I was the one in whom he delighted" (translation of LXX text). Wisdom thus becomes an hypostasis (a self-subsistent entity), independent of God, but remaining very closely associated with Him…

"But in the personalized or hypostasized sense the Logos is found only in the Prologue to John's Gospel (1:1–18), to which reference is made in two subsequent writings of the Johannine community (1 John 1:1; Rev 19:13). The opening sentence of the Prologue (1:1) reads: "In the beginning was the Logos, and the Logos was with (the) God, and the Logos was God." The first phrase very clearly recollects both the opening words of the Torah (Gen 1:1) and the description of the pre-existent Wisdom of Prov 8:22. The second phrase emphasizes the intimacy of the Logos' relation to God (cf. Prov 8:31, also John 1:18 "in the bosom of the →Father"). The third phrase is climactic. "John intends that the whole of his gospel shall be read in the light of this verse. The deeds and words of Jesus are the deeds and words of God" (C. K. BARRETT, The Gospel according to St. John [London 1978²] 156). The predicative use of theos without the article is striking. "The Johannine hymn is bordering on the usage of "God" for the →Son, but by omitting the article it avoids any suggestion of personal identifcation of the Word with the Father. And for Gentile readers the line also avoids any suggestion that the Word was a second God in any Hellenistic sense."

D. T. Runia, "Logos," ed. Karel van der Toorn, Bob Becking, and Pieter W. van der Horst, Dictionary of Deities and Demons in the Bible (Leiden; Boston; Köln; Grand Rapids, MI; Cambridge: Brill; Eerdmans, 1999), 525–529.

[3] **Forever, everlasting covenant**: see Exodus 12:14, Leviticus 3:17, Leviticus 23:21, Deut 12:1.

Psalm 105:8–11
8 He remembers his covenant forever,
the word that he commanded, for a thousand generations,

9 the covenant that he made with Abraham,
his sworn promise to Isaac,

10 which he confirmed to Jacob as a statute,
to Israel as an everlasting covenant,

11 saying, "To you I will give the land of Canaan
as your portion for an inheritance."

[4] Ekklesia translated as "congregation" or "assembly" rather than "church":

"English translations have obscured the biblical and historical meaning of ekklēsia by translating it as "church" rather than "assembly" or "congregation." It's unfortunate that John Wycliffe (c. 1324–1384) and the translators of the Geneva Bible (1560) chose to translate ekklēsia as "church" rather than the more accurate "assembly" or "congregation." And it's a shame that the scholars who were chosen to develop what has come to us as the King James Version were forced to translate ekklēsia as "church." The English word "church" is not related to the Greek word ekklēsia but is derived from the Greek kyriake (oikia) "Lord's (house)," from kyrios "ruler, lord."…

"It's my contention that the use of "church" instead of "congregation" or "assembly" has gone a long way to create the myth of an Israel-Church distinction because it was viewed as a new thing rather than an extension of what the Old Testament had made obvious, both in the Hebrew and its Greek translation, the Septuagint. In all of the many definitional uses of ekklēsia in the New Testament – Melvin Elliott lists six – not one of them fits the definition given by dispensationalists as an newly created category of believers that had the result of creating an Israel-Church distinction."

Gary DeMar, 10 Popular Prophecy Myths Exposed: The Last Days Might Not Be as near as You Think (Powder Springs, GA: American Vision, 2010), 167–168.

[5] Ebionites as Judaizers:

"Those who are called Ebionites agree that the world was made by God; but their opinions with respect to the Lord are similar to those of Cerinthus and Carpocrates. They use the Gospel according to Matthew only, and repudiate the Apostle Paul, maintaining that he was an apostate from the law. As to the prophetical writings, they endeavour to expound them in a somewhat singular manner: they practise circumcision, persevere in the observance of those customs which are enjoined by the law, and are so Judaic in their style of life, that they even adore Jerusalem as if it were the house of God."

Irenaeus of Lyons, "Irenæus against Heresies," 1.26.2 in The Apostolic Fathers with Justin Martyr and Irenaeus, ed. Alexander Roberts, James Donaldson, and A. Cleveland Coxe, vol. 1, The Ante-Nicene Fathers (Buffalo, NY: Christian Literature Company, 1885), 352.

From Eusebius: "These, indeed, thought on the one hand that all the epistles of the apostles ought to be rejected, calling him an apostate from the law, but on the other, only using the gospel according to the Hebrews, they esteem the others as of but little value. They also observe the Sabbath and other discipline of the Jews, just like them, but on the other hand, they also celebrate the Lord's days very much like us, in commemoration of his resurrection. Whence, in consequence of such a course, they have also received their epithet, the name of Ebionites, exhibiting the poverty of their intellect. For it is thus that the Hebrews call a poor man..."

Hans-Joachim Schoeps, trans., Douglas R.A. Hare, Jewish Christianity: Factional Disputes in the Early Church (Philadelphia: Fortress Press, 1969), 14.

"The theology taught by Paul viewed Jesus' death as sacrificial. This proved to be a disruptive doctrine among the Ebionites. They nurtured a tremendous dislike for Paul and all of Pauline soteriology. Having completely rejected the sacrificial cult, they found no reconciliation in Jesus dying on the cross for the sins of the world...

"Characteristically, unlike Jesus, the Ebionites pushed towards staunch legalism. They carried the idea of eating anything still containing its own blood beyond the rabbinic requirement of draining the blood. They completely abstained from meats. Bloodshed of any kind was inappropriate to the Ebionites. This also widened the gap between the Ebionites and Paul. Poverty became a virtue, and the manner in which they followed the purity regulations was extremely strict and legalistic.

"The Ebionites maintained much of the Pharisaic halakhah and expanded upon it."

Randall A. Weiss, *Jewish Sects of the New Testament Era* (Cedar Hill, TX: Cross Talk, 1994).

Ebionites were linked to the Nazoreans, and sometimes considered synonymous:

"This heresy of the Nazoraeans exists in Beroea around Coele Syria, and in the Decapolis around the area of Pella, and in Basanitis in the so-called Kokabe (but the so-called Chochabe in Hebrew). 8. For from there it originated after the migration from Jerusalem, after all the disciples had settled in Pella, because Christ had told them to leave Jerusalem and to depart, since it was about to suffer siege; and for this reason, after settling in Perea, they were living there, as I said. There the Nazoraean heresy had its beginning.

"A second reference to the Pella flight occurs in the Panarion 30.2.7 in a discussion of the Ebionites: [The Ebionites] originated after the capture of Jerusalem. For at that time all who believed in Christ had settled predominantly in Perea, in a certain city called Pella of the Decapolis, of which it is written in the gospel [that it is near] the region of Batanaea and Basanitis. At that time, after having and while they were living there, from this [place] Ebion's."...

"that Epiphanius saw the refugees from Jerusalem as orthodox Christians who later fell prey to heresy. could hold such a position because he, like Eusebius, assumed that the group that went to Pella included no apostles, whom he considered to be the guardians of orthodoxy. The fugitives to Pella included "all the disciples" (Pan. 29.7.8), which meant "all who believed in Christ" (30.2.7). They were "the disciples of the apostles" rather than the apostles themselves...

"The Ebionites claimed that their name, meaning "the poor," derived from a time when they sold their longings and laid the money at the feet of the apostles (Pan. 30.17.2). Epiphanius denied this, insisting that their identity derived from Ebion, their founder. The Ebionites had noncanonical books bearing the names of apostles (30.23. 1-2). Epiphanius attacked these writings by telling a story to show that the apostle John knew of Ebion and considered him heretical. He concluded: "It is clear to everyone that the apostles disowned the faith of Ebion and considered it foreign to the character of their own preaching" (30.24.7)...

Craig Koester, "The Origin and Significance of the Flight to Pella Tradition," *The Catholic Biblical Quarterly*, Vol. 51, No. 1 (January, 1989), 92-93, 96.

Epiphanius does not consider the Nazoraeans to be sufficiently orthodox, however:

"They are different from Jews, and different from Christians, only in the following. They disagree with Jews because they have come to faith in Christ; but since they are still fettered by the Law – circumcision, the Sabbath, and the rest – they are not in accord with Christians...

Jeffrey J. Bütz and James D. Tabor, The Secret Legacy of Jesus: The Judaic Teachings That Passed from James the Just to the Founding Fathers (Inner Traditions, 2009), 335.

Epiphanius is quite correct when he dates the origin of the Ebionites and Nazoreans at the time of the capture of Jerusalem (Pan. 30.2.7; 29.5.4). And yet it is not a contradiction when he at the same time attributes the beginnings of the Nazoreans to the earliest period of the primitive church in Jerusalem, directly after the death of Jesus (29.7). Both dates are correct, depending upon whether one is speaking of the beginning of Ebionitism as an institution or of its spiritual beginnings.

Hans-Joachim Schoeps, trans., Douglas R.A. Hare, *Jewish Christianity: Factional Disputes in the Early Church* (Philadelphia: Fortress Press, 1969), 18.

"The Sacrificial Cult. Of primary importance is the bloody animal sacrifice, abolished by Jesus. According to Recognitions 1.35 ff., the real point of Jesus' mission is the annulling of the sacrificial law combined with complete loyalty to and affirmation of the rest of the Mosaic law. Animal sacrifice, it is claimed, was permitted on a temporary basis by Moses only because of the people's hardness of heart; Jesus abolished it and replaced the blood of sacrificial animals with the water of baptism. Thus the logion of Matthew 5:17 reads in the Gospel of the Ebionites, with a characteristic alteration: "I have come to annul sacrifice, and if you will not cease to sacrifice the wrath will not turn from you."

Hans-Joachim Schoeps, trans., Douglas R.A. Hare, *Jewish Christianity: Factional Disputes in the Early Church* (Philadelphia: Fortress Press, 1969), 82.

[6] Symeon misquotes Paul:

> 1 Timothy 2:12
> [12] I do not permit a woman to teach or to exercise authority over a man; rather, she is to remain quiet.

[7] Cassandra is drawing about false teachers from:

> 2 Peter 2:10–22
> [10] and especially those who indulge in the lust of defiling passion and despise authority. Bold and willful, they do not tremble as they blaspheme the glorious ones, [11] whereas angels, though greater in might and power, do not pronounce a blasphemous judgment against them before the Lord. [12] But these, like irrational animals, creatures of instinct, born to be caught and destroyed, blaspheming about matters of which they are ignorant, will also be destroyed in their destruction, [13] suffering wrong as the wage for their wrongdoing. They count it pleasure to revel in the daytime. They are blots and blemishes, reveling in their deceptions, while they feast with you. [14] They have eyes full of adultery, insatiable for sin. They entice unsteady souls. They have hearts trained in greed. Accursed children! [15] Forsaking the right way, they have gone astray. They have followed the way of Balaam, the son of Beor, who loved gain from wrongdoing, [16] but was rebuked for his own transgression; a speechless donkey spoke with human voice and restrained the prophet's madness. [17] These are waterless springs and mists driven by a storm. For them the gloom of utter darkness has been reserved. [18] For, speaking loud boasts of folly, they entice by sensual passions of the flesh those who are barely escaping from those who live in error. [19] They promise them freedom, but they themselves are slaves of corruption. For whatever overcomes a person, to that he is enslaved. [20] For if, after they have escaped the defilements of the world through the knowledge of our Lord and Savior Jesus Christ, they are again entangled in them and overcome, the last state has become worse for them than the first. [21] For it would have been better for them never to have known the way of righteousness than after knowing it to turn back from the holy commandment delivered to them. [22] What the true proverb says has happened to them: "The dog returns to its own vomit, and the sow, after washing herself, returns to wallow in the mire."

[8] **Cassandra quotes from**: Ephesians 2:14–15

[9] Temple as microcosm of heavens and earth:

"YHWH is building a new Temple, therefore creating a new world, and vice versa. In light of Gosta Ahlstrom's astute argument that Syro-Palestinian temples were meant to be "heaven and earth," I am led to wonder whether "heaven and earth" in Isa. 65:17 and elsewhere is not functioning as a name for the Jerusalem Temple. The Sumerian parallels are strong. The Temple at Nippur (and elsewhere) was called Duranki, "bond of heaven and earth," and in Babylon we find Etemenanki, "the house where the foundation of heaven and earth is."64 Perhaps it is not coincidence that the Hebrew Bible begins with an account of the creation of heaven and earth by the command of God (Gen. 1:1) and ends with the command of the God of heaven "to build him a Temple in Jerusalem" (2 Chron. 35:23). It goes from creation (Temple) to Temple (creation) in twenty four books."

Jon Levenson, "The Temple and the World," *The Journal of Religion*, Vol. 64, No. 3 (Jul., 1984), pp. 295.

Flavius Josephus, *The Wars of the Jews*, 5.5.5
"Now, the seven lamps signified the seven planets; for so many there were springing out of the candlestick. Now, the twelve loaves that were upon the table signified the circle of the zodiac and the year; (218) but the altar of incense, by its thirteen kinds of sweet-smelling spices with which the sea replenished it, signified that God is the possessor of all things that are both in the uninhabitable and habitable parts of the earth, and that they are all to be dedicated to his use."

Flavius Josephus and William Whiston, *The Works of Josephus: Complete and Unabridged* (Peabody: Hendrickson, 1987), 707.

Flavius Josephus, *The Antiquities of the Jews*, 3.7.7

"Moses distinguished the tabernacle into three parts, and allowed two of them to the priests, as a place accessible and common, he denoted the land and the sea, these being of general access to all; but he set apart the third division for God, because heaven is inaccessible to men. (182) And when he ordered twelve loaves to be set on the table, he denoted the year, as distinguished into so many months. By branching out the candlestick into seventy parts, he secretly intimated the Decani, or seventy divisions of the planets; and as to the seven lamps upon the candlesticks, they referred to the course of the planets, of which that is the number. (183) The veils, too, which were composed of four things, they declared the four elements; for the fine linen was proper to signify the earth, because the flax grows out of the earth; the purple signified the sea, because that color is dyed by the blood of a sea shell fish; the blue is fit to signify the air; and the scarlet will naturally be an indication of fire. (184) Now the vestment of the high priest being made of linen, signified the earth; the blue denoted the sky, being like lightning in its pomegranates, and in the noise of the bells resembling thunder. And for the ephod, it showed that God had made the universe of four [elements]; and as for the gold interwoven, I suppose it related to the splendor by which all things are enlightened. (185) He also appointed the breastplate to be placed in the middle of the ephod, to resemble the earth, for that has the very middle place of the world. And the girdle which encompassed the high priest round, signified the ocean, for that goes round about and includes the universe. Each of the sardonyxes declare to us the sun and the moon; those, I mean, that were in the nature of buttons on the high priest's shoulders. (186) And for the twelve stones, whether we understand by them the months, or whether we understand the like number of the signs of that circle which the Greeks call the Zodiac, we shall not be mistaken in their meaning."

Flavius Josephus and William Whiston, *The Works of Josephus: Complete and Unabridged* (Peabody: Hendrickson, 1987), 90–91.

"This "age to come" was the new covenant age. Paul wrote elsewhere that the gospel (the new covenant) was "hidden for ages, but now revealed to his saints (Col 1:26). In 1 Corinthians 10:11, he wrote that the old covenant events occurred as an example "for our instruction upon whom the end of the ages has come." Did you catch that? The temple had not yet been destroyed, and Paul was saying that his generation was at the end of the ages! He said that it had come upon that first century of believers. The end of the age is not a future event that hasn't happened yet; it occurred in the first century with the coming of the new covenant, confirmed in the destruction of the temple. But Paul isn't the only one who wrote that in the New Testament.

"Hebrews 9:26 says that Jesus suffered on the cross, "once for all at the end of the ages to put away sin by the sacrifice of himself." The end of the ages is not the end of history or the end of the world as we understand it. The end of the ages had already occurred at the time of the crucifixion of Christ. The end of the ages was the end of the old covenant era and the beginning of the new covenant in Christ's blood!

"But get this: that same writer of Hebrews talked about the new covenant in Christ being superior to the old covenant in Hebrews 8. He quoted Jeremiah confirming that the prophets predicted the arrival of the new covenant age. And then he said, "In speaking of a new covenant, he makes the first one obsolete. And what is becoming obsolete and growing old is ready to vanish away" (8:13).

"What was growing old and ready to vanish at that time?

"It blew my theology when I realized that he was talking about the destruction of the temple as the final culmination of the new covenant replacement of the old covenant! He was writing in the time period after Christ's death and resurrection and right before the temple had been destroyed. So the new covenant had been established in Christ's blood, but it was not consummated with historical finality. Like Paul, the writer believed they were at the end of the ages. The new covenant would make the old covenant obsolete. But take a closer look at the language he used. He said that the old is "becoming obsolete and is ready to vanish away," as if the old covenant had not vanished yet. It was only in the process of becoming obsolete. "Becoming," not "had become," and not "would become" thousands of years in the future. What could that mean?

"Well, the writer was writing within the generation that Jesus said would see the destruction of the temple. The temple had not yet been destroyed. Hebrews 8 says that they were in a time period of change between covenants and that change had not yet been fully or historically consummated. That first century generation was in the transition period between ages or covenants. So, what would be the event that would embody the theological claim that the old covenant was obsolete and the new covenant had replaced it? The destruction of the symbol of the old covenant, the temple! The old covenant would not be obsolete until its symbolic incarnation, the temple, was made desolate."

Brian Godawa, *End Times Bible Prophecy: It's Not What They Told You* (Los Angeles, CA: Embedded Pictures Publishing, 2017), 72-74.

[10] **Jesus greater than Moses, angels, Aaron**: This is the message of Hebrews 1-5.

[11] **Torah fulfilled in Christ**: 2Corinthians 1:20. Also…

> Romans 10:4–10
> [4] For Christ is the end of the law for righteousness to everyone who believes. [5] For Moses writes about the righteousness that is based on the law, that the person who does the commandments shall live by them. [6] But the righteousness based on faith says, …"The word is near you, in your mouth and in your heart" (that is, the word of faith that we proclaim); [9] because, if you confess with your mouth that Jesus is Lord and believe in your heart that God raised him from the dead, you will be saved. [10] For with the heart one believes and is justified, and with the mouth one confesses and is saved.

> Galatians 3:23–29
> [23] Now before faith came, we were held captive under the law, imprisoned until the coming faith would be revealed. [24] So then, the law was our guardian until Christ came, in order that we might be justified by faith. [25] But now that faith has come, we are no longer under a guardian, [26] for in Christ Jesus you are all sons of God, through faith. [27] For as many of you as were baptized into Christ have put on Christ. [28] There is neither Jew nor Greek, there is neither slave nor free, there is no male and female, for you are all one in Christ Jesus. [29] And if you are Christ's, then you are Abraham's offspring, heirs according to promise.

> Romans 7:1–6
> [1] Or do you not know, brothers – for I am speaking to those who know the law – that the law is binding on a person only as long as he lives? [2] For a married woman is bound by law to her husband while he lives, but if her husband dies she is released from the law of marriage. [3] Accordingly, she will be called an adulteress if she lives with another man while her husband is alive. But if her husband dies, she is free from that law, and if she marries another man she is not an adulteress. [4] Likewise, my brothers, you also have died to the law through the body of Christ, so that you may belong to another, to him who has been raised from the dead, in order that we may bear fruit for God. [5] For while we were living in the flesh, our sinful passions, aroused by the law, were at work in our members to bear fruit for death. [6] But now we are released from the law, having died to that which held us captive, so that we serve in the new way of the Spirit and not in the old way of the written code.

Torah abolished:

> Ephesians 2:13–15
> [13] But now in Christ Jesus you who once were far off have been brought near by the blood of Christ. [14] For he himself is our peace, who has made us both one and has broken down in his flesh the dividing wall of hostility [15] **by abolishing the law of commandments expressed in ordinances**, that he might create in himself one new man in place of the two, so making peace,

[12] **Cassandra quotes from**: Ephesians 2:19-22.

[13] **Symeon quotes from**: Genesis 17:4-8.

CHAPTER 36

[1] **Description of the Antonia fortress**: Flavius Josephus 5.5.8, The Wars of the Jews, §238-247.

[2] Daniel speaks of Rome as the trampling beast of iron jaws:

> Daniel 7:7
> [7] After this I saw in the night visions, and behold, a fourth beast, terrifying and dreadful and exceedingly strong. It had great iron teeth; it devoured and broke in pieces and stamped what was

left with its feet. It was different from all the beasts that were before it, and it had ten horns.

[3] Two Messiahs and a prophet in the Dead Sea Scrolls:

CD–B Col. xix:10
"These shall escape in the age of the visitation; but those that remain shall be delivered up to the sword when there comes the messiah of Aaron and Israel."

Florentino García Martínez and Eibert J. C. Tigchelaar, "*The Dead Sea Scrolls Study Edition (translations)*" (Leiden; New York: Brill, 1997–1998), 577.

1QS Col. ix:11
"until the prophet comes, and the Messiahs of Aaron and Israel."

Florentino García Martínez and Eibert J. C. Tigchelaar, "*The Dead Sea Scrolls Study Edition (translations)*" (Leiden; New York: Brill, 1997–1998), 93.

1QS Col. ix:10
"shall be ruled by the first directives which the men of the Community began to be taught until the prophet comes, and the Messiahs of Aaron and Israel."

Florentino García Martínez and Eibert J. C. Tigchelaar, "*The Dead Sea Scrolls Study Edition (translations)*" (Leiden; New York: Brill, 1997–1998), 93.

See also: CD–B Col. xx:1; 4Q266 Frag. 10 i:11. CD–A Col. xii:22-xiii:1.

Priestly Messiah and Kingly Messiah: 1Q28a ii:11-21.

[4] Messiah saving his Remnant at the Day of the Lord for Israel:

Zechariah 8:6–8
[6] Thus says the LORD of hosts: If it is marvelous in the sight of **the remnant** of this people in those days, should it also be marvelous in my sight, declares the LORD of hosts? [7] Thus says the LORD of hosts: Behold, I will save my people from the east country and from the west country, [8] and I will bring them to dwell in the midst of Jerusalem. And they shall be my people, and I will be their God, in faithfulness and in righteousness."

Paul claimed that this prophecy was fulfilled in the New Covenant:

2 Corinthians 6:16
[16] What agreement has the temple of God with idols? For we are the temple of the living God; as God said, "I will make my dwelling among them and walk among them, and I will be their God, and they shall be my people.

Hebrews 8:10
[10] For this is the covenant that I will make with the house of Israel after those days, declares the Lord: I will put my laws into their minds, and write them on their hearts, and I will be their God, and they shall be my people.

CHAPTER 37

[1] **Marduk splitting Tiamat**: In the Babylonian myth The Enuma Elish, Marduk splits the dragon of chaos, named Tiamat in half to create the heavens and earth.

[2] "Victor" the battering ram:

Flavius Josephus, *The Wars of the Jews* 5.7.2, §298-299.
"So they retired out of the reach of the darts, and did no longer endeavor to hinder the impression of their rams, which, by continually beating upon the wall, did gradually prevail against it; (299) so that the wall already gave way to the Nico ("Victor"), for by that name did the Jews themselves call the greatest of their engines, because it conquered all things."

Flavius Josephus and William Whiston, *The Works of Josephus: Complete and Unabridged* (Peabody:

Hendrickson, 1987), 712.

[3] Israel has become a symbolic Babylon, Sodom, Egypt:

> Revelation 11:8 ...and their dead bodies will lie in the street of the great city that symbolically is called Sodom and Egypt, where their Lord was crucified.

Israel called by the name of Sodom: Isaiah 3:8–9; Jeremiah 23:14; Lamentations 4:6; Ezekiel 16:46, 48–49, 55–56; Amos 4:11; John 11:8 Matthew 10:15; 11:23–24).

Israel likened to Egypt: Amos 4:10-11.

The Great City of Babylon in Revelation 17 is Jerusalem:

> Revelation 18:21–24 [21] "So will Babylon the great city be thrown down with violence, and will be found no more;.. [24] And in her was found the blood of prophets and of saints, and of all who have been slain on the land."

The Great City was previously introduced as the place of the crucifixion, which is Jerusalem.

> Revelation 11:8 ...and their dead bodies will lie in the street of the great city that symbolically is called Sodom and Egypt, where their Lord was crucified.

Jerusalem was the one guilty of the "blood of all the prophets and saints who have been slain on the land." (Rev 18:24):

> Matthew 23:35–37 [35] so that on you [Jerusalem] may come all the righteous blood shed on the land.... [37] "O Jerusalem, Jerusalem, the city that kills the prophets and stones those who are sent to it!!

Old Testament prophets call Jerusalem the Great City: Jeremiah 22:8 " 'And many nations will pass by this city, and every man will say to his neighbor, "Why has the LORD dealt thus with this great city?"

> Lamentations 1:1 How lonely sits the city that was full of people! How like a widow has she become, she who was great among the nations! She who was a princess among the provinces has become a slave.

Josephus calls Jerusalem a great city: "This was the end which Jerusalem came to by the madness of those that were for innovations; a city otherwise of great magnificence, and of mighty fame among all mankind." Flavius Josephus, The Wars of the Jews, 7.4.

"And where is now that great city, the metropolis of the Jewish nation, which was fortified by so many walls round about, which had so many fortresses and large towers to defend it, which could hardly contain the instruments prepared for the war, and which had so many ten thousands of men to fight for it? (376) Where is this city that was believed to have God himself inhabiting therein?" Flavius Josephus, Jewish Wars 7:8:7 §375.

Roman historians Tacitus and Pliny call Jerusalem a great city: "However, as I am about to describe the last days of a famous city, it seems proper for me to give some account of its origin." Tacitus, Histories 5.2

"Jerusalem, by far the most famous city, not of Judæa only, but of the East, and Herodium, with a celebrated town of the same name." Pliny the Elder, The Natural History, 15.15, ed. John Bostock (Medford, MA: Taylor and Francis, Red Lion Court, Fleet Street, 1855), 1428.

The Great City is Jerusalem. Extra biblical sources: Sibylline Oracles 5:154, 226, 413.

Babylon in Revelation 17 and 18 is Jerusalem, not Rome: "Several textual indicators suggest that John is focusing on Jerusalem rather than Rome (cp. Provan 1996: 94). (1) In this very Judaic book the language of religious defilement in 18:2 would suggest a Jewish city is in view. (2) Babylon's double punishment reflects the Old Testament prophetic witness against Jerusalem (18:6; see below). (3) The "great city" (18:10, 16, 18, 19, 21; cp. 18:2) was previously introduced as the place of the crucifixion (11:8). (4) In 18:24 the killing of the prophets by Babylon reflects a familiar sin of Jerusalem (Neh 9:26; cp. 1Ki 19:10, 14; 21:13; 2Ch 24:19, 21; 36:14-16; Isa 1:15; Jer 2:30; 25:4; 26:20-23). (5) The bowl judgments in Revelation 16 are being expanded upon in Revelation 17-18. In the latter bowls "Babylon the great" was distinguished from the cities of the nations (16:19)."Kenneth L. Gentry, Jr., *The Divorce of Israel: A Redemptive-Historical Interpretation of Revelation Vol. 2* (Dallas, GA: Tolle Lege Press, 2016), 506-507.

"It might be objected that the great city in Revelation appears too important among the nations to be identified with Jerusalem rather than Rome. However, Jerusalem was thought to be the "navel" or center of the earth (Gen R 59:5), "destined to become the metropolis of all countries" (Exod R 23:10), and the Psalms (e.g. 48:2–3, 50:2); Lamentations (e.g. 1:1, 2:15) and Prophets (e.g. Zech 14:16–21, Isa 2:2–4, Micah 4:1–3) speak in the loftiest terms of Jerusalem's place among the nations. Rev 17:18 is probably a similar hyperbole; cf. 4QLam which describes her as "princess of all nations." J. Massyngberde Ford, *Revelation: Introduction, Translation, and Commentary, vol. 38, Anchor Yale Bible* (New Haven; London: Yale University Press, 2008), 285.

[4] **Fighting for their lives**: Remember, the judgment of the Watchers in Psalm 82 is "death" like any human prince.

[5] Agrippa's archers:

Flavius Josephus, *The Wars of the Jews* 3.4.2, §68
"A considerable number of auxiliaries got together, that came from the kings Antiochus, and Agrippa, and Sohemus, each of them contributing one thousand footmen that were archers, and a thousand horsemen. Malchus also, the king of Arabia, sent a thousand horsemen, besides five thousand footmen, the greatest part of whom were archers."

[6] **The source for this battle**: The spiritual warfare is obviously creative license. The human story of what really happened here can be found in Flavius Josephus, *The Wars of the Jews* 5.8.1-2, §331-347. The Romans ended up taking this wall five days later, but I have altered that for purposes of brevity and avoiding redundancy.

CHAPTER 38

[1] Cut off, condition of the Abrahamic covenant:

Genesis 17:9, 14
[9] And God said to Abraham, "As for you, you shall keep my covenant, you and your offspring after you throughout their generations.
[14] Any uncircumcised male who is not circumcised in the flesh of his foreskin shall be cut off from his people; he has broken my covenant."

[2] **To see a fuller fleshed out biblical argument for Jesus fulfilling all the promises of Abraham:** See Brian Godawa, *Israel in Bible Prophecy: The New Testament Fulfillment of the Promise to Abraham*, (Los Angeles, Embedded Pictures Publishing, 2017).

CHAPTER 39

[1] **This incident is described in:** chapter 53 of *Resistant: Revolt of the Jews*, Chronicles of the Apocalypse Book 3 by Brian Godawa.

[2] **Prince of desolation**: Titus, the prince to come on the wing of abomination.

Daniel 9:26–27
[26] And after the sixty-two weeks, an anointed one shall be cut off and shall have nothing. And the people of the prince who is to come shall destroy the city and the sanctuary. Its end shall come with a flood, and to the end there shall be war. Desolations are decreed. [27] And he shall make a strong covenant with many for one week, and for half of the week he shall put an end to sacrifice and offering. And on the wing of abominations shall come one who makes desolate, until the decreed end is poured out on the desolated."

CHAPTER 40

[1] **Jesus fulfilled all the Jewish feasts**: Special thanks to David Curtis of Berean Bible Church for his

teaching on this topic. You can get his free teachings on these at:
http://www.bereanbiblechurch.org/studies/leviticus.php

[2] Feast of Weeks:

> Leviticus 23:15–16
> [15] "You shall count seven full weeks from the day after the Sabbath, from the day that you brought the sheaf of the wave offering. [16] You shall count fifty days to the day after the seventh Sabbath. Then you shall present a grain offering of new grain to the LORD.

[3] **See chapter 14** for the theological explanation of the covenant in terms of "heaven and earth."

[4] The Restoration of Israel is embodied in the book of Acts:

The following is an excerpt from my book, Brian Godawa, *Israel in Bible Prophecy: The New Testament Fulfillment of the Promise to Abraham*, (Los Angeles, Embedded Pictures Publishing, 2017), 59-61.

In Acts 2, we read about the first explosion of the Gospel with the first baptism of the Holy Spirit. It was the thing that Jesus had told them to wait for, which would launch them into all the world with the Good News (Acts 1:4). Pentecost would be the historical inauguration of the heavenly New Covenant achieved by the death, resurrection and ascension of Christ. It would be the pouring out of God's Spirit upon his people (Isa 32:12-19; 44:5; Ezek 36:25-28; 37:14).

The disciples asked Jesus if this was the time of the restoration of Israel (1:6), the very thing we have been discussing in this work. Jesus told them that the restoration of Israel would begin occurring when the Holy Spirit came upon them, but they were not to worry themselves with the timing (1:8).

And what was the restoration, but the pouring out of God's Spirit and the regathering of Jews from all over the known earth in a spiritual metaphorical resurrection? (Ezek 37). So when the disciples were baptized with the Spirit at Pentecost and began to speak in foreign tongues, that was the fulfillment of God's pouring out of his Spirit. Pouring is a form of baptizing (Heb 9:10, 13, 19, 21). But it was also the beginning of the regathering of Jews because "there were dwelling in Jerusalem Jews, devout men from every nation under heaven" (Acts 2:5). The list of nations that are described (Acts 2:9-11) just happens to be a representative sampling of the seventy nations of Genesis 10. To the ancient Jews, those seventy were "all the nations" to which the Jews were scattered (Amos 9:9). According to the apostle Luke, Pentecost of AD 30 was transformed into the beginning of the gathering of Jews from all the nations.

And that gathering of Jews included the Gentiles. It was a gathering of two bodies into one that was occurring all throughout the book of Acts. Notice these passages that say that the evangelism of Acts is the very fulfillment of the promise to gather the Gentiles with the Jews as his people:

> Acts 15:13–19
> [13] After they finished speaking, James replied, "Brothers, listen to me. [14] Simeon has related how God first visited the Gentiles, to take from them a people for his name. [15] And with this the words of the prophets agree, just as it is written.

> Acts 26:23
> [Paul:] [23] that the Christ must suffer and that, by being the first to rise from the dead, he would proclaim light both to our people and to the Gentiles."

The "ingathering" was based upon the unity of belief in Jesus as Messiah. Isaiah had prophesied that when Messiah first came (the branch of Jesse), *in that very day*, the Lord would "recover the remnant that remains of his people," from all the nations. "In that day," the root of Jesse would be "raised (resurrected) as a signal for the nations," and would "assemble the banished of Israel and gather the dispersed of Judah from the four corners of the earth" (Isa 11:1-2, 10-12). According to the prophecy, the gathering of the remnant and the Gentiles would occur at the *first coming* of Messiah, when Jesus was resurrected, not the second coming. *In that day* of Messiah's arrival and resurrection (his raising as a signal), he would draw both the remnant of Israel as well as Gentile believers. This will not start in our future, it already started in the book of Acts! Paul likened that raising of the signal to Christ's resurrection, and confirmed this Isaianic promise as already being fulfilled *during his ministry*:

Romans 15:8–9, 12

8 For I tell you that <u>Christ became a servant</u> to the circumcised to show God's truthfulness, <u>in order to confirm the promises given to the patriarchs,</u> 9 and in order that the Gentiles might glorify God for his mercy...12 And again <u>Isaiah says, "The root of Jesse will come, even he who arises to rule the Gentiles; in him will the Gentiles hope.</u>

What were the promises given to the patriarchs that Paul says were confirmed ("verified") in Christ's resurrection? All of them, including the regathering (Acts 3:24; 32; 15:13-15; 24:24; 26:6). In fact, most of the prophecies about the regathering of Israel almost always add the inclusion of Gentiles as a simultaneous event (See more below). But the point is that the book of Romans says explicitly that the Isaianic prophecy about the gathering of the remnant along with the Gentiles was already being fulfilled *in his own day*. This is not an eschatological system demanding something must be fulfilled in the future, this is the New Testament itself saying the prophecy was fulfilled in the first century, *in that day*.

5 **Believers as the new covenant temple of God**: I have already explained this in previous footnotes.

Ephesians 2:19–22

19 So then you are no longer strangers and aliens, but you are fellow citizens with the saints and members of the household of God, 20 built on the foundation of the apostles and prophets, Christ Jesus himself being the cornerstone, 21 in whom the whole structure, being joined together, grows into a holy temple in the Lord. 22 In him you also are being built together into a dwelling place for God by the Spirit.

1 Peter 2:4–5

4 As you come to him, a living stone rejected by men but in the sight of God chosen and precious, 5 you yourselves like living stones are being built up as a spiritual house, to be a holy priesthood, to offer spiritual sacrifices acceptable to God through Jesus Christ.

6 **This parable is a paraphrase of Jesus' parables of the end of the age**: Matthew 13:24-30, 36-43. But it also integrates with John the baptizer's warning about the separation of the wheat and chaff at the end of the age as well:

Matthew 3:11–12

11 "I baptize you with water for repentance, but he who is coming after me is mightier than I, whose sandals I am not worthy to carry. He will baptize you with the Holy Spirit and fire. 12 His winnowing fork is in his hand, and he will clear his threshing floor and gather his wheat into the barn, but the chaff he will burn with unquenchable fire."

7 **This is a reference to**: Revelation 14:14-16. It fits in with Jesus' parable about the end of the age and John the baptizer's parable as well. In Revelation 14, the first harvest is of believers in Jesus to protect them from judgment. But the second harvest right after it is a harvest of grapes for the winepress of God's wrath. This is the judgment on apostate Jews. Revelation 14:17-20.

8 **God used Babylonians to perform his judgment destroying the first temple 587 BC**

Jeremiah 4:12–27

<u>Now it is I who speak in judgment upon them.</u>" 13 Behold, he <u>comes up like clouds</u>; his chariots like the whirlwind; his horses are swifter than eagles... Warn the nations that <u>he is coming</u>; announce to Jerusalem, <u>"Besiegers come from a distant land</u>; they shout against the cities of Judah...27 For thus says the LORD, "The whole land shall be a desolation; yet I will not make a full end.

God uses Nebuchadnezzar as his tool to judge Egypt

Ezekiel 30:24–26

24 And I will <u>strengthen the arms of the king of Babylon and put my sword in his hand,</u> but I will break the arms of Pharaoh, and he will groan before him like a man mortally wounded. 25 I will strengthen the arms of the king of Babylon, but the arms of Pharaoh shall fall. <u>Then they shall know that I am the LORD, when I put my sword into the hand of the king of Babylon and he stretches it out against the land of Egypt</u>. 26 And I will scatter the Egyptians among the nations and disperse them throughout the countries. Then they will know that I am the LORD."

392

God uses the Medes to destroy Babylon in 539 BC

Isa. 13:1
The oracle concerning Babylon ...The LORD of hosts is mustering the army for battle. 5 They are coming from a far country, From the farthest heavens, The LORD and His instruments of indignation, To destroy the whole earth. ...11 Thus I will punish the world for its evil..17 Behold, I am going to stir up the Medes against them..

[9] **Moshe is quoting from**: Zechariah 14:12-13.

Here is an interesting possibility for an interpretation of that judgment on Rome:

This is the plague with which the LORD will strike all the nations that fought against Jerusalem: Their flesh will rot while they are still standing on their feet, their eyes will rot in their sockets, and their tongues will rot in their mouths.

"In Zechariah 14:2, the prophet predicts that "all the nations [will be gathered] to Jerusalem to fight against it." This seems to have been fulfilled when the Roman legions and auxiliaries consisting of a vast array of ethnic groups from all over the known world attacked Jerusalem in A.D. 70...

"In v. 12 the Lord threatens to "strike all the nations that fought against Jerusalem [such that t]heir flesh will rot while they are still standing on their feet, their eyes will rot in their sockets, and their tongues will rot in their mouths." A couple years after Israel's war with Rome, Mount Vesuvius erupted releasing a colossal surge cloud that engulfed the surrounding Roman cities of Pompeii, Herculaneum, Stabiae and Oplontis in an incendiary cloud of smoke, lava and ash. Burning at approximately one thousand degrees Fahrenheit, this volcanic ash would have killed the people in these cities in roughly three to five seconds – their flesh beginning to be consumed before their bodies even hit the ground. Zechariah 14 closes with the following prediction: "And on that day there will no longer be a Canaanite in the house of the LORD Almighty."2 In A.D. 70, the Romans destroyed the Temple, the "house of the LORD Almighty," making it impossible for anyone to physically enter...

"Under Titus's leadership, Jerusalem was attacked and destroyed. Nine years after this military victory, Titus succeeded his father as emperor of Rome. During this time, I believe God patiently waited to fulfill the plague described in v. 12. After Titus, the Roman general responsible for Jerusalem's desolation, had at last become emperor of Rome in June of A.D. 79, the scourge of Zechariah 14:12 may have been released.

"In August of that year, Mount Vesuvius erupted destroying Pompeii, Herculaneum, Stabiae and Oplontis. When Mount Vesuvius erupted, a colossal surge cloud rushed down the mountain engulfing the surrounding cities in an incendiary cloud of smoke, lava and ash. Burning at approximately one thousand degrees Fahrenheit, five times hotter than boiling water, this volcanic ash would have killed the people of Pompeii and the surrounding cities in roughly three to five seconds. The flesh of many of these people would have begun to be consumed even before their bodies dropped to the ground fulfilling v.12: "Their flesh will rot while they are still standing on their feet, their eyes will rot in their sockets, and their tongues will rot in their mouths." Concerning the magnitude of this eruption and its aftermath, Cassius Dio writes:

Indeed, the amount of dust, taken all together, was so great that some of it reached Africa and Syria and Egypt, and it also reached Rome, filling the air overhead and darkening the sun. . . .These ashes, now, did the Romans no great harm at the time, though later they brought a terrible pestilence upon them.29

"Concerning the plague induced by the ashes of Vesuvius, Suetonius writes that it was "one of the worst outbreaks of plague that had ever been known." Cassius Dio also says that this ash "wrought much injury of various kinds. . . ."31 The plague described in v. 12 may be the fifth plague of Revelation 16:11, the plague of boils. Perhaps this burning ash and the subsequent pestilence it caused also brought about tissue necrosis, rotting the flesh of those affected, as is suggested in v. 12 and Revelation 16:11? ...

"Volcanic eruptions often release great amounts of sulfuric dioxide into the atmosphere. When this gas reacts with water vapor it forms sulfuric acid which falls to the ground as acid rain. Could the tissue rot mentioned in Zechariah 14:12 and the "pains" and "sores" of Revelation 16:11 have also been induced by especially-caustic acid rain?...

13 On that day men will be stricken by the LORD with great panic. Each man will seize the hand

of another, and they will attack each other. 14 Judah too will fight at Jerusalem. The wealth of all the surrounding nations will be collected – great quantities of gold and silver and clothing.

"Describing the panic induced by the eruption of Mt. Vesuvius, Cassius Dio writes in fulfillment of v. 13: "Therefore they fled, some from the houses into the streets, others from the outside into the houses, now from the sea to the land and now from the land to the sea; for in their excitement they regarded any place where they were not as safer than where they were."32 In the next verse, Cassius Dio states that the citizens of Pompeii were seated at the theater when the eruption took place.33 Were the people of Pompeii watching Jewish prisoners of war forced to dual to the death? Were they watching gladiatorial combat or any other type of hand to hand combat as was commonly presented in Roman theaters in fulfillment of v. 13: "Each man will seize the hand of another, and they will attack each other"?"

"Zechariah 14 Fulfilled–including the splitting of the Mount of Olives!" on RevelationRevolution.org online: https://revelationrevolution.org/zechariah-14-fulfilled-a-preterist-commentary/

Also consider:

"[D]uring the period of the Jewish War (AD 67–70) judgments befell Rome: the specific manifestation of the beast, Nero, committed suicide (June, AD 68) and the Roman civil wars erupted (AD 68-69) causing the death throes of the generic concept of the beast.

"Tacitus records the (generic) beast's circumstances:

The history on which I am entering is that of a period rich in disasters, terrible with battles, torn by civil struggles, horrible even in peace. Four emperors fell by the sword; there were three civil wars, more foreign wars and often both at the same time. There was success in the East [i.e., the Jewish War], misfortune in the West. Illyricum was disturbed, the Gallic provinces wavering, Britain subdued and immediately let go. The Sarmatae and Suebi rose against us; the Dacians won fame by defeats inflicted and suffered; even the Parthians were almost roused to arms through the trickery of a pretended Nero. Moreover, Italy was distressed by disasters unknown before or returning after the lapse of ages. . . . Rome was devastated by conflagrations, in which her most ancient shrines were consumed and the very Capitol fired by citizens' hands. Sacred rites were defiled; there were adulteries in high places. The sea was filled with exiles, its cliffs made foul with the bodies of the dead. In Rome there was more awful cruelty. High birth, wealth, the refusal or acceptance of office – all gave ground for accusations, and virtues caused the surest ruin. The rewards of the informers were no less hateful than their crimes; for some, gaining priesthoods and consulships as spoils, others, obtaining positions as imperial agents and secret influence at court, made havoc and turmoil everywhere, inspiring hatred and terror. Slaves were corrupted against their masters, freedmen against their patrons; and those who had no enemy were crushed by their friends. . . . Besides the manifold misfortunes that befell mankind, there were prodigies in the sky and on the earth, warnings given by thunderbolts, and prophecies of the future, both joyful and gloomy, uncertain and clear. For never was it more fully proved by awful disasters of the Roman people or by indubitable signs that gods care not for our safety, but for our punishment. (Hist. 1:2–3)

"Josephus himself observes that "about this time it was that heavy calamities came about Rome on all sides" (J.W. 4:10:1 §585) with thousands dying (J.W. 4:9:9 §545–555; 4:11:4 §645–55; Tac., Hist. 1:2). General Vespasian was tormented by the horrible news: "And as this sorrow of his was violent, he was not able to support the torments he was under, nor to apply himself further in other wars when his native country was laid waste" (J.W. 4:10:2). In addition, the Jewish War was extremely costly to the Romans, requiring four legions (which sustained thousands of casualties) and more than three years of effort and resources (Barker 311)."

In 19:19-20 John finally gets to the fate of the beast.

Kenneth L. Gentry, Jr., The Divorce of Israel: A Redemptive-Historical Interpretation of Revelation Vol. 2 (Dallas, GA: Tolle Lege Press, 2016), 619-620.

CHAPTER 41

[1] **Achan is a single man who disobeyed Yahweh during the Conquest**, resulting in the suffering of the whole nation until he was found and punished. His story is in Joshua 7.

CHAPTER 42

[1] Boaz refers to:

Hebrews 8:13
[13] In speaking of a new covenant, he makes the first one obsolete. And what is becoming obsolete and growing old is ready to vanish away.

[2] **Stoicheia:** In every place that *stoicheion* shows up in the New Testament it means elementary principle rudiments of a worldview, sometimes a godless worldview (Col. 2:8), but more often the elementary principles of the Old Covenant law described as a "cosmos" (Gal. .4:3; 9; Col. 2:20; Heb. 5:12).[2]

Remember how the cosmic language of creating heavens and earth was used to describe the cosmic significance of God establishing a covenant? And remember how in the Old Testament, the destruction of covenants, nations, and peoples was described in *decreation* terms as the collapsing of the universe?

That is the case in these passages as well, with the term "cosmos" being used metaphorically for the "universe" of God's covenantal order as embodied in the Old Covenant laws of Jewish separation: Circumcision, dietary restrictions and Sabbaths. Paul is telling his readers that the *stoicheion* of the Old Covenant *cosmos* are no longer over them because the people of God are under new *stoicheion*, the elementary principles of faith (Gal. 4:1-11).

Peter means the same thing. When he says that the heavens will pass away and the *stoicheion* will be burned up, he is claiming that when the Temple in Jerusalem is destroyed, it will be the final passing away of the Old Covenant cosmos, along with all the elementary principles tied to that physical sacramental structure, the laws that once separated Jew and Gentile. The new cosmos is one in which both Jew and Gentile "by God's power are being guarded through faith for a salvation ready to be revealed in the last time" (1 Pet. 1:5).

Leithart, Peter J. *The Promise of His Appearing: An Exposition of Second Peter*. Moscow, ID: Canon Press, 2004, p.101. Bauckham argues that "The heavenly bodies (sun, moon and stars) is the interpretation favored by most commentators," for *stoicheion*. But then we are right back to the sun, moon, and stars as figurative language of covenantal elements. Bauckham, *2 Peter, Jude*, 316. But I doubt this interpretation because the clear words for "heavenly bodies" are not stoicheion, but epouranios soma (1 Cor. 15:40-41).

[3] **Boaz quotes**: Hebrews 12:26-29.

[4] Symeon, son of Clopas became a bishop of Jerusalem after the war:

"Hegesippus writes that the election of Symeon happened "after the martyrdom of James and the capture of Jerusalem, which instantly followed" (see chapter 6), thus suggesting that the election of Symeon happened following the Jewish War."

Jeffrey J. Bütz and James D. Tabor, The Secret Legacy of Jesus: The Judaic Teachings That Passed from James the Just to the Founding Fathers (Inner Traditions, 2009), 213.

CHAPTER 43

[1] **Thelonius quotes**: Revelation 18:10.

[2] **Thelonius quotes**: Romans 1:21-25.

[3] **Thelonius quotes**: Colossians 1:13-14.

CHAPTER 44

[1] Titus crucified Jews at the city walls:

Flavius Josephus, *The Wars of the Jews* 5.11.1, §449-451

[captured Jews] were first whipped, and then tormented with all sorts of tortures before they died, and were then crucified before the wall of the city. (450) This miserable procedure made Titus greatly to pity them, while they caught every day five hundred Jews; nay, some days they caught more; yet did it not appear to be safe for him to let those that were taken by force go their way; and to set a guard over so many, he saw would be to make such as guarded them useless to him. The main reason why he did not forbid that cruelty was this, that he hoped the Jews might perhaps yield at that sight, out of fear lest they might themselves afterwards be liable to the same cruel treatment. (451) So the soldiers out of the wrath and hatred they bore the Jews, nailed those they caught, one after one way, and another after another, to the crosses, by way of jest; when their multitude was so great, that room was wanting for the crosses, and crosses wanting for the bodies."

Flavius Josephus and William Whiston, *The Works of Josephus: Complete and Unabridged* (Peabody: Hendrickson, 1987), 720.

CHAPTER 46

[1] **Titus's knowledge of Judaism**: The Roman historian Tacitus gives a glimpse of the fascinating misunderstanding of Judaism that the Romans had. In his *Histories* 5.2-5 we read of Tacitus' understanding of Judaism as a mixture of truth and bizarre fiction drawn from gossip. Here is just a small section of that passage.

[4] In order to secure the allegiance of his people in the future, Moses prescribed for them a novel religion quite different from those of the rest of mankind. Among the Jews all things are profane that we hold sacred; on the other hand they regard as permissible what seems to us immoral. In the innermost part of the Temple, they consecrated an image of the animal which had delivered them from their wandering and thirst, choosing a ram as beast of sacrifice to demonstrate, so it seems, their contempt for Hammon. The bull is also offered up, because the Egyptians worship it as Apis. They avoid eating pork in memory of their tribulations, as they themselves were once infected with the disease to which this creature is subject.. They still fast frequently as an admission of the hunger they once endured so long, and to symbolize their hurried meal the bread eaten by the Jews is unleavened. We are told that the seventh day was set aside for rest because this marked the end of their toils. In course of time the seductions of idleness made them devote every seventh year to indolence as well. Others say that this is a mark of respect to Saturn, either because they owe the basic principles of their religion to the Idaei, who, we are told, were expelled in the company of Saturn and became the founders of the Jewish race, or because, among the seven stars that rule mankind, the one that describes the highest orbit and exerts the greatest influence is Saturn. A further argument is that most of the heavenly bodies complete their path and revolutions in multiples of seven.

Tacitus, *Histories*, 5.4. See the rest of the this passage at:
http://www.livius.org/sources/content/tacitus/tacitus-on-the-jews/

CHAPTER 47

[1] **Woes of Moshe**: These were the words of the man in Josephus' Wars of the Jews who prophesied against the city. I have made that man into my Moshe character. Flavius Josephus, *The Wars of the Jews* 6.5.3, §309.

[2] **Ellihu quotes from**: Revelation 11:14. Technically this occurs after the Witnesses ascend to heaven. I am using this prophecy proleptically.

[3] **Three-and-a-half years**: This is the length of the ministry of the Two Witnesses in Revelation 11:2-3.

Revelation 11:2–3
2 [Rome] will trample the holy city for forty-two months. 3 And I will grant authority to my two witnesses, and they will prophesy for 1,260 days, clothed in sackcloth."

Notice that this also matches the "time, times and a half time (3 1/2 years) of the siege of Jerusalem by Titus:

Daniel 12:6–7
6 "How long shall it be till the end of these wonders?" 7 ... it would be for a time, times, and half a

time, and that when the shattering of the power of the holy people comes to an end all these things would be finished.

CHAPTER 47

[4] The death of the Two Witnesses:

Revelation 11:7–13
[7] And when they have finished their testimony, the beast that rises from the bottomless pit will make war on them and conquer them and kill them, [8] and their dead bodies will lie in the street of the great city that symbolically is called Sodom and Egypt, where their Lord was crucified. [9] For three-and-a-half days some from the peoples and tribes and languages and nations will gaze at their dead bodies and refuse to let them be placed in a tomb, [10] and those who dwell on the earth will rejoice over them and make merry and exchange presents, because these two prophets had been a torment to those who dwell on the earth. [11] But after the three-and-a-half days a breath of life from God entered them, and they stood up on their feet, and great fear fell on those who saw them. [12] Then they heard a loud voice from heaven saying to them, "Come up here!" And they went up to heaven in a cloud, and their enemies watched them. [13] And at that hour there was a great earthquake, and a tenth of the city fell. Seven thousand people were killed in the earthquake, and the rest were terrified and gave glory to the God of heaven.

In previous books of this series, I have created a fictionalized version of the witnesses that I tied into Josephus' history of the war. He spoke of one prophet named Jesus or Joshua ben Ananus who preached similarly to the Two Witnesses, so I made him into one of them (changed his name to Moshe). Josephus was not inside the walls so he was writing from other people's accounts. Just because he speaks of one man, does not mean there could not have been two in reality. Just like the resurrection accounts speak of one man at the tomb and another of two. Both can be true.

Here is the passage from Josephus that tells of Joshua ben Ananus.

Flavius Josephus, *The Wars of the Jews* 6.5.3, §300-309
"Jesus, the son of Ananus, a plebeian and a husbandman, who, four years before the war began, and at a time when the city was in very great peace and prosperity, came to that feast whereon it is our custom for everyone to make tabernacles to God in the temple, (301) began on a sudden cry aloud, "A voice from the east, a voice from the west, a voice from the four winds, a voice against Jerusalem and the holy house, a voice against the bridegrooms and the brides, and a voice against this whole people!" This was his cry, as he went about by day and by night, in all the lanes of the city. (302) However, certain of the most eminent among the populace had great indignation at this dire cry of his, and took up the man, and gave him a great number of severe stripes; yet did not he either say anything for himself, or anything peculiar to those that chastised him, but still he went on with the same words which he cried before. (303) Hereupon our rulers supposing, as the case proved to be, that this was a sort of divine fury in the man, brought him to the Roman procurator; (304) where he was whipped till his bones were laid bare; yet did he not make any supplication for himself, nor shed any tears, but turning his voice to the most lamentable tone possible, at every stroke of the whip his answer was, "Woe, woe to Jerusalem!" (305) And when Albinus (for he was then our procurator) asked him who he was, and whence he came, and why he uttered such words; he made no manner of reply to what he said, but still did not leave off his melancholy ditty, till Albinus took him to be a madman, and dismissed him. (306) Now, during all the time that passed before the war began, this man did not go near any of the citizens, nor was seen by them while he said so; but he every day uttered these lamentable words, as if it were his premeditated vow, "Woe, woe, to Jerusalem!" (307) Nor did he give ill words to any of those that beat him every day, nor good words to those that gave him food; but this was his reply to all men, and indeed no other than a melancholy presage of what was to come. (308) This cry of his was the loudest at the festivals; and he continued this ditty for seven years and five months, without growing hoarse, or being tired therewith, until the very time that he saw his presage in earnest fulfilled in our siege, when it ceased; (309) for as he was going round upon the wall, he cried out with his utmost force, "Woe, woe, to the city again, and to the people, and to the holy house!" And just as he added at the last, – "Woe, woe, to myself also!" there came a stone out of one of the engines, and smote him, and killed him immediately; and as he was uttering the very same presages, he gave up the ghost."

Flavius Josephus and William Whiston, *The Works of Josephus: Complete and Unabridged* (Peabody: Hendrickson, 1987), 742–743.

CHAPTER 48

[1] This chapter is taken from:

Revelation 11:7–14
[7] And when [the Two Witnesses] have finished their testimony, the beast that rises from the bottomless pit will make war on them and conquer them and kill them, [8] and their dead bodies will lie in the street of the great city that symbolically is called Sodom and Egypt, where their Lord was crucified. [9] For three-and-a-half days some from the peoples and tribes and languages and nations will gaze at their dead bodies and refuse to let them be placed in a tomb, [10] and those who dwell on the earth will rejoice over them and make merry and exchange presents, because these two prophets had been a torment to those who dwell on the earth. [11] But after the three-and-a-half days a breath of life from God entered them, and they stood up on their feet, and great fear fell on those who saw them. [12] Then they heard a loud voice from heaven saying to them, "Come up here!" And they went up to heaven in a cloud, and their enemies watched them. [13] And at that hour there was a great earthquake, and a tenth of the city fell. Seven thousand people were killed in the earthquake, and the rest were terrified and gave glory to the God of heaven. [14] The second woe has passed; behold, the third woe is soon to come.

[2] 42 months, 1260 days is also the "time, times, and a half times" of Daniel:

Revelation 11:1–3
[1] Then I was given a measuring rod like a staff, and I was told, "Rise and measure the temple of God and the altar and those who worship there, [2] but do not measure the court outside the temple; leave that out, for it is given over to the nations, and they will trample the holy city for forty-two months. [3] And I will grant authority to my two witnesses, and they will prophesy for 1,260 days, clothed in sackcloth."

Daniel 12:6–7
[6] And someone said to the man clothed in linen, who was above the waters of the stream, "How long shall it be till the end of these wonders?" [7] And I heard the man clothed in linen, who was above the waters of the stream; he raised his right hand and his left hand toward heaven and swore by him who lives forever that it would be for a time, times, and half a time, and that when the shattering of the power of the holy people comes to an end all these things would be finished.

[3] First Woe corresponds to the fifth trumpet:

Revelation 9:1–12
[1] And the fifth angel blew his trumpet, and I saw a star fallen from heaven to earth, and he was given the key to the shaft of the bottomless pit. [2] He opened the shaft of the Abyss, and from the shaft rose smoke like the smoke of a great furnace, and the sun and the air were darkened with the smoke from the shaft. [3] Then from the smoke came locusts on the earth, and they were given power like the power of scorpions of the earth… [12] The first woe has passed; behold, two woes are still to come.

The Second Woe corresponds to the sixth trumpet:

Revelation 11:11–14
[11] But after the three-and-a-half days a breath of life from God entered them, and they stood up on their feet, and great fear fell on those who saw them. [12] Then they heard a loud voice from heaven saying to them, "Come up here!" And they went up to heaven in a cloud, and their enemies watched them. [13] And at that hour there was a great earthquake, and a tenth of the city fell. Seven thousand people were killed in the earthquake, and the rest were terrified and gave glory to the God of heaven. [14] The second woe has passed; behold, the third woe is soon to come.

[4] Resurrection in Daniel 12:2:

"[Options for interpreting Daniel 12:2 resurrection]:A fifth possibility is that this refers to the emptying of sheol into heaven when Christ ascended there. This is a concept less familiar to us today, and will be explained below.

"And a sixth possibility is that the resurrection here is a national resurrection like the one portrayed in Ezekiel 37. This is the only credible possibility.

"Looking first at the fifth possibility, ascension to heaven: Until Jesus went into heaven, nobody went into heaven. Those who died from Adam to Christ went to sheol, which the New Testament calls hades. The righteous went to Abraham's Bosom, also called in theology Limbus Patrum, while the wicked went to an uncomfortable place. After Jesus' death He descended to sheol and sorted the dead. When Jesus ascended into heaven, He emptied Abraham's bosom and brought all the righteous dead to heaven with Him. The wicked in sheol, however, are not brought up to heaven until the end of time, when they are cast into the lake of fire that is before the throne of God (Revelation 14:9–11; 20:10–15).

"It is possible that the first resurrection of Revelation 20:4–6 refers to the ascension of the Old Covenant saints to heaven, to be seated with Christ at the right hand of the Father, and to reign with Him as kings and priests for a thousand years. Meanwhile, Christ and the Church on earth are binding Satan from deceiving the nations for the same thousand years (Rev. 20:1–2; Matt. 16:18–19). On the basis of Revelation 6:9–11, and the fact that Revelation 20 comes after Revelation 19, my guess is that the ascension of the Old Covenant saints to reign with Christ happened in AD 70, not AD 30.

"It is likely that Daniel 12:13 refers to this event. Daniel is told that he will enter into rest and then rise for his allotted portion at the end of the days. In context, the end of the latter days refers to the coming of Christ, for throughout Daniel the prophetic period is the Restoration Era, and that is what "latter days" and "time of the end" refer to.

"Thus, possibly the resurrection of Daniel 12:2 refers to this same event, especially since it appears right after the statement about the Great Tribulation to come. We have to discard this possibility, however, since Revelation 20 says that the wicked in sheol do not rise for their judgment until after the millennium, at the last judgment.

"In context, those who sleep in the dust of the earth are parallel to Daniel, who fell into deep sleep with his face to the earth when God appeared to him at the beginning of this vision. Daniel's resurrection is a type and foreshadowing of the resurrection spoken of here.

"The resurrection of verse 2 seems to connect to the evangelistic and teaching ministry spoken of in verse 3; thus, it is some kind of historical resurrection that is spoken of, a resurrectional event in this world, in our history.

"The solution to our difficulty is found in Ezekiel 37. There the prophet is told to prophesy to the dead bones of the idolaters scattered all over the mountains of Israel (see Ezekiel 6:5). Ezekiel prophesies and the bones come to life again. This is explained in Ezekiel 37:11 as the national resurrection of Israel after the captivity. The language used by God is very "literal sounding," to wit: "I will open your graves and cause you to come up out of your graves" (vv. 12–13). Yet, this graphic language refers to the spiritual resurrection of the nation.

"Now clearly, the resurrection of the whole nation does not mean the salvation of each individual. Thus, Daniel 12:2 tells us that in the days of Jesus the nation will undergo a last spiritual resurrection, but some will not persevere and their resurrection will only be unto destruction. The Parable of the Soils fits here (Matthew 13:3–23): three different kinds of people come to life, but only one of the three kinds is awakened to persevering, everlasting life.

"During His ministry, Jesus raised the nation back to life. He healed the sick, cleansed the unclean, brought dead people back to life, restored the Law, entered the Temple as King, etc. Then, as always, the restored people fell into sin, and crucified Him.

"Thus, a resurrection of Israel is in view. The wicked are raised, but do not profit from it, and are destroyed. The saints experience a great distress, and live with God forever and ever."

James B. Jordan, *The Handwriting on the Wall: A Commentary on the Book of Daniel* (Powder Springs, GA: American Vision, 2007), 617–619.

From Kenneth Gentry on Daniel 12:

"In Daniel 12:1–2 we find a passage that clearly speaks of the great tribulation in AD 70: "Now at that time Michael, the great prince who stands guard over the sons of your people, will arise. And there will be a time of distress such as never occurred since there was a nation until that time; and at that time your people, everyone who is found written in the book, will be rescued" (12:1). But it also seems to speak of the resurrection occurring at that time: "And many of those who sleep in the dust of the ground will awake, these to everlasting life, but the others to disgrace and everlasting contempt" (12:2).

"How are we to understand this passage? Does Daniel teach that the eschatological, consummate resurrection occurs during the great tribulation in AD 70? No, he does not. Let me explain.

"Daniel appears to be presenting Israel as a grave site under God's curse: Israel as a corporate body is in the "dust" (Da 12:2; cp. Ge 3:14, 19; Job 7:21; 20:11; 21:26; Ps 7:5; 22:15; 90:3; 104:29; Ecc 3:20; 12:7; Isa 26:9). In this he follows Ezekiel's pattern in his vision of the dry bones, which represent Israel's "death" in the Babylonian dispersion (Eze 37). In Daniel's prophecy many will awaken, as it were, during the great tribulation to suffer the full fury of the divine wrath, while others will enjoy God's grace in receiving everlasting life. Luke presents similar imagery in Luke 2:34 in a prophecy about the results of Jesus's birth for Israel: "And Simeon blessed them, and said to Mary His mother, 'Behold, this Child is appointed for the fall and rise of many in Israel, and for a sign to be opposed.'"

"Though in AD 70 elect Jews will flee Israel and will live (Mt 24:22), the rest of the nation will be a corpse: "wherever the corpse is, there the vultures will gather" (Mt 24:28). Indeed, in AD 70 we see in the destruction of the city of Jerusalem (Mt 22:7) that "many are called, but few are chosen" (Mt 22:14).18 Elsewhere he employs the imagery of "regeneration" to the arising of the new Israel from out of dead, old covenant Israel in AD 70: "You who have followed Me, in the regeneration when the Son of Man will sit on his glorious throne, you also shall sit upon twelve thrones, judging the twelve tribes of Israel" (Mt 19:28).

"Returning now to Daniel, it appears that Daniel is drawing from the hope of the future, literal resurrection and applying it symbolically to the first century leading up to the tribulation in AD 70. That is, he is portraying God's separating believing Jews out of Israel through the winnowing of Israel in AD 70. Again, this is much like Ezekiel's practice in his vision of the valley of dry bones.20 Though Ezekiel's prophecy is concerned with Israel as a whole, whereas Daniel shows that Israel's hope is the believing remnant."

Ken Gentry, *He Shall Have Dominion, Second Edition* (Draper, VA: Apologetics Group Media, 1992, 1997), 579-580.

5 Some thoughts on the Two Witnesses:

For this entire Chronicles of the Apocalypse I have depicted the Two Witnesses as literal people who may even have ties to real persons written of by Josephus. But these are theological novels. My ultimate goal is truth told entertainingly. Therefore, I have used creative license. What matters most is not whether they were literally alive but what the symbolism means in the vision. Here are some arguments for that theological proposition drawn from Gentry's Divorce of Israel:

"Though Jesus' two witnesses have the power to plague their opponents "as often as they desire" (11:6c) for purposes of self-defense, now things change and they themselves are killed. This turn of events occurs only after they have finished their testimony (11:7a), that is, after they have completed their appointed time for prophetic ministry (1,260 days, 11:3). Their ministry was specifically linked temporally with God's judgment on Israel during the Jewish War with Rome (cp. 11:2) and involved their prophecy of the temple's destruction (see above). So when the temple fell, their ministry was over…

"As Prigent observes regarding the "three-and-a-half days" (11:9a; cp. 11:11a) of their exposure: "This death is placed under the same symbolic sign as the prophetic ministry: half of a sevenfold cycle." Thus as Campbell expresses it, this period is "parodying the duration of their testimony." This time frame seems intentionally to parallel the three-and-a-half years of the Jewish War (11:2) during which the prophets witnessed to Jerusalem (11:3). John is apparently emphasizing the brief time of their public abuse in comparison to the much longer time of God's wrath upon Jerusalem that it is likely that John relied directly on Ezekiel at this point."..

On the death and resurrection of the Witnesses:

"We should probably not understand this episode as an actual public, visible, bodily resurrection. Rather it is reminiscent of Ezekiel 37 which speaks of the revival of Israel after her Babylonian judgment. Consequently, even though these witnesses are two individuals, they probably are representatives of Christianity. They would therefore picture Christianity's "resurrection" as the true, living new covenant Israel from out of the false, dead old covenant Israel (cp. 2:9; 3:9 and the synagogue's "lie"). This non-literal imagery occurs elsewhere in Scripture. Not only do we see it in Ezekiel's vision, but Isaiah spoke of Israel's return from Babylon as a resurrection (Isa 26:13–19). Daniel 12:2 probably uses resurrection metaphorically to speak of a remnant arising from within dead Israel.127 Similarly, Paul also speaks of his hope for Israel's future conversion as if it were a resurrection (Ro 11:16–21). Luke 2:34 even uses anastasis ("resurrection") to indicate that "those who accept him in faith are headed for vindication."

"Just as John himself heard the call from God's throne to "come up here" (4:1), so the two witnesses are called into heaven. We have already seen that the two prophets are modeled upon Elijah and Moses (cf. 11:6), but they also reflect Christ's death, resurrection, and ascension. "The two witnesses . . . are an incarnation of the witness which the church renders to Christ (together with the law and the prophets)129 in the face of a hostile and unbelieving Judaism" (Feuillet 1964: 247). Biblical revelation informs us of Elijah's literal cloud ascension (2 Ki 2:11), and Jewish and Christian tradition (though not Scripture) has Moses ascending to heaven in a cloud (Beale 598-99; Osborne 430)…

"As in their resurrection (11:11), this additional imagery indicates God accepts them into heaven, blesses their witness, and vindicates their deaths (cp. 6:10–11; 14:13; 20:4–6), just as he does the "faithful witness" of Jesus "the first-born of the dead" (1:5; cp. Ac 1:8–11). Thus, "the fate of the church rests on that of her founder". As Terry interprets the matter: "Their resurrection and triumphant going up into heaven is an apocalyptic picture of what Jesus had repeatedly assured his followers (Matt. x, 16–32; xxiv, 9–13; Luke xxi, 12–19), and corresponds to the triumph of the martyrs in chap. xx, 4–6, which is there called 'the first resurrection."

Kenneth L. Gentry, Jr., The Divorce of Israel: A Redemptive-Historical Interpretation of Revelation Vol. 1 (Dallas, GA: Tolle Lege Press, 2016),

CHAPTER 49

[1] The third seal and the price of food during the siege of Jerusalem:

"Josephus actually mentions that during the siege, the Jews paid a talent for a measure of wheat (J.W. 5:13:7 §571). A talent "was the largest unit of weight" (ISBE2 4:1052) and therefore represents enormously high prices. In fact, Josephus speaks much about famine prices for food during the siege (J.W. 5:10:2 §427; 6:3:3– 5 §198–219; cp. Dio 66:5:4). He even specifically notes the difference in wheat and barley, as per Revelation 6:6: "Many there were indeed who sold what they had for one measure; it was of wheat, if they were of the richer sort; but of barley, if they were poor" (J.W. 5:10:2 §427). This removal of food from Jerusalem during the Jewish War seems to be another feature of God's divorce judgment against her. After all, "the responsibility of the husband is to provide his wife with the necessities of life, such as food, clothing, and dwelling."

Kenneth L. Gentry, Jr., The Divorce of Israel: A Redemptive-Historical Interpretation of Revelation Vol. 1 (Dallas, GA: Tolle Lege Press, 2016), 588.

[2] For these stories in this chapter, I used the following testimonies of famine inside the city walls from: Flavius Josephus, The Wars of the Jews 5.10.1-5, §420-445; 5.12.3-4, §512-518; 6.3.3, §193-198.

[3] The story about Syrians and Arabs cutting coins out of Jewish intestines comes from:

Flavius Josephus, The Wars of the Jews 5.10.1, §421
"They had a great inclination to desert to the Romans; (421) accordingly, some of them sold what they had, and even the most precious things that had been laid up as treasures by them, for a very small matter, and swallowed down pieces of gold, that they might not be found out by the robbers; and when they had escaped to the Romans, went to stool, and had wherewithal to provide plentifully for themselves"

Flavius Josephus and William Whiston, The Works of Josephus: Complete and Unabridged (Peabody: Hendrickson, 1987), 718.

Flavius Josephus, The Wars of the Jews 5.13.4, §550-561
"Yet did another plague seize upon those that were thus preserved; for there was found among the Syrian

deserters a certain person who was caught gathering pieces of gold out of the excrements of the Jews' bellies…

"But when this contrivance was discovered in one instance, the fame of it filled their several camps, that the deserters came to them full of gold. So the multitude of the Arabians, with the Syrians, cut up those that came as supplicants, and searched their bellies. (552) Nor does it seem to me that any misery befell the Jews that was more terrible than this, since in one night's time about two thousand of these deserters were thus dissected.

"When Titus came to the knowledge of this wicked practice, he had like to have surrounded those that had been guilty of it with his horse, and have shot them dead; and he had done it, had not their number been so very great, and those that were liable to this punishment would have been manifold, more than those whom they had slain. (554) However, he called together the commanders of the auxiliary troops he had with him, as well as the commanders of the Roman legions (for some of his own soldiers had been also guilty herein, as he had been informed)…

"Titus then threatened that he would put such men to death, if any of them were discovered to be so insolent as to do so again; moreover, he gave it in charge to the legions, that they should make a search after such as were suspected, and should bring them to him."

Flavius Josephus and William Whiston, *The Works of Josephus: Complete and Unabridged* (Peabody: Hendrickson, 1987), 726.

CHAPTER 50

[1] Jews throwing dead bodies outside the wall instead of burying them:

Flavius Josephus, *The Wars of the Jews* 5.12.3, §2
"Now the seditious at first gave orders that the dead should be buried out of the public treasury, as not enduring the stench of their dead bodies. But afterwards, when they could not do that, they had them cast down from the walls into the valleys beneath."

Flavius Josephus and William Whiston, *The Works of Josephus: Complete and Unabridged* (Peabody: Hendrickson, 1987), 724.

Flavius Josephus, *The Wars of the Jews* 5.12.3, §514
"As for burying them, those that were sick themselves were not able to do it; and those that were hearty and well were deterred from doing it by the great multitude of those dead bodies, and by the uncertainty there was how soon they should die themselves, for many died as they were burying others, and many went to their coffins before that fatal hour was come!"

Flavius Josephus, *The Wars of the Jews* 6.1.1, §518
"And indeed the multitude of carcasses that lay in heaps one upon another, was a horrible sight, and produced a pestilential stench, which was a hindrance to those that would make sallies out of the city and fight the enemy: but as those were to go in battle-array, who had been already used to ten thousand murders, and must tread upon those dead bodies as they marched along."

Flavius Josephus and William Whiston, *The Works of Josephus: Complete and Unabridged* (Peabody: Hendrickson, 1987), 723, 727.

[2] **Gehenna as the Valley of Slaughter**: Most Christians think references to Gehenna, translated sometimes in the NT as "hell," is a reference to the final judgment of unbelievers. But the context indicates that the passages where Jesus refers to Gehenna are applied to the judgment of Jerusalem in AD 70, because the phrase is a duplication of the original reference used of the first destruction of the temple in 586 BC.

"Witherington notes that the word *geenna* refers to the Hinnom Valley, south of the city of Jerusalem, that this place was associated in the Old Testament with the idolatrous practice of child sacrifice, that it was, therefore, a "place of uncleanness and horror in the Jewish imagination", and that it was a wet and dry rubbish dump where maggots abounded and the fires never went out. So he concludes: "It's a graphic image, and Jesus uses it to describe the eternally stinking, hot place that no one in their right mind would want to visit, much less dwell in."

402

"This account, however, overlooks a critical part of the interpretive background. Witherington cites the two places in the Old Testament where human sacrifice in the Valley of Hinnom is mentioned: the original account of the offence (2 Chron. 28:3; 33:6), and Jeremiah's reference to the abhorrent practice (Jer. 7:31; 19:2-6). But he does not stop to consider what Jeremiah is actually saying here.

"The two texts are part of a proclamation of judgment on Jerusalem – not least because Ahaz and Manasseh burned their sons in the Valley of Hinnom. So the days are coming when "it will no more be called Topheth, or the Valley of the Son of Hinnom, but the Valley of Slaughter; for they will bury in Topheth, because there is no room elsewhere" (Jer. 7:32).

> And in this place I will make void the plans of Judah and Jerusalem, and will cause their people to fall by the sword before their enemies, and by the hand of those who seek their life. I will give their dead bodies for food to the birds of the air and to the beasts of the earth. And I will make this city a horror, a thing to be hissed at. Everyone who passes by it will be horrified and will hiss because of all its wounds. And I will make them eat the flesh of their sons and their daughters, and everyone shall eat the flesh of his neighbor in the siege and in the distress, with which their enemies and those who seek their life afflict them. (Jer. 19:7-9)

"What Jeremiah describes is the impending Babylonian invasion and the destruction of Jerusalem, attended by dreadful suffering and loss of life. The Valley of Hinnom is a metonymy for this catastrophic judgment on Judah and Jerusalem; it becomes a symbol for God's wrath against his people.

"So if Jesus warns the Jews – not all humankind – that they risk being thrown into Gehenna, and if we allow that elsewhere he prophesied the destruction of Jerusalem and the temple within a few decades, why not make the historical assumption that in his mind Gehenna was no less a symbol of concrete judgment on Israel than it was for Jeremiah? Why should we allow theology to overrule the historical reading at this point?"

Perriman, Andrew. *Hell and Heaven in Narrative Perspective* (K-Locations 398-418). P.OST. K-Edition.

CHAPTER 51

[1] There are a few different interpretations of when the 1290 days of Daniel 12:11 occurs:

The ceasing of the daily sacrifice and the abomination being set up in the holy land are two starting points for the 1290 days that ends in the shattering of the power of the holy people. So the ceasing of the sacrifice on behalf of Caesar, which started the war, is the first part in mid-AD 66. But the 1290 days does not start until the second part, the abomination of desolation, is "set up" in the holy land in AD 67. I am basically using the first one, but the second one is just as viable.

"TWO STARTING POINTS FOR THE 1,290 DAYS: Daniel 12:11 gives two starting points to the 1,290 days, seemingly without an end point: "And from the time that the daily sacrifice is taken away, and the abomination of desolation is set up, there shall be one thousand two hundred and ninety days." Because it is unusual to have two beginning points, some view the taking away of the sacrifice as the beginning of the 1,290 days, with the abomination of desolation happening at the end of the 1,290 days. J. E. H. Thomson notes the following on how the grammatical construction of this verse does not support this interpretation:

> And the abomination that maketh desolate set up. At first sight the reader is inclined to… regard this as a statement of the terminus ad quem [end point]. The grammatical difficulties against this view are forcible…Yet it seems strange that two termini a quo [starting points] should be assigned and no terminus ad quem.

That Daniel 12:11 gives two starting points for the 1,290 days (the daily sacrifice taken away and the abomination of desolation) is not as strange as it first seems. The end point has already been supplied in v. 7; it would be the shattering of Daniel's people. Thus, the glorious Man was saying from the time that the daily sacrifice was removed and the one who would make the Jewish nation desolate came (the abomination of desolation) to the shattering of the Jewish nation would be 1,290 days or 43 months.

"I believe the removal of the daily sacrifice that Daniel 12:11 speaks of is not the cessation of sacrifice that happened near the end of the Jewish war (in late July of AD 70) but the removal of the sacrifice the Jews offered twice a day on behalf of the emperor (Josephus, The Jewish War 2, 10, 4); this occurred in the summer of AD 66. This change in the sacrifice marked the beginning of the Jewish war with Rome."

McKenzie PhD, Duncan W.. *The Antichrist and the Second Coming: A Preterist Examination Volume I* (K-Locations 3672-3685). Xulon Press. K-Edition.

"The primary indicator of the Jewish rebellion involved the leaders of the revolt refusing to allow any sacrifices in the Temple from Gentiles. This resulted in the taking away of the daily sacrifice that was being offered for the emperor. According to Josephus, "This action laid the foundation of the war with Rome; for they renounced in consequence the sacrifices offered for Rome and the emperor."

"The outcome of this taking away of the daily sacrifice for the emperor was the coming of the one who would make the Jewish nation desolate; this was the abomination of desolation (Dan. 9:27). Responding to Nero's order to crush the Jewish rebellion, Titus marched the fifteenth legion from Egypt up the length of the Holy Land to rendezvous with his father at Ptolemais on the western border of Galilee. This coming of Titus happened around February of AD 67 as he marched a wing of the Roman army through the sacred land of Israel. This was the abomination of desolation that Jesus warned those in Judea to flee from; all hell literally broke loose at this time (Matt. 24:15-24; cf. Rev. 6).

"Titus's coming was the beginning of the great tribulation; this culminated in the shattering of the Jewish nation 1,290 days later, in August/September of AD 70 (Dan. 12:1-7).

"I thus propose that the starting point for the 1,290 days of Daniel 12:11 involved two stages. The first stage was the taking away of the daily sacrifice for the emperor (c. August AD 66); this marked the beginning of the Jewish rebellion. The second stage (which happened about six months later, c. February AD 67) was the abomination of desolation, the coming of the one who would make Israel desolate (Dan. 9:27). It was 1,290 days after Titus's coming to the Holy Land that the Jewish nation was shattered and dispersed into the nations. We thus see the meaning of Daniel 12:11 as follows: From the time that the daily sacrifice is taken away and the abomination of desolation is set up [i.e., the coming of the one who would make Israel desolate, Dan. 9:27], [to the time of the end, the shattering of the Jewish nation, Dan. 12:6-8] there shall be one thousand two hundred and ninety days."

McKenzie PhD, Duncan W.. *The Antichrist and the Second Coming: A Preterist Examination Volume I* (K-Locations 3705-3714). Xulon Press. K-Edition.

A second possibility for the 1290 days:

"It is to be noted that the two measures of time here given, 1290 days and 1335 days, both fall within the period of three years and a part, given in verse 7 as the full measure of the time of the end. This tends still further to confirm the view that by "a time, times, and a part" is meant three full rounds of the annual feasts of the Jews, and part of a fourth.

"It will further be seen from this answer that Daniel's question had reference to the very last epoch of Jewish history; for it was in that very last stage of their national existence that the daily sacrifice was caused to cease, which was by them regarded (when it came to pass in the days of the siege of Jerusalem, as we shall presently show) the harbinger of some dire calamity.

"THE TAKING AWAY OF THE DAILY SACRIFICE

"We take the marginal reading (which is the more literal) as giving the sense, the words of the margin being "and to set up the abomination, " &c. This reading would make the 1290 days the measure of time between the two specified events. But we have lately seen an interpretation, based on the text of the A. V., which makes the taking away of the daily sacrifice, and the setting up of the abomination that maketh desolate, simultaneous events, both governed by the preposition "from." But this obviously leaves the verse without meaning; for it gives a measure of time from two specified events, without stating to what that measure brings us.

"The "daily sacrifice" was the sacrifice of a lamb every morning and evening. This was to be kept up by the children of Israel throughout all their generations, and a special promise was given upon condition that this offering be continued (Ex 29: 38-45). (It should be observed that the causing of the sacrifice and oblation to cease, as foretold in (Da 9: 27), is a very different thing.)

"Now, as a matter of historic fact, the daily sacrifice was taken away during the siege of Jerusalem; and this was counted by the Jews an event of such importance, and such a portent of approaching disaster, that Josephus has recorded the very date on which it occurred, saying: "And now Titus gave orders to his soldiers that were with him to dig up the foundations of the tower of Antonia, and make a ready passage for his army to come up, while he himself had Josephus brought to him; for he had been informed that, on that very day, which was the seventeenth day of Panemus, the sacrifice called 'the daily sacrifice' had failed, and had not been offered to God for want of men to offer it; and that the people were grievously troubled at it" (Wars, VI. 2.1.)."

"The Roman army, which, by comparison of the Lord's words in (Mt 24: 15,16 Lu 21: 20,21,) is clearly seen to be "the abomination which maketh desolate, " encompassed Jerusalem before the failure of the daily sacrifice; whereas it might appear from the wording of the prophecy that those events occurred in the reverse order. But Mr. Farquharson shows that "there is nothing whatever in the verbs of the sentence to indicate which of the events should precede the other; the interval of time between them only is expressed."

"The first approach of the Roman armies under Cestius is described by Josephus in his book of Wars, II 17, 10. This was in the month corresponding to our November, A.D. 66. The taking away of the daily sacrifice was in the month Panemus, corresponding to the Hebrew Tammuz, and our July, A.D. 70 (Hartwell Horne's Chronological Table). Thus the measure of time between the two events was three years, and part of a fourth.

"But more than this: the measure 1290 days is exactly 43 great months (30 days each, according to the Hebrew method of reckoning), and inasmuch as their practice was to reckon by even weeks, months, and years the fulfilment of this part of the prophecy is seen in the fact that it is just 43 even months between the two events, ignoring the parts of the two months in which the events severally occurred."

Mauro, Philip. *The Seventy Weeks and the Great Tribulation* (K-Locations 2288-2319). K-Edition.

A third view is that the Abomination of desolation being set up is the Roman armies surrounding Jerusalem:

"Around the 6th of Av of A.D. 66, Eleazar terminated the daily sacrifice to Caesar fulfilling part of v. 11.12 According to Josephus, this act "was the true beginning of our war with the Romans." Hearing about this act of sedition, Agrippa immediately dispatched three thousand horsemen who seized the upper city, Mt. Zion, where they attacked the Jewish rebels who possessed the lower city and Temple. The Roman army with their idols to Zeus, Caesar and Rome is the abomination that causes desolation... Thus immediately after Eleazar put an end to the daily sacrifice to Caesar, Roman auxiliaries, the abomination that causes desolation, entered Jerusalem. Thus the starting point of the 1,290 days is the termination of the daily sacrifice to Caesar and the consequent abomination that causes desolation which occurred immediately thereafter.

"Counting 1290 days from these two events ends on Shabat of A.D. 70. This is the month in which the Roman army arrived outside of Jerusalem to begin preparations for what would end up being the final siege of Jerusalem. Remember, the Roman army with their idols to Zeus, Caesar and Rome is the abomination that causes desolation. Here one can see that there appears to have been 1,290 days from the cessation of the daily sacrifice to Caesar and the resulting abomination that causes desolation when the Roman auxiliaries fought the rebels inside Jerusalem until the Roman army, the abomination that causes desolation, arrived outside of Jerusalem again in preparation for their final assault on the city."

Daniel Chapter 12: A Preterist Commentary online. http://revelationrevolution.org/daniel-chapter-12-a-preterist-commentary/

[2] John of Gischala distributed the gold of the temple and its sacred foodstuffs to his men: Flavius Josephus, The Wars of the Jews 5.13.6, §562-566.

[3] The infamous story of cannibalism in Jerusalem during the siege:

Flavius Josephus, *The Wars of the Jews* 6.3.3-4, §199-213
There was a certain woman that dwelt beyond Jordan, her name was Mary...What she had treasured up besides, as also what food she had contrived to save, had been also carried off by the rapacious guards, who came every day running into her house for that purpose... She then attempted a most unnatural thing; (205) and snatching up her son, who was a child sucking at her breast, she said, "O, thou miserable infant! For whom shall I preserve thee in this war, this famine, and this sedition? (206) As to the war with the Romans, if they preserve our lives, we must be slaves! This famine also will destroy us, even before that slavery comes upon us: – yet are these seditious rogues more terrible than both the other. (207) Come on; be thou my food,

and be thou a fury to these seditious varlets and a byword to the world, which is all that is now wanting to complete the calamities of us Jews." (208) As soon as she had said this she slew her son; and then roasted him, and ate the one half of him, and kept the other half by her concealed. (209) Upon this the seditous came in presently, and smelling the horrid scent of this food, they threatened her, that they would cut her throat immediately if she did not show them what food she had gotten ready. She replied, that she had saved a very fine portion of it for them; and withal uncovered what was left of her son. (210) Hereupon they were seized with a horror and amazement of mind, and stood astonished at the sight; when she said to them, "This is my own son; and what hath been done was mine own doing! Come, eat of this food; for I have eaten of it myself! (211) Do not you pretend to be either more tender than a woman, or more compassionate than a mother; but if you be so scrupulous and do abominate this my sacrifice, as I have eaten the one half, let the rest be reserved for me also." (212) After which, those men went out trembling, being never so much affrighted at anything as they were at this, and with some difficulty they left the rest of that meat to the mother."

Flavius Josephus and William Whiston, *The Works of Josephus: Complete and Unabridged* (Peabody: Hendrickson, 1987), 737–738.

⁴ **A haunt for unclean spirits**: This phraseology was often used to pronounce judgment on places like Babylon and Edom. And then in Revelation it is used of Jerusalem.

Take a look at these prophecies of Isaiah referencing the destruction of Edom and Babylon.

Isaiah 34:11–15 (The destruction of Edom)
¹¹But the hawk and the porcupine shall possess it, the owl and the raven shall dwell in it…
¹³Thorns shall grow over its strongholds, nettles and thistles in its fortresses. It shall be the haunt of jackals, an abode for ostriches. ¹⁴And wild animals shall meet with hyenas; the wild goat (*seirim*) shall cry to his fellow; indeed, there the night bird settles and finds for herself a resting place. ¹⁵There the owl nests and lays and hatches and gathers her young in her shadow; indeed, there the hawks are gathered, each one with her mate.

Isaiah 13:21–22 (The destruction of Babylon)
²¹But wild animals will lie down there, and their houses will be full of howling creatures; there ostriches will dwell, and there wild goats (*seirim*) will dance. ²²Hyenas will cry in its towers, and jackals in the pleasant palaces; its time is close at hand and its days will not be prolonged.

The passages above speak of God's judgment upon the nations of Babylon and Edom (symbols of all that is against Israel and Yahweh). A cursory reading of the texts seem to indicate a common word picture of Yahweh destroying these nations so thoroughly that they end up a desert wasteland with wild animals and birds inhabiting them because the evil people will be no more.

I explain in my book *When Giants Were Upon the Earth*, that these animals are symbols of demons.

A look at the Septuagint (LXX) translation into Greek made by ancient Jews in the second century before Christ, reveals the hint of that different picture.

Isaiah 34:13-14 (LXX)
¹¹and for a long time birds and hedgehogs, and ibises and ravens shall dwell in it: and the measuring line of desolation shall be cast over it, and satyrs shall dwell in it…¹³And thorns shall spring up in their cities, and in her strong holds: and they shall be habitations of monsters, and a court for ostriches. ¹⁴And devils shall meet with satyrs, and they shall cry one to the other: there shall satyrs rest, having found for themselves *a place of* rest.

Isaiah 13:21-22 (LXX)
But wild beasts shall rest there; and the houses shall be filled with howling; and monsters shall rest there, and devils shall dance there, ²² and satyrs shall dwell there.

The Hebrew for the words "wild animals" and "hyenas" are not readily identifiable, so the ESV translators simply guessed according to their anti-mythical bias and filled in their translations with naturalistic words like "wild animals" and "hyenas." But of these words, Bible commentator Hans Wildberger says,

"Whereas (jackals) and (ostriches), mentioned in v. 13, are certainly well-known animals, the creatures that are mentioned in v. 14 cannot be identified zoologically, not because we are not provided with enough information, but because they refer to fairy tale and mythical beings. *Siyyim* are demons, the kind that do their mischief by the ruins of Babylon, according to [Isaiah] 13:21. They are mentioned along with the *iyyim* (goblins) in this passage.

The demons and goblins that Wildberger makes reference to in Isaiah 13:21-22 and 34:14 are the Hebrew words *siyyim* and *iyyim*, a phonetic play on words that is echoed in Jeremiah's prophecy against Babylon as well:

> Jeremiah 50:39
> 39 "Therefore wild beasts (*siyyim*) shall dwell with hyenas (*iyyim*) in Babylon, and ostriches shall dwell in her. She shall never again have people, nor be inhabited for all generations.

The Dictionary of Biblical Languages (DBL) admits that another interpretation of *iyyim* other than howling desert animals is "spirit, ghost, goblin, i.e., a night demon or dead spirit (Isa. 13:22; 34:14; Jer. 50:39), note: this would be one from the distant lands, i.e., referring to the nether worlds." One could say that *siyyim and iyyim* are similar to our own play on words, "ghosts and goblins."

The proof of this demon interpretation is in the Apostle John's inspired reuse of the *same exact language* when pronouncing judgment upon first century Israel as a symbolic "Mystery Babylon."

> Revelation 18:2
> 2"Fallen, fallen is Babylon the great! She has become a dwelling place for demons, a haunt for every unclean spirit, a haunt for every unclean bird, a haunt for every unclean and detestable beast."

Because of the exile under the Babylonians, Jews would use Babylon as the ultimate symbol of evil. So when John attacks his contemporaries in Israel for rejecting Messiah, he describes them as demonic Babylon worthy of the same judgment as that ultimate evil nation.

But regardless of one's eschatological interpretation, the "wild beasts" or "monsters" and "hyenas" of Isaiah and Jeremiah are interpreted as demons, unclean spirits and detestable beasts, along with the unclean animals that will scavenge over the ruins of the judged nation. The Old Testament "haunt of jackals" is the New Testament equivalent of the "haunt of demons." The "dwelling of hyenas and ostriches" is the "dwelling of demons."

So in Revelation, Babylon, or Jerusalem is a haunt for demons.

CHAPTER 56

1 **Gischala quotes from**: Isaiah 61:1-2. This passage was quoted by Jesus as referring to himself in Luke 4:16-21.

CHAPTER 57

1 The visitation of Yahweh promised:.

> Luke 19:41–44
> 41 And when he drew near and saw the city, he wept over it, 42 saying, "Would that you, even you, had known on this day the things that make for peace! But now they are hidden from your eyes. 43 For the days will come upon you, when your enemies will set up a barricade around you and surround you and hem you in on every side 44 and tear you down to the ground, you and your children within you. And they will not leave one stone upon another in you, because you did not know **the time of your visitation**."

"Luke's point, however, does not concern timing, but effects. The thrust is not 'no, the kingdom is not coming for a long time'; the point is 'the kingdom is indeed coming – but it will mean judgment, not blessing, for Israel'. It ought to be clear from his next two paragraphs that Luke intends this: in verses 28–40, Jesus approaches Jerusalem in a quasi-royal manner, and in verses 41–4, as the crowd descends the Mount of Olives, he bursts into tears and solemnly announces judgment on the city for failing to recognize 'its time of visitation'. YHWH is visiting his people, and they do not realize it; they are therefore in imminent danger of judgment, which will take the form of military conquest and devastation. This is not a denial of the imminence of the kingdom. It is a warning about what that imminent kingdom will entail. The parable functions, like so many, as a devastating redefinition of the kingdom of God. Yes, the kingdom does mean the return of YHWH to Zion. Yes, this kingdom is even now about to appear. But no, this will not be a cause of celebration for nationalist Israel."

N. T. Wright, *Jesus and the Victory of God, Christian Origins and the Question of God* (London: Society for Promoting Christian Knowledge, 1996), 635–636.

"The second-Temple Jewish hope for YHWH's return has not received as much attention as I believe it should. This hope is, I think, the truth behind the point that Bruce Chilton has stressed in various works: that 'the kingdom of god' denotes the coming of Israel's god in person and in power. Whether or not it is true, as Chilton argues, that Jesus made actual use of an early Jewish commentary on Isaiah (the Isaiah Targum), it is certainly the case that the theme of announcing the kingdom, and the phrase 'the kingdom of god' itself, both of which feature in that commentary but not elsewhere in non-Christian Jewish literature, are central features of what we most securely know about Jesus. And in the announcement of the dawning kingdom we find the persistent emphasis that now, at last, YHWH is returning to Zion. He will do again what he did at the exodus, coming to dwell in the midst of his people.

"This theme is not usually highlighted in this way. For this reason I shall make the point by setting out the main passages quite fully:

> On that day the branch of YHWH shall be beautiful and glorious, and the fruit of the land shall be the pride and glory of the survivors of Israel … Then YHWH will create over the whole site of Mount Zion and over its places of assembly a cloud by day and smoke and the shining of a flaming fire by night. Indeed over all the glory there will be a canopy. It will serve as a pavilion, a shade by day from the heat, and a refuge and a shelter from the storm and rain.
>
> Then the moon will be abashed, and the sun ashamed;
> for YHWH of hosts will reign on Mount Zion and in Jerusalem,
> and before his elders he will manifest his glory.
> Isa. 24:23.
>
> It will be said on that day,
> Lo, this is our god; we have waited for him, so that he might save us.
> This is YHWH, for whom we have waited;
> let us be glad and rejoice in his salvation.
> For the hand of YHWH will rest on this mountain.
> Isa. 25:9–10
>
> Strengthen the weak hands,
> and make firm the feeble knees.
> Say to those who are of a fearful heart,
> 'Be strong, do not fear!'
> Here is your God.
> He will come with vengeance,
> with terrible recompense.
> He will come and save you.
>
> Then the eyes of the blind shall be opened,
> and the ears of the deaf unstopped;
> then the lame shall leap like a deer,
> and the tongue of the speechless sing for joy …
> And the ransomed of YHWH shall return,
> and come to Zion with singing;
> everlasting joy shall be upon their heads;
> they shall obtain joy and gladness,
> and sorrow and sighing shall flee away.
> Isa. 35:3–6, 10.
>
> A voice cries out:

'In the wilderness prepare the way of YHWH,
make straight in the desert a highway for our god.
Every valley shall be lifted up,
and every mountain and hill be made low;
the uneven ground shall become level,
and the rough places a plain.
Then the glory of YHWH shall be revealed,
and all people shall see it together,
for the mouth of YHWH has spoken.'

Get you up to a high mountain,
O Zion, herald of good tidings;
lift up your voice with strength,
O Jerusalem, herald of good tidings,
lift it up, do not fear;
say to the cities of Judah,
'Here is your god!'
See, the Lord YHWH comes with might,
and his arm rules for him;
his reward is with him,
and his recompense before him.
He will feed his flock like a shepherd
and carry them in his bosom,
and gently lead the mother sheep.
Isa. 40:3–5, 9–11.

N. T. Wright, *Jesus and the Victory of God, Christian Origins and the Question of God* (London: Society for Promoting Christian Knowledge, 1996), 615–617.

[2] **This is quoted from**: Daniel 9:24. The phrase that I have translated "most holy one" is a controversial one. Some believe it refers to the "most holy place" or the holy of holies. But the original language is just "most holy."

This from Ken Gentry on Daniel's seventy weeks:

"The phrase "most holy" speaks of the Messiah who is "that Holy One who is to be born" (Luke 1:35). Isaiah prophesies of Christ in the ultimate redemptive Jubilee: "The Spirit of the Lord GOD is upon Me, because the LORD has anointed Me to preach good tidings to the poor; He has sent Me to heal the brokenhearted, to proclaim liberty to the captives, and the opening of the prison to those who are bound; to proclaim the acceptable year of the LORD" (Isa. 61:1-2a; cp. Luke 4:17-21).

"At his baptismal anointing the Spirit comes upon Him (Mark 1:9-11) to prepare Him for his ministry, of which we read three verses later: "Jesus came to Galilee, preaching the gospel of the kingdom of God, and saying, 'The time is fulfilled [the sixty-ninth week?], and the kingdom of God is at hand. Repent, and believe in the gospel'" (Mark 1:14-15). Christ is preeminently the Anointed One (Psa. 2:2; 132:10; Isa. 11:2; 42:1; Hab. 3:13; Acts 4:27; 10:38; Heb. 1:9)."

Kenneth L. Gentry, "What is the Goal of Daniel 9:24?" online:
https://postmillennialworldview.com/2013/11/15/what-is-the-goal-of-daniel-924/#more-1114

[3] **This strategy was taken from**: Flavius Josephus, *The Wars of the Jews* 3.7.20, §222-228. Josephus had used the tactic at Jotapata.

CHAPTER 58

[1] **This strategy was taken from**: Flavius Josephus, *The Wars of the Jews* 3.7.20, §222-228. Josephus had used the tactic at Jotapata.

[2] **This story is based loosely on the following**: Though it was John, not Simon who destroyed the tunnels below.

Flavius Josephus, *The Wars of the Jews* 6.1.3, §28

"…the wall suddenly fell in, for it had been shaken by the rams at the point where John had dug beneath it while undermining the former earthworks."

Paul L. Maier, editor and translator, *Josephus: The Essential Writings* (Grand Rapids, MI: Kregel, 1988), 351.

CHAPTER 59

[1] **Dwelt upon the land**: This phrase, translated in Young's Literal Translation as "those who live upon the land, is translated in other versions as "land-dwellers" or "those dwell on the land." It is used of the Israelites throughout Revelation. Rev 3:10; 6:10; 8:13; 11:10;13:8, 14; 14:6; 17:2, 8

Same Greek phrase used of Israelites in OT: Jeremiah 1:14; 10:18; Ezekiel 7:7; 36:17; Hosea 4:1, 3; Joel 1:2, 14; 2:1; Zephaniah 1:8

It is also the Greek phrase used by Josephus of Jews: Wars 4.5.3 (324).

[2] This winepress and harvest comes from:

> Revelation 14:17–20
> [17] Then another angel came out of the temple in heaven, and he too had a sharp sickle. [18] And another angel came out from the altar, the angel who has authority over the fire, and he called with a loud voice to the one who had the sharp sickle, "Put in your sickle and gather the clusters from the vine of the earth, for its grapes are ripe." [19] So the angel swung his sickle across the earth and gathered the grape harvest of the earth and threw it into the great winepress of the wrath of God. [20] And the winepress was trodden outside the city, and blood flowed from the winepress, as high as a horse's bridle, for 1,600 stadia.

"The vine can be a figure for Israel, as in Isa 5, Ps 80, but this does not preclude other meanings. However, there are two striking points in vs. 20 which suggest that the author did have Israel in mind. First, the trampling of the winepress is performed outside the city. The author will reach the destruction of the city in chs. 17, 18, but now he is concerned only about those "outside the city." Second, the amount of bloodshed is enormous. The measurement of one thousand six hundred stadia is approximately the distance from Tyre to El Arish, two hundred miles. On a historical level one might suggest that the author predicted, or his work reflected, conditions in Palestine. In A.D. 66 Vespasian (with Titus), after strengthening his forces, captured nearly all the cities in Galilee which were held by the Zealots. Then he marched to Caesarea and Jerusalem. It was at this time that the whole of Palestine suffered bloodshed, with the exception of the Holy City. It may be this kind of situation to which the vision of the vintaging of the land addressed itself."

J. Massyngberde Ford, Revelation: Introduction, Translation, and Commentary, vol. 38, Anchor Yale Bible (New Haven; London: Yale University Press, 2008), 250.

"Josephus's Jewish War records various particularly bloody battles: "the whole space of ground whereon they fought ran with blood, and the wall might have been ascended over by the bodies of the dead carcasses" (J. W. 3:7:23 §249); "the sea was bloody a long way" (3:9:3 §426); "one might then see the lake all bloody, and full of dead bodies" (3:10:9 §529); "the whole of the country through which they had fled was filled with slaughter, and Jordan could not be passed over, by reason of the dead bodies that were in it" (4:7:6; §437). Even in Jerusalem itself we learn that eventually "blood ran down over all the lower parts of the city, from the upper city" (4:1:10 §72); "the outer temple was all of it overflowed with blood" (4:5:1 §313); "the blood of all sorts of dead carcases stood in lakes in the holy courts" (5:1:3 §18); and "the whole city ran down with blood, to such a degree indeed that the fire of many of the houses was quenched with these men's blood" (6:8:5 §406)."

Kenneth L. Gentry, Jr., The Divorce of Israel: A Redemptive-Historical Interpretation of Revelation Vol. 2 (Dallas, GA: Tolle Lege Press, 2016), 323.

[3] **The Marriage Supper of the Lamb**: The imagery of marriage was used in the Old Testament for Yahweh marrying Israel. Now, that woman has become a harlot. God is divorcing her and marrying a new bride, the body of Christ. Consider the parables of Chris about the wedding feast. The Jews are invited, and they refuse to come, so God rejects them and offers the wedding feast to others:

Matthew 8:11–12

[11] I tell you, many will come from east and west and recline at table with Abraham, Isaac, and Jacob in the kingdom of heaven, [12] while the sons of the kingdom will be thrown into the outer darkness. In that place there will be weeping and gnashing of teeth."

Matthew 22:1–10

[1] And again Jesus spoke to them in parables, saying, [2] "The kingdom of heaven may be compared to a king who gave a wedding feast for his son, [3] and sent his servants to call those who were invited to the wedding feast, but they would not come. [4] Again he sent other servants, saying, 'Tell those who are invited, "See, I have prepared my dinner, my oxen and my fat calves have been slaughtered, and everything is ready. Come to the wedding feast." ' [5] But they paid no attention and went off, one to his farm, another to his business, [6] while the rest seized his servants, treated them shamefully, and killed them. [7] The king was angry, and he sent his troops and destroyed those murderers and burned their city. [8] Then he said to his servants, 'The wedding feast is ready, but those invited were not worthy. [9] Go therefore to the main roads and invite to the wedding feast as many as you find.' [10] And those servants went out into the roads and gathered all whom they found, both bad and good. So the wedding hall was filled with guests.

"Another OT passage which speaks dramatically of Jerusalem as the bride of God is Ezek 16:8–10. God says, "… yea, I plighted my troth to you and entered into a covenant with you, says the Lord God, and you became mine … I swathed you in fine linen and covered you with silk" (RSV). Like the bride in Ezekiel, the bride in Rev 19:8 is dressed in fine linen. So are the martyrs in 6:11 and the angels in 15:6. The two epithets, "bright" and "clean," are in contrast to the clothing of the harlot as is also the simplicity of the bride's clothes compared with the multicolored ones of the harlot. There is no doubt that the bride takes the place of the harlot, and with Carrington we may say, "It is impossible any longer to maintain that the harlot means Rome; the antithesis must lie between the old Israel and the new, the false Israel and the true, the Israel that is to appear so soon as the new Jerusalem." The symbolism of linen as the just deeds of the saints confirms this."

J. Massyngberde Ford, *Revelation: Introduction, Translation, and Commentary, vol. 38, Anchor Yale Bible* (New Haven; London: Yale University Press, 2008), 317–318.

Messianic marriage and war coupled:

"Marriage is a metaphor for the covenant relationship, but it should not cause surprise that the marriage theme is associated with war. Two OT texts show the same alignment, Ps 45 and Wisd Sol 18 (see p. 319). Ps 45 is a royal psalm probably composed on the occasion of the marriage of an Israelite king to a foreign princess (vss. 11–13). The king is praised for his virtue and his military ability. Ps 45:3 mentions the sword upon the thigh (cf. Rev 19:15, 16); 45:4 refers to riding on in victory and majesty; 45:2 speaks of grace upon the king's lips; 45:5 mentions conquest of peoples (cf. Rev 19:15); 45:6 refers to the royal throne and the royal scepter. Ps 45 was converted into messianic prophecy and the bridegroom was portrayed as both king and conqueror; after slaying his enemies he claimed the bride; Carrington, p. 308. This psalm, therefore, presents a "military bridegroom" carrying a sword, riding (either on horse or chariot), a victor conquering people and acquiring a royal throne and scepter. His speech (lips) are gracious. The rider on the white horse also is a military figure. He has royal insignia (diadems and royal title), he conquers and/or rules nations, and his speech is unique."

J. Massyngberde Ford, Revelation: Introduction, Translation, and Commentary, vol. 38, Anchor Yale Bible (New Haven; London: Yale University Press, 2008), 318.

"The context for the coming of the wedding feast is significant, fitting my overall thesis that Revelation is dealing with God's divorce of Israel so that a new bride, the church, may be taken. As Chilton (473) well notes: "The destruction of the Harlot and the marriage of the Lamb and the Bride – the divorce and the wedding – are correlative events. The existence of the Church as the congregation of the New Covenant marks an entirely new epoch in the history of redemption" (cp. Terry 440; Leonard 139). Though joyful feasting – as in a wedding banquet – seems to clash with a scene of wrathful judgment, we actually see this combination of images elsewhere. Note especially the Lord's own teaching in Matthew 8:11-12. There the image shows faithful people from all over reclining at feast with Abraham while the Jews ("the sons of the kingdom") are cast out and sorely judged. Jesus' parable of the wedding banquet in Matthew 22:2-13 also combines the themes of a festive banquet and tormenting judgment. Such images are built on the messianic

411

feast in Isaiah 25:6-12 where the "lavish banquet / for all peoples" occurs in the context of the statement against Moab that "the unassailable fortifications of your walls He will bring down, / Lay low, and cast to the ground, even to the dust." Therefore, "Rev 19 links the gamos [wedding] of the Lamb with the destruction of Babylon and the vindication of Christ and his church, not with a remote future event. Salvation from the oppression by the great harlot opens the marital festivities" (Smolarz 253). Thus, "we would also submit the thesis that the marriage theme is developed throughout the battle of Armageddon."

Kenneth L. Gentry, Jr., The Divorce of Israel: A Redemptive-Historical Interpretation of Revelation Vol. 2 (Dallas, GA: Tolle Lege Press, 2016), 592.

The Messianic marriage Psalm:

Psalm 45:4–17

4 In your majesty ride out victoriously
for the cause of truth and meekness and righteousness;
let your right hand teach you awesome deeds!

5 Your arrows are sharp
in the heart of the king's enemies;
the peoples fall under you.

6 Your throne, O God, is forever and ever.
The scepter of your kingdom is a scepter of uprightness;

7 you have loved righteousness and hated wickedness.
Therefore God, your God, has anointed you
with the oil of gladness beyond your companions;

13 All glorious is the princess in her chamber, with robes interwoven with gold.

14 In many-colored robes she is led to the king,
with her virgin companions following behind her.

[4] The armies of heaven:

"Though all of those redeemed by the Lamb – from all lands and in all ages – will enjoy the fullness of Christ's redemptive provision, Revelation is a judicial drama focusing on his judgment of first-century Israel. It is explaining those things "which must shortly take place" (1:1; 22:6) because "the time is near" (1:3; 22:10). It is highlighting the formal and permanent establishment of the new covenant kingdom as Christ overthrows his people's first and most dangerous enemy, their mother Israel (11:15; 12:10; 19:6). Given this temporal and dramatic focus of Revelation, these armies must be composed of first-century saints, who have all been subjected to Israel's persecuting wrath – whether directly by the Jews themselves or through Israel's manipulation of the Roman beast.""

Kenneth L. Gentry, Jr., The Divorce of Israel: A Redemptive-Historical Interpretation of Revelation Vol. 2 (Dallas, GA: Tolle Lege Press, 2016), 610.

[5] Dipped in the blood of his enemies:

"Our local context compels us to view the blood as that of his enemies, for the following reasons: (1) The vision presents war (19:11, 14, 15, 19) leading to the death of his enemies (19:17-18, 21). (2) It employs the imagery of the wine press (19:15c) which suggests the blood of those trodden down (as in 14:20). (3) John's primary Old Testament source material is Isaiah 63:1-3 where we read: "Why is Your apparel red, / And Your garments like the one who treads in the wine press? I have trodden the wine trough alone / . . . And their lifeblood is sprinkled on My garments, / And I stained all My raiment." (4) This is appropriate to a context where we recently heard that his enemies are to be paid back even for what they had done (18:6) – and their guilt is taking the blood of the saints (19:2; cp. 6:10; 17:6; 18:20, 24).""

Kenneth L. Gentry, Jr., The Divorce of Israel: A Redemptive-Historical Interpretation of Revelation Vol. 2 (Dallas, GA: Tolle Lege Press, 2016), 609.

[6] Sword in the mouth of Christ:

"Surely it cannot be that "the sword that comes from his mouth is the gospel message that defeats evil by showing the love of God in revealing the gift of eternal life" (L. Michaels 1999: 113). Rather the sword represents judgment, just as do both the rod (2:27; 12:5; cp. Ps 2:9; 11:4) and the winepress (14:19-20; 16:19). In 1:16 the sword pictures an instrument of judgment…

"Hosea 6:5 parallels the judgment word of the prophets with words coming out of God's mouth: "Therefore I have hewn them in pieces by the prophets; / I have slain them by the words of My mouth; / And the judgments on you are like the light that goes forth" (cp. Isa 49:2). As Mounce (355) puts it: "the sharp sword symbolizes the lethal power of his word of judgment. We are not to envision a literal sword but a death-dealing pronouncement that goes forth like a sharp blade from the lips of Christ." The Lord prophesied Israel's judgment in several contexts, most dramatically in his Olivet Discourse (Mt 24:2-34ff)."

Kenneth L. Gentry, Jr., The Divorce of Israel: A Redemptive-Historical Interpretation of Revelation Vol. 2 (Dallas, GA: Tolle Lege Press, 2016), 612.

[7] **This is all drawn from**: Revelation 19:11-16.

[8] The coming of Christ on the white horse:

"Though most commentators associate this with the second advent at the close of history, it is surely a response to first-century events surrounding the destruction of Babylon-Jerusalem. This must be so in light of the following: (1) The primary focus of Revelation is on soon-occurring events (1:1, 3; 22:6, 10). (2) The theme of Revelation regards the destruction of Jerusalem in response to the crucifixion of Christ occurring there (1:7; cf. 11:8; Exc. 3 at 1:7), hence Revelation's dominant character is the slaughtered Lamb (5:6, 12; 13:8; cp. 5:8, 13; 6:1; 7:9, 14, 17; 12:11; 14:1, 4, 10; 15:3; 17:14; 19:7, 9; 21:9, 14, 22; 22:1, 3). (3) The Babylonian harlot is an image of Jerusalem, not Rome or some end-time foe (Exc. 13 at 17:1). (4) In the Old Testament an announcement that God reigns often resulted from the historical overthrow of some enemy of Israel (e.g., Ex 15:1-5, 18; cp. Ps 10:15-18; 47:3, 8; 96:10, 13; 97:1-3; Isa 52:7-10), and Revelation is strongly influenced by the Old Testament. (5) This approach fits well with the earlier announcements of the beginning of the reign of Christ (11:15) and God (11:17) at the destruction of the first-century temple (11:1-2) which destruction opened the heavenly temple (11:19). (6) This also comports nicely with God's promise to vindicate the first-century slaughtered saints in just a "little while" (6:10-11). Why should we expect them to wait centuries, especially in light of all the near term indicators in Revelation? (7) It seems strange that the evidence of God reigning would wait until the final act of history."

Kenneth L. Gentry, Jr., The Divorce of Israel: A Redemptive-Historical Interpretation of Revelation Vol. 2 (Dallas, GA: Tolle Lege Press, 2016), 591.

CHAPTER 60

[1] Seraphim:

"In Isa 6, the seraphim appear in connection with the enthroned heavenly king, →Yahweh Zebaoth. The following may be said about their position, form, number and function. Their position, ʽōmĕdîm mimma' al lô, "standing above" Yahweh (v 2), lends itself to comparison with the raised uraei on the chapel friezes, where the uraei are however without wings. Whether their shape is serpentine or more humanoid is a matter of dispute. As for number, there are probably two seraphim in Isa 6 (cf. v 3a). Concerning their function Isa 6 displays a noteworthy mutation of the uraeus motif (KEEL 1977: 113): instead of protecting Yahweh the seraphim need their wings to cover themselves from head to feet from Yahweh's consuming holiness; Yahweh does not need their protection. Isaiah thus uses the seraphim to underscore the supreme holiness of the God on the throne.

"The seraphim occur a number of times in the pseudepigrapha and later Jewish literature (see OTP 2, index sub seraphim and J. MICHEL, RAC 5, 60–97). The seraphim, →cherubim and ophanim are described as "the sleepless ones who guard the throne of his glory" (1 Enoch 71:7)."

T. N. D. Mettinger, "Seraphim," ed. Karel van der Toorn, Bob Becking, and Pieter W. van der Horst, *Dictionary of Deities and Demons in the Bible* (Leiden; Boston; Köln; Grand Rapids, MI; Cambridge: Brill; Eerdmans, 1999), 743.

"The prophet Isaiah had an exalted vision of the Lord sitting on his heavenly throne high and lifted up with the glorious train of his robe filling the temple. But there were also some other chimeric creatures in his presence:

> Isaiah 6:2–7
> Above him stood the seraphim. Each had six wings: with two he covered his face, and with two he covered his feet, and with two he flew. And one called to another and said: "Holy, holy, holy is the LORD of hosts; the whole earth is full of his glory!"… Then one of the seraphim flew to me, having in his hand a burning coal.

"The meaning of the Hebrew word for seraphim is "fiery serpent." It was used to describe the fiery serpents in the wilderness whose poisonous burning venom was God's punishment for Israel's grumbling and complaining (Num. 21:6). God's balm of healing forgiveness was obtained by looking to a brass serpent (seraph) image raised on a pole called Nehushtan (Num. 21:8).

"But this is not the only use of seraph that sheds light on the meaning of the angelic seraphim. The Brown-Driver-Briggs Hebrew Lexicon points out that Isaiah 14:29 and 30:6 refer to a "flying fiery serpent" (seraph) in the wilderness that originated in mythically conceived winged serpent deities. The term is unavoidably serpentine in all its cognates.

"Some deny this serpentine essence by pointing out that the Isaianic seraphim are described as having human heads, wings, hands and feet. But Karen Randolph Joines has persuasively argued that the Egyptian winged ureus (upright cobra) that guarded the Pharaoh's tombs and thrones with its "fiery" venom is demonstrably the equivalent of the Hebrew seraph. Like the seraphim in Isaiah, the ureus was also commonly described as having a human face, wings, hands and feet when it was necessary for it to accomplish tasks like those of Isaiah 6. But it remained a winged serpent.

"ANE scholar Michael S. Heiser goes one step further and provisionally considers a literary overlapping of all these elements of fiery serpents, flying, humanoid features, and divinity to be variations of descriptions for the "Watcher paradigm":

> "Seraphim, then, are reptilian/serpentine beings – they are the Watchers (the "watchful ones" who diligently guard God's throne, which is carried [cf. Ezekiel 1, 10] by the cherubim, who may also serve as guardians). There are "good" serpentine beings (seraphim) who guard God's throne (so Isaiah 6's seraphim), and there are fallen, wicked serpentine beings (seraphim) who rebelled against the Most High at various times, and who became the pagan gods of the other nations."

Brian Godawa, When Giants Were Upon the Earth: The Watchers, the Nephilim, and the Biblical Cosmic War of the Seed (Los Angeles, CA: Embedded Pictures Publishing, 2014), 143-144.

[2] Cherubim:

"The term 'cherubim' occurs 91 times in the Hebrew Bible. It denotes the Israelite counterpart of the sphinx known from the pictorial art of the ancient Near East. In the Bible the cherubim occur essentially in two functions: as guardians of a sacred tree or as guardians and carriers of a throne…

T. N. D. Mettinger, "Cherubim," ed. Karel van der Toorn, Bob Becking, and Pieter W. van der Horst, *Dictionary of Deities and Demons in the Bible* (Leiden; Boston; Köln; Grand Rapids, MI; Cambridge: Brill; Eerdmans, 1999), 189–190.

> Ezekiel 1:4–14
> [4] As I looked, behold, a stormy wind came out of the north, and a great cloud, with brightness around it, and fire flashing forth continually, and in the midst of the fire, as it were gleaming metal. [5] And from the midst of it came the likeness of four living creatures. And this was their appearance: **they had a human likeness** ('shape"), [6] **but each had four faces, and each of them had four wings**. [7] **Their legs were straight, and the soles of their feet were like the sole of a calf's foot. And they sparkled like burnished bronze**. [8] Under their wings on their four sides they had human hands. And the four had their faces and their wings thus: [9] their wings touched one another. Each one of them went straight forward, without turning as they went. [10] As for the likeness of their faces, each had a human face. The four had the face of a lion on the right side, the four had the face of an ox on the left side, and the four had the face of an eagle. [11] Such were their faces. And their wings were spread out above. Each creature had two wings, each of which touched the wing of another, while two covered their bodies. [12] And each went straight forward. Wherever the spirit would go, they went, without turning as they went. [13] As for the

likeness of the living creatures, their appearance was like burning coals of fire, like the appearance of torches moving to and fro among the living creatures. And the fire was bright, and out of the fire went forth lightning. [14] And the living creatures darted to and fro, like the appearance of a flash of lightning.

Ophanim:

Not much is known about ophanim. Some scholars suggest they may be the "wheels" in Ezekiel's vision. They show up in 2nd temple literature.

> 1Enoch 61:10
> And he will summon all the forces of the heavens, and all the holy ones above, and the forces of the Lord – the cherubim, seraphim, ophanim, all the angels of governance."

> 1Enoch 71:7
> Moreover, seraphim, cherubim, and ophanim – the sleepless ones who guard the throne of his glory – also encircled it.

I have chosen to portray them as the "flame of the whirling sword" that accompanies the Cherubim because they have the same kind of presence as the wheels of Ezekiel.

Genesis 3:24 says that the cherubim guard the Tree of Life with "the flame of the whirling sword." Scholar Ronald Hendel has argued that "the 'flame' is an animate divine being, a member of Yahweh's divine host, similar in status to the cherubim; the 'whirling sword' is its appropriate weapon, ever-moving, like the flame itself."

Scholar P.D. Miller appeals to passages such as Psalm 104:4 where "fire and flame" are described as "Yahweh's ministers" to conclude a convergence of imagery with ancient Ugaritic texts that describe "fire and flame" as armed deities with flashing swords. He writes that "the cherubim and the flaming sword are probably to be recognized as a reflection of the Canaanite fiery messengers."

CHAPTER 61

[1] On Ba'al's two weapons:

One as a hammer like mace and the other "Ginsberg (1935:328) identified *ṣmdm* with the two-pieced maces excavated at Ugarit. The weapon consists of two pieces, a head latched onto a handle, specifically in Ginsberg's words (1935:328) "a mace with a stone head drilled through to adjust the wooden shaft, to which it is lashed tightly with thongs; and hence the name from the root ṣmd, 'to bind.' Such mace heads are found frequently in excavations."…

"A famous stele from Ugarit, sometimes called the "Baal au foudre" stele and housed in the Louvre, depicts Baal wielding two weapons. The weapon in his right hand is sometimes characterized as a mace (Amiet 1980:201).204 In his left hand Baal holds "tree-lightning" (Vanel 1965:84; Williams-Forte 1983:28, 30). Other examples of second millennium iconography of the storm-god depict him with a weapon (Vanel 1965:esp. 108; Seeden 1980:esp. 102), which appears at times as "branch-like lightning" (Williams-Forte 1983:26)."…

Comparative evidence drawn from Mediterranean and Near Eastern myths comports with the meteorological character of ṣmdm (Thespis 164–65). Zeus pelts Typhon with thunderbolts at Mons Cassius, the Latin name for Mount Sapan (Apollodorus, The Library, 1.6.3; Frazer 1921:48–49). Zeus's thunderbolts made by Cyclopes, the son of the craftsman-god Hephaistos, have been compared with Baal's weapons fashioned by Kothar (Walcot 1969:115)…."

Mark S. Smith, The Ugaritic Baal Cycle: Introduction with Text, Translation and Commentary of KTU 1.1-1.2, vol. 1 (Leiden; New York; Köln: E.J. Brill, 1994), 339–340.

The actual text of the Baal cycle where Kothar-wa-Hasis crafts the two weapons, Yagarrish/Yagrush ("Driver") and Ayyamarri/Ayamur ("Expeller") for Baal to defeat Yamm (Sea) and River (Nahar) is KTU 1.2.11-25:

Kothar fashions the weapons,
And he proclaims their names:
"Your name, yours, is Yagarrish:

Yagarrish, drive Yamm,
Drive Yamm from his throne,
[Na]har from the seat of his dominion.
"Your name, yours, is Ayyamarri:
Ayyamarri, expel Yamm,
Expel Yamm from his throne,
Nahar from the seat of his dominion.
Leap from Baal's hand,
Like a raptor from his fingers.
Strike the head of Prince Yamm,
Between the eyes of Judge River.
May Yamm sink and fall to the earth."
The weapon leaps from Baal's hand,
[Like] a raptor from his fingers,
It strikes the head of Prince [Yamm,]
Between the eyes of Judge River.

Mark S. Smith and Simon B. Parker, *Ugaritic Narrative Poetry, vol. 9, Writings from the Ancient World* (Atlanta, GA: Scholars Press, 1997), 103–104.

"The most important textual witnesses to the weapons of the storm god of Aleppo [Ba'al] are found in the Old Babylonian letters from the Mari archives From these letters we learn that the weapons that were housed in the temple of the storm god in Aleppo were brought to the Mariote city of Terqa during Zimri-Lim's reign. While the letters seem to allude to the conflict myth that we find in fuller form later on in the Baal-Cycle from Ugarit, the weapons in the letters appear to be real weapons used as cultic objects." Joanna Töyräänvuori, "Weapons of the Storm God in Ancient Near Eastern and Biblical Traditions," Studia Orientalia, volume 112 (Helsinki, Finnish Oriental Society, 2012), 154, 160.

"In the text of the Ugaritic Baal-Cycle, the weapons forged by the smith Kothar-wa-Ḥasis, and wielded by Baal in the battle against Yamm, were clubs called by the names ygrš and aymr and traslated as 'driver' and 'chaser,' respectively. A club (or a hammer, also a smiting weapon) could certainly have been one of the storm god's weapons, as the association seems to have had a cross-cultural mythological foundation. Many Syrian and Anatolian reliefs depict the weather god (Adad or Tarhunt) holding a lightning weapon in one hand and a hammer or a smiting weapon in the other hand."

Joanna Töyräänvuori, "Weapons of the Storm God in Ancient Near Eastern and Biblical Traditions," *Studia Orientalia, vol. 112*, (Finnish Oriental Society, 2012) 166

Marduk's weapons:

Enuma Elish Tablet IV:27-59:

When the gods his fathers saw what he had commanded,
Joyfully they hailed, "Marduk is king!"
They bestowed in full measure scepter, throne, and staff,
(30) They gave him unopposable weaponry that vanquishes enemies.
"Go, cut off the life of Tiamat,
Let the winds bear her blood away as glad tidings!"
The gods, his fathers, ordained the Lord's destiny,
On the path to success and authority did they set him marching.
(35) He made the bow, appointed it his weapon,
He mounted the arrow, set it on the string.
He took up the mace, held it in his right hand,
Bow and quiver he slung on his arm.
Thunderbolts he set before his face,
(40) With raging fire he covered his body.
Then he made a net to enclose Tiamat within,
He deployed the four winds that none of her might escape:
South Wind, North Wind, East Wind, West Wind,

Gift of his grandfather Anu; he fastened the net at his side.
(45) He made ill wind, whirlwind, cyclone,
Four–ways wind, seven–ways wind, destructive wind, irresistible wind:
He released the winds which he had made, the seven of them,
Mounting in readiness behind him to roil inside Tiamat.
Then the Lord raised the Deluge, his great weapon.
(50) He mounted the terrible chariot, the unopposable Storm Demon,
He hitched to it the four–steed team, he tied them at his side:
"Slaughterer," "Merciless," "Overwhelmer," "Soaring."
Their lips are curled back, their teeth bear venom,
They know not fatigue, they are trained to trample down.
(55) He stationed at his right gruesome battle and strife,
At his left the fray that overthrows all formations.
He was garbed in a ghastly armored garment,
On his head he was covered with terrifying auras.
The Lord made straight and pursued his way,

William W. Hallo and K. Lawson Younger, *The Context of Scripture* (Leiden; New York: Brill, 1997–), 397.

CHAPTER 62

[1] This confrontation between Titus and Simon is creative license.

[2] God's providence over the acts of evil in Revelation:

Revelation 9:1
[1] And the fifth angel blew his trumpet, and I saw a star fallen from heaven to earth, and **he was given** the key to the shaft of the bottomless pit.

Revelation 6:2
And I looked, and behold, a white horse! And its rider had a bow, and **a crown was given to him**, and he came out conquering, and to conquer.

Revelation 6:4
And out came another horse, bright red. **Its rider was permitted** to take peace from the earth, so that people should slay one another, and he was given a great sword.

Revelation 6:8
And I looked, and behold, a pale horse! And its rider's name was Death, and Hades followed him. And **they were given authority** over a fourth of the earth, to kill with sword and with famine and with pestilence and by wild beasts of the earth.

Revelation 9:3
Then from the smoke came locusts on the earth, and **they were given power** like the power of scorpions of the earth.

Revelation 13:5
And the beast was given a mouth uttering haughty and blasphemous words, and it was allowed to exercise authority for forty-two months.

Revelation 13:7
Also it was allowed to make war on the saints and to conquer them. And authority was given it over every tribe and people and language and nation,

Revelation 13:14–15
[14] and by the **signs that it is allowed to work** in the presence of the beast it deceives those who dwell on earth, telling them to make an image for the beast that was wounded by the sword and yet lived. [15] **And it was allowed to give breath** to the image of the beast, so that the image of the beast might even speak and might cause those who would not worship the image of the beast to be slain.

Revelation 16:8
The fourth angel poured out his bowl on the sun, and **it was allowed to scorch people** with fire.

[3] Titus believed that the temple was no longer protected by a deity:

Flavius Josephus, *The Wars of the Jews* 6.2.4, §127
"I appeal to the gods of my own country, and to every god that ever had any regard to this place (for I do not suppose it to be now regarded by any of them); I also appeal to my own army, and to those Jews that are now with me, and even to you yourselves, that I do not force you to defile this your sanctuary; (128) and if you will but change the place whereon you will fight, no Roman shall either come near your sanctuary, or offer any affront to it; nay, I will endeavor to preserve you your holy house, whether you will or not."

Flavius Josephus and William Whiston, *The Works of Josephus: Complete and Unabridged* (Peabody: Hendrickson, 1987), 733.

[4] **Josephus' story of Simon's capture**: I have used creative license in the ending of Simon's and Gischala's stories. According to Josephus, Simon went and hid in the tunnels beneath the city. He was captured trying to trick the Romans. He was then brought to Rome for the triumphal procession. See Flavius Josephus, *The Wars of the Jews* 7.2.1, §26-36.

John of Gischala had actually hid in the tunnels as well before being captured by the Romans. Flavius Josephus, *The Wars of the Jews* 6.9.4, §433-434.

CHAPTER 63

[1] The previous final sequence of the Romans taking the Antonia and then the temple mount has been telescoped from a month into a day for creative license.

[2] **This story is taken from:** Flavius Josephus, *The Wars of the Jews* 6.5.2, §283-287. Six thousand die burned alive in the cloisters because they were following a false prophet awaiting their deliverance.

[3] **Gischala's death here is creative license**. He was actually captured in the tunnels and brought to Rome for the Triumphal procession.

Flavius Josephus, *The Wars of the Jews* 6.9.4, §433-434
"As for John, he wanted food, together with his brethren, in these caverns, and begged that the Romans would now give him their right hand for his security, which he had often proudly rejected before; but for Simon, he struggled hard with the distress he was in, till he was forced to surrender himself, as we shall relate hereafter; (434) so he was reserved for the triumph, and to be then slain: as was John condemned to perpetual imprisonment; and now the Romans set fire to the extreme parts of the city, and burnt them down, and entirely demolished its walls."

[4] The burning of the holy house:

Flavius Josephus, *The Wars of the Jews* 6.4.5, §250
"But, as for that [holy] house, God had for certain long ago doomed it to the fire; and now that fatal day was come, according to the revolution of ages; it was the tenth day of the month Lous [Ab], upon which it was formerly burnt by the king of Babylon."

CHAPTER 64

[1] Gold of the temple melting:

"When at last the walls were breached Titus tried to preserve the Temple by giving orders to his soldiers not to destroy or burn it. But the anger of the soldiers against the Jews was so intense that, maddened by the resistance they encountered, they disobeyed the order of their general and set fire to the Temple. There were great quantities of gold and silver there which had been placed in the Temple for safekeeping. This melted and ran down between the rocks and into the cracks of the stones. When the soldiers captured the Temple area, in their greed to obtain this gold and silver they took long bars and pried apart the massive stones. Thus, quite literally, not one stone was left standing upon another. The Temple itself was totally destroyed, though the wall supporting the area upon which the Temple was built was left partially intact and a portion of it

418

remains to this day, called the Western Wall."

This was supposedly taken from Jossipon's account of the war.

It can be found in Ray C. Stedman, *What's This World Coming To? (An expository study of Matthew 24-26, the Olivet Discourse).* Discovery Publications, 3505 Middlefield Rd., Palo Alto, CA 94306. 1970

http://www.templemount.org/destruct2.html#anchor615789

[2] The Romans raise their standards in the temple and sacrifice to Titus:

Flavius Josephus, *The Wars of the Jews* 6.6.1, §316
"And now the Romans, upon the flight of the seditious into the city, and upon the burning of the holy house itself, and of all the buildings round about it, brought their ensigns to the temple, and set them over against its eastern gate; and there did they offer sacrifices to them, and there did they make Titus imperator, with the greatest acclamations of joy."

Flavius Josephus and William Whiston, *The Works of Josephus: Complete and Unabridged* (Peabody: Hendrickson, 1987), 743.

Roman standards: "The Roman Standard (Latin: Signum or Signa Romanum) was a pennant, flag, or banner, suspended or attached to a staff or pole, which identified a Roman legion (infantry) or Equites (cavalry). The Standard of a cavalry unit was emblazoned with the symbol of the serpent (Draconarius) while a legion of infantry was represented by a totemic animal. The most famous of these is the eagle (Aquila)...

"Besides the Serpent and Eagle symbols, there were also the Imago (a Standard displaying the image of the emperor), the Manus (an open hand at the top of the banner), the Vexillum (a rectangular cut cloth of a certain color, sometimes with a number, attached to a pole), and Banners which designated military hierarchy (a red banner, for example, would designate a general). The Vexillum designated the type of unit (legion or cohort) and which legion it was. The Manus of the open hand symbolized the loyalty of the soldiers and the trust they had in their leaders. The Imago reminded the troops of the emperor they fought for and symbolically stood for the will of Rome among them. A Standard would have more than one banner on it except for the Vexillum which was used to direct the troops' movements." "Roman Standard," *Ancient History Encyclopedia* Online http://www.ancient.eu/Roman_Standard/

Roman standards ("ensigns") were considered idolatrous by the Jews: Flavius Josephus, *The Wars of the Jews* 2.9.2 §169-170 "Now Pilate, who was sent as procurator into Judea by Tiberius, sent by night those images of Caesar that are called Ensigns, into Jerusalem. (170) This excited a very great tumult among the Jews when it was day; for those that were near them were astonished at the sight of them, as indications that their laws were trodden underfoot: for those laws do not permit any sort of image to be brought into the city." Flavius Josephus and William Whiston, *The Works of Josephus: Complete and Unabridged* (Peabody: Hendrickson, 1987), 608.

[3] Titus's pompous blasphemous words and deeds in the temple:

Babylonian Talmud Gittin 5:6, I.12.A–D

I.12 A. He went and sent Titus, who said, " 'Where is their God, the rock in whom they trusted?' (Deut. 32:37)."

B. This is that wicked Titus, who blasphemed and raged against Heaven. What did he do? He took a whore by her hand, and went into the house of the Holy of Holies; he spread out a scroll of the Torah, and on it he f****d her.

C. He took a sword and slashed the curtain.

D. A miracle was done, and blood spurted out. He thought he had killed himself: "Your adversaries have roared in the midst of your assembly, they have set up their ensigns for signs" (Ps. 74:4)...

G. What did he do? He took the veil and made it into a kind of basket, and he brought all the utensils that were in the sanctuary and put them in it, and he set them onto a boat to go to serve in his triumph his city...

I. A gale arose at sea, to swamp him. He said, "It appears to me that the god of these people is mighty only through water. Pharaoh came along, and he drowned him in water. Sisera came along, and he drowned him

419

in water. So he's now standing against me to drown me in water. So if he's so mighty, let him come up onto dry land and make war with me there."

Jacob Neusner, *The Babylonian Talmud: A Translation and Commentary, vol. 11b* (Peabody, MA: Hendrickson Publishers, 2011), 243–244.

http://www.come-and-hear.com/gittin/gittin_56.html

[4] Titus kills all the surviving priests:

Flavius Josephus, *The Wars of the Jews* 6.6.1, §316, 321
"And now all the soldiers had such vast quantities of the spoils which they had gotten by plunder, that in Syria a pound weight of gold was sold for half its former value. (318) But as for those priests that kept themselves still upon the wall of the holy house…

On the fifth day afterward, the priests that were pined with the famine came down, and when they were brought to Titus by the guards, they begged for their lives; (322) but he replied, that the time of pardon was over as to them; and that this very holy house, on whose account only they could justly hope to be preserved, was destroyed; and that it was agreeable to their office that priests should perish with the house itself to which they belonged. So he ordered them to be put to death."

Flavius Josephus and William Whiston, *The Works of Josephus: Complete and Unabridged* (Peabody: Hendrickson, 1987), 743–744.

The False Prophet destroyed:

In this book, I take the False Prophet as a symbol of the office of the High Priest, who, because they rejected Messiah, had become the unholy opposite of a Biblical prophet. Though Ananus the high priest and others had been killed earlier in the siege, all representing this destruction, Titus nonetheless slaughtered the last of the priests after taking the temple, which represented that final blow.

CHAPTER 66

[1] Fleeing citizens finding refuge in the tunnels beneath the city:

Flavius Josephus, *The Wars of the Jews* 6.9.4, §429-430
"and others they made search for underground, and when they found where they were, they broke up the ground and slew all they met with. (430) There were also found slain there above two thousand persons, partly by their own hands, and partly by one another, but chiefly destroyed by the famine."

Flavius Josephus and William Whiston, *The Works of Josephus: Complete and Unabridged* (Peabody: Hendrickson, 1987), 749.

The Jewish soldier defenders of the city also sought refuge in the tunnels beneath the city:

Flavius Josephus, *The Wars of the Jews* 6.7.3, §370-373
3. (370) So now the last hope which supported the tyrants and that crew of robbers who were with them, was in the caves and caverns underground; whither, if they could once fly, they did not expect to be searched for; but endeavored, that after the whole city should be destroyed, and the Romans gone away, they might come out again, and escape from them. (371) This was no better than a dream of theirs; for they were not able to lie hid either from God or from the Romans. (372) However, they depended on these underground subterfuges,

Flavius Josephus and William Whiston, *The Works of Josephus: Complete and Unabridged* (Peabody: Hendrickson, 1987), 746.

CHAPTER 67

[1] **The details of the taking of the Upper City can be found in**: Flavius Josephus, *The Wars of the Jews* 6.6.1-6.8.5, § 316-408.

[2] Titus's comment about destroying the temple as subverting both Judaism and Christianity:

Sulpicius Severus, *The Sacred History* 2.30.6-7

"Titus is said, after calling a council, to have first deliberated whether he should destroy the temple, a structure of such extraordinary work. For it seemed good to some that a sacred edifice, distinguished above all human achievements, ought not to be destroyed, inasmuch as, if preserved, it would furnish an evidence of Roman moderation, but, if destroyed, would serve for a perpetual proof of Roman cruelty. But on the opposite side, others and Titus himself thought that the temple ought specially to be overthrown, in order that the religion of the Jews and of the Christians might more thoroughly be subverted; for that these religions, although contrary to each other, had nevertheless proceeded from the same authors; that the Christians had sprung up from among the Jews; and that, if the root were extirpated, the offshoot would speedily perish. Thus, according to the divine will, the minds of all being inflamed, the temple was destroyed."

Sulpicius Severus, "The Sacred History Of Sulpitius Severus," in *Sulpitius Severus*, Vincent of Lérins, John Cassian, ed. Philip Schaff and Henry Wace, trans. Alexander Roberts, vol. *11, A Select Library of the Nicene and Post-Nicene Fathers of the Christian Church, Second Series* (New York: Christian Literature Company, 1894), 111.

[3] **Titus orders the destruction of the Temple**: Josephus paints a picture of Titus reluctantly allowing the destruction only after unruly soldiers started the flames. But Josephus was a paid collaborator of Flavius Vespasian who took on his patron's Flavian name, so he was an untrustworthy apologist for Titus. Titus ultimately "gave orders that they should now demolish the entire city and temple" (J.W. 7:1:1 §1).

"As an important consequence, Feuillet (229) states that "the Jewish war and the destruction of Jerusalem… are of tremendous importance because they mark the definitive independence of the Christian religion from that of Israel, thereby preparing the way for the advance of the Church among the pagans of the Gentile world." It is likely, however, that Titus actually intended the opposite effect: to destroy Christianity in the process. Since apostolic Christianity was so tied up with Israel and the temple, Titus apparently hoped to crush both Judaism and Christianity with the destruction of the temple. According to Sulpicius Severus (ca. AD 400), whose "authority is undoubtedly Tacitus," we learn that "Titus is said, after calling a council, to have first deliberated whether he should destroy the temple, a structure of such extraordinary work. For it seemed good to some that a sacred edifice, distinguished above all human achievements, ought not to be destroyed…But on the opposite side, others and Titus himself thought that the temple ought specially to be overthrown in order that the religion of the Jews and of the Christians might more thoroughly be subverted; for that these religions, although contrary to each other, had nevertheless proceeded from the same authors; that the Christians had sprung up from among the Jews; and that, if the root were extirpated, the offshoot would speedily perish" (Severus 2:30). Tommaso Leoni notes that "very few have doubts… that the version of the Christian chronographer [Severus] should be preferred" over Josephus' account, which states that Titus tried to prevent the burning of the temple (Jos., J.W. 6:4:3 §236–43).44 J. Barclay (1996: 353) argues that "this notorious feature of Josephus' account is certainly 'economical with the truth' and possibly a complete fabrication." Kenneth L. Gentry, Jr., The Divorce of Israel: A Redemptive-Historical Interpretation of Revelation Vol. 2 (Dallas, GA: Tolle Lege Press, 2016), 57-58.

"Most historians agree that Josephus whitewashed many of Titus's activities and motivations regarding his hostility toward the Jewish religion. Commenting on the unlikely assertion that the Temple was destroyed contrary to Titus's wishes, Paul Spilsbury writes: The Jewish War's description of the events surrounding the fateful burning of the Temple is notorious for its disingenuousness. Josephus reports that on the night before the event itself Titus held a council of war in which he argued against the advice of most of those present that the Temple should be spared. In the actual event, though, the Temple was burned to the ground after an unruly soldier, "moved by some supernatural impulse," (War 6.252) threw a firebrand into the sanctuary. Titus's personal efforts to extinguish the fire, we are told, were thwarted by the recalcitrance of his men (War 6.260). The majority of modern historians find this account of events implausible.

"G. Alon, Jews, Judaism and the Classical World. Studies in Jewish History in the Times of the Second Temple and Talmud, trans. Abrahams (Jerusalem: Magnes Press, 1977), 253] states unambiguously that "we cannot avoid the almost certain conclusion that the Temple was put to the torch at Titus's behest." [emphasis original to Alon]. His argument is based on: (1) comparison with other sources, most notably Sulpicius Severus' Chronica, perhaps derived from Tacitus' lost Histories, which attributes the decision to burn the Temple to Titus himself; (2) examination of the events immediately preceding and following the burning of the Temple, which indicate that it was always part of the Roman intention; and (3) indication in other parts of Josephus' works where he seems to betray that he knew Titus was to blame for the burning of the Temple (e.g., War 7.1; Ant 20.250). Alon's conclusion is that Josephus distorted the truth and "adjusted" his history to meet "the demands of his benefactors" [Vespasian and Titus].41 Roman historian Dio Cassius presents a very different picture of Titus's intentions concerning the Temple. Dio said the Roman troops were afraid to violate the sanctity of the Temple and that it was Titus who compelled them to enter it: "... the Temple was now laid open to the Romans. Nevertheless, the soldiers because of their superstition did not immediately rush in; but at last, under compulsion from Titus, they made their way inside."

"The suggestion that the Temple was destroyed by out-of-control troops is especially unlikely when you read Josephus' own description of how disciplined the Roman army was: "Military law demands the death penalty not only for desertion of the ranks but even some slight neglect of duty...." Burning the Temple in violation of a (supposed) direct order from Titus Caesar would have been far worse than some slight neglect of duty. Technically, this would have made the troops' actions worthy of death. An example of an obvious omission of Titus's actions by Josephus can be found in his failure to even mention Titus's relationship with the Jewish queen Bernice. Titus met Bernice in AD 67 when he first came to Judea. She lived with Titus and essentially became his common law wife, and yet Josephus fails to mention her or their scandalous relationship. The reason for this is that, since the time of Mark Antony's disastrous relationship with Cleopatra, the Roman public was very leery of alliances between its leaders and foreign queens. If one depends only on Josephus' record, the relationship between Titus and Bernice (who has been referred to as the "little Cleopatra") never happened. This should make one suspicious of what other items Josephus left out of his account of Titus's actions during this time."

McKenzie PhD, Duncan W.. *The Antichrist and the Second Coming: A Preterist Examination Volume I* (K-Locations 2035-2045). Xulon Press. K-Edition.

"[T]he Temple was now laid open to the Romans. Nevertheless, the soldiers because of their superstition did not immediately rush in; but at last, under compulsion from Titus, they made their way inside."

Dio Cassius, *Roman History* 15.6.2, in Dio's Roman History, vol. VIII, trans. Earnest Cary (Cambridge, MA: Harvard University Press, 1982), 269 Quoted in McKenzie PhD, Duncan W.. *The Antichrist and the Second Coming: A Preterist Examination Volume I* (Kindle Locations 7543-7545). Xulon Press. Kindle Edition.

4 Shattering of the holy people and the end of days:

> Daniel 12:7–13
> 7 And I heard the man clothed in linen, who was above the waters of the stream; he raised his right hand and his left hand toward heaven and swore by him who lives forever that it would be for a time, times, and half a time, and that when the shattering of the power of the holy people comes to an end all these things would be finished... But go your way till the end. And you shall rest and shall stand in your allotted place at the end of the days."

CHAPTER 68

1 The Feast of Trumpets:

> Leviticus 23:23–25 (NASB95)
> 23 Again the LORD spoke to Moses, saying, 24 "Speak to the sons of Israel, saying, 'In the seventh month on the first of the month you shall have a rest, a reminder by blowing *of trumpets,* a holy convocation. 25 'You shall not do any laborious work, but you shall present an offering by fire to the LORD.' "

"No man knows the day or the hour" of the beginning of the Feast of Trumpets: Thanks to David Curtis from Berean Bible church for his online sermons on the Feasts of the Lord.
http://www.bereanbiblechurch.org/transcripts/topical/feasts_lord_02.htm

2 Matthew 24:36–44

3 Joel 2:1.

4 Pentecost, Joel and the Day of the Lord:

"In Acts 2, Peter was preaching on the day of Pentecost. Jews from many nations had been filled with the Spirit of God and began to speak gospel truth in their own tongues. The nations were beginning to stream into the mountain of the house of the Lord, the new covenant. Unbelievers accused them of being drunk and Peter

422

responded.

Acts 2:15–20
For these people are not drunk, as you suppose, since it is only the third hour of the day. [16] But this is what was uttered through the prophet Joel: [17] "And in the last days it shall be, God declares, that I will pour out my Spirit on all flesh, and your sons and your daughters shall prophesy, and your young men shall see visions, and your old men shall dream dreams; [18] even on my male servants and female servants in those days I will pour out my Spirit, and they shall prophesy. [19] And I will show wonders in the heavens above and signs on the earth below, blood, and fire, and vapor of smoke; [20] the sun shall be turned to darkness and the moon to blood, before the day of the Lord comes, the great and magnificent day."

"Look at what I underlined. Peter said that the Spirit of God falling on "all flesh" at Pentecost (another figurative, nonliteral expression for Gentiles and the nations outside of Israel) was the fulfillment of Joel's prophecy about *the last days*!

"That had always bothered me because I wondered how he could say that the last days were his own days when the day of the Lord was not for another few thousand years? What about the sun and moon turning dark? Was that all just a metaphor, or did he literally mean what he said?

"He was an apostle who spoke with God's authority and he said that the last days prophecy was being fulfilled in his own day, not thousands of years later. We have already discussed the notion that in the Old Testament the cosmic catastrophes of sun, moon, and stars were poetic metaphors for the fall of earthly and spiritual powers. And we also learned that the day of the Lord was not necessarily the end of history but a day of judgment on a nation or people or city.

"And the temple and Jerusalem had not yet been destroyed as Jesus predicted. So the Spirit of God being poured out on the nations began to be fulfilled at Pentecost, and that happened just years before the heavenly and earthly power of Israel was abolished in the destruction of the holy city and temple. The last days were the last days of the old covenant that was replaced by the new covenant mountain of God, finalized in the destruction of the Jewish temple and holy city."

Brian Godawa, *End Times Bible Prophecy: It's Not What They Told You* (Los Angeles, CA: Embedded Pictures Publishing, 2017), 85.

[5] Jesus as the end goal of Torah:

Romans 10:4
[4] For Christ is the end [final goal] of the law for righteousness to everyone who believes.

All God's promises fulfilled in Jesus:

2 Corinthians 1:20
[20] For all the promises of God find their Yes in him.

Jesus ends sacrifice and vision and prophecy:

Daniel 9:24-27
[24] "Seventy weeks are decreed about your people and your holy city, to finish the transgression, to put an end to sin, and to atone for iniquity, to bring in everlasting righteousness, to seal both vision and prophet, and to anoint a most holy place...[27] And he shall make a strong covenant with many for one week, and for half of the week he shall put an end to sacrifice and offering.

[6] Fleeing citizens and soldiers in the tunnels beneath the city were found by Romans and killed:

Flavius Josephus, *The Wars of the Jews* 6.9.4, §429-430
"and others they made search for underground, and when they found where they were, they broke up the ground and slew all they met with. (430) There were also found slain there above two thousand persons, partly by their own hands, and partly by one another, but chiefly destroyed by the famine."

Flavius Josephus and William Whiston, *The Works of Josephus: Complete and Unabridged* (Peabody: Hendrickson, 1987), 749.

Flavius Josephus, *The Wars of the Jews* 6.7.3, §370-373
3. (370) So now the last hope which supported the tyrants and that crew of robbers who were with them, was in the caves and caverns underground; whither, if they could once fly, they did not expect to be searched for; but endeavored, that after the whole city should be destroyed, and the Romans gone away, they might come out again, and escape from them. (371) This was no better than a dream of theirs; for they were not able to lie hid either from God or from the Romans. (372) However, they depended on these underground subterfuges,

Flavius Josephus and William Whiston, *The Works of Josephus: Complete and Unabridged* (Peabody: Hendrickson, 1987), 746.

CHAPTER 69

[1] Demoniacal experience in Jerusalem:

"Although Josephus does not mention demonic activity during the War, the cruel barbarity of the Jews' internal strife strongly suggests such.14 As Henderson (1903: 374) expresses the situation: "That unhappy city during all this year of grace had been prey to the most bloody anarchy and demoniacal fanaticism." Or as Rudolf Stier (cited in Farrar 1884: 454) puts it (though speaking more broadly than of the final five month siege): "In the period between the Resurrection and the Fall of Jerusalem the Jewish nation acted as if possessed by seven thousand demons. The whole age had upon it a stamp of the infernal." Terry (351) summarizes this whole fifth trumpet scenery as "an apocalyptic symbolizing of the demoniacal possessions and mad fury which came upon the Jewish people, and especially upon their leaders, during the last bitter struggle with Rome." By "leaders," Terry probably does not mean the high-priestly aristocracy (many of whom had their throats cut by the Sicarii, J.W. 7:8:1 §267), but the forces of the rebel leaders, hell. Josephus writes: "For the present sedition, one should not mistake if he called it a sedition begotten by another sedition, and to be like a wild beast grown mad, which, for want of food from abroad, fell now upon eating its own flesh" (J.W. 5:1:1 §4)."

Kenneth L. Gentry, Jr., The Divorce of Israel: A Redemptive-Historical Interpretation of Revelation Vol. 1 (Dallas, GA: Tolle Lege Press, 2016), 737.

[2] Day of Atonement:

Leviticus 23:26–32
[26] And the LORD spoke to Moses, saying, [27] "Now on the tenth day of this seventh month is the Day of Atonement. It shall be for you a time of holy convocation, and you shall afflict yourselves and present a food offering to the LORD. [28] And you shall not do any work on that very day, for it is a Day of Atonement, to make atonement for you before the LORD your God. [29] For whoever is not afflicted on that very day shall be cut off from his people. [30] And whoever does any work on that very day, that person I will destroy from among his people. [31] You shall not do any work. It is a statute forever throughout your generations in all your dwelling places. [32] It shall be to you a Sabbath of solemn rest, and you shall afflict yourselves. On the ninth day of the month beginning at evening, from evening to evening shall you keep your Sabbath."

Numbers 29:7–11
[7] "On the tenth day of this seventh month you shall have a holy convocation and afflict yourselves. You shall do no work, [8] but you shall offer a burnt offering to the LORD, a pleasing aroma: one bull from the herd, one ram, seven male lambs a year old: see that they are without blemish. [9] And their grain offering shall be of fine flour mixed with oil, three tenths of an ephah for the bull, two tenths for the one ram, [10] a tenth for each of the seven lambs: [11] also one male goat for a sin offering, besides the sin offering of atonement, and the regular burnt offering and its grain offering, and their drink offerings.

Also, thanks to David Curtis from Berean Bible church for his online sermons on the Feasts of the Lord.
http://www.bereanbiblechurch.org/transcripts/topical/feasts_lord_02.htm

The scapegoat ritual:

Leviticus 16:6–10
[6] "Aaron shall offer the bull as a sin offering for himself and shall make atonement for himself and for his house. [7] Then he shall take the two goats and set them before the LORD at the entrance of

424

the tent of meeting. [8] And Aaron shall cast lots over the two goats, one lot for the LORD and the other lot for Azazel. [9] And Aaron shall present the goat on which the lot fell for the LORD and use it as a sin offering, [10] but the goat on which the lot fell for Azazel shall be presented alive before the LORD to make atonement over it, that it may be sent away into the wilderness to Azazel.

The Holy of Holies ritual:

Leviticus 16:15–19
[15] "Then he shall kill the goat of the sin offering that is for the people and bring its blood inside the veil and do with its blood as he did with the blood of the bull, sprinkling it over the mercy seat and in front of the mercy seat. [16] Thus he shall make atonement for the Holy Place, because of the uncleannesses of the people of Israel and because of their transgressions, all their sins. And so he shall do for the tent of meeting, which dwells with them in the midst of their uncleannesses. [17] No one may be in the tent of meeting from the time he enters to make atonement in the Holy Place until he comes out and has made atonement for himself and for his house and for all the assembly of Israel. [18] Then he shall go out to the altar that is before the LORD and make atonement for it, and shall take some of the blood of the bull and some of the blood of the goat, and put it on the horns of the altar all around. [19] And he shall sprinkle some of the blood on it with his finger seven times, and cleanse it and consecrate it from the uncleannesses of the people of Israel.

[3] Christ as high priest entered the heavenly Holy Place:

Hebrews 8:1–2
[1] Now the point in what we are saying is this: we have such a high priest, one who is seated at the right hand of the throne of the Majesty in heaven, [2] a minister in the holy places, in the true tent that the Lord set up, not man.

Hebrews 9:11–12
[11] But when Christ appeared as a high priest of the good things that have come, then through the greater and more perfect tent (not made with hands, that is, not of this creation) [12] he entered once for all into the holy places, not by means of the blood of goats and calves but by means of his own blood, thus securing an eternal redemption.

[4] The earthly temple must be destroyed for the new covenant access to be complete:

Hebrews 9:8–9 (NASB95)
[8] The Holy Spirit *is* signifying this, that the way into the holy place has not yet been disclosed while the outer tabernacle is still standing, [9] which *is* a symbol for the present time.

Hebrews 8:13
[13] In speaking of a new covenant, he makes the first one obsolete. And what is becoming obsolete and growing old is ready to vanish away.

The book of Hebrews was written before the temple was destroyed in AD 70. The writer and his Christian audience knew the desolation was coming because Jesus had foretold it (Matt 23:37-24:1). They were in a transition period between covenants. The New Covenant had been spiritually inaugurated at Christ's death, resurrection and ascension. But the earthly elements of the Old Covenant were still standing. The Old Covenant was becoming obsolete as the New Covenant was taking its place. The Old Covenant was about to finally and fully vanish away – when the earthly incarnation of that Old Covenant was destroyed: the holy city and temple.

Hebrews 8:13
[13] In speaking of a new covenant, he makes the first one obsolete. And what is becoming obsolete and growing old is ready to vanish away.

Hebrews was written in a transition period. In an earthly sense, the New Covenant had been inaugurated, but not consummated until the Old Covenant had been completely done away by the destruction of the earthly incarnation of that Old Covenant. When the Roman armies destroyed the earthly city of Jerusalem and its temple, that marked God historically consummating the New Covenant that he had previously spiritually inaugurated.

Hebrews 9:26 says that Jesus suffered on the cross, "once for all at the end of the ages to put away sin by the sacrifice of himself." The end of the ages is not the end of history or the end of the world as we understand it. The end of the ages had already occurred at the time of the crucifixion of Christ. The end of the ages was the end of the old covenant era and the beginning of the new covenant in Christ's blood!

But get this: that same writer of Hebrews talked about the new covenant in Christ being superior to the old covenant in Hebrews 8. He quoted Jeremiah confirming that the prophets predicted the arrival of the new covenant age. And then he said, "In speaking of a new covenant, he makes the first one obsolete. And what is becoming obsolete and growing old is ready to vanish away" (8:13).

What was growing old and ready to vanish at that time?

It blew my theology when I realized that he was talking about the destruction of the temple as the final culmination of the new covenant replacement of the old covenant! He was writing in the time period after Christ's death and resurrection and right before the temple had been destroyed. So the new covenant had been established in Christ's blood, but it was not consummated with historical finality. Like Paul, the writer believed they were at the end of the ages. The new covenant would make the old covenant obsolete. But take a closer look at the language he used. He said that the old is "becoming obsolete and is ready to vanish away," as if the old covenant had not vanished yet. It was only in the process of *becoming* obsolete. "Becoming," not "had become," and not "would become" thousands of years in the future. What could that mean?

Well, the writer was writing within the generation that Jesus said would see the destruction of the temple. The temple had not yet been destroyed. Hebrews 8 says that they were in a time period of change between covenants and that change had not yet been fully or historically consummated. That first century generation was in the transition period between ages or covenants. So, what would be the event that would embody the theological claim that the old covenant was obsolete and the new covenant had replaced it? The destruction of the symbol of the old covenant, the temple! The old covenant would not be obsolete until its symbolic incarnation, the temple, was made desolate.

Brian Godawa, *End Times Bible Prophecy: It's Not What They Told You* (Los Angeles, CA: Embedded Pictures Publishing, 2017), 79-80.

[5] High Priest, holy place, atonement in the OT:

"Under the Mosaic law, until the High Priest came out of the Most Holy Place in the temple and announced that the sacrifice had been accepted by God, the atonement wasn't complete. After the cross, Jesus took his sacrifice to heaven, the real Most Holy Place. The sacrifice was accepted, and Jesus as our High Priest came out of the Most Holy Place and announced that salvation was complete. This is what Jesus was about to do in Heb. 9.27-28: 27

> And inasmuch as it is appointed unto men once to die, and after this cometh judgment; 28 so Christ also, having been once offered to bear the sins of many, shall appear a second time, apart from sin, to them that wait for him, unto salvation.

The word "time" is not in the original. The passage literally says that Jesus would appear "out of second." Second what? Notice verses 2, 6, 8, where "the first" is in reference to the Holy Place, which tells us that the "second" was the real Most Holy Place, heaven. This is a picture of Christ coming out of heaven to announce that salvation was complete."

Dawson, Samuel G., *The Resurrection: Israel's Old Testament Hope in Chronological Order* (Kindle Locations 1288-1297). SGD Press. K-Edition.

[6] These fulfillments are taken from: Daniel 9:24-27

[7] **The missing ark of the covenant**: Michael Heiser examines 9 theories of where the ark is and concludes that the most likely biblical evidence is that the ark of the covenant was destroyed when Babylon destroyed the temple and took its vessels. The Naked Bible podcast #158 The Fate of the Ark of the Covenant. https://www.nakedbiblepodcast.com/naked-bible-158-the-fate-of-the-ark-of-the-covenant/

Though not explicit, this is implied in several Scriptures. First...

Ezekiel prophesies the jealousy of God (and therefore, the ark of God's presence) departing when

Babylon destroys the ark: Ezekiel 16:41–42 And they shall burn your houses and execute judgments upon you in the sight of many women. I will make you stop playing the whore, and you shall also give payment no more. 42 So will I satisfy my wrath on you, and my jealousy shall depart from you. I will be calm and will no more be angry.

Jeremiah implies that the ark is gone (Yahweh's footstool and glory), but will not be missed with the coming of Messiah and the new covenant: Jeremiah 3:16 And when you have multiplied and been fruitful in the land, in those days, declares the LORD, they shall no more say, "The ark of the covenant of the LORD." It shall not come to mind or be remembered or missed; it shall not be made again.

The ark is Yahweh's footstool Jeremiah implies again that it is gone and will not be remembered: Lamentations 2:1 How the Lord in his anger has set the daughter of Zion under a cloud! He has cast down from heaven to earth the splendor of Israel; he has not remembered his footstool in the day of his anger.

When Babylon came and destroyed the temple: 2 Esdras 10:22 Our psaltery is laid on the ground, our song is put to silence, our rejoicing is at an end, the light of our candlestick is put out, the ark of our covenant is spoiled, our holy things are defiled. The Apocrypha: King James Version (Bellingham, WA: Logos Research Systems, Inc., 1995), 2 Esd 10:22.

Revelation says that the ark of the covenant was in heaven in the first century: Revelation 11:19 Then God's temple in heaven was opened, and the ark of his covenant was seen within his temple. There were flashes of lightning, rumblings, peals of thunder, an earthquake, and heavy hail.

"According to some Jewish traditions, the Babylonians removed the vessels of gold, silver, and bronze, but Jeremiah removed the ark and the sacred tablets and hid them from the Babylonians. This tradition may be traced at least to the historian Eupolemus (see Eusebius, Praep. Evang. 9.39). A similar account is related by Alexander Polyhistor of Miletus in the 1st century B.C.E., but he was probably dependent on Eupolemus for this story. In a variant of this account, Jeremiah hid the tent, the ark, and the altar of incense in a cave on the mountain from which Moses saw the Promised Land (2 Macc 2:4–8). Another source has it that Josiah hid the ark under a rock "in its place" (b. Yoma 53b–54a; m. Šeqal. 6:1–2). According to a legend, an angel descended from heaven during the destruction of Jerusalem and removed the sacred vessels from the temple (2 Bar. 6:7). These accounts are obviously ways of coping with the unthinkable destruction of the ark of divine presence at the hands of Gentile invaders. More credible is the lament over the desecration of the temple and plundering of the ark during the destruction of the First Temple (2 Esdr 10:20–23). In any case, all traditions point to the exilic period for the disappearance of the ark. It appears that the ark was not rebuilt for the Second Temple. Jeremiah declared that it was not to be made again (Jer 3:16)."

C. L. Seow, "Ark of the Covenant," ed. David Noel Freedman, *The Anchor Yale Bible Dictionary* (New York: Doubleday, 1992), 390–391.

[8] The ark in heaven:

Revelation 11:15–19
Then the seventh angel blew his trumpet, and there were loud voices in heaven, saying, "The kingdom of the world has become the kingdom of our Lord and of his Christ, and he shall reign forever and ever." And the twenty-four elders who sit on their thrones before God fell on their faces and worshiped God, saying,

"We give thanks to you, Lord God Almighty,
who is and who was,
for you have taken your great power
and begun to reign.

18 The nations raged,
but your wrath came,

and the time for the dead to be judged,
and for rewarding your servants, the prophets and saints,
and those who fear your name,
both small and great,

and for destroying the destroyers of the Land."

19 Then God's temple in heaven was opened, and the ark of his covenant was seen within his temple. There were flashes of lightning, rumblings, peals of thunder, an earthquake, and heavy hail.

[9] Daniel's night visions: Daniel 7.

[10] The throne room vision:

This scene is an integration of: Daniel 7:9-27 and Revelation 4.

[11] Martyrs on thrones:

Revelation 20:4–6
4 Then I saw thrones, and seated on them were those to whom the authority to judge was committed. Also I saw the souls of those who had been beheaded for the testimony of Jesus and for the word of God, and those who had not worshiped the beast or its image and had not received its mark on their foreheads or their hands. They came to life and reigned with Christ for a thousand years. 5 The rest of the dead did not come to life until the thousand years were ended. This is the first resurrection. 6 Blessed and holy is the one who shares in the first resurrection! Over such the second death has no power, but they will be priests of God and of Christ, and they will reign with him for a thousand years.

Jesus said that the first generation of apostate Jews would be guilty of all the blood of the prophets spilled in the holy land. That was why the temple was destroyed.

Matthew 23:32–24:2
[Jesus:] 32 "Fill up, then, the measure of your fathers. 33 You serpents, you brood of vipers, how are you to escape being sentenced to hell? 34 Therefore I send you prophets and wise men and scribes, some of whom you will kill and crucify, and some you will flog in your synagogues and persecute from town to town, 35 so that on you may come all the righteous blood shed on earth, from the blood of righteous Abel to the blood of Zechariah the son of Barachiah, whom you murdered between the sanctuary and the altar. 36 Truly, I say to you, all these things will come upon this generation. 37 "O Jerusalem, Jerusalem, the city that kills the prophets and stones those who are sent to it! How often would I have gathered your children together as a hen gathers her brood under her wings, and you were not willing! 38 See, your house is left to you desolate. 39 For I tell you, you will not see me again, until you say, 'Blessed is he who comes in the name of the Lord.' " 1 Jesus left the temple and was going away, when his disciples came to point out to him the buildings of the temple. 2 But he answered them, "You see all these, do you not? Truly, I say to you, there will not be left here one stone upon another that will not be thrown down."

Revelation proclaims the judgment of Jerusalem as Babylon is for the blood of the martyrs:

Revelation 6:9–10
9 When he opened the fifth seal, I saw under the altar the souls of those who had been slain for the word of God and for the witness they had borne. 10 They cried out with a loud voice, "O Sovereign Lord, holy and true, how long before you will judge and avenge our blood on those who dwell on the earth?"

Revelation 17:5–6
5 And on her forehead was written a name of mystery: "Babylon the great, mother of prostitutes and of earth's abominations." 6 And I saw the woman, drunk with the blood of the saints, the blood of the martyrs of Jesus. When I saw her, I marveled greatly.

Revelation 18:20
Rejoice over her, O heaven, and you saints and apostles and prophets, for God has given judgment for you against her!"

Revelation 18:21
Then a mighty angel took up a stone like a great millstone and threw it into the sea, saying, "So will Babylon the great city be thrown down with violence, and will be found no more;

Revelation 18:24
And in her was found the blood of prophets and of saints, and of all who have been slain on earth."

The Martyrs on thrones judging:

""The millennium is the millennium of the martyrs" which "is in direct line with the many other references to the martyrs (6:9–11; 7:13–17; 11:4–13; 12:11–12; 14:1–5; 15:2–4)" (McKelvey 2001: 97). John's statement alludes to formal judicial sanctions that were levied on earth against these who are now enthroned in heaven: (1) As in 1:9 and 6:9, "because (dia) of the word of God" gives the reason for the negative sanction in view. (2) The idea of "beheading" shows he is not concerned with saints who die in their sleep. (3) The term pepelekismenōn literally means "killed with an ax" (pelekus = ax), and was a Roman means of judicial execution, not (for instance) of death in battle (Mt 14:10; Polyb. 1:7:12; 11:20:2; Diod. S. 19:101, 3; Strabo 16:2:18; Jos., Ant. 14:7:4 §125; 14:8:4 §140; 15:1:2 §8–9; 20:5:4 §).6677 BAGD (794) states that the word means: "normally an act of capital punishment.""...

"John, in fact, states that they "had been beheaded," which requires their physical death by judicial sanction. In this extremely Old Testament-oriented work employing much temple imagery, he frequently emphasizes the saints' bloodshed (6:10; 16:6; 17:6; 18:24;19:2) and the blood of the Lamb (1:5; 5:9; 7:14; 12:11), while reflecting on the Lamb's vengeance upon the temple and its high-priestly aristocracy...

"This text seems clearly to reflect 6:9–11 (Mounce 365; Beale 997; Smalley 507) – even more directly than Daniel 7. And that text speaks of "the souls of those who had been slain." These did not just fall over and die in exile; they were slaughtered (esphagmenōn, Rev 6:9). They are crying out for God to avenge [ekdikeis] their blood on those who "dwell in the Land [tēs gēs]" (6:10). Aune (1087–88) argues that 20:4 and 6:9 are doublets, based on replicated wording and strong parallels:

20:4
And I saw the souls of those who had been beheaded because of the testimony of Jesus and because of the word of God.

6:9
I saw underneath the altar the souls of those who had been slain because of the word of God, and because of the testimony which they had maintained.

"I would argue that these two passages represent promise and fulfillment: In 6:9 the souls are beneath the earthly altar praying for vindication and receiving the promise of such. In 20:4 they actually receive their vindication by being given the right to sit in judgment over their enemies (cp. 19:2). To those caught up in the earthly terror, the martyrs would seem to be tragically destroyed and altogether lost in the struggle (cp. 11:9–10; 13:7, 15). "What happens when Christians are viciously put to death? It appears to the world that they have been decisively defeated. The persecuting authorities are very much alive and as powerful as ever, while Christians have been simply wiped out" (Poythress 181). But John characteristically provides a heavenly insight, showing that these are actually enthroned with Christ because of their faithfulness to him...

"As Jesus explained to those who would be caught up in the war that led to the temple's destruction: "the one who endures to the end, he shall be saved" (24:13; cp. 24:34). This, of course, fits well with Revelation's overarching theme (1:7), within its specific time frame ("soon" and "near"; 1:1, 3; 22:6, 10), and with its recurring concern for judging the slayers of the saints (12:10–11; 13:7–10; 14:9–13; 15:2–4; 16:5–7; 17:1–6, 14; 18:20, 24; 19:2)."

Kenneth L. Gentry, Jr., The Divorce of Israel: A Redemptive-Historical Interpretation of Revelation Vol. 2 (Dallas, GA: Tolle Lege Press, 2016), 678, 680-681.

[12] The Millennium and the first resurrection:

"Concurrent with Satan's binding comes the rule of the martyrs (Rev 20:4–6). Although the vast majority of Revelation focuses on events that will occur "soon" (Rev 1:1, 3), this section on the thousand years begins, but is not completed, in the first century. It projects itself into the distant future, allowing a glimpse of the end result of the events beginning in the apostolic era.

"In Rev 20:4 John focuses on the martyred saints, who participate in Christ's heavenly rule (Rev 20:4): "the souls of those who had been beheaded for their witness and those who had not worshiped the beast."[64]

Given John's time frame concern (cf. Rev 1:3, 9), his focus is on the martyrs of the first-century era.65 In fact, 20:4 is the answer to the plea of the martyrs in Rev 6:9–11, as we can see from the strong parallels between the passages:

Rev 20:4
And I saw the souls of those who had been beheaded because of the testimony of Jesus and because of the word of God.

Rev 6:9
I saw underneath the altar the souls of those who had been slain because of the word of God, and because of the testimony which they had maintained.

"In Revelation 20:1–3 John explicates the first phase of Christ's triumph over Satan: he is spiritually bound, being restricted from successfully accomplishing his evil design in history. In Revelation 20:7–10 we witness the second and concluding phase of Christ's triumph: Satan is personally punished, being tormented in the eternal flames of the lake of fire. John employs this two-fold pattern of spiritual/physical realities followed by initial/conclusive realities in the resurrection reference in Revelation 20, as well.

"The "first resurrection" secures the participation of the martyred saints in Christ's rule (Rev 20:4–6). The context suggests that this resurrection may not be literal. After all, we see a chain binding Satan and a key locking the abyss. As in the case of the two-fold triumph over Satan, this is the initial, spiritual victory-resurrection. That is, it refers to the spiritual resurrection of the martyrs who are born again by God's grace and enter heaven to new life. After all, elsewhere Scripture speaks of salvation as a spiritual resurrection: "We know that we have passed from death to life, because we love the brethren. He who does not love his brother abides in death" (1Jn 3:14).67 For dramatic purposes John ties this resurrection to the martyr's vindication in AD 70.

"Elsewhere John, Revelation's author, speaks of a non-literal resurrection that occurs at the moment of salvation, much like Rev 20 associates a non-literal resurrection with the martyrs' vindication in AD 70. He presents this in such a way that it serves as an advance indication of the final eschatological resurrection:

"Most assuredly, I say to you, he who hears My word and believes in Him who sent Me has everlasting life, and shall not come into judgment, but has passed from death into life. Most assuredly, I say to you, the hour is coming, and now is, when the dead will hear the voice of the Son of God; and those who hear will live. For as the Father has life in Himself, so He has granted the Son to have life in Himself, and has given Him authority to execute judgment also, because He is the Son of Man. Do not marvel at this; for the hour is coming in which all who are in the graves will hear His voice and come forth; those who have done good, to the resurrection of life, and those who have done evil, to the resurrection of condemnation. (Jn 5:24–29)

"John presents the martyrs' vindication metaphorically as their being resurrected to enthronement, which does not require a physical resurrection. This non-literal enthronement should not surprise us in that earlier he more broadly states that he "has made us kings and priests to His God and Father, to Him be glory and dominion forever and ever" (Rev 1:6). After all, Christians are "overcomers" (cf. 1Jn 2:13–14; 4:4; 5:4–5) and sit with Christ in heavenly rule: "To him who overcomes I will grant to sit with Me on My throne, as I also overcame and sat down with My Father on His throne" (Rev 3:21). As Paul puts it, Christ "raised us up together, and made us sit together in the heavenly places in Christ Jesus" (Eph 2:6). The "rest of the dead" do not participate in this first century, spiritual resurrection. In fact, they "do not live again until the thousand years" is finished (Rev 20:5). For John's purposes, these dead probably refer to "the rest," who were killed in Revelation 19:21. In the future they will be physically resurrected (implied) in order to experience "the second death" (eternal torment in both body and soul, Mt 10:28), which occurs on Judgment Day (Rev 20:11–15)."

Kenneth L. Gentry, Jr., Th.M., Th.D., *He Shall Have Dominion: A Postmillennial Eschatology, Third Edition: Revised and Expanded* (Draper: VA, Apologetics Group, 1992, 1997, 2009), 457-458

13 Daniel's Parousia cloud coming:

"There is a third cloud motif in Scripture. The reference is found in Daniel 7:13–14, the passage that Jesus quotes in Matthew 24:30. Notice that the coming of the Son of Man in Daniel 7 is not down but up! The Son of Man, Jesus, comes up "with the clouds of heaven" to "the Ancient of Days and was presented before Him."

"In Daniel's vision, coming on the clouds means that the Son of Man was coming onstage, into the scene. It is not a coming toward Daniel or toward earth, but a coming seen from the standpoint of God, since Daniel uses three verbs that all indicate this: "coming … approached … was led to" the Ancient of Days. This is no picture of the Second Coming, because the Son of man is going the wrong way for that. His face is turned, not toward earth, but toward God. His goal is not to receive His saints, but to receive His kingdom (Cf. 1 Peter 3:22; Luke 19:12; Acts 2:32–36; 3:22; 5:31; Col. 3:1; Rev. 3:21.).

"Jesus had Daniel 7 in mind as He described His enthronement: "The key verse in Daniel 7:13 that predicts the triumph of the Son of Man represents Him as coming into the presence of the Ancient of Days 'with the clouds of heaven,' a phrase that is repeated in Matthew 26:64; Mark 14:62; Revelation 14:14. Clouds are much more closely associated with the glory and throne of God than they are connected with the earth."

"Being familiar with the Hebrew Scriptures, Jesus' disciples understood the context of His words and grasped their meaning. Jesus spoke against the backdrop of the Old Testament.

"Our discussion of the meaning of Daniel 7:13 in its Old Testament context led us to the conclusion that its keynote is one of vindication and exaltation to an everlasting dominion, and that the "coming" of verse 13 was a coming to God [the Ancient of Days] to receive power, not a "descent" to earth. When we studied Jesus' use of these verses, we found that in every case this same theme was the point of the allusion, and, in particular, that nowhere (unless here) was verse 13 [in Dan. 7] interpreted of his coming to earth at the Parousia. In particular, the reference to Mark 14:62, where the wording is clearly parallel to that in the present verse [Mark 13:26], was to Jesus' imminent vindication and power, with a secondary reference to a manifestation of that power in the near future. Thus, the expectation that Jesus would in fact use Daniel 7:13 in the sense in which it was written is amply confirmed by his actual allusions. He saw in that verse a prediction of his imminent exaltation to an authority which supersedes that of the earthly powers which have set themselves against God.… Jesus is using Daniel 7:13 as a prediction of that authority which he exercised when in AD 70 the Jewish nation and its leaders, who had condemned him, were overthrown, and Jesus was vindicated as the recipient of all power from the Ancient of Days.

"At His trial, Jesus told Caiaphas the high priest and the Sanhedrin that they would see "the Son of Man sitting at the right hand of power and coming on the clouds of heaven" (Matt. 26:64). When would this take place? "The phrase … 'from now on' means exactly what it says …, and refers not to some distant event but to the imminent vindication of Jesus which will shortly be obvious to those who have sat in judgement over him." What did they "see"? Certainly not an event that was thousands of years in the future. N.T. Wright comments:

"Jesus is not, then, suggesting that Caiaphas will witness the end of the space-time order. Nor will he look out of the window one day and observe a human figure flying downwards on a cloud. It is absurd to imagine either Jesus, or Mark, or anyone in between, supposing the words to mean that. Caiaphas will witness the strange events which follow Jesus' crucifixion: the rise of a group of disciples claiming that he has been raised from the dead, and the events which accelerate towards the final clash with Rome, in which, judged according to the time-honoured test, Jesus will be vindicated as a true prophet. In and through it all, Caiaphas will witness events which show that Jesus was not, after all, mistaken in his claim, hitherto implicit, now at last explicit: he is the Messiah, the anointed one, the true representative of the people of Israel, the one in and through whom the covenant God is acting to set up his kingdom.

"At His ascension, Jesus had come up to the Ancient of Days "with the clouds of heaven" to receive the kingdom from His Father (Mark 16:19; Acts 1:9). Jesus' reception of the kingdom gave Him possession so that He could do with it as He pleased."

Gary DeMar, Last Days Madness: Obsession of the Modern Church, Fourth revised edition (Powder Springs, GA: American Vision, 1999), 161–163.

[14] This paragraph comes from:

Daniel 7:26
[26] But the court shall sit in judgment, and his [the Little Horn's] dominion shall be taken away, to be consumed and destroyed to the end.

[15] **Nero as the Little Horn of Daniel, or as some call it, the Antichrist**: I am not dead set on this interpretation as I consider there to be a pretty good argument for Titus as the little horn. However, in writing a novel, I have to commit to a specific view so I chose this one because it makes narrative sense with my story. I have included the theory for Titus as the little horn right after it.

I considered the horns, and, behold, there came up among them another little horn, before whom there were three of the first horns plucked up by the roots: and, behold, in this horn were eyes like the eyes of man, and a mouth speaking great things (Daniel 7:8).

"This speaks of Nero Caesar. He is the little horn "among them." Nero was the sixth of the ten emperors. Thus he is "another little horn" – one of many. Note that the passage says, "Three of the first horns plucked up by the roots." Nero was born on December 15th, AD 37. Three emperors ruled in his lifetime, Tiberius, Caligula and Claudius. Roman historians tell us that each one was assassinated to make way for Nero, who was not in the line of succession. Although some have doubted the Tiberius assassination story recorded by Tacitus and Suetonius as a mere rumor, Nero was born in the year of Tiberius' death and survived the emperors Caligula and Claudius. He lived in an era when political assassinations of those in the Julio-Claudian line had become the norm...

"Daniel 7 is important because the language here closely parallels Revelation 13 and 17. If we are to "count the number of the beast" (Revelation 13:18), then we need to know who is the Little Horn. Daniel 7 must be consistent with a preterist interpretation of Revelation 13 and 17...

11. I beheld then because of the voice of the great words which the horn spake: I beheld even till the beast was slain, and his body destroyed, and given to the burning flame.

The beast was slain – This speaks of both the destruction of the Roman Empire and of Nero who committed suicide with a military sword that killed many people before him.

12. As concerning the rest of the beasts, they had their dominion taken away: yet their lives were prolonged for a season and time.

"As concerning the rest of the beasts – After Nero's death, other rulers governed the Roman Empire, but the power of their throne began to weaken. They had their dominion taken away – At this point, the kingdom of God began to grow in all the earth.

"Yet their lives were prolonged for a season and time – There are several possible interpretations from a preterist perspective. A general interpretation has the rest of the beasts symbolizing the Gentile nations, including the realms held by the Babylonian, Persian and Greek kingdoms, that will remain in rebellion to God for an unspecified period of time until the kingdom of God gradually fills the whole world, as in chapter 2. This is the interpretation I favor, but there are two others that are interesting and worth considering.

"A more specific interpretation is that the rest of the beasts symbolize the remaining four Roman kings who ruled after Nero. The "Year of the Four Emperors" lasted a little more than a year from the death of Nero on June 8th of AD 68 to the accession of Vespasian on July 1st, 69. In this space of time, Nero, Galba, Otho and Vespasian ruled in turn.

"On the other hand, if "a season and a time" is interpreted to be exactly "three months and one year," then Vespasian's reign as emperor began on July 1st of AD 69 and the destruction of Jerusalem took place on September 24th, AD 70. This is a one year and three month period. In fact, it is exactly 360 days (a year) plus 90 days (a season) according to the Babylonian calendar in use at that time.

13. I saw in the night visions, and, behold, one like the Son of man came with the clouds of heaven, and came to the Ancient of days, and they brought him near before him...

The Son of Man – This speaks of Jesus Christ, the Son of God who is fully God and fully man. In the Gospels, Jesus identities himself as the "Son of man" in order to identify himself as the Messiah.

14. And there was given him dominion, and glory, and a kingdom, that all people, nations, and languages, should serve him: his dominion is an everlasting dominion, which shall not pass away, and his kingdom that which shall not be destroyed.

"Dominion, and glory, and a kingdom – Christ was given the keys to the kingdom by God the Father when he sat down at the right hand of God after His resurrection and ascension. This kingdom is not a future kingdom. It began in the days of the Roman Empire. It overcame Rome and will overcome all the kingdoms of this world. It will last forever...

20. And of the ten horns that were in his head, and of the other which came up, and before whom three fell; even of that horn that had eyes, and a mouth that spake very great things, whose look

was more stout than his fellows.

"Before whom three fell – Nero was born in AD 37, the same year as the death of Tiberius Caesar. Three Caesars were assassinated to clear the way for him. These were Tiberius, Caligula and Claudius. Tacitus and Suetonius record that Tiberius was smothered by Caligula and Macro and the crowd in Rome hearing the news rejoiced. Some consider this story to be spurious, but this is the consensus of the ancient historians. Caligula was murdered by his own guardsmen at the behest of a rival faction. Claudius was poisoned and it is thought that his fourth wife, Agrippina, committed the deed in order to make way for her son, Nero, whom Claudius had adopted as his step-son and heir.

"Many interpret the Little Horn as the "eleventh" horn. Of course, the number eleven is mentioned nowhere in the text. The Little Horn does not come after the ten horns, but as it has been translated as "in the midst of them" or "among them." Thus if the Little Horn is Nero, he is the sixth of the ten.

21. I beheld, and the same horn made war with the saints, and prevailed against them;

"The same horn made war with the saints – Nero began a persecution of the saints which began in AD 64 and lasted until his death on June 9th, AD 68.

22. Until the Ancient of days came, and judgment was given to the saints of the most High; and the time came that the saints possessed the kingdom. 23. Thus he said, The fourth beast shall be the fourth kingdom upon earth, which shall be diverse from all kingdoms, and shall devour the whole earth, and shall tread it down, and break it in pieces. 24. And the ten horns out of this kingdom are ten kings that shall arise: and another shall rise after them; and he shall be diverse from the first, and he shall subdue three kings. Another shall rise after them

– Nero was not in the direct line of succession, but three emperors were assassinated to make way for him.

25. And he shall speak great words against the most High, and shall wear out the saints of the most High, and think to change times and laws: and they shall be given into his hand until a time and times and the dividing of time.

"Until a time and times and the dividing of time – Literally, "time, times, half a time." If we understand a "time "to mean a year, then it is three-and a-half years. Nero's persecution of the Church lasted from about December AD 64 until his death in June AD 68. Although neither Suetonius not Tacitus give us the exact date when the persecution began, we can safely assume it was late 64 and lasted until Nero's death.

26. But the judgment shall sit, and they shall take away his dominion, to consume and to destroy it unto the end. 27. And the kingdom and dominion, and the greatness of the kingdom under the whole heaven, shall be given to the people of the saints of the most High, whose kingdom is an everlasting kingdom, and all dominions shall serve and obey him. 28. Hitherto is the end of the matter. As for me Daniel, my cogitations much troubled me, and my countenance changed in me: but I kept the matter in my heart.

"An everlasting kingdom – The purpose of this passage, and the entire prophecy of Daniel, is to give the Jews a correct understanding of the time when the Messiah would come. The purpose is to declare when the kingdom of God would come on earth. Jesus alluded to Daniel when He said to His disciples, "Assuredly, I say to you, there are some standing here who shall not taste death till they see the Son of Man coming in His kingdom." (Matthew 16:28)."

Jay Rogers, In the Days of These Kings: The Book of Daniel in Preterist Perspective (Clermont, FL, Media House Intl., 2017), 101, 54-57

Titus as the Little Horn of Daniel:

"Keeping in mind that the Antichrist was ultimately the demonic ruler from the abyss that worked through Titus (cf. Rev. 11:7; 17:8), the following are the prophecies of Daniel concerning the Antichrist that were fulfilled in Titus:

1. Although Titus would become the eleventh Caesar of Rome (the fourth beast), he was only a general when he destroyed the Jewish nation, hence his designation as a little (eleventh) horn (Dan. 7:7-8). This agrees with the traditional Jewish understanding of the little horn of Daniel 7 (e.g., Rashi).

433

2. Vespasian and Titus were victorious over three rulers (Galba, Otho, and Vitellius) in their takeover of the Roman Empire in AD 69 (the year of four emperors). These were the three horns removed before the little eleventh horn (Dan. 7:8). According to Roman historians, Titus was a major force behind the Flavian takeover of the empire.

3. The little eleventh horn was to speak great blasphemies against the Most High God (Dan. 7:8, 11, 20, 25). Jewish sources say that Titus spoke extraordinary blasphemies against God when he captured the Temple (cf. Dan. 11:36-37; 2 Thess. 2:4; Rev. 13:5-6).

4. The Antichrist was to have a three-and-a-half-year reign of terror (Dan. 7:25; Rev. 13:5). Titus persecuted Daniel's people for a time, times, and half a time (three-and-a-half years, or forty-two months), from March/April AD 67 to August/September AD 70 (cf. Rev. 11:2). This time period ended with the shattering of the Jewish nation (Dan. 12:7).

5. Titus and his father changed the times of religious observance and rules of Jewish law when they set up the equivalent of a new Sanhedrin in Yavneh (Dan.7:25).

6. Titus was the one who the demonic prince to come worked through in his destruction of Jerusalem and the Temple (Dan. 9:26).

7. The coming of Titus was associated with abominations (i.e., idols). He came on the wing of an army full of abominations (the images of Caesar on the Roman standards); this resulted in the Jewish nation being made desolate (Dan. 9:27; cf. 12:6-11).

8. Titus exalted himself above every god when his troops sacrificed to his name/image as they worshiped the Roman standards in the Temple (Dan. 11:36-37; cf. 2 Thess. 2:4).

9. The destruction of the Jews by Titus was assisted by the help of a foreign god named Sarapis; this god was not one of Titus's ancestors' gods. In recognition of this, Sarapis was elevated to the position of one of the Roman gods (Dan. 11:38-39).

10. After Titus's destruction of the Jewish nation in AD 70, the land of Israel was divided up by the Romans and leased out for profit (Dan. 11:39).

11. Titus first invaded the Holy Land in AD 67 with his father. In late AD 69 Titus and Vespasian were in Egypt securing its precious things to help finance their takeover of the Roman Empire (Dan. 11:40-43).

12. In mid-AD 69 Titus was given sole authority over Syria (the domain of the king of the North) as well as Judea. In the spring of AD 70, with tidings from the north (a revolt in Germany) and east (the continuing revolt in Judea) troubling him, Titus invaded the Holy Land from Egypt (Dan. 11:44). This was the Antichrist's second coming to the Holy Land.

13. In the final siege of Jerusalem, Titus set up his camp between the Mediterranean Sea and the glorious holy mountain of God (Dan. 11:45; cf. 9:26). It was at Jerusalem that the demonic king of the North (cf. Dan. 10:13), the spirit of Antichrist working through Titus (cf. 1 John 4:3), met its end as it was destroyed in the lake of fire (Dan. 7:11; cf. Rev. 19:20).

14. The length of time between the abomination of desolation (the coming to sacred Jewish soil of the one who would make desolate, Dan. 9:27 NKJV) until the shattering of the power of the Jews was 1,290 days (Dan. 12:6-11). Titus came to the Holy Land around February of AD 67; 1,290 days later the Jewish nation was left shattered."

McKenzie PhD, Duncan W.. *The Antichrist and the Second Coming: A Preterist Examination Volume I* (K-Locations 4181-4216). Xulon Press. K-Edition.

[16] **The spiritual principality behind the earthly beast**: Revelation talks about the Beast as a fluid image that sometimes represents the empire (Rev 17:9-10), sometimes an individual (Rev 17:11; 13:18), and sometimes a spiritual entity that seems to empower the earthly beast (Rev 11:7; 17:8).

Revelation 11:7
And when they have finished their testimony, the beast that rises from the bottomless pit will make war on them and conquer them and kill them,

Revelation 17:8
The beast that you saw was, and is not, and is about to rise from the bottomless pit and go to destruction. And the dwellers on earth whose names have not been written in the book of life from the foundation of the world will marvel to see the beast, because it was and is not and is to come.

The destruction of Azazel as the spiritual principality behind the beast: The book of Revelation does not say that Azazel is the "beast that came out of the Abyss." I have made that creative choice for the theological connections it helps to make. But this should not be considered a doctrinal claim on my part but rather theological speculation.

Daniel 7:11–12
[11] "I looked then because of the sound of the great words that the horn was speaking. And as I looked, the beast was killed, and its body destroyed and given over to be burned with fire. [12] As for the rest of the beasts, their dominion was taken away, but their lives were prolonged for a season and a time.

"When earthly rulers battle on earth, the Bible describes the host of heaven battling with them in spiritual unity. In Daniel 10, hostilities between Greece and Persia is accompanied by the battle of heavenly Watchers over those nations (described as "princes").

Daniel 10:13, 20-21
The prince of the kingdom of Persia withstood me twenty-one days, but Michael, one of the chief princes, came to help me, for I was left there with the kings of Persia." …Then he said, "Do you know why I have come to you? But now I will return to fight against the prince of Persia; and when I go out, behold, the prince of Greece will come. 21 But I will tell you what is inscribed in the book of truth: there is none who contends by my side against these except Michael, your prince.

"When Sisera fought with Israel, the earthly kings and heavenly authorities (host of heaven) are described interchangeably in unity.

Judges 5:19–20
"The kings came, they fought; then fought the kings of Canaan…From heaven the stars fought, from their courses they fought against Sisera.

"When God punishes earthly rulers, he punishes them along with the heavenly rulers ("host of heaven") above and behind them.

Isaiah 24:21–22
On that day the LORD will punish the host of heaven, in heaven, and the kings of the earth, on the earth. They will be gathered together as prisoners in a pit; they will be shut up in a prison, and after many days they will be punished.

"Though this notion of territorial archons or spiritual rulers is Biblical and carries over into intertestamental literature such as the Book of Enoch (1 En. 89:59, 62-63; 67) and others, it seems to lessen at the time of the New Testament.

"Walter Wink points out that the picture of Watchers over nations is hinted at in 1 Cor. 4:9 where the apostle explains their persecution has "become a spectacle (theatre) to the world, to angels and to men." He explains that "the image of the Roman theater conjures up hostile and jeering crowds," and the angels are "heavenly representatives of the Gentile nations and people, who watch, not without malicious glee, the tribulations endured by the apostle in their peoples."

"The epistles speak of the spiritual principalities and powers that are behind the earthly rulers and powers to be sure (Eph. 6:12-13), but it appears to be more generic in reference. And after the death, resurrection, and ascension of Christ, these spiritual powers have been disarmed and overthrown (Col. 2:15, Luke 10:18), at least legally losing their hegemony (Eph. 1:20-23)."

Brian Godawa, When Giants Were Upon the Earth: The Watchers, the Nephilim, and the Biblical Cosmic War of the Seed (Los Angeles, CA: Embedded Pictures Publishing, 2014), 278-279.

[17] Daniel's resurrection as typological:

Daniel 12:2–3

[2] And many of those who sleep in the dust of the earth shall awake, some to everlasting life, and some to shame and everlasting contempt. [3] And those who are wise shall shine like the brightness of the sky above; and those who turn many to righteousness, like the stars forever and ever.

"The resurrection of verse 2 seems to connect to the evangelistic and teaching ministry spoken of in verse 3; thus, it is some kind of historical resurrection that is spoken of, a resurrectional event in this world, in our history.

"The solution to our difficulty is found in Ezekiel 37. There the prophet is told to prophesy to the dead bones of the idolaters scattered all over the mountains of Israel (see Ezekiel 6:5). Ezekiel prophesies and the bones come to life again. This is explained in Ezekiel 37:11 as the national resurrection of Israel after the captivity. The language used by God is very "literal sounding," to wit: "I will open your graves and cause you to come up out of your graves" (vv. 12–13). Yet, this graphic language refers to the spiritual resurrection of the nation.

"Now clearly, the resurrection of the whole nation does not mean the salvation of each individual. Thus, Daniel 12:2 tells us that in the days of Jesus the nation will undergo a last spiritual resurrection, but some will not persevere and their resurrection will only be unto destruction. The Parable of the Soils fits here (Matthew 13:3–23): three different kinds of people come to life, but only one of the three kinds is awakened to persevering, everlasting life.

"During His ministry, Jesus raised the nation back to life. He healed the sick, cleansed the unclean, brought dead people back to life, restored the Law, entered the Temple as King, etc. Then, as always, the restored people fell into sin, and crucified Him.

"Thus, a resurrection of Israel is in view. The wicked are raised, but do not profit from it, and are destroyed. The saints experience a great distress, and live with God forever and ever."

James B. Jordan, *The Handwriting on the Wall: A Commentary on the Book of Daniel* (Powder Springs, GA: American Vision, 2007), 618–619.

"Many of them that sleep in the dust of the earth shall awake – This refers primarily to the Gospel being preached. Many who sleep in the dust, both Jews and Gentiles, shall be awakened by the preaching of the Gospel out of their heathenism. It has a secondary application to a future resurrection when the multitude that sleep in the dust shall awake; many shall arise to life, and many to shame.

"Is this referring to the First Resurrection in which we receive eternal life through regeneration?

"Or does it refer to the Final Resurrection that will occur at the Second Coming of Jesus when we will be raised as spiritual bodies and glorified with Christ?

"This is one of the verses in Daniel that creates a lot questions from a preterist perspective. In the context of the following verses, I believe it refers to awakening of God's chosen people at the preaching of the Gospel. However, like other apocalyptic passages in the Bible, there is also a "telescoping" aspect of this imagery. The Final Resurrection is projected onto the historical events of the first century. We see in the dawning light of the Gospel during the first century a prefiguring of the final glorious state of the kingdom of God at the Second Coming of Christ and the Resurrection of the saints.

> Daniel 12:3 – And they that be wise shall shine as the brightness of the firmament; and they that turn many to righteousness as the stars for ever and ever.

"They that be wise shall shine – Just as the kingdom of God is in the here and now, but won't be revealed in all its glory until Christ returns, so the born-again believers in Jesus Christ are seated in heavenly places reigning with Christ in the present (Ephesians 2:4-7). This began to be made manifest when Jesus first began to preach the kingdom of God…

"There are two aspects of our resurrection just as there are two aspects of Christ's coming in the glory of His kingdom. We are even now raised with Christ and seated with Him. Spiritual death has been defeated."

Jay Rogers, In the Days of These Kings: The Book of Daniel in Preterist Perspective (Clermont, FL, Media House Intl., 2017) 477-478.

[18] The Regeneration:

"The "regeneration" (palingenesia) of which Jesus speaks in Matthew 19:28 appears in Revelation 21–22. As we shall see this refers to the renewal of God's kingdom in the coming of new covenant Christianity. Later in Luke 22:30 Christ uses similar language to underscore Christianity's new covenantal emphasis, for there he utters it while establishing the Lord's Supper (Lk 22:28–29), the new covenant's sacramental meal (Lk 22:20). The paligenesia need not refer to the consummate new heavens and new earth found in 2 Peter 3:10.63 In fact, both Philo (Mos 2:65) and Clement (1 Clem 9:4) use the word to speak of the world as it exists after Noah's Flood. Josephus (Ant. 11:3:9 §66) uses it when referring to Israel's renewal after her exile: "when they heard the same, [they] gave thanks also to God that he restored the land of their forefathers to them again." The word signifies a radical re-orientation or a new beginning. This fits perfectly with the conception that new covenant Christianity would supplant old covenant Israel as the focus of divine activity. This is not only an important point in Revelation (indeed, its very theme), but is also the basic argument of Hebrews (Heb 1:1–4; 3:1–6; 8:1–13; 9:15–28; 10:19–22; 12:18–29) as well."

Kenneth L. Gentry, Jr., The Divorce of Israel: A Redemptive-Historical Interpretation of Revelation Vol. 1 (Dallas, GA: Tolle Lege Press, 2016), 674.

[19] The great white throne judgment:

> Revelation 20:11–15
> [11] Then I saw a great white throne and him who was seated on it. From his presence earth and sky fled away, and no place was found for them. [12] And I saw the dead, great and small, standing before the throne, and books were opened. Then another book was opened, which is the book of life. And the dead were judged by what was written in the books, according to what they had done. [13] And the sea gave up the dead who were in it, Death and Hades gave up the dead who were in them, and they were judged, each one of them, according to what they had done. [14] Then Death and Hades were thrown into the lake of fire. This is the second death, the lake of fire. [15] And if anyone's name was not found written in the book of life, he was thrown into the lake of fire.

CHAPTER 70

[1] **The first words of the Copper Scroll**: Florentino García Martínez and Eibert J. C. Tigchelaar, "The Dead Sea Scrolls Study Edition (translations)" (Leiden; New York: Brill, 1997–1998), 233.

[2] The Copper Scroll as presented here:

"COPPER SCROLL (3Q15 = 3QTreasure). Thinly rolled metal sheets of copper discovered among the Dead Sea Scrolls; engraved with a list of directions to hidden treasure across Judaea and Galilee. Also known as "Copper Plaque," "Copper Rolls," and occasionally "Bronze Scrolls.""

Justin David Strong, "Copper Scroll," ed. John D. Barry et al., The Lexham Bible Dictionary (Bellingham, WA: Lexham Press, 2016).

"The purpose of the Scroll remains a puzzle. There are three main theories. The first is that it is a record of the Qumran community's possessions which were cached in various places just before the Romans advanced upon their 'monastery' in 68 A.D. Against this, however, it has been objected that the amount of the treasure listed is prodigiously disproportionate to the probable resources of an ascetic brotherhood!

"The second theory is that the treasure is that of the Sec-ond Temple, committed for safekeeping to the desert community when the sacred edifice fell, or was about to fall, to the Roman forces. But this too is not without its diffi. culties. According to Josephus, (War, vi.5, §2) the main treasure of the Temple was still in the building when it fell, and this happened in 70 A.D., whereas, according to the archaeological evidence, the Qumran monastery had already been abandoned two years earlier. Moreover, if the censorious references to the Jerusalemitan priesthood which we find in the Scrolls really represent a contemporary attitude, it is not very likely that those officials would have turned to the Qumran brotherhood for the safekeeping of their sacred vessels!

"A third hypothesis is that the Scroll registers the treasure not of the Second but of the First (Solomonic) Temple, removed from Jerusalem when it fell to Nebuchadnezzar in 586 B.C. Opinion is divided, however, as to whether the list is factual or fictitious, seeing that accounts of somewhat similar character indeed appear in later Jewish legend.

"Perhaps there is room for a fourth theory. May not the Scroll represent an unconscionable fraud (or even a cruel practical joke) perpetrated by some cynical outsider upon the naive and innocent minds of the ascetics of Qumran? The fraud (or joke) would have been founded upon time-honored legends about the buried treasure of the First Temple and have been calculated especially to appeal to the hearts and minds of men who were looking to an imminent restoration of the past glories of Israel."

Theodor H. Gaster, *The Dead Sea Scriptures, 3rd Edition* (NY: Anchor Books, 1976) Online: https://thebibleisnotholy.files.wordpress.com/2010/06/dead-sea-scriptures.pdf

CHAPTER 72

[1] The parable of the ten virgins: Mattehw 25:1-13.

[2] Parable of the Wedding Feast: Matthew 22:1-14.

[3] **The Feast of Tabernacles**: See Numbers 29:12-38.

> Leviticus 23:33–36
> 33 And the LORD spoke to Moses, saying, 34 "Speak to the people of Israel, saying, On the fifteenth day of this seventh month and for seven days is the Feast of Booths to the LORD. 35 On the first day shall be a holy convocation; you shall not do any ordinary work. 36 For seven days you shall present food offerings to the LORD. On the eighth day you shall hold a holy convocation and present a food offering to the LORD. It is a solemn assembly; you shall not do any ordinary work.

[4] Jesus fulfilled Tabernacles:

> Revelation 21:3
> 3 And I heard a loud voice from the throne saying, "Behold, the dwelling place of God is with man. He will dwell with them, and they will be his people, and God himself will be with them as their God.

> John 1:14
> 14 And the Word became flesh and dwelt ("tabernacled") among us, and we have seen his glory, glory as of the only Son from the Father, full of grace and truth.

Jesus fulfilled all the Jewish feasts: Special thanks to David Curtis of Berean Bible Church for his teaching on this topic. You can get his free teachings on these at: http://www.bereanbiblechurch.org/studies/leviticus.php

EPILOGUE

[1] **Josephus' statement of the dead and captives**: Flavius Josephus, The Wars of the Jews 6.9.3-4, §420, 429.

[2] **The story of Masada is told by Josephus in**: Flavius Josephus, *The Wars of the Jews* 7.6.1-4, §163-209

[3] **Simon's death in Rome:** (Historically, John of Gischala was also captured and imprisoned in Rome until his death. I used creative license in this story by having Gischala die in the fire of the temple.)

Flavius Josephus, *The Wars of the Jews* 7.5.6, §153-155
"Now the last part of this pompous show was at the temple of Jupiter Capitolinus, whither when they were come, they stood still; for it was the Romans' ancient custom to stay, till somebody brought the news that the general of the enemy was slain. (154) This general was Simon, the son of Gioras, who had then been led in this triumph among the captives; a rope had also been put upon his head, and he had been drawn into a proper place in the forum, and had withal been tormented by those that drew him along, and the law of the Romans required that malefactors condemned to die should be slain there. (155) Accordingly, when it was related that there was an end of him, and all the people had sent up a shout for joy, they then began to offer those sacrifices which they had consecrated, in the prayers used in such solemnities; which when they had finished, they went away to the palace."

Flavius Josephus and William Whiston, *The Works of Josephus: Complete and Unabridged* (Peabody:

Hendrickson, 1987), 758.

[4] **The Triumphal Procession in Rome**: Flavius Josephus, *The Wars of the Jews* 7.5.3-6, §121-157

The Temple spoils in the triumph:

Flavius Josephus, *The Wars of the Jews* 7.5.6, §148-152
"and for the other spoils, they were carried in great plenty. But for those that were taken in the temple of Jerusalem, they made the greatest figure of them all; that is, the golden table, of the weight of many talents; the candlestick also, that was made of gold, though its construction were now changed from that which we made use of: (149) for its middle shaft was fixed upon a basis, and the small branches were produced out of it to a great length, having the likeness of a trident in their position, and had every one a socket made of brass for a lamp at the tops of them. These lamps were in number seven, and represented the dignity of the number seven among the Jews; (150) and the last of all the spoils was carried the Law of the Jews. (151) After these spoils passed by a great many men, carrying the images of Victory, whose structure was entirely either of ivory or of gold. (152) After which Vespasian marched in the first place, and Titus followed him."

Flavius Josephus and William Whiston, *The Works of Josephus: Complete and Unabridged* (Peabody: Hendrickson, 1987), 757–758.

[5] Vespasian after the war:

"Vespasian diligently promoted his dynastic plans in his speeches and on his coins. Titus was carefully groomed to succeed; and for the greater part of the reign was effectively the deputy-emperor. Some senators disapproved of the dynastic concept, but most accepted that it removed the danger of civil war among rival contenders. Moderation and accessibility were Augustan qualities practiced by Vespasian and much approved after the regal trappings of a Nero. He was able to pursue this policy largely because Titus, as Praetorian Prefect, efficiently crushed any plots and opposition before they could mature. The success of Vespasian's consolidation of his and his family's power can be seen in the smooth and undisputed succession of Titus…

"When Vespasian died in 79 A.D., he was immediately deified by the Senate – a genuine mark of its respect and admiration for the man and his work. The coins which he struck during his reign proclaimed "The Augustan Peace," "Rome Rising Anew," and "The Happiness of the People." These were not empty phrases. Even "Liberty Restored" had a certain plausibility. For though Vespasian was no less an autocrat than Nero had been, his modest, down-to-earth manner, his affability, and his accessibility at least helped to conceal the realities of power. His shrewd judgement, combined with a quick wit and keen humor, enabled him to avoid or deflect difficult and unpleasant situations. He had deserved well of Rome, for he had ended a calamitous civil war, brought back order and prosperity and, above all, had restored confidence in Rome and its system of government. He has been called "the common-sense emperor"; but in Vespasian it was the common-sense of genius."

R. D. Milns, "Vespasian (Emperor)," ed. David Noel Freedman, *The Anchor Yale Bible Dictionary* (New York: Doubleday, 1992), 852-853.

[6] Titus after the war:

"On Titus's return to Rome in June 71, Vespasian granted him powers so extensive that he was almost coruler. But he soon acquired a reputation for ruthlessness, extravagance, and licentiousness. As commander of the praetorian guard, he was "somewhat arrogant and tyrannical" (Suetonius Titus 6.1), crushing any opposition…

"Men feared that on his accession, he would be a second Nero (Suetonius Titus 7.1).

"Their fears proved groundless, according to our sources. On becoming emperor, Titus dismissed Berenice when she returned to Rome (Dio 66.18.1), executed no senators or anyone else (Dio 66.19.1), and declared that a day when he had conferred no favors was a day wasted (Suetonius Titus 8). Clearly, he intended to project an image of moderation, affability, and generosity…

"After a brief reign of twenty-six months, Titus died suddenly on Sept. 13, 81, apparently of natural causes, and was immediately deified. Suggestions that he was murdered by Domitian seem unfounded. For

Suetonius, Titus was "the darling of the human race" (Titus 1), a view shared by non-Jewish writers of antiquity. Brave and intellectually capable, he gathered all the accomplishments of a highly educated Roman noble of his time. His bland charm and diplomatic skill served to conceal both his efficiency and his ruthlessness.

Brian W. Jones, "Titus (Emperor)," ed. David Noel Freedman, *The Anchor Yale Bible Dictionary* (New York: Doubleday, 1992), 581.

[7] Berenice in Rome:

Cassius Dio, *Roman History*, 65.15.3-4
"Berenice was at the very height of her power and consequently came to Rome along with her brother Agrippa. 4 The latter was given the rank of praetor, while she dwelt in the palace, cohabiting with Titus. She expected to marry him and was already behaving in every respect as if she were his wife; but when he perceived that the Romans were displeased with the situation, he sent her away."

http://penelope.uchicago.edu/Thayer/E/Roman/Texts/Cassius_Dio/65*.html

[8] Herod Agrippa II after the war:

"When Vespasian had established himself as emperor and the Jewish revolt had been crushed, Agrippa was rewarded for his loyalty with additional territory (details are lacking; see HJP[2], 478). In Rome in A.D. 75 Agrippa was awarded the symbols of praetorian rank. Thereafter he all but disappears from history. Josephus tells us that Agrippa corresponded with him on the subject of his book on the Jewish War, praising its accuracy and admitting that he owned a copy (Life 65; AgAp 1.9). Agrippa seems to have died in the reign of Vespasian's younger son, Domitian, about A.D. 93 (HJP[2], 480–83). His attitude toward the Romans, in part at least, is summed up in the speech which Josephus attributed to him. If Agrippa did not actually deliver this speech in trying to quell the revolt, he apparently later read and approved of it. The main point of the speech seems notably well-reasoned: namely, that the Romans were simply too strong to succumb to any uprising which Jewish revolutionaries could mount (War 2.345ff.).

Agrippa seems not to have married and not to have fathered any children. It was rumored that his relationship with his sister Bernice was incestuous."

David C. Braund, "Agrippa (Person)," ed. David Noel Freedman, *The Anchor Yale Bible Dictionary* (New York: Doubleday, 1992), 100.

[9] Josephus:

"In Rome Josephus resided in an apartment within the emperor's house and devoted much of his time to writing. In part his works were addressed to his fellow Jews, justifying to them not only Roman conduct during the Jewish War, but also his own personal conduct in switching loyalties. However, his writings were also designed to justify Jewish culture and religion to an interested and sometimes sympathetic Roman audience. The earliest of his extant writings is the Bellum Judaicarum (or Jewish War), which was apparently drafted initially in Aramaic and then translated into Greek 5 to 10 years after the 70 C.E. destruction of Jerusalem. His second work, Antiquitates Judaicae (or Jewish Antiquities), was published more than a decade later; it was much longer, and recounts Jewish history from creation to the Jewish War, and contains some valuable historical information. His last two works, probably published shortly before his death, include the Vita (or Life), an autobiography intended primarily to defend his conduct during the Jewish War 30 years earlier, and Contra Apionem (or Against Apion), an apologetic defense of Judaism against a wave of anti-Semitism emanating from Alexandria. Josephus probably died ca. 100 C.E., several years after Trajan had become emperor in Rome. His writings, while generally ignored by fellow Jews, were preserved by Christians."

Louis H. Feldman, "Josephus (Person)," ed. David Noel Freedman, *The Anchor Yale Bible Dictionary* (New York: Doubleday, 1992), 982.

[10] Johannan ben Zakkai:

"Rabbinic Judaism pictures Yohanan as the person most responsible for the survival of Judaism after the Great Roman War of 66 C.E.–73 C.E., and the destruction of the Jerusalem Temple in 70 C.E. By establishing a school in Jamnia/Yavneh, Yohanan – a legislative innovator, a mystic, and a creative biblical exegete – made it possible for Judaism to survive despite the destruction of its physical and spiritual centers."

Gary G. Porton, "Yohanan Ben Zakkai," ed. David Noel Freedman, *The Anchor Yale Bible Dictionary* (New York: Doubleday, 1992), 1024.

[11] The Dead Sea community of Qumran:

"The identification of the Qumran community as an Essene settlement is well established. See ESSENES. Yet the character of the community as it emerges from the scrolls is very different from that conveyed by Philo and Josephus in their descriptions of the Essenes. The ascetic tendencies of the community arise not from the pursuit of philosophical mysticism or from the dualism of mind and body but from the observance of priestly purity laws, the dualism of light and darkness, and the expectation of divine judgment.

"The priestly character of the community is pervasive and is reflected in its leadership and even in the name "sons of Zadok." (See Davies 1987: 51–72, on the limitations of what can be inferred from this term.) It is also reflected in the sense of participation in the angelic world…

"We have repeatedly noted the eschatological orientation of the scrolls. Several documents attest a periodization of history, culminating in the penultimate age of wrath, in which the community lived. The settlement in the desert was supposed to prepare the imminent way of the Lord (1Q58), and rule books were prepared for the community of the end of days (1QSa) and for the final war. The scrolls frequently refer to the coming of the messiahs of Aaron and Israel – the eschatological counterparts of the priest and the overseer of the actual community…

"While the War Scroll cannot be simply assigned to the Roman period, the late copies of it show the continued vitality of eschatological hope. Whether that hope led the community to participate in the revolt against Rome in the belief that the day of vengeance had come, remains a tantalizing but unanswerable question…

"The scrolls attest another Jewish community which, like the early Christians, lived in the belief that the end of days was at hand and that its struggle was with principalities and powers, and which reinterpreted the Scriptures in that context."

John J. Collins, "Dead Sea Scrolls," ed. David Noel Freedman, *The Anchor Yale Bible Dictionary* (New York: Doubleday, 1992), 99-100.

[12] Not one stone left upon another:

Matthew 23:36–24:2
[36] Truly, I say to you, all these things will come upon this generation. [37] "O Jerusalem, Jerusalem, the city that kills the prophets and stones those who are sent to it! How often would I have gathered your children together as a hen gathers her brood under her wings, and you were not willing! [38] See, your house is left to you desolate. [39] For I tell you, you will not see me again, until you say, 'Blessed is he who comes in the name of the Lord.' " [1] Jesus left the temple and was going away, when his disciples came to point out to him the buildings of the temple. [2] But he answered them, "You see all these, do you not? Truly, I say to you, there will not be left here one stone upon another that will not be thrown down."

"The disciples were surprised when Jesus told them that the temple was going to be destroyed, with not one stone left on top of another (Matt. 24:2). In response, they asked this multifaceted question: "Tell us, when will these things be, and what will be the sign of Your coming, and of the end of the age" (24:3)? It is crucial that we pay close attention to when Jesus said these events would take place.

"Jesus told the scribes and Pharisees, "Truly I say to you, all these things shall come upon this generation," that is, the destruction of their temple and city will be realized before the then-existing generation passes into history (23:36). It was the generation of those who rejected Jesus who would experience His wrath. The "this generation" of Matthew 23:36 is the generation upon whom Jesus pronounced judgment.

"But what of those who say that the Olivet Discourse is a prophecy about a still-future temple that must be rebuilt in Jerusalem and destroyed like the temple that was destroyed by the Roman military leader Titus in A.D. 70? This supposed future temple would have to be rebuilt with the same stones that made up the temple that was destroyed. Not just any stones will do. Jesus said that "not one stone here shall be left upon another, which will not be torn down" (Matt. 24:2).

441

"The temple that Jesus said would be destroyed is the same temple with the same stones that were pointed out by Jesus to His disciples. No future temple is in view. Jesus gives no indication that He has a future rebuilt temple in mind. Certainly Jesus' disciples would not be thinking of a rebuilt temple when they were looking at an existing temple that Jesus said would be destroyed! But what if the Jews are able to rebuild the temple? Such a temple will have nothing to do with the fulfillment of any part of this prophecy."

Gary DeMar, Last Days Madness: Obsession of the Modern Church, Fourth revised edition (Powder Springs, GA: American Vision, 1999), 52–53.

"And He answered and said to them, 'Do you not see all these things? Truly I say to you, not one stone here shall be left upon another, which will not be torn down' " (Matt. 24:2).

"Notice that Jesus says, "not one stone here shall be left upon another." Jesus is not describing what will happen to some future rebuilt temple. No mention is ever made in the New Testament about a rebuilt temple. Those who claim that the temple must be rebuilt during a future period of "great tribulation" cannot point to one verse in the New Testament that describes such a rebuilding program. Even those who teach that the temple will be rebuilt admit, "There are no Bible verses that say, 'There is going to be a third temple.' " The temple under discussion throughout the Olivet Discourse is the one that was standing during the time of Jesus' ministry, the same temple that was destroyed by the Romans in A.D. 70."

Gary DeMar, Last Days Madness: Obsession of the Modern Church, Fourth revised edition (Powder Springs, GA: American Vision, 1999), 67–68.

For more details on the lack of a rebuilt temple, see the chapter, "The Myth that the Temple Needs to be Rebuilt" in Gary DeMar, 10 Popular Prophecy Myths Exposed: The Last Days Might Not Be as near as You Think (Powder Springs, GA: American Vision, 2010), 103-118.

[13] **Fall of the Roman Empire**: Because of the modern prejudice and bigotry of academia against Christianity, many scholars have sought to deny that Christianity was a significant factor in the fall of the Roman Empire. But famous historian, Edward Gibbon, an unbeliever, made a powerful argument that supported the thesis of Christianity leading to the fall:

"A candid but rational inquiry into the progress and establishment of Christianity may be considered as a very essential part of the history of the Roman empire. While that great body was invaded by open violence, or undermined by slow decay, a pure and humble religion gently insinuated itself into the minds of men, grew up in silence and obscurity, derived new vigour from opposition, and finally erected the triumphant banner of the Cross on the ruins of the Capitol. Nor was the influence of Christianity confined to the period or to the limits of the Roman empire. After a revolution of thirteen or fourteen centuries, that religion is still professed by the nations of Europe, the most distinguished portion of human kind in arts and learning as well as in arms. By the industry and zeal of the Europeans it has been widely diffused to the most distant shores of Asia and Africa; and by the means of their colonies has been firmly established from Canada to Chili, in a world unknown to the ancients.

Edward Gibbon, The Decline And Fall Of The Roman Empire, Chapter 15 (Online Christian Classics Ethereal Library) https://www.ccel.org/g/gibbon/decline/volume1/chap15.htm

[14] The kingdom that never ends and grows as a mountain to fill the earth:

Daniel 2:44–45
[44] And in the days of those kings the God of heaven will set up a kingdom that shall never be destroyed, nor shall the kingdom be left to another people. It shall break in pieces all these kingdoms and bring them to an end, and it shall stand forever, [45] just as you saw that a stone was cut from a mountain by no human hand, and that it broke in pieces the iron, the bronze, the clay, the silver, and the gold. A great God has made known to the king what shall be after this. The dream is certain, and its interpretation sure."

Daniel 2:35
But the stone that struck the image became a great mountain and filled the whole earth.

442

Made in the USA
Middletown, DE
17 March 2024

51666068R00255